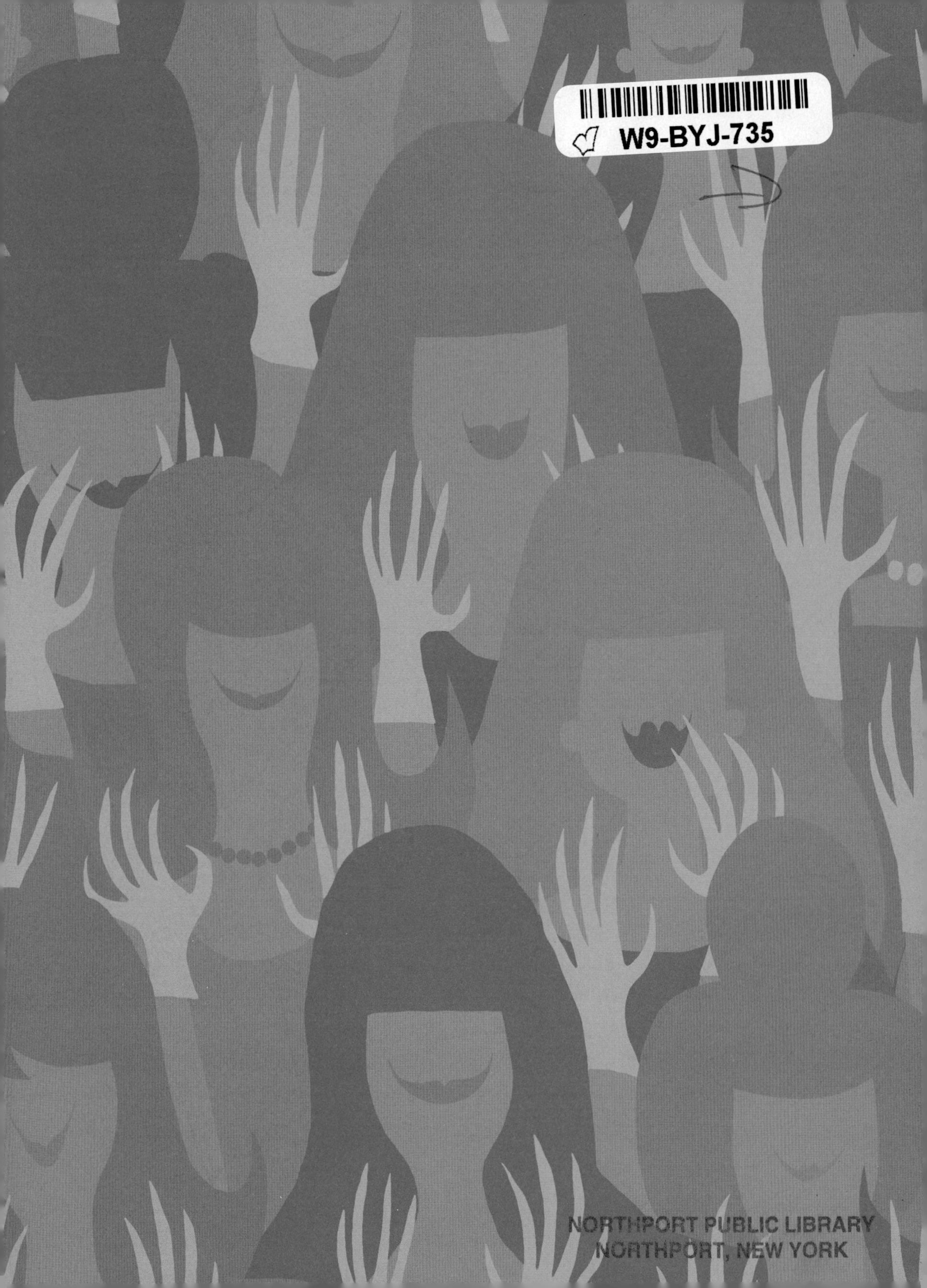

THE WITCHES

THE GRAPHIC NOVEL

ROALD DAHL

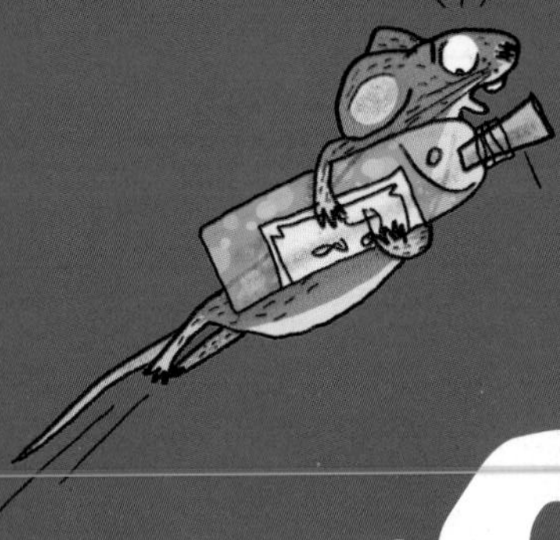

THE WITCHES

THE GRAPHIC NOVEL

Adapted and Illustrated by

PÉNÉLOPE BAGIEU

graphix

An Imprint of

SCHOLASTIC

This graphic novel adaptation of *The Witches* was originally published in France by Gallimard Bande Dessinée in 2020 under the title *Sacrées Sorcières*.

Library of Congress Control Number: 2020937404

ISBN 978-1-338-67744-7 (hardcover)
ISBN 978-1-338-67743-0 (paperback)

10 9 8 7 6 5 4 3 2 20 21 22 23 24

Printed in the U.S.A. 113
This edition first printing, September 2020

Translated from the French by Montana Kane
Edited by Emily Clement
Lettering by John Martz
Creative Director: Phil Falco
Publisher: David Saylor

To my dear grandmother
— P.B.

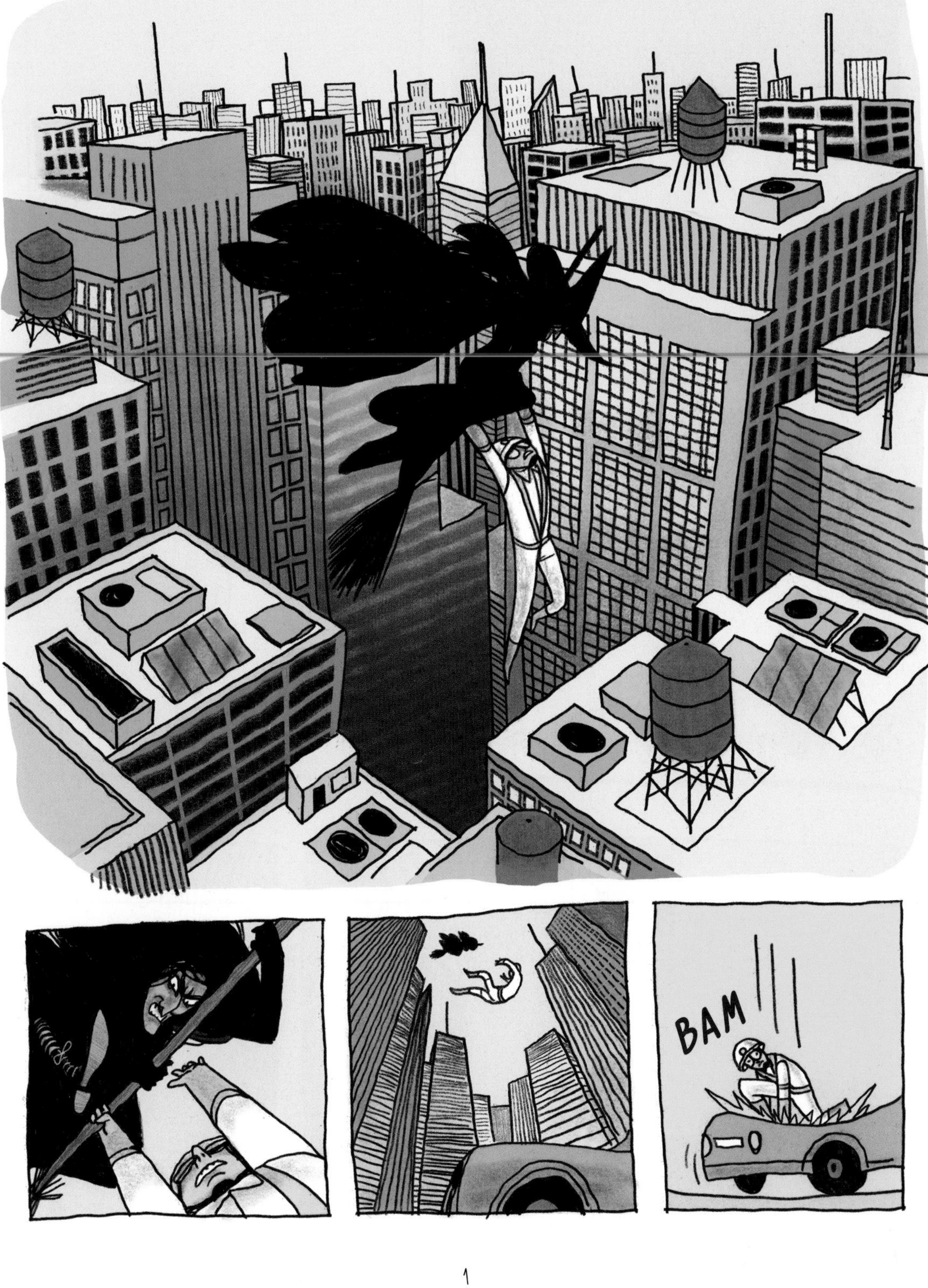
BAM

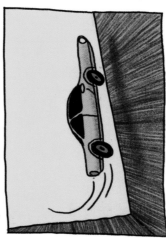

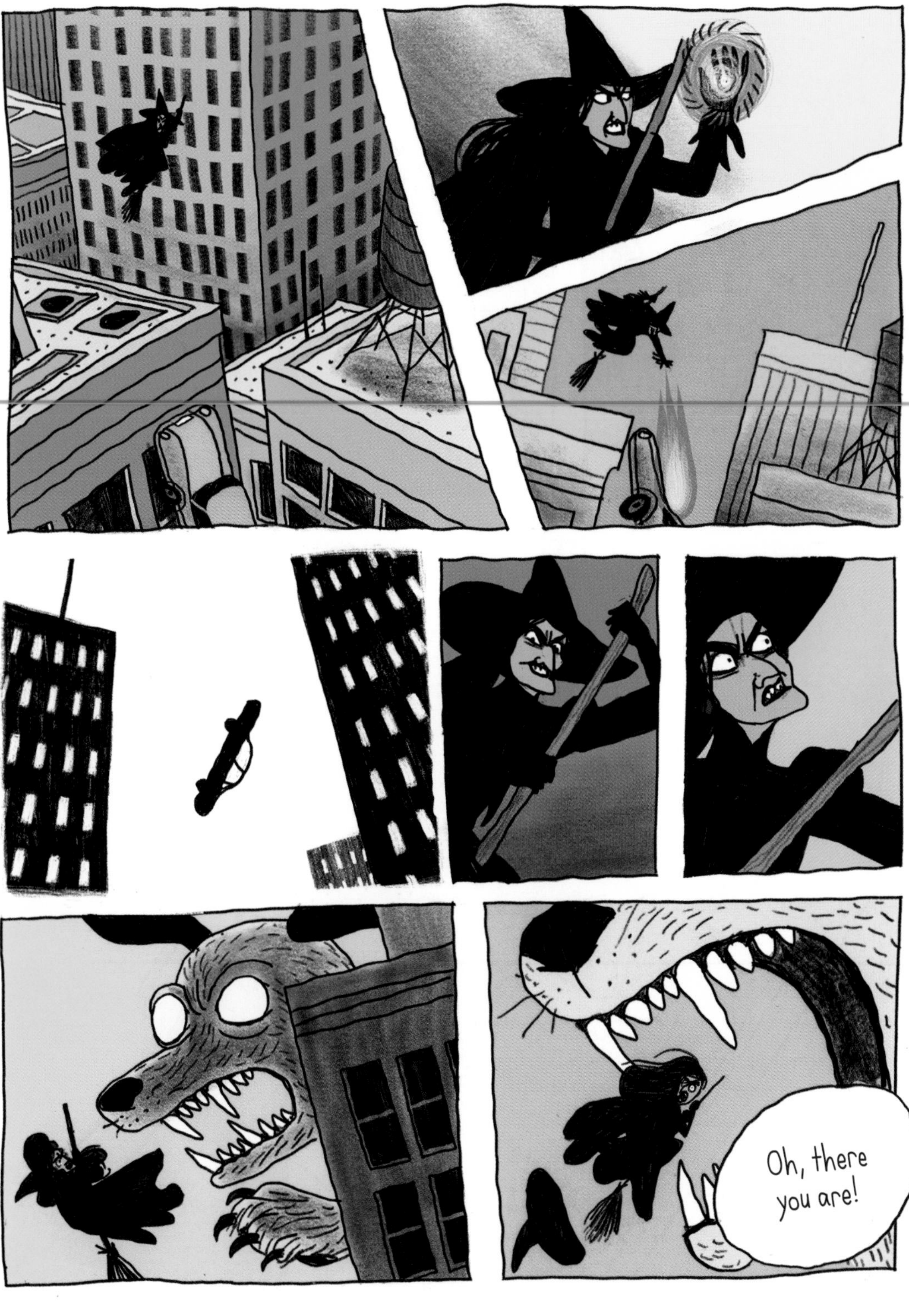
Oh, there you are!

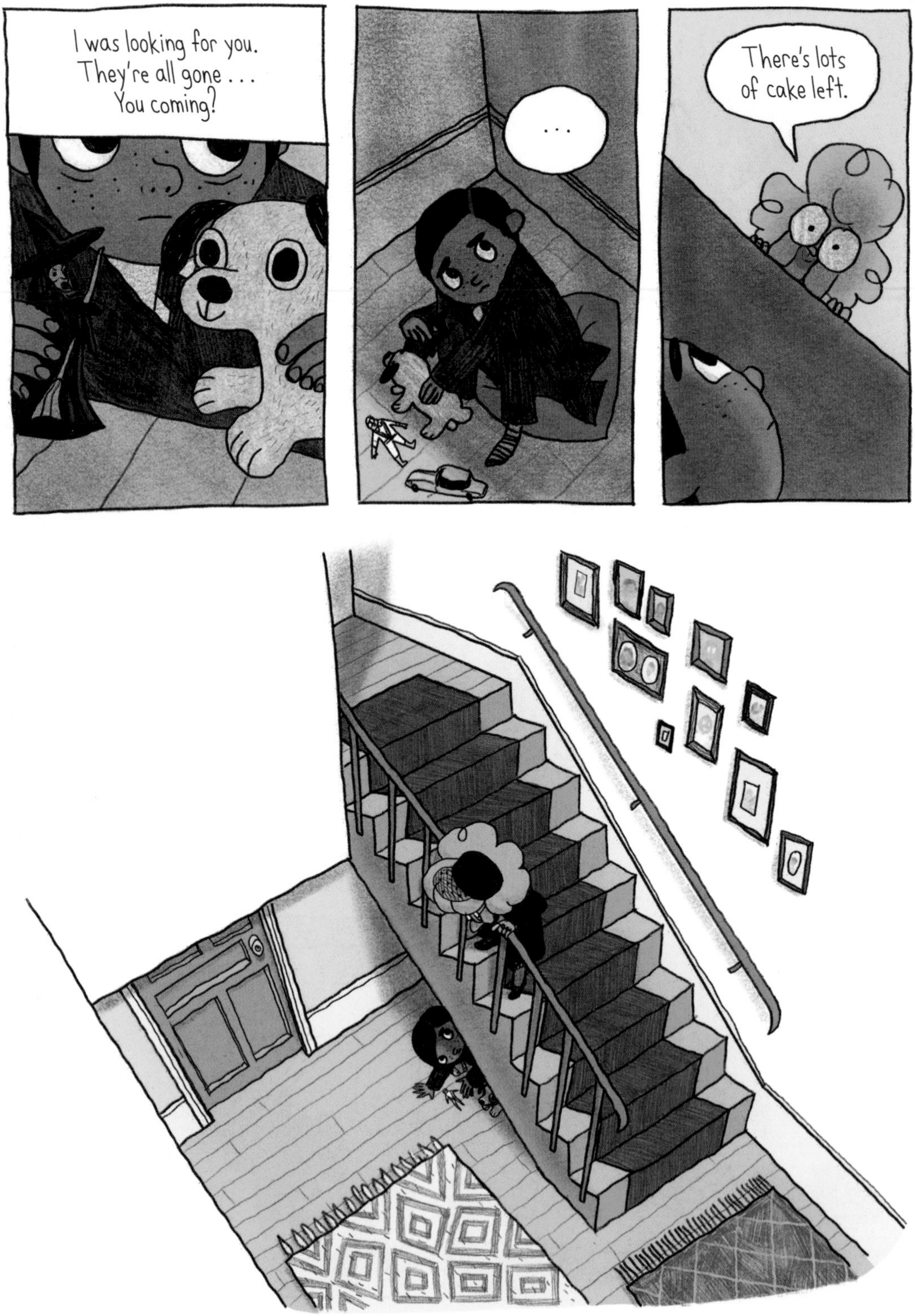
I was looking for you. They're all gone . . . You coming?
. . .
There's lots of cake left.

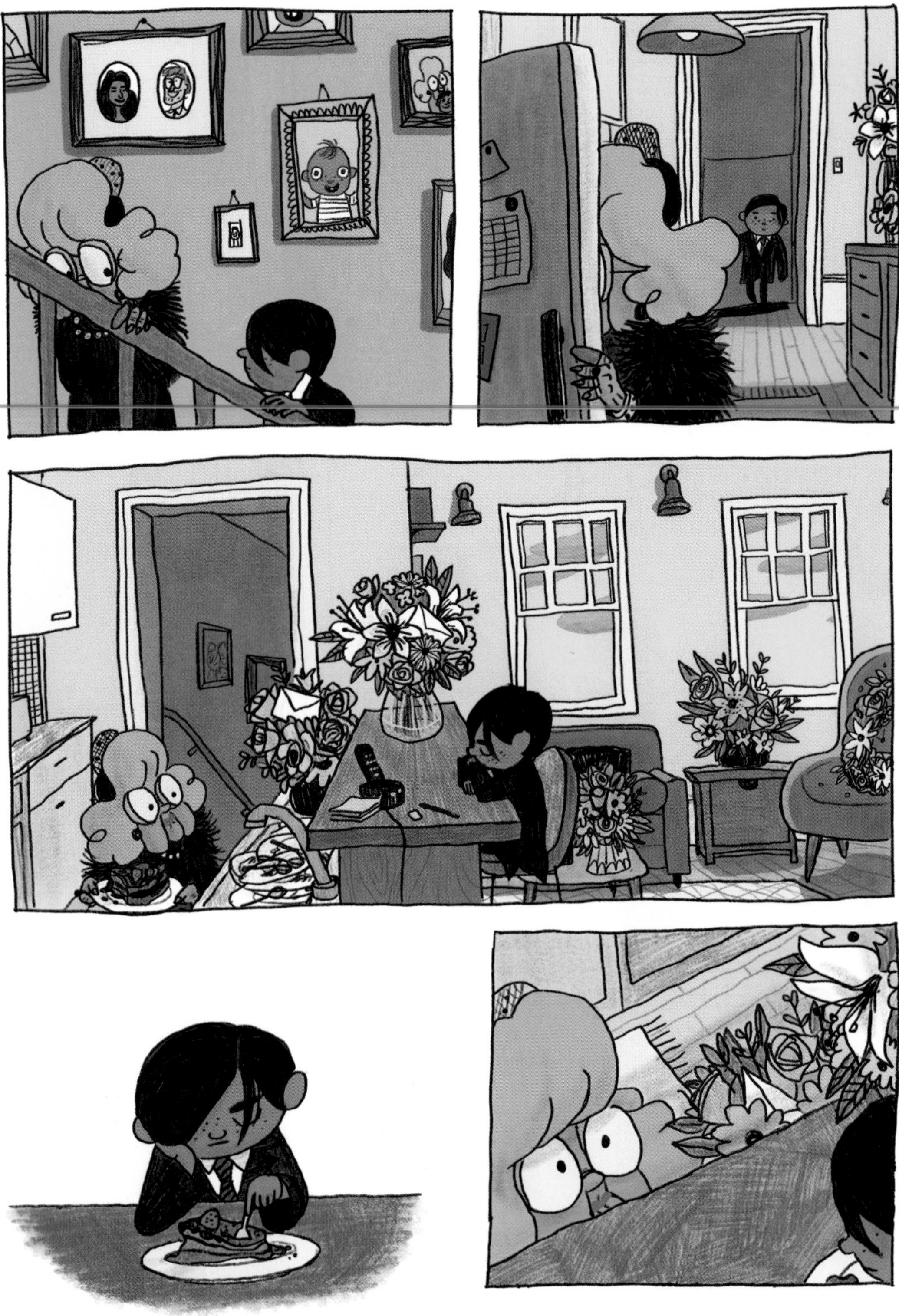

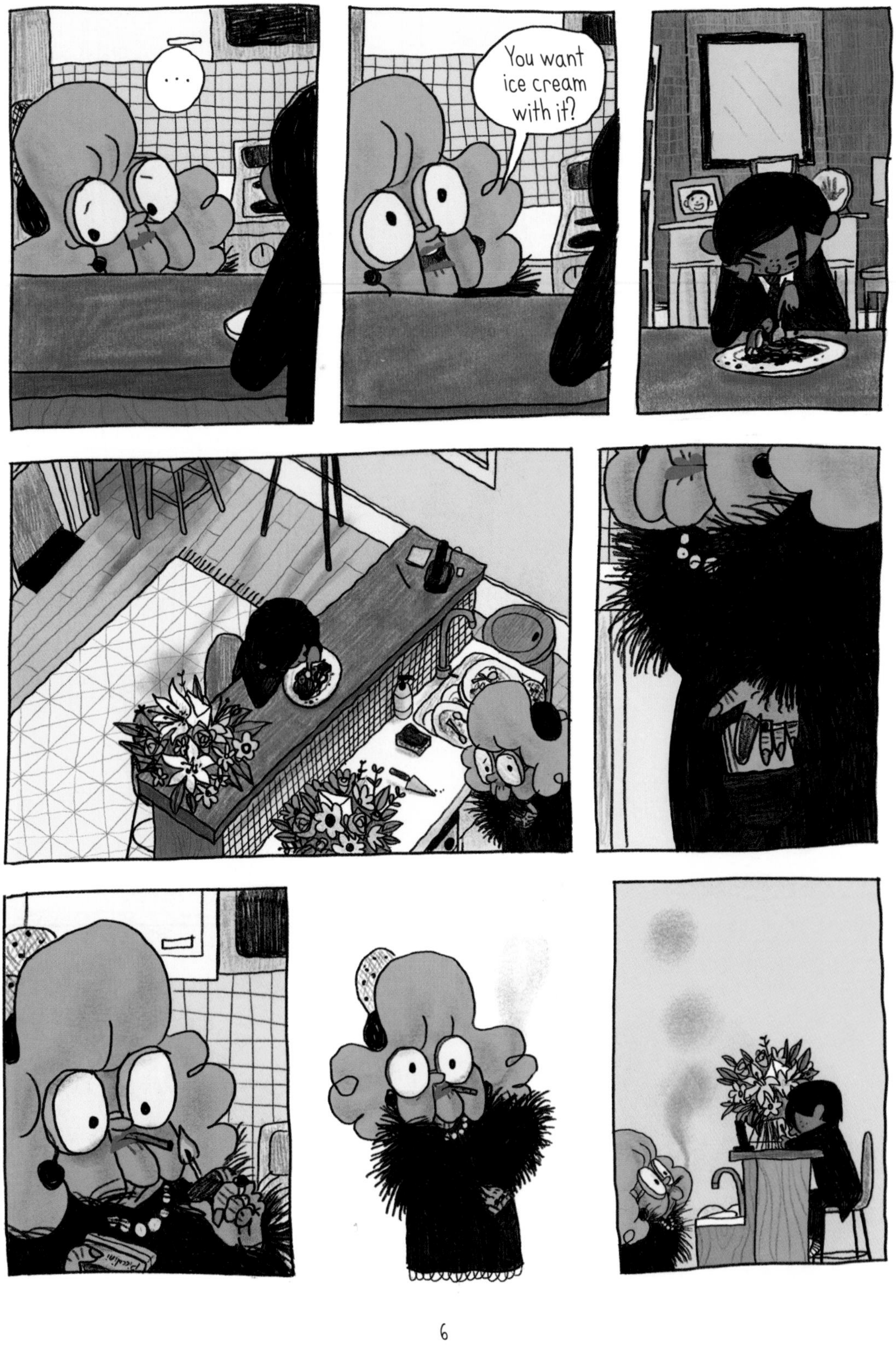
. . .
You want ice cream with it?

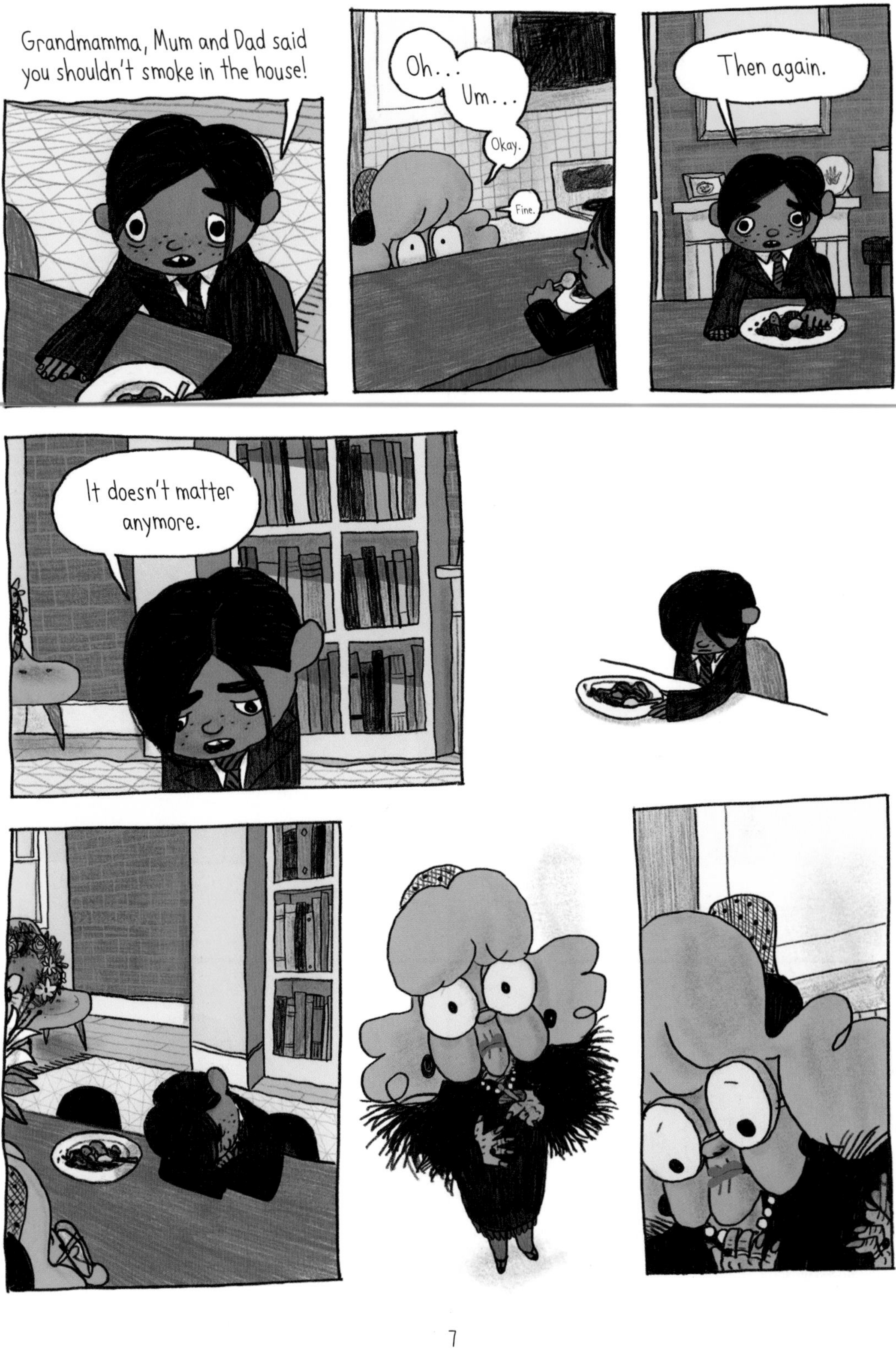

Grandmamma, Mum and Dad said you shouldn't smoke in the house!
Oh...
Um...
Okay.
Fine.
Then again.
It doesn't matter anymore.

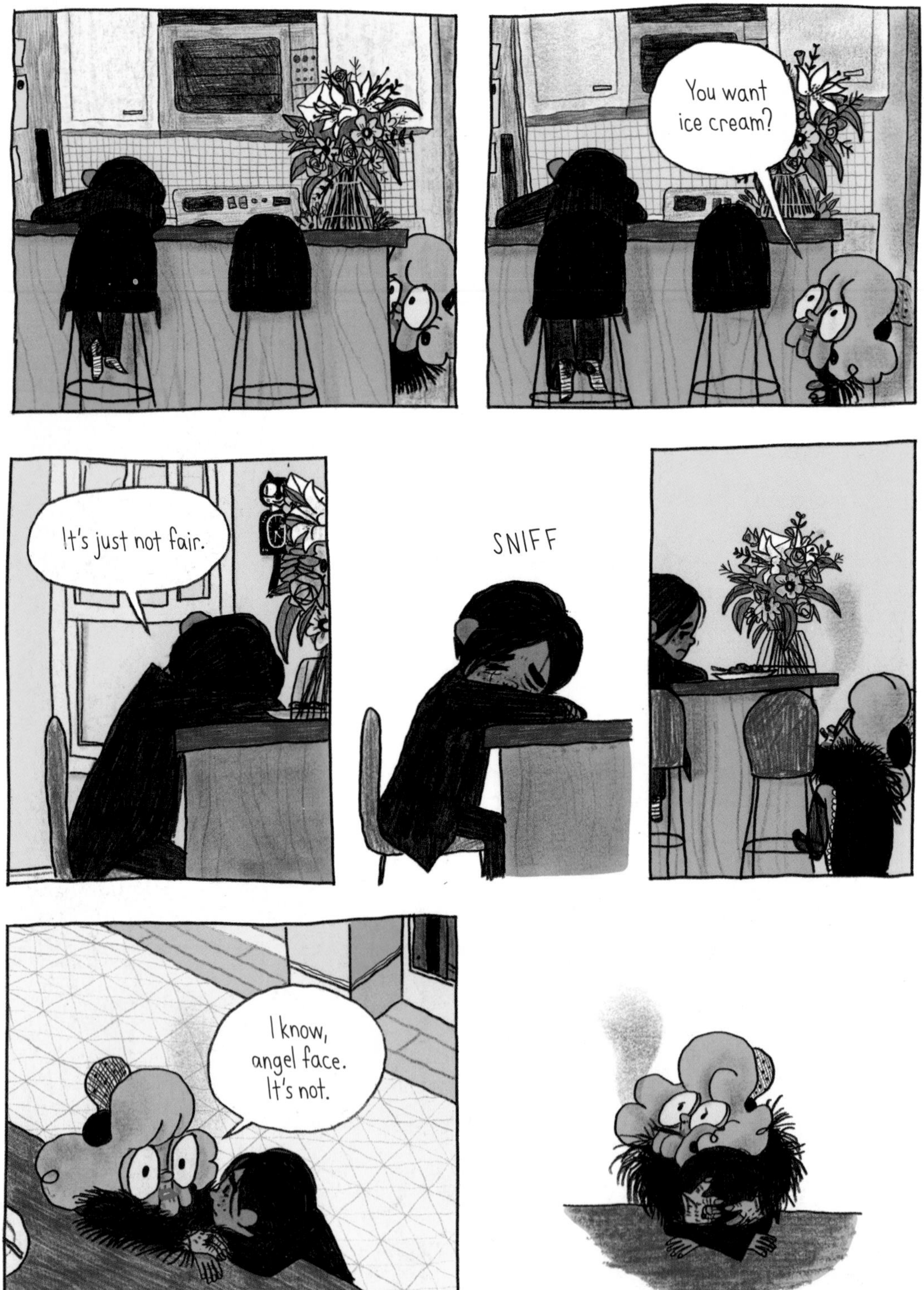
You want ice cream?
It's just not fair.
SNIFF
I know, angel face. It's not.

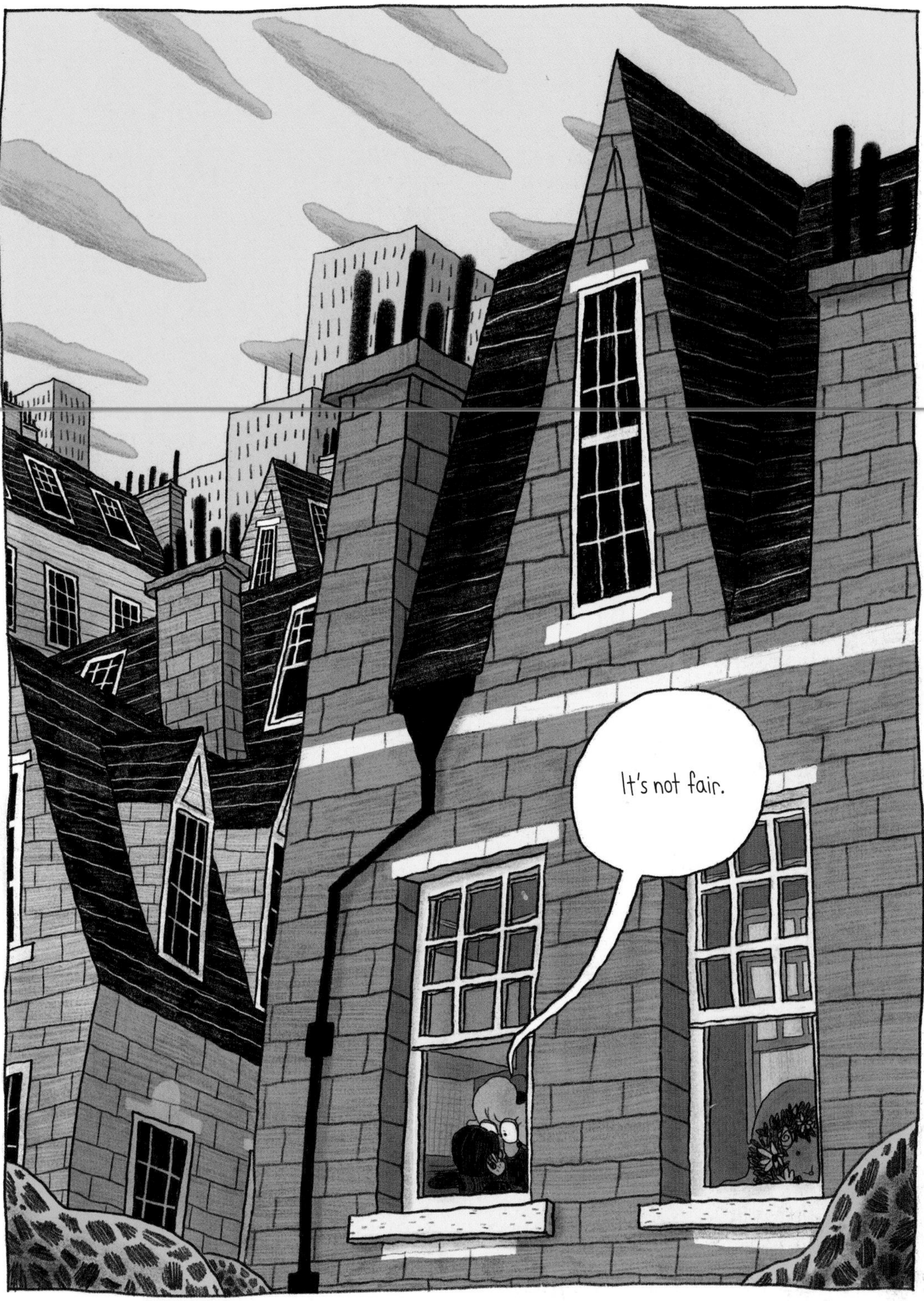
It's not fair.

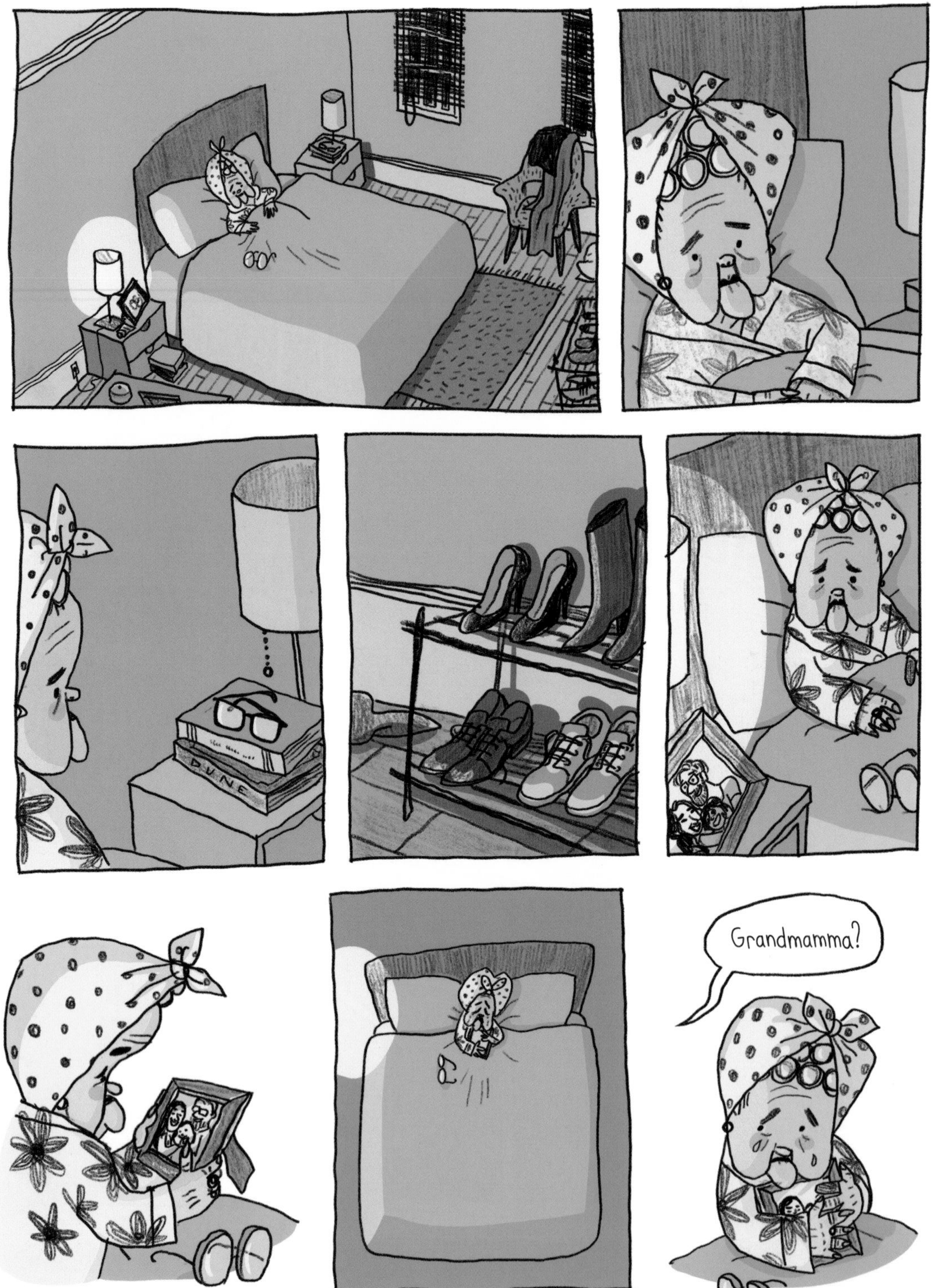
DUNE
Grandmamma?

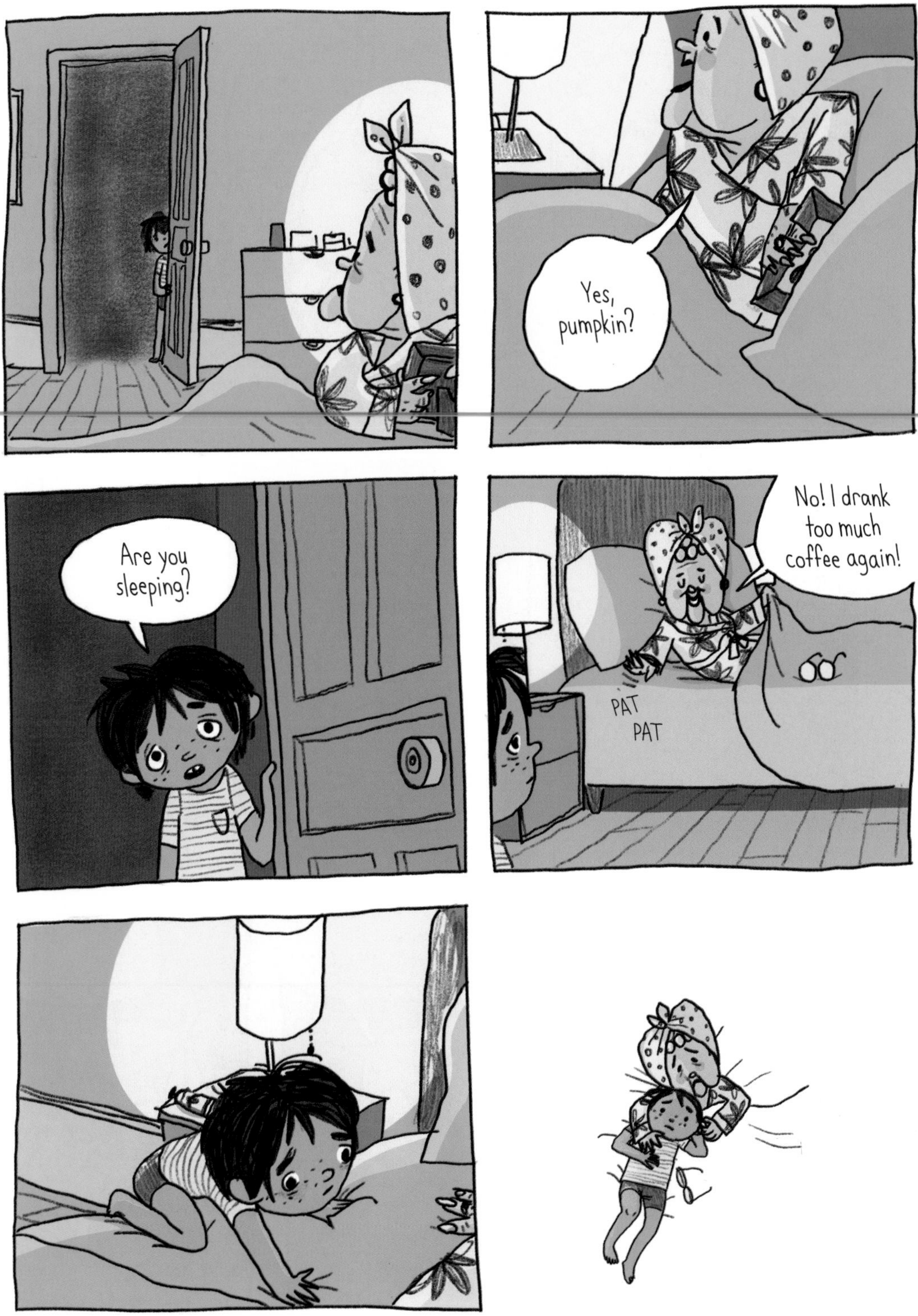
Yes, pumpkin?
Are you sleeping?
No! I drank too much coffee again!
PAT
PAT

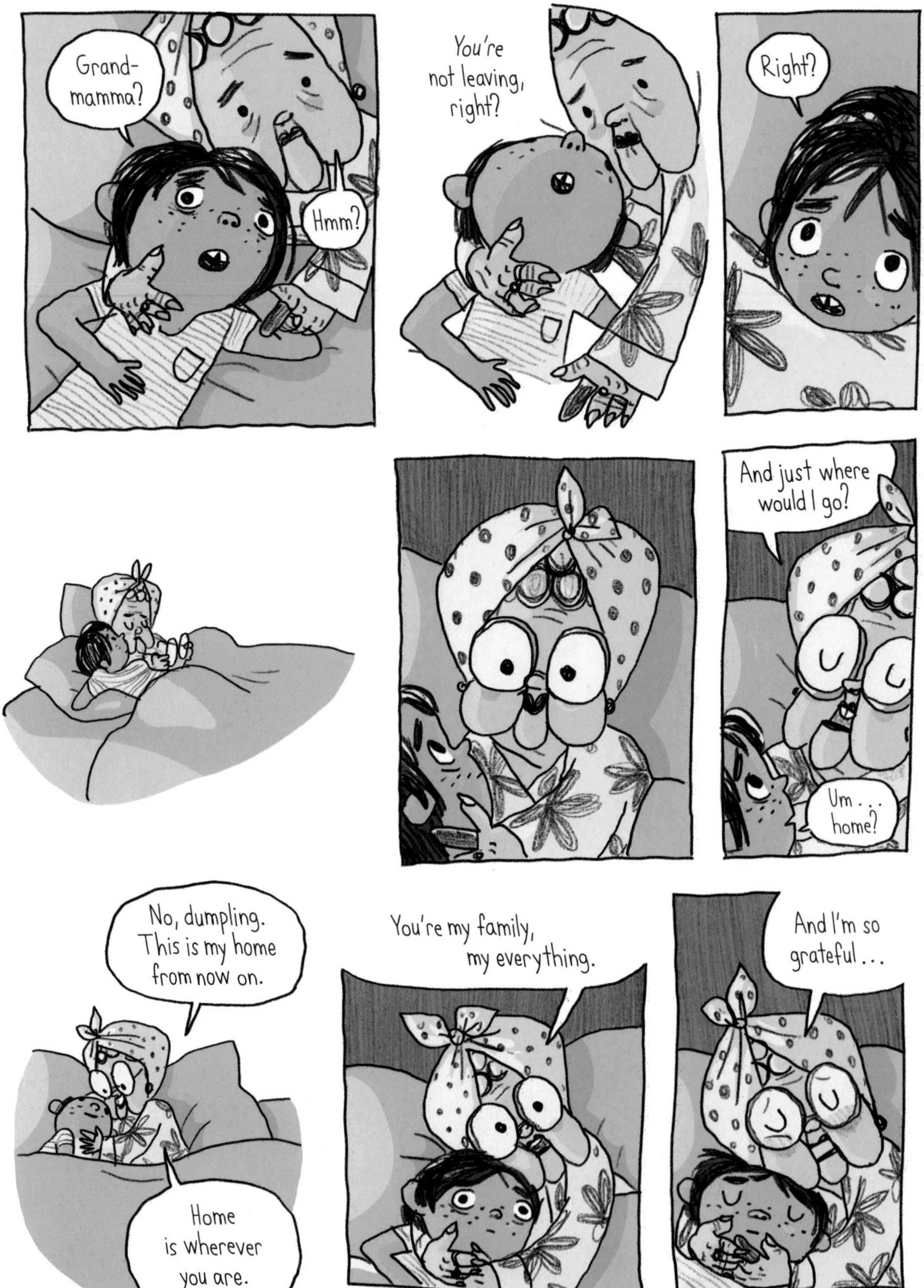

Grand-mamma?
Hmm?
You're not leaving, right?
Right?
And just where would I go?
Um . . . home?
No, dumpling. This is my home from now on.
Home is wherever you are.
You're my family, my everything.
And I'm so grateful . . .

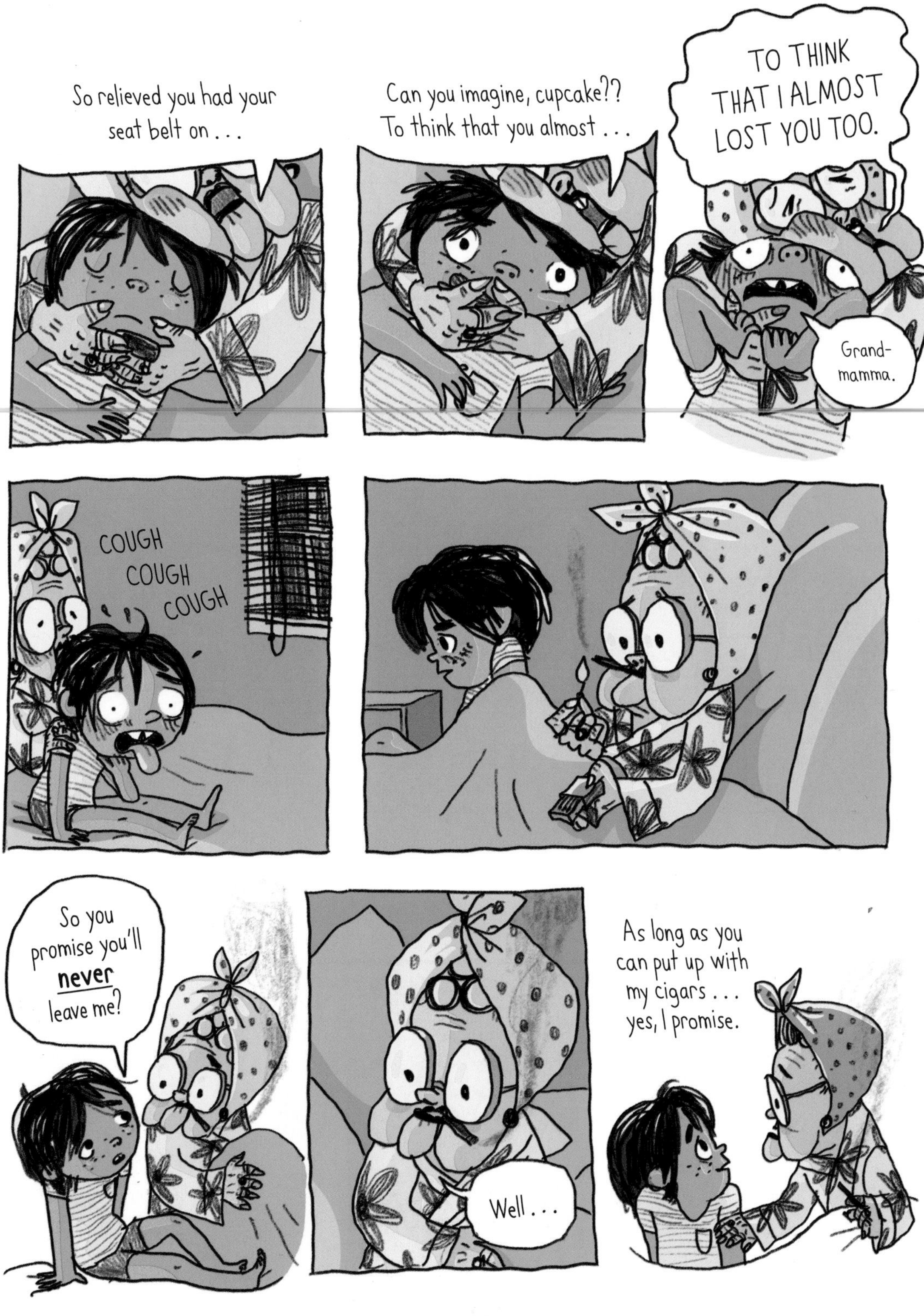

So relieved you had your seat belt on . . .
Can you imagine, cupcake?? To think that you almost . . .
TO THINK THAT I ALMOST LOST YOU TOO.
Grand-mamma.
COUGH COUGH COUGH
So you promise you'll **never** leave me?
Well . . .
As long as you can put up with my cigars . . . yes, I promise.

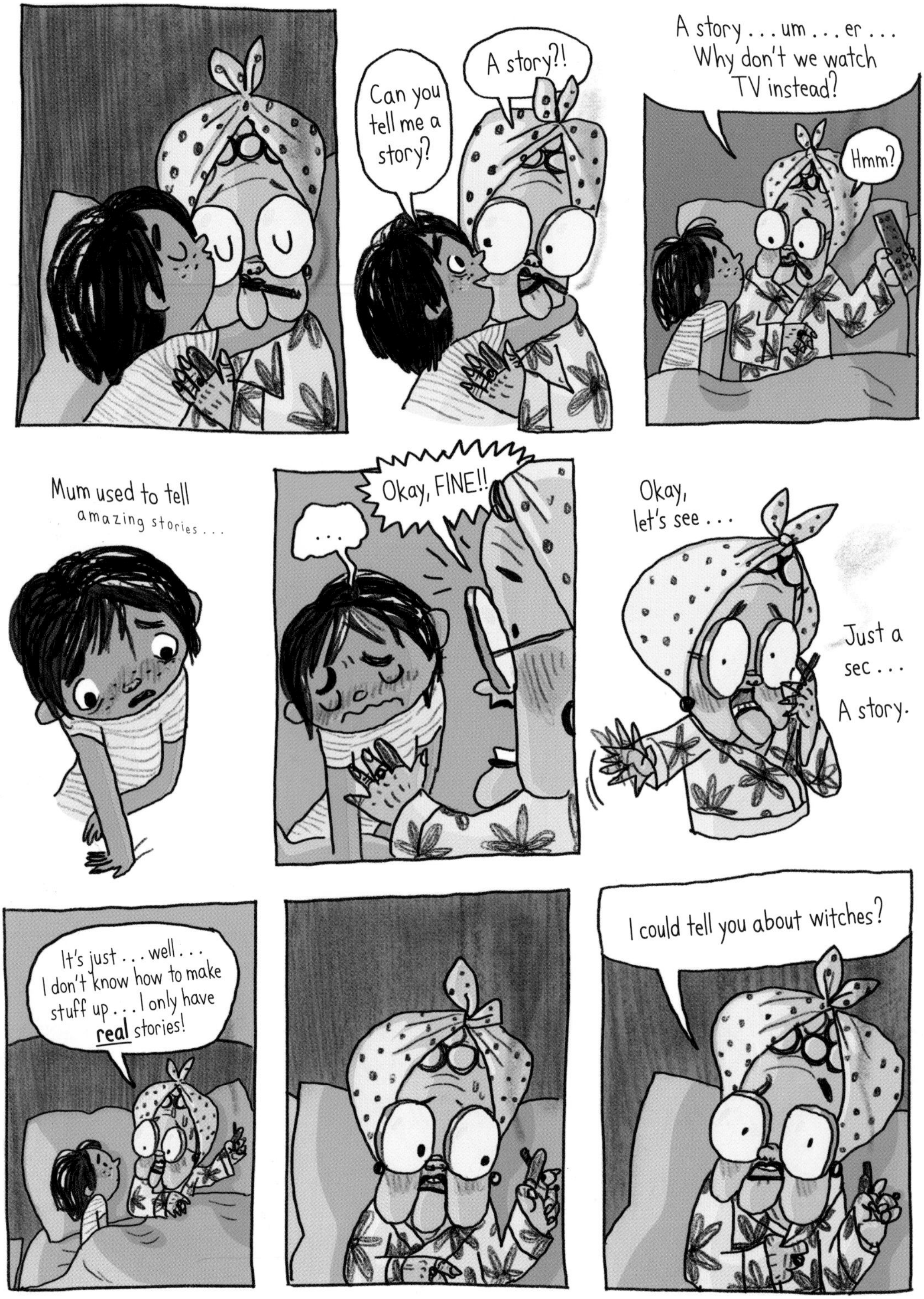
Can you tell me a story?
A story?!
A story . . . um . . . er . . . Why don't we watch TV instead?
Hmm?
Mum used to tell amazing stories . . .
. . .
Okay, FINE!!
Okay, let's see . . .
Just a sec . . .
A story.
It's just . . . well . . . I don't know how to make stuff up . . . I only have **real** stories!
I could tell you about witches?

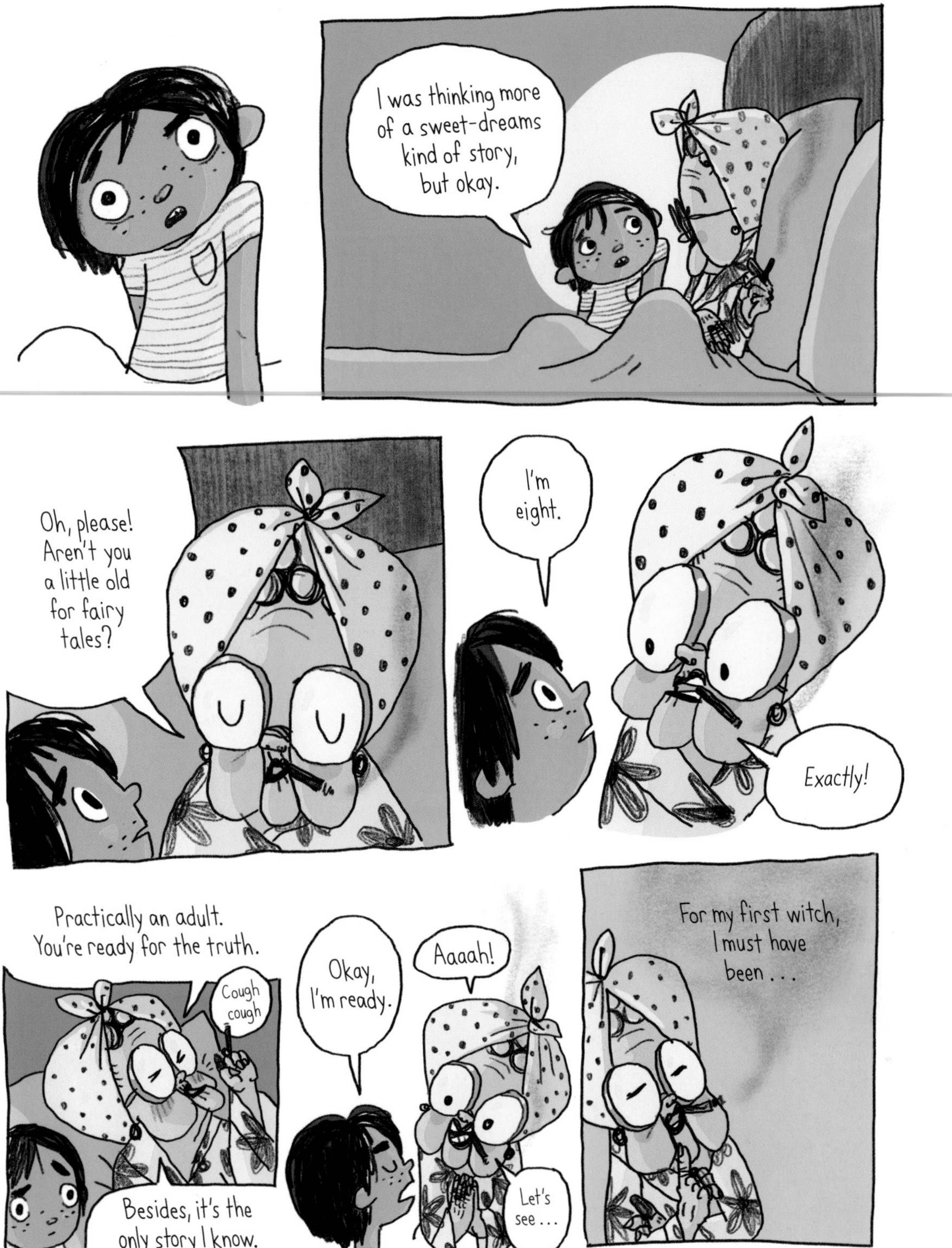
I was thinking more of a sweet-dreams kind of story, but okay.
Oh, please! Aren't you a little old for fairy tales?
I'm eight.
Exactly!
Practically an adult. You're ready for the truth.
Cough cough
Besides, it's the only story I know.
Okay, I'm ready.
Aaaah!
Let's see . . .
For my first witch, I must have been . . .

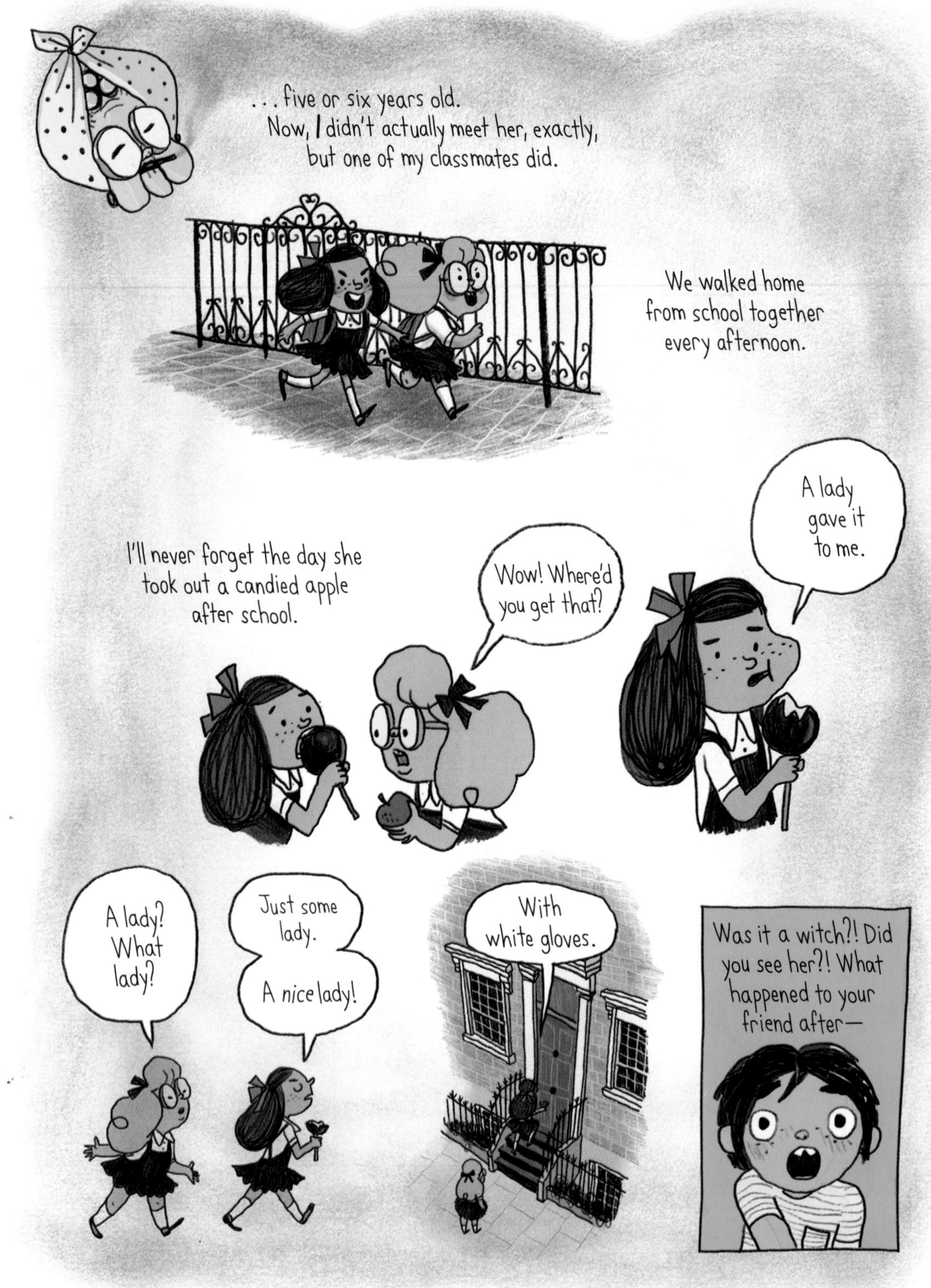

. . . five or six years old.
Now, I didn't actually meet her, exactly, but one of my classmates did.
We walked home from school together every afternoon.
I'll never forget the day she took out a candied apple after school.
Wow! Where'd you get that?
A lady gave it to me.
A lady? What lady?
Just some lady.
A *nice* lady!
With white gloves.
Was it a witch?! Did you see her?! What happened to your friend after—

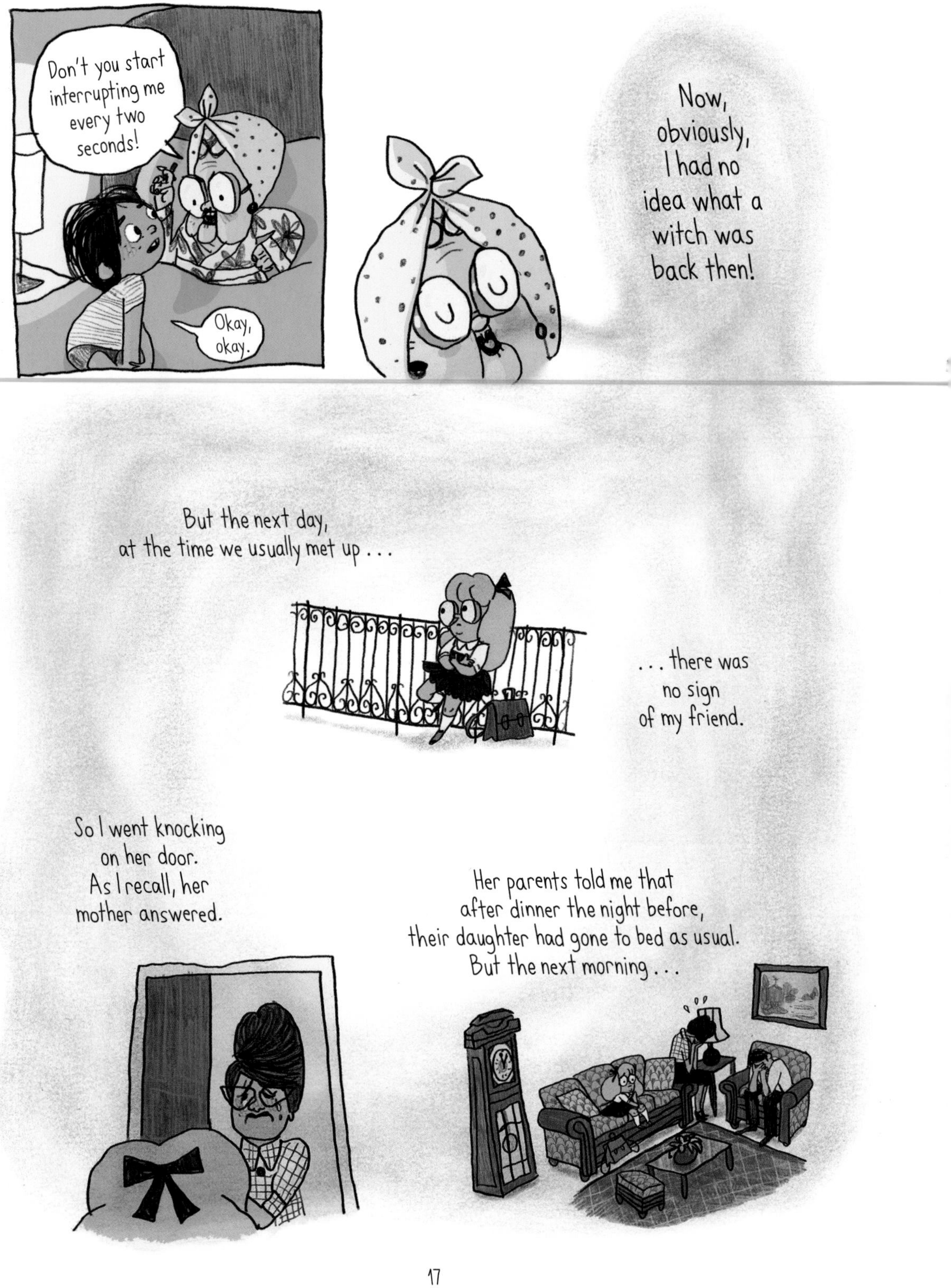
Don't you start interrupting me every two seconds!
Okay, okay.
Now, obviously, I had no idea what a witch was back then!
But the next day, at the time we usually met up . . .
. . . there was no sign of my friend.
So I went knocking on her door. As I recall, her mother answered.
Her parents told me that after dinner the night before, their daughter had gone to bed as usual. But the next morning . . .

... she wasn't
in her bed ...

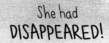
She had
DISAPPEARED!

Now, I know
what you're
going to say:

But

"People don't just
suddenly DISAPPEAR!"

Well, my friend **did**.
The police looked for her everywhere,
for weeks.

She had simply vanished <u>into thin air</u>.

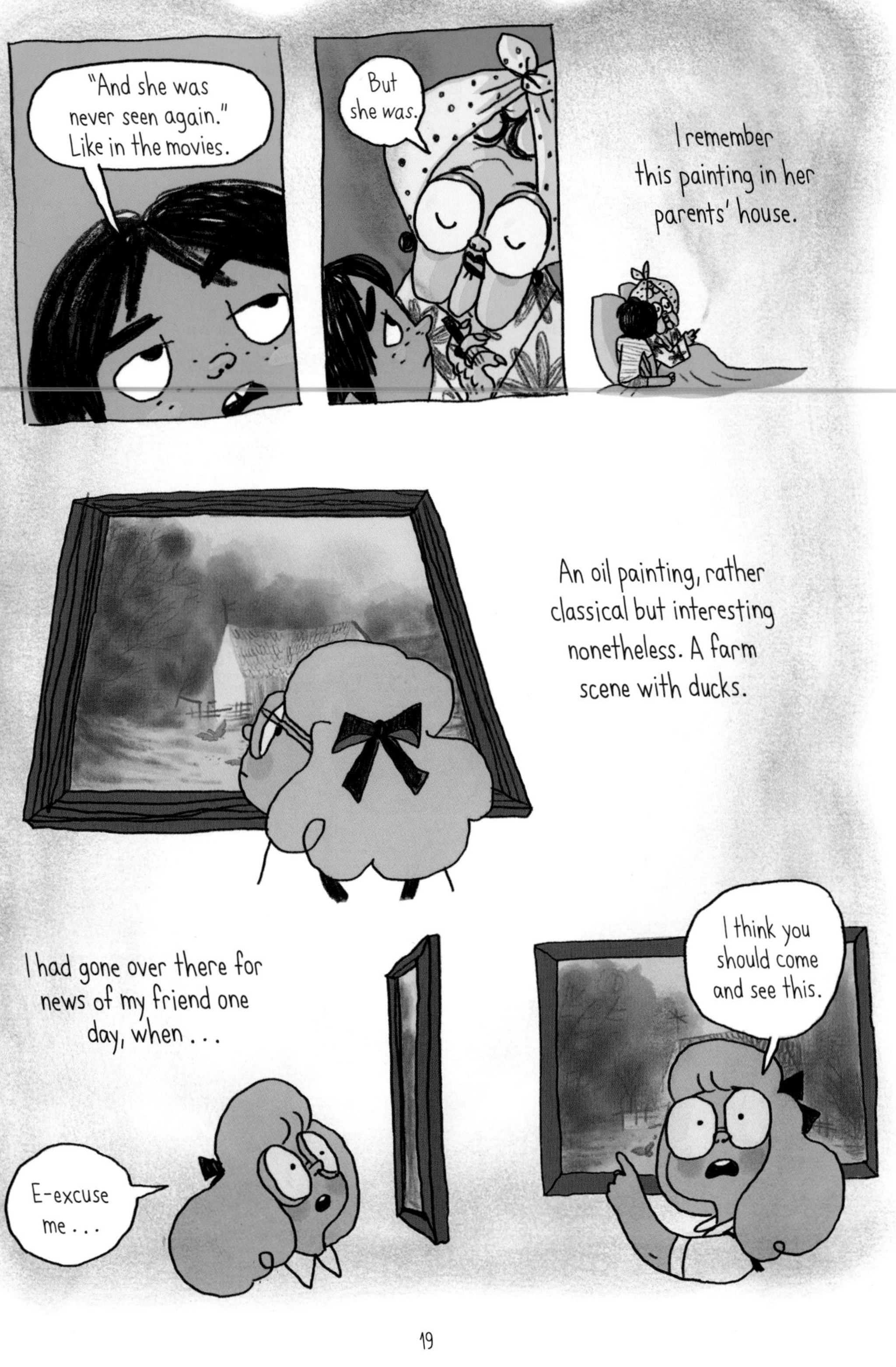

"And she was never seen again." Like in the movies.
But she was.
I remember this painting in her parents' house.
An oil painting, rather classical but interesting nonetheless. A farm scene with ducks.
I had gone over there for news of my friend one day, when . . .
E-excuse me . . .
I think you should come and see this.

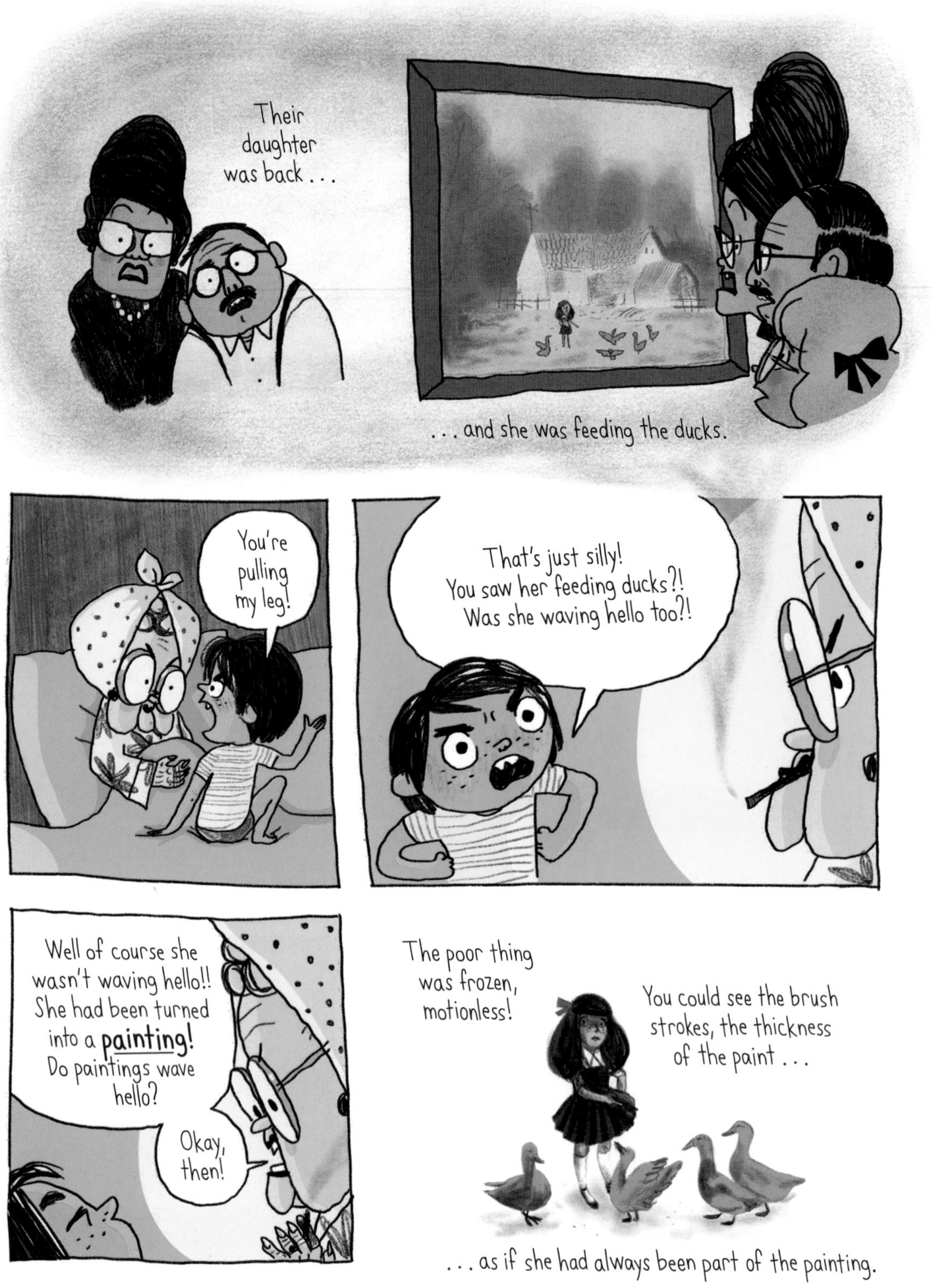

Their daughter was back . . .
. . . and she was feeding the ducks.
You're pulling my leg!
That's just silly! You saw her feeding ducks?! Was she waving hello too?!
Well of course she wasn't waving hello!! She had been turned into a **painting**! Do paintings wave hello?
Okay, then!
The poor thing was frozen, motionless!
You could see the brush strokes, the thickness of the paint . . .
. . . as if she had always been part of the painting.

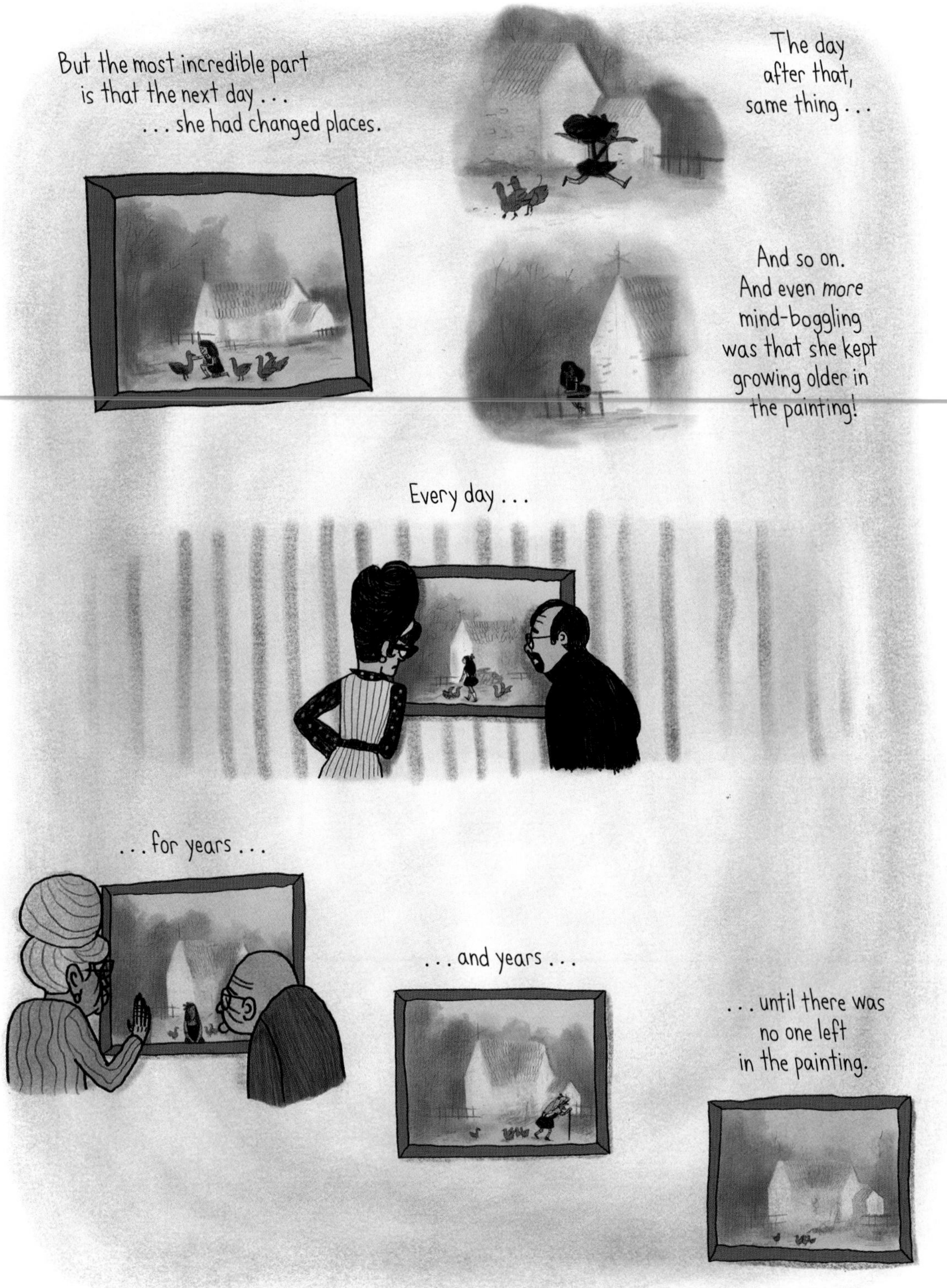
But the most incredible part is that the next day . . .
. . . she had changed places.
The day after that, same thing . . .
And so on. And even *more* mind-boggling was that she kept growing older in the painting!
Every day . . .
. . . for years . . .
. . . and years . . .
. . . until there was no one left in the painting.

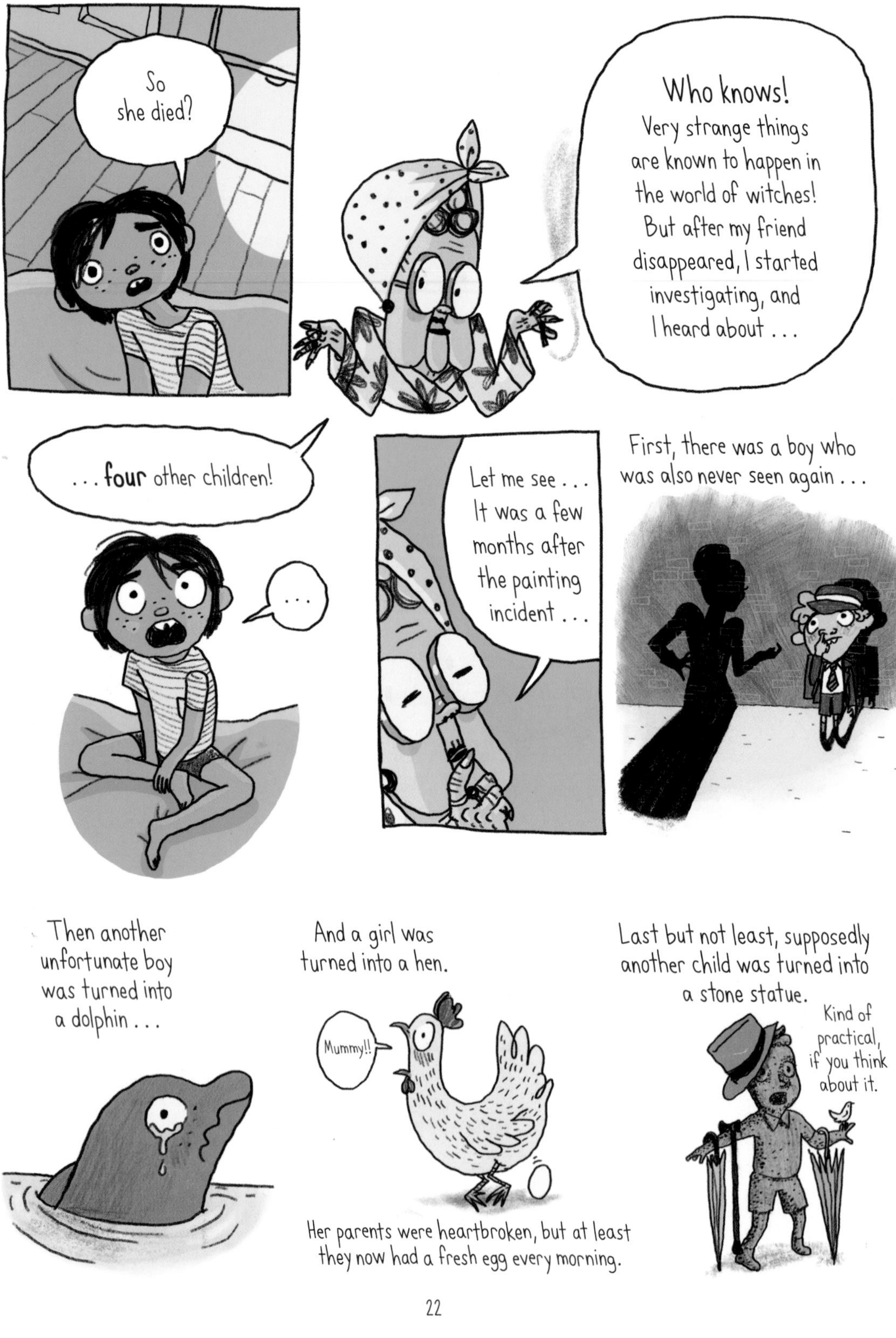

So she died?
Who knows! Very strange things are known to happen in the world of witches! But after my friend disappeared, I started investigating, and I heard about . . .
. . . **four** other children!
. . .
Let me see . . . It was a few months after the painting incident . . .
First, there was a boy who was also never seen again . . .
Then another unfortunate boy was turned into a dolphin . . .
And a girl was turned into a hen.
Mummy!!
Her parents were heartbroken, but at least they now had a fresh egg every morning.
Last but not least, supposedly another child was turned into a stone statue.
Kind of practical, if you think about it.

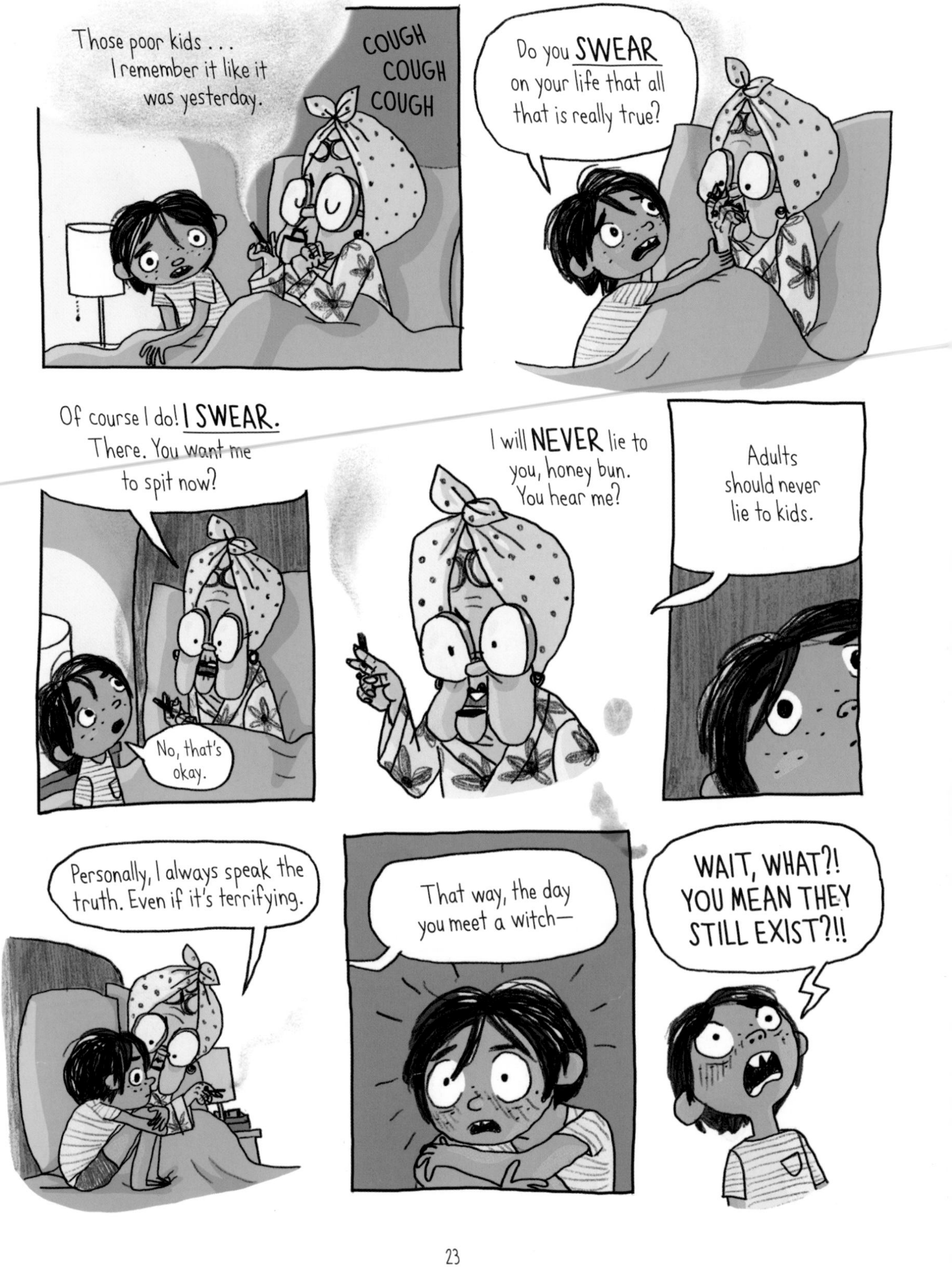

Those poor kids . . . I remember it like it was yesterday.
COUGH COUGH COUGH
Do you SWEAR on your life that all that is really true?
Of course I do! I SWEAR. There. You want me to spit now?
No, that's okay.
I will NEVER lie to you, honey bun. You hear me?
Adults should never lie to kids.
Personally, I always speak the truth. Even if it's terrifying.
That way, the day you meet a witch—
WAIT, WHAT?! YOU MEAN THEY STILL EXIST?!!

I THOUGHT IT WAS ONLY WHEN **YOU** WERE LITTLE!

LIKE, 100 YEARS AGO!

Nope. No such luck.

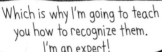

Which is why I'm going to teach you how to recognize them. I'm an expert!

But . . . but what if a witch climbs in through our window *tonight*?!

Nah!

No witch is silly enough to climb up the side of the house, my boy.

CLICK

You will <u>ALWAYS</u> be safe with me.

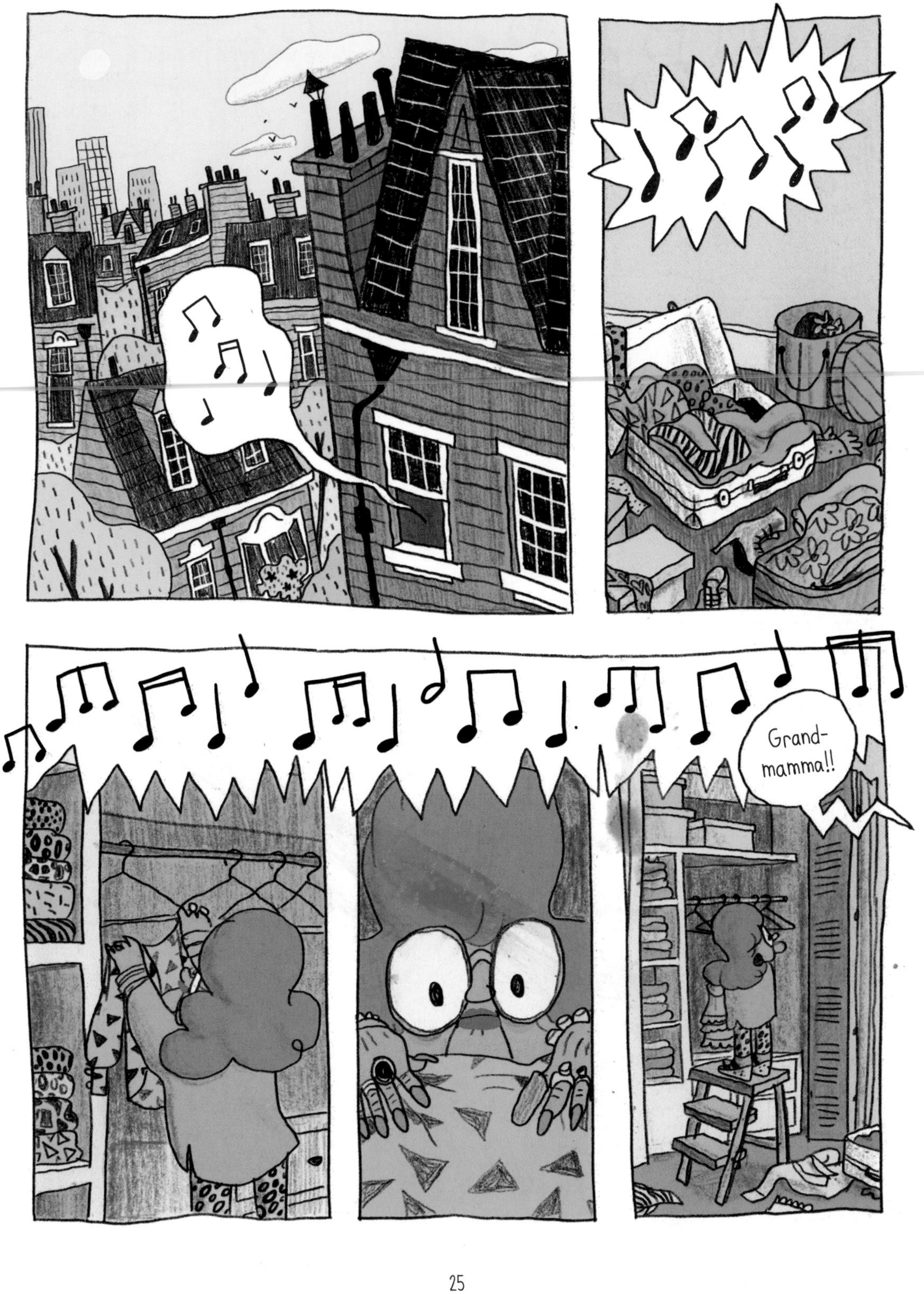
Grand-
mamma!!

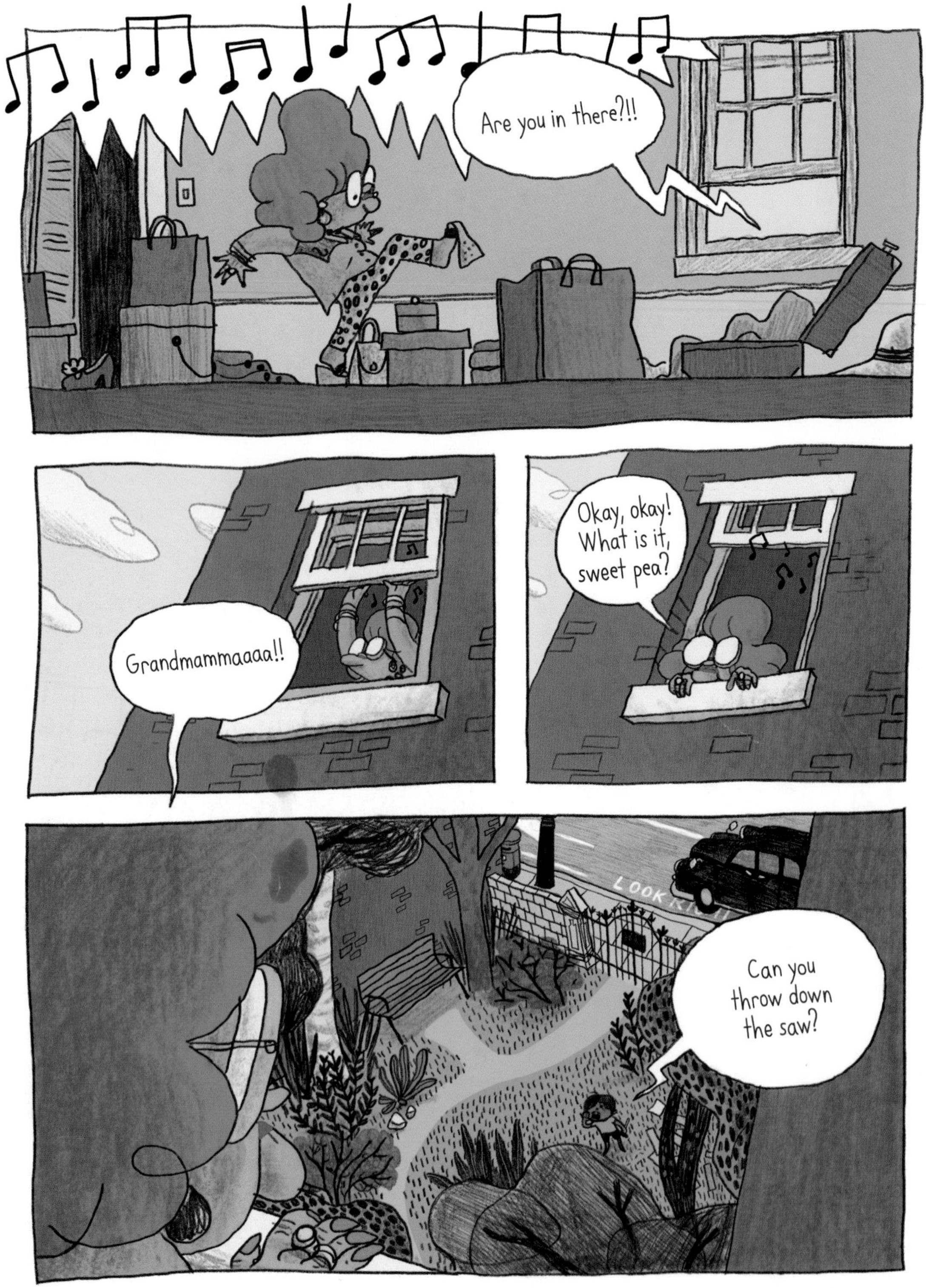
Are you in there?!!
Grandmammaaaa!!
Okay, okay! What is it, sweet pea?
LOOK
Can you throw down the saw?

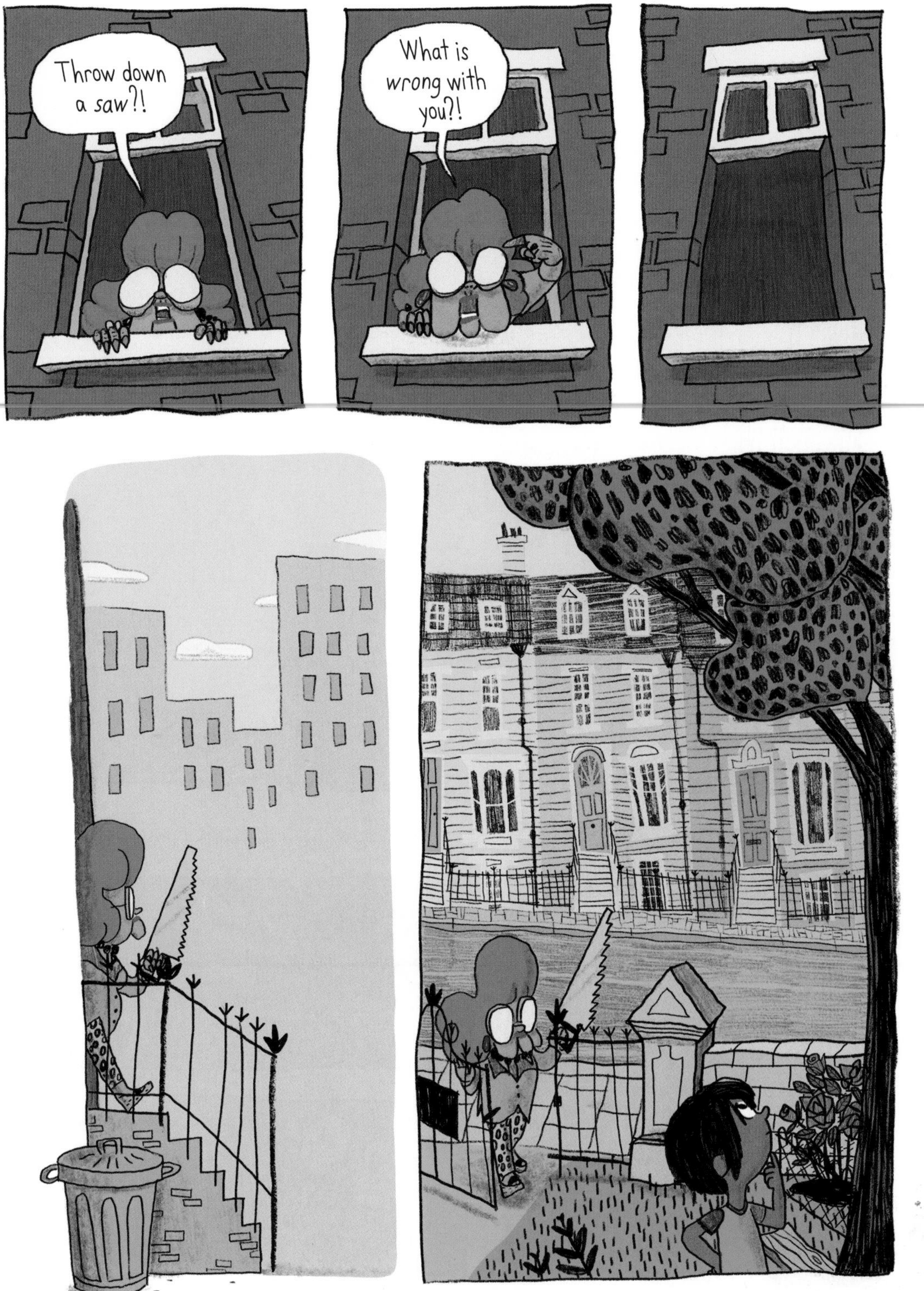
Throw down a saw?!
What is wrong with you?!

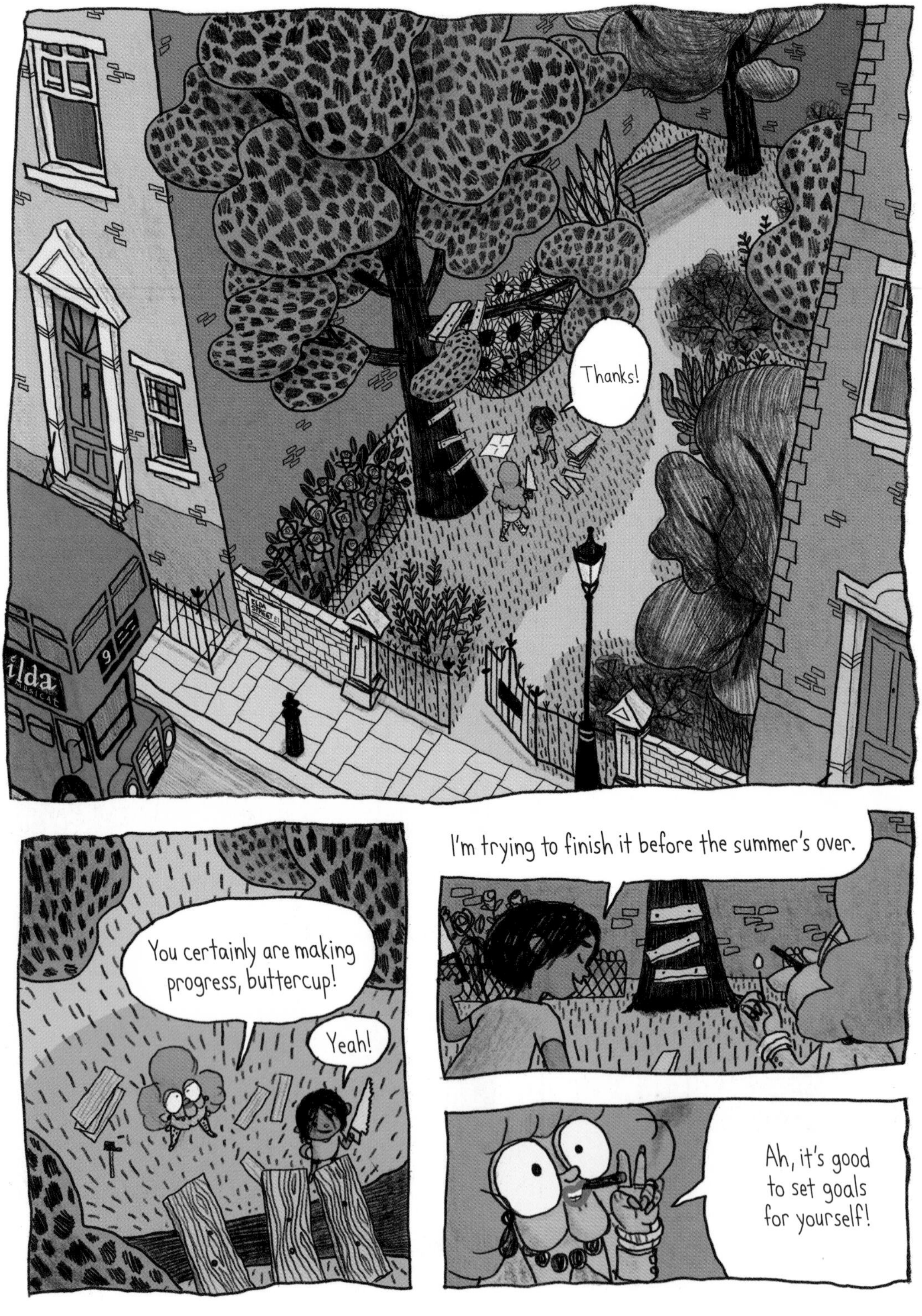
Thanks!
You certainly are making progress, buttercup!
Yeah!
I'm trying to finish it before the summer's over.
Ah, it's good to set goals for yourself!

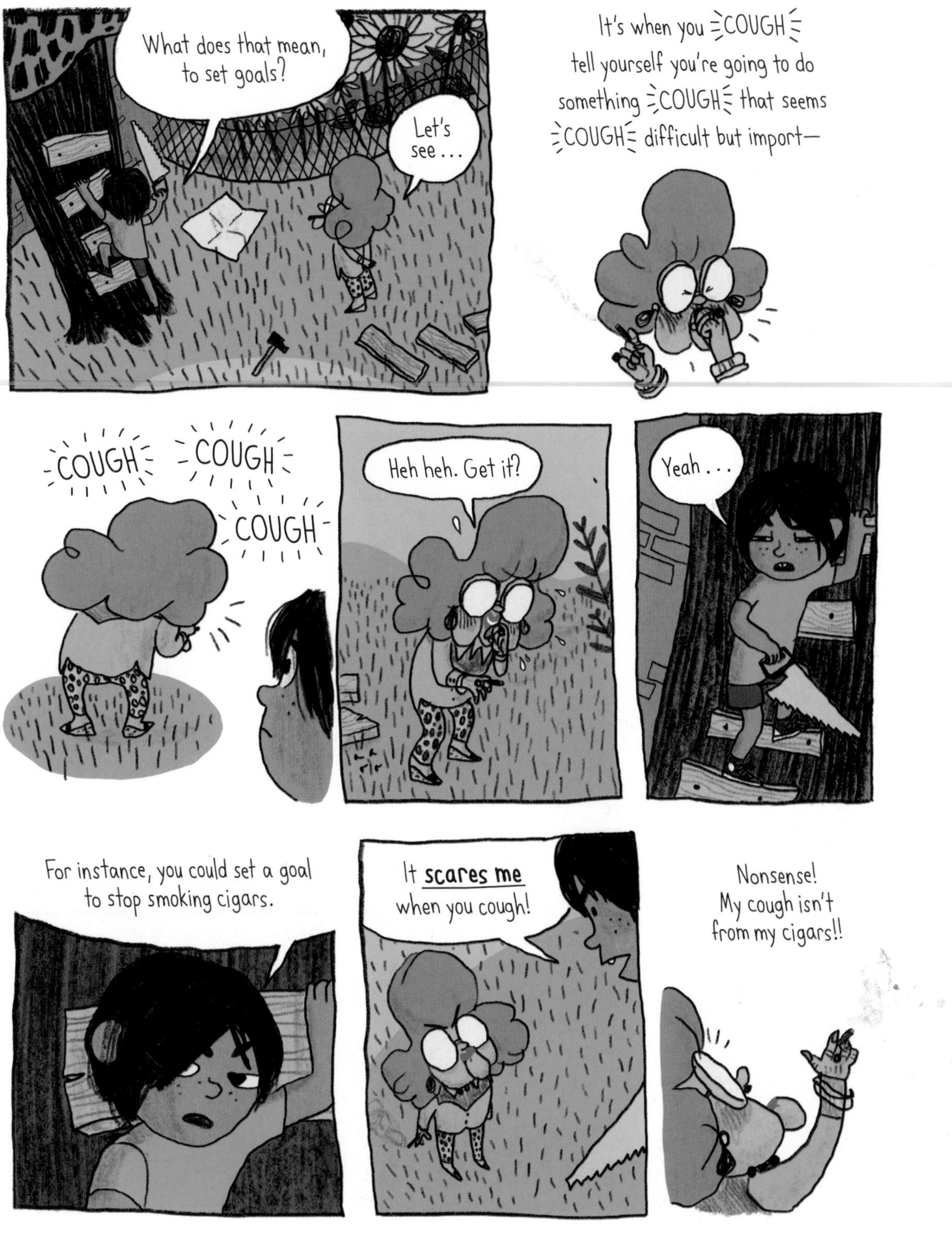

What does that mean, to set goals?
Let's see . . .
It's when you COUGH tell yourself you're going to do something COUGH that seems COUGH difficult but import—
COUGH
COUGH
COUGH
Heh heh. Get it?
Yeah . . .
For instance, you could set a goal to stop smoking cigars.
It **scares me** when you cough!
Nonsense! My cough isn't from my cigars!!

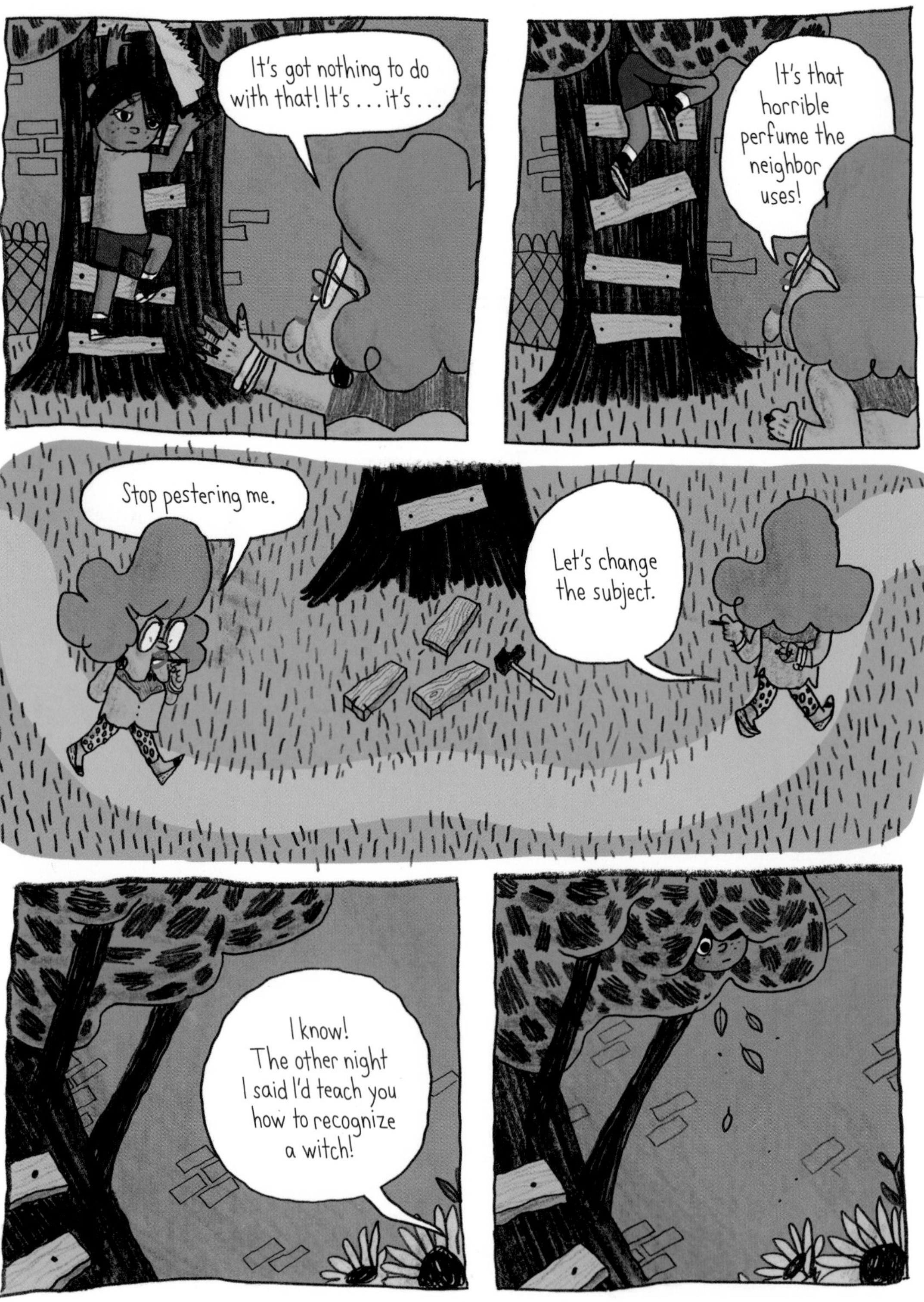
It's got nothing to do with that! It's . . . it's . . .
It's that horrible perfume the neighbor uses!
Stop pestering me.
Let's change the subject.
I know! The other night I said I'd teach you how to recognize a witch!

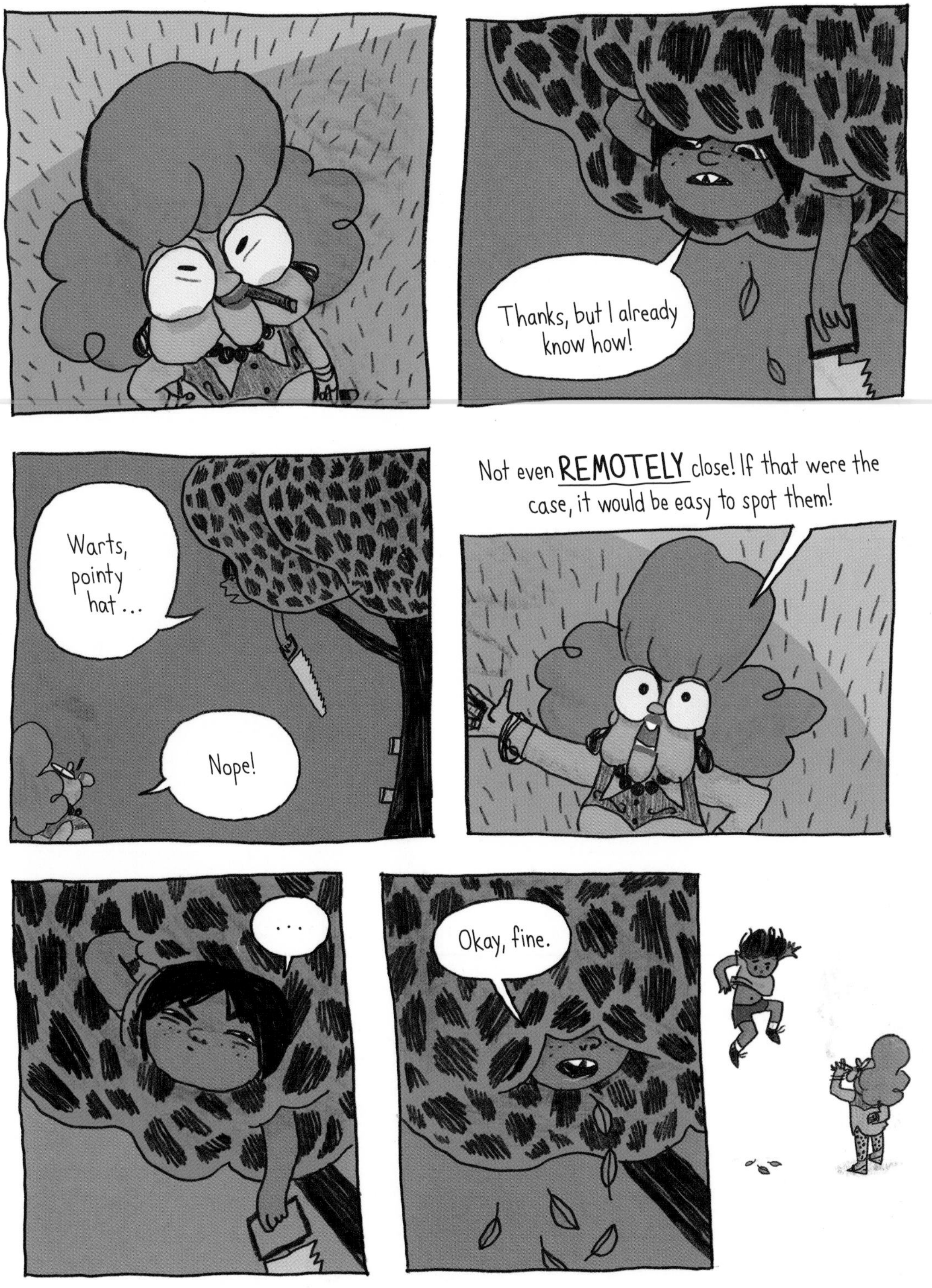
Thanks, but I already know how!
Warts, pointy hat...
Nope!
Not even REMOTELY close! If that were the case, it would be easy to spot them!
...
Okay, fine.

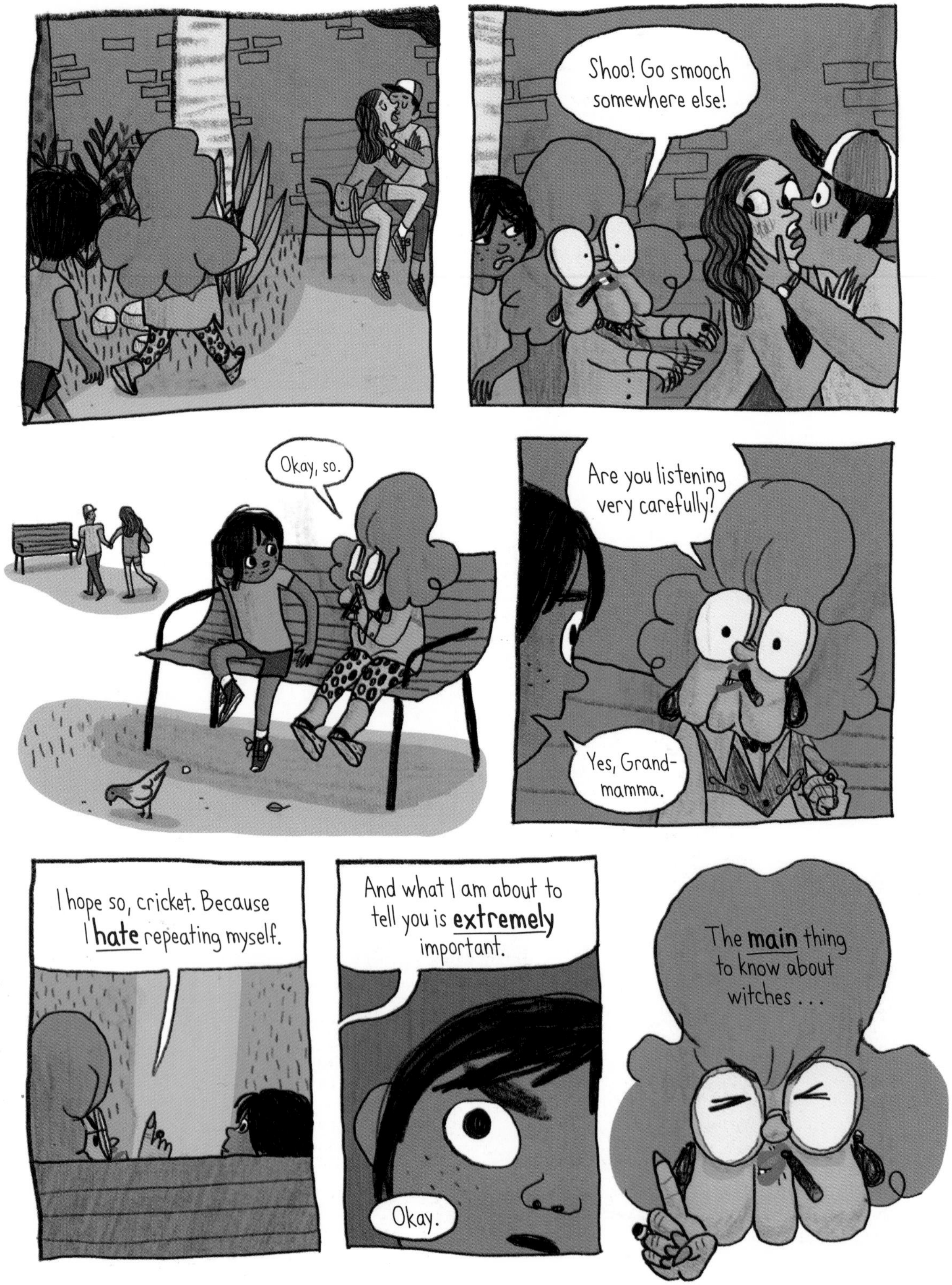
Shoo! Go smooch somewhere else!
Okay, so.
Are you listening very carefully?
Yes, Grand-mamma.
I hope so, cricket. Because I **hate** repeating myself.
And what I am about to tell you is **extremely** important.
Okay.
The **main** thing to know about witches . . .

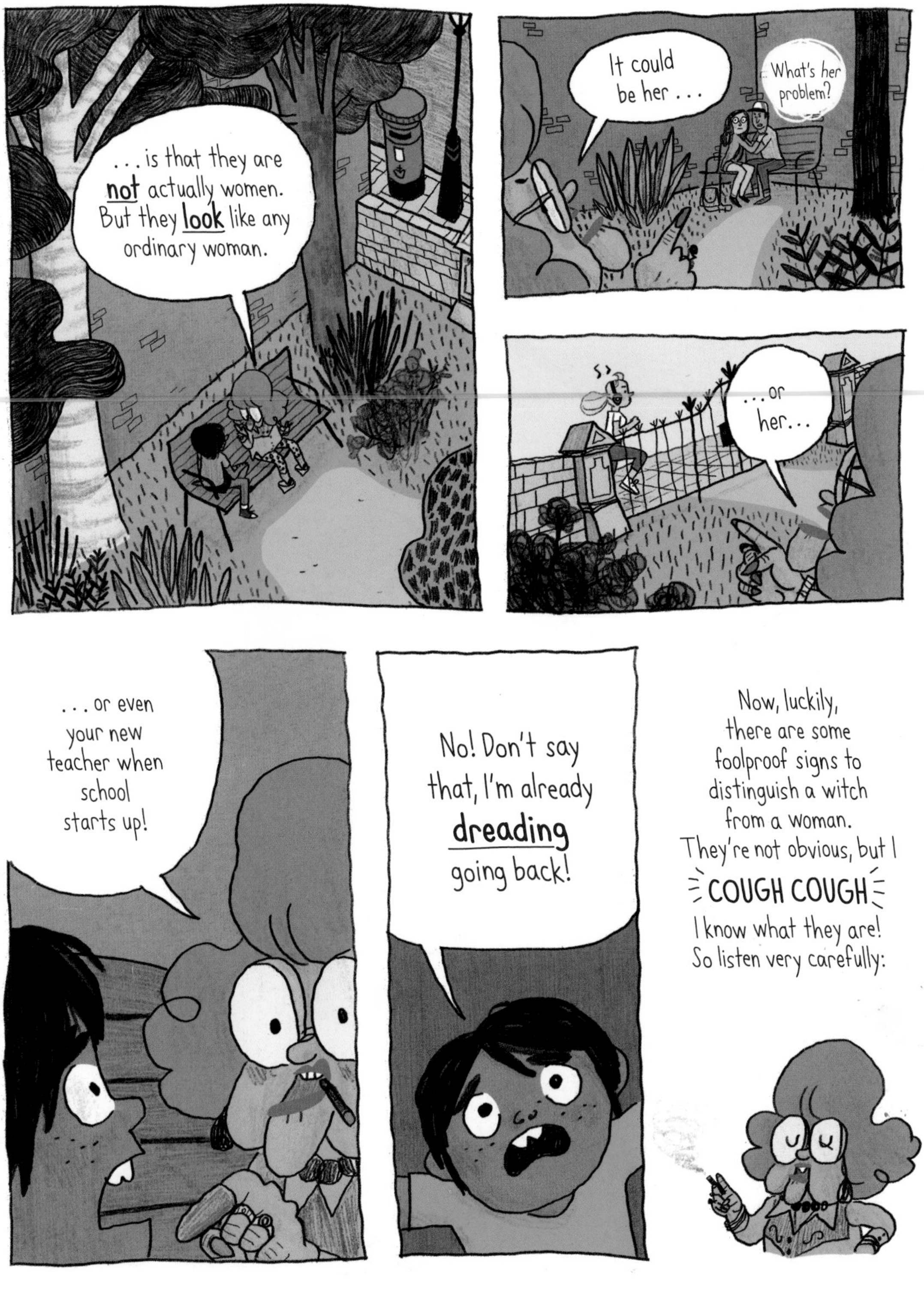
. . . is that they are **not** actually women. But they **look** like any ordinary woman.
It could be her . . .
What's her problem?
. . . or her . . .
. . . or even your new teacher when school starts up!
No! Don't say that, I'm already **dreading** going back!
Now, luckily, there are some foolproof signs to distinguish a witch from a woman. They're not obvious, but I
COUGH COUGH
I know what they are! So listen very carefully:

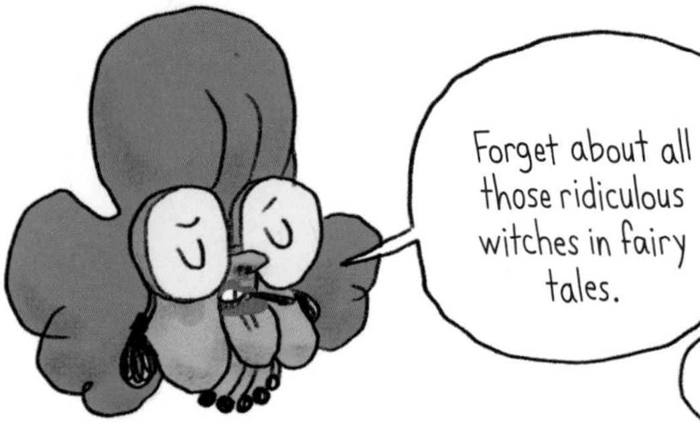
Forget about all those ridiculous witches in fairy tales.

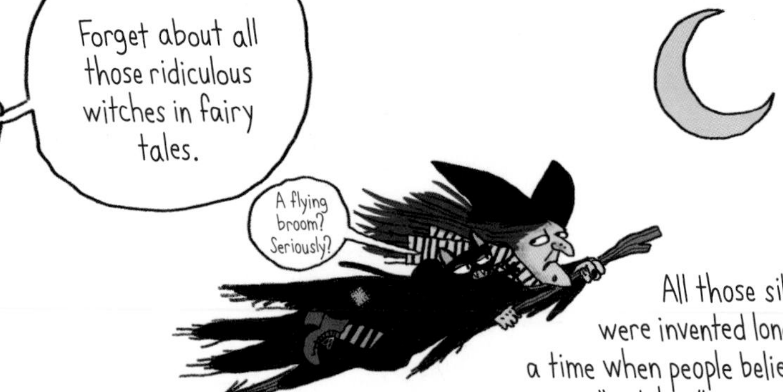
A flying broom? Seriously?

All those silly ideas were invented long ago, at a time when people believed they were seeing "witches" everywhere . . . It didn't take much for a woman to be accused of being a witch. People were suspicious of unruly old women and believed they had evil powers!

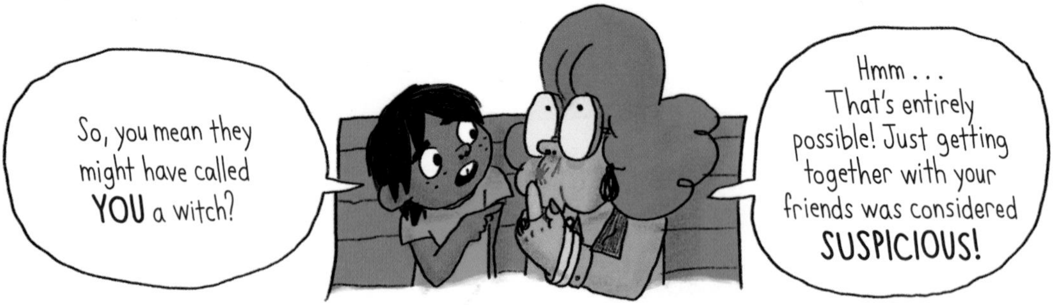
So, you mean they might have called YOU a witch?
Hmm . . . That's entirely possible! Just getting together with your friends was considered SUSPICIOUS!

Simply not having a husband or treating your cold with herbal remedies . . .

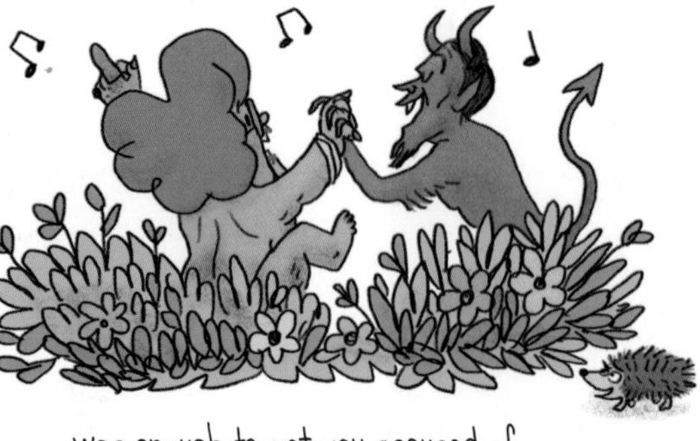

. . . was enough to get you accused of DANCING NAKED WITH THE DEVIL.

In order to "prove" you were definitely a witch, they would throw you in the water to see if you would float.

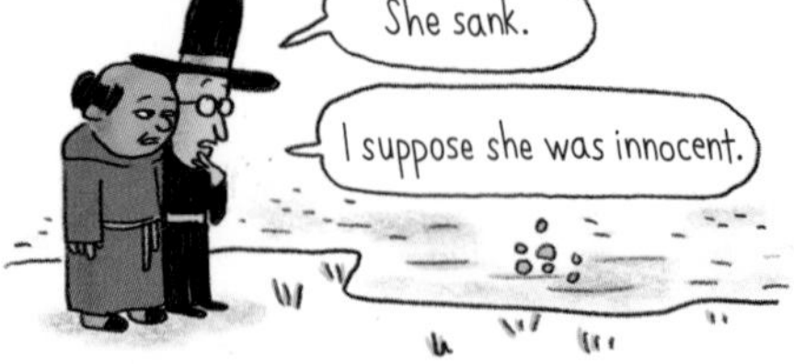
She sank.
I suppose she was innocent.

And they'd find very persuasive ways to get you to confess.

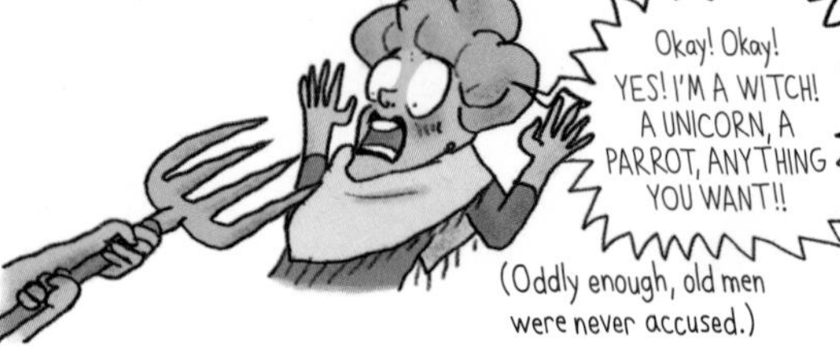
Okay! Okay! YES! I'M A WITCH! A UNICORN, A PARROT, ANYTHING YOU WANT!!

(Oddly enough, old men were never accused.)

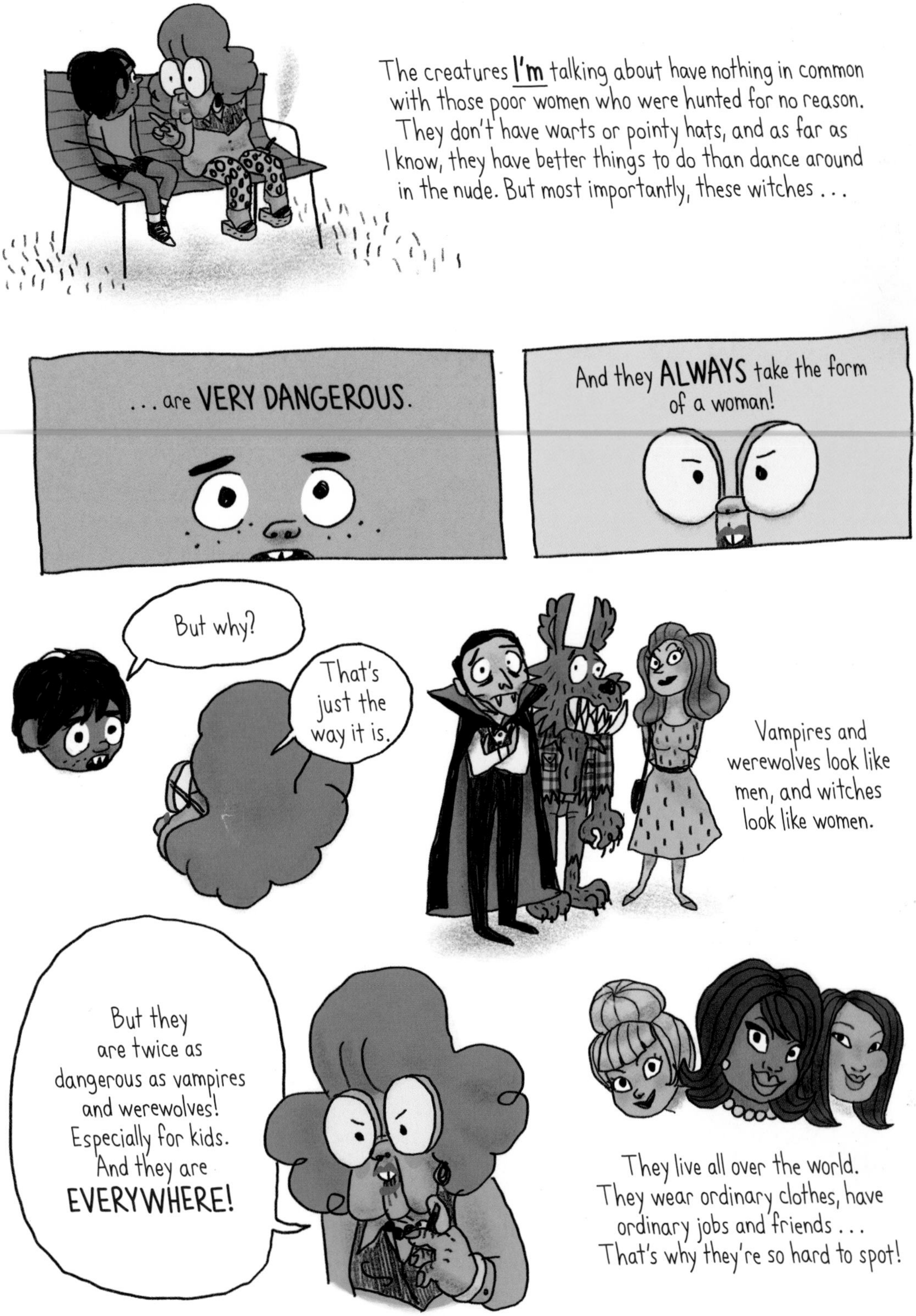

The creatures I'm talking about have nothing in common with those poor women who were hunted for no reason. They don't have warts or pointy hats, and as far as I know, they have better things to do than dance around in the nude. But most importantly, these witches . . .
. . . are VERY DANGEROUS.
And they ALWAYS take the form of a woman!
But why?
That's just the way it is.
Vampires and werewolves look like men, and witches look like women.
But they are twice as dangerous as vampires and werewolves! Especially for kids. And they are EVERYWHERE!
They live all over the world. They wear ordinary clothes, have ordinary jobs and friends . . . That's why they're so hard to spot!

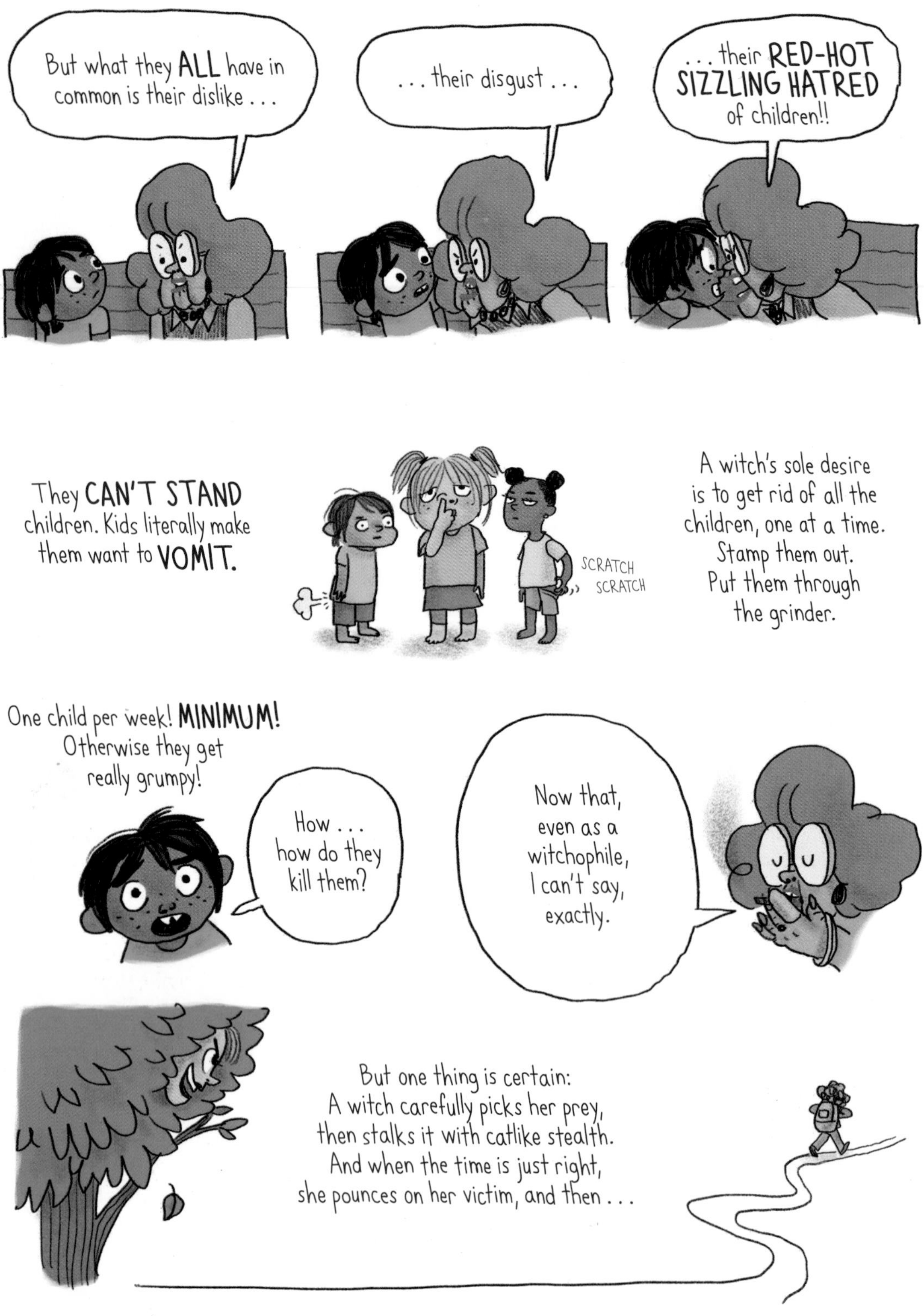
But what they ALL have in common is their dislike . . .
. . . their disgust . . .
. . . their RED-HOT SIZZLING HATRED of children!!
They CAN'T STAND children. Kids literally make them want to VOMIT.
SCRATCH SCRATCH
A witch's sole desire is to get rid of all the children, one at a time. Stamp them out. Put them through the grinder.
One child per week! MINIMUM! Otherwise they get really grumpy!
How . . . how do they kill them?
Now that, even as a witchophile, I can't say, exactly.
But one thing is certain: A witch carefully picks her prey, then stalks it with catlike stealth. And when the time is just right, she pounces on her victim, and then . . .

The child vanishes!

What? HOW??

I have no idea. At any rate, no witch has ever been caught by the police. Or gone to prison.

Luckily, there aren't too many around nowadays.

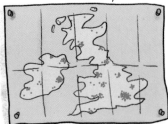

I'd say there are about 100 in England alone.

They live in EVERY single country in the world, but they all obey the same queen, the most powerful one of all:

THE GRAND HIGH WITCH!

She is very mysterious and only rarely makes an appearance. Besides, to the human eye, she too would look just like a perfectly ordinary woman.

So how can we spot them, then?

Well, like I said, they're creatures that have to constantly wear a disguise in order to pass for ordinary women.

But easier said than done, for them! There are still some things that betray them! That can help unmask them!

It's no guarantee, alas. But based on my research, here are a few details that could be useful to you:

HANDS

Fig. 1
With gloves

Fig. 2
Without gloves

Witches wear gloves all year long, no matter the season, in order to hide their claws and their wrinkly fingers.

HEAD

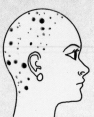

Fig. 1   **Fig. 2**

Witches are totally bald (Fig. 1). They wear wigs (Fig. 2). But the chafing on their scalp 365 days a year drives them crazy, and they are prone to what we call "the itch."

Witch succumbing to "the itch."

FEET

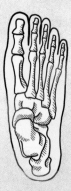

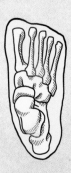

Woman   **Witch**

Witches don't have toes. Their feet are square. They hide their feet year-round in closed-toe, pointy shoes, which are very uncomfortable.

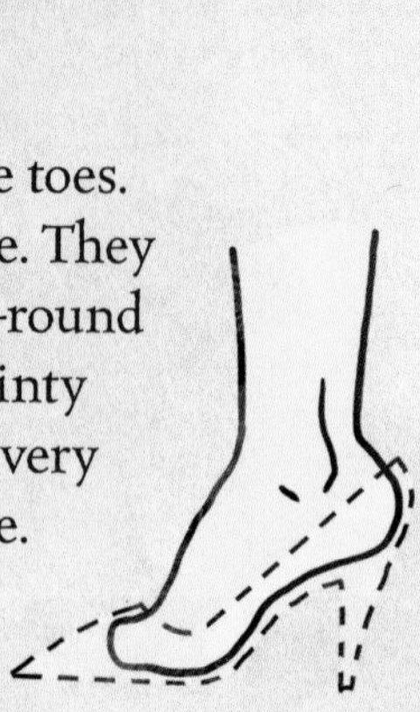

SMILE

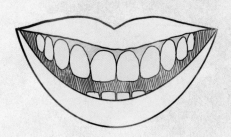

Witches have blue spit (blue as a blueberry), which gives their teeth a slight blue tinge.

EYES

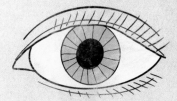

Fig. 1

While human eyes have ordinary black pupils (Fig. 1), a witch's pupils are full of dancing ice crystals and fire (Fig. 2).

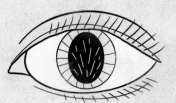

Fig. 2

NOSE

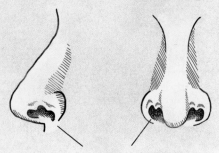

Witch Nostril

Witches have large, twitchy nostrils for sniffing out children.

Riiight . . .
Let me guess . . .

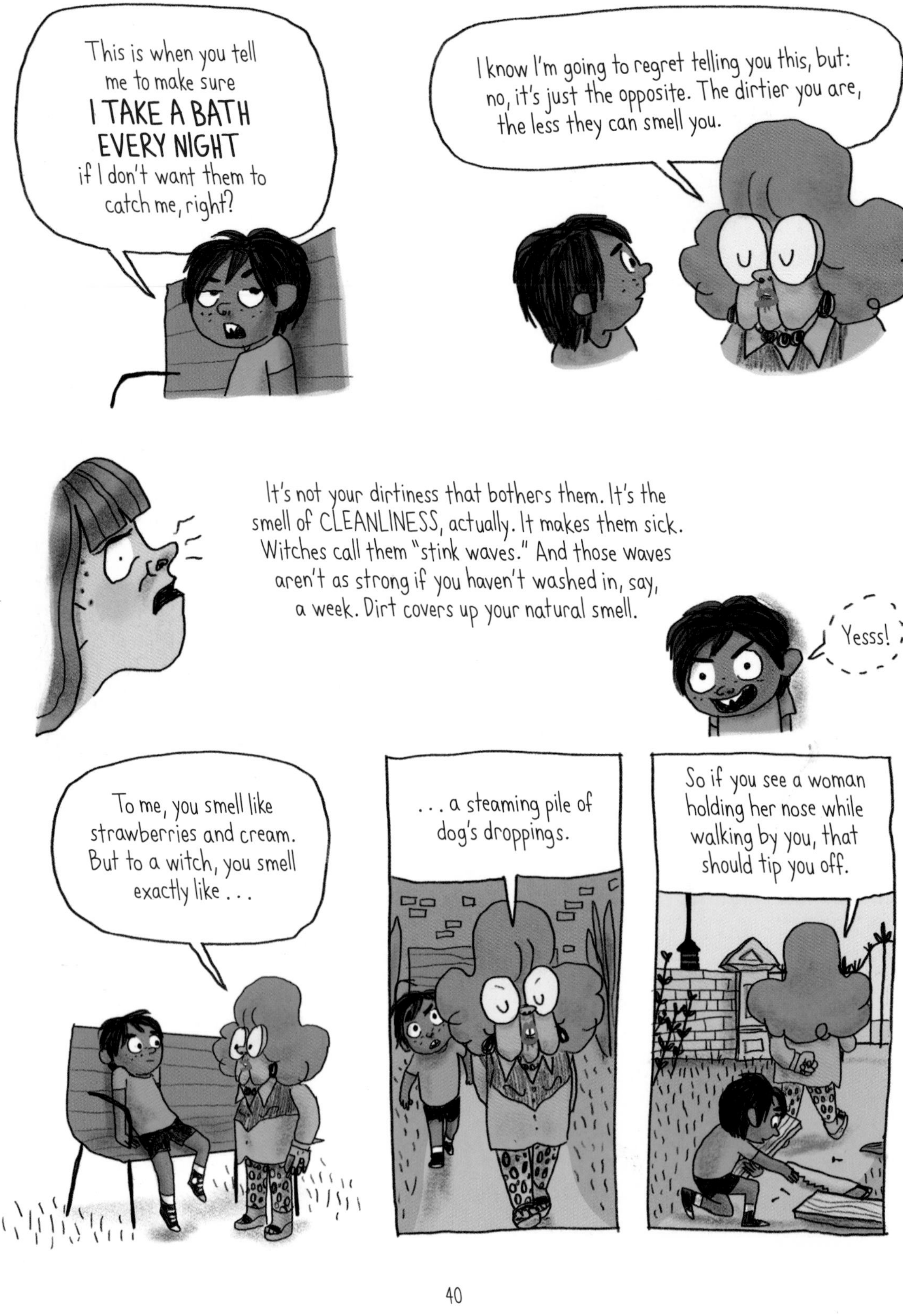

This is when you tell me to make sure I TAKE A BATH EVERY NIGHT if I don't want them to catch me, right?
I know I'm going to regret telling you this, but: no, it's just the opposite. The dirtier you are, the less they can smell you.
It's not your dirtiness that bothers them. It's the smell of CLEANLINESS, actually. It makes them sick. Witches call them "stink waves." And those waves aren't as strong if you haven't washed in, say, a week. Dirt covers up your natural smell.
Yesss!
To me, you smell like strawberries and cream. But to a witch, you smell exactly like . . .
. . . a steaming pile of dog's droppings.
So if you see a woman holding her nose while walking by you, that should tip you off.

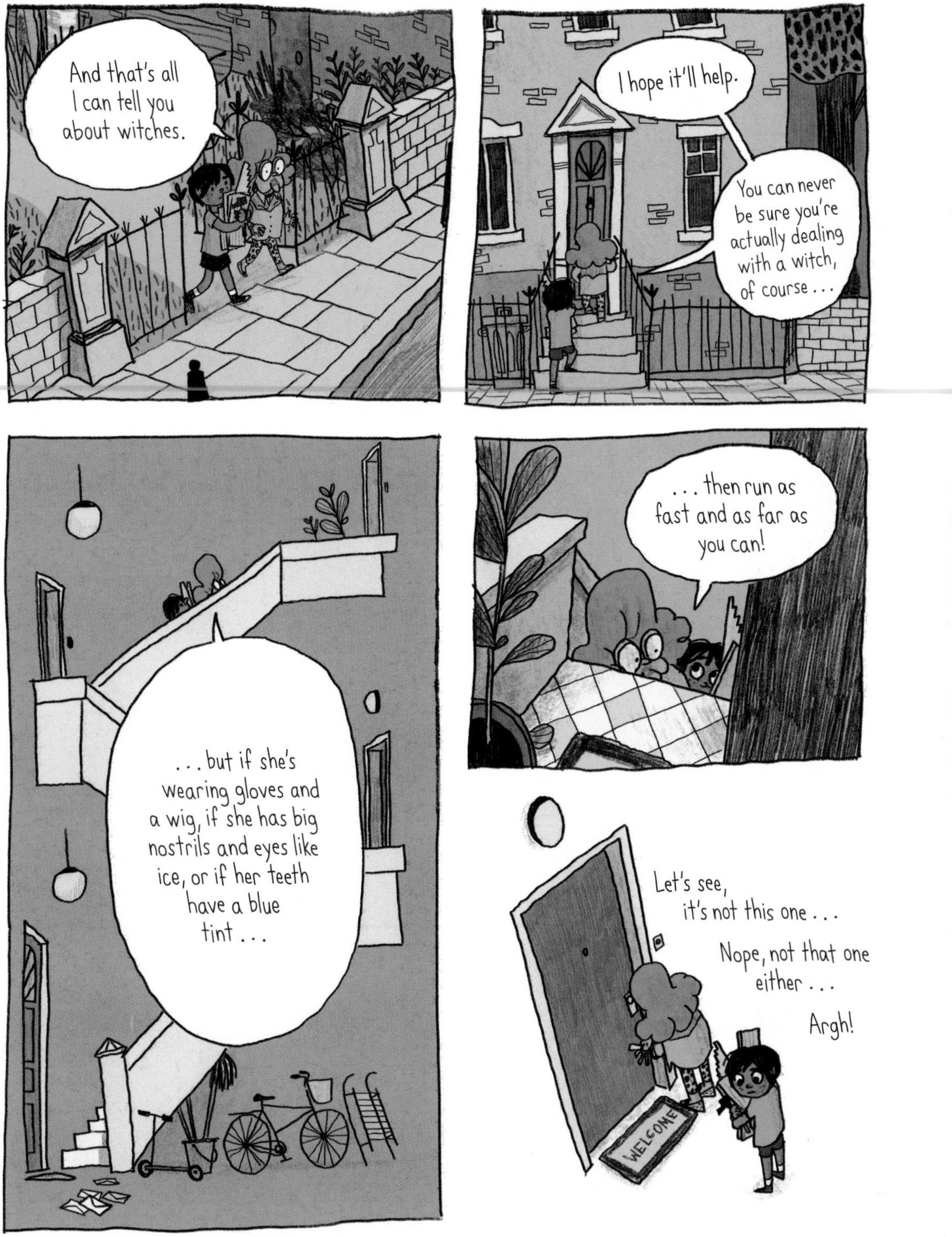
And that's all I can tell you about witches.
I hope it'll help.
You can never be sure you're actually dealing with a witch, of course . . .
. . . but if she's wearing gloves and a wig, if she has big nostrils and eyes like ice, or if her teeth have a blue tint . . .
. . . then run as fast and as far as you can!
Let's see, it's not this one . . .
Nope, not that one either . . .
Argh!
WELCOME

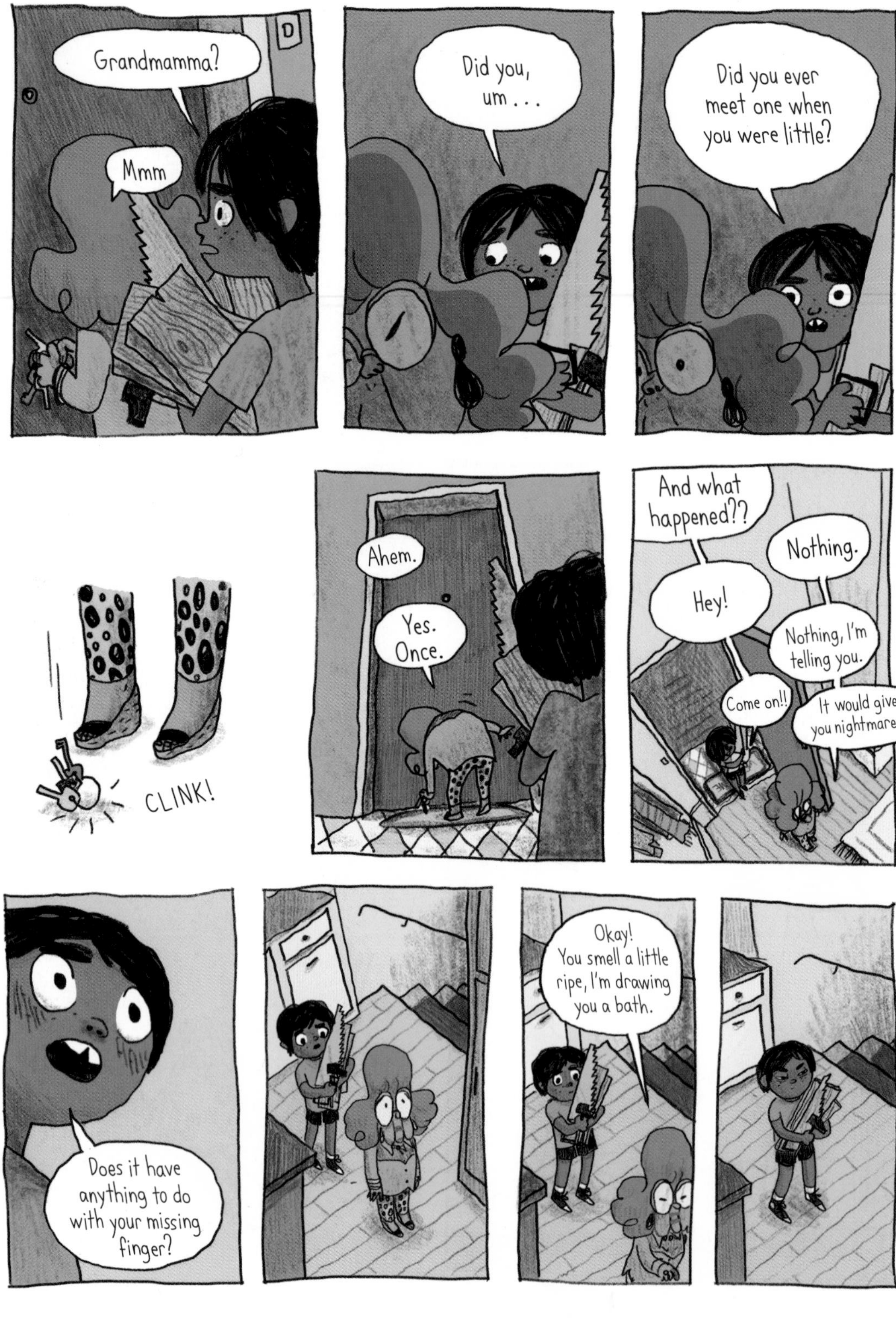

Grandmamma?
Mmm
Did you, um . . .
Did you ever meet one when you were little?
CLINK!
Ahem.
Yes. Once.
And what happened??
Nothing.
Hey!
Nothing, I'm telling you.
Come on!!
It would give you nightmares.
Does it have anything to do with your missing finger?
Okay! You smell a little ripe, I'm drawing you a bath.

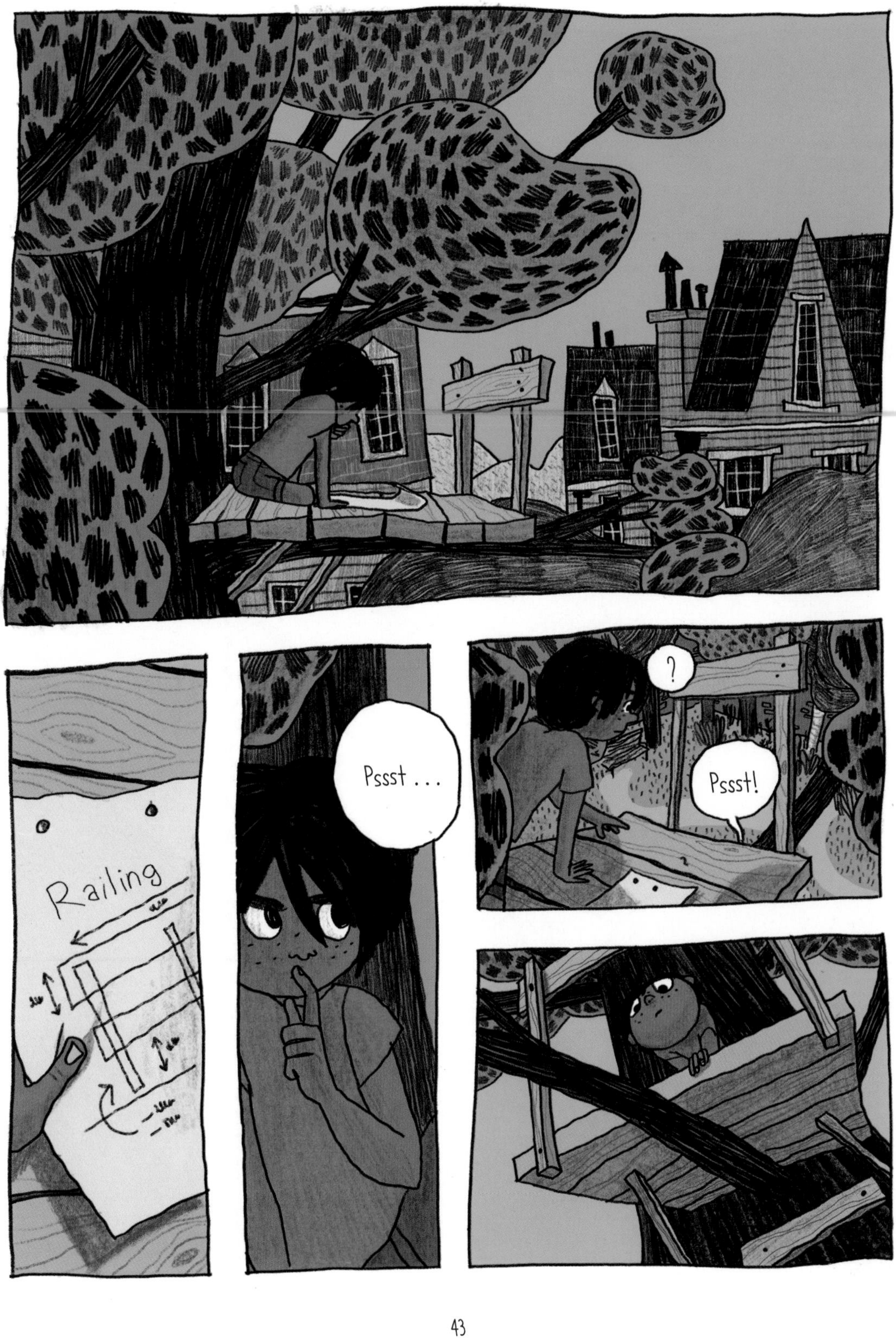
Railing
Pssst . . .
?
Pssst!

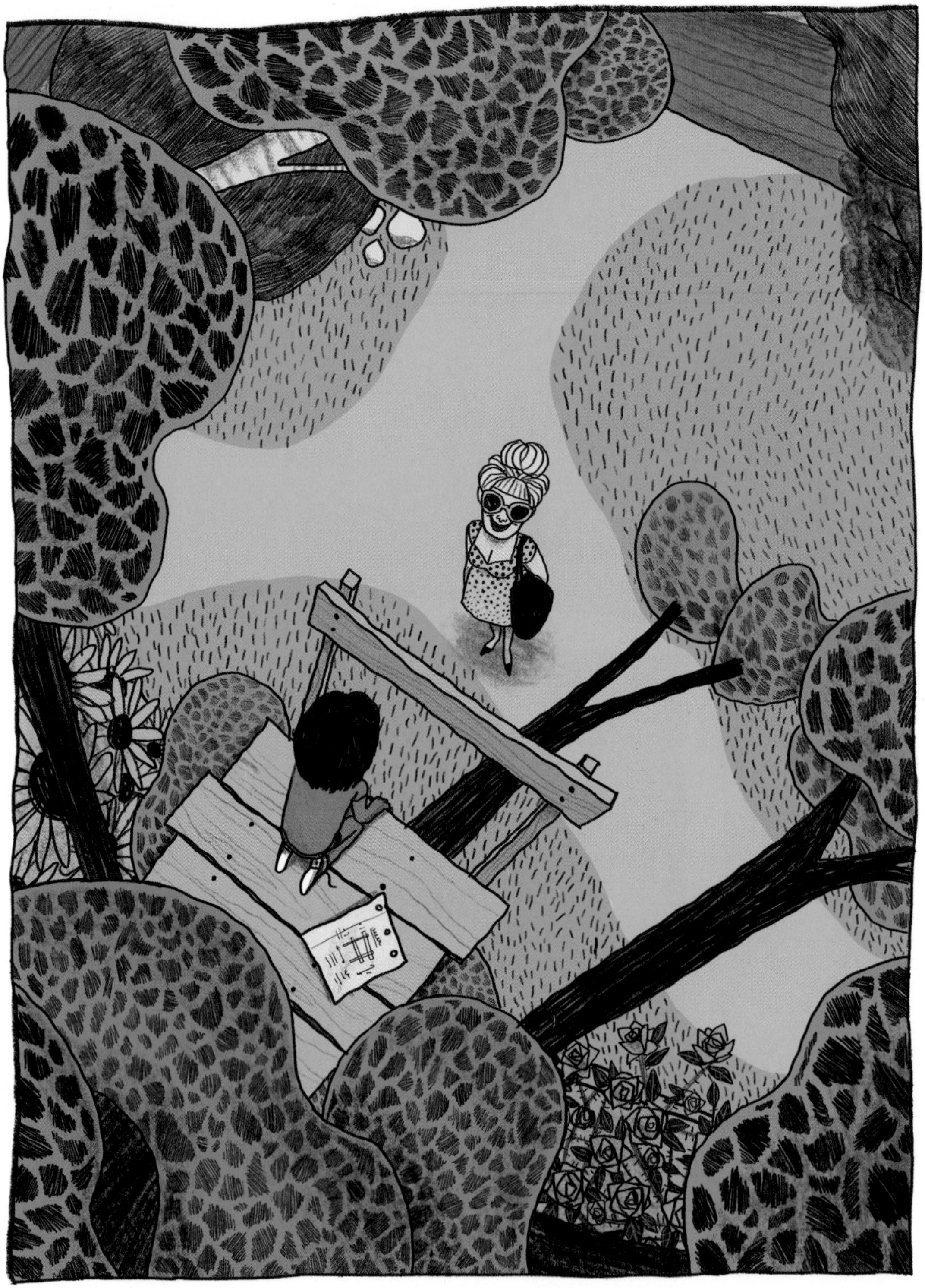

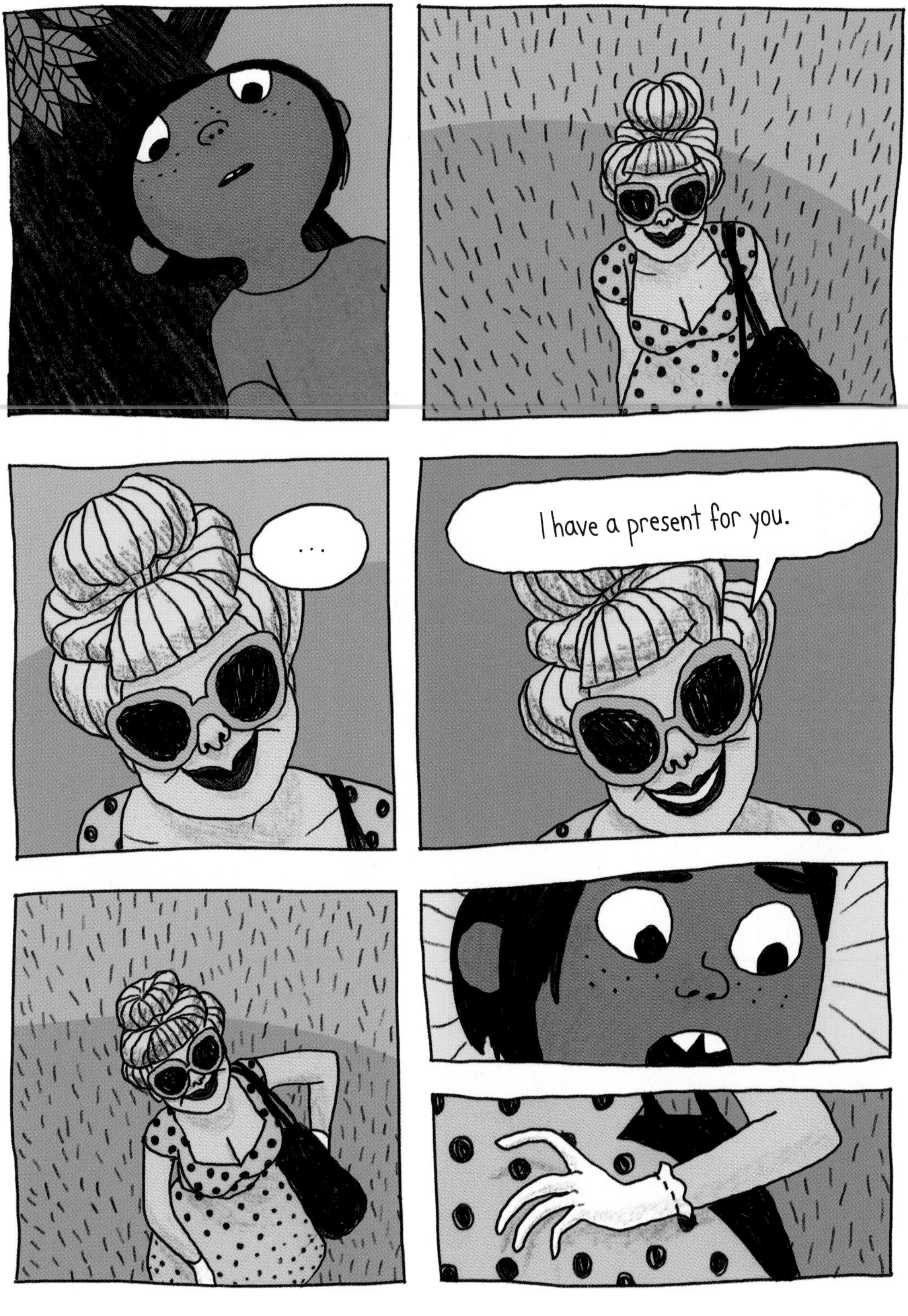
...
I have a present for you.

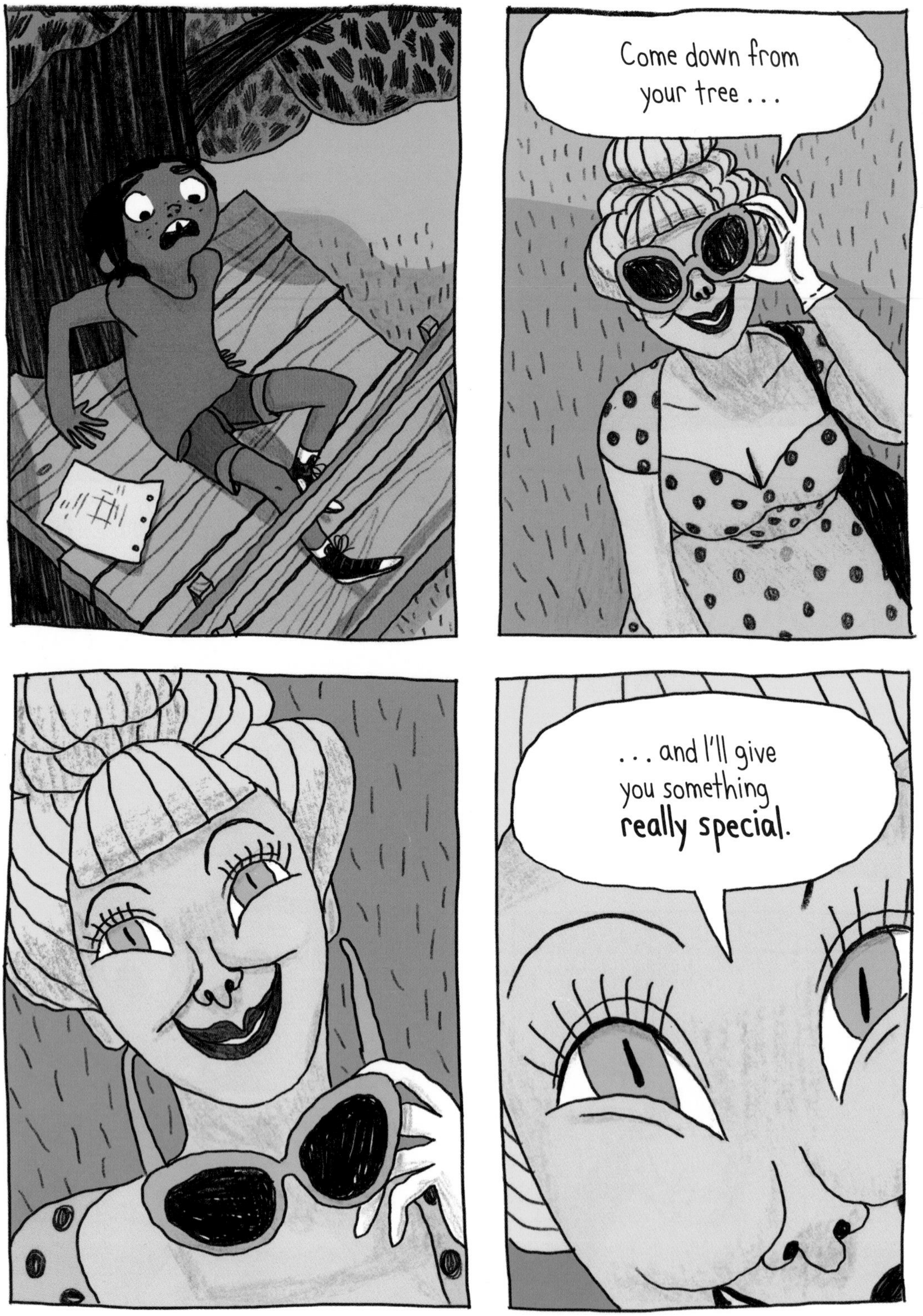
Come down from your tree . . .
. . . and I'll give you something **really special**.

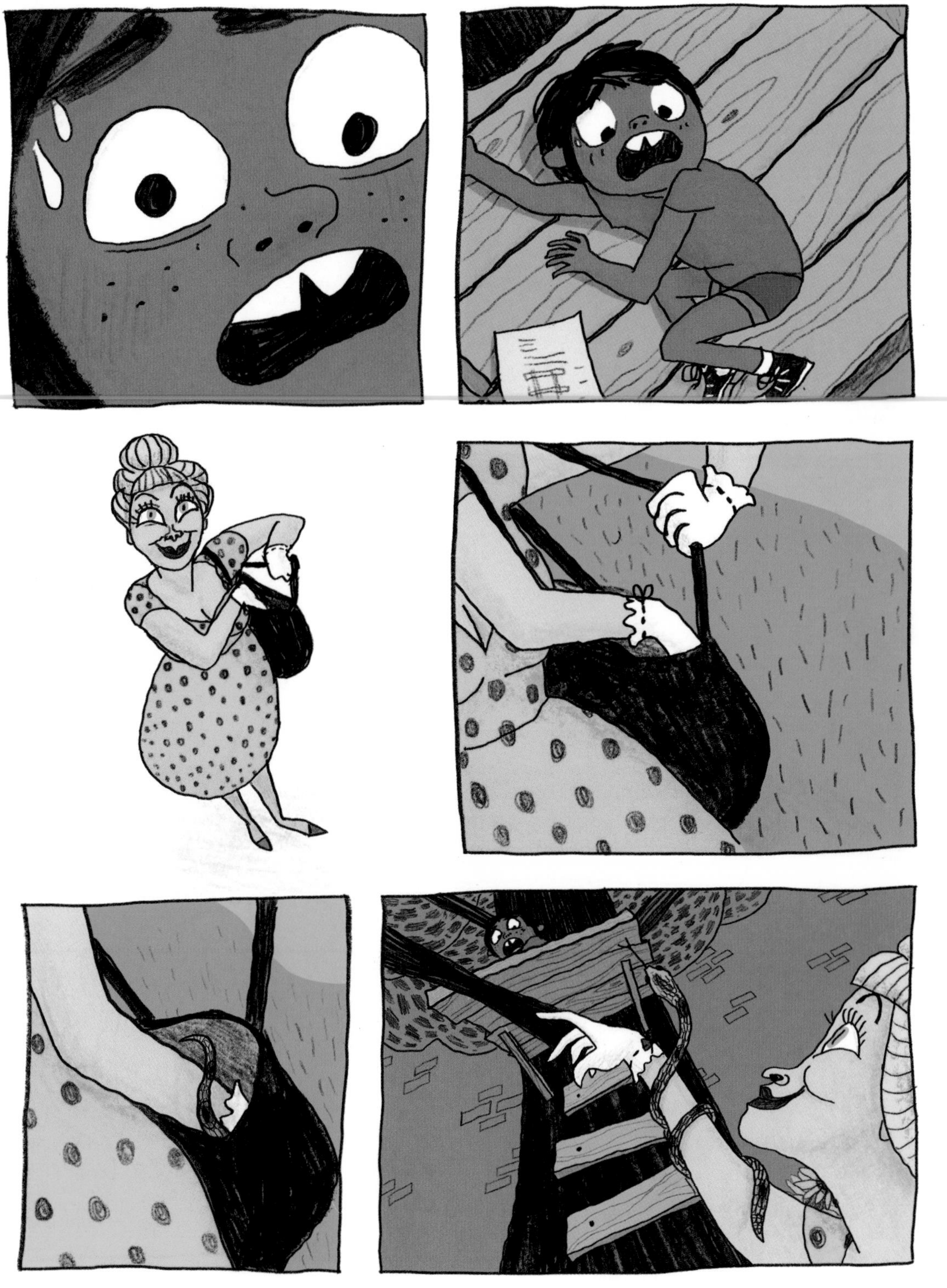

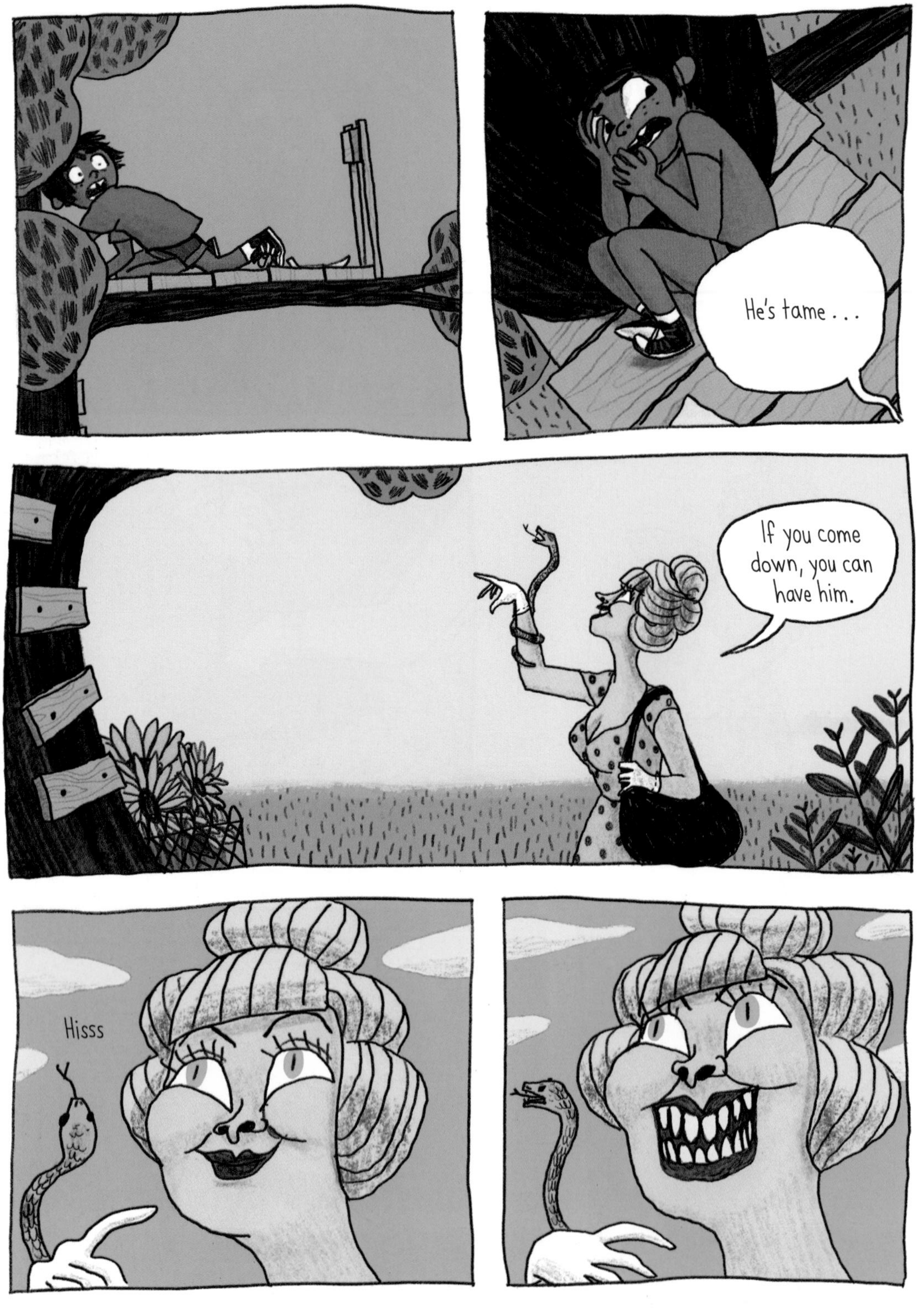
He's tame . . .
If you come down, you can have him.
Hisss

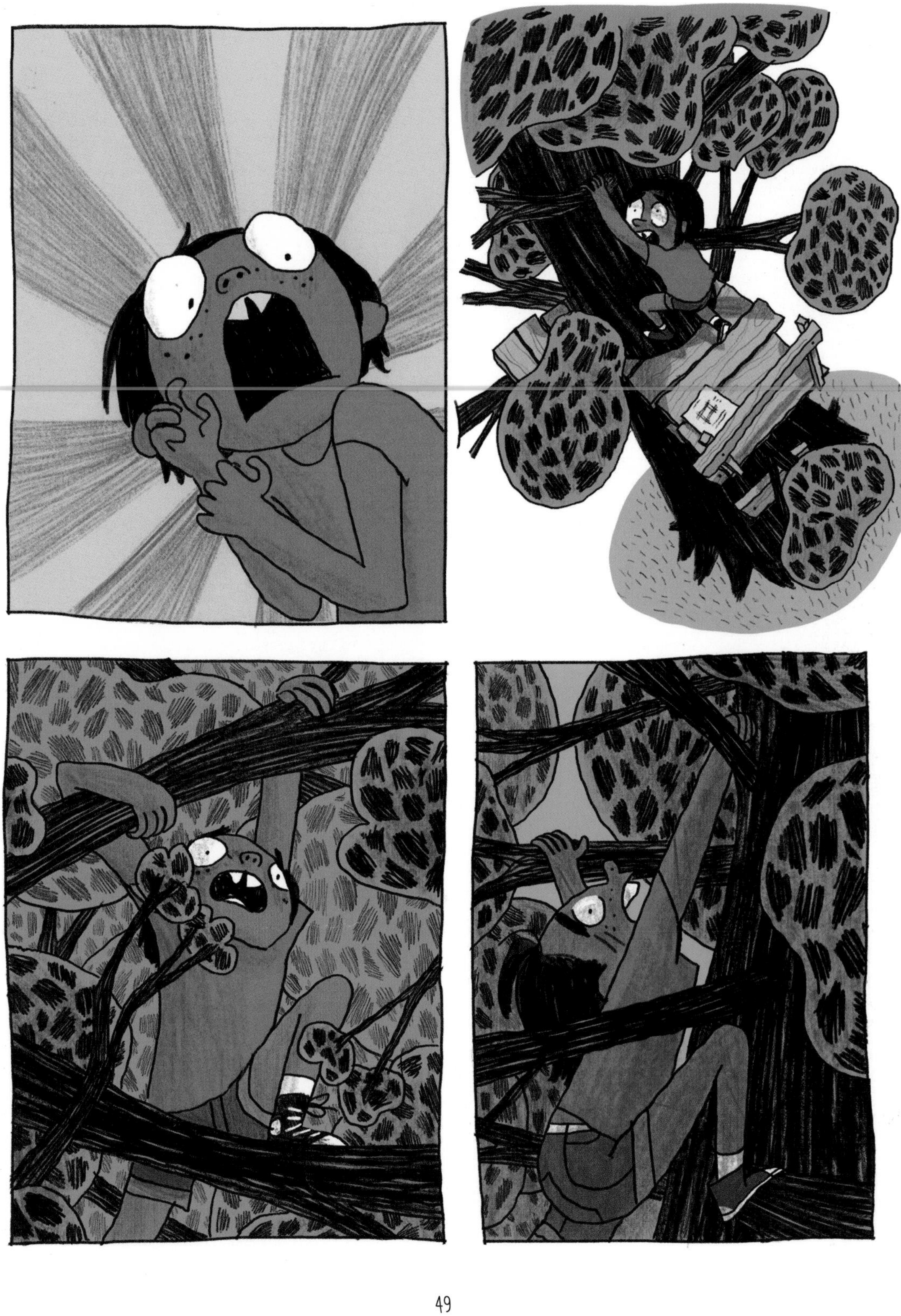

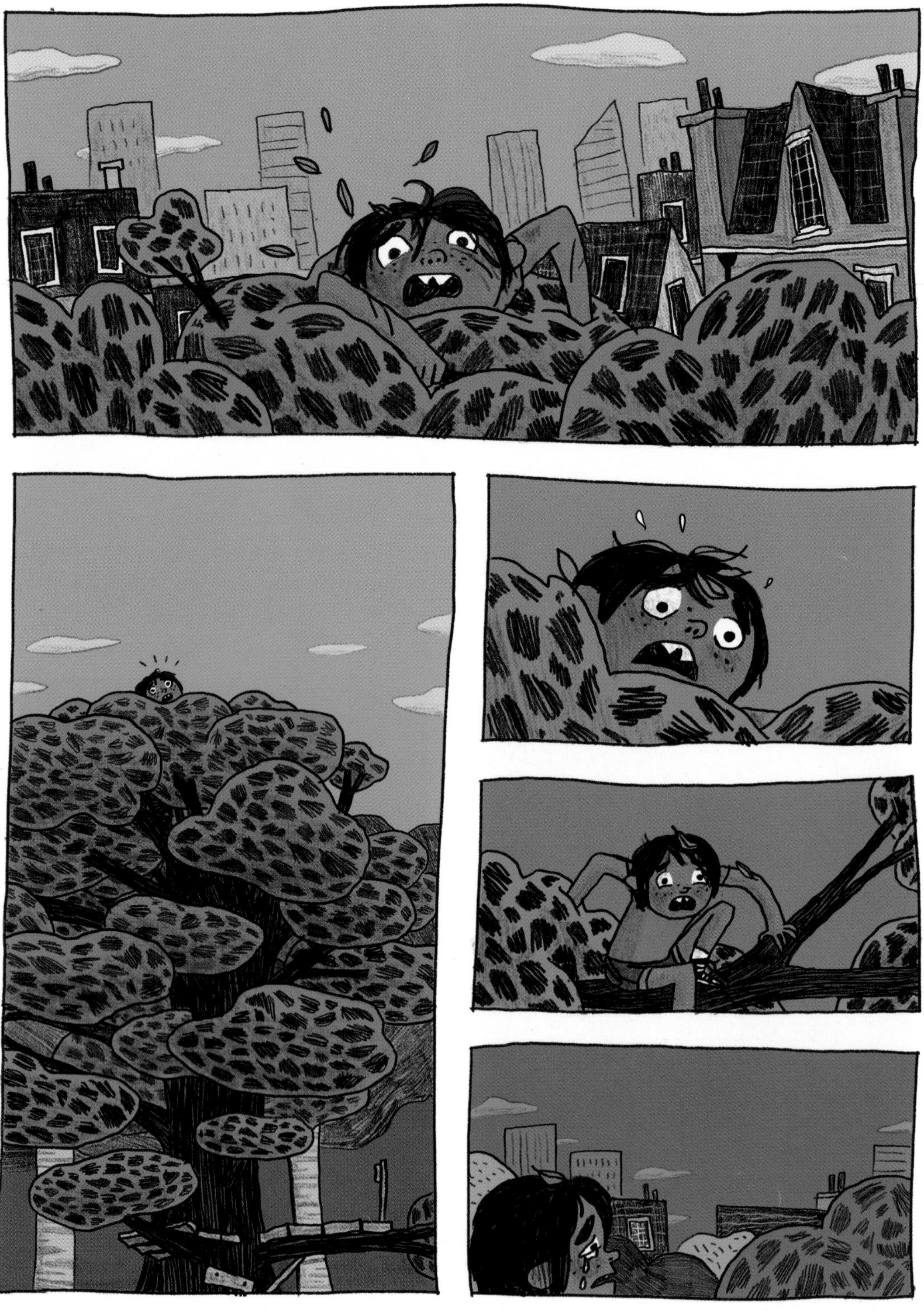

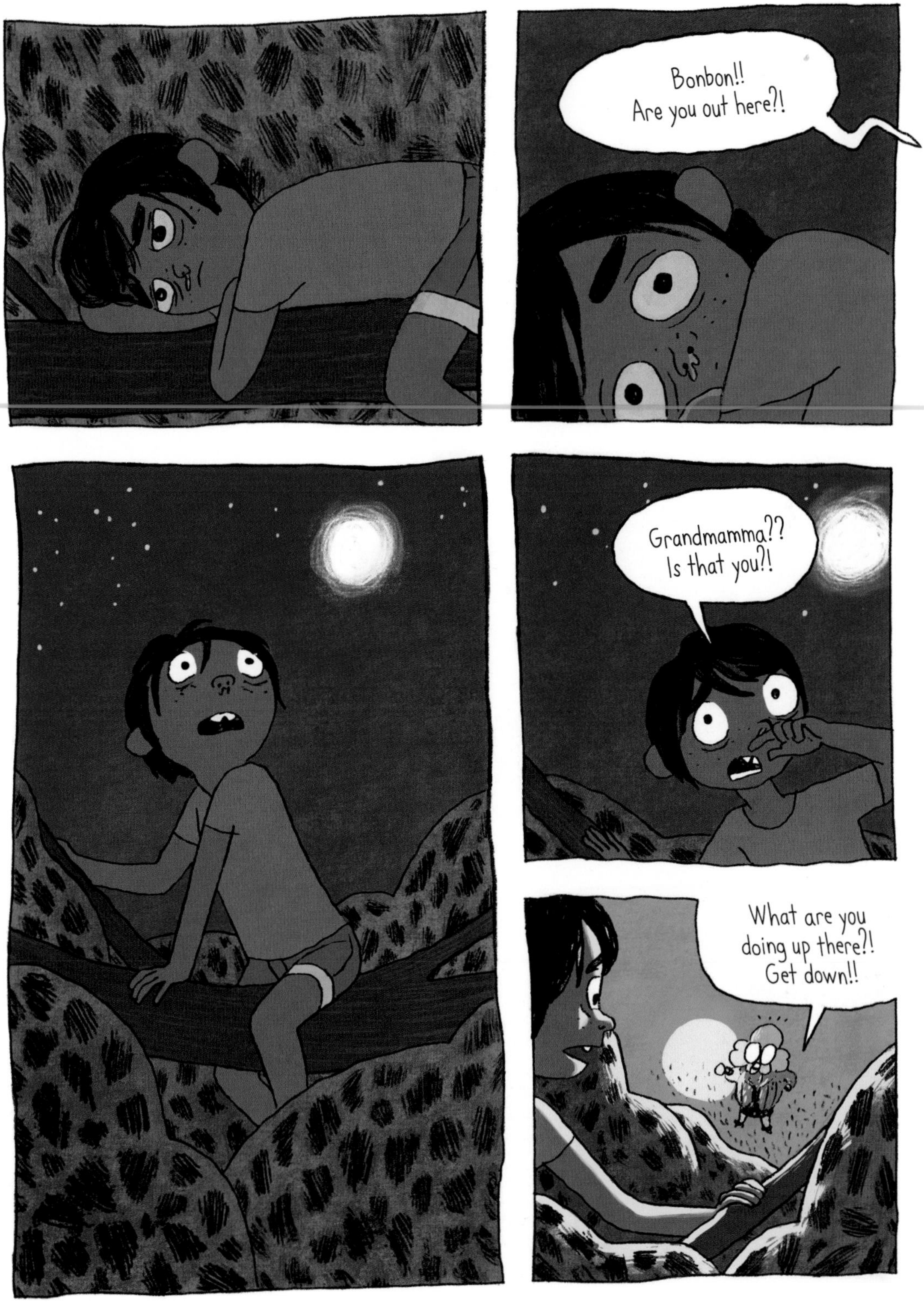
Bonbon!!
Are you out here?!
Grandmamma??
Is that you?!
What are you doing up there?! Get down!!

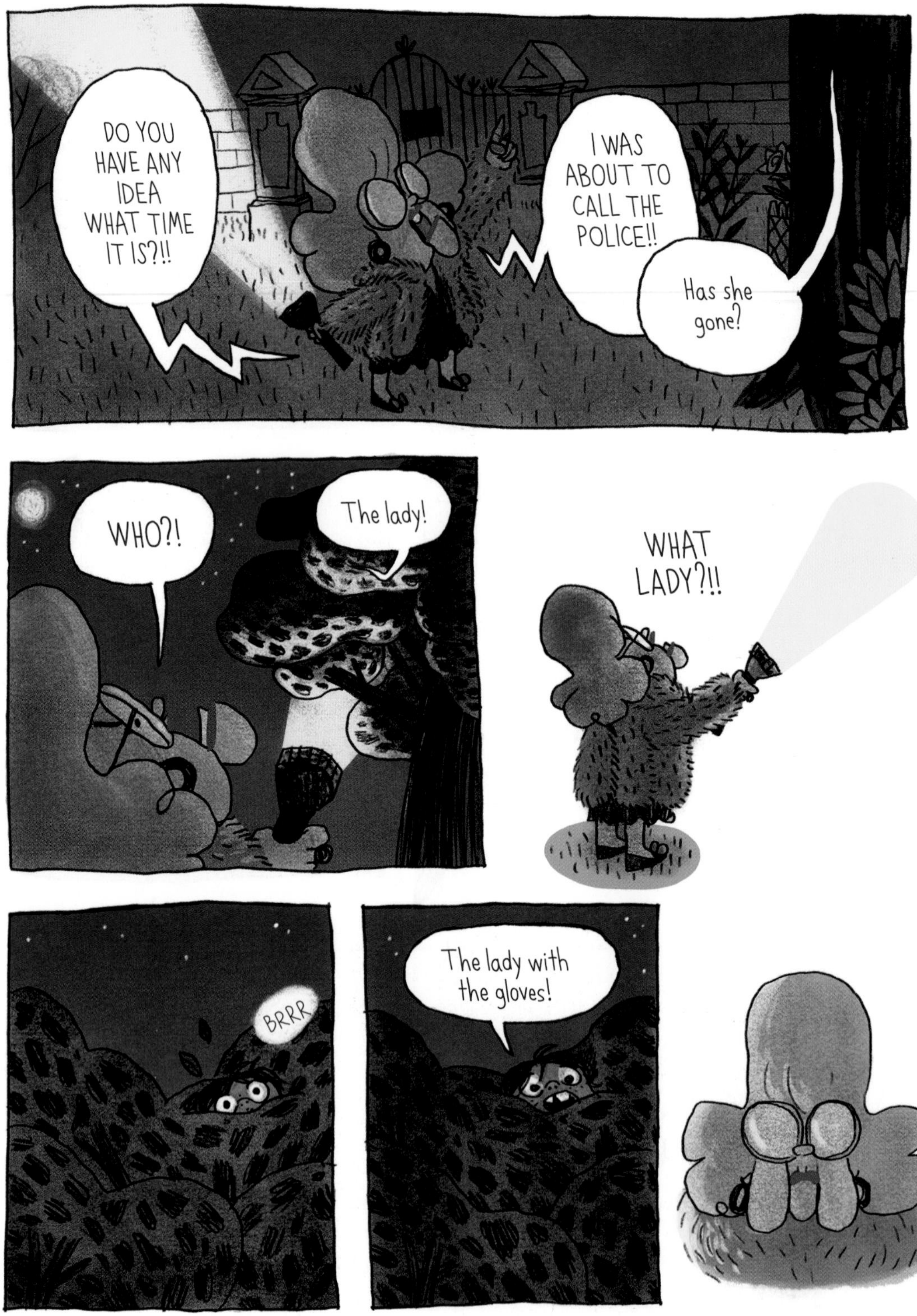
DO YOU HAVE ANY IDEA WHAT TIME IT IS?!!
I WAS ABOUT TO CALL THE POLICE!!
Has she gone?
WHO?!
The lady!
WHAT LADY?!!
BRRR
The lady with the gloves!

Was she a witch? Was she, Grand-mamma??

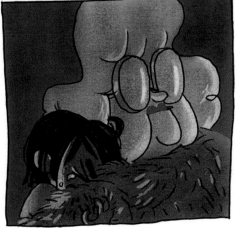

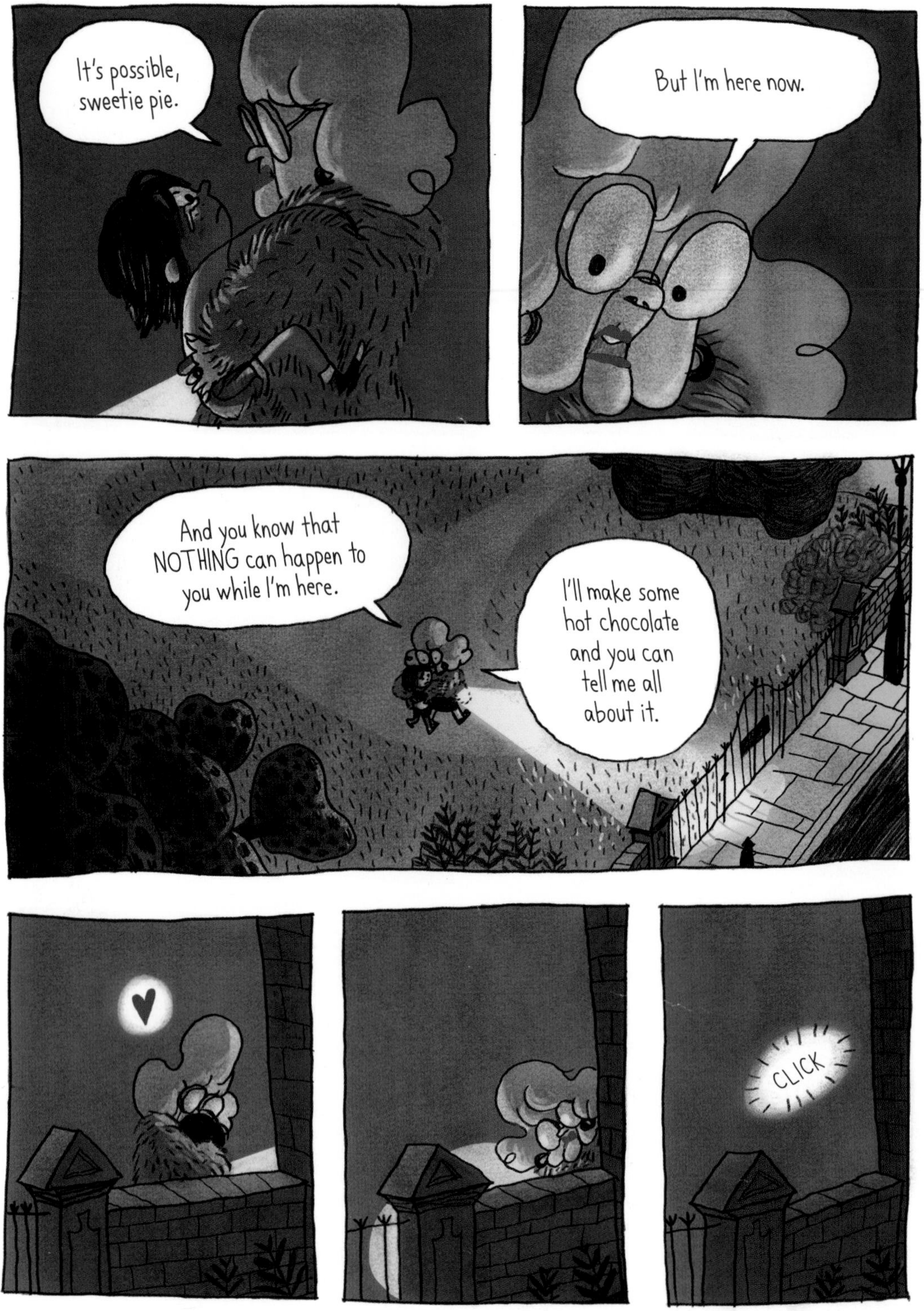
It's possible, sweetie pie.
But I'm here now.
And you know that NOTHING can happen to you while I'm here.
I'll make some hot chocolate and you can tell me all about it.
CLICK

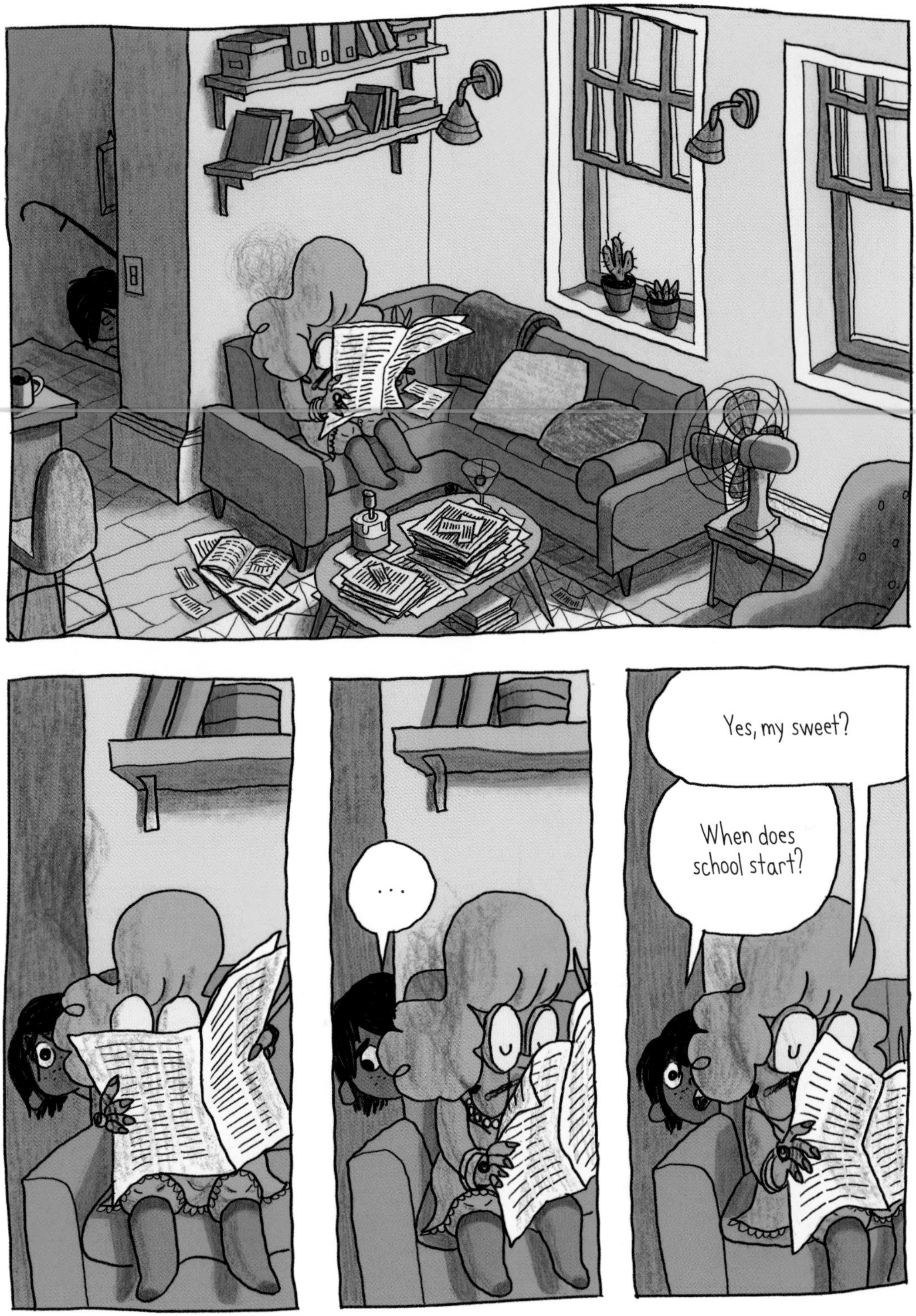

. . .
Yes, my sweet?
When does school start?

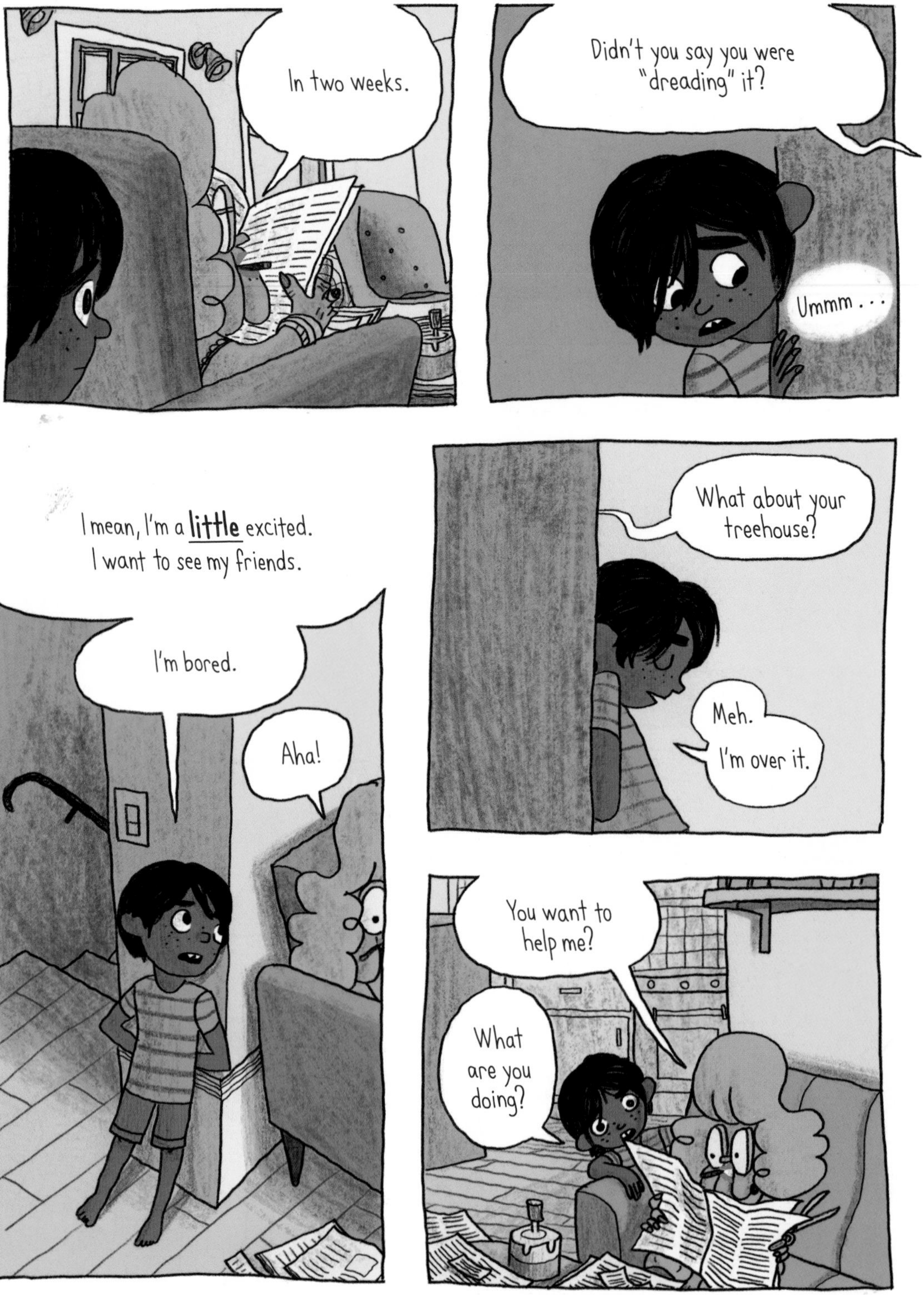
In two weeks.
Didn't you say you were "dreading" it?
Ummm . . .
I mean, I'm a little excited. I want to see my friends.
What about your treehouse?
Meh.
I'm over it.
I'm bored.
Aha!
You want to help me?
What are you doing?

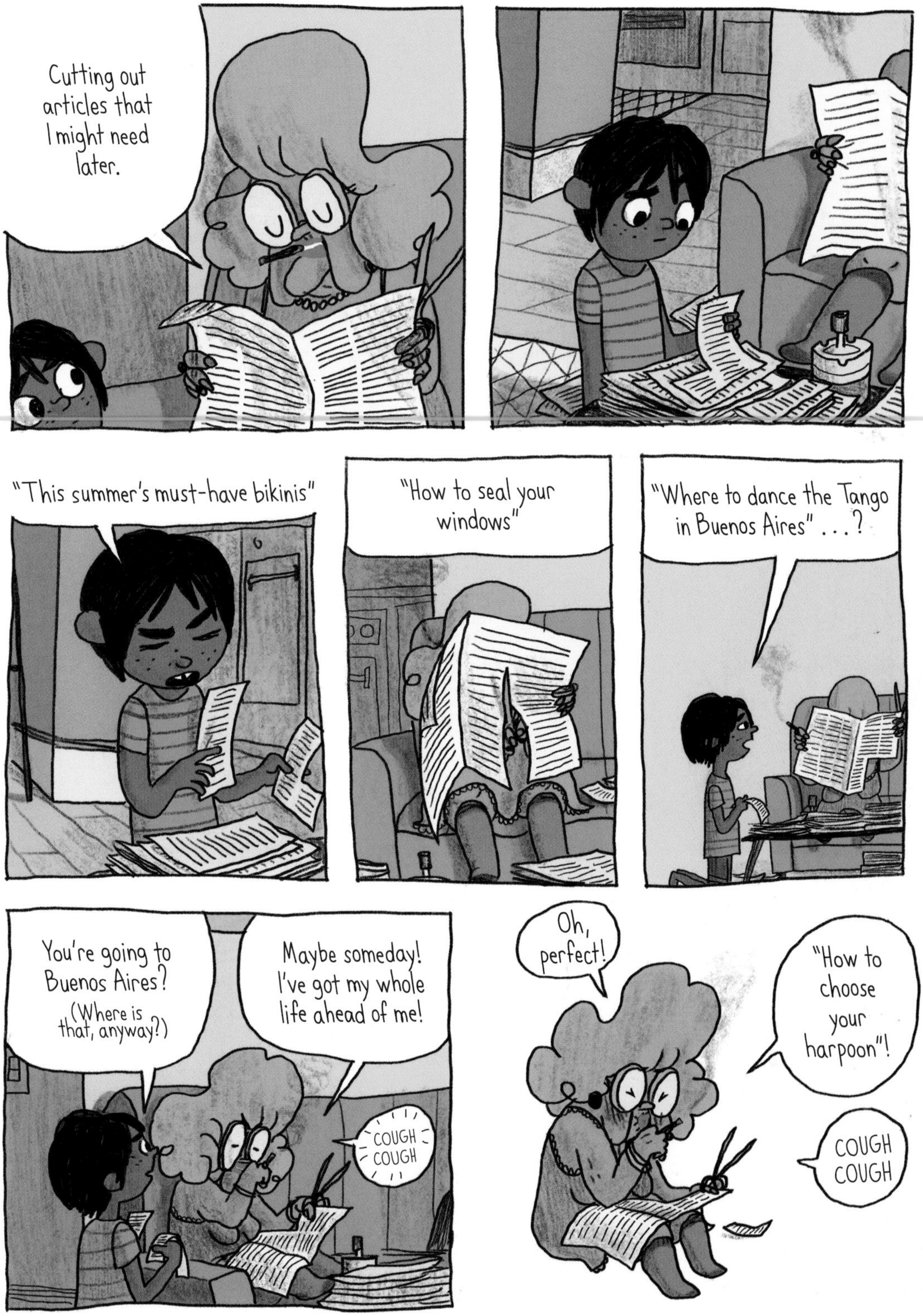
Cutting out articles that I might need later.
"This summer's must-have bikinis"
"How to seal your windows"
"Where to dance the Tango in Buenos Aires" . . . ?
You're going to Buenos Aires? (Where is that, anyway?)
Maybe someday! I've got my whole life ahead of me!
COUGH COUGH
Oh, perfect!
"How to choose your harpoon"!
COUGH COUGH

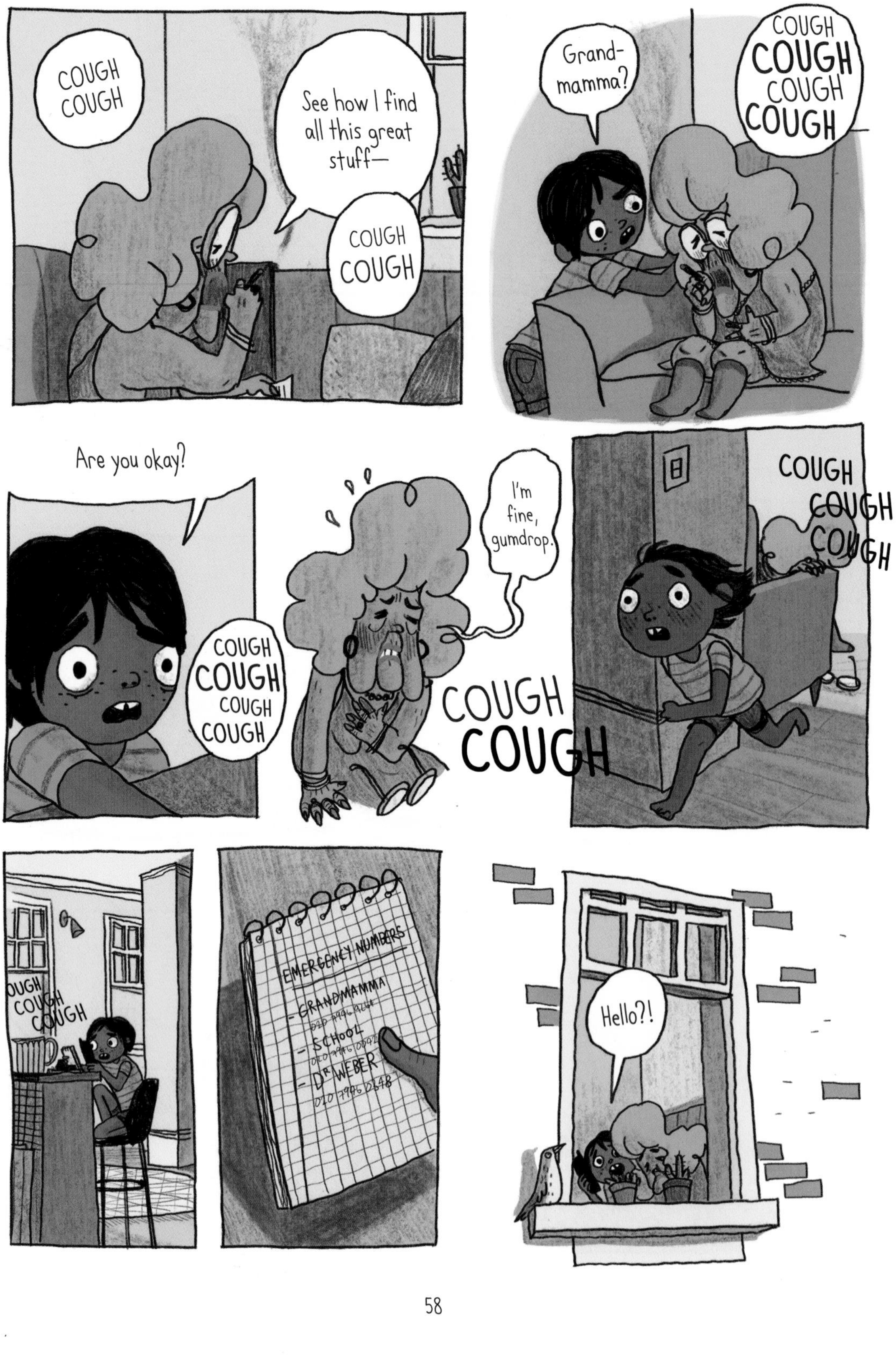
COUGH COUGH
See how I find all this great stuff—
COUGH COUGH
Grand-mamma?
COUGH COUGH COUGH COUGH
Are you okay?
COUGH COUGH COUGH COUGH
I'm fine, gumdrop.
COUGH COUGH
COUGH COUGH COUGH
OUGH COUGH COUGH
EMERGENCY NUMBERS
GRANDMAMMA
SCHOOL
Dr WEBER
Hello?!

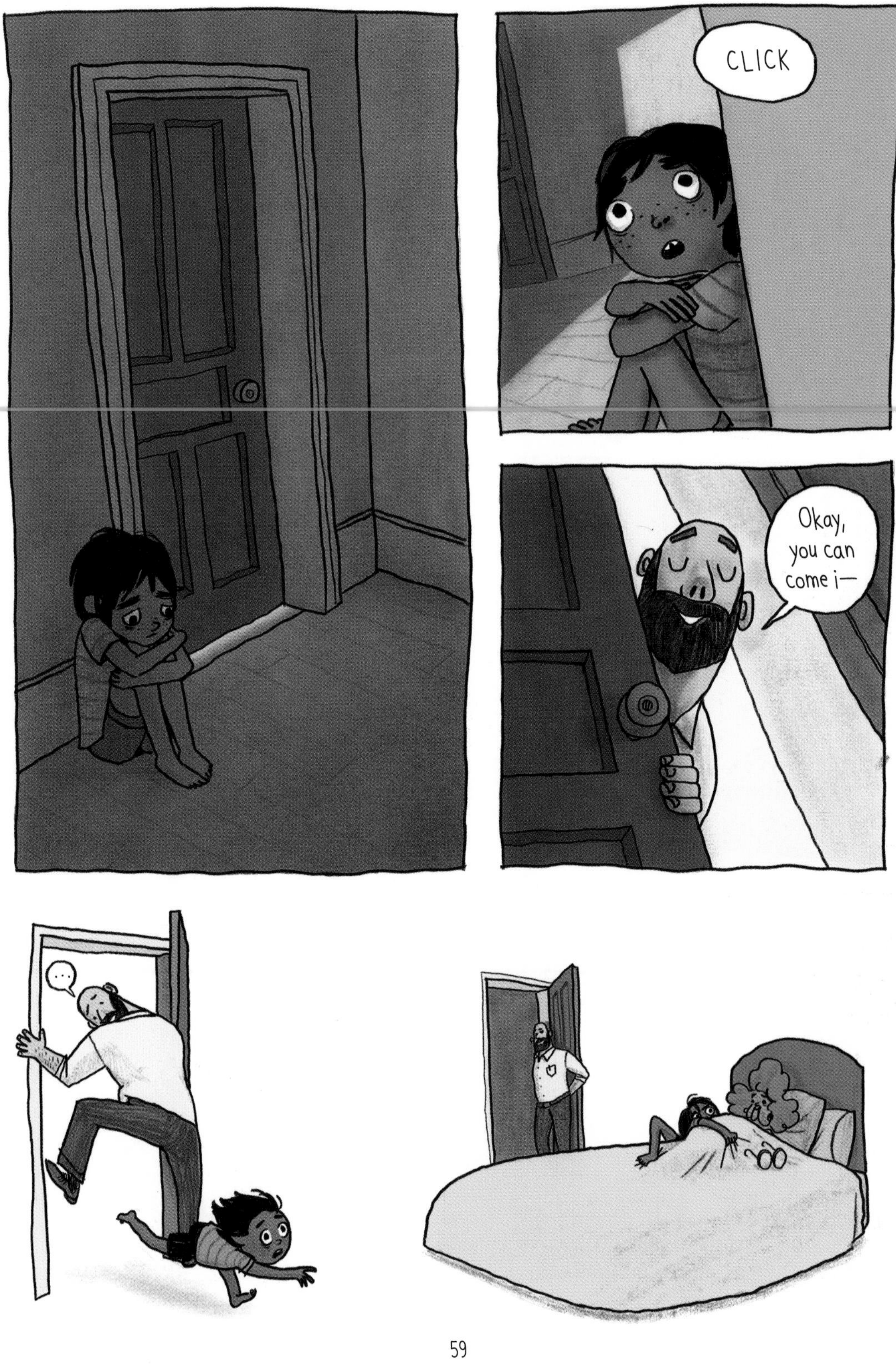
CLICK
Okay, you can come i—
...

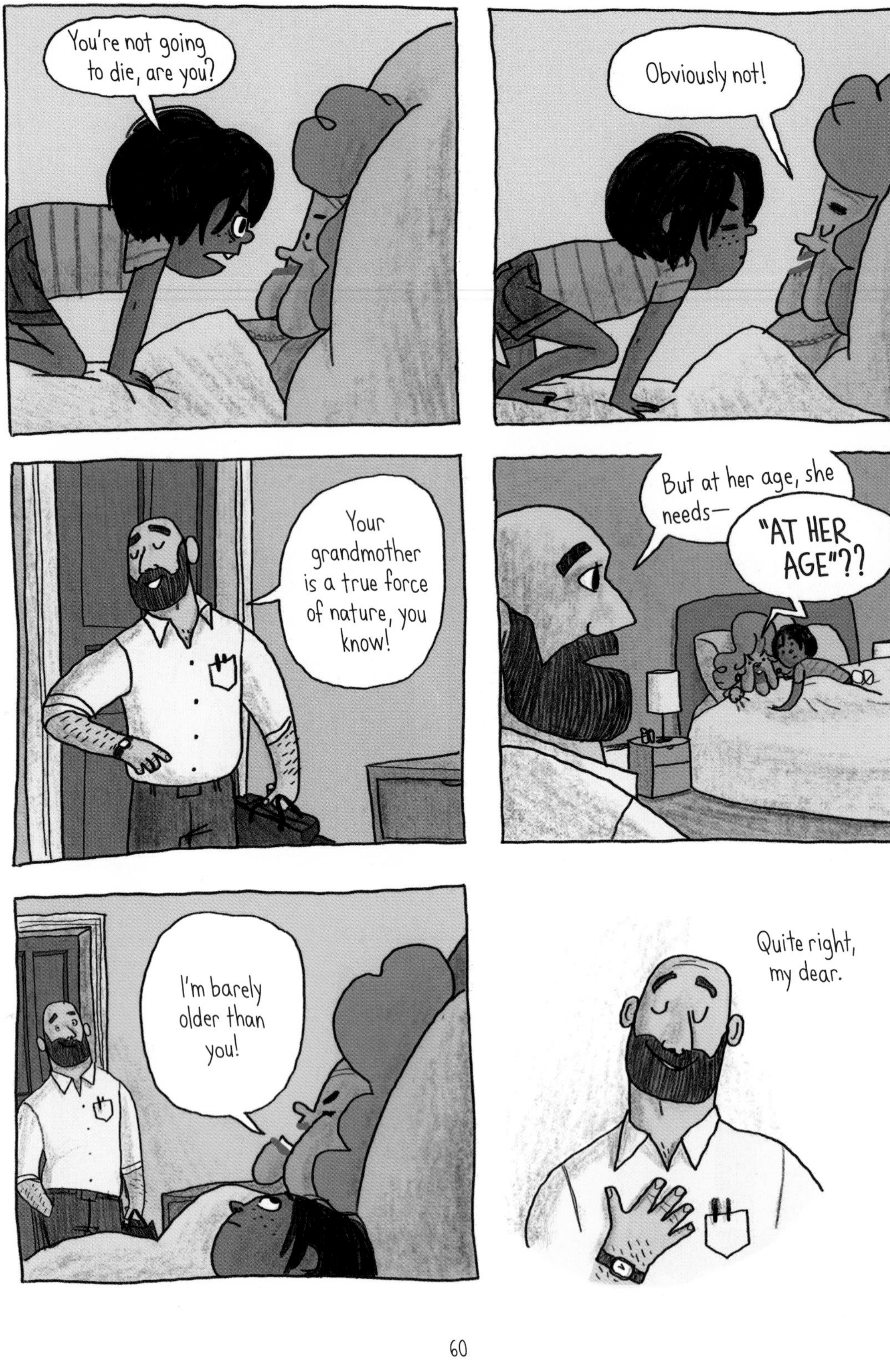

You're not going to die, are you?
Obviously not!
Your grandmother is a true force of nature, you know!
But at her age, she needs—
"AT HER AGE"??
I'm barely older than you!
Quite right, my dear.

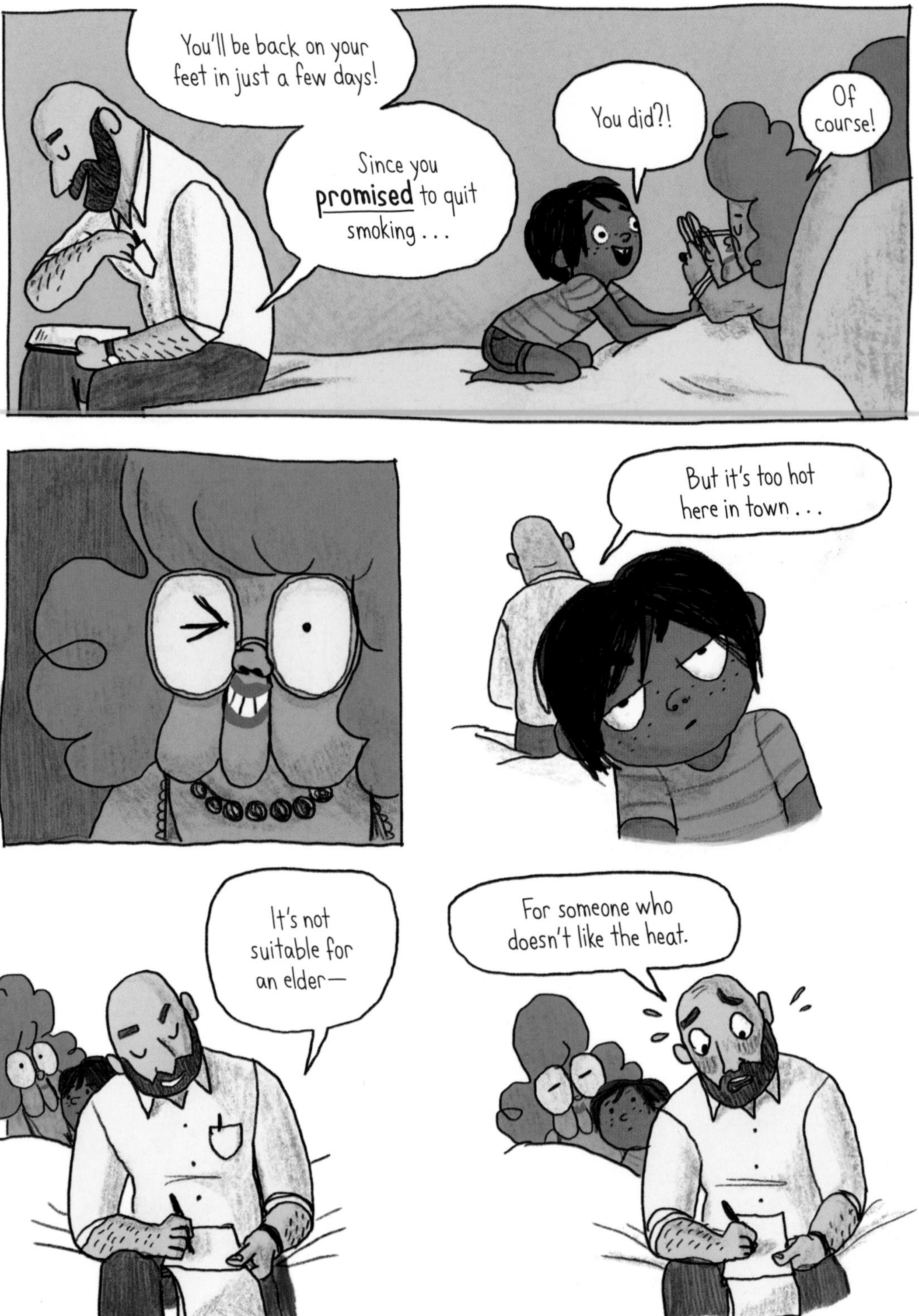
You'll be back on your feet in just a few days!
Since you **promised** to quit smoking . . .
You did?!
Of course!
But it's too hot here in town . . .
It's not suitable for an elder—
For someone who doesn't like the heat.

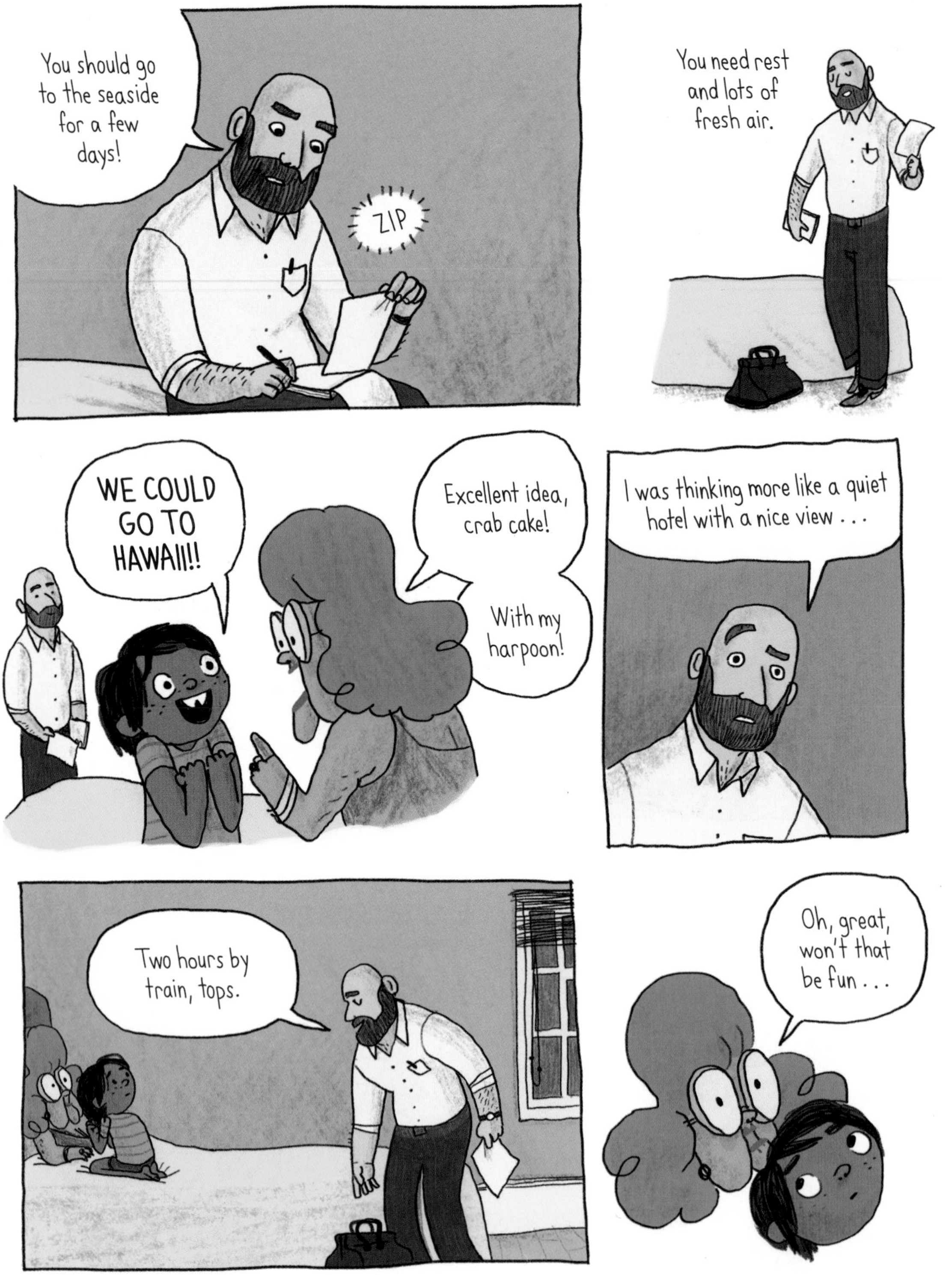
You should go to the seaside for a few days!
ZIP
You need rest and lots of fresh air.
WE COULD GO TO HAWAII!!
Excellent idea, crab cake!
With my harpoon!
I was thinking more like a quiet hotel with a nice view . . .
Two hours by train, tops.
Oh, great, won't that be fun . . .

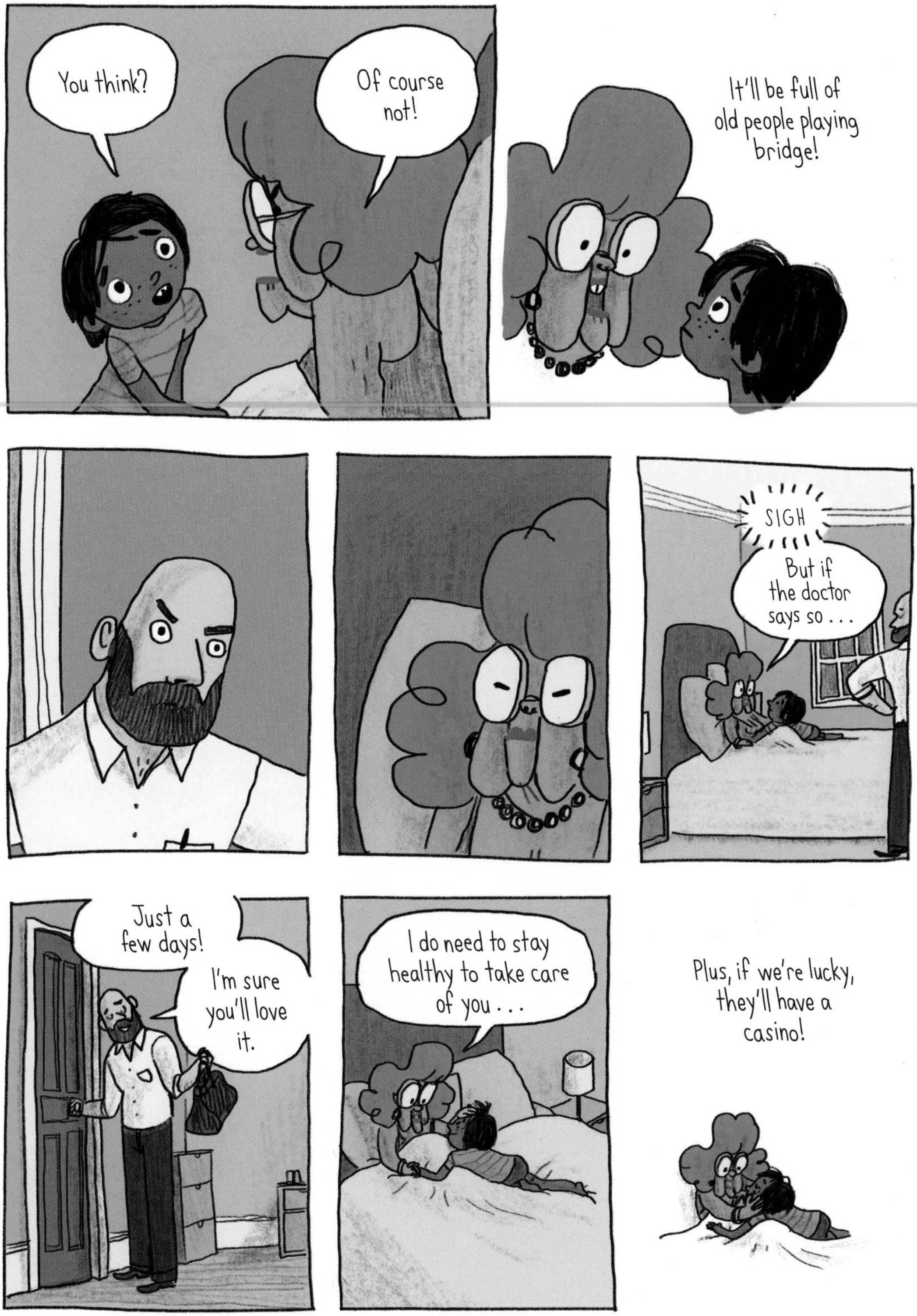
You think?
Of course not!
It'll be full of old people playing bridge!
SIGH
But if the doctor says so . . .
Just a few days!
I'm sure you'll love it.
I do need to stay healthy to take care of you . . .
Plus, if we're lucky, they'll have a casino!

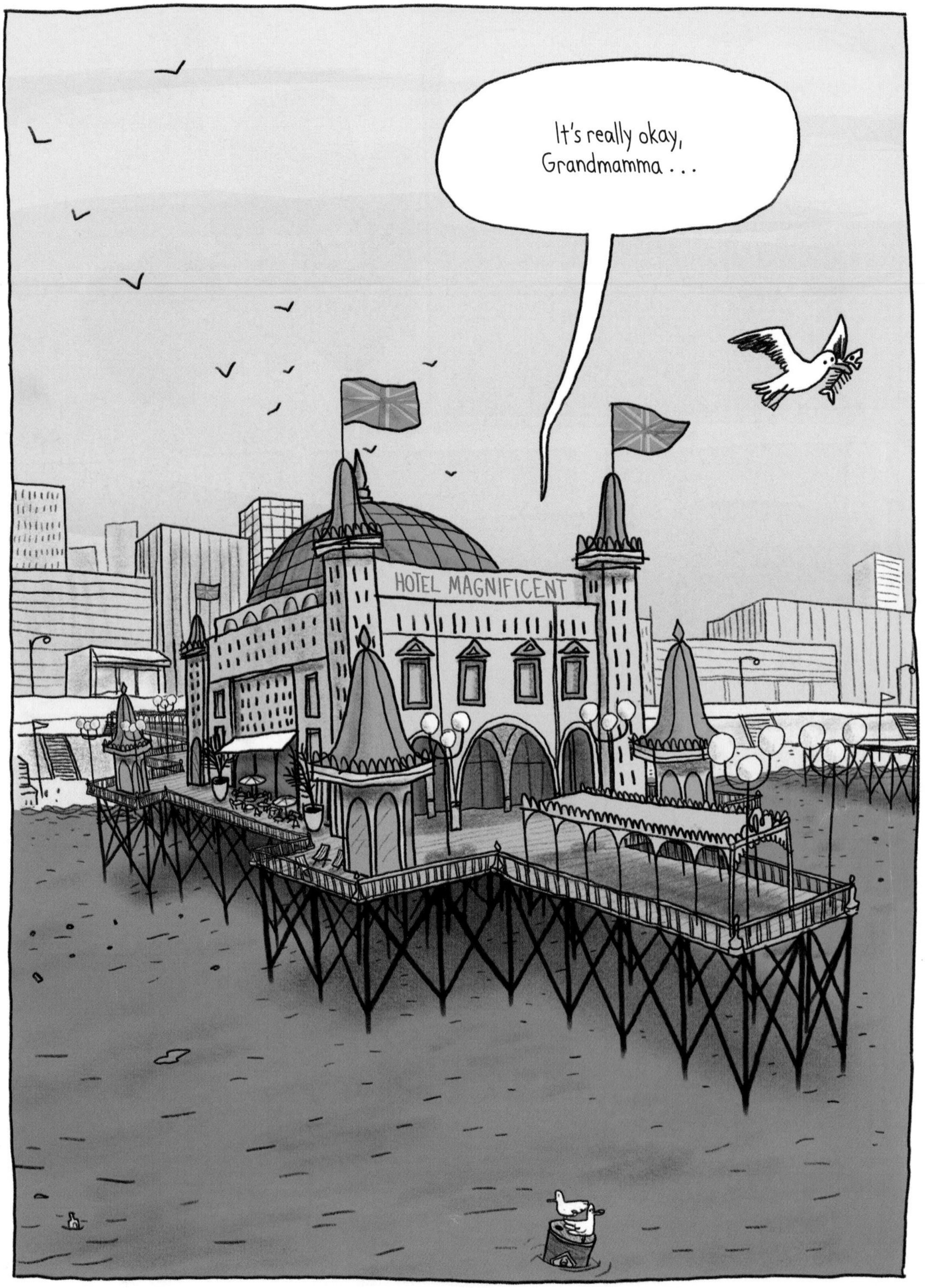
It's really okay, Grandmamma . . .
HOTEL MAGNIFICENT

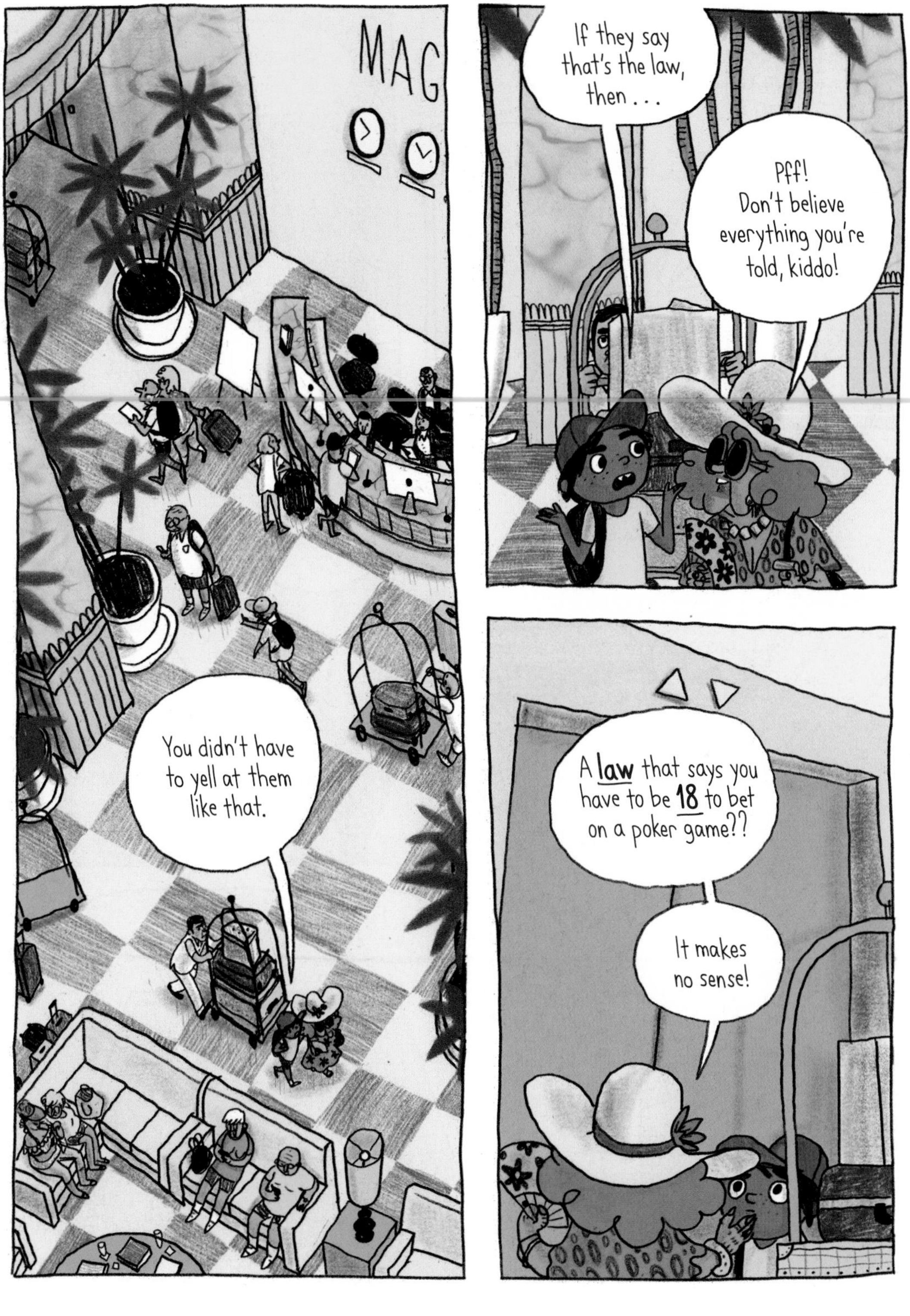

MAG
You didn't have to yell at them like that.
If they say that's the law, then . . .
Pff! Don't believe everything you're told, kiddo!
A law that says you have to be 18 to bet on a poker game??
It makes no sense!

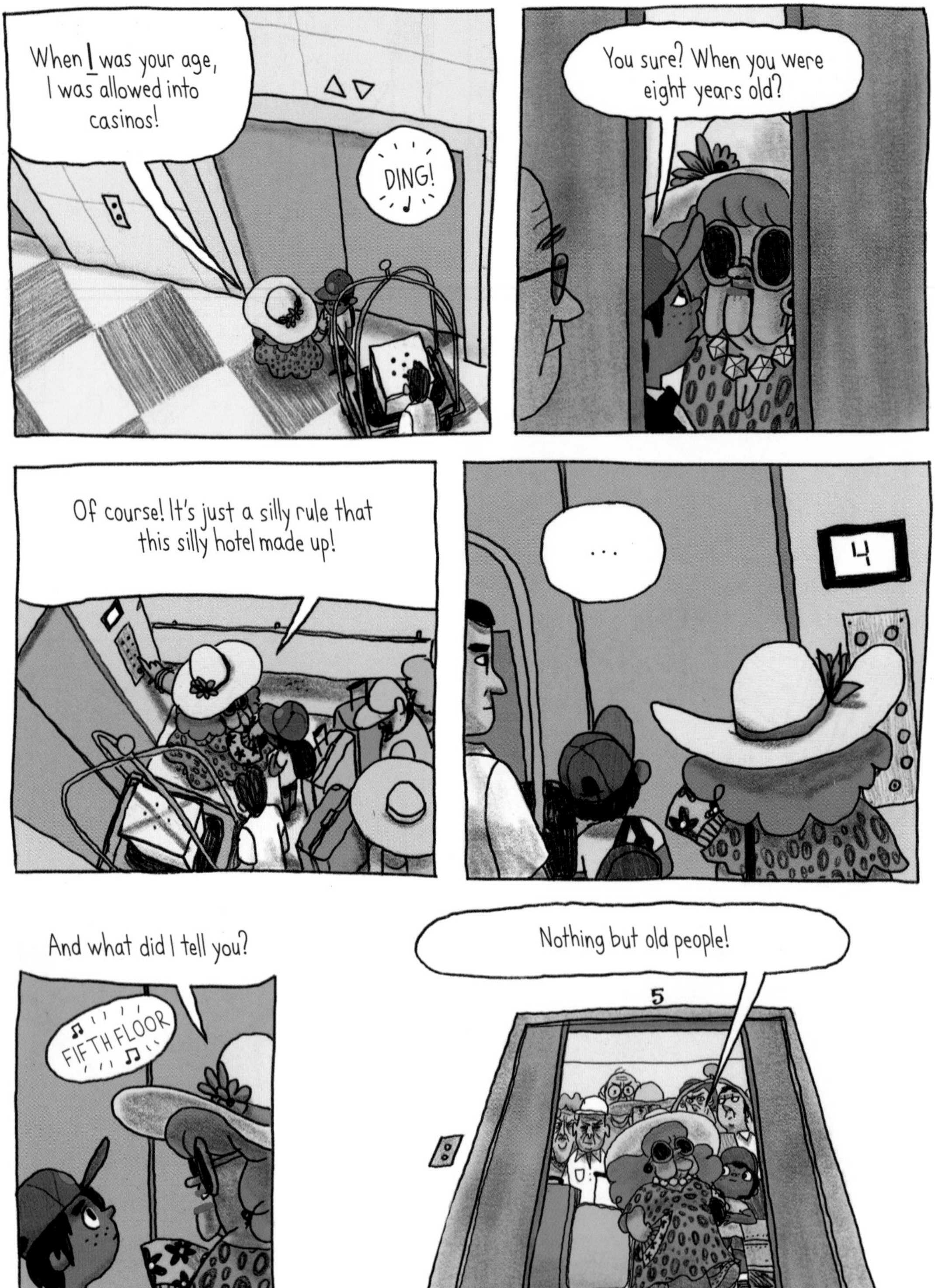
When I was your age, I was allowed into casinos!
DING!
You sure? When you were eight years old?
Of course! It's just a silly rule that this silly hotel made up!
...
4
And what did I tell you?
FIFTH FLOOR
Nothing but old people!
5

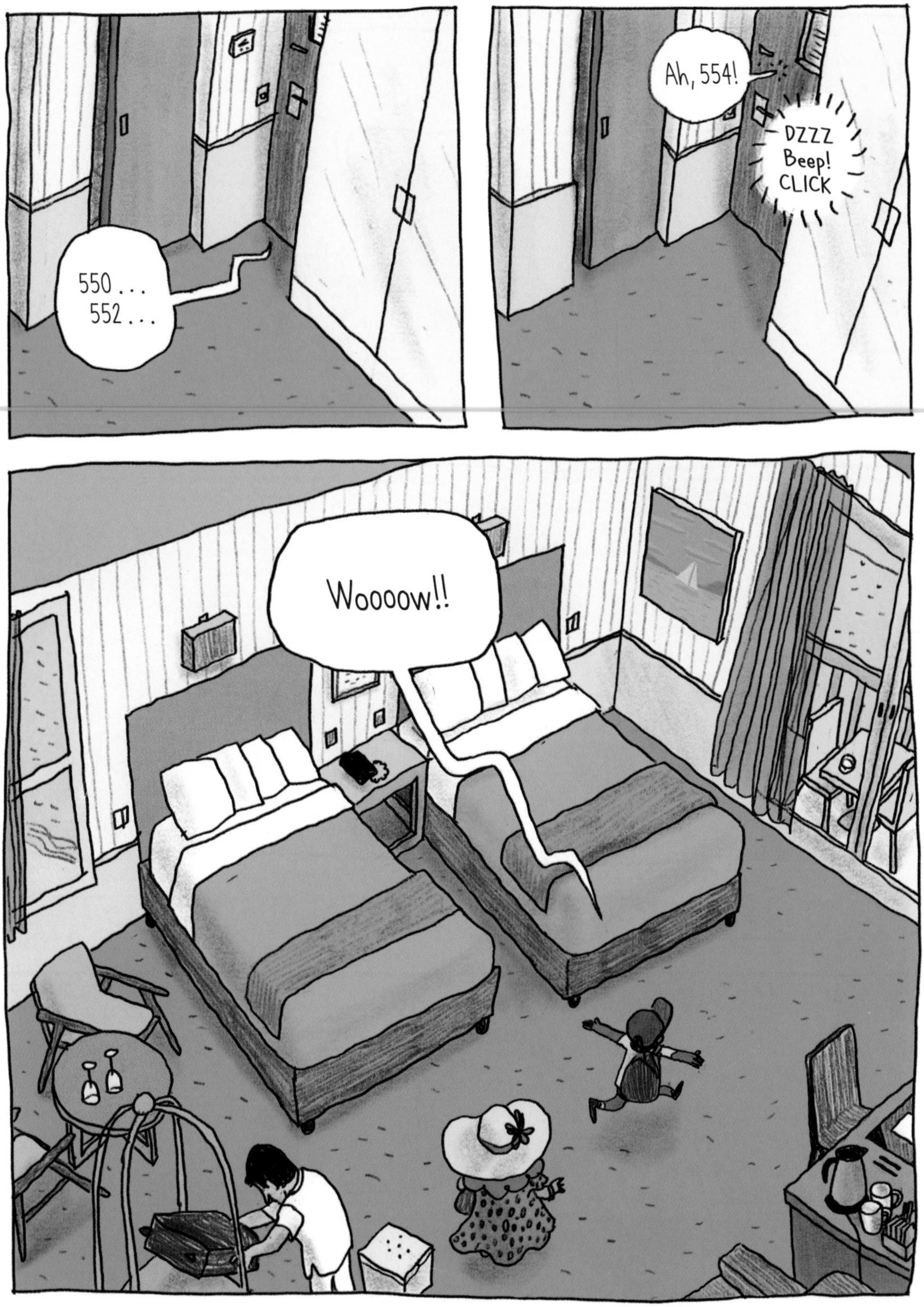
550 . . .
552 . . .
Ah, 554!
DZZZ Beep! CLICK
Woooow!!

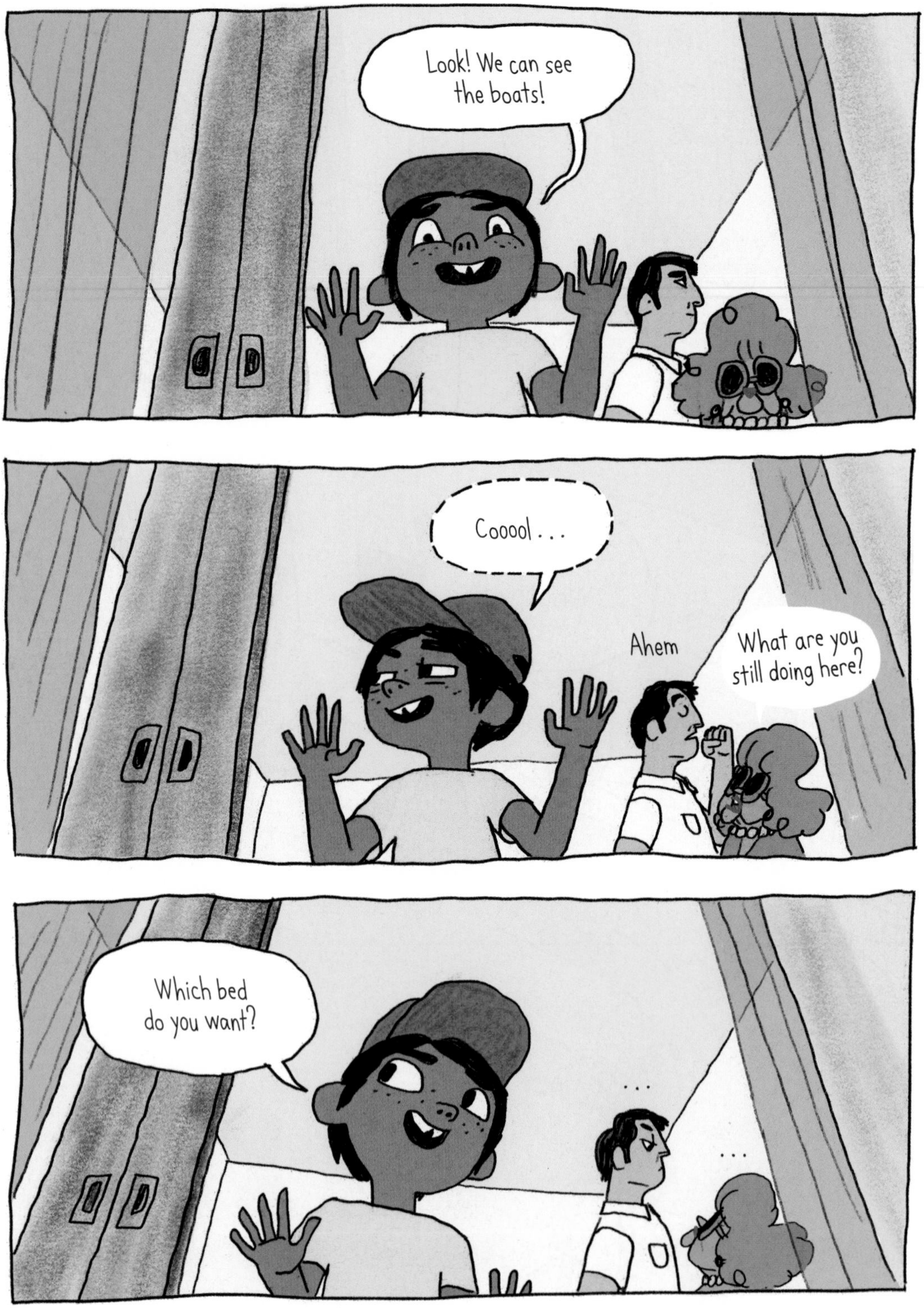
Look! We can see the boats!
Cooool . . .
Ahem
What are you still doing here?
Which bed do you want?
. . .
. . .

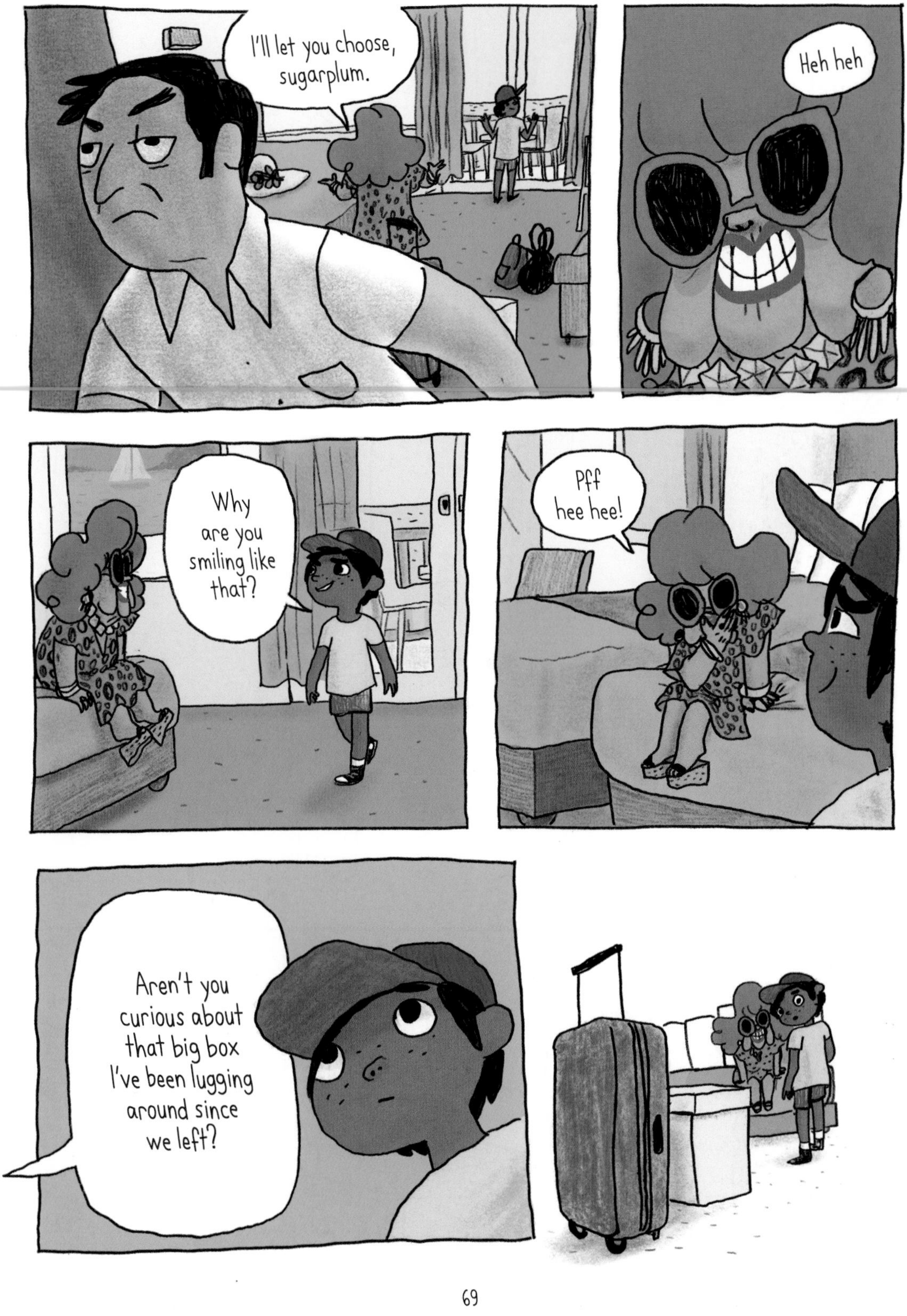
I'll let you choose, sugarplum.
Heh heh
Why are you smiling like that?
Pff hee hee!
Aren't you curious about that big box I've been lugging around since we left?

Um I thought it was your makeup case . . .

WRONG!!

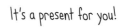

It's a present for you!

. . .

Well? Aren't you going to open it?!

!!!

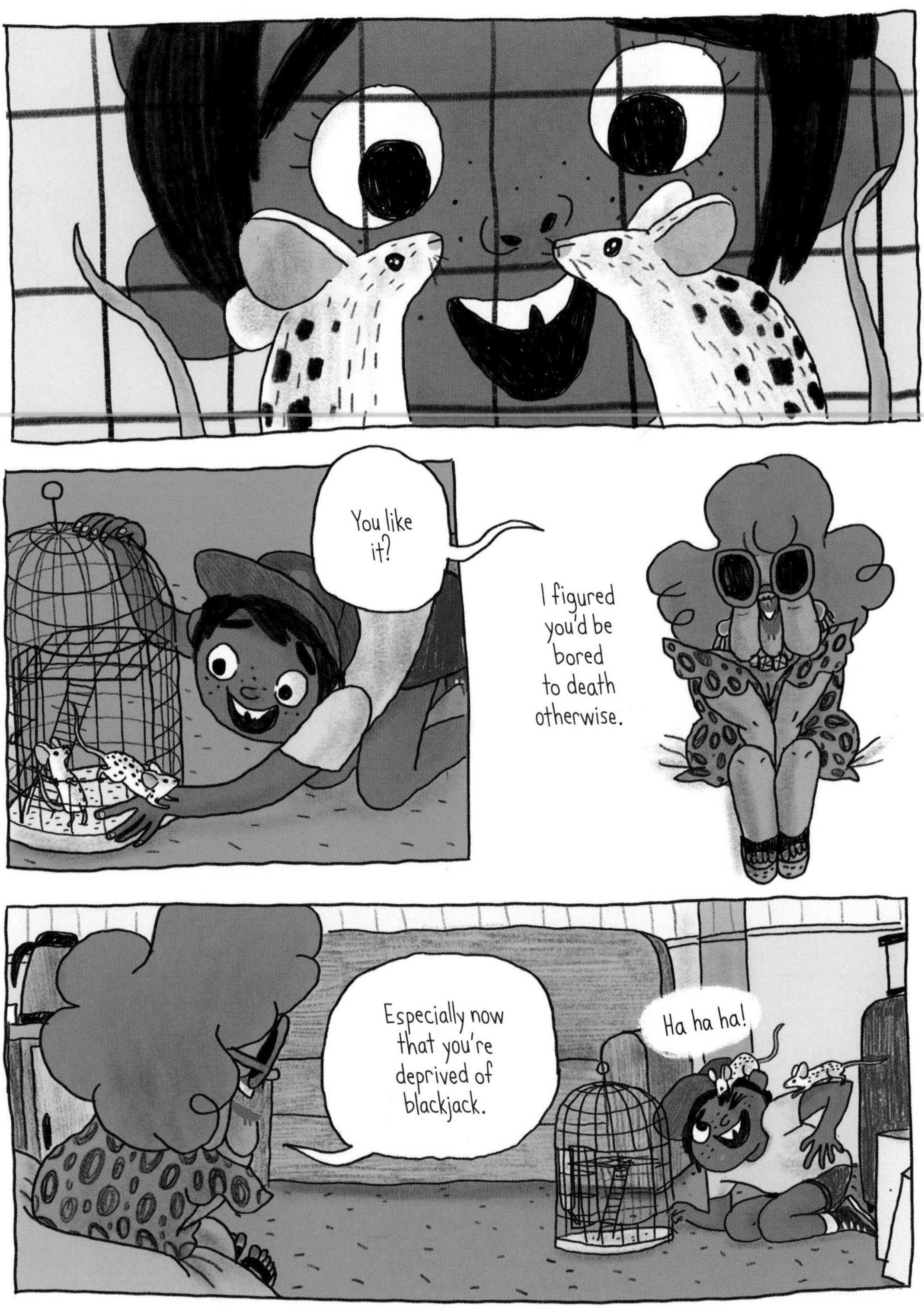
You like it?
I figured you'd be bored to death otherwise.
Especially now that you're deprived of blackjack.
Ha ha ha!

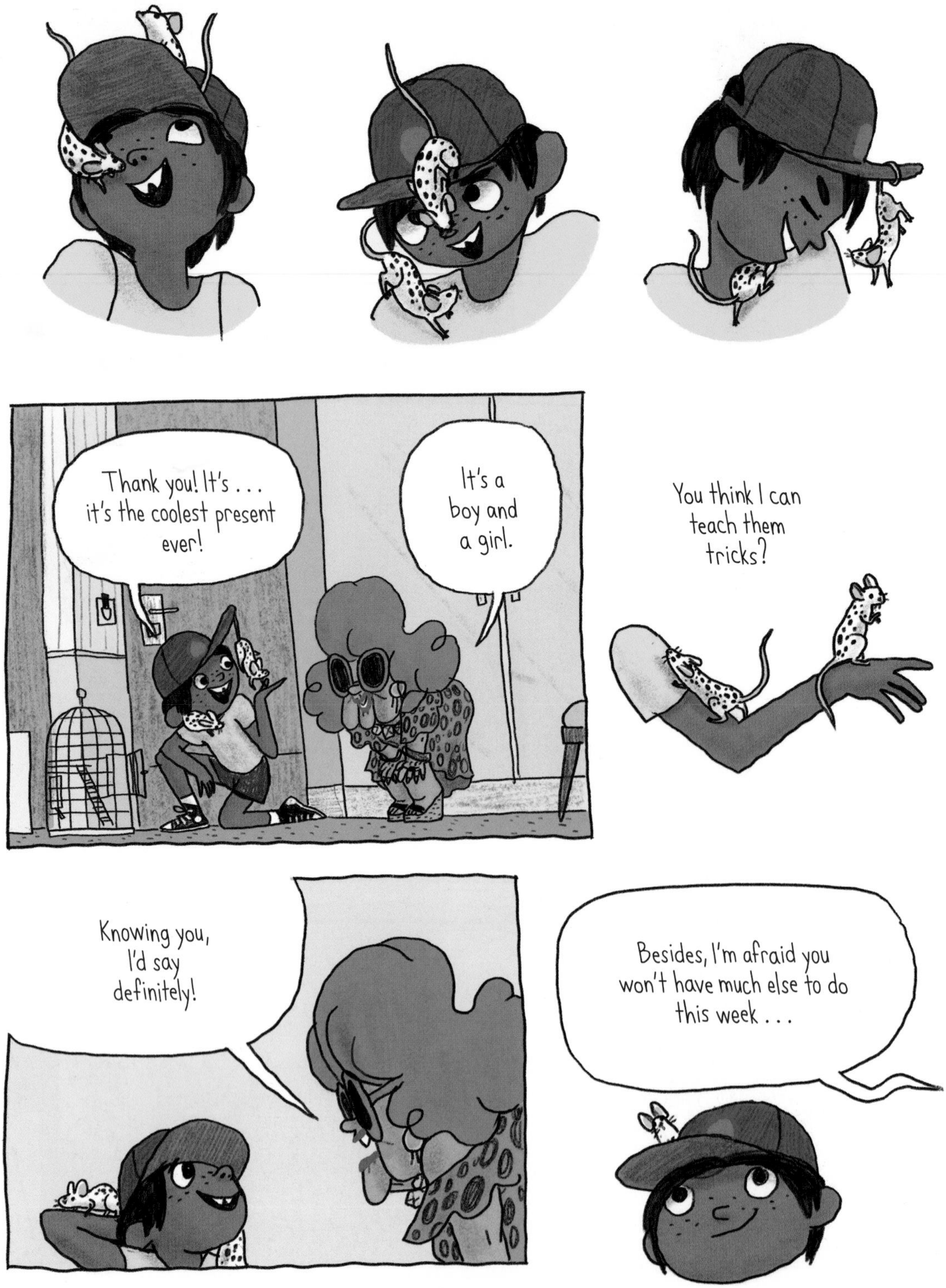
Thank you! It's . . . it's the coolest present ever!
It's a boy and a girl.
You think I can teach them tricks?
Knowing you, I'd say definitely!
Besides, I'm afraid you won't have much else to do this week . . .

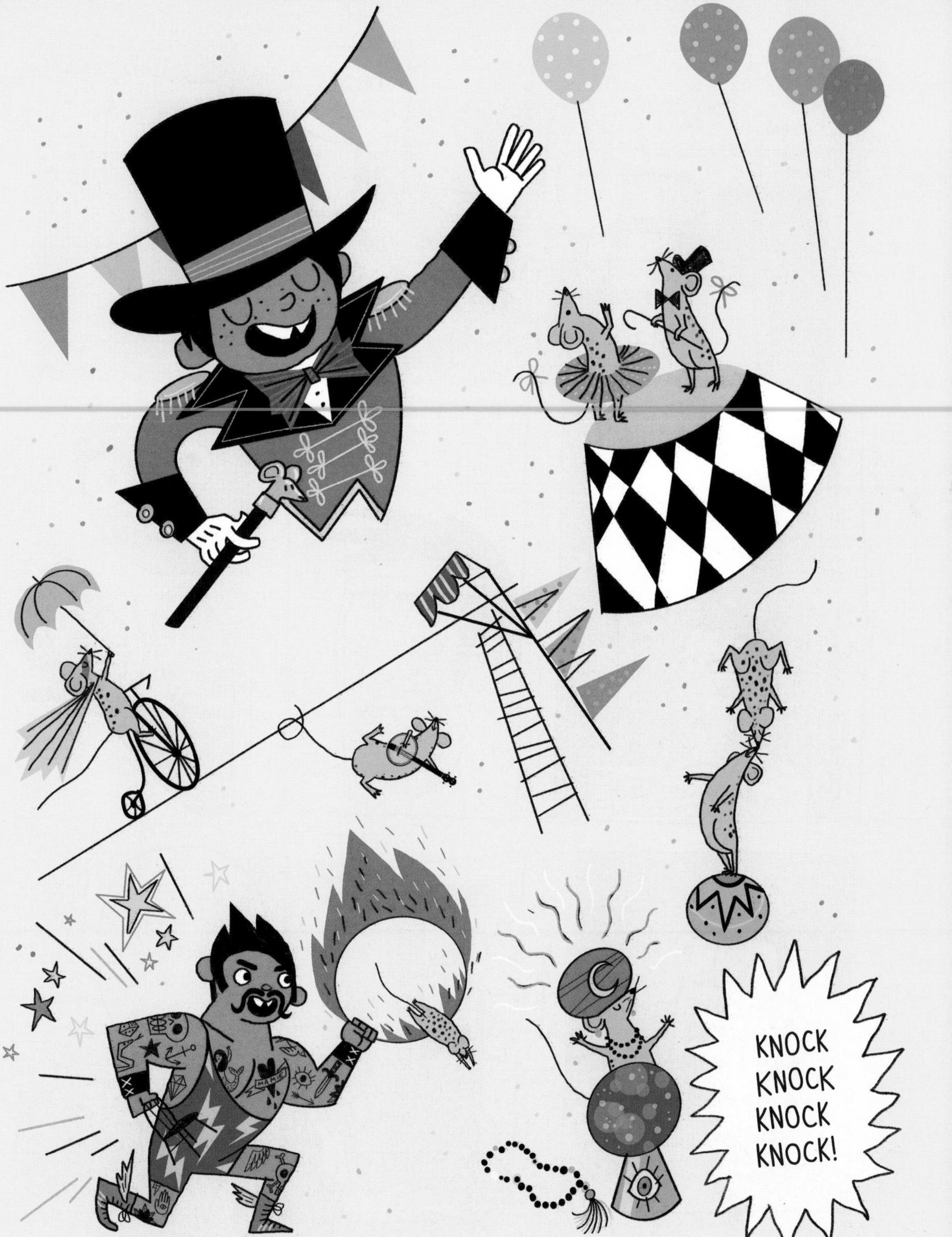
MAMIE
KNOCK
KNOCK
KNOCK
KNOCK!

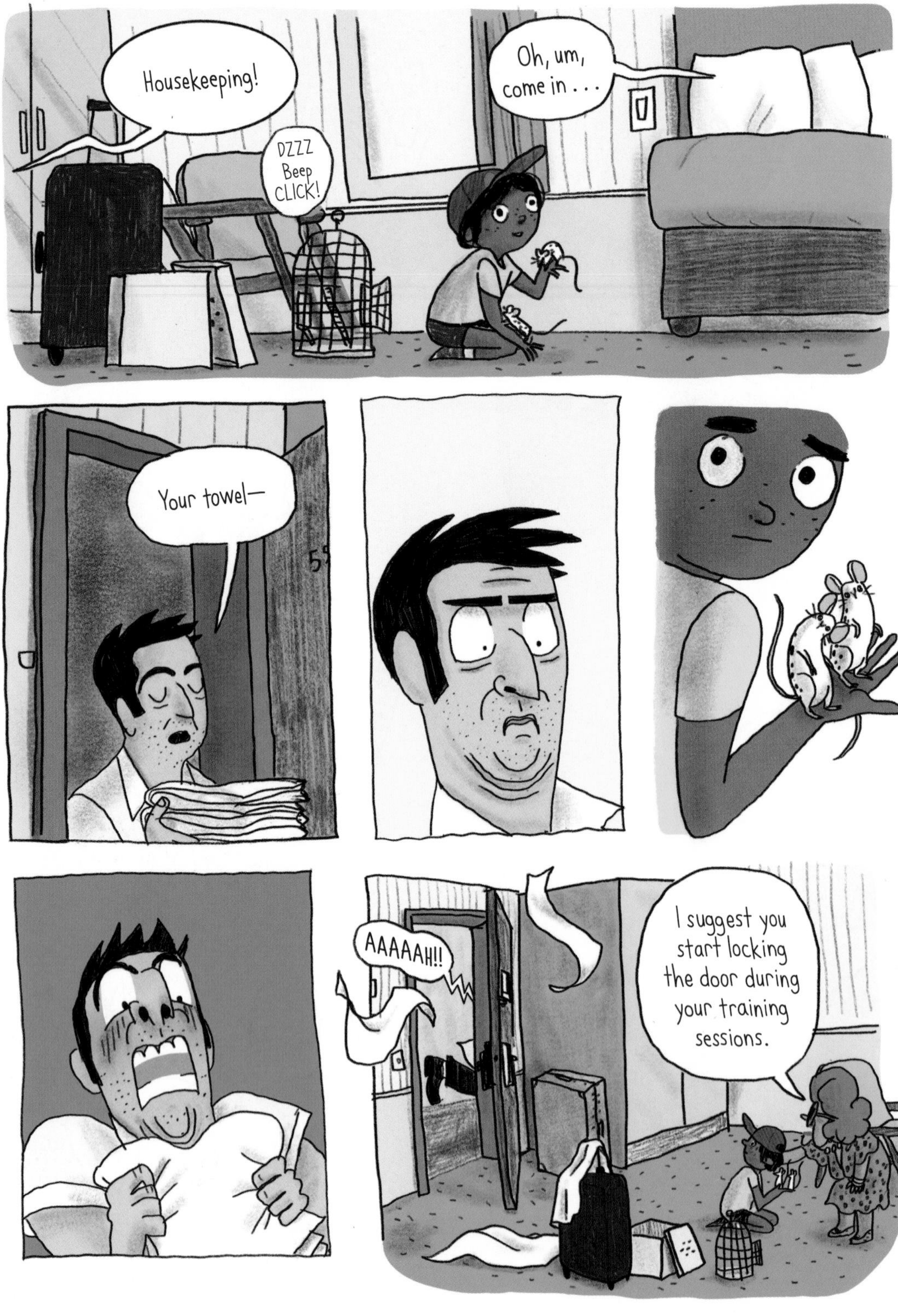
Housekeeping!
DZZZ Beep CLICK!
Oh, um, come in . . .
Your towel—
AAAAAH!!
I suggest you start locking the door during your training sessions.

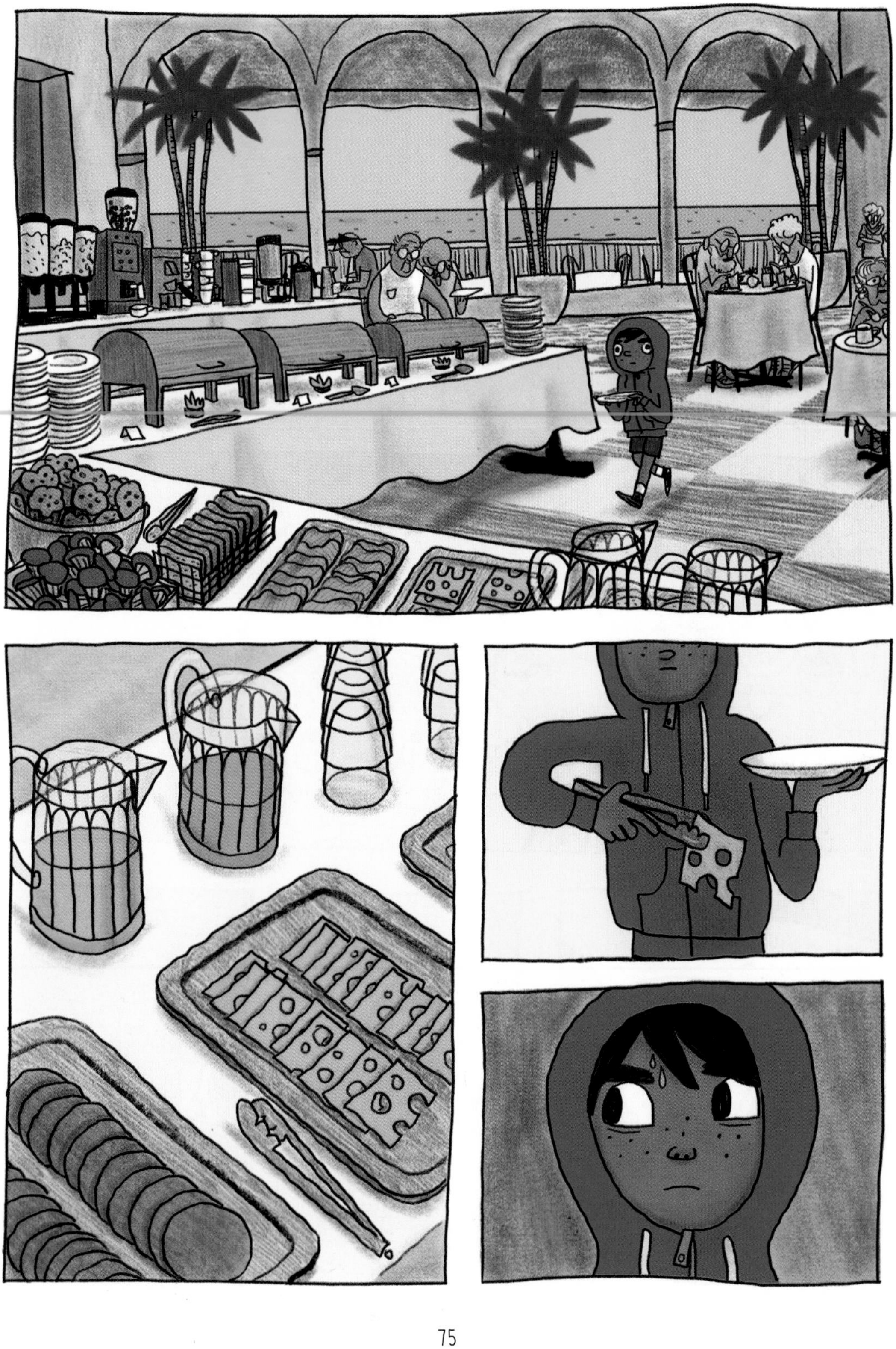

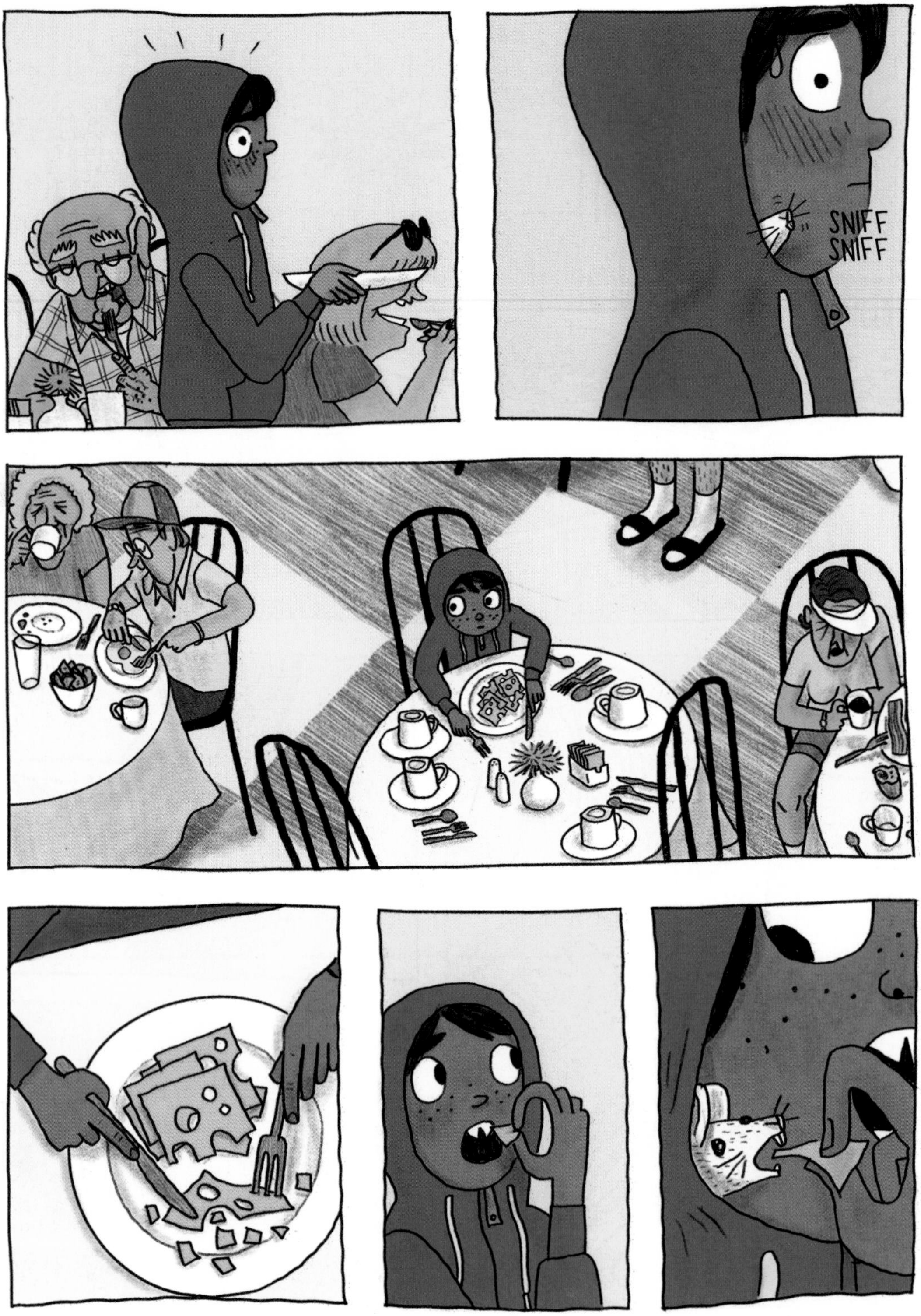
SNIFF
SNIFF

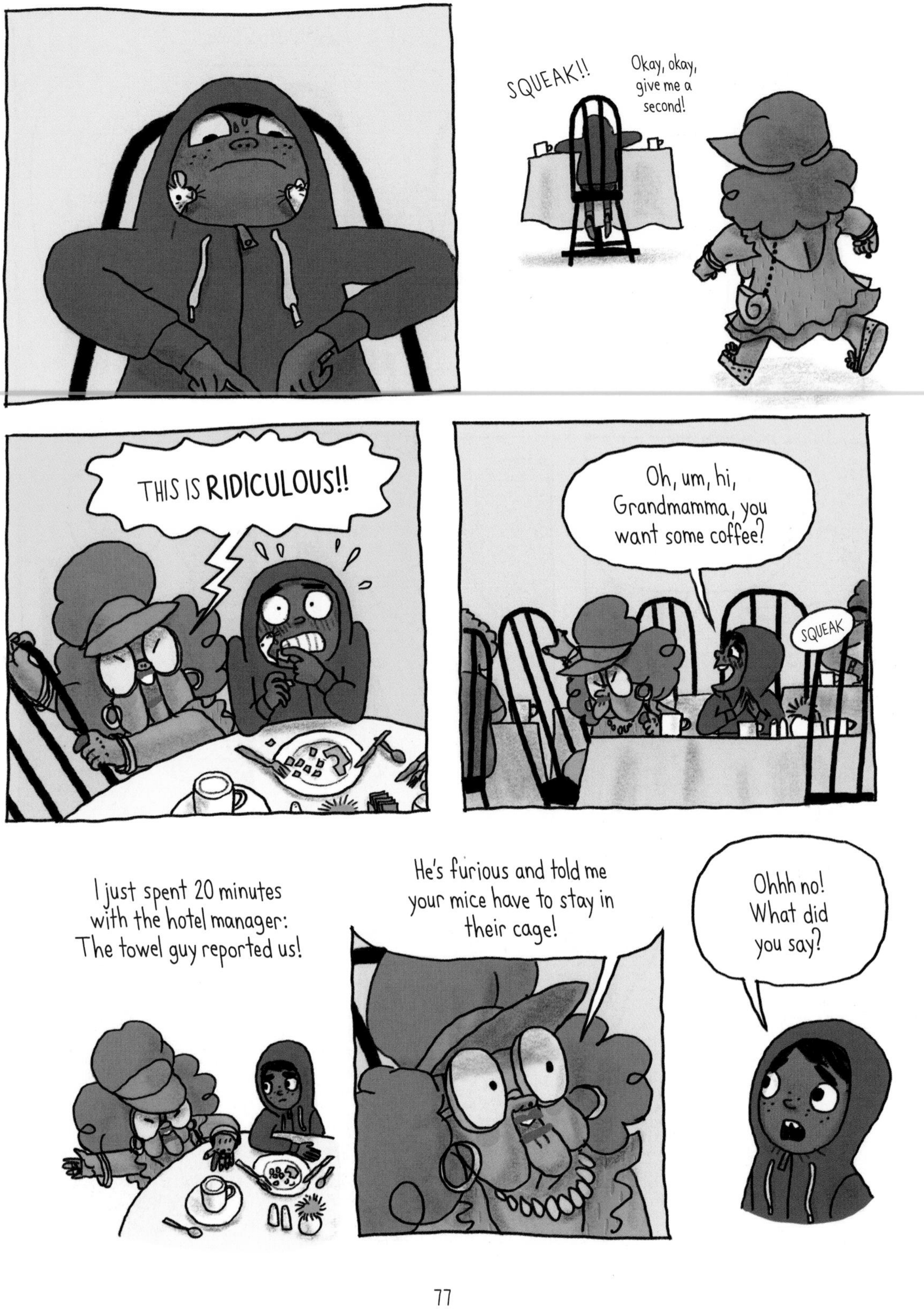
SQUEAK!!
Okay, okay, give me a second!
THIS IS RIDICULOUS!!
Oh, um, hi, Grandmamma, you want some coffee?
SQUEAK
I just spent 20 minutes with the hotel manager: The towel guy reported us!
He's furious and told me your mice have to stay in their cage!
Ohhh no! What did you say?

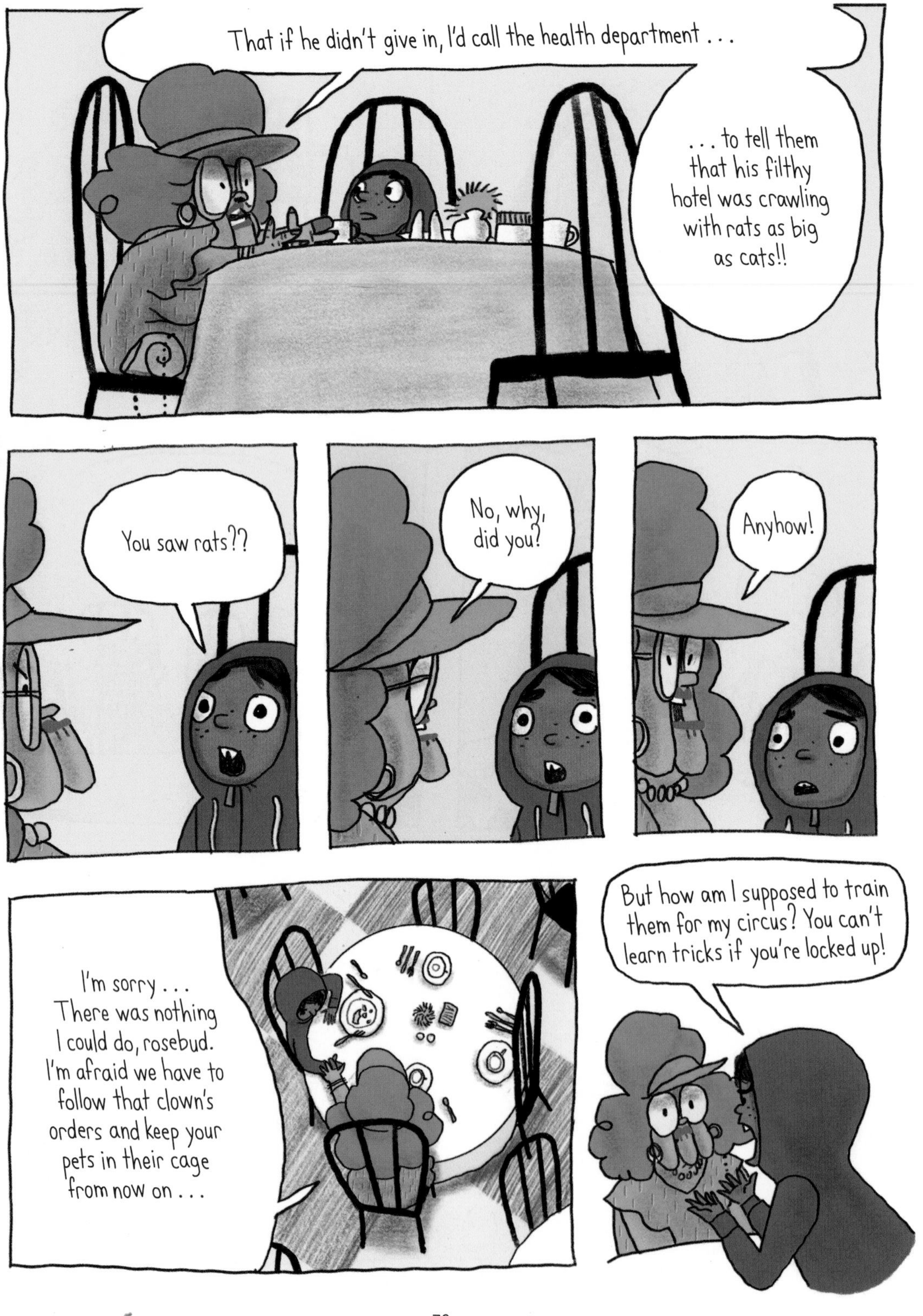
That if he didn't give in, I'd call the health department . . .
. . . to tell them that his filthy hotel was crawling with rats as big as cats!!
You saw rats??
No, why, did you?
Anyhow!
I'm sorry . . . There was nothing I could do, rosebud. I'm afraid we have to follow that clown's orders and keep your pets in their cage from now on . . .
But how am I supposed to train them for my circus? You can't learn tricks if you're locked up!

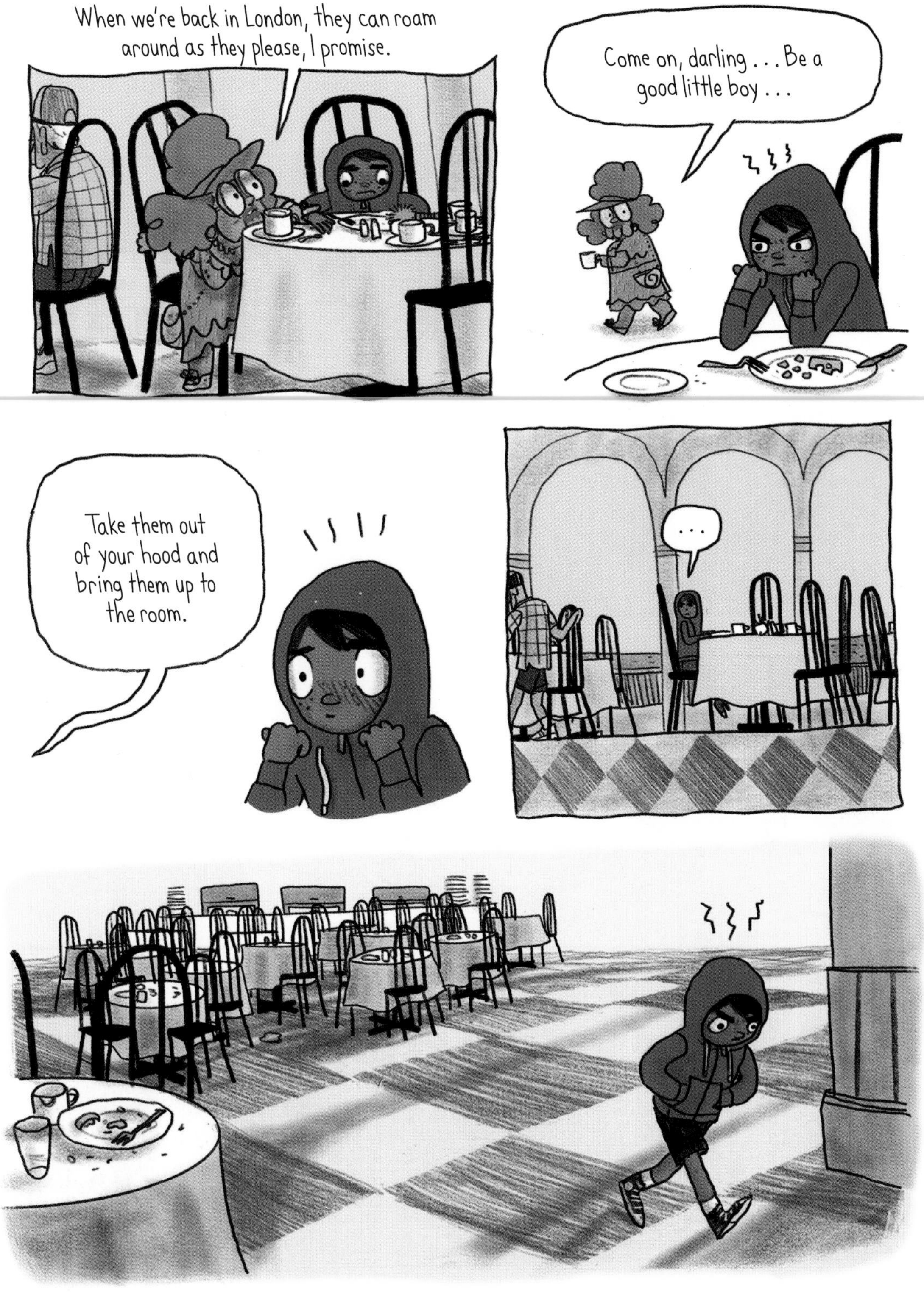
When we're back in London, they can roam around as they please, I promise.
Come on, darling . . . Be a good little boy . . .
Take them out of your hood and bring them up to the room.
. . .

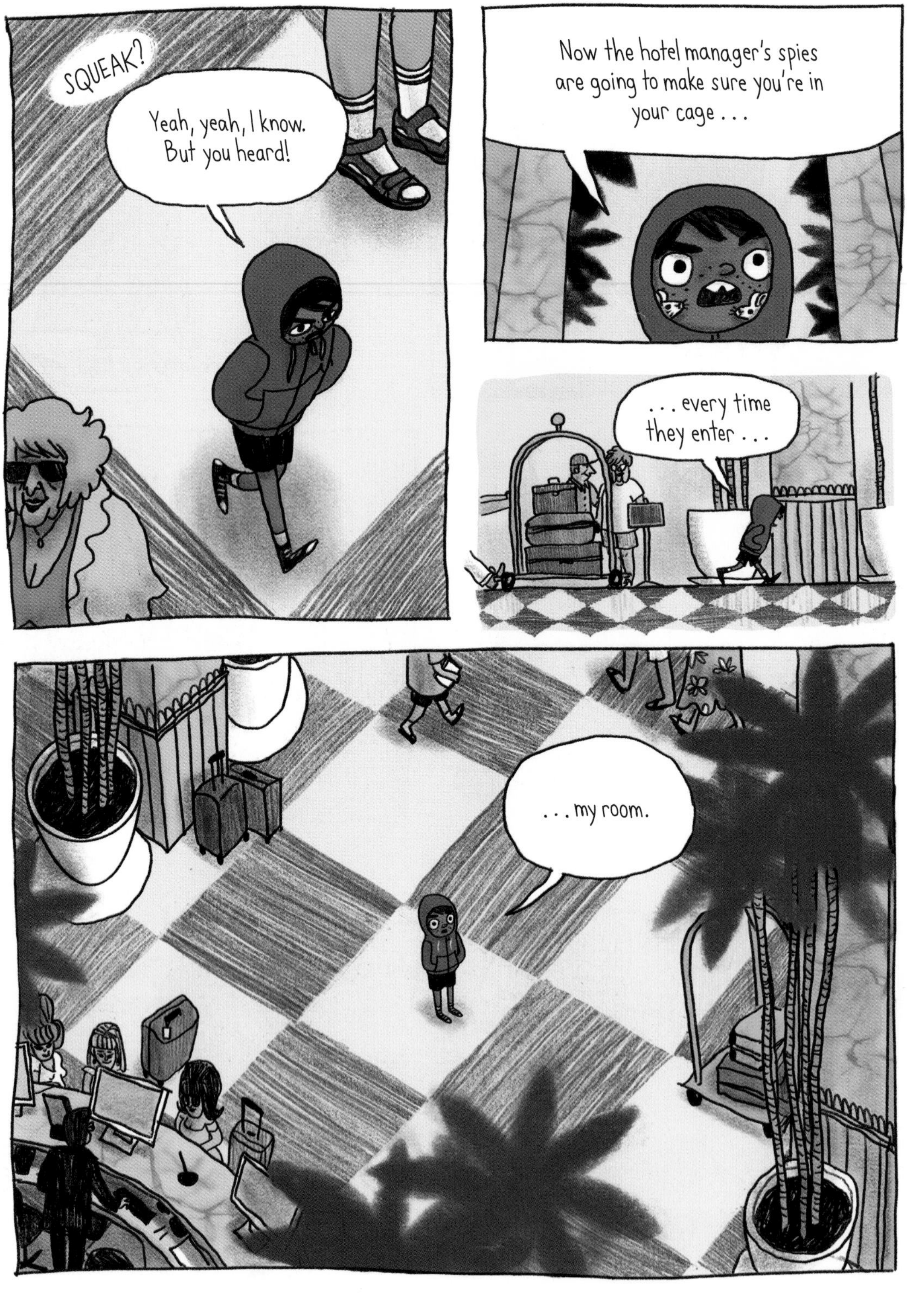
SQUEAK?
Yeah, yeah, I know. But you heard!
Now the hotel manager's spies are going to make sure you're in your cage . . .
. . . every time they enter . . .
. . . my room.

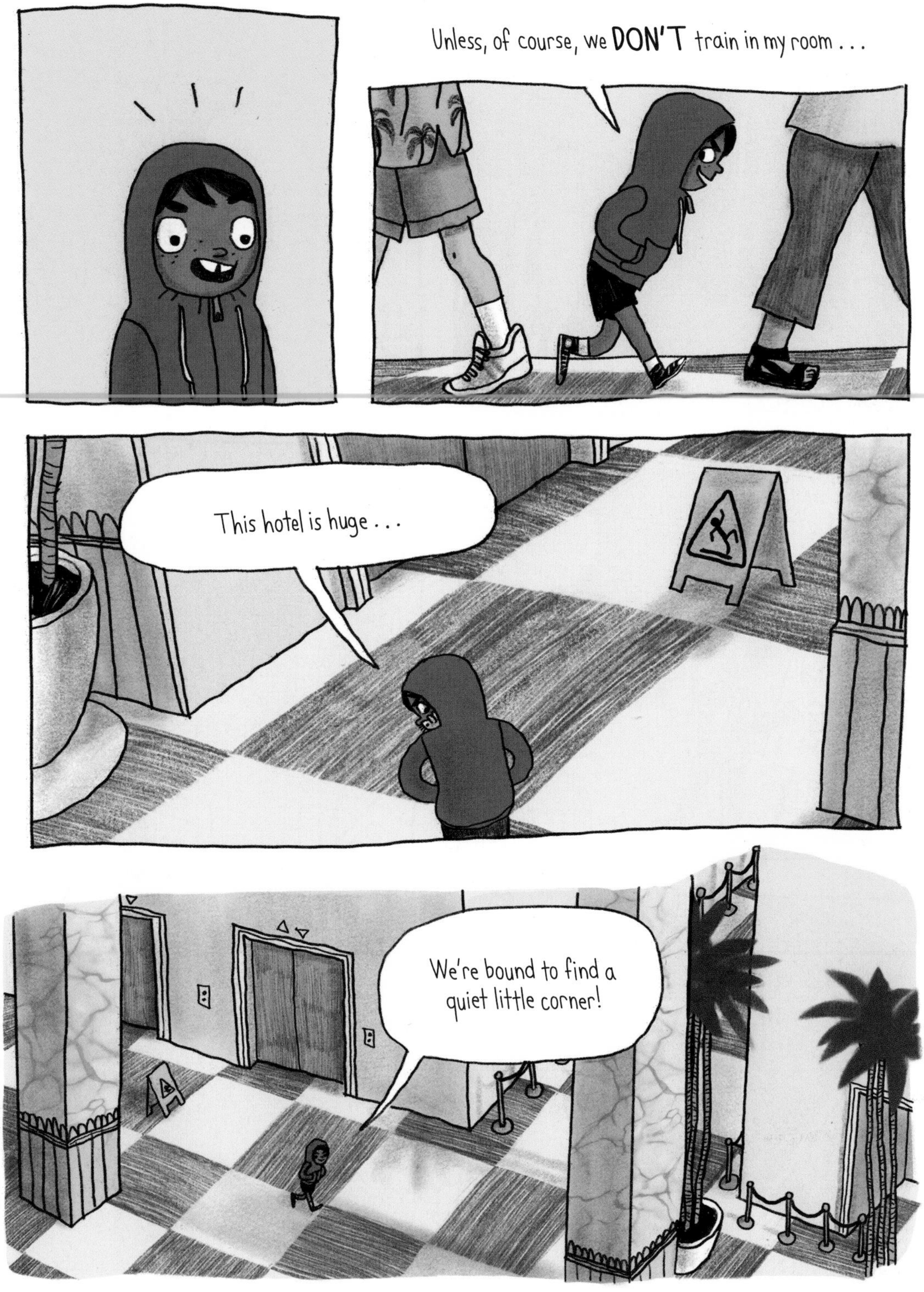
Unless, of course, we DON'T train in my room . . .
This hotel is huge . . .
We're bound to find a quiet little corner!

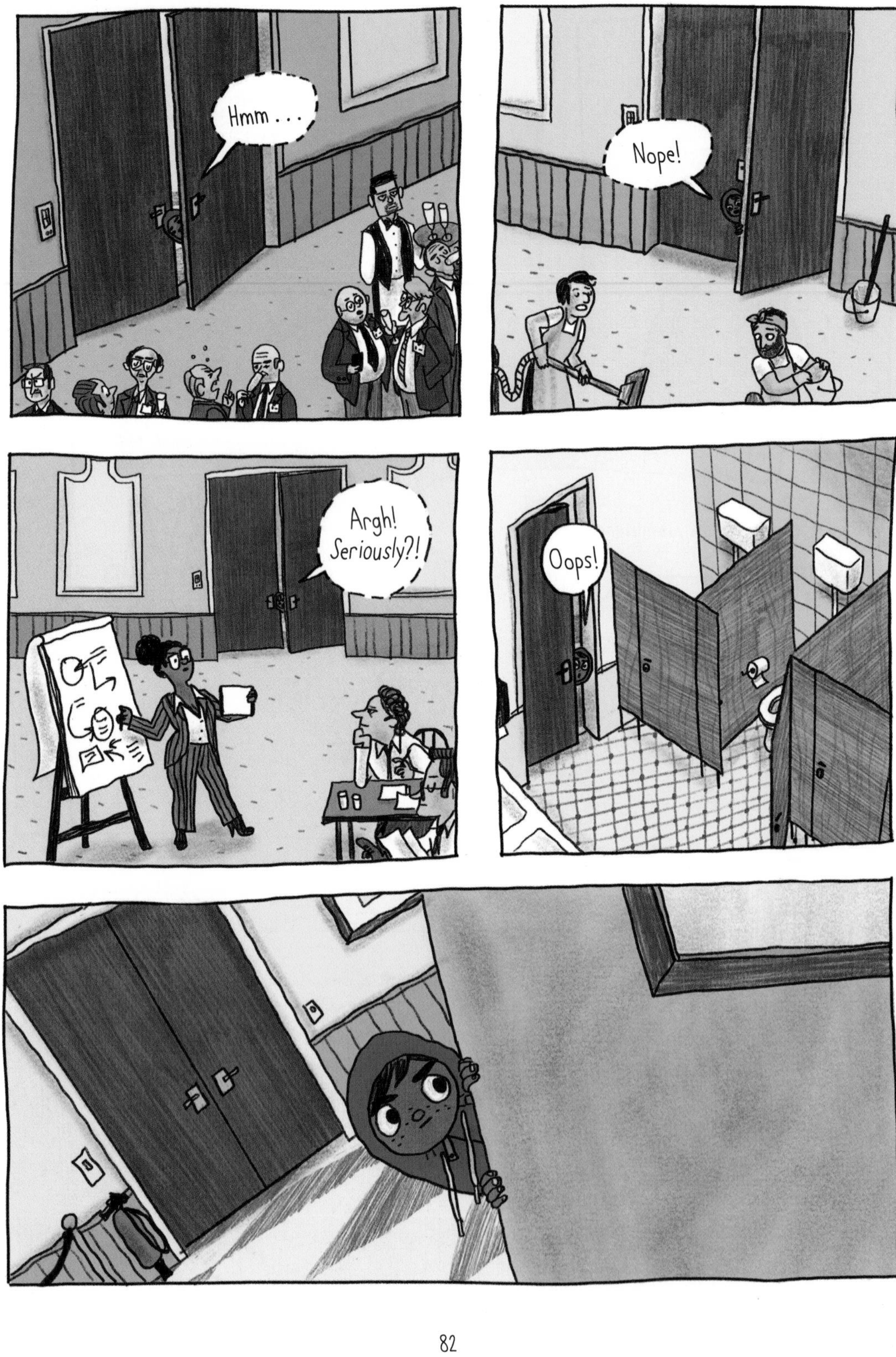
Hmm . . .
Nope!
Argh! Seriously?!
Oops!

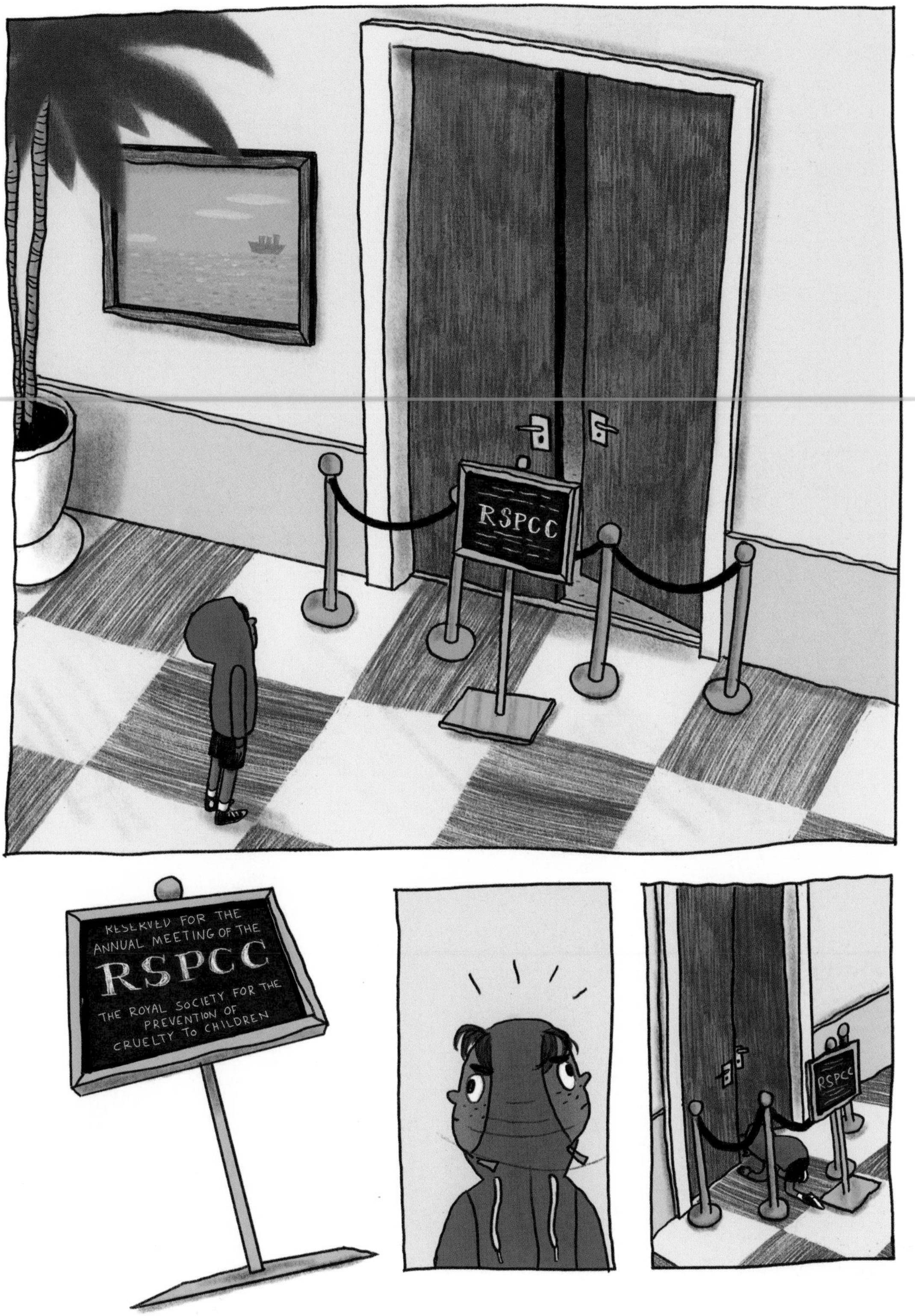
RSPCC
RESERVED FOR THE ANNUAL MEETING OF THE
RSPCC
THE ROYAL SOCIETY FOR THE PREVENTION OF CRUELTY TO CHILDREN
RSPCC

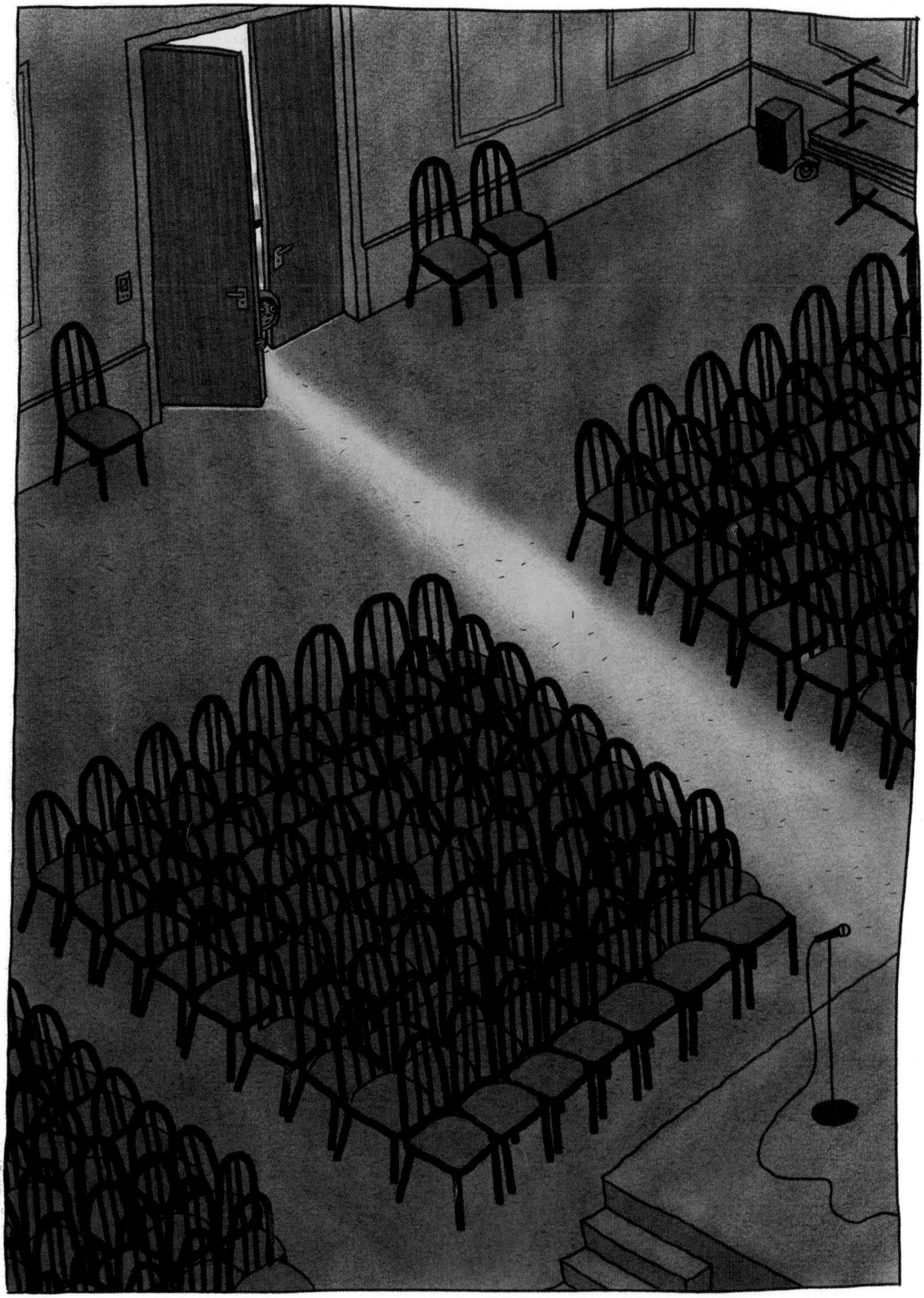

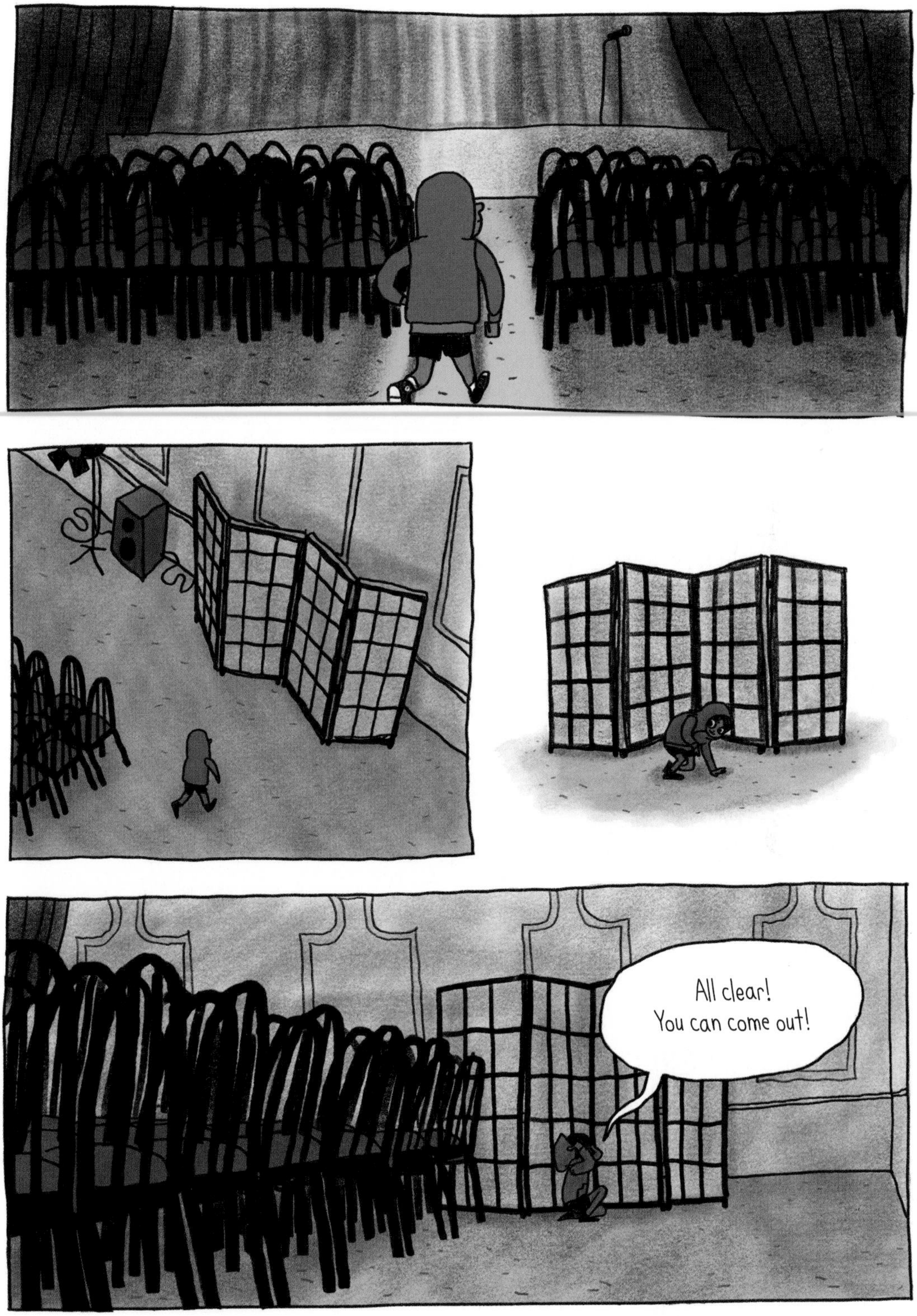
All clear!
You can come out!

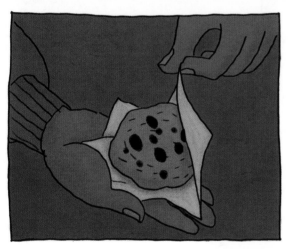

Okay, now it's time . . .

. . . to concentrate!

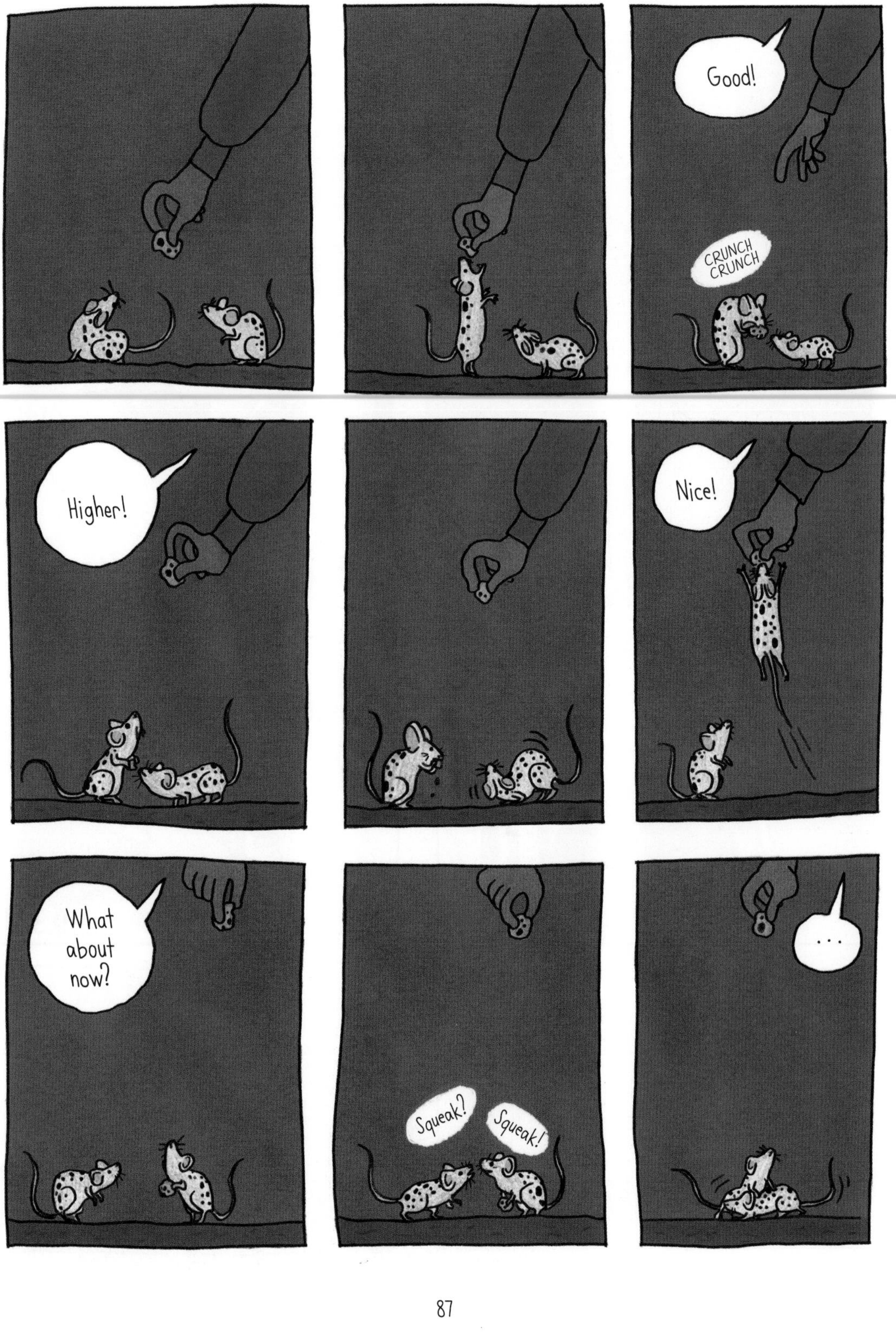
Good!
CRUNCH CRUNCH
Higher!
Nice!
What about now?
Squeak?
Squeak!
...

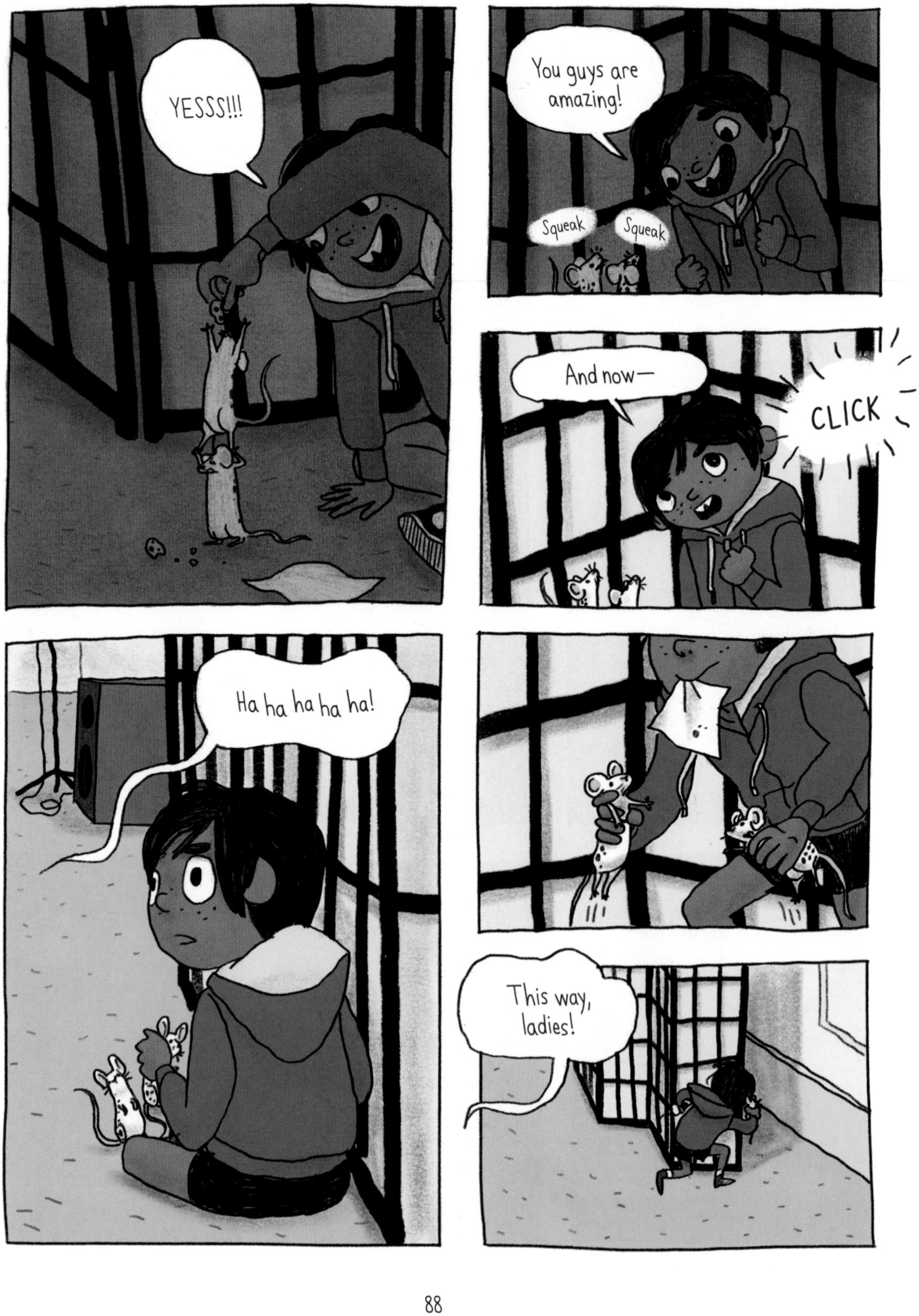
YESSS!!!
You guys are amazing!
Squeak
Squeak
And now—
CLICK
Ha ha ha ha ha!
This way, ladies!

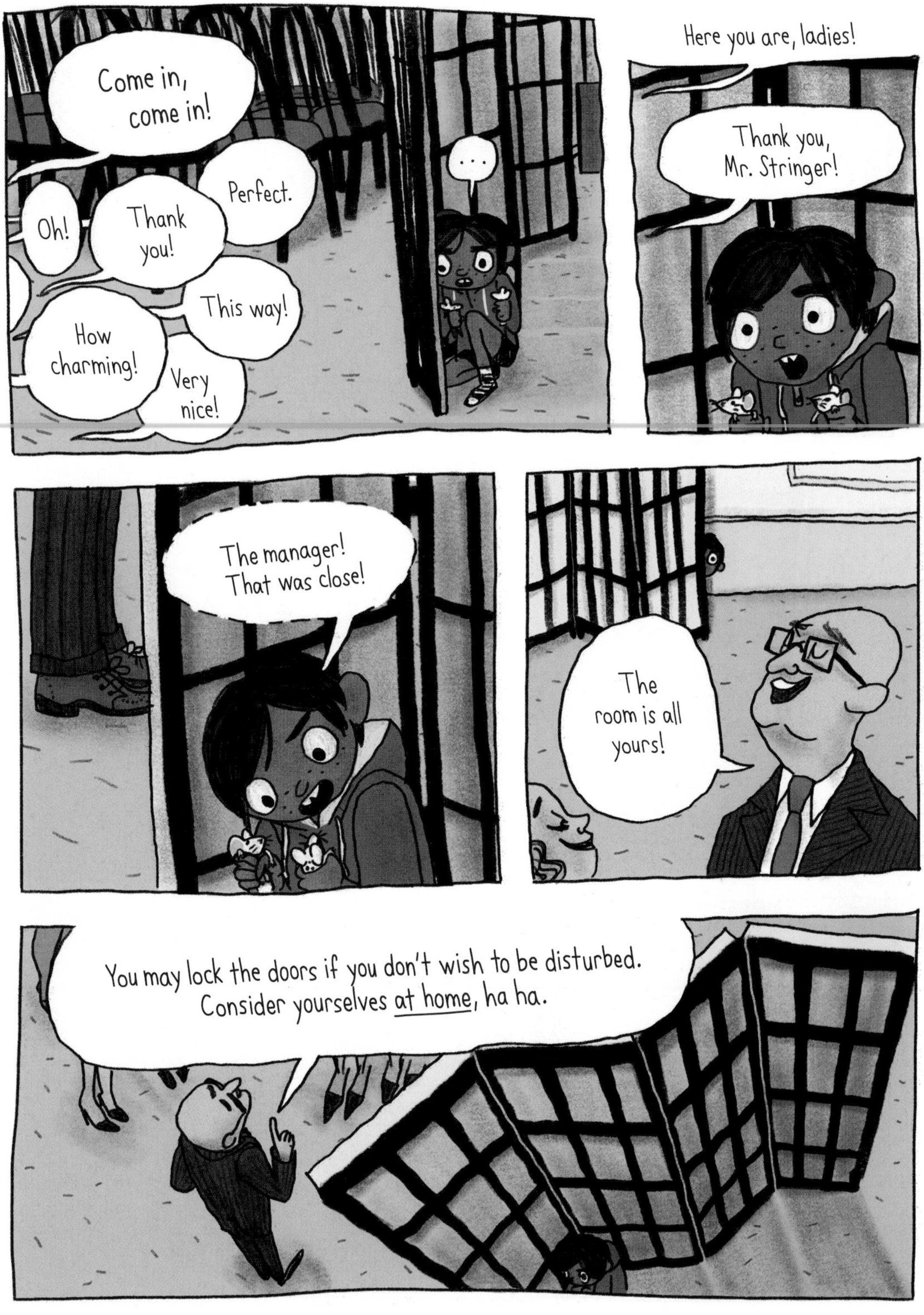
Come in, come in!
Oh!
Thank you!
Perfect.
How charming!
This way!
Very nice!
. . .
Here you are, ladies!
Thank you, Mr. Stringer!
The manager! That was close!
The room is all yours!
You may lock the doors if you don't wish to be disturbed. Consider yourselves at home, ha ha.

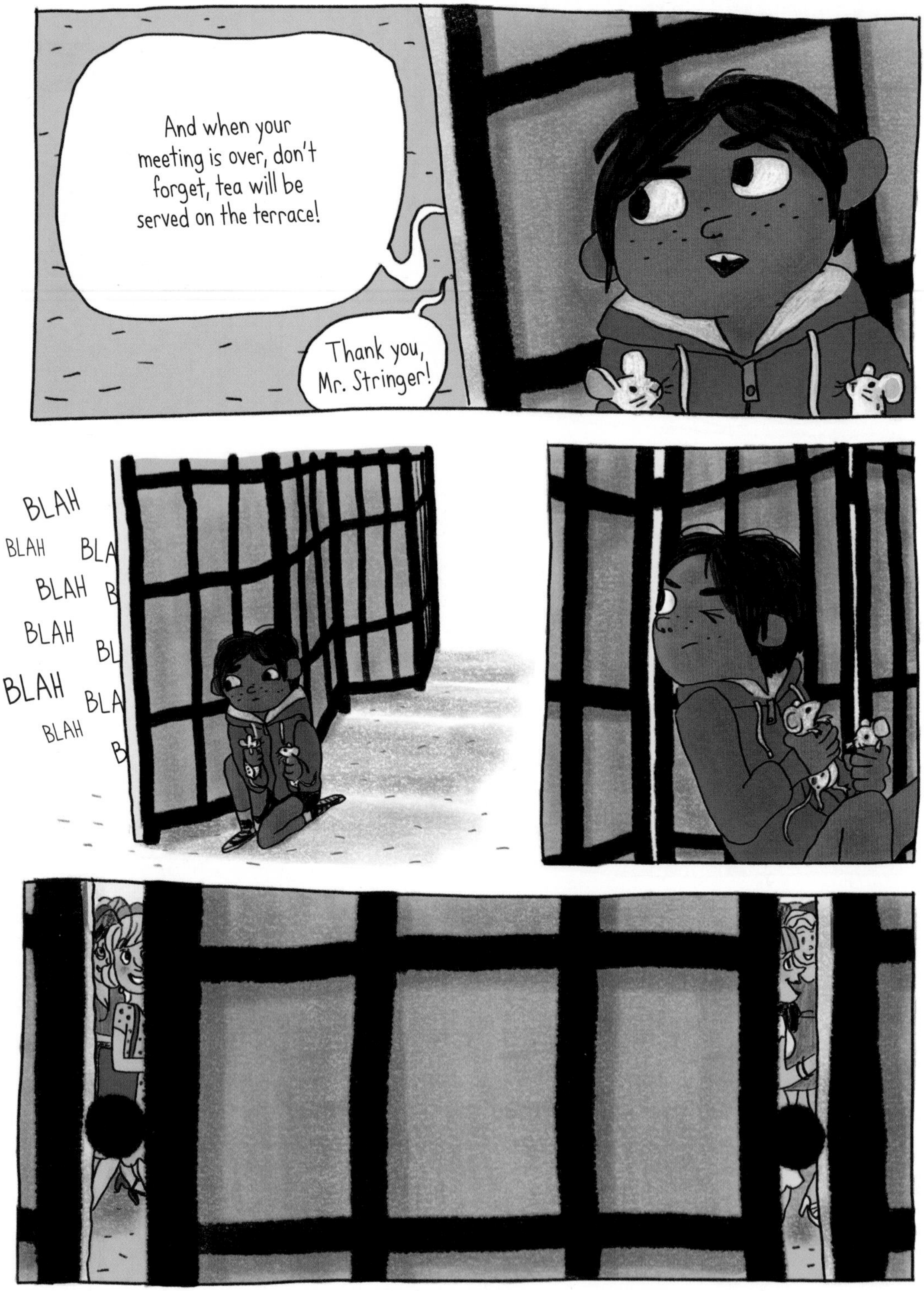

And when your meeting is over, don't forget, tea will be served on the terrace!
Thank you, Mr. Stringer!
BLAH
BLAH
BLA
BLAH
BLAH
BLAH
BLA
BLAH

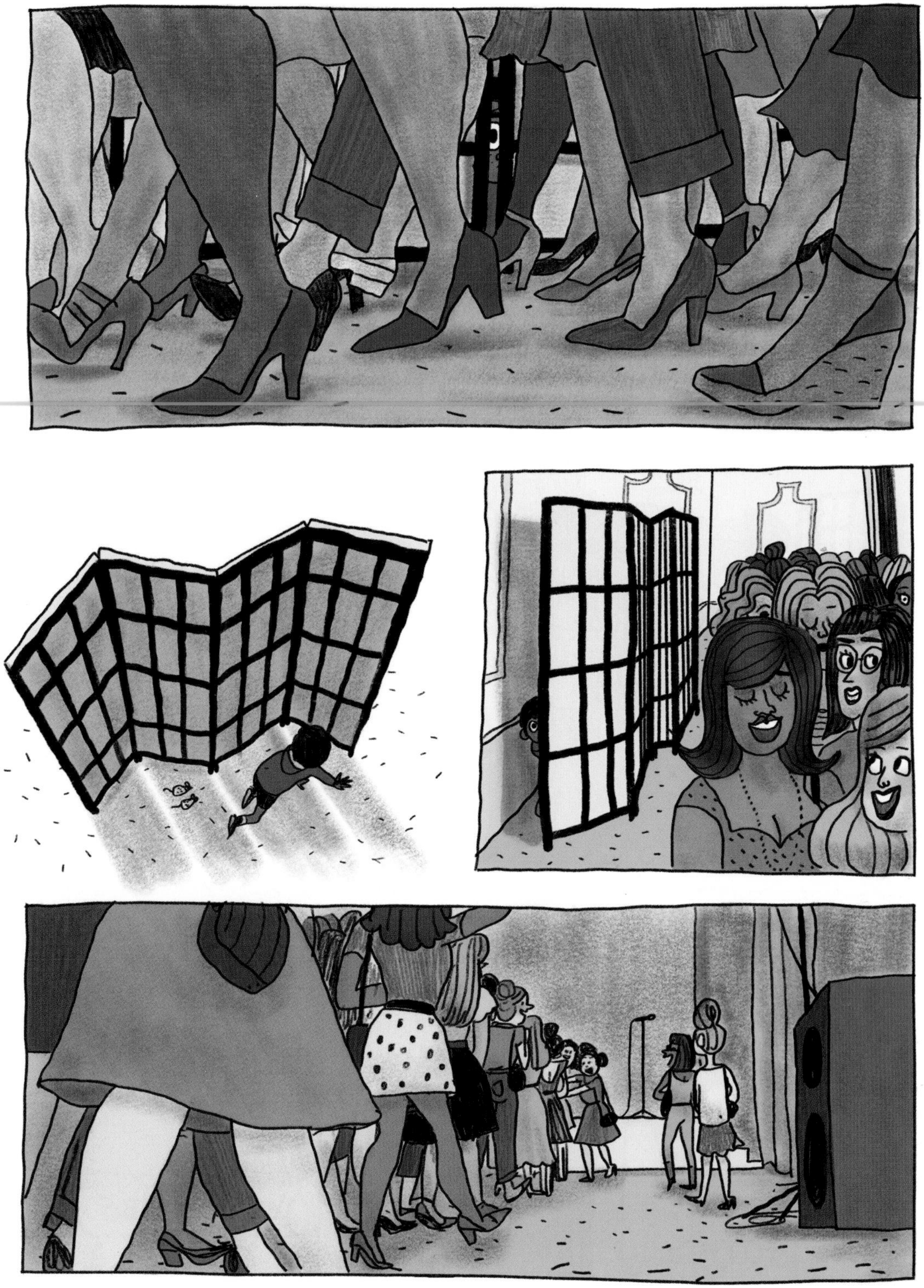

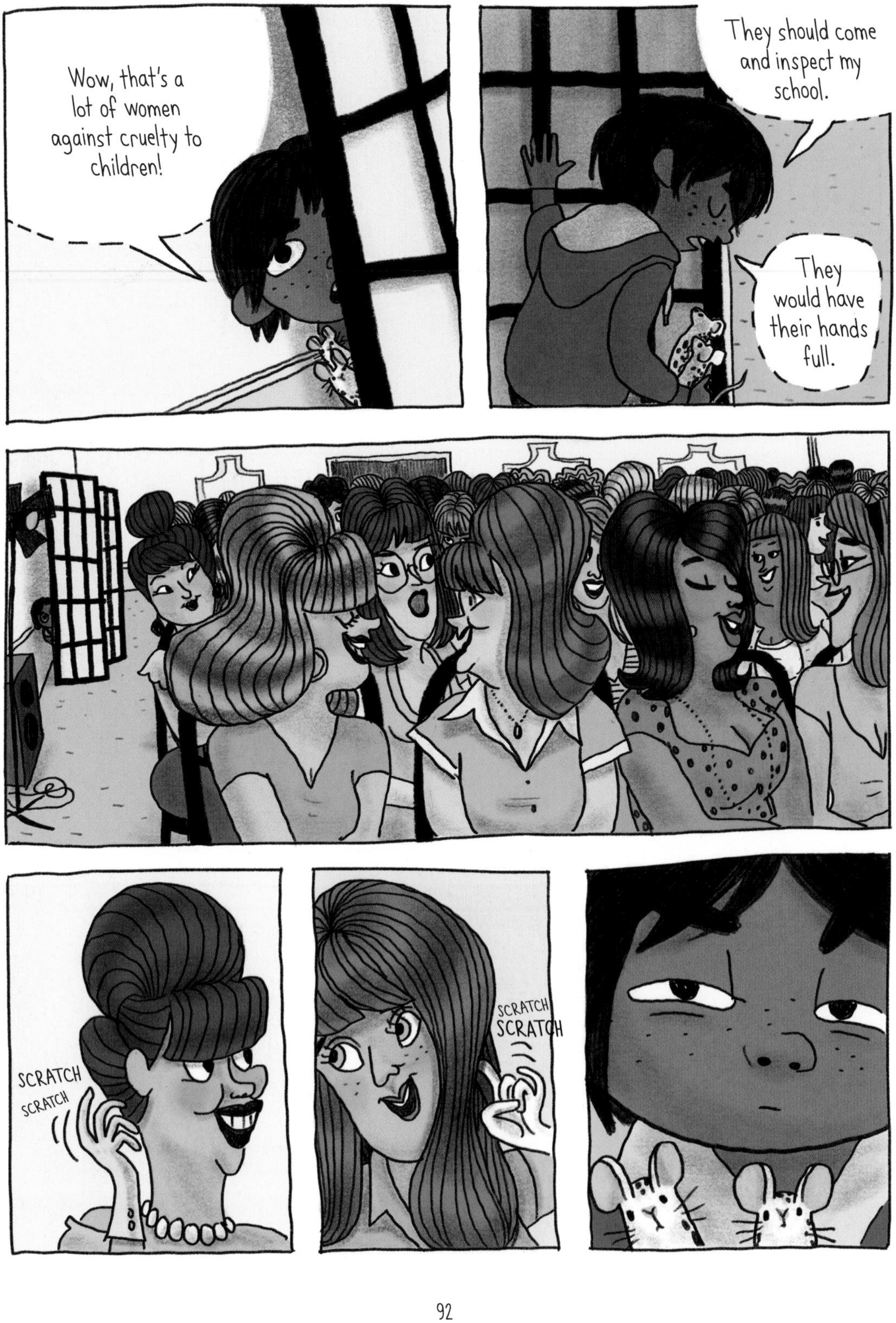
Wow, that's a lot of women against cruelty to children!
They should come and inspect my school.
They would have their hands full.
SCRATCH
SCRATCH
SCRATCH
SCRATCH

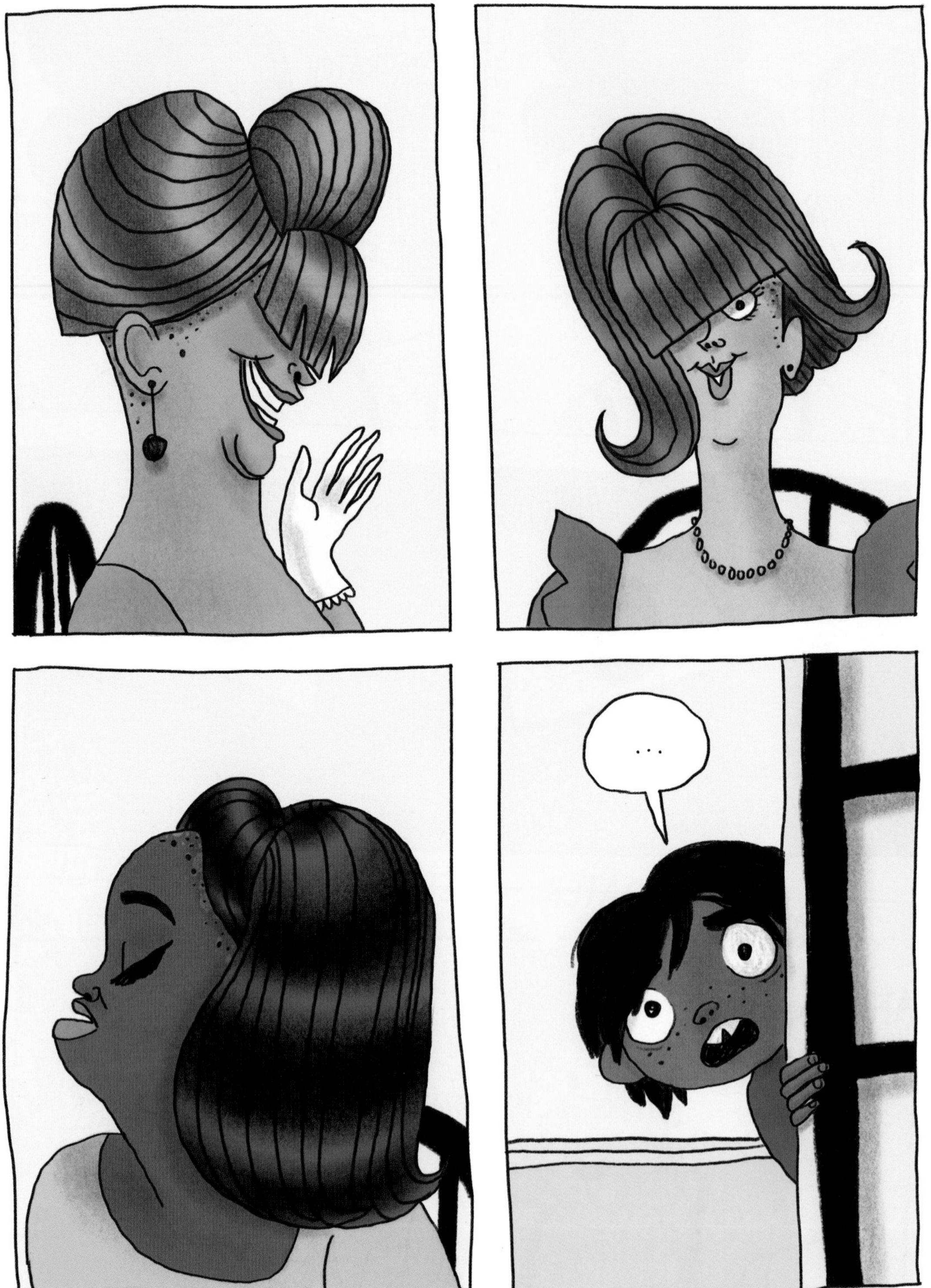
...

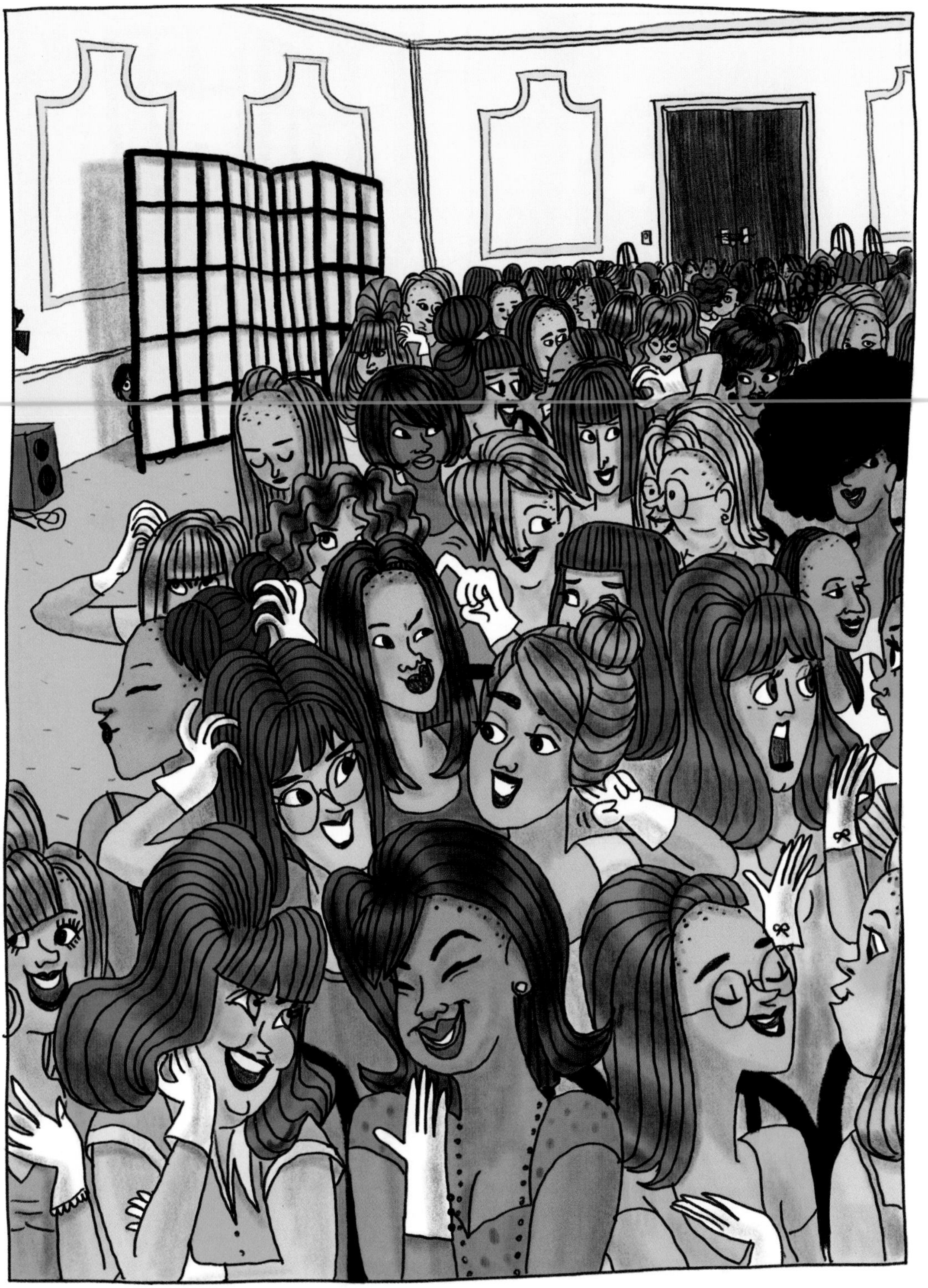

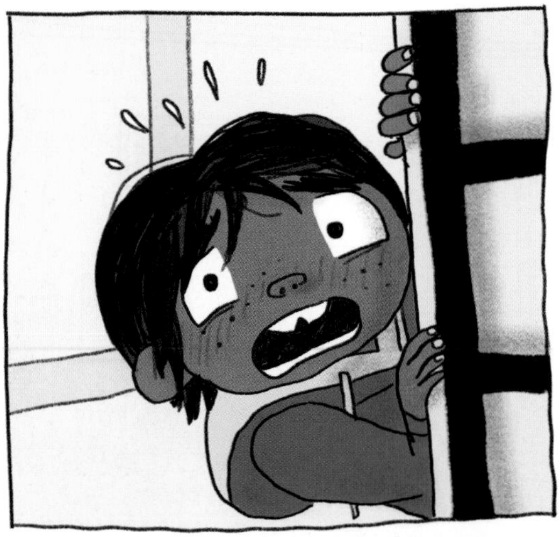

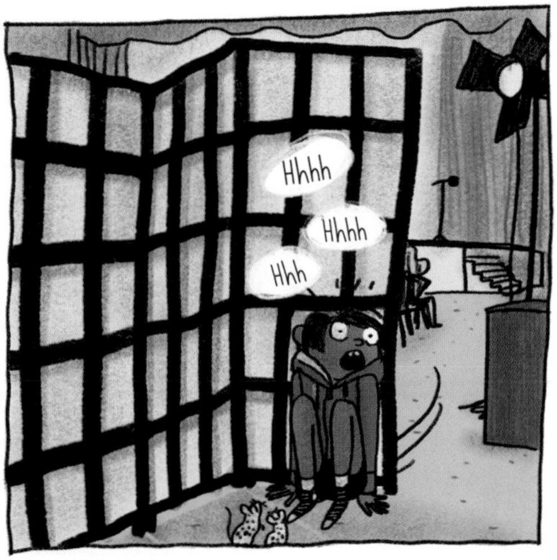
Hhhh
Hhhh
Hhh

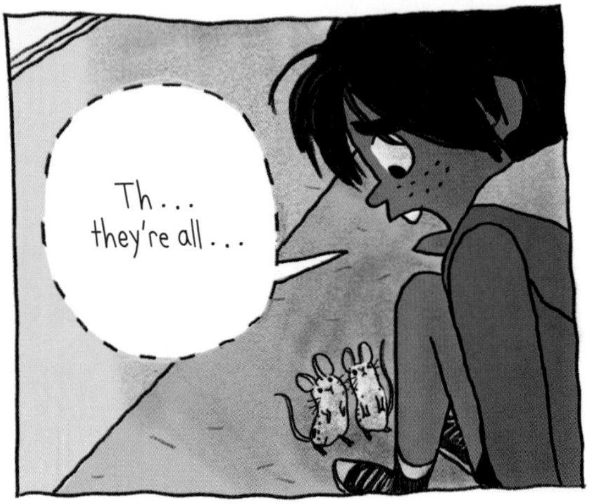
Th . . .
they're all . . .

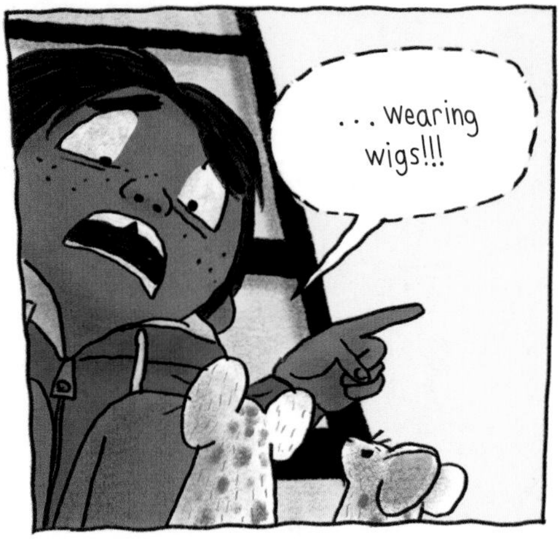
. . . wearing
wigs!!!

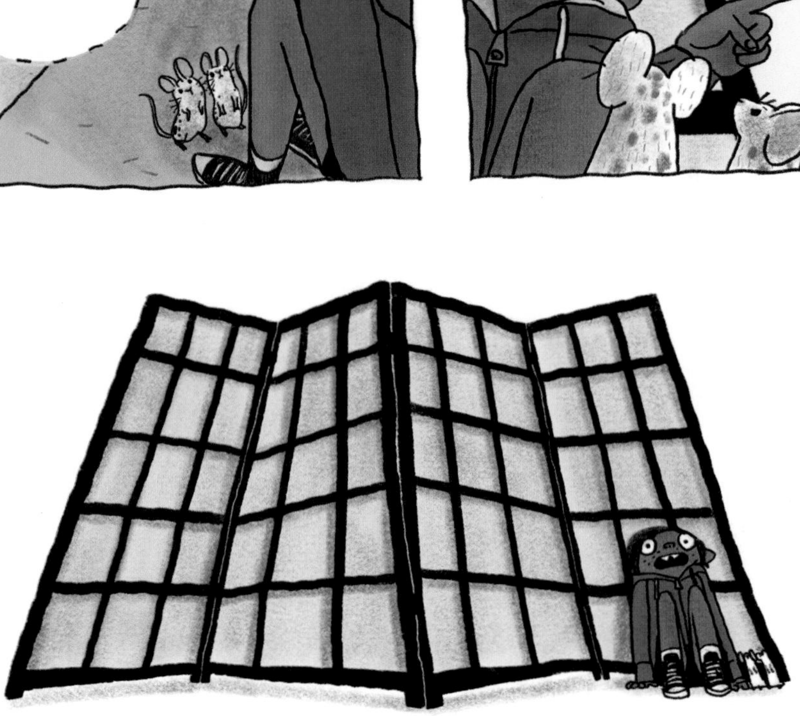

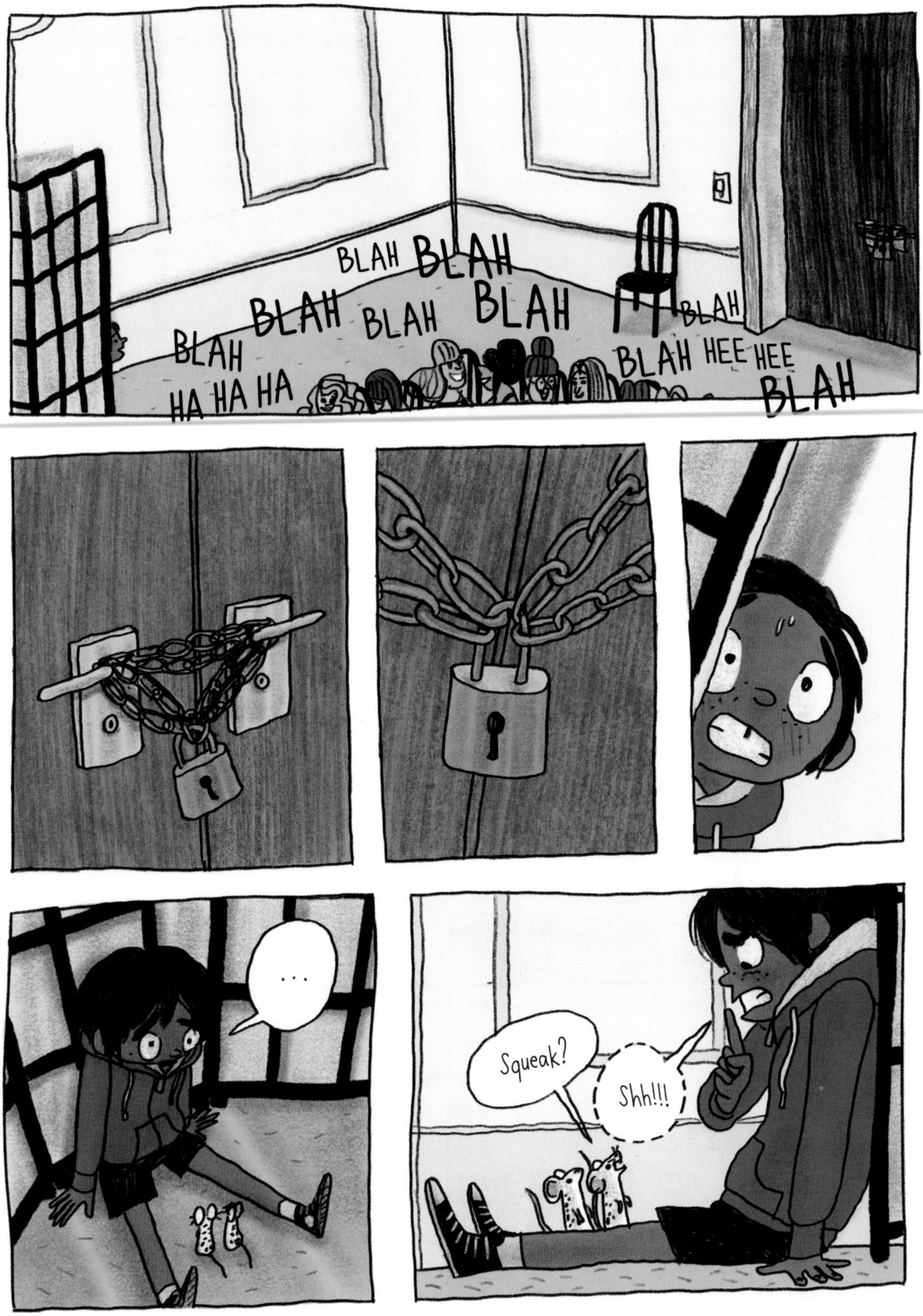
BLAH BLAH
BLAH BLAH BLAH BLAH
BLAH
HA HA HA
BLAH
BLAH HEE HEE
BLAH
. . .
Squeak?
Shh!!!

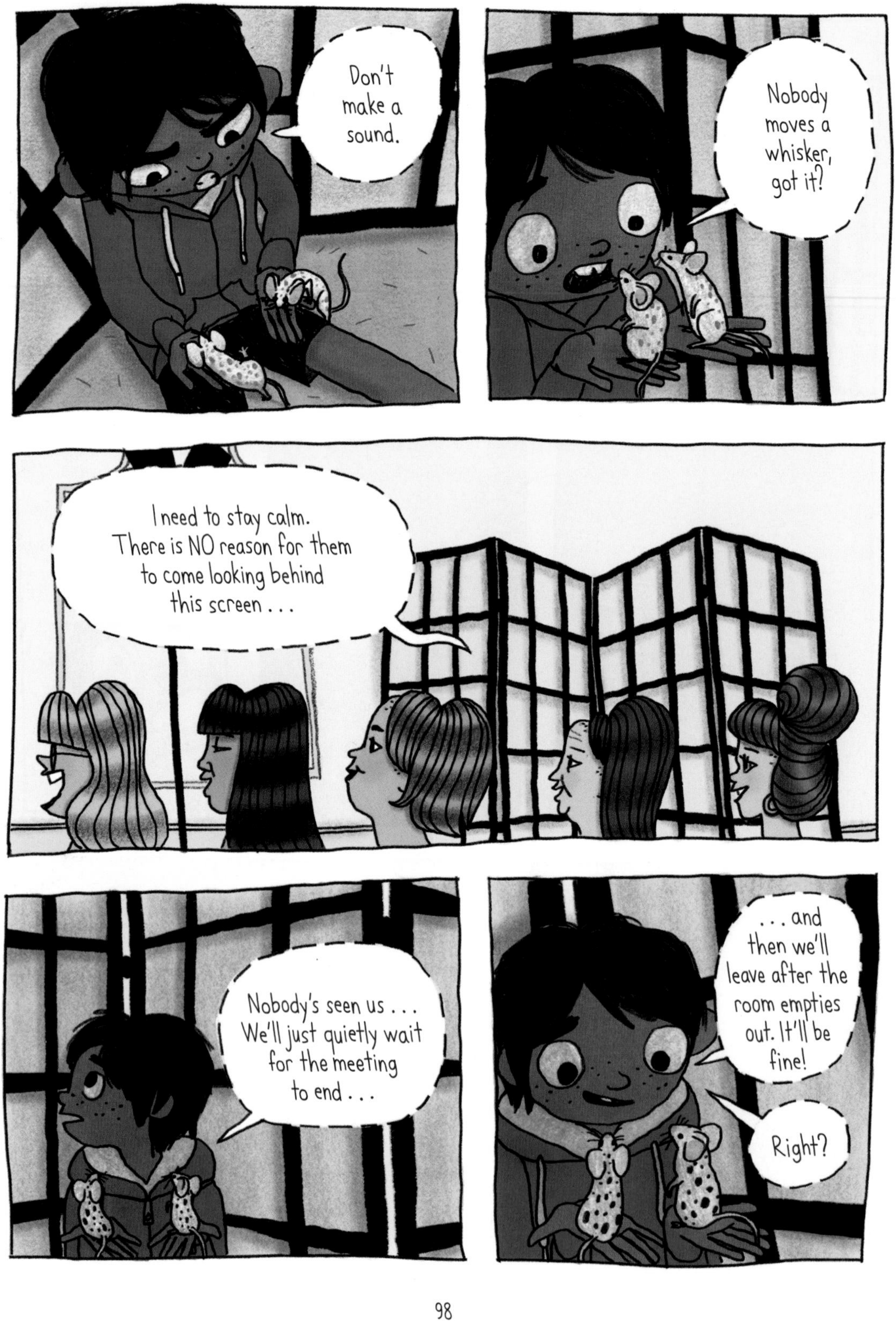
Don't make a sound.
Nobody moves a whisker, got it?
I need to stay calm. There is NO reason for them to come looking behind this screen . . .
Nobody's seen us . . . We'll just quietly wait for the meeting to end . . .
. . . and then we'll leave after the room empties out. It'll be fine!
Right?

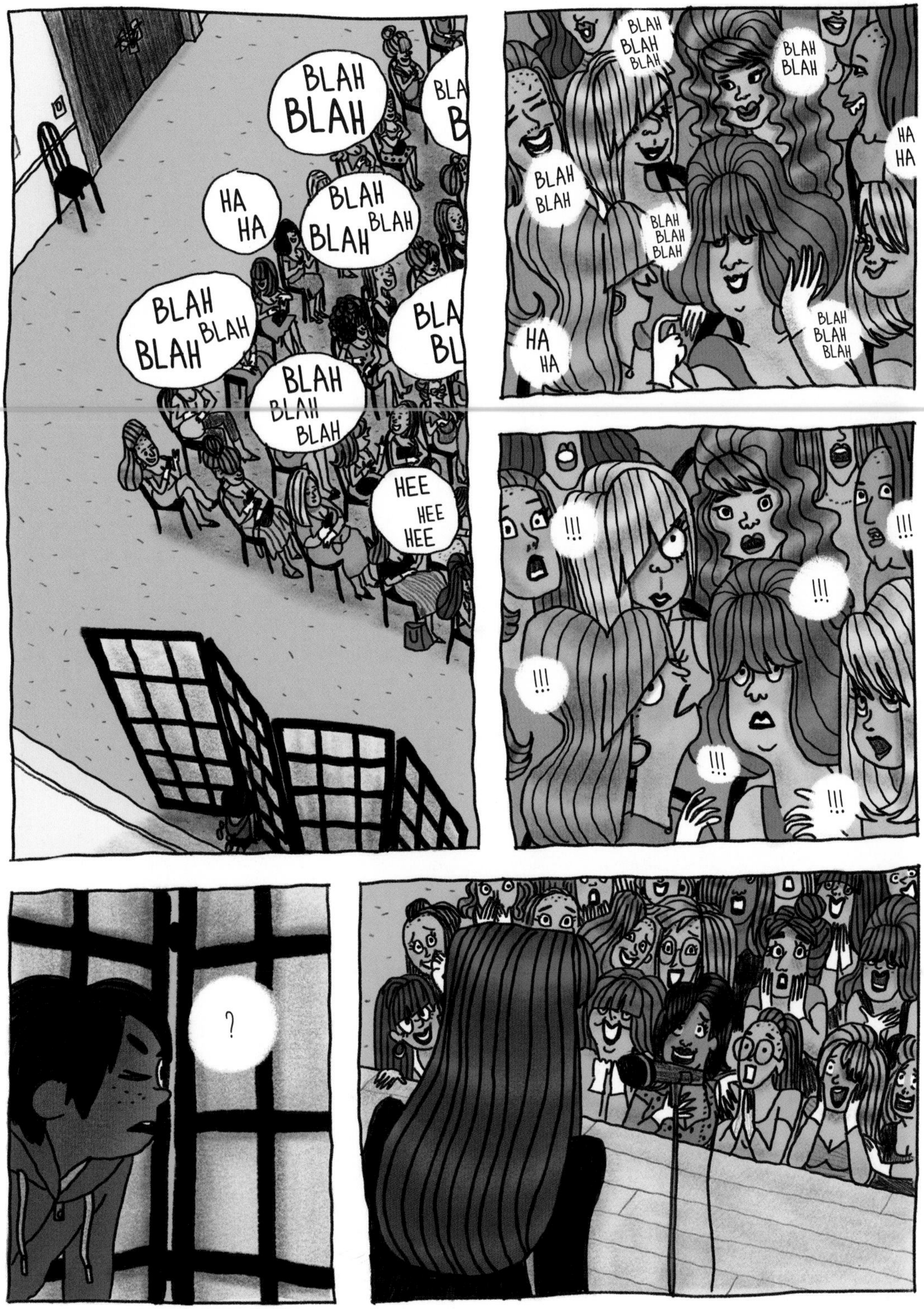
BLAH BLAH
BLAH BLAH
HA HA
BLAH BLAH BLAH
BLAH BLAH BLAH
BLAH BLAH BLAH
HEE HEE HEE
BLAH BLAH BLAH
BLAH BLAH
HA HA
BLAH BLAH
BLAH BLAH BLAH
HA HA
BLAH BLAH BLAH
!!!
!!!
!!!
!!!
!!!
!!!
?

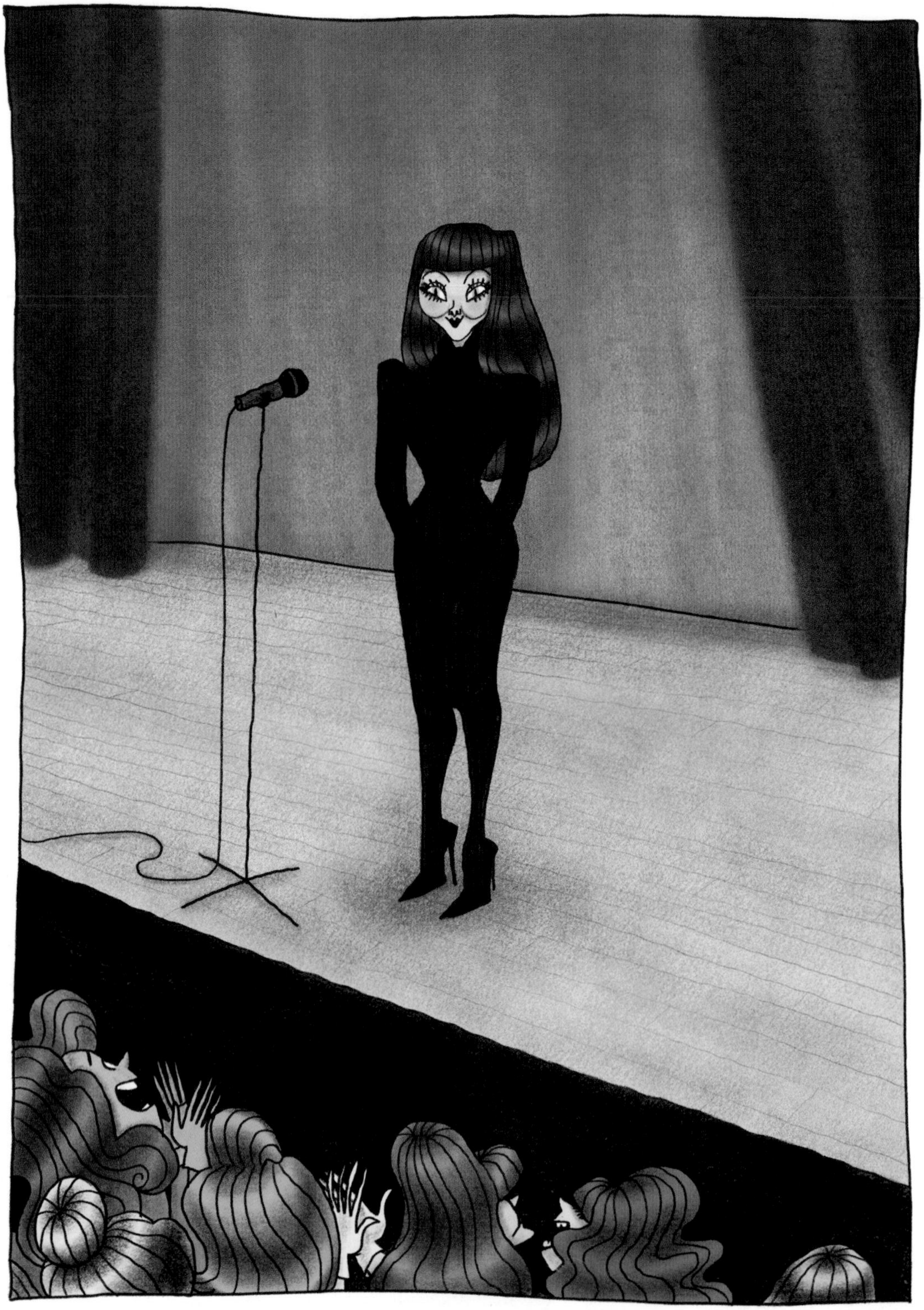

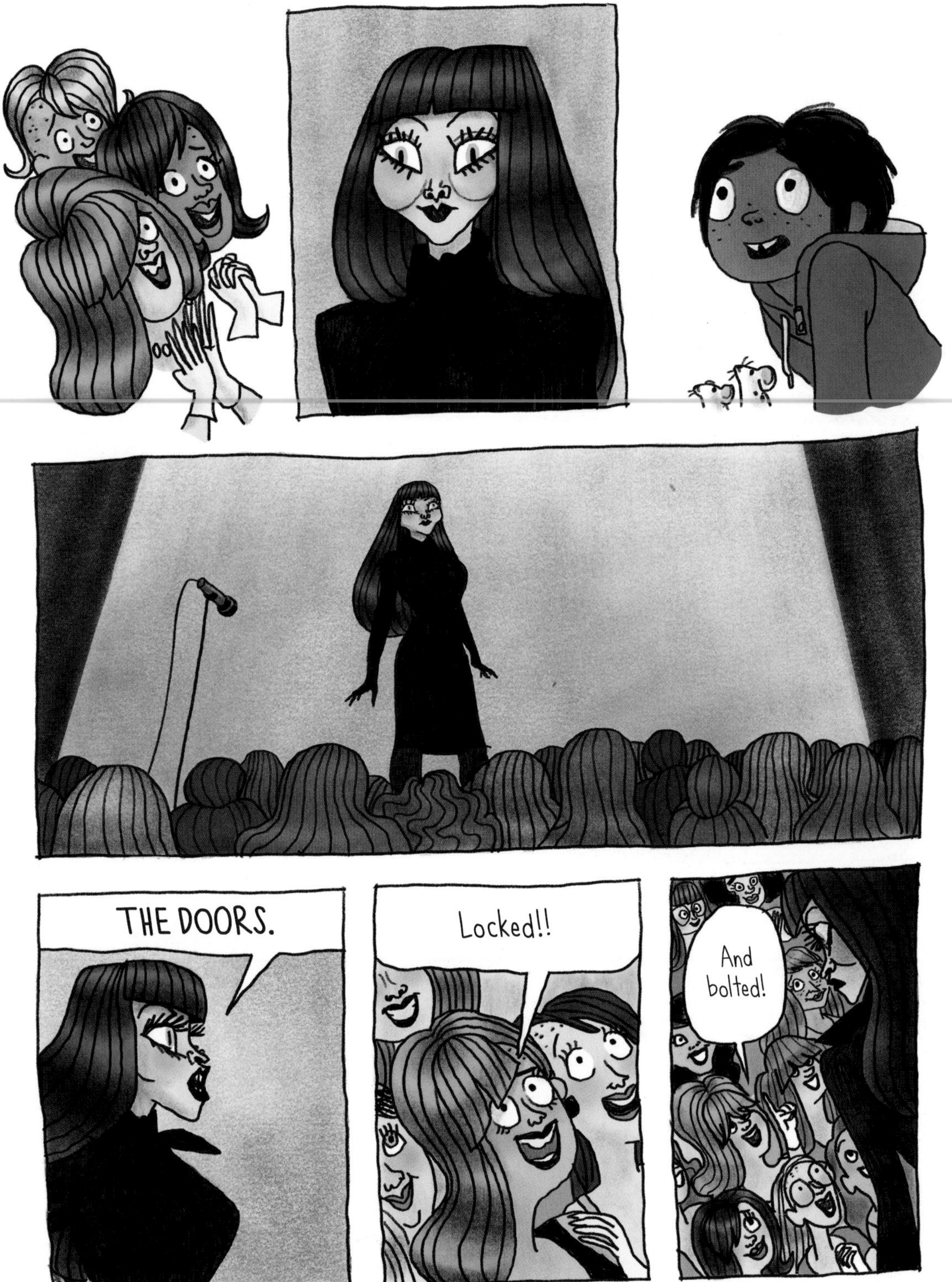
THE DOORS.
Locked!!
And bolted!

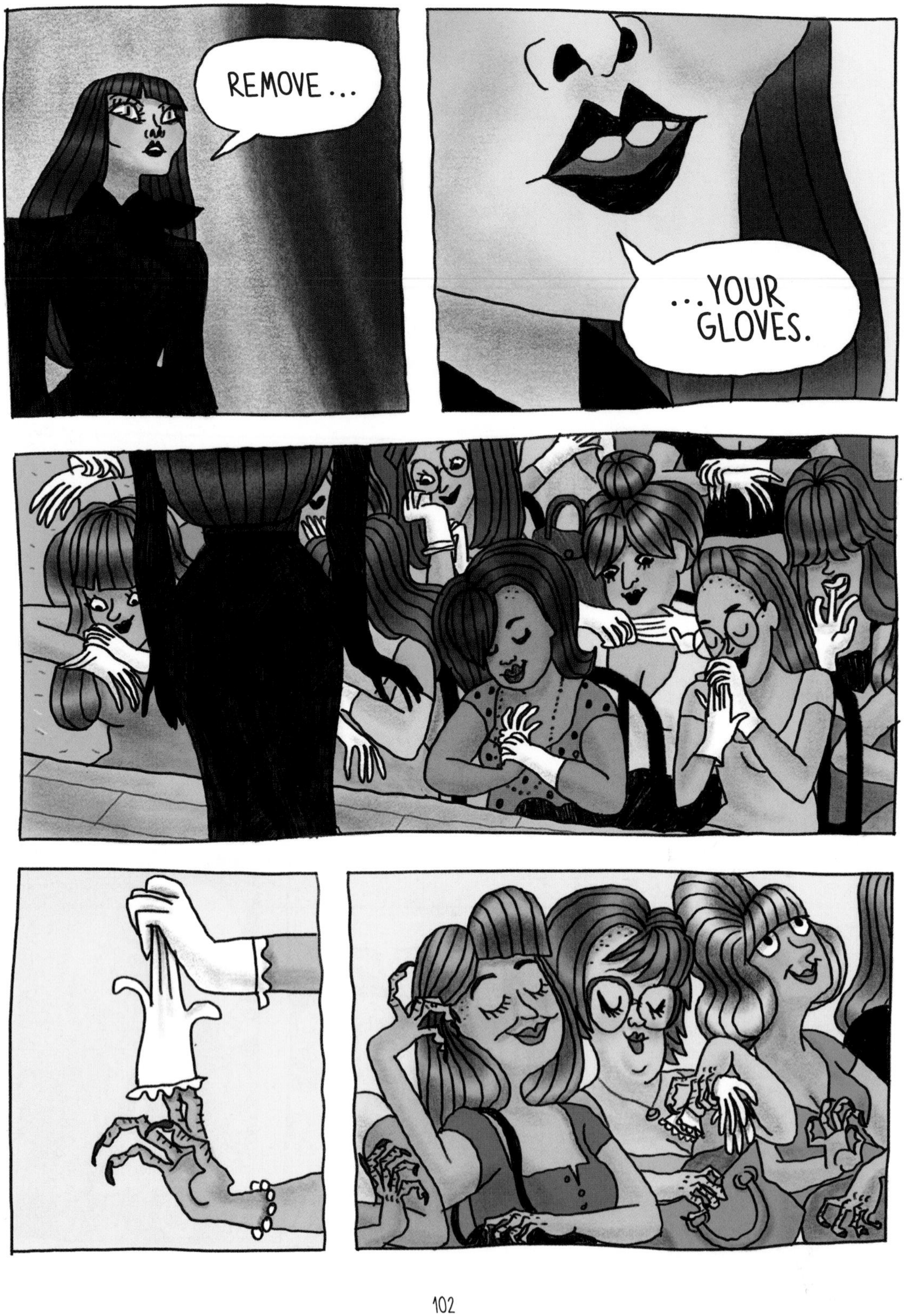
REMOVE...
...YOUR GLOVES.

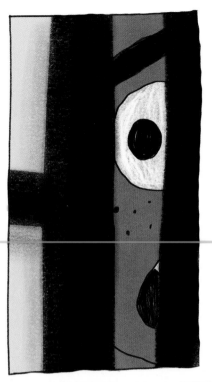

REMOVE . . .

. . . YOUR SHOES.

Ooh, thank goodness!

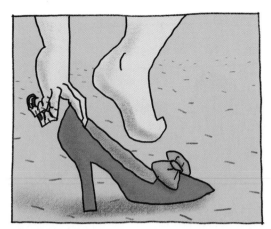
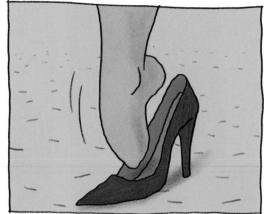
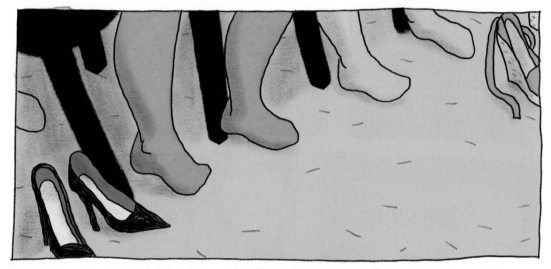

AND NOW ...

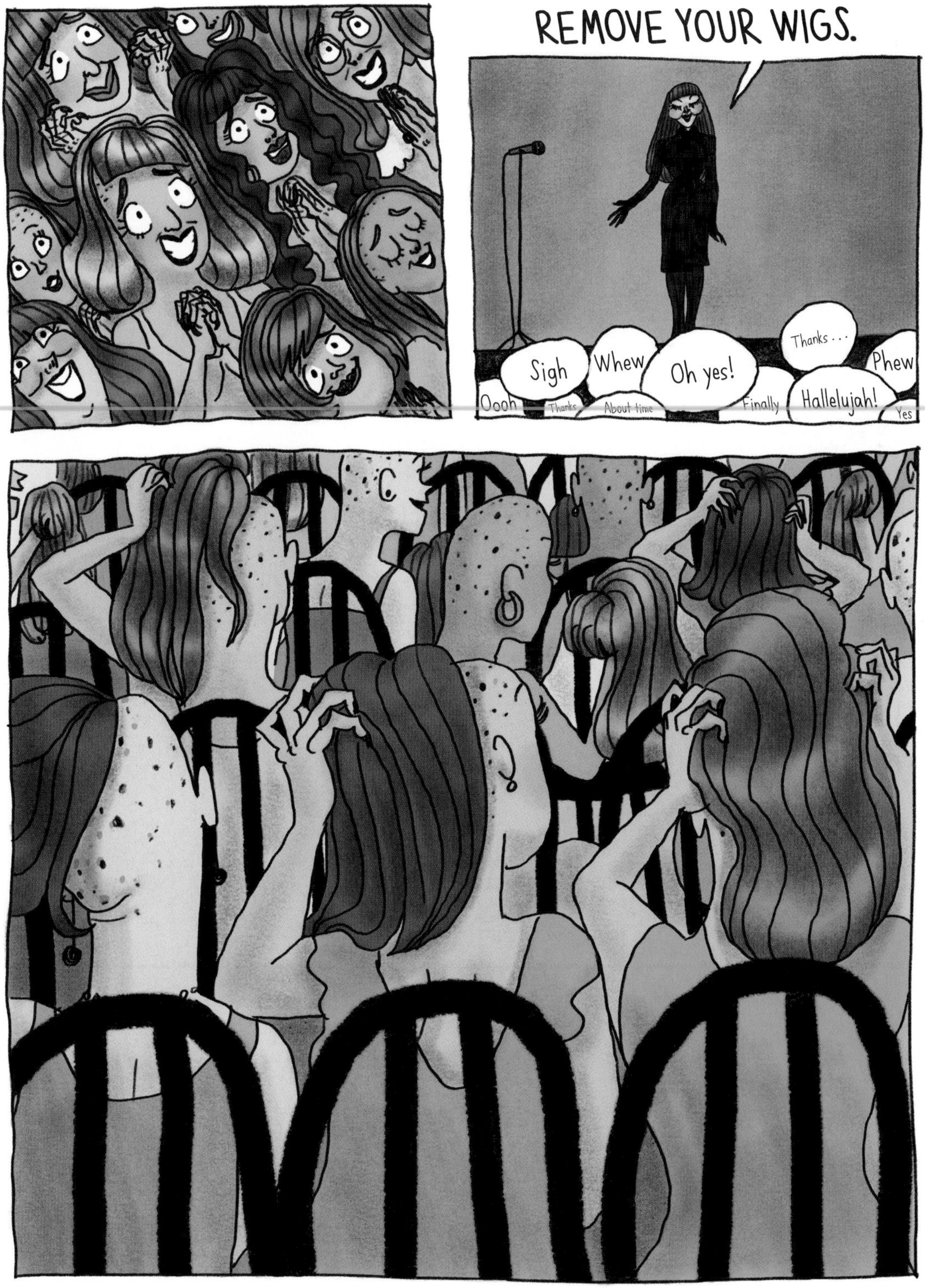
REMOVE YOUR WIGS.
Sigh
Whew
Oh yes!
Thanks . . .
Phew
Oooh
Thanks
About time
Finally
Hallelujah!
Yes

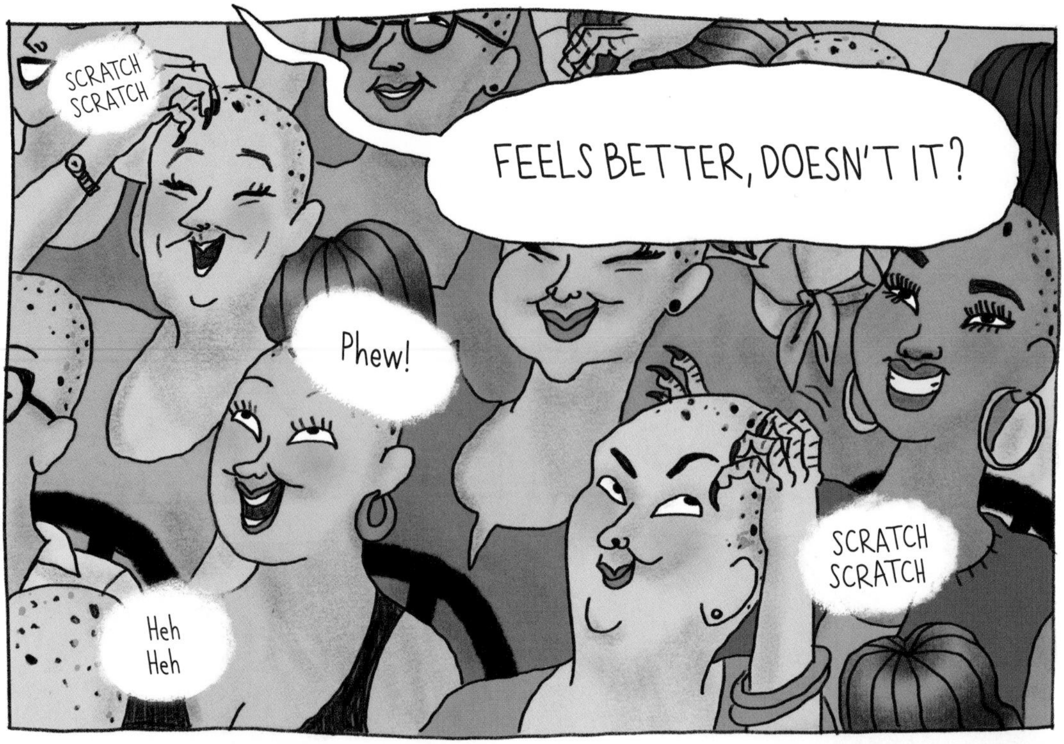
SCRATCH
SCRATCH
FEELS BETTER, DOESN'T IT?
Phew!
SCRATCH
SCRATCH
Heh
Heh

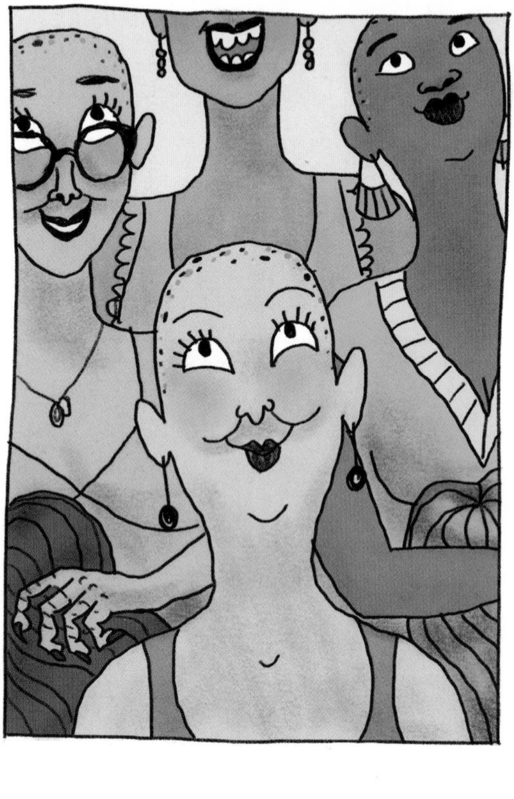

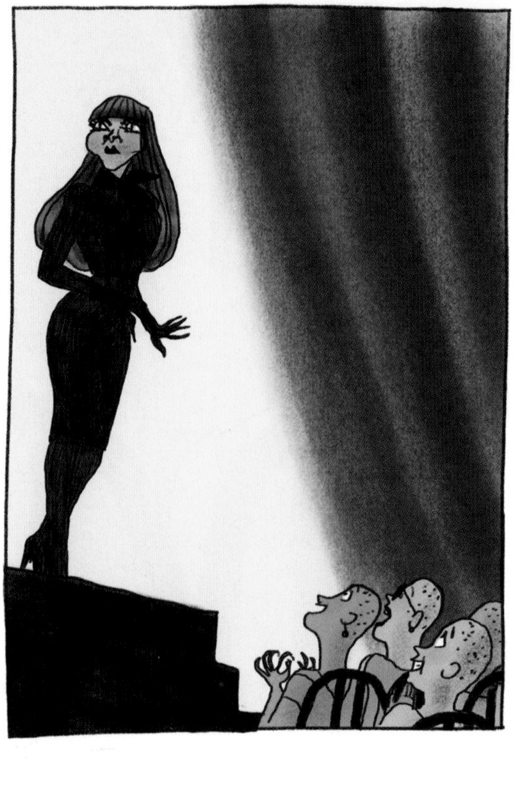

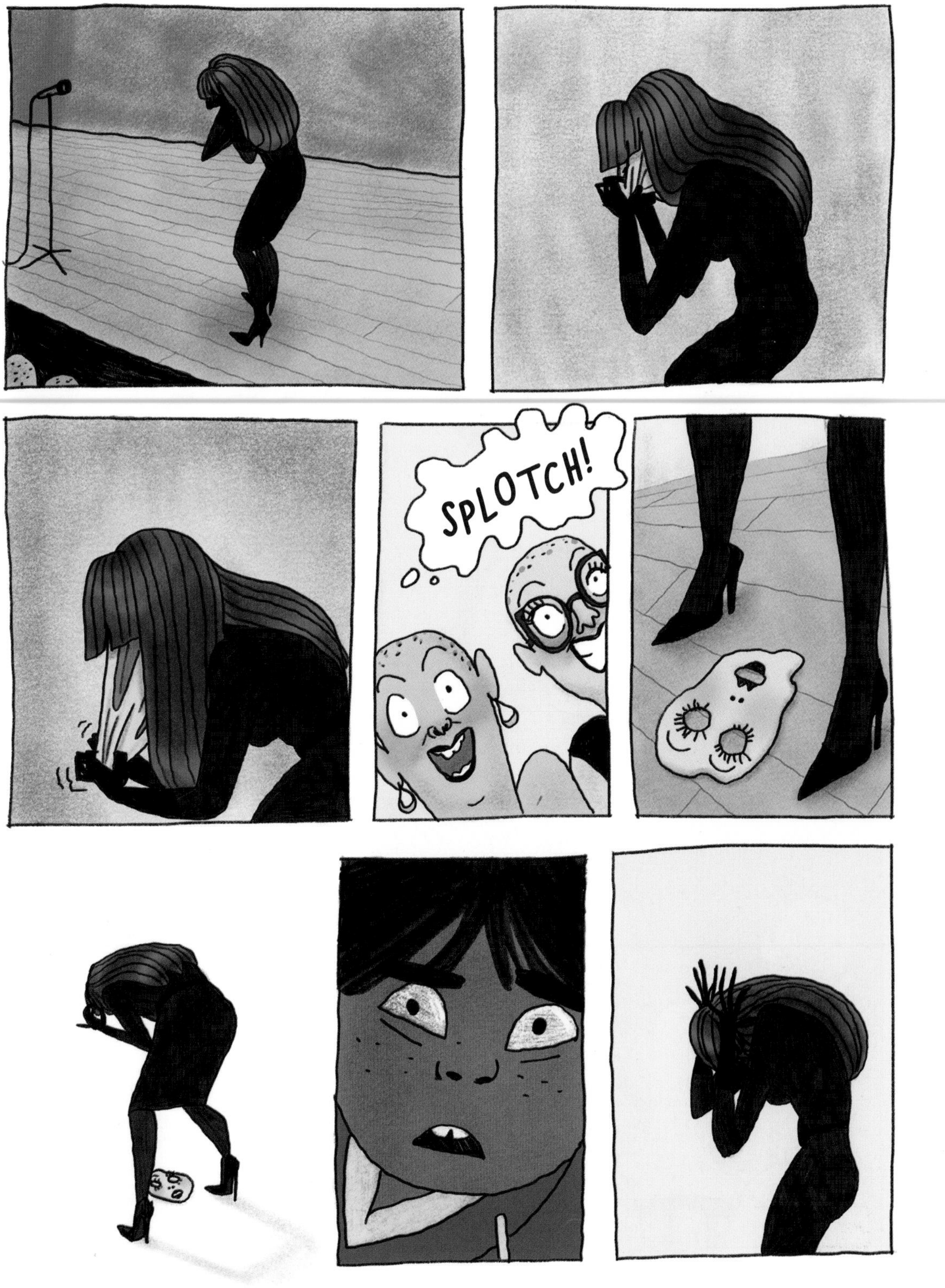
SPLOTCH!

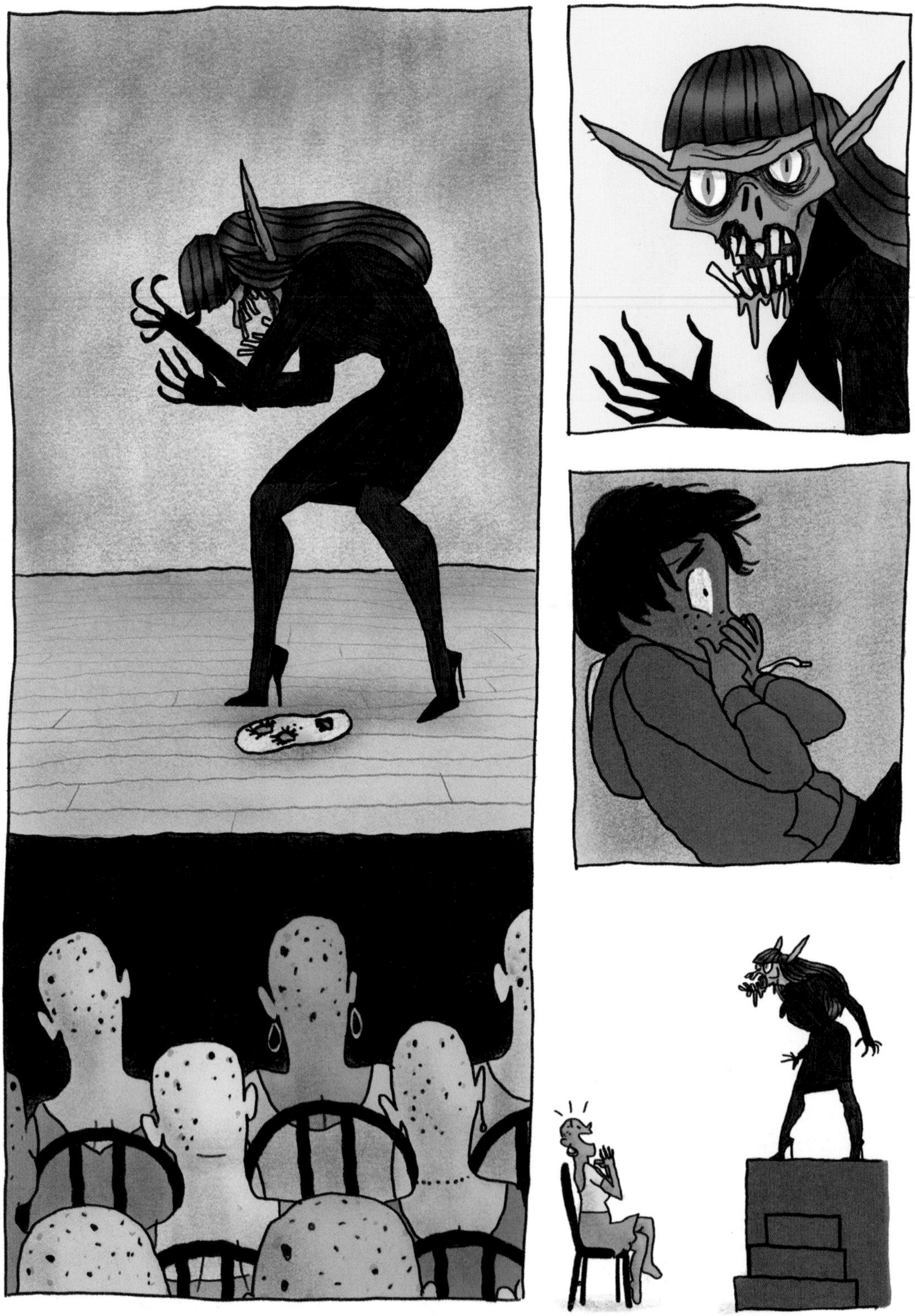

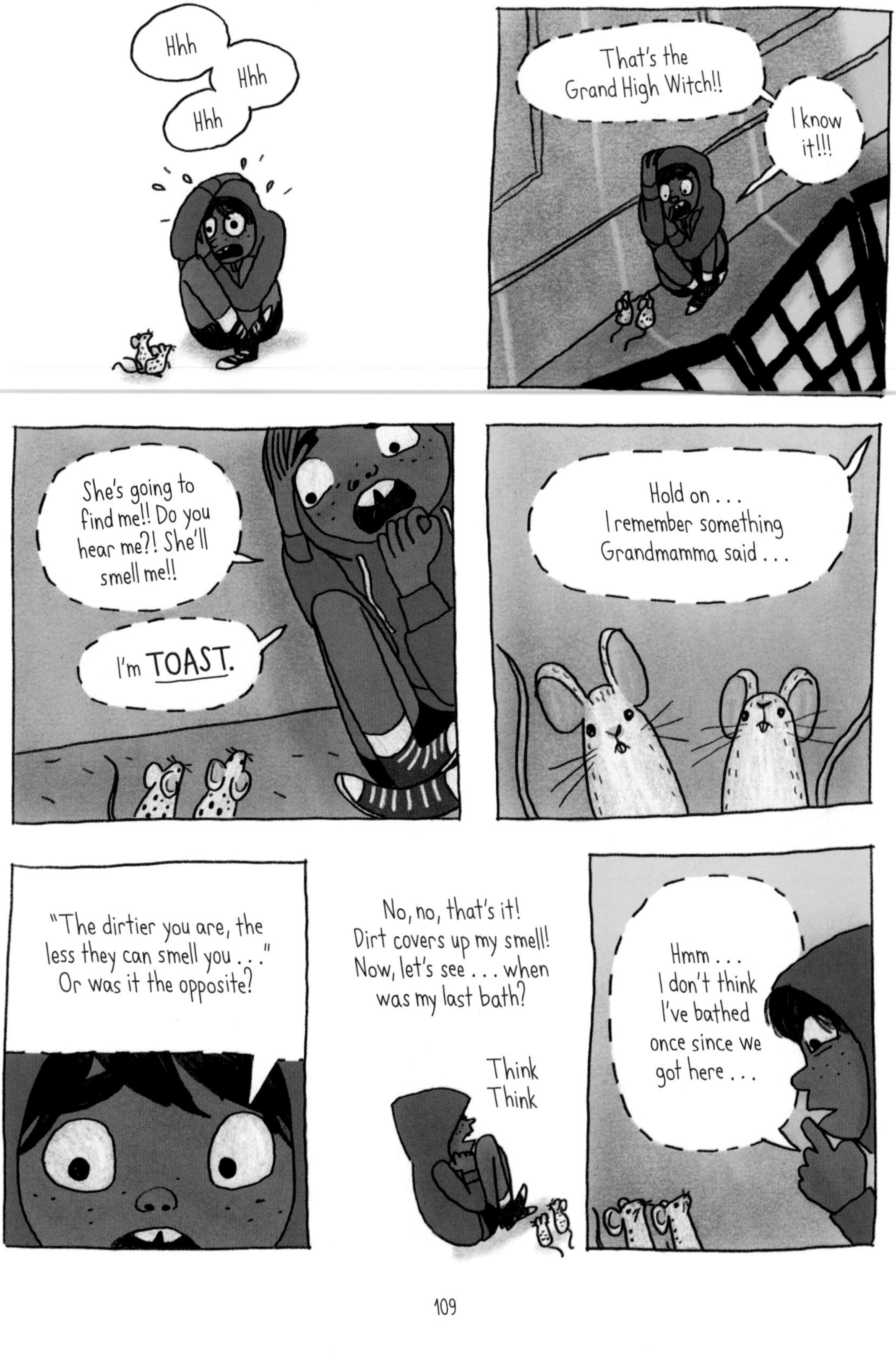
Hhh
Hhh
Hhh
That's the Grand High Witch!!
I know it!!!
She's going to find me!! Do you hear me?! She'll smell me!!
I'm TOAST.
Hold on . . . I remember something Grandmamma said . . .
"The dirtier you are, the less they can smell you . . ." Or was it the opposite?
No, no, that's it! Dirt covers up my smell! Now, let's see . . . when was my last bath?
Think
Think
Hmm . . . I don't think I've bathed once since we got here . . .

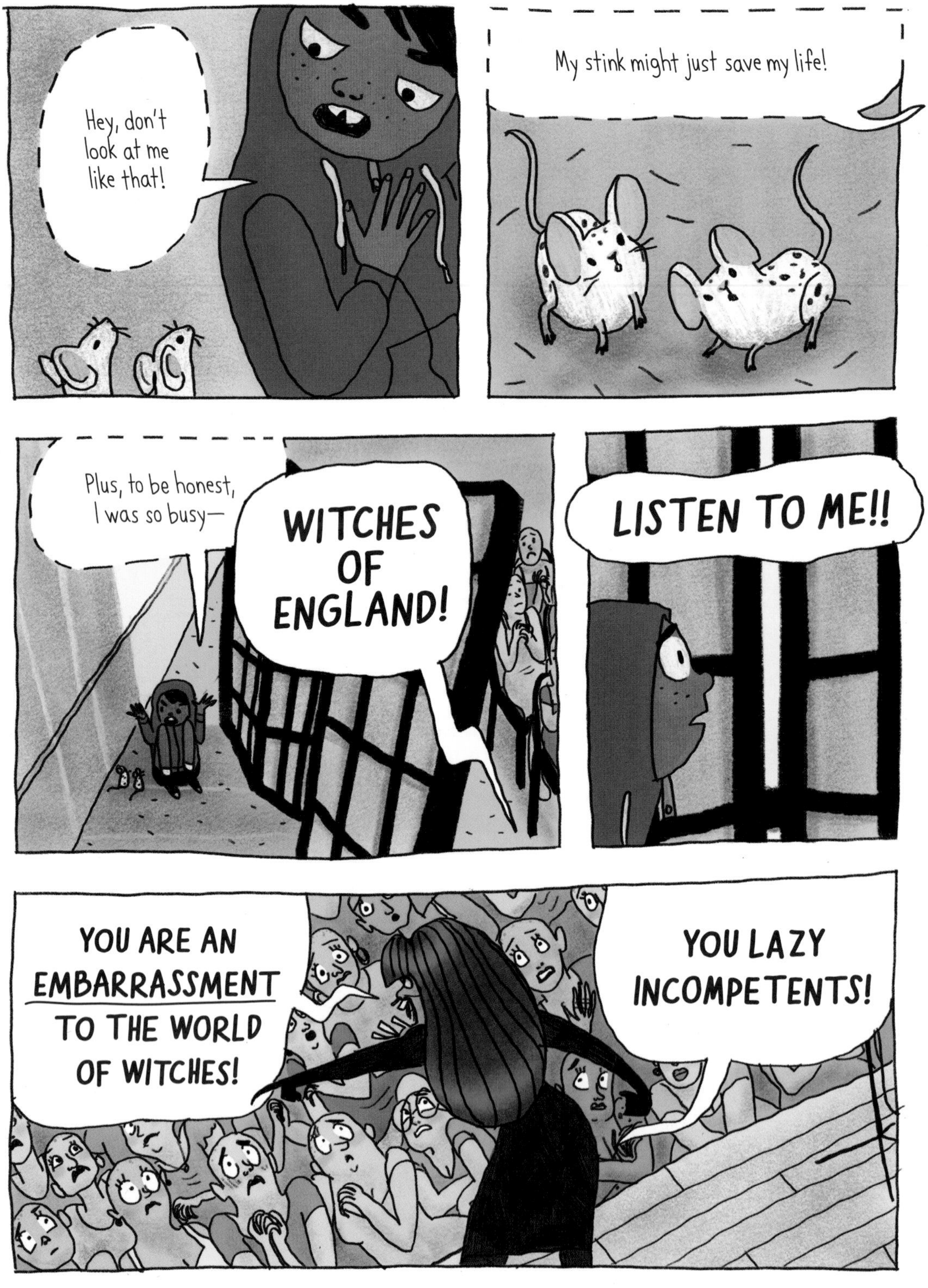
Hey, don't look at me like that!
My stink might just save my life!
Plus, to be honest, I was so busy—
WITCHES OF ENGLAND!
LISTEN TO ME!!
YOU ARE AN EMBARRASSMENT TO THE WORLD OF WITCHES!
YOU LAZY INCOMPETENTS!

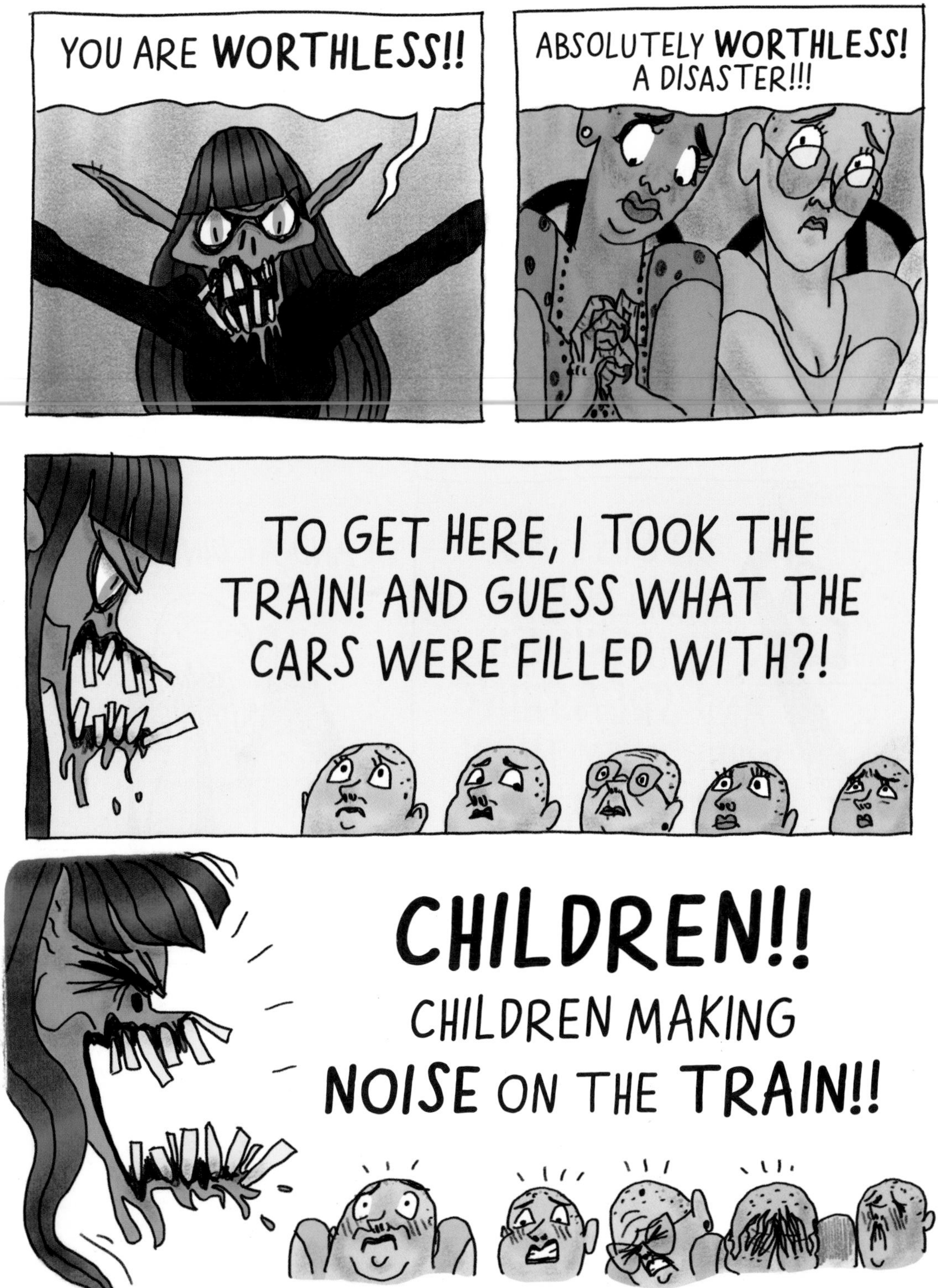
YOU ARE WORTHLESS!!
ABSOLUTELY WORTHLESS! A DISASTER!!!
TO GET HERE, I TOOK THE TRAIN! AND GUESS WHAT THE CARS WERE FILLED WITH?!
CHILDREN!!
CHILDREN MAKING NOISE ON THE TRAIN!!

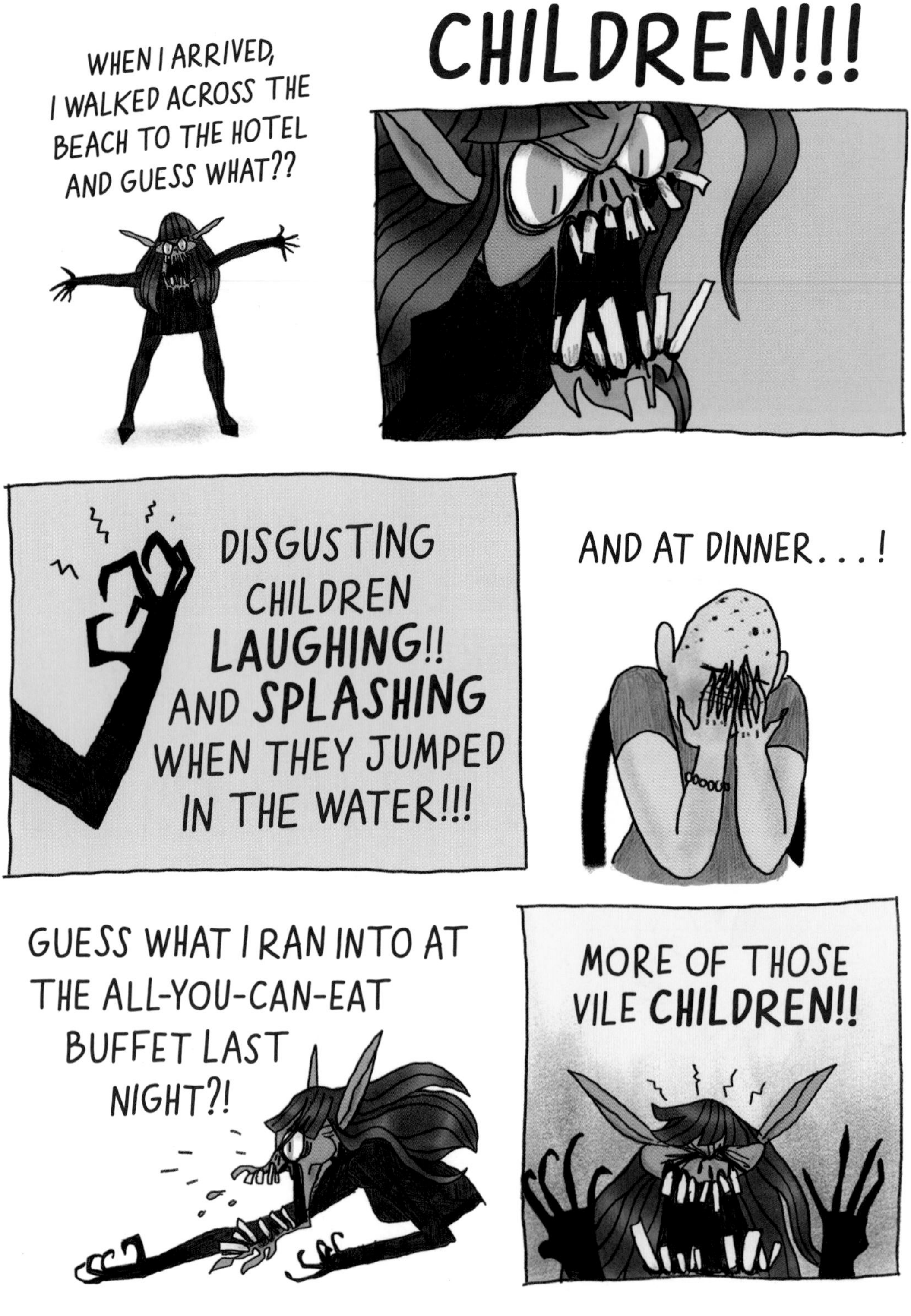
WHEN I ARRIVED, I WALKED ACROSS THE BEACH TO THE HOTEL AND GUESS WHAT??
CHILDREN!!!
DISGUSTING CHILDREN LAUGHING!! AND SPLASHING WHEN THEY JUMPED IN THE WATER!!!
AND AT DINNER...!
GUESS WHAT I RAN INTO AT THE ALL-YOU-CAN-EAT BUFFET LAST NIGHT?!
MORE OF THOSE VILE CHILDREN!!

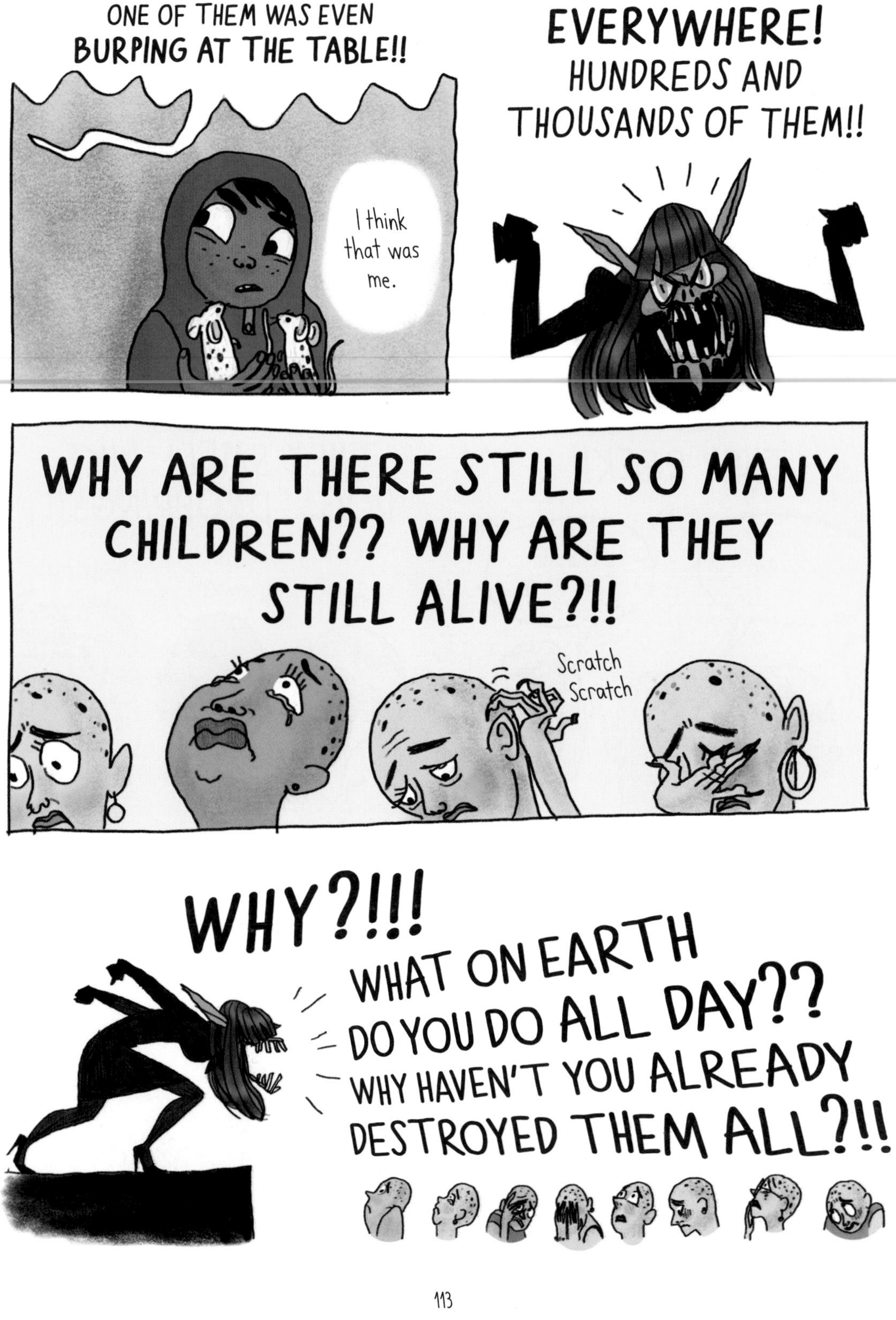
ONE OF THEM WAS EVEN BURPING AT THE TABLE!!
I think that was me.
EVERYWHERE! HUNDREDS AND THOUSANDS OF THEM!!
WHY ARE THERE STILL SO MANY CHILDREN?? WHY ARE THEY STILL ALIVE?!!
Scratch Scratch
WHY?!!!
WHAT ON EARTH DO YOU DO ALL DAY?? WHY HAVEN'T YOU ALREADY DESTROYED THEM ALL?!!

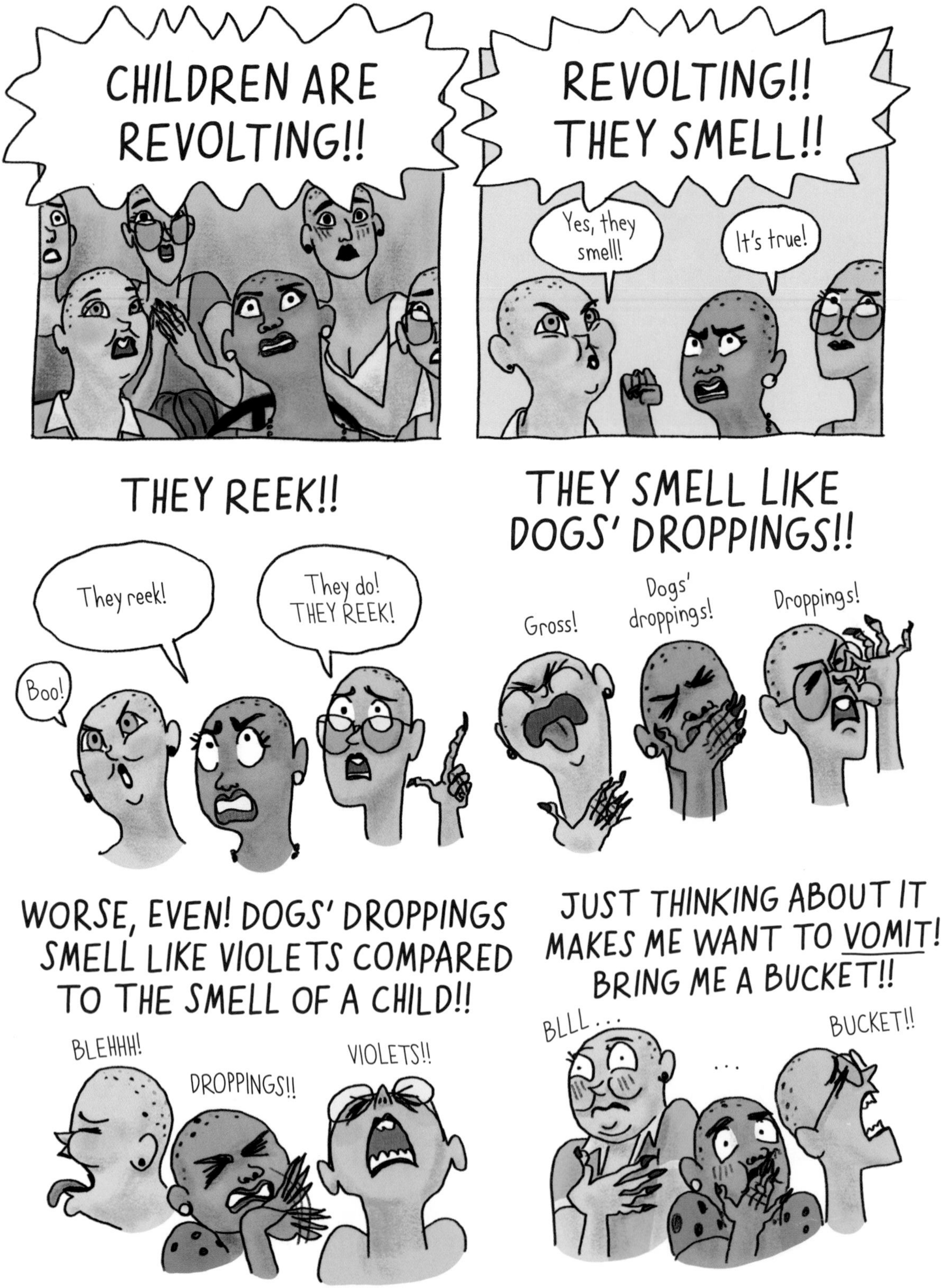
CHILDREN ARE REVOLTING!!
REVOLTING!! THEY SMELL!!
Yes, they smell!
It's true!
THEY REEK!!
Boo!
They reek!
They do! THEY REEK!
THEY SMELL LIKE DOGS' DROPPINGS!!
Gross!
Dogs' droppings!
Droppings!
WORSE, EVEN! DOGS' DROPPINGS SMELL LIKE VIOLETS COMPARED TO THE SMELL OF A CHILD!!
BLEHHH!
DROPPINGS!!
VIOLETS!!
JUST THINKING ABOUT IT MAKES ME WANT TO VOMIT! BRING ME A BUCKET!!
BLLL . . .
. . .
BUCKET!!

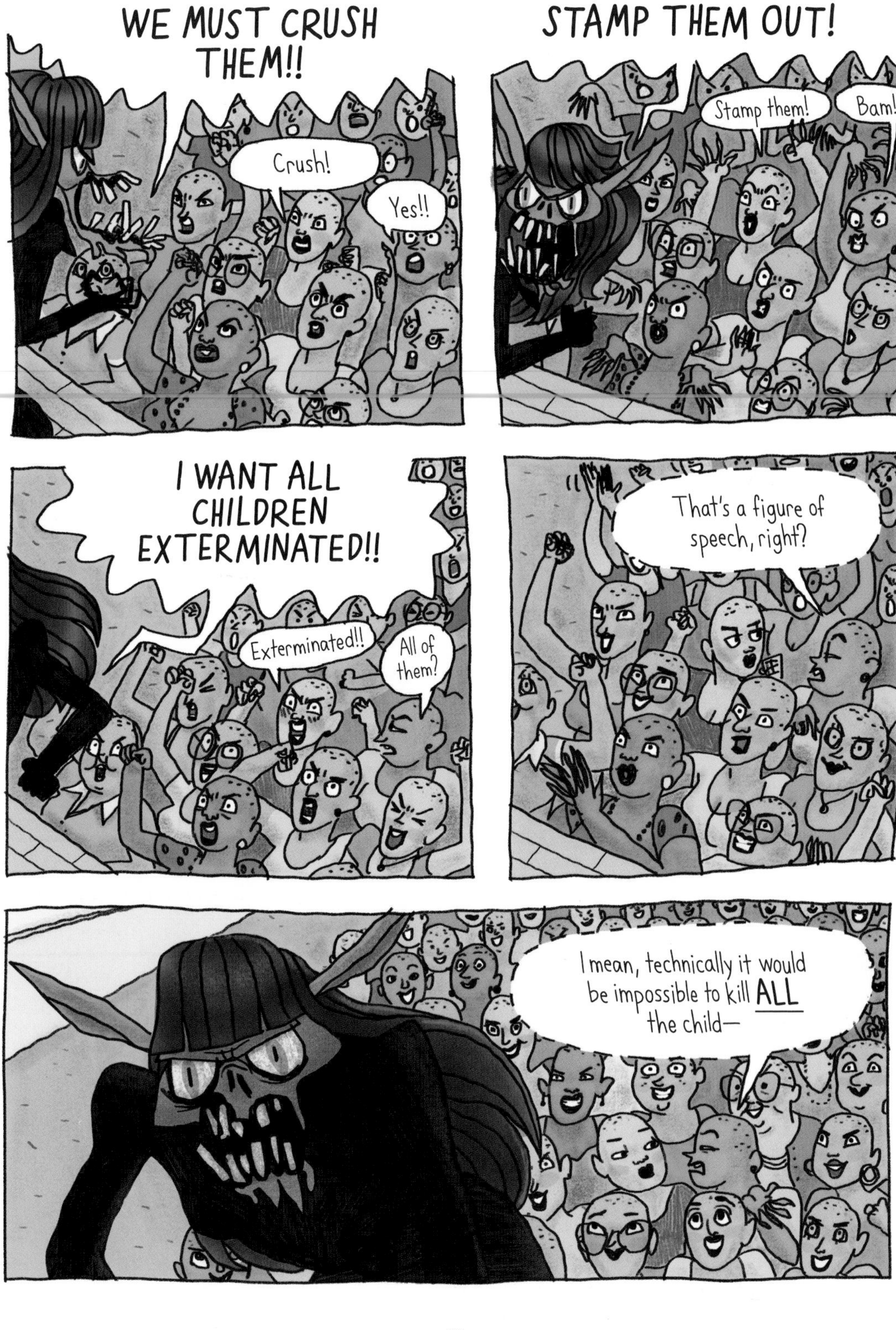
WE MUST CRUSH THEM!!
Crush!
Yes!!
STAMP THEM OUT!
Stamp them!
Bam!!!
I WANT ALL CHILDREN EXTERMINATED!!
Exterminated!!
All of them?
That's a figure of speech, right?
I mean, technically it would be impossible to kill ALL the child—

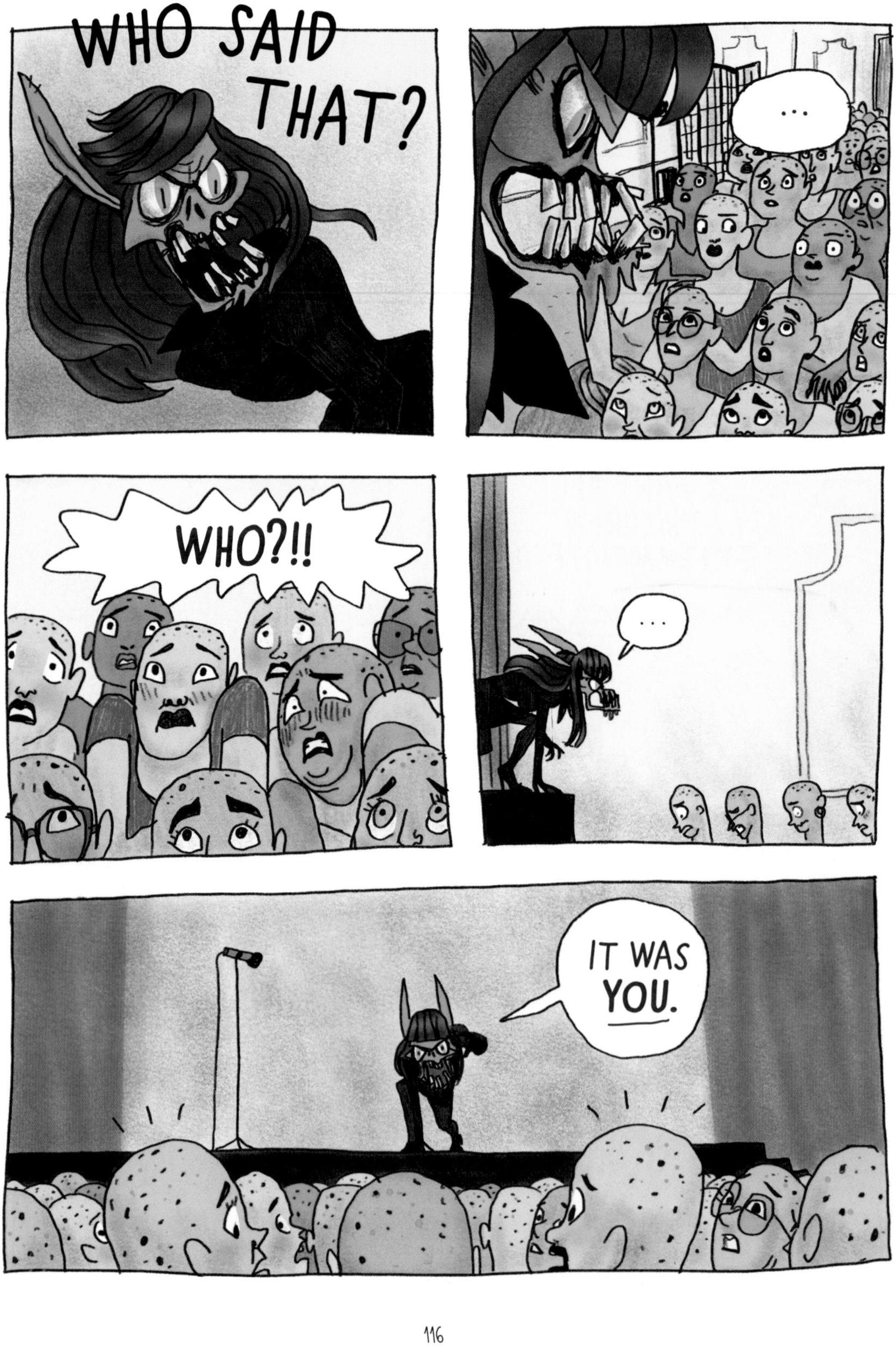
WHO SAID THAT?
...
WHO?!!
...
IT WAS YOU.

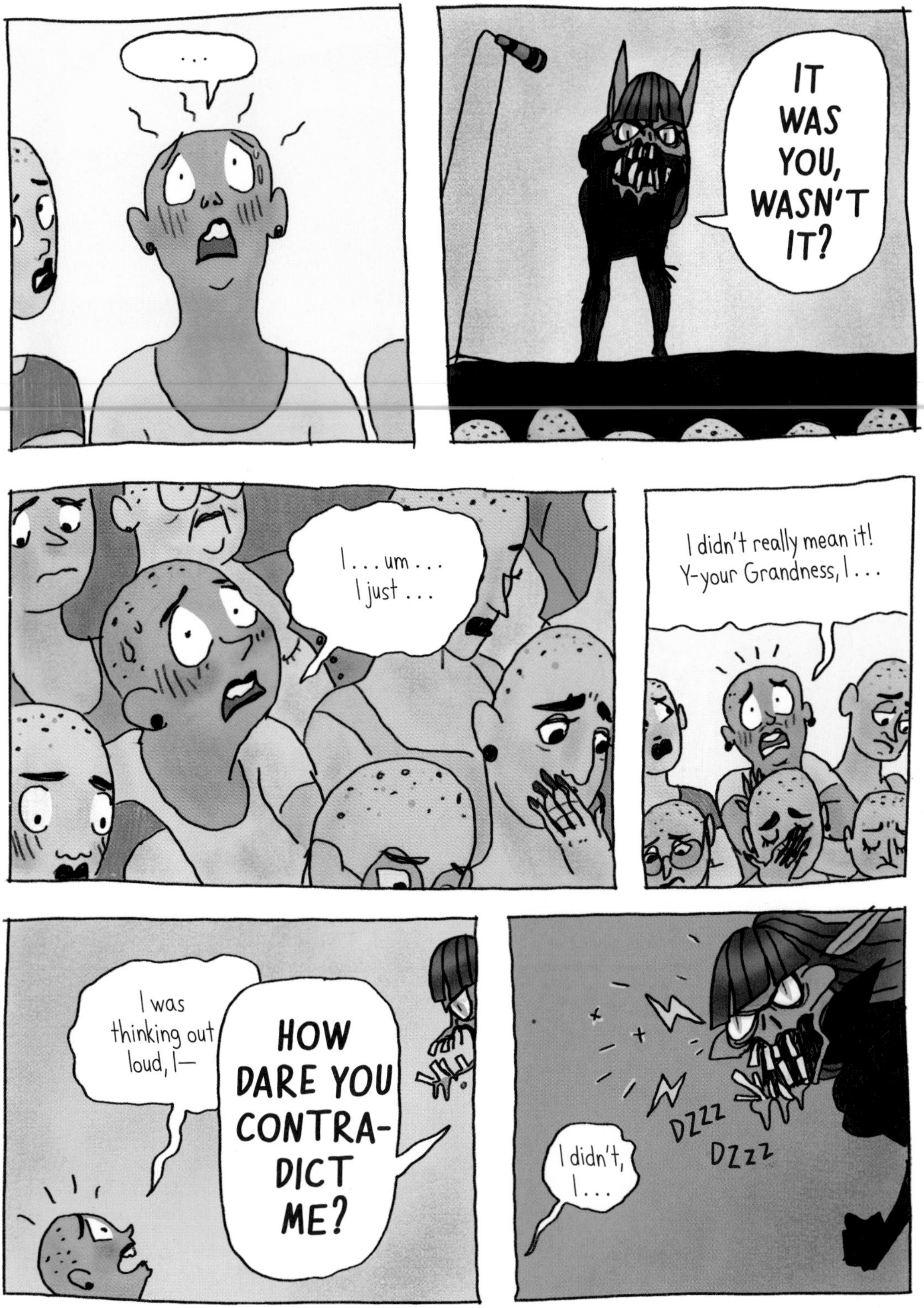
. . .
IT WAS YOU, WASN'T IT?
I . . . um . . . I just . . .
I didn't really mean it! Y-your Grandness, I . . .
I was thinking out loud, I—
HOW DARE YOU CONTRA-DICT ME?
I didn't, I . . .
DZZZ DZZZ

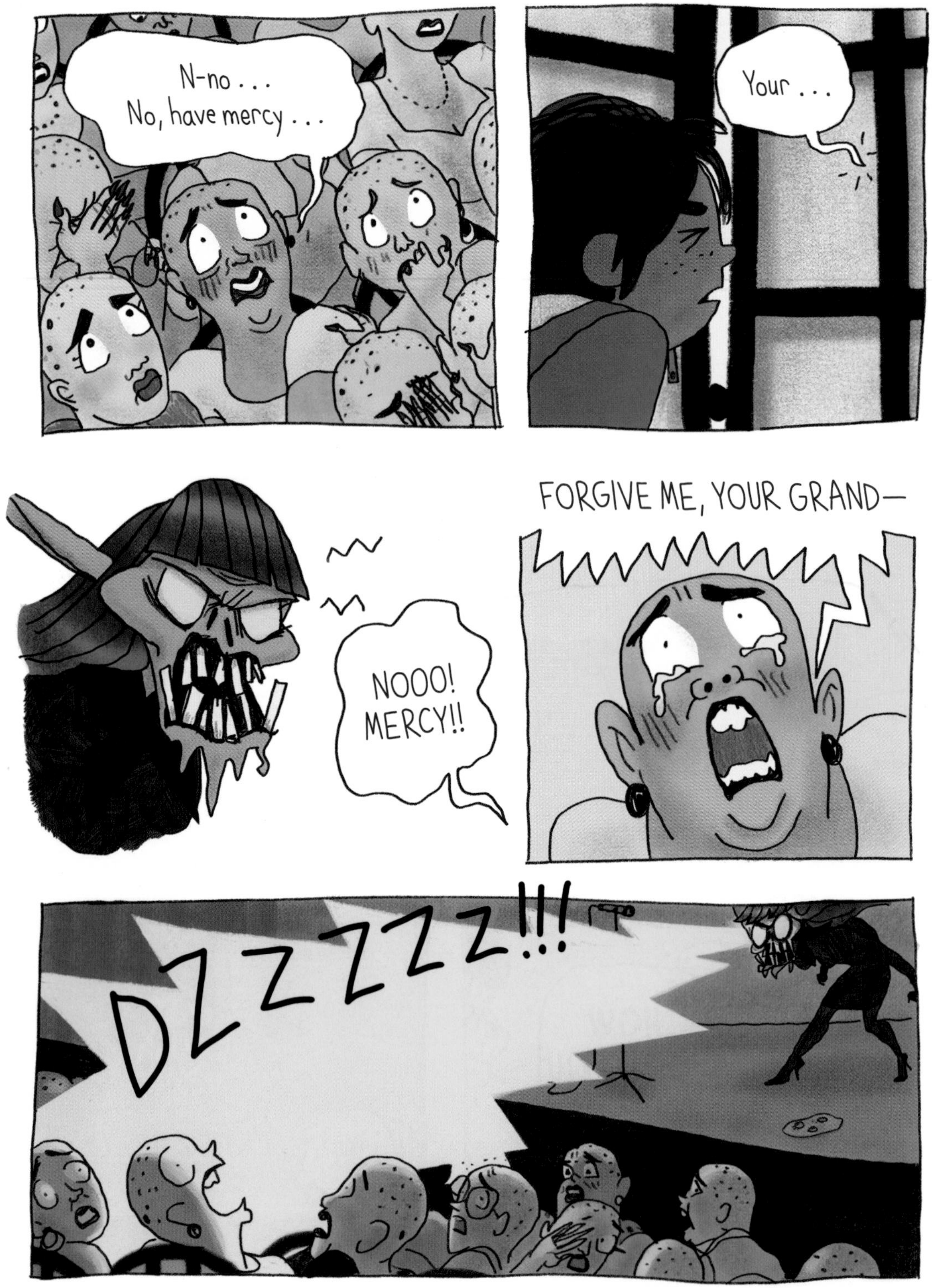
N-no . . .
No, have mercy . . .
Your . . .
NOOO! MERCY!!
FORGIVE ME, YOUR GRAND—
DZZZZZZ!!!

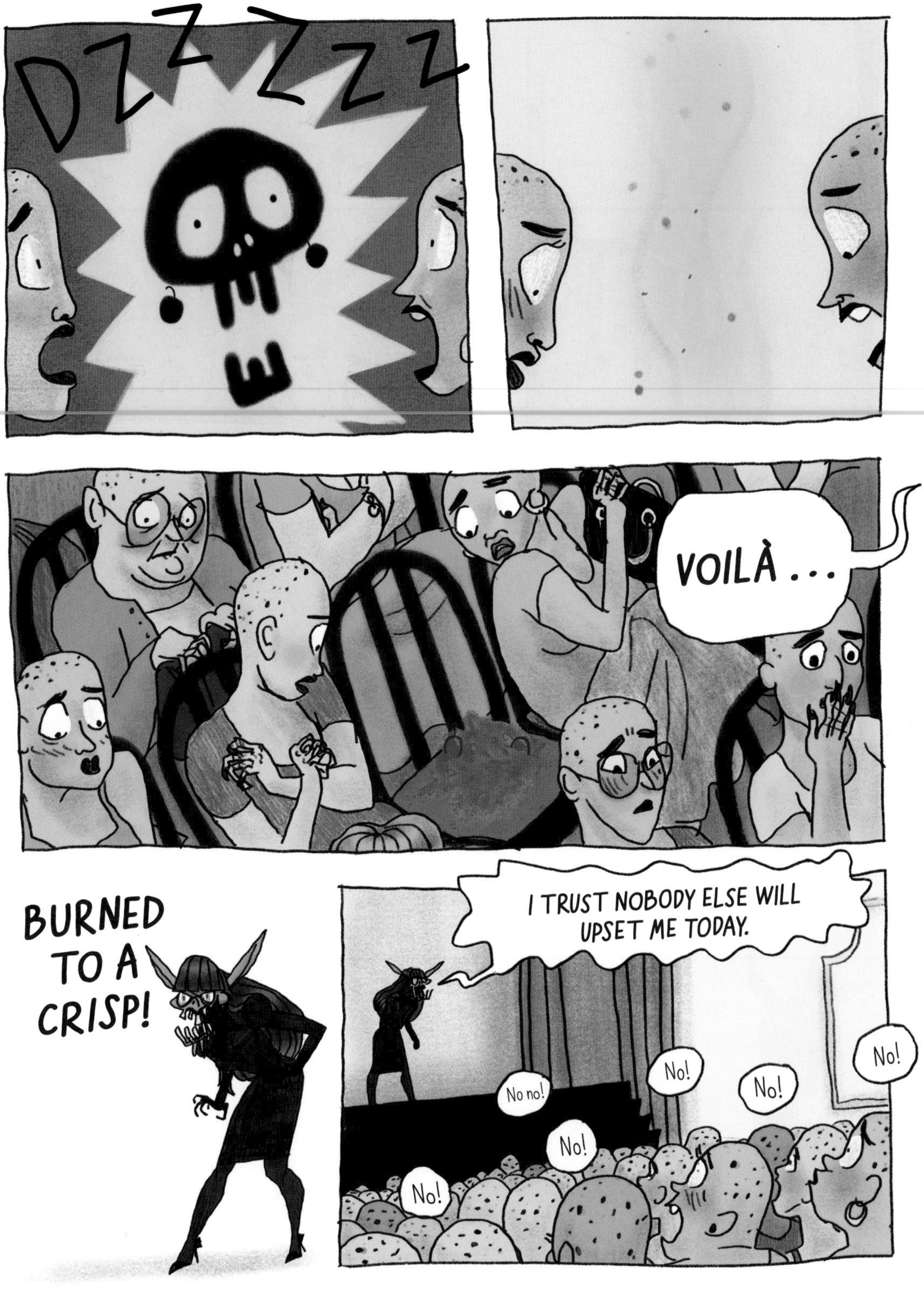
DZZZZZZ
VOILÀ ...
BURNED TO A CRISP!
I TRUST NOBODY ELSE WILL UPSET ME TODAY.
No no!
No!
No!
No!
No!
No!

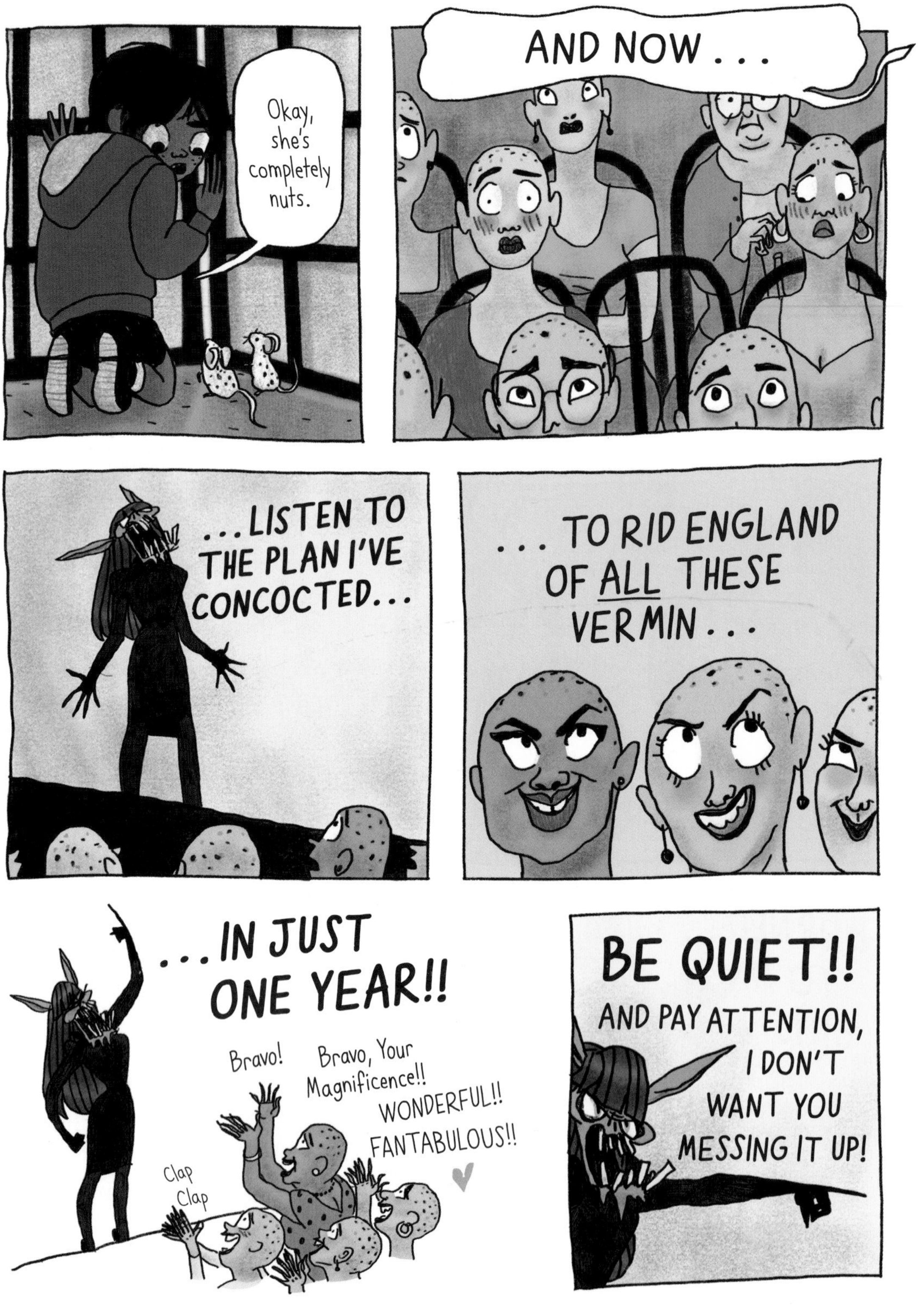
Okay, she's completely nuts.
AND NOW . . .
. . . LISTEN TO THE PLAN I'VE CONCOCTED . . .
. . . TO RID ENGLAND OF ALL THESE VERMIN . . .
. . . IN JUST ONE YEAR!!
Bravo!
Bravo, Your Magnificence!!
WONDERFUL!!
FANTABULOUS!!
Clap
Clap
BE QUIET!!
AND PAY ATTENTION, I DON'T WANT YOU MESSING IT UP!

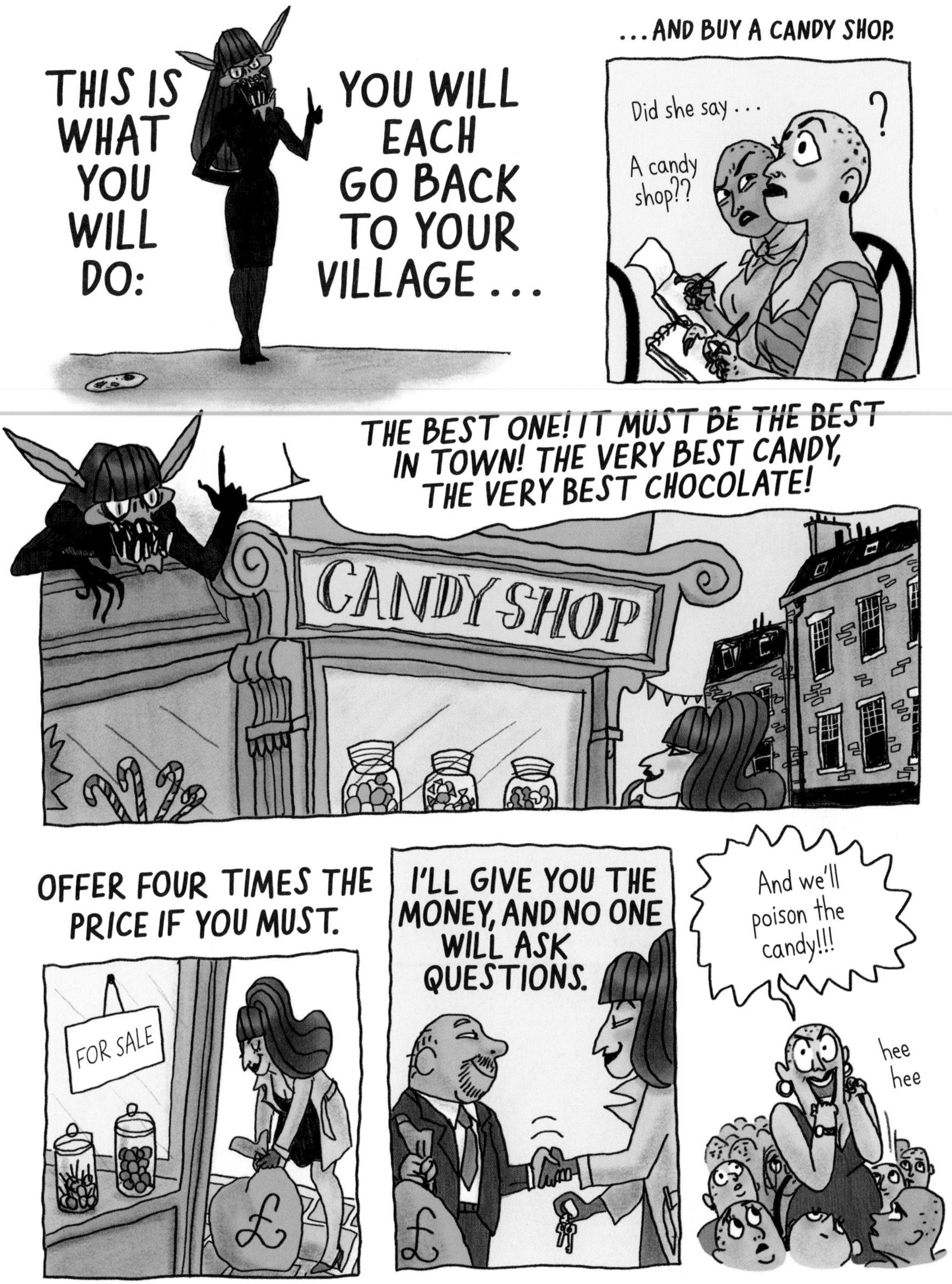
THIS IS WHAT YOU WILL DO:
YOU WILL EACH GO BACK TO YOUR VILLAGE . . .
. . . AND BUY A CANDY SHOP.
Did she say . . .
?
A candy shop??
THE BEST ONE! IT MUST BE THE BEST IN TOWN! THE VERY BEST CANDY, THE VERY BEST CHOCOLATE!
CANDY SHOP
OFFER FOUR TIMES THE PRICE IF YOU MUST.
FOR SALE
I'LL GIVE YOU THE MONEY, AND NO ONE WILL ASK QUESTIONS.
And we'll poison the candy!!!
hee hee

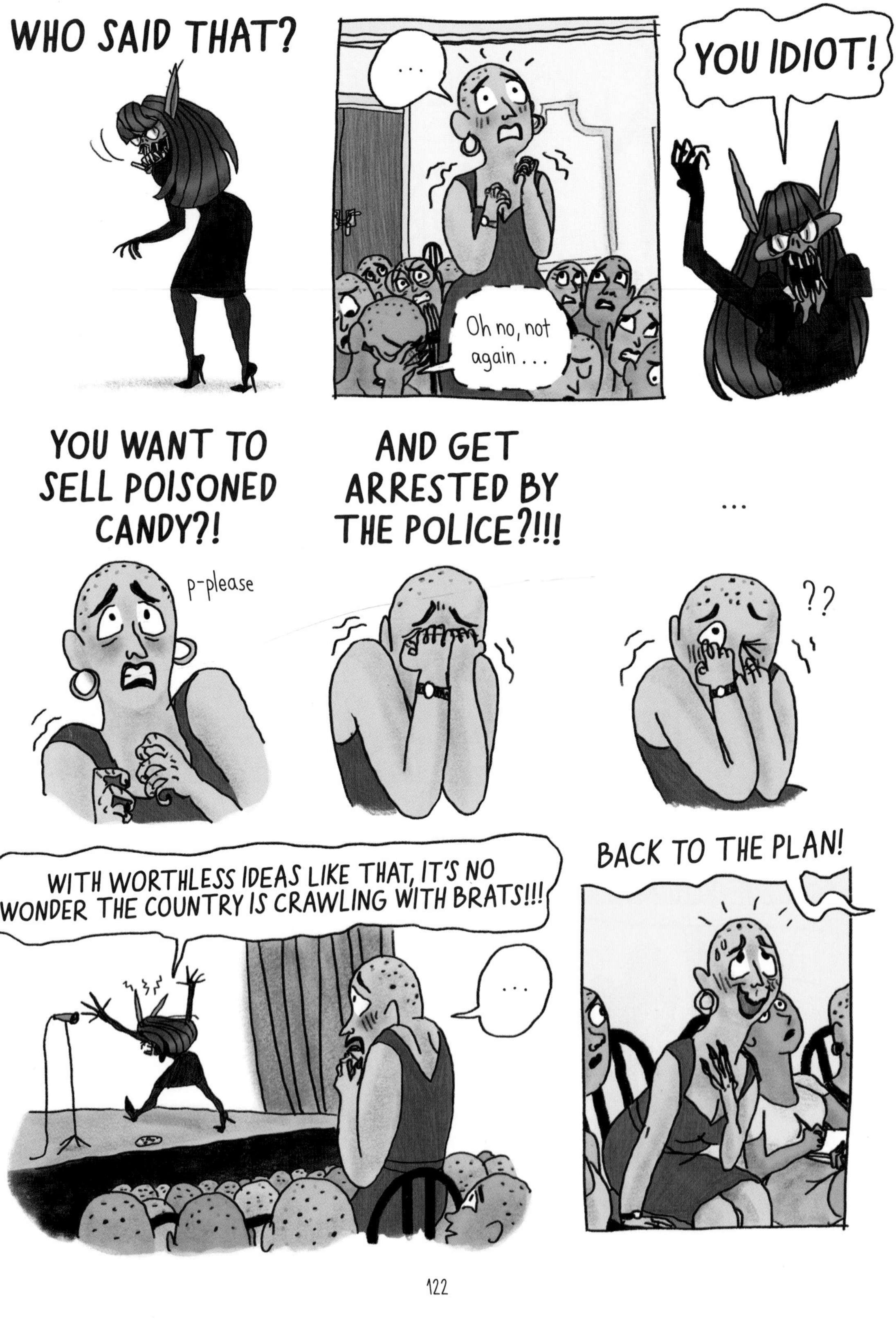
WHO SAID THAT?
. . .
Oh no, not again . . .
YOU IDIOT!
YOU WANT TO SELL POISONED CANDY?!
p-please
AND GET ARRESTED BY THE POLICE?!!!
. . .
??
WITH WORTHLESS IDEAS LIKE THAT, IT'S NO WONDER THE COUNTRY IS CRAWLING WITH BRATS!!!
. . .
BACK TO THE PLAN!

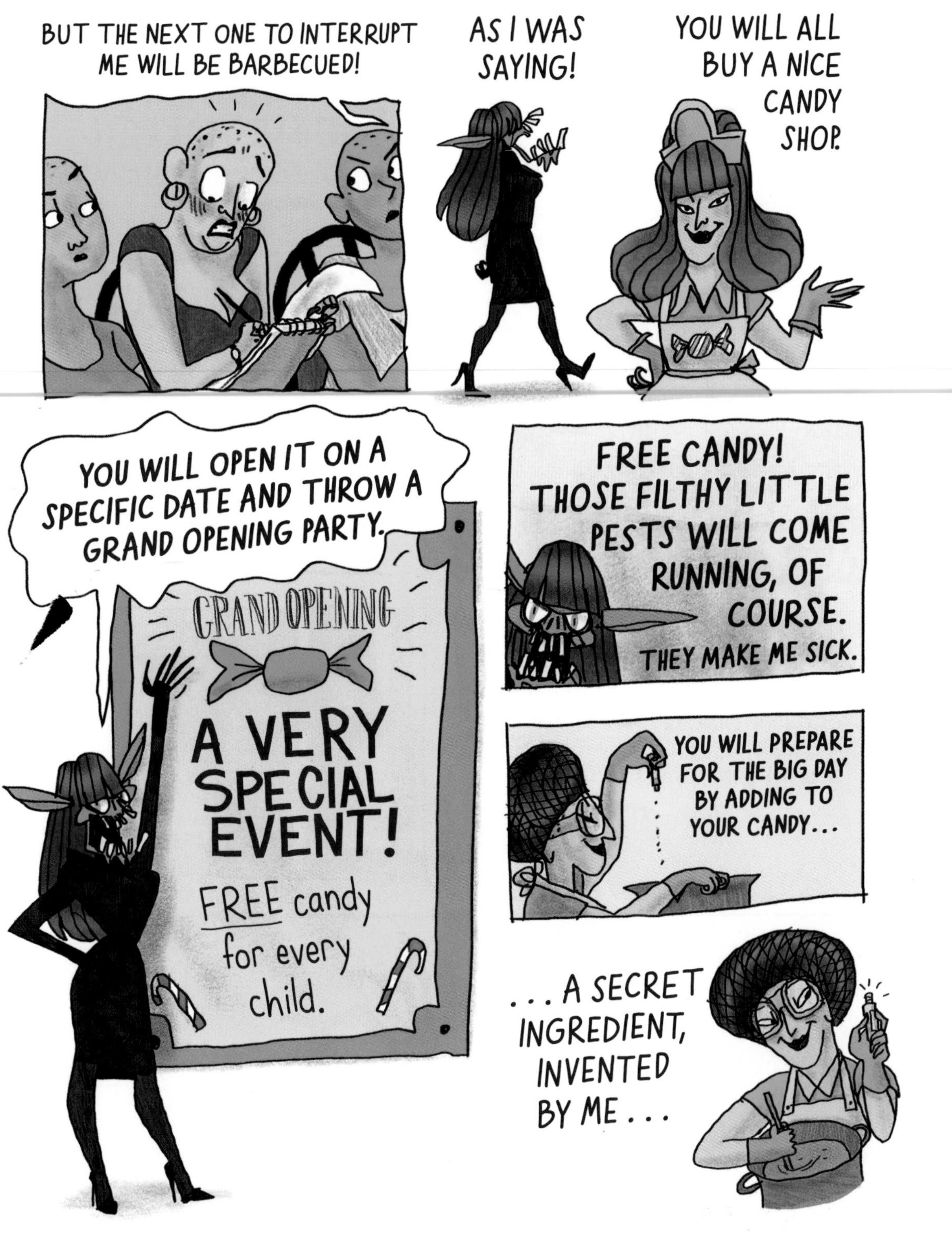
BUT THE NEXT ONE TO INTERRUPT ME WILL BE BARBECUED!
AS I WAS SAYING!
YOU WILL ALL BUY A NICE CANDY SHOP.
YOU WILL OPEN IT ON A SPECIFIC DATE AND THROW A GRAND OPENING PARTY.
GRAND OPENING
A VERY SPECIAL EVENT!
FREE candy for every child.
FREE CANDY! THOSE FILTHY LITTLE PESTS WILL COME RUNNING, OF COURSE.
THEY MAKE ME SICK.
YOU WILL PREPARE FOR THE BIG DAY BY ADDING TO YOUR CANDY...
...A SECRET INGREDIENT, INVENTED BY ME...

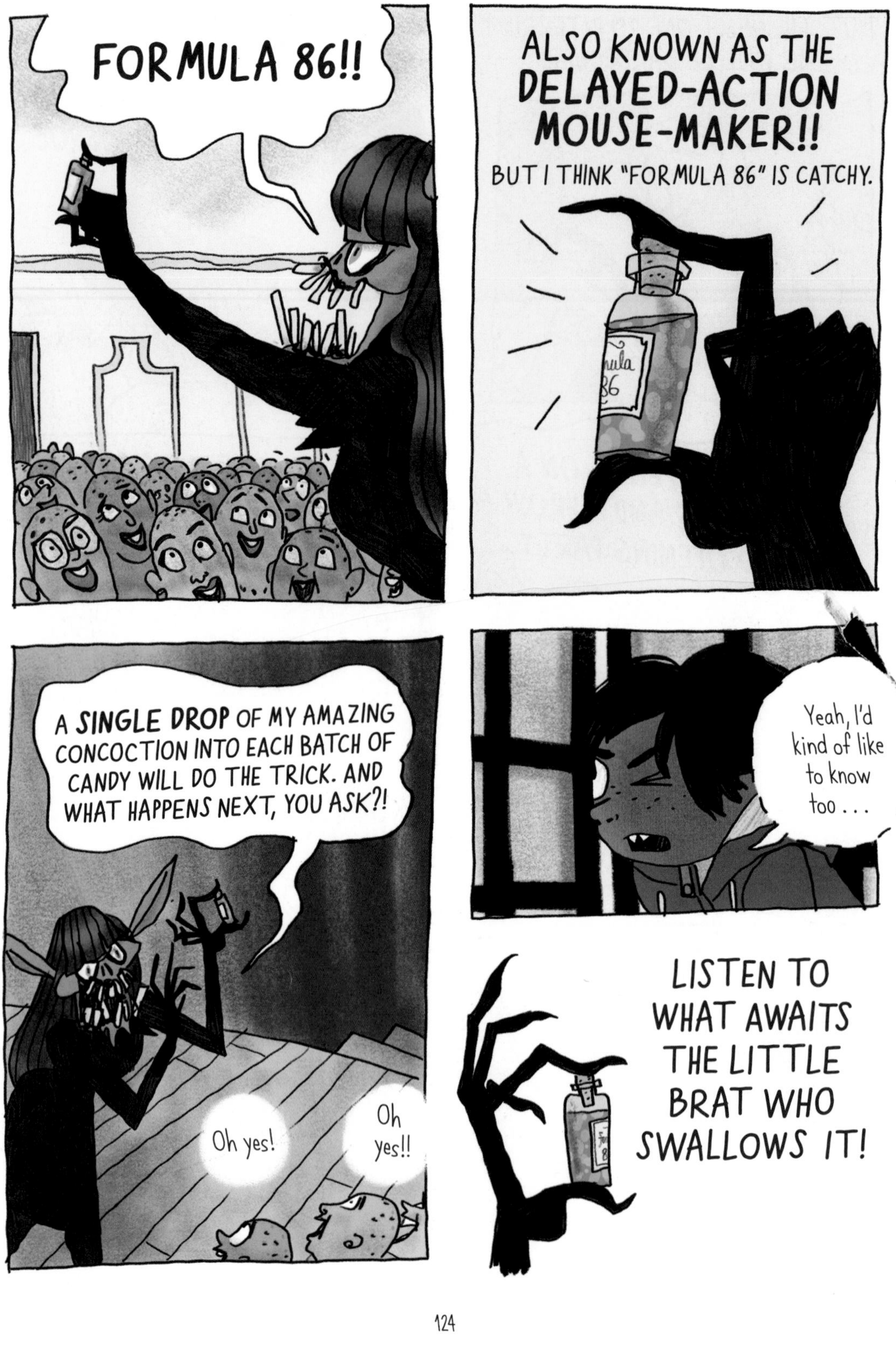
FORMULA 86!!
ALSO KNOWN AS THE DELAYED-ACTION MOUSE-MAKER!!
BUT I THINK "FORMULA 86" IS CATCHY.
A SINGLE DROP OF MY AMAZING CONCOCTION INTO EACH BATCH OF CANDY WILL DO THE TRICK. AND WHAT HAPPENS NEXT, YOU ASK?!
Oh yes!
Oh yes!!
Yeah, I'd kind of like to know too . . .
LISTEN TO WHAT AWAITS THE LITTLE BRAT WHO SWALLOWS IT!

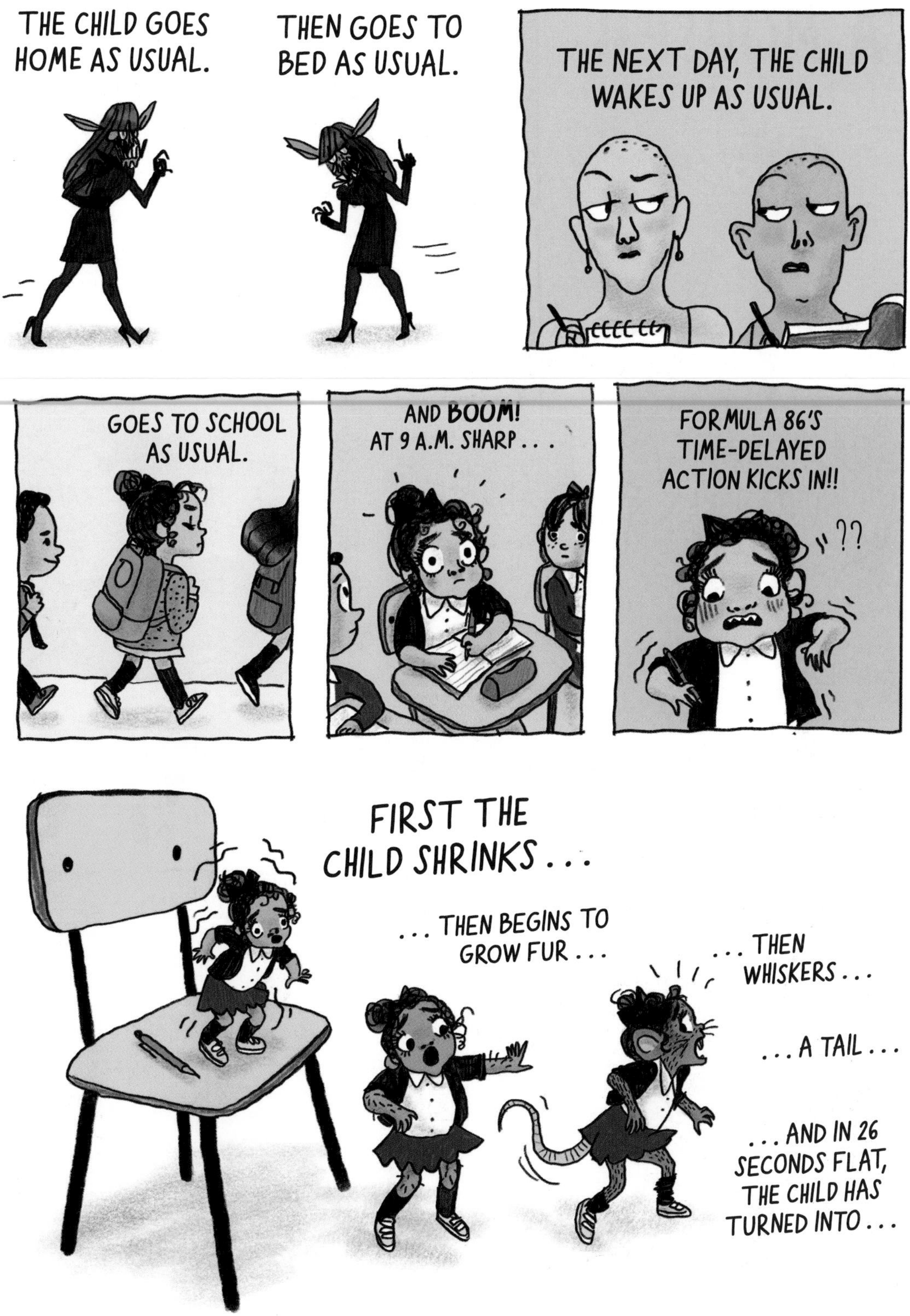
THE CHILD GOES HOME AS USUAL.
THEN GOES TO BED AS USUAL.
THE NEXT DAY, THE CHILD WAKES UP AS USUAL.
GOES TO SCHOOL AS USUAL.
AND BOOM! AT 9 A.M. SHARP . . .
FORMULA 86'S TIME-DELAYED ACTION KICKS IN!!
??
FIRST THE CHILD SHRINKS . . .
. . . THEN BEGINS TO GROW FUR . . .
. . . THEN WHISKERS . . .
. . . A TAIL . . .
. . . AND IN 26 SECONDS FLAT, THE CHILD HAS TURNED INTO . . .

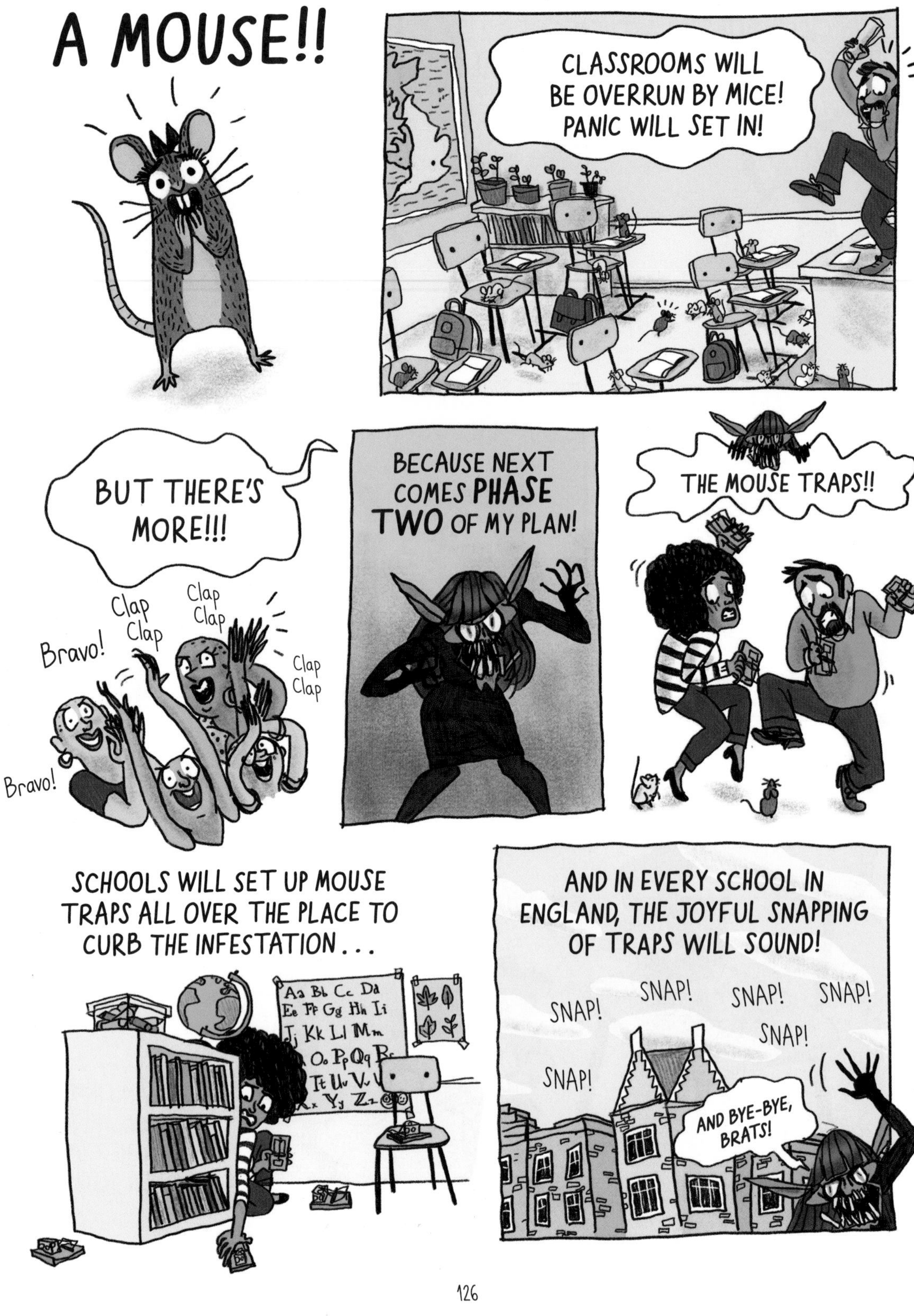
A MOUSE!!
CLASSROOMS WILL BE OVERRUN BY MICE! PANIC WILL SET IN!
BUT THERE'S MORE!!!
Bravo!
Clap Clap
Clap Clap
Clap Clap
Bravo!
BECAUSE NEXT COMES PHASE TWO OF MY PLAN!
THE MOUSE TRAPS!!
SCHOOLS WILL SET UP MOUSE TRAPS ALL OVER THE PLACE TO CURB THE INFESTATION . . .
AND IN EVERY SCHOOL IN ENGLAND, THE JOYFUL SNAPPING OF TRAPS WILL SOUND!
SNAP!
SNAP!
SNAP!
SNAP!
SNAP!
SNAP!
AND BYE-BYE, BRATS!

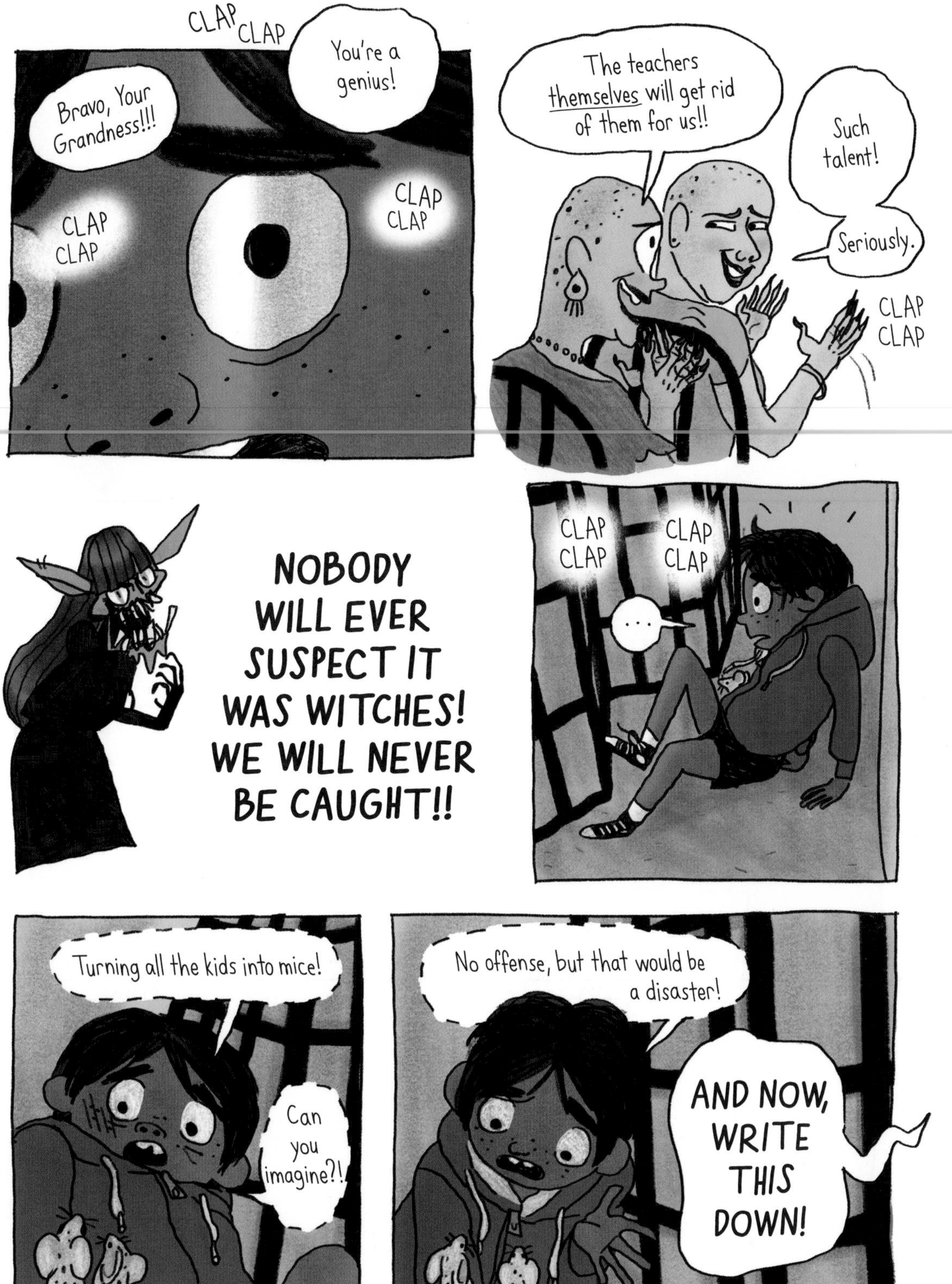
CLAP CLAP
Bravo, Your Grandness!!!
You're a genius!
CLAP CLAP
CLAP CLAP
The teachers themselves will get rid of them for us!!
Such talent!
Seriously.
CLAP CLAP
NOBODY WILL EVER SUSPECT IT WAS WITCHES! WE WILL NEVER BE CAUGHT!!
CLAP CLAP
CLAP CLAP
. . .
Turning all the kids into mice!
Can you imagine?!
No offense, but that would be a disaster!
AND NOW, WRITE THIS DOWN!

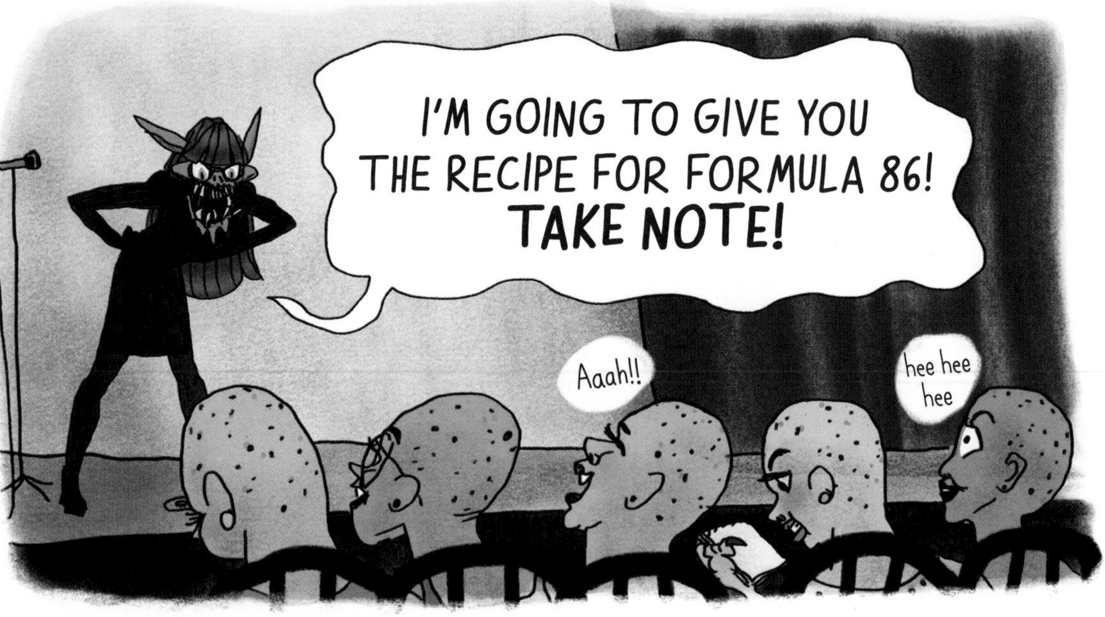
I'M GOING TO GIVE YOU THE RECIPE FOR FORMULA 86! TAKE NOTE!
Aaah!!
hee hee hee

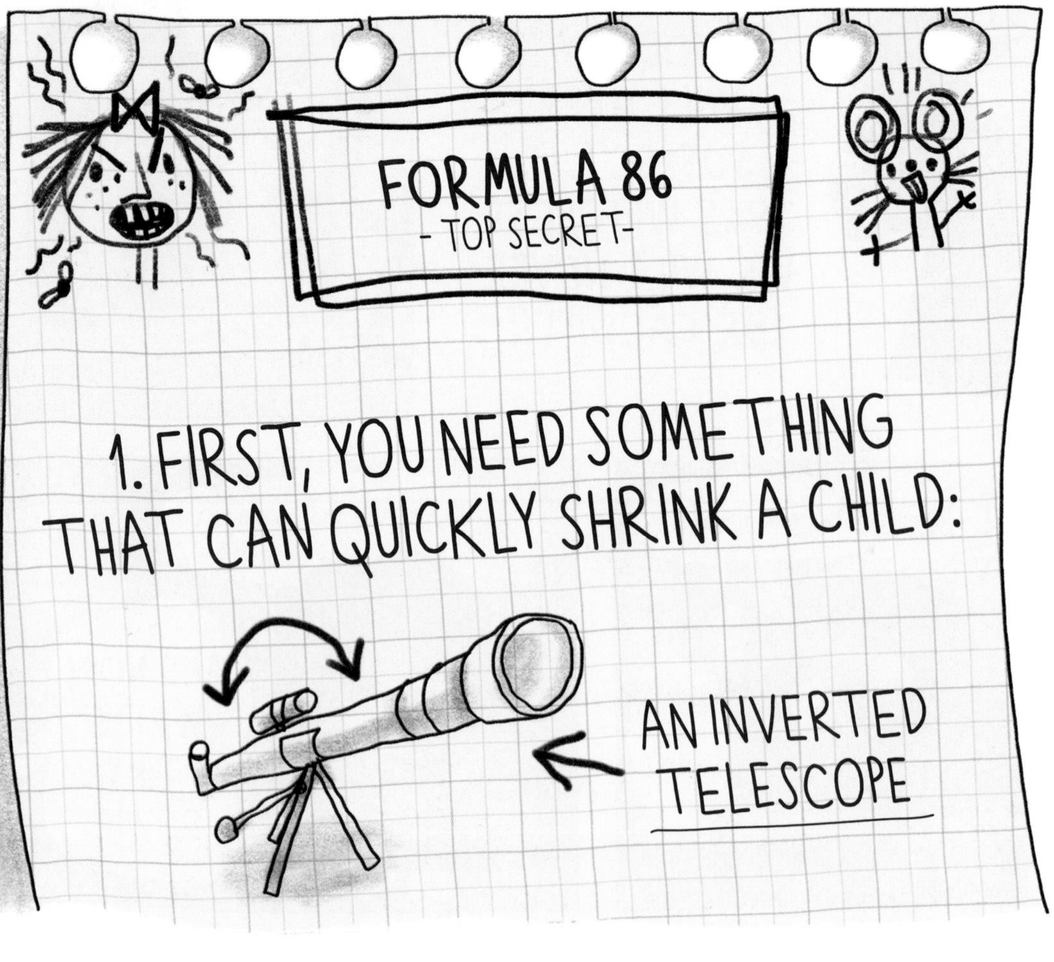
FORMULA 86
- TOP SECRET -
1. FIRST, YOU NEED SOMETHING THAT CAN QUICKLY SHRINK A CHILD:
AN INVERTED TELESCOPE

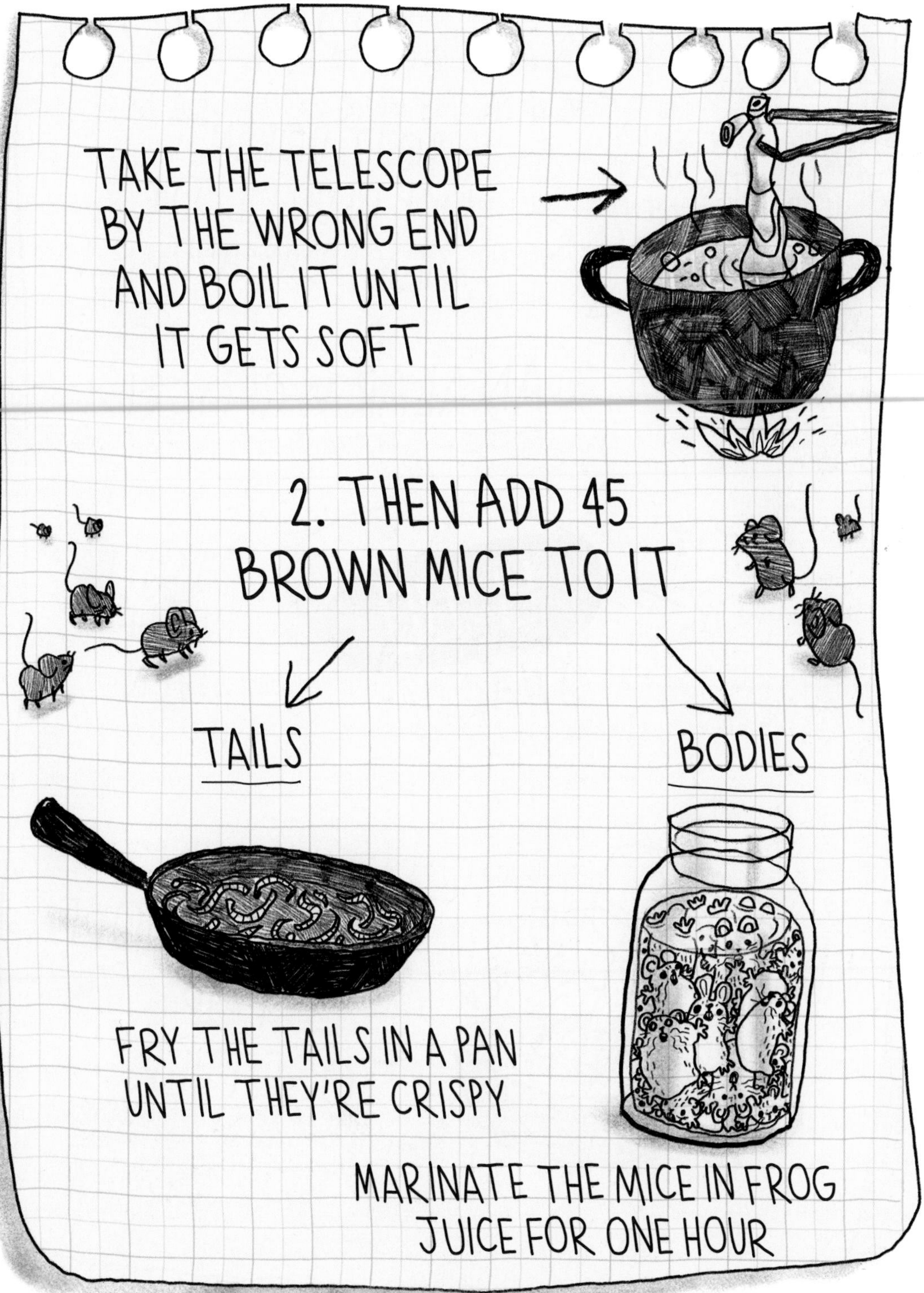
TAKE THE TELESCOPE BY THE WRONG END AND BOIL IT UNTIL IT GETS SOFT
2. THEN ADD 45 BROWN MICE TO IT
TAILS
BODIES
FRY THE TAILS IN A PAN UNTIL THEY'RE CRISPY
MARINATE THE MICE IN FROG JUICE FOR ONE HOUR

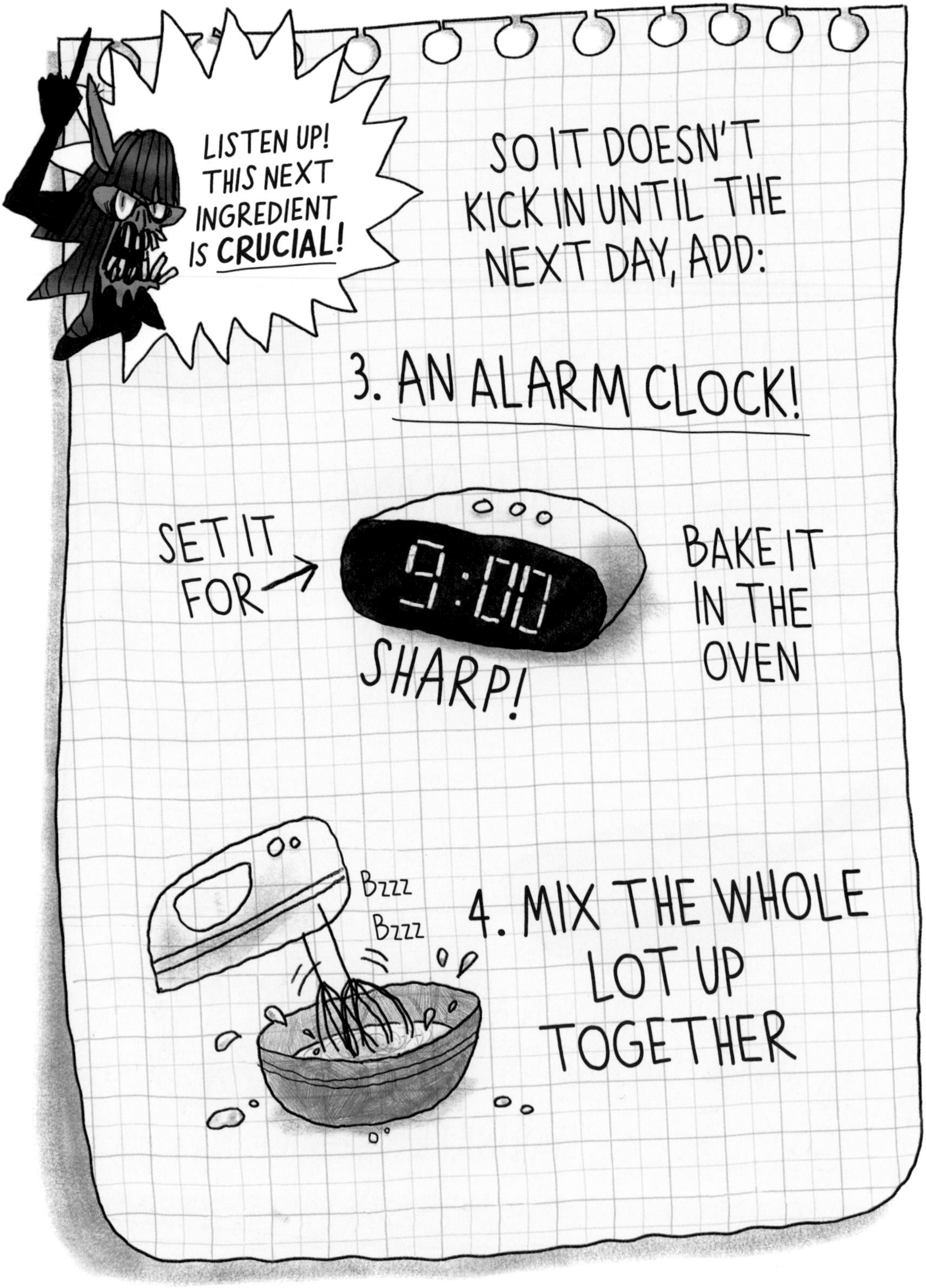
LISTEN UP! THIS NEXT INGREDIENT IS CRUCIAL!
SO IT DOESN'T KICK IN UNTIL THE NEXT DAY, ADD:
3. AN ALARM CLOCK!
SET IT FOR
9:00
SHARP!
BAKE IT IN THE OVEN
Bzzz
Bzzz
4. MIX THE WHOLE LOT UP TOGETHER

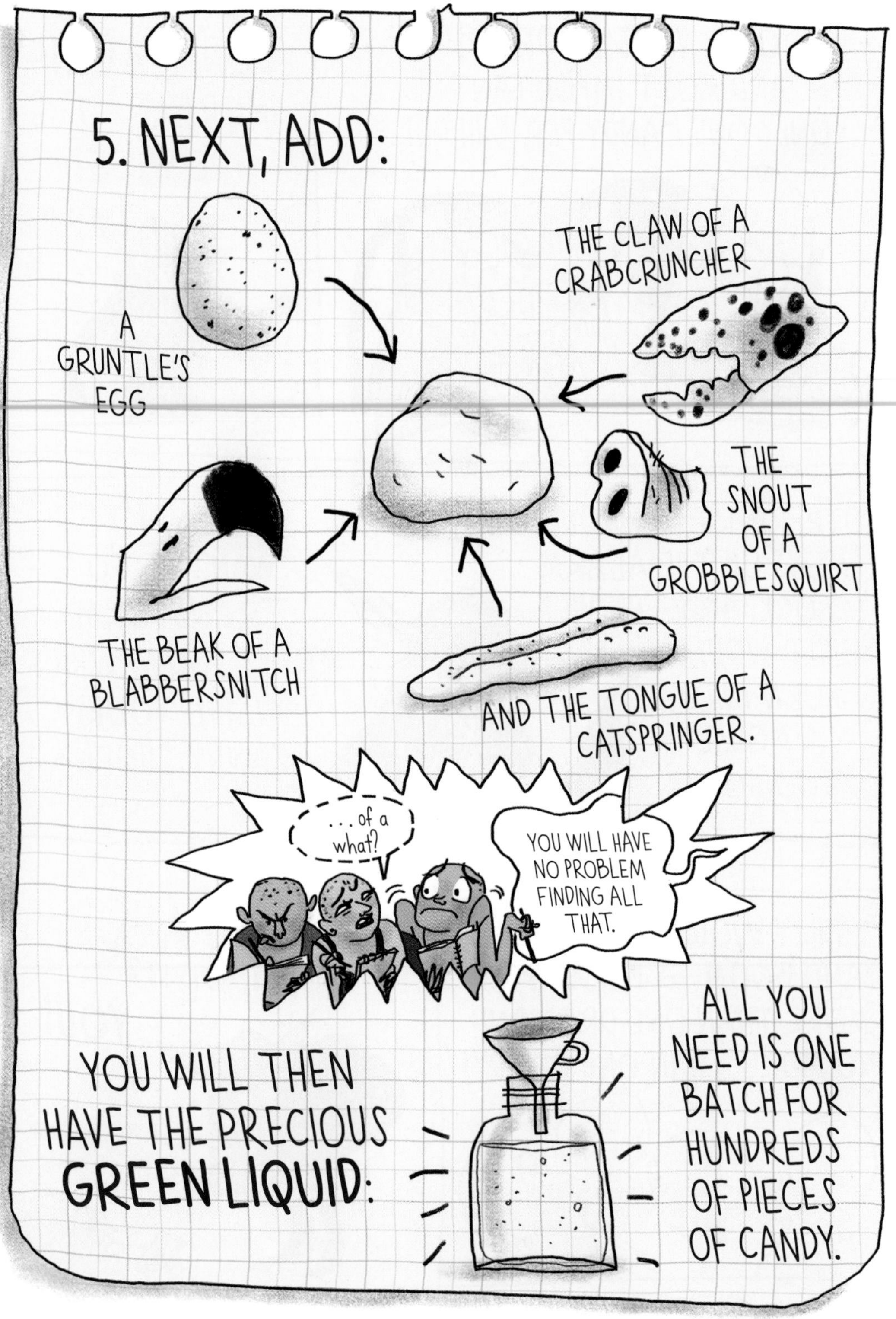
5. NEXT, ADD:
A GRUNTLE'S EGG
THE CLAW OF A CRABCRUNCHER
THE SNOUT OF A GROBBLESQUIRT
THE BEAK OF A BLABBERSNITCH
AND THE TONGUE OF A CATSPRINGER.
. . . of a what?
YOU WILL HAVE NO PROBLEM FINDING ALL THAT.
YOU WILL THEN HAVE THE PRECIOUS **GREEN LIQUID**:
ALL YOU NEED IS ONE BATCH FOR HUNDREDS OF PIECES OF CANDY.

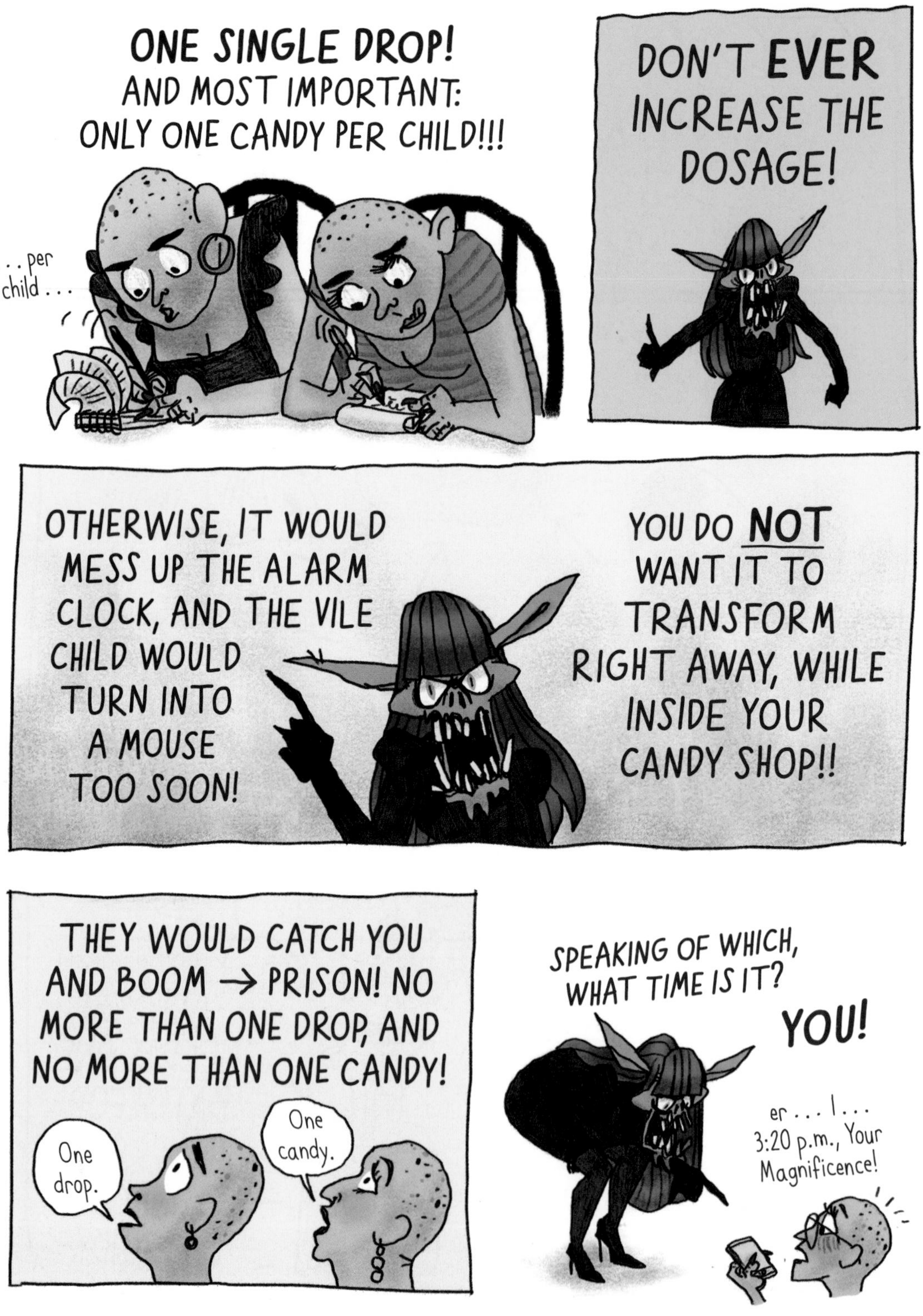
ONE SINGLE DROP!
AND MOST IMPORTANT:
ONLY ONE CANDY PER CHILD!!!
. . . per child . . .
DON'T EVER INCREASE THE DOSAGE!
OTHERWISE, IT WOULD MESS UP THE ALARM CLOCK, AND THE VILE CHILD WOULD TURN INTO A MOUSE TOO SOON!
YOU DO NOT WANT IT TO TRANSFORM RIGHT AWAY, WHILE INSIDE YOUR CANDY SHOP!!
THEY WOULD CATCH YOU AND BOOM → PRISON! NO MORE THAN ONE DROP, AND NO MORE THAN ONE CANDY!
One drop.
One candy.
SPEAKING OF WHICH, WHAT TIME IS IT?
YOU!
er . . . I . . . 3:20 p.m., Your Magnificence!

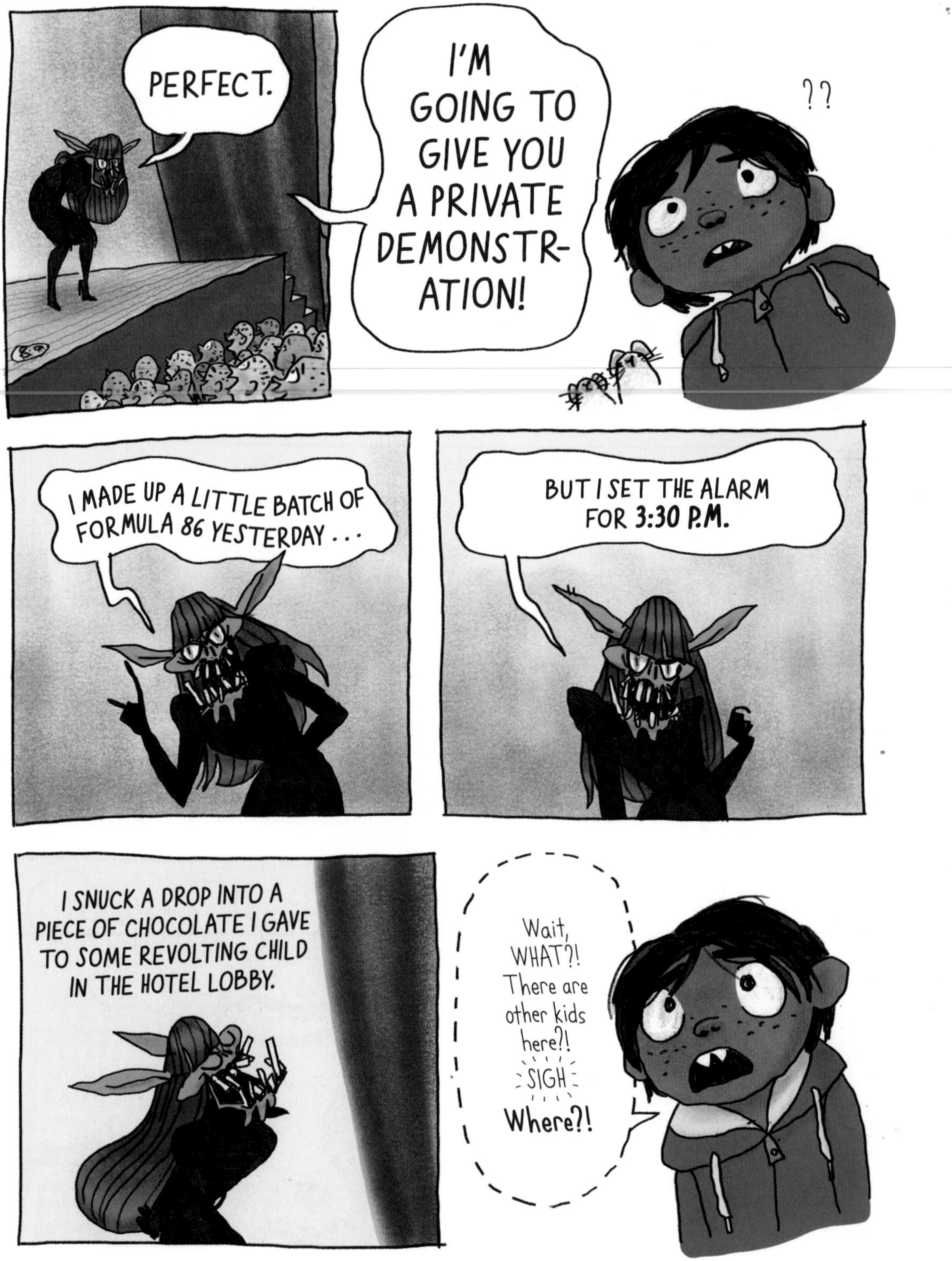
PERFECT.
I'M GOING TO GIVE YOU A PRIVATE DEMONSTR-ATION!
??
I MADE UP A LITTLE BATCH OF FORMULA 86 YESTERDAY . . .
BUT I SET THE ALARM FOR 3:30 P.M.
I SNUCK A DROP INTO A PIECE OF CHOCOLATE I GAVE TO SOME REVOLTING CHILD IN THE HOTEL LOBBY.
Wait, WHAT?! There are other kids here?! SIGH Where?!

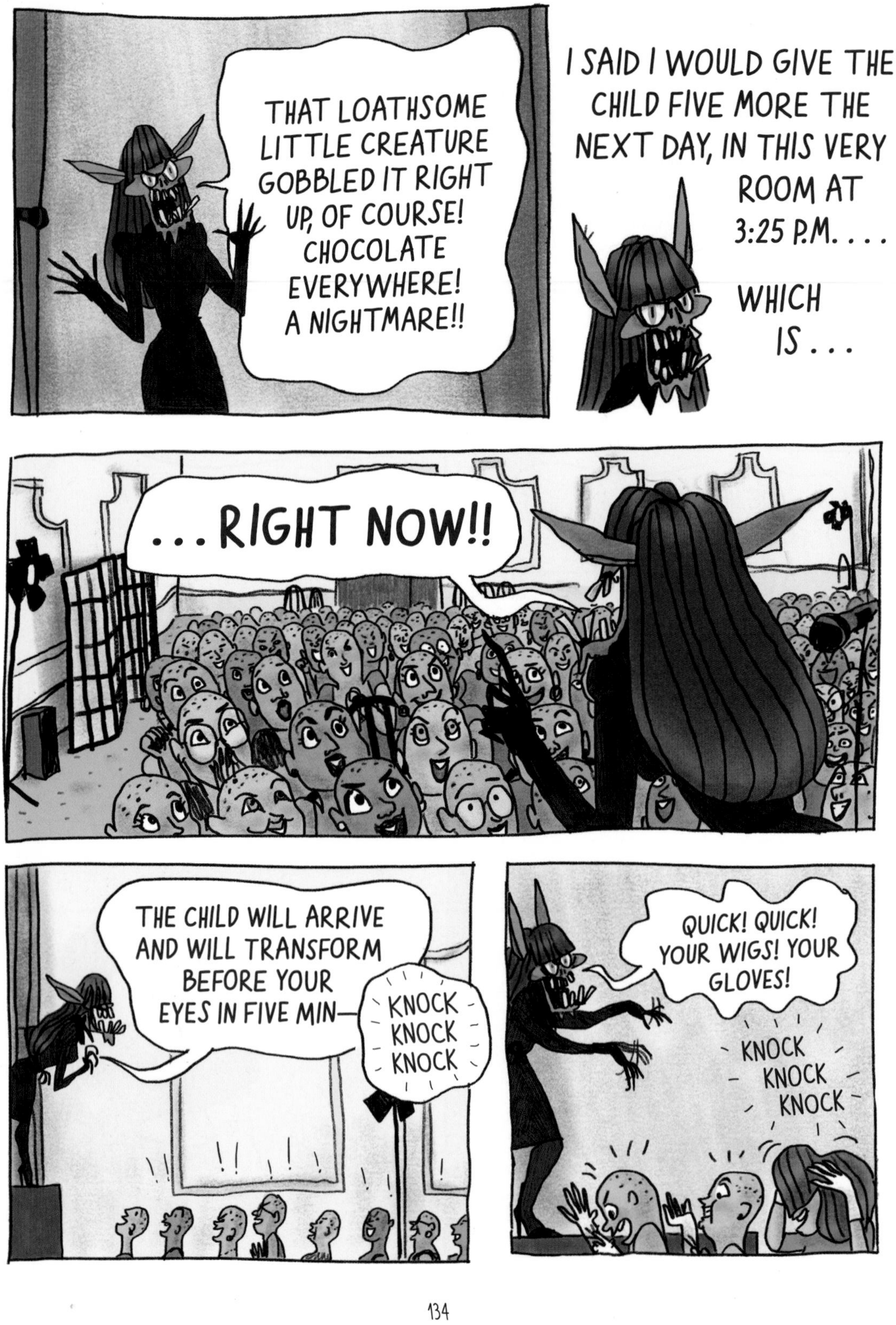
THAT LOATHSOME LITTLE CREATURE GOBBLED IT RIGHT UP, OF COURSE! CHOCOLATE EVERYWHERE! A NIGHTMARE!!
I SAID I WOULD GIVE THE CHILD FIVE MORE THE NEXT DAY, IN THIS VERY ROOM AT 3:25 P.M. . . .
WHICH IS . . .
. . . RIGHT NOW!!
THE CHILD WILL ARRIVE AND WILL TRANSFORM BEFORE YOUR EYES IN FIVE MIN—
KNOCK KNOCK KNOCK
QUICK! QUICK! YOUR WIGS! YOUR GLOVES!
KNOCK KNOCK KNOCK

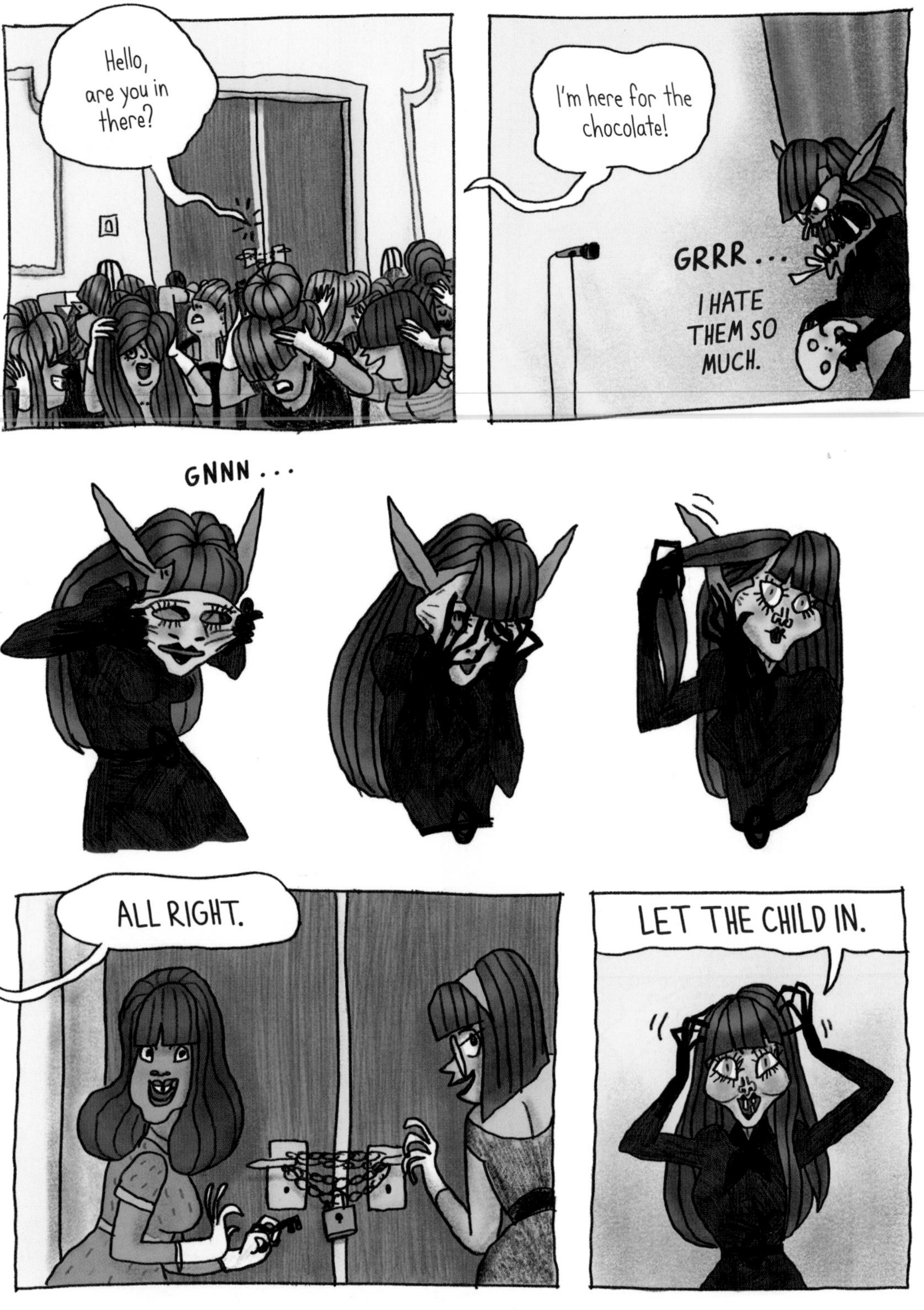
Hello,
are you in
there?
I'm here for the
chocolate!
GRRR...
I HATE
THEM SO
MUCH.
GNNN...
ALL RIGHT.
LET THE CHILD IN.

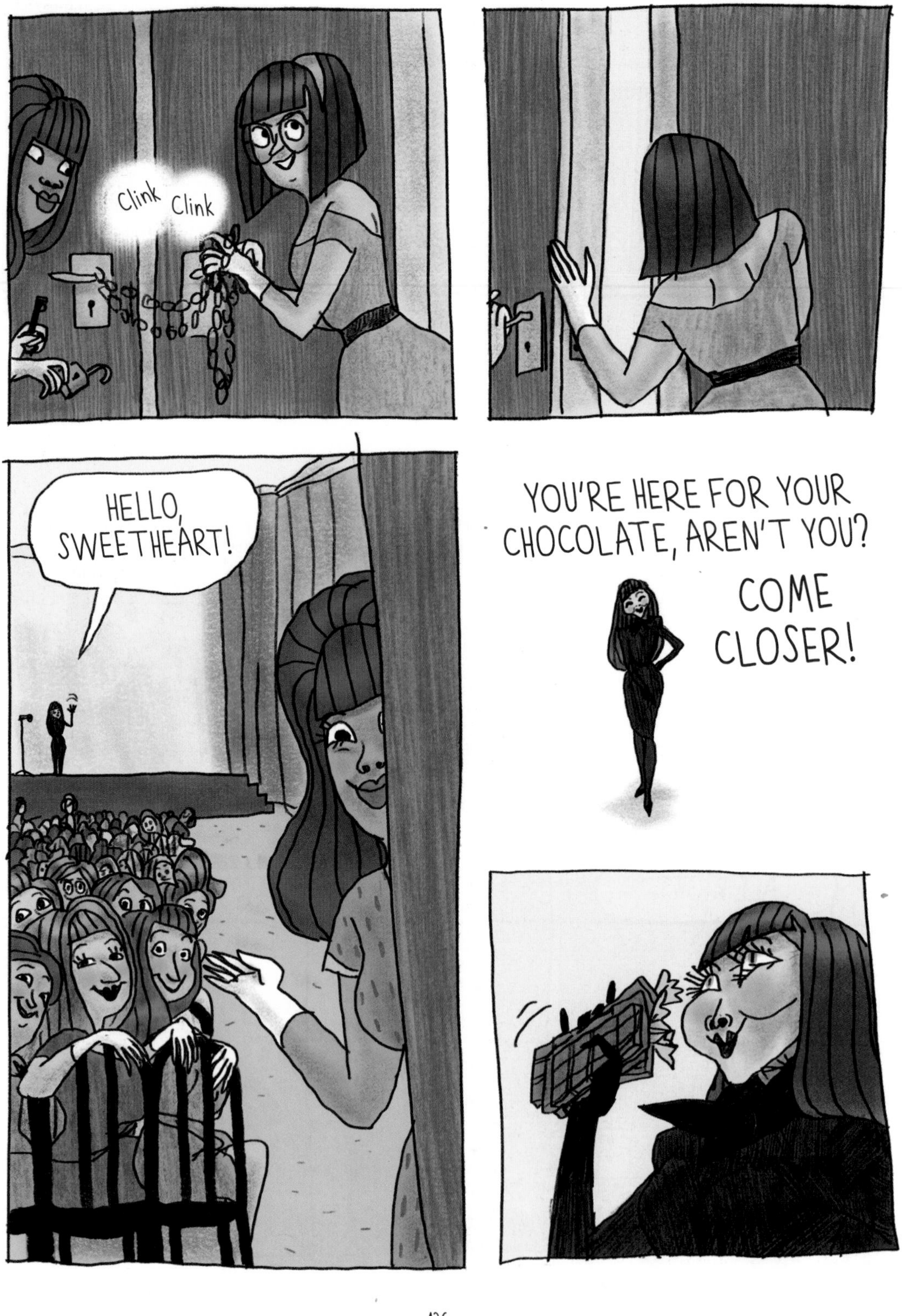
Clink Clink
HELLO, SWEETHEART!
YOU'RE HERE FOR YOUR CHOCOLATE, AREN'T YOU?
COME CLOSER!

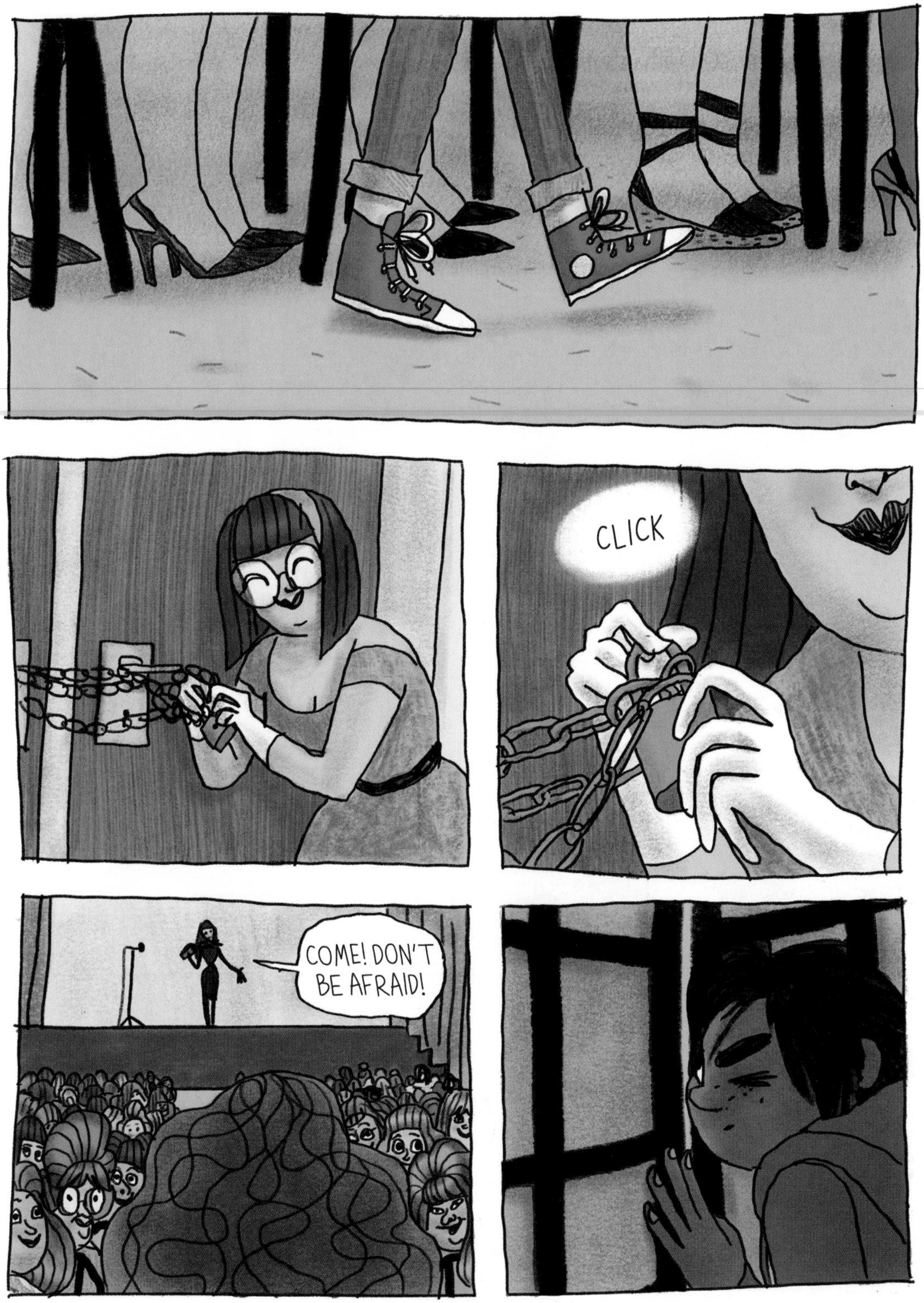
CLICK
COME! DON'T BE AFRAID!

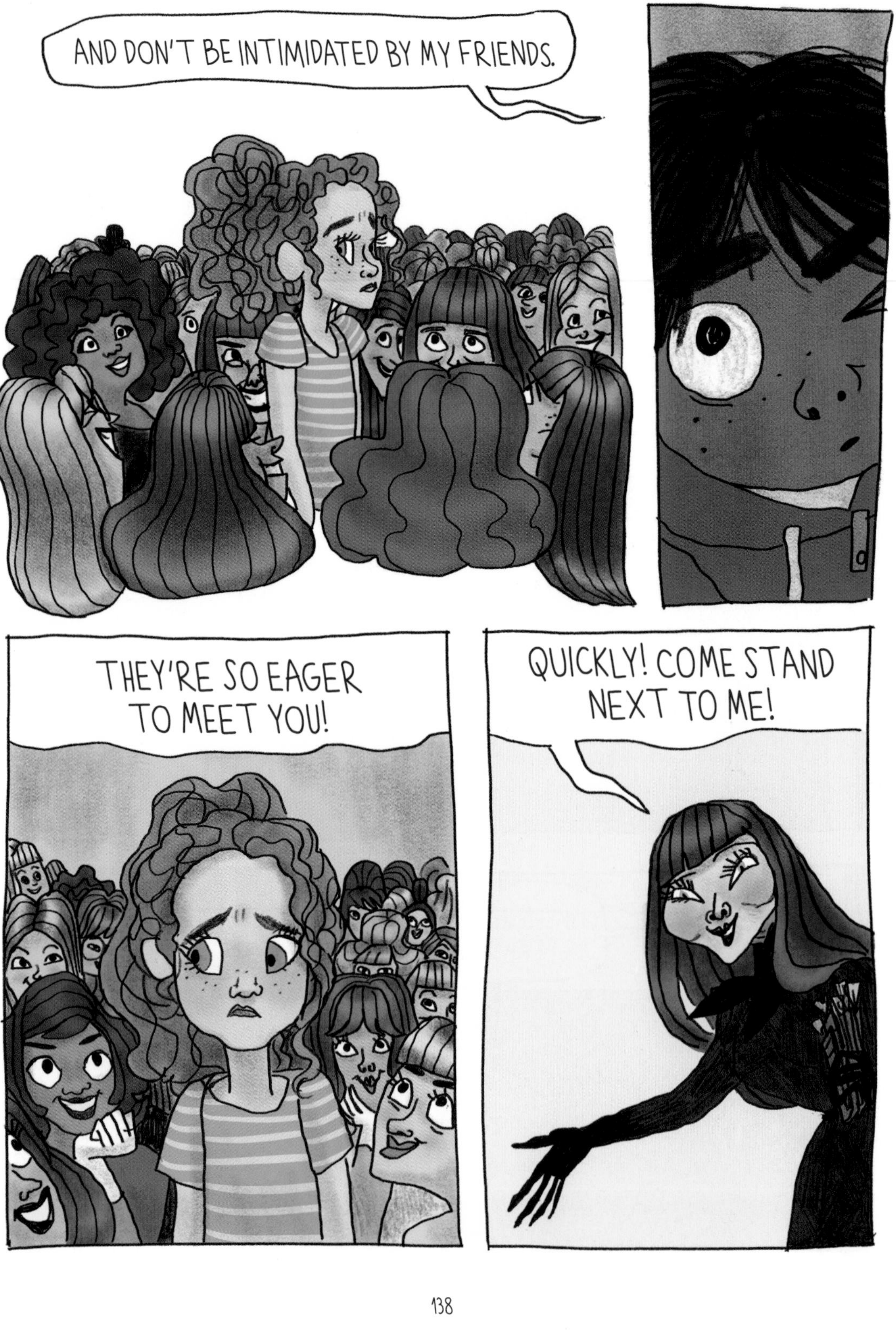
AND DON'T BE INTIMIDATED BY MY FRIENDS.
THEY'RE SO EAGER TO MEET YOU!
QUICKLY! COME STAND NEXT TO ME!

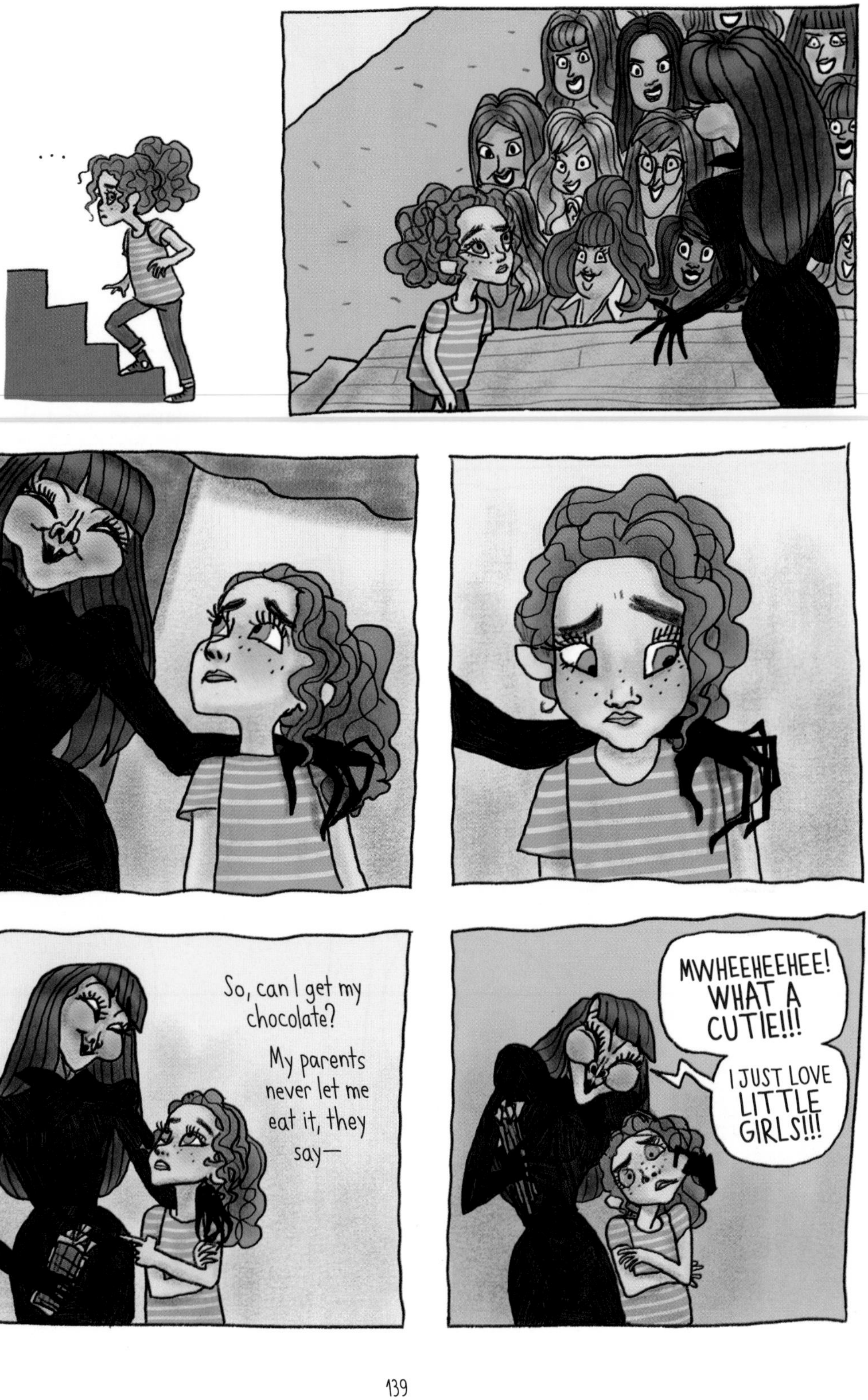
...
So, can I get my chocolate?
My parents never let me eat it, they say—
MWHEEHEEHEE! WHAT A CUTIE!!!
I JUST LOVE LITTLE GIRLS!!!

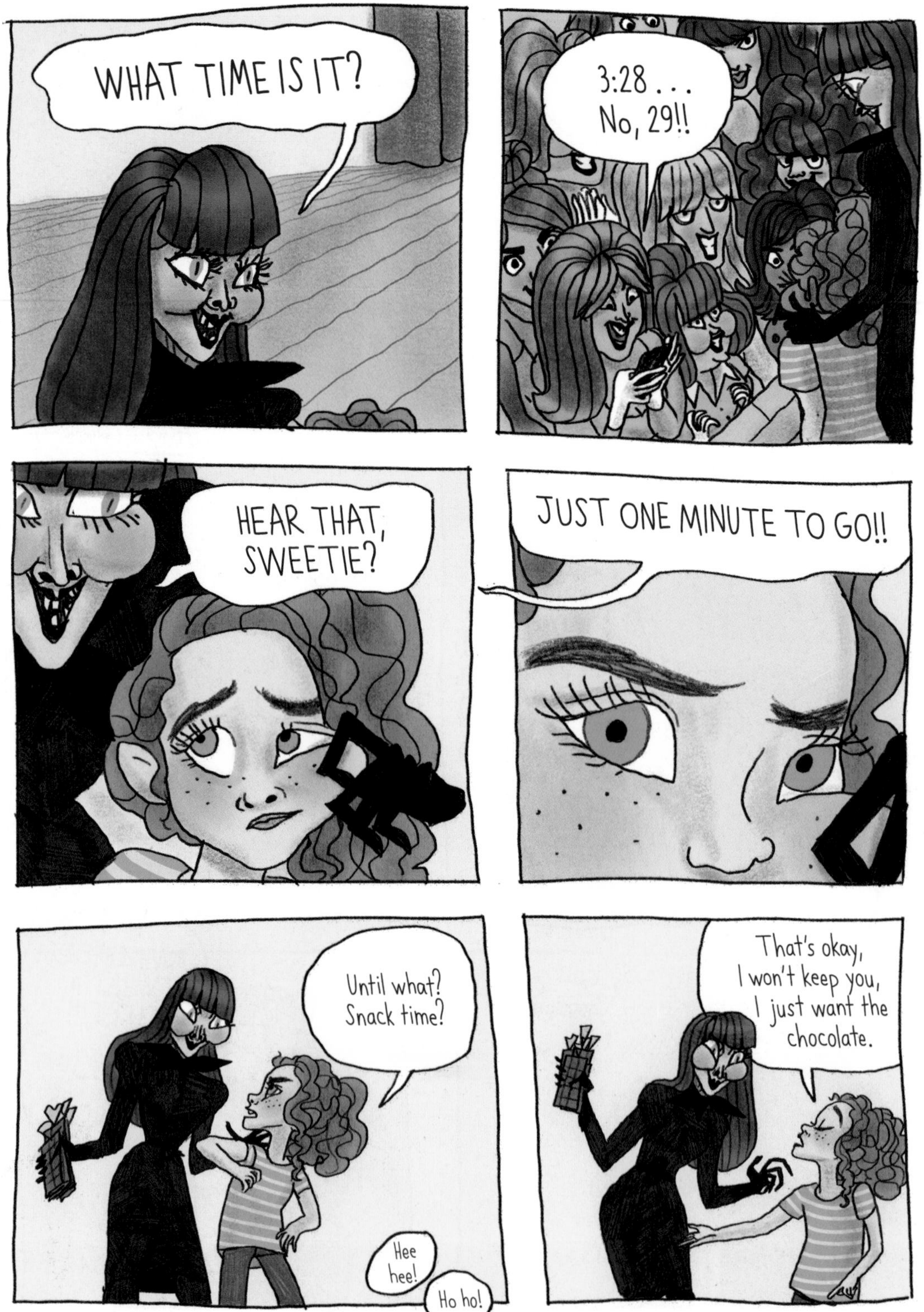
WHAT TIME IS IT?
3:28 . . . No, 29!!
HEAR THAT, SWEETIE?
JUST ONE MINUTE TO GO!!
Until what? Snack time?
Hee hee!
Ho ho!
That's okay, I won't keep you, I just want the chocolate.

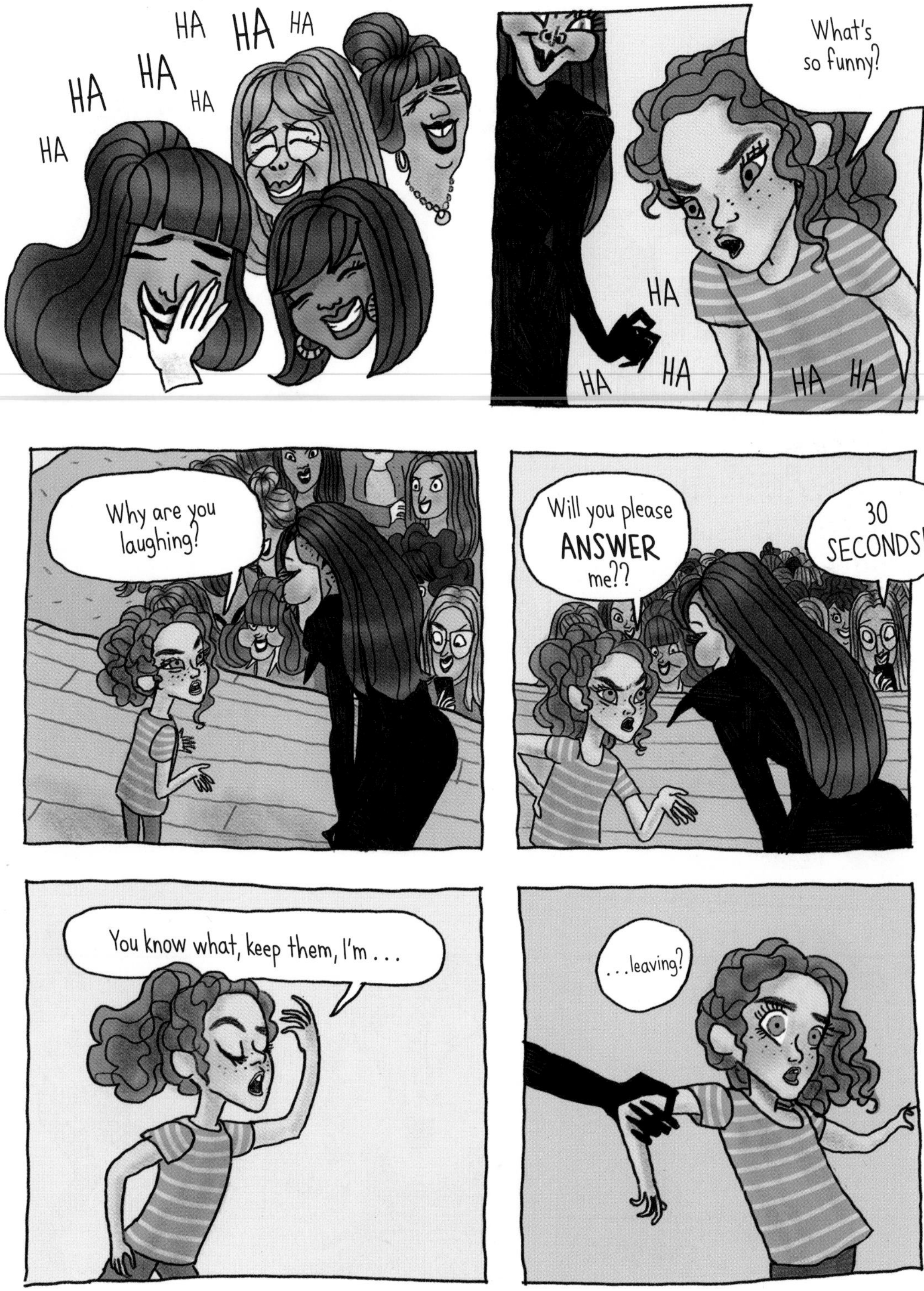
HA
HA
HA
HA
HA
HA
HA
What's so funny?
HA
HA
HA
HA
HA
Why are you laughing?
Will you please ANSWER me??
30 SECONDS!
You know what, keep them, I'm . . .
. . . leaving?

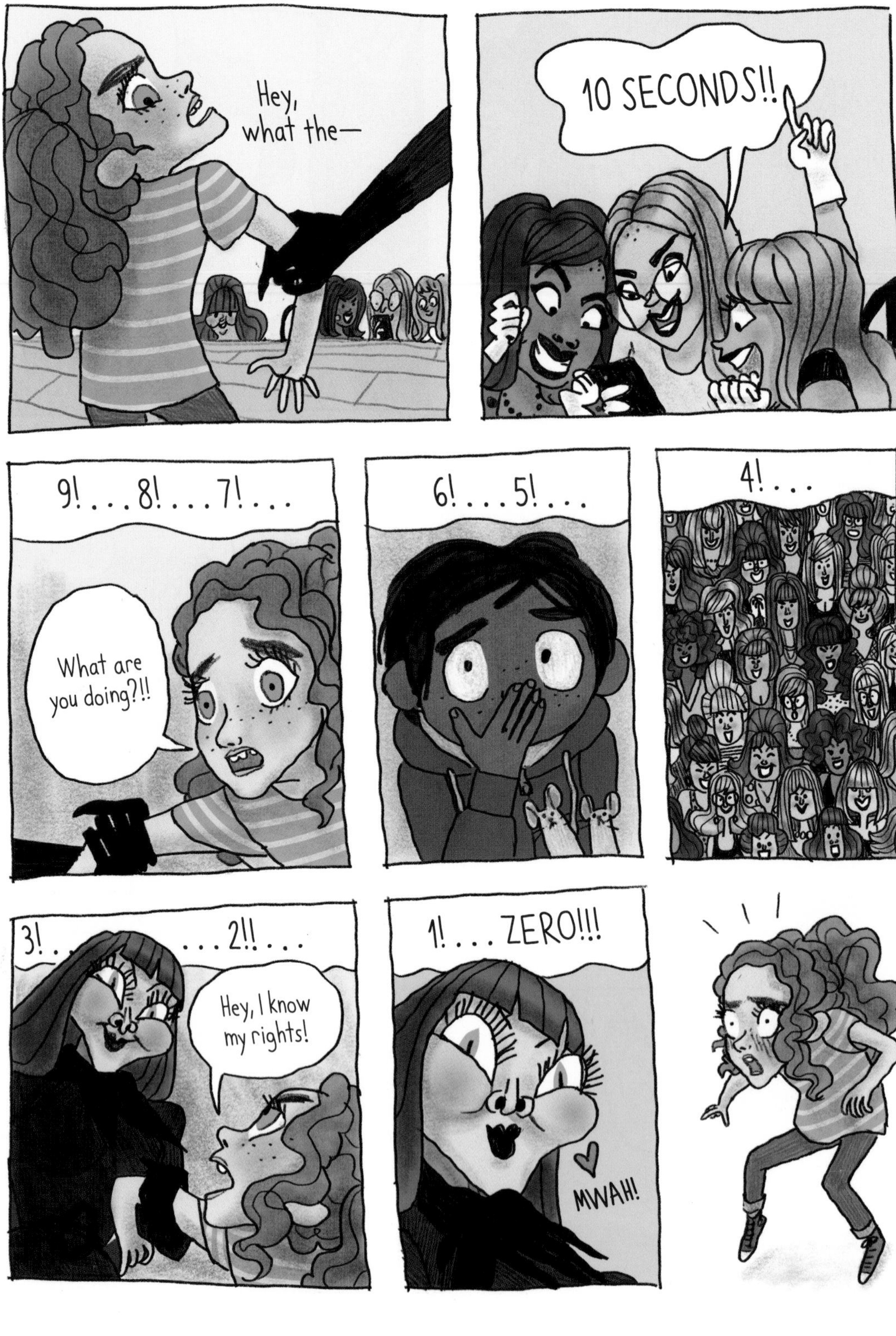

Hey, what the—
10 SECONDS!!
9! . . . 8! . . . 7! . . .
What are you doing?!!
6! . . . 5! . . .
4! . . .
3! . . .
. . . 2!! . . .
Hey, I know my rights!
1! . . . ZERO!!!
MWAH!

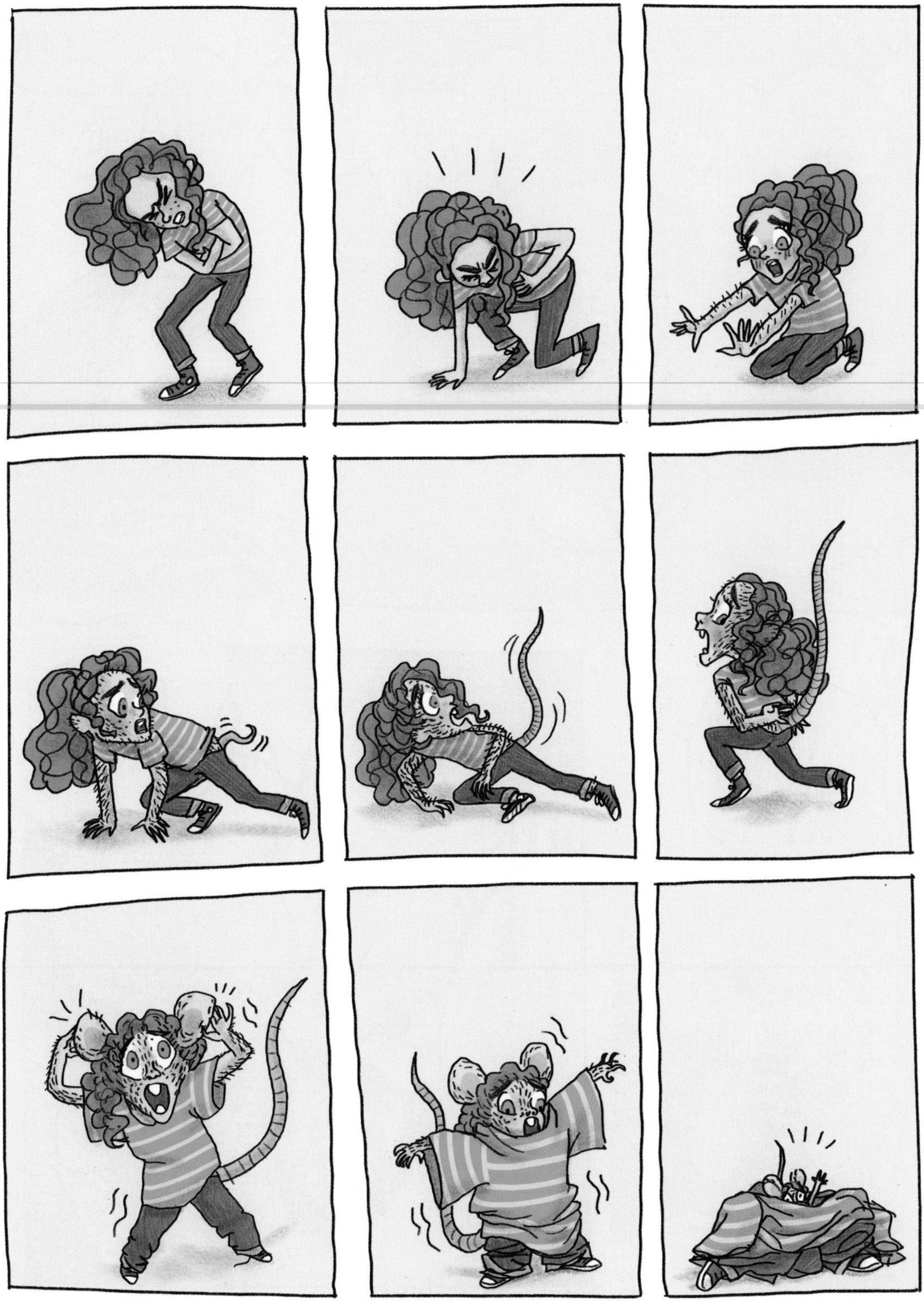

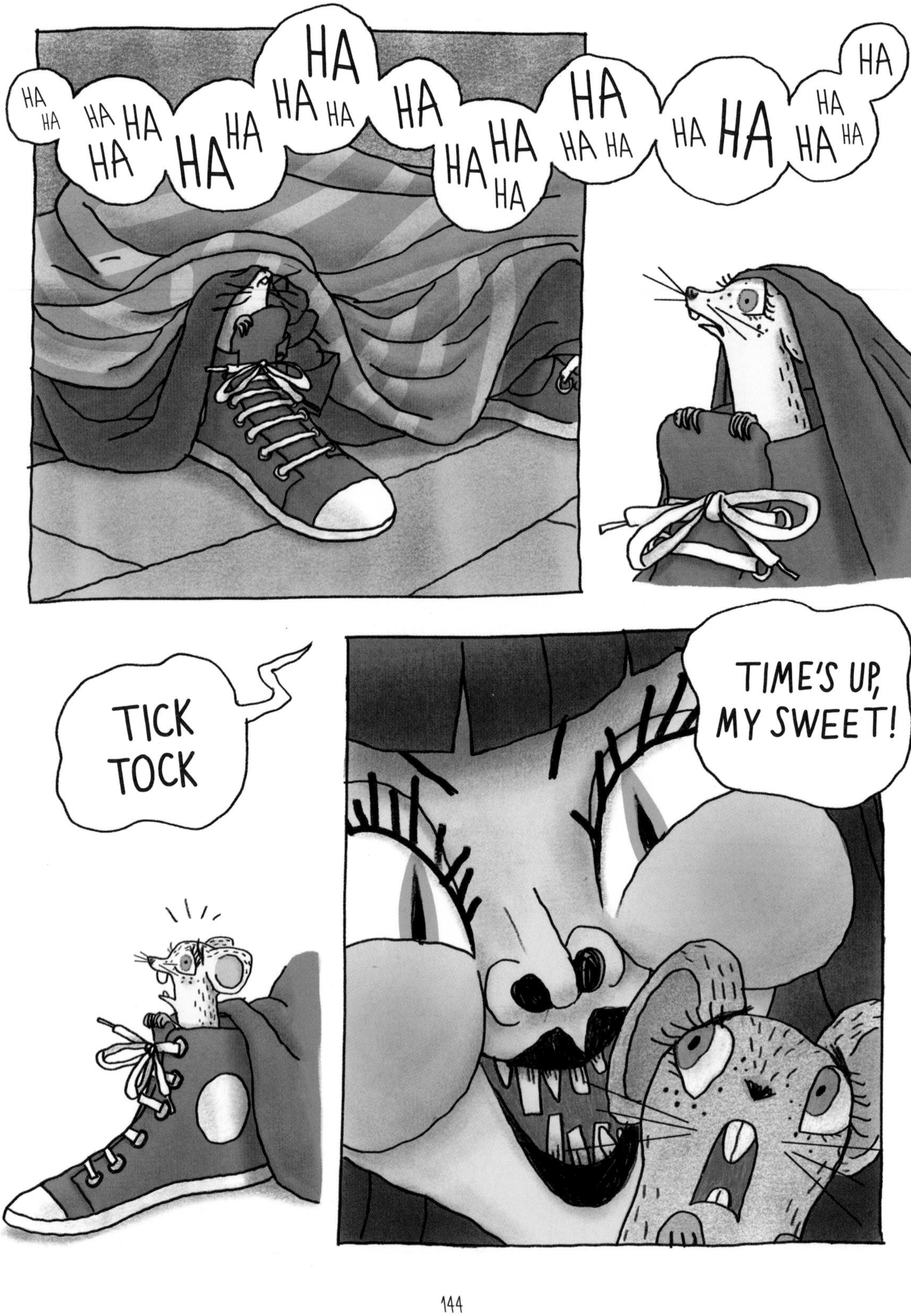
HA HA
HA HA HA
HA HA
HA HA HA
HA
HA HA HA
HA HA HA
HA HA
HA HA HA HA
HA
TICK TOCK
TIME'S UP, MY SWEET!

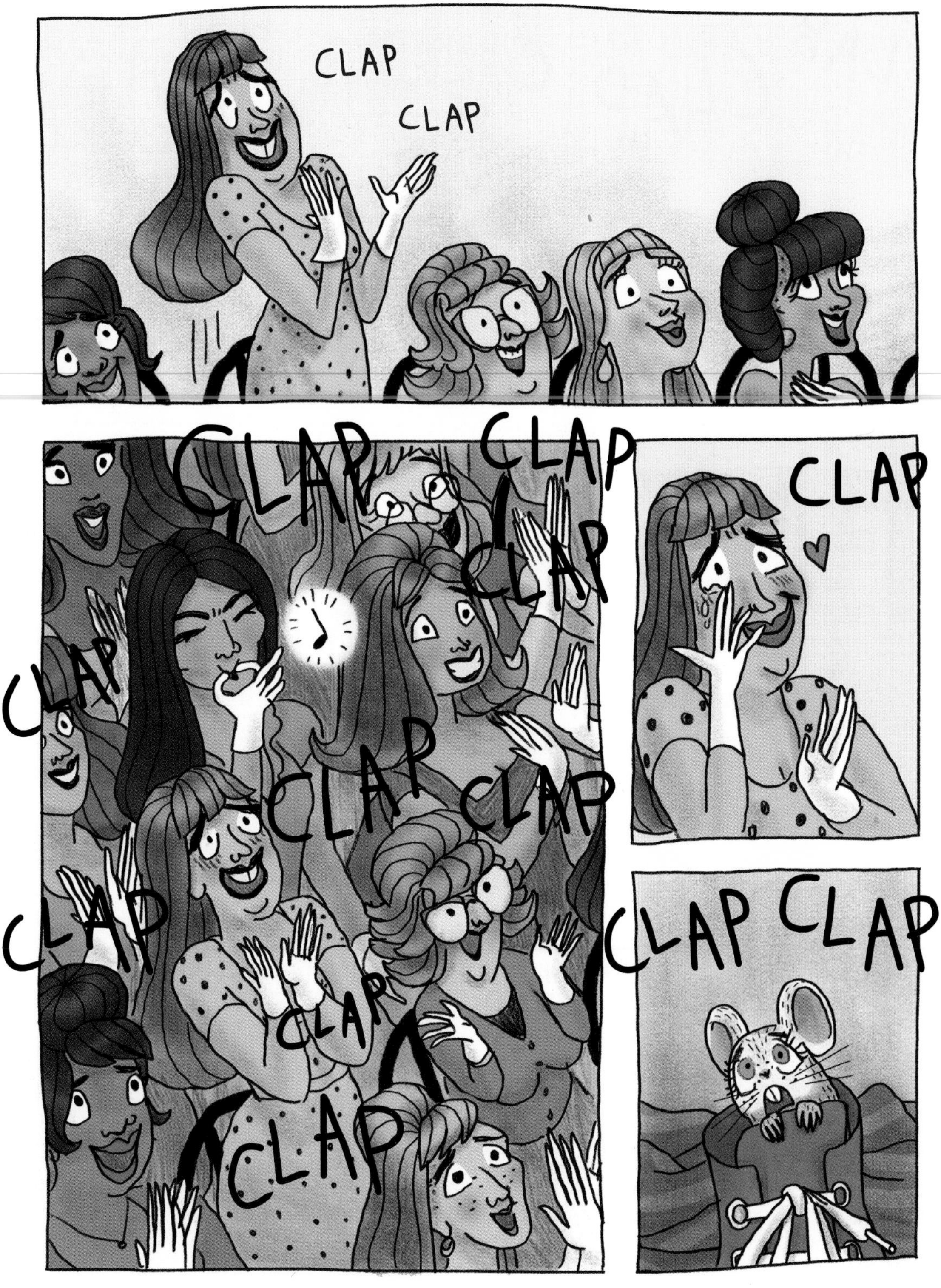
CLAP
CLAP
CLAP
CLAP
CLAP
CLAP
CLAP
CLAP
CLAP
CLAP
CLAP
CLAP
CLAP CLAP

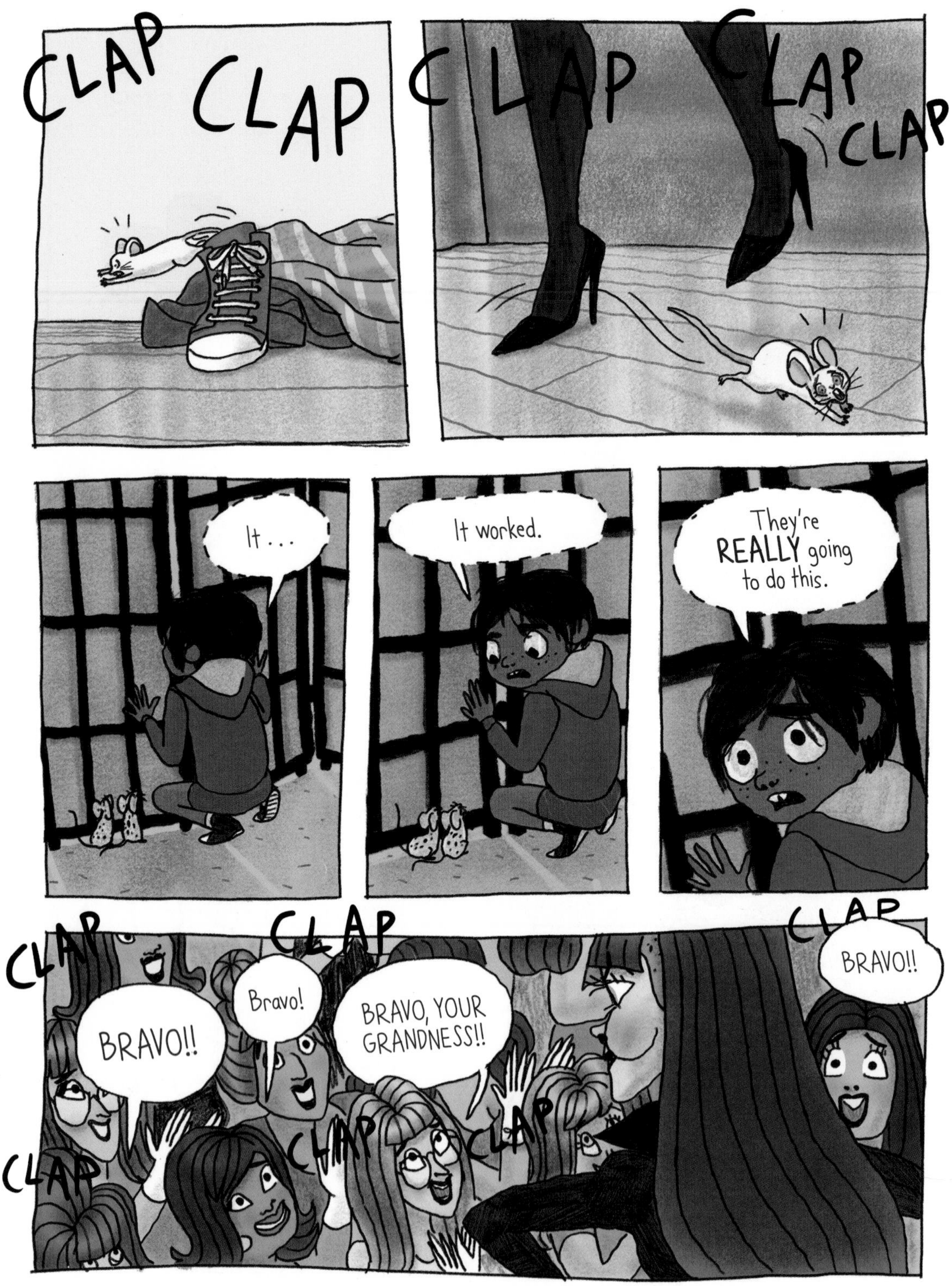
CLAP
CLAP
CLAP
CLAP
CLAP
It . . .
It worked.
They're REALLY going to do this.
CLAP
CLAP
CLAP
BRAVO!!
Bravo!
BRAVO, YOUR GRANDNESS!!
BRAVO!!
CLAP
CLAP
CLAP

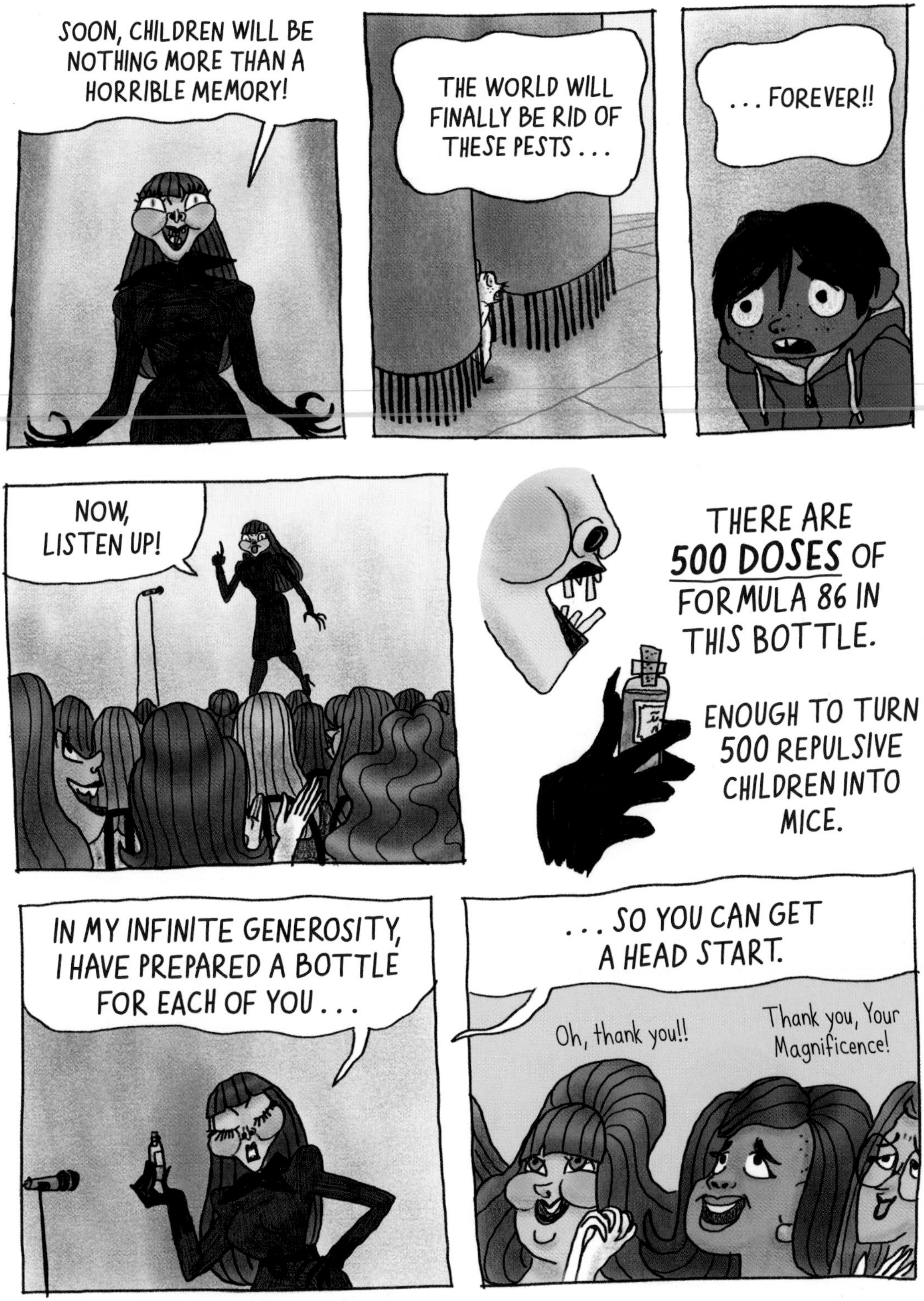

SOON, CHILDREN WILL BE NOTHING MORE THAN A HORRIBLE MEMORY!
THE WORLD WILL FINALLY BE RID OF THESE PESTS . . .
. . . FOREVER!!
NOW, LISTEN UP!
THERE ARE 500 DOSES OF FORMULA 86 IN THIS BOTTLE.
ENOUGH TO TURN 500 REPULSIVE CHILDREN INTO MICE.
IN MY INFINITE GENEROSITY, I HAVE PREPARED A BOTTLE FOR EACH OF YOU . . .
. . . SO YOU CAN GET A HEAD START.
Oh, thank you!!
Thank you, Your Magnificence!

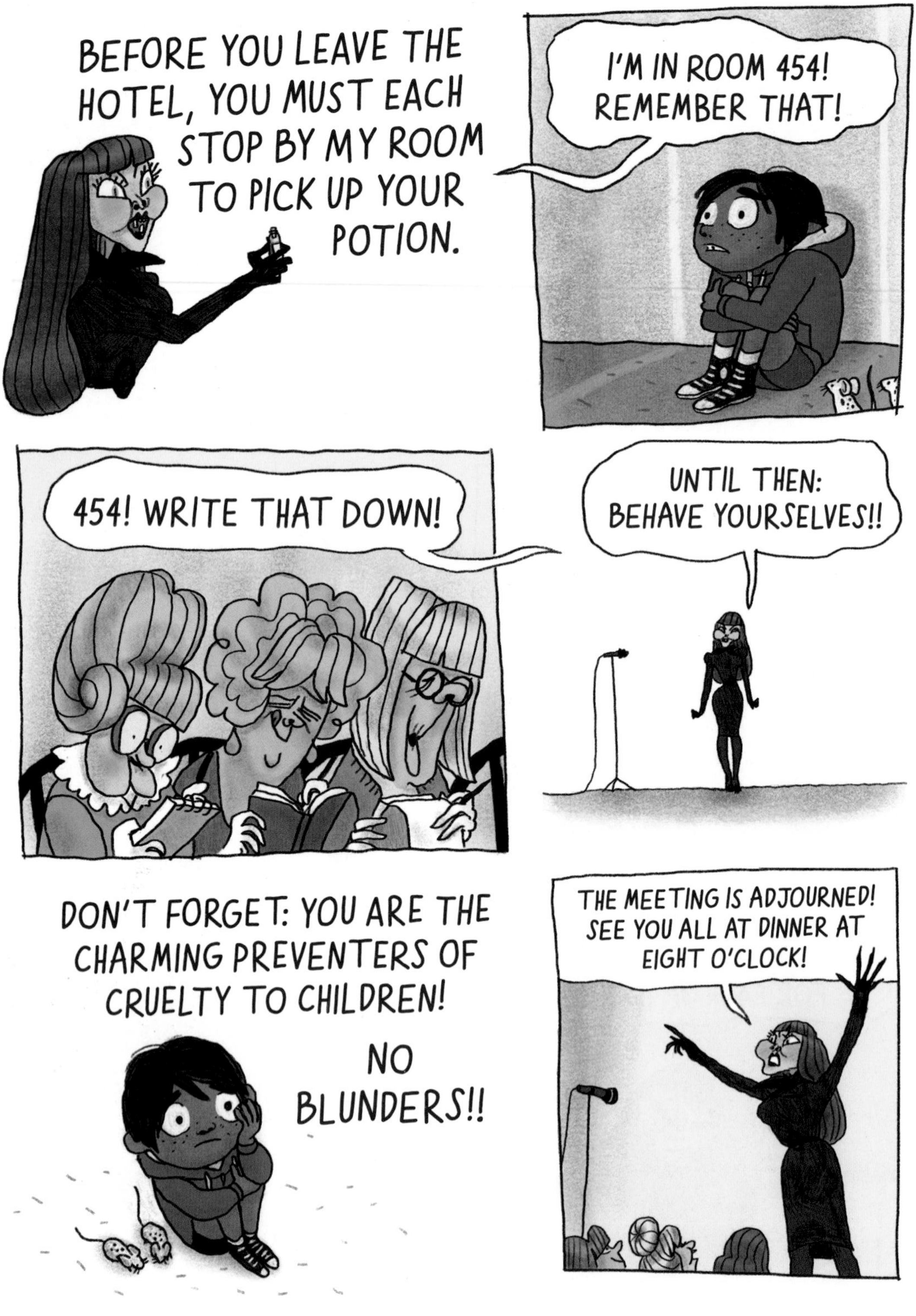
BEFORE YOU LEAVE THE HOTEL, YOU MUST EACH STOP BY MY ROOM TO PICK UP YOUR POTION.
I'M IN ROOM 454! REMEMBER THAT!
454! WRITE THAT DOWN!
UNTIL THEN: BEHAVE YOURSELVES!!
DON'T FORGET: YOU ARE THE CHARMING PREVENTERS OF CRUELTY TO CHILDREN!
NO BLUNDERS!!
THE MEETING IS ADJOURNED! SEE YOU ALL AT DINNER AT EIGHT O'CLOCK!

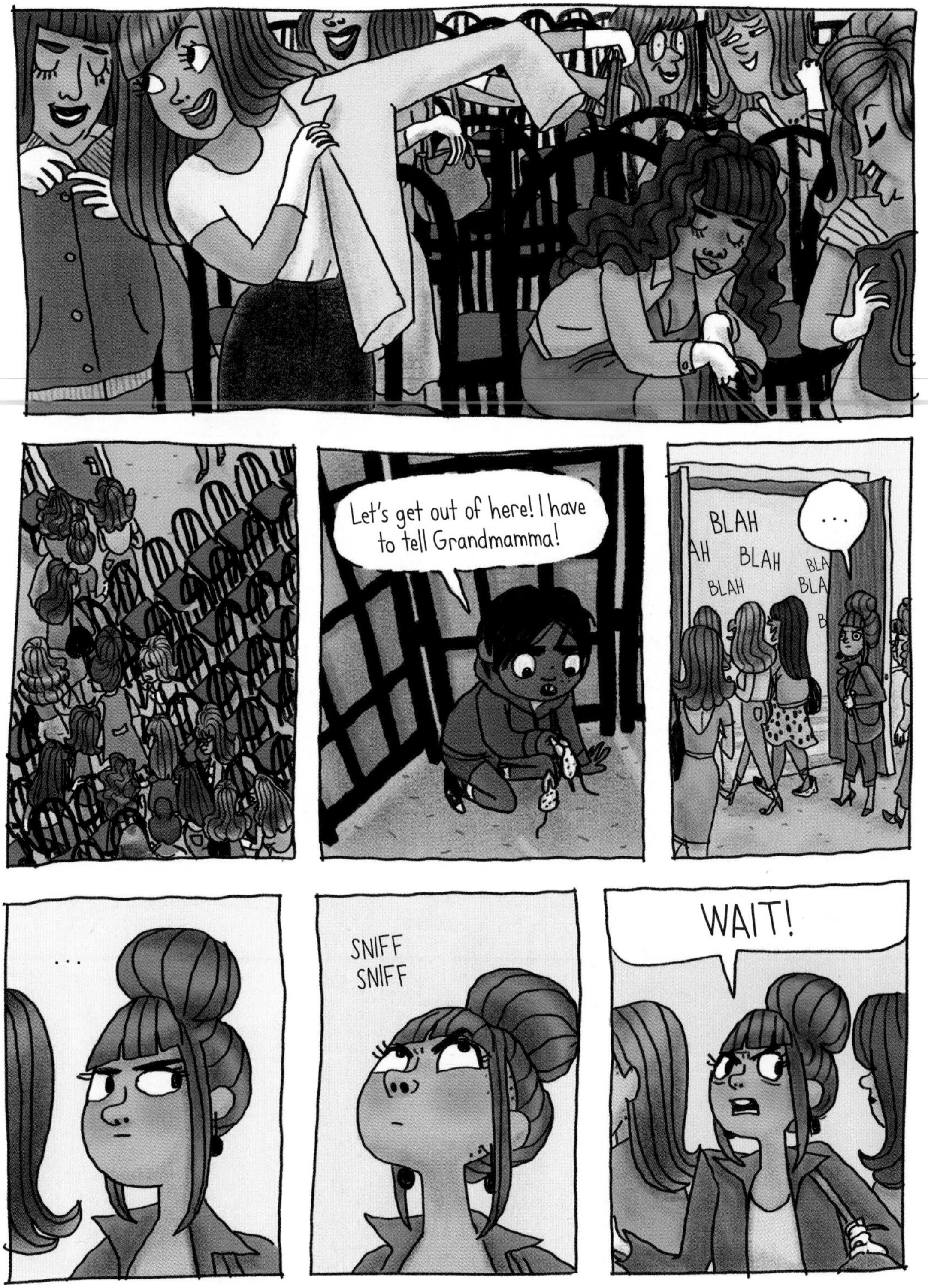
Let's get out of here! I have to tell Grandmamma!
BLAH
AH
BLAH
BLA
BLAH
BLA
B
...
...
SNIFF
SNIFF
WAIT!

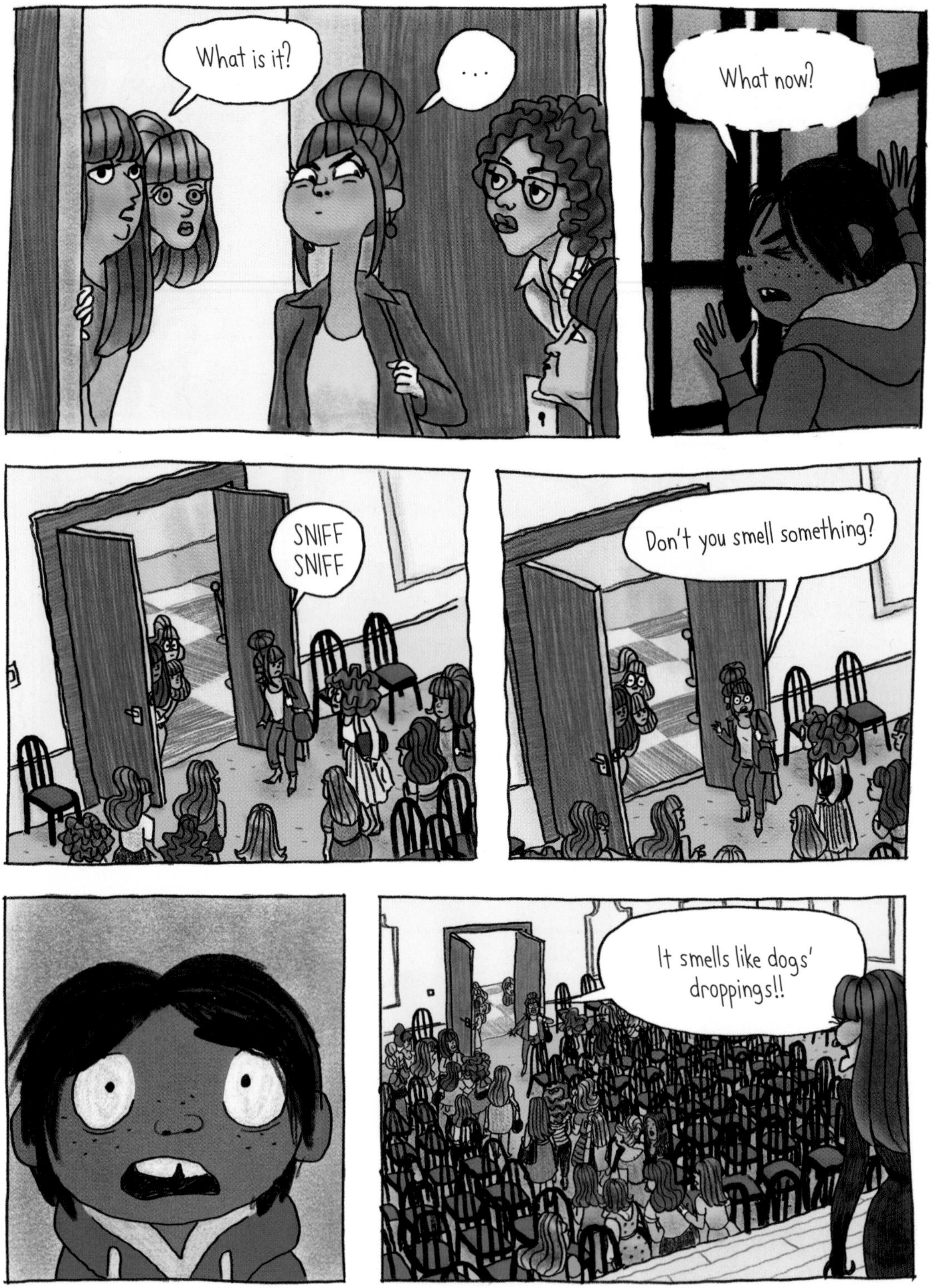
What is it?
...
What now?
SNIFF SNIFF
Don't you smell something?
It smells like dogs' droppings!!

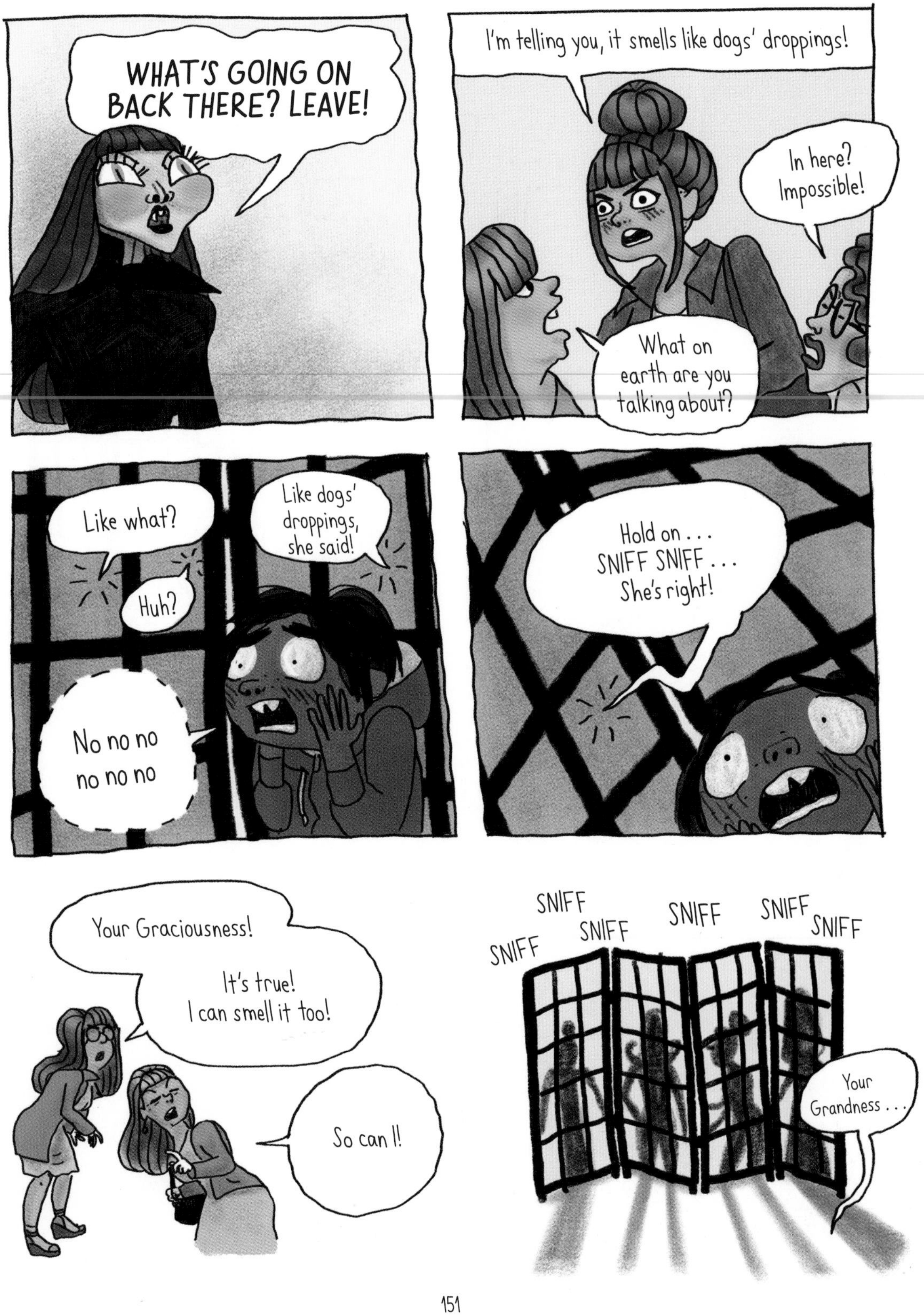
WHAT'S GOING ON BACK THERE? LEAVE!
I'm telling you, it smells like dogs' droppings!
In here? Impossible!
What on earth are you talking about?
Like what?
Like dogs' droppings, she said!
Huh?
No no no no no no
Hold on . . . SNIFF SNIFF . . . She's right!
Your Graciousness!
It's true! I can smell it too!
So can I!
SNIFF
SNIFF
SNIFF
SNIFF
SNIFF
SNIFF
Your Grandness . . .

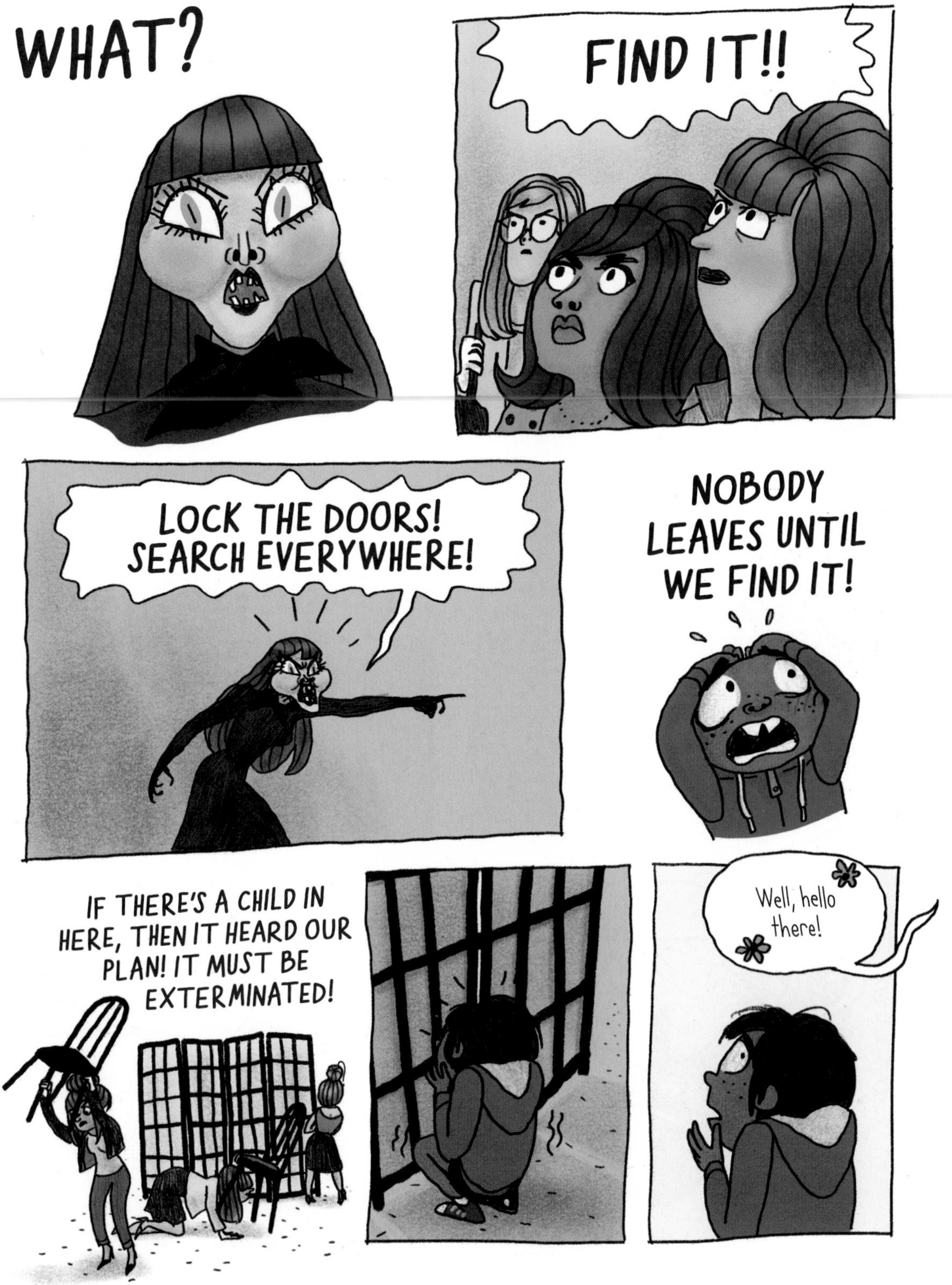
WHAT?
FIND IT!!
LOCK THE DOORS! SEARCH EVERYWHERE!
NOBODY LEAVES UNTIL WE FIND IT!
IF THERE'S A CHILD IN HERE, THEN IT HEARD OUR PLAN! IT MUST BE EXTERMINATED!
Well, hello there!

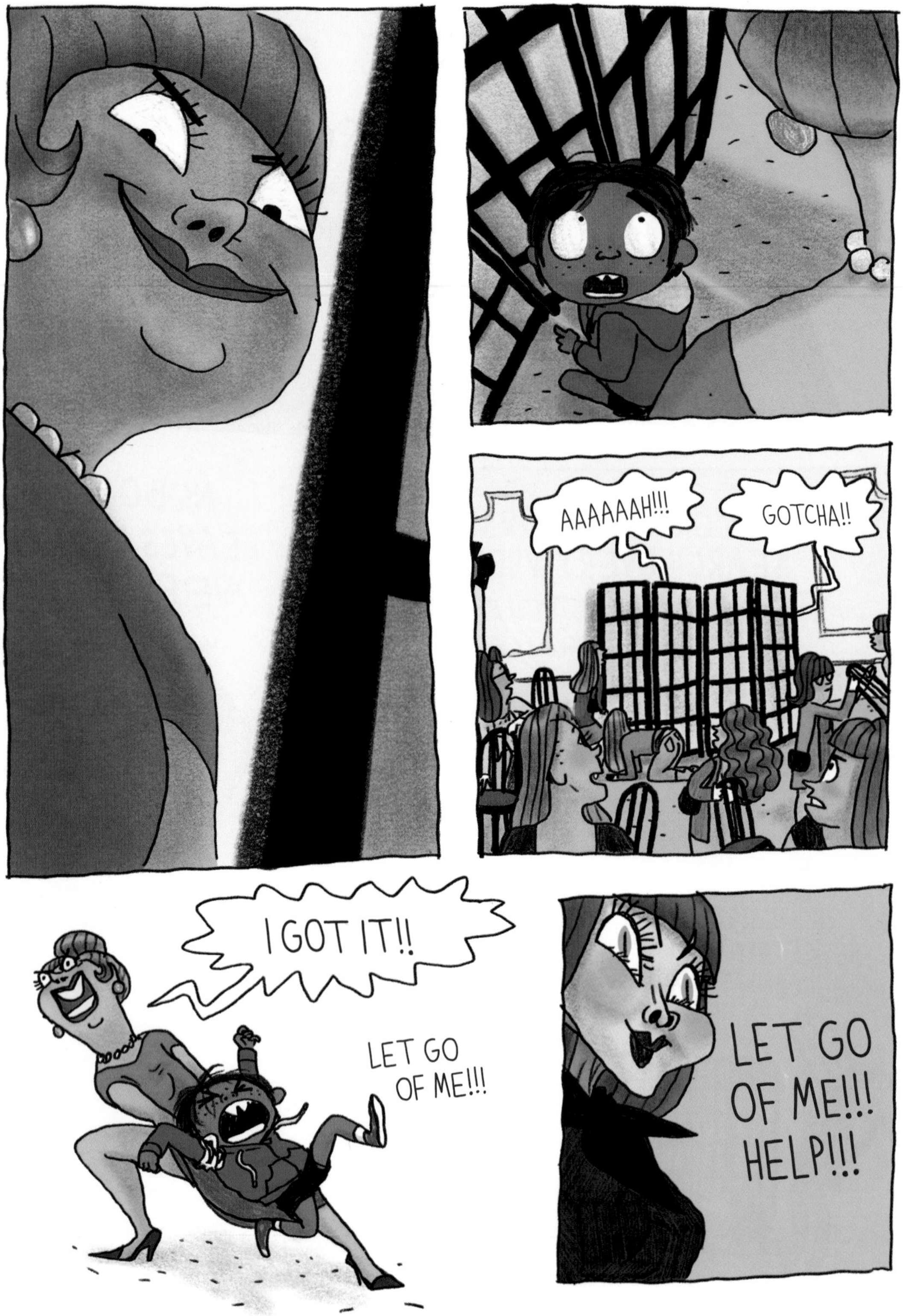
AAAAAAH!!!
GOTCHA!!
I GOT IT!!
LET GO OF ME!!!
LET GO OF ME!!! HELP!!!

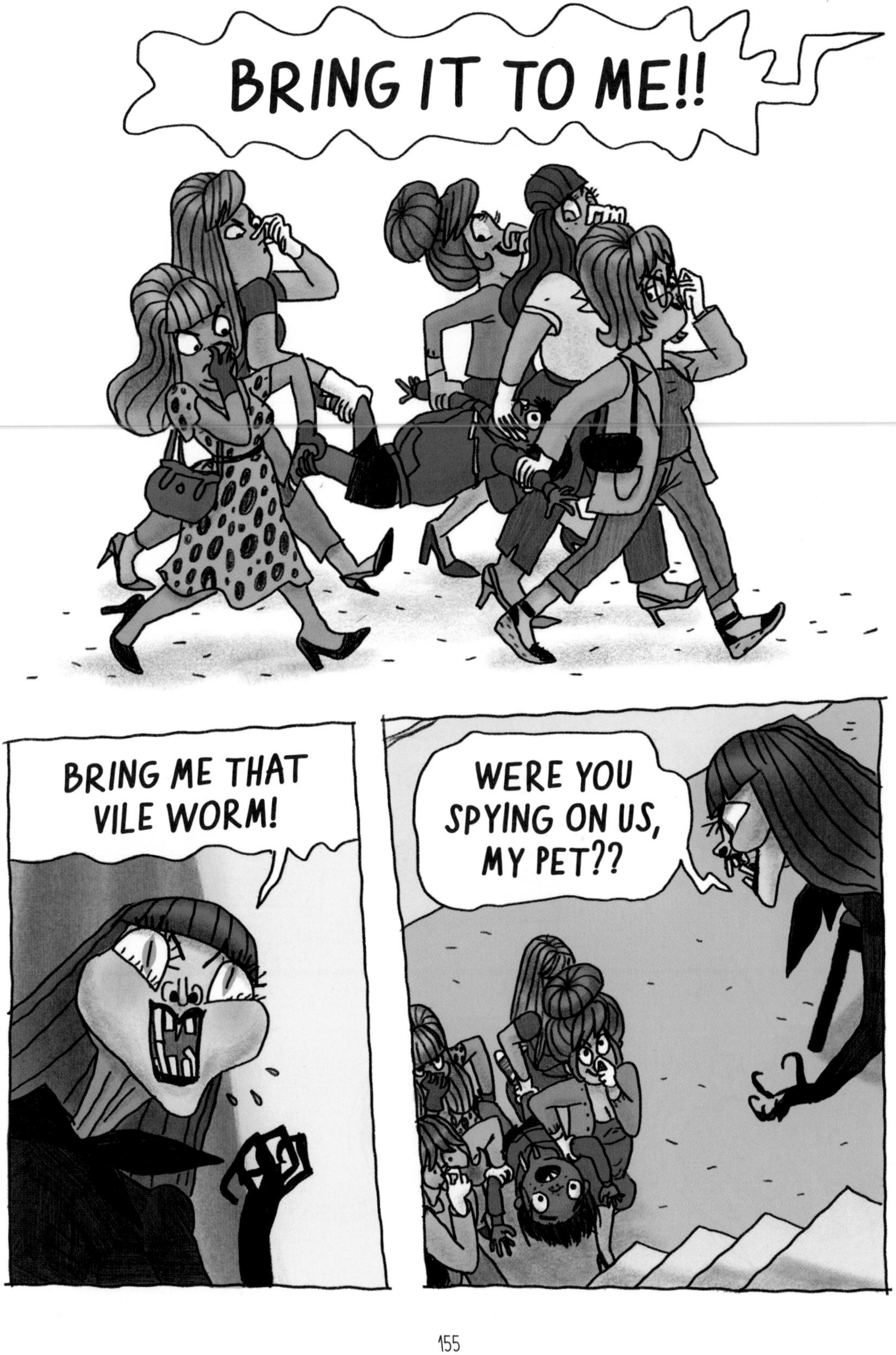
BRING IT TO ME!!
BRING ME THAT VILE WORM!
WERE YOU SPYING ON US, MY PET??

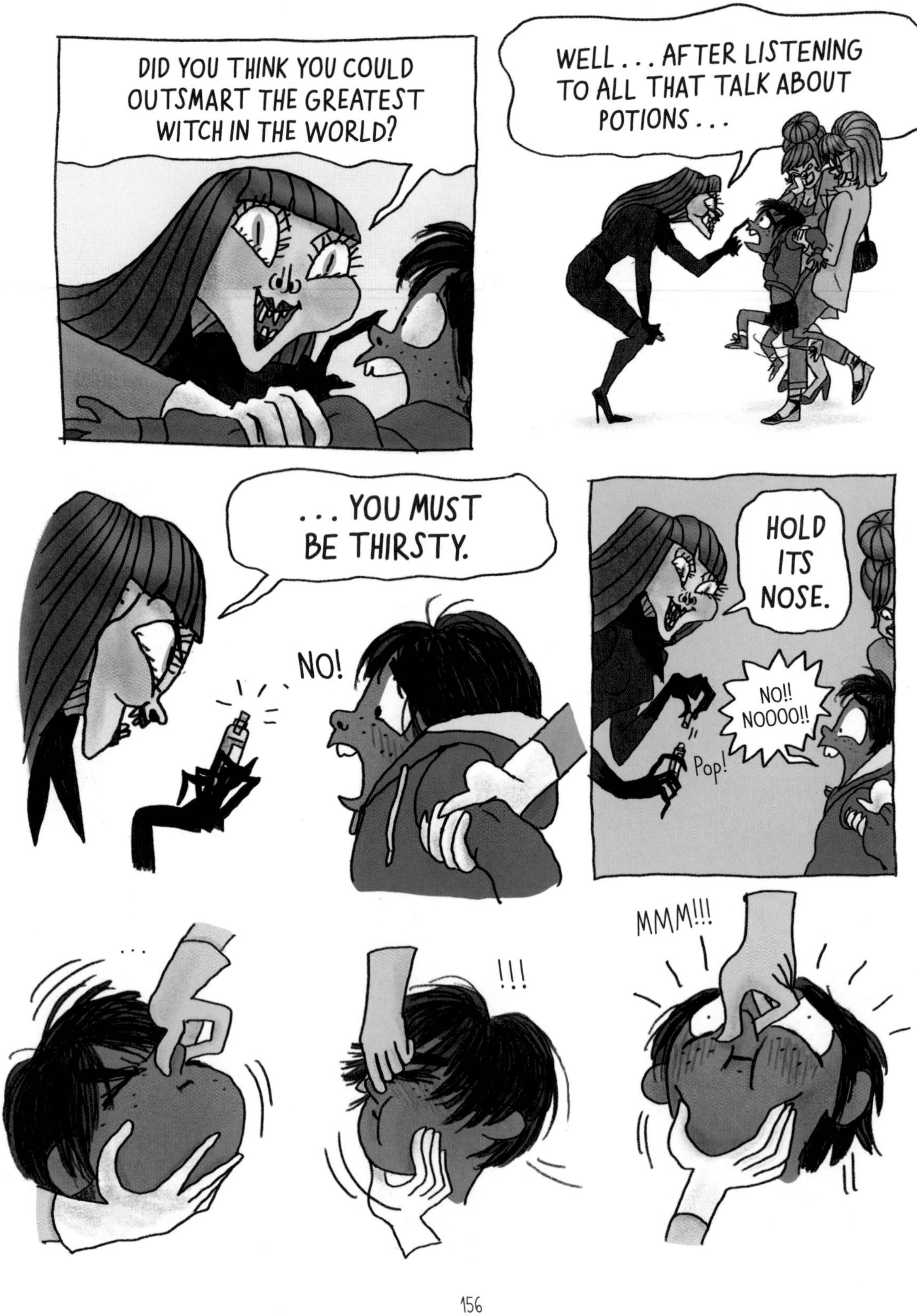

DID YOU THINK YOU COULD OUTSMART THE GREATEST WITCH IN THE WORLD?
WELL . . . AFTER LISTENING TO ALL THAT TALK ABOUT POTIONS . . .
. . . YOU MUST BE THIRSTY.
NO!
HOLD ITS NOSE.
NO!! NOOOO!!
Pop!
...
!!!
MMM!!!

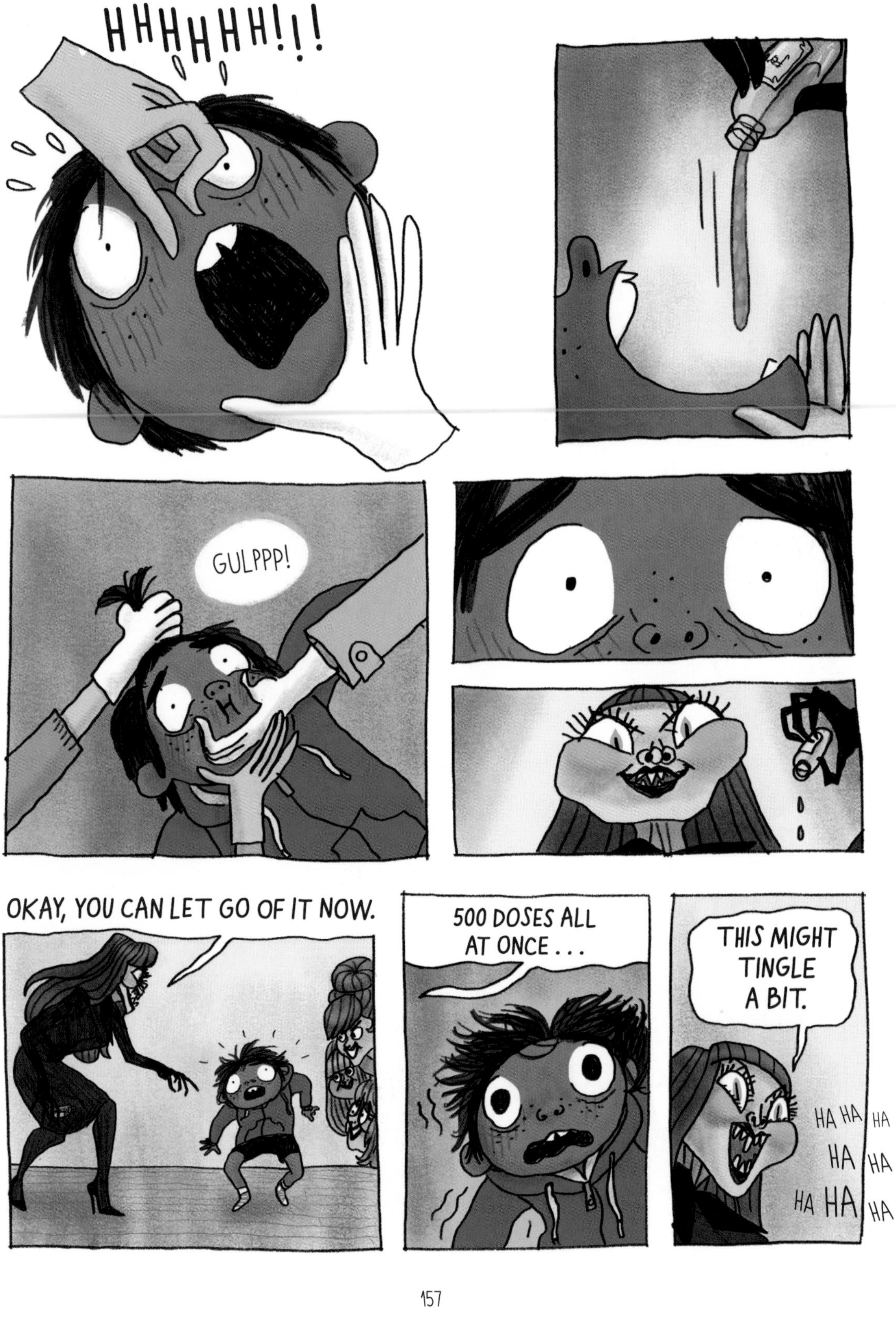
HHHHHH!!!
GULPPP!
OKAY, YOU CAN LET GO OF IT NOW.
500 DOSES ALL AT ONCE . . .
THIS MIGHT TINGLE A BIT.
HA HA HA HA HA HA HA HA

AAAAAAAAAAAAAAAA

AAAAAAA

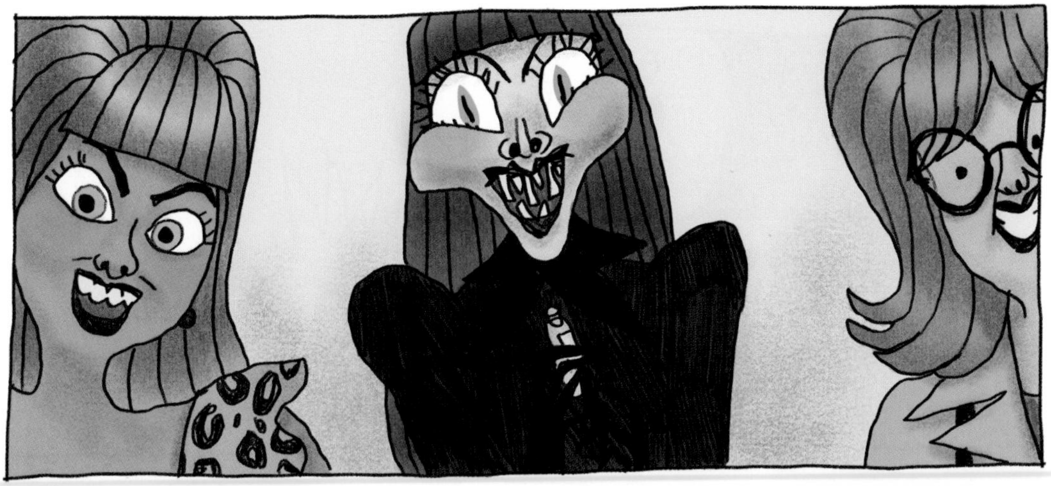

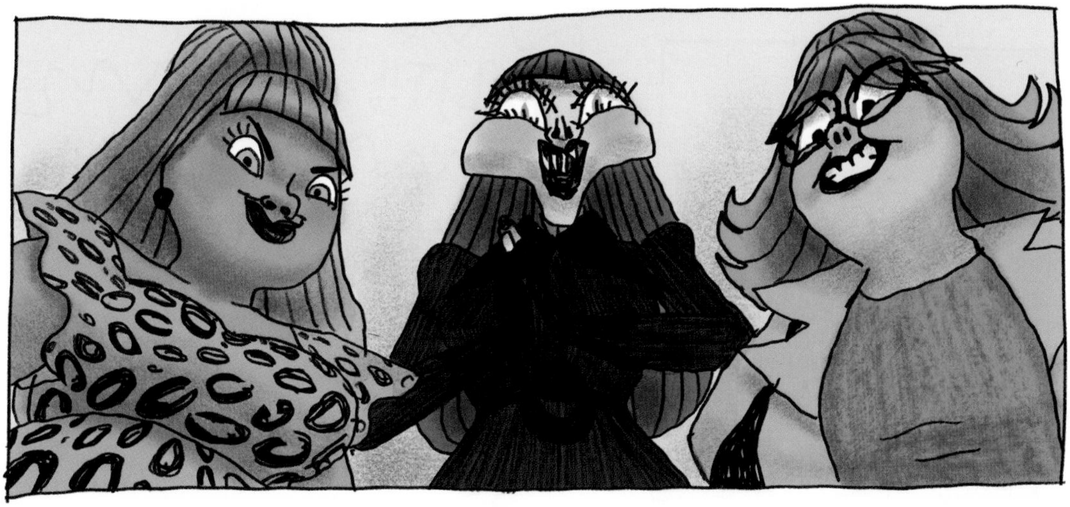

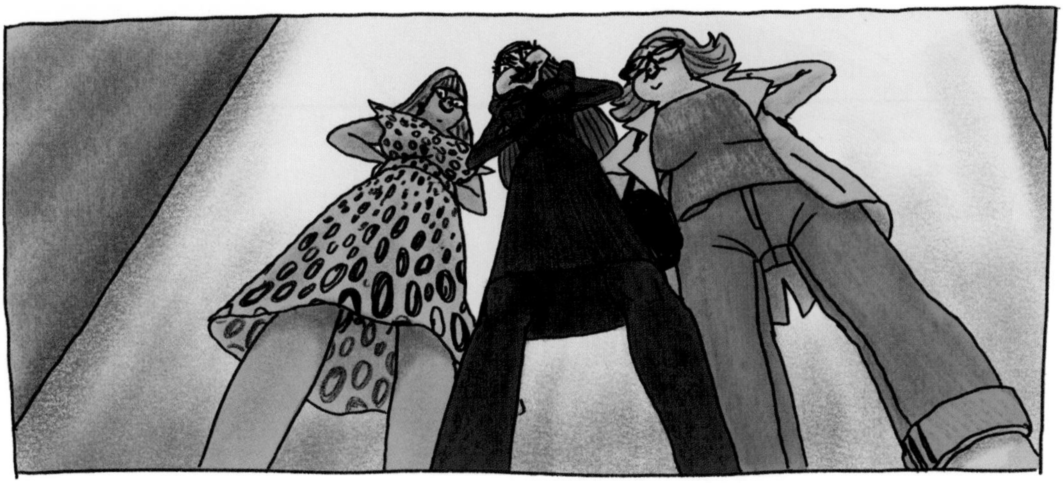

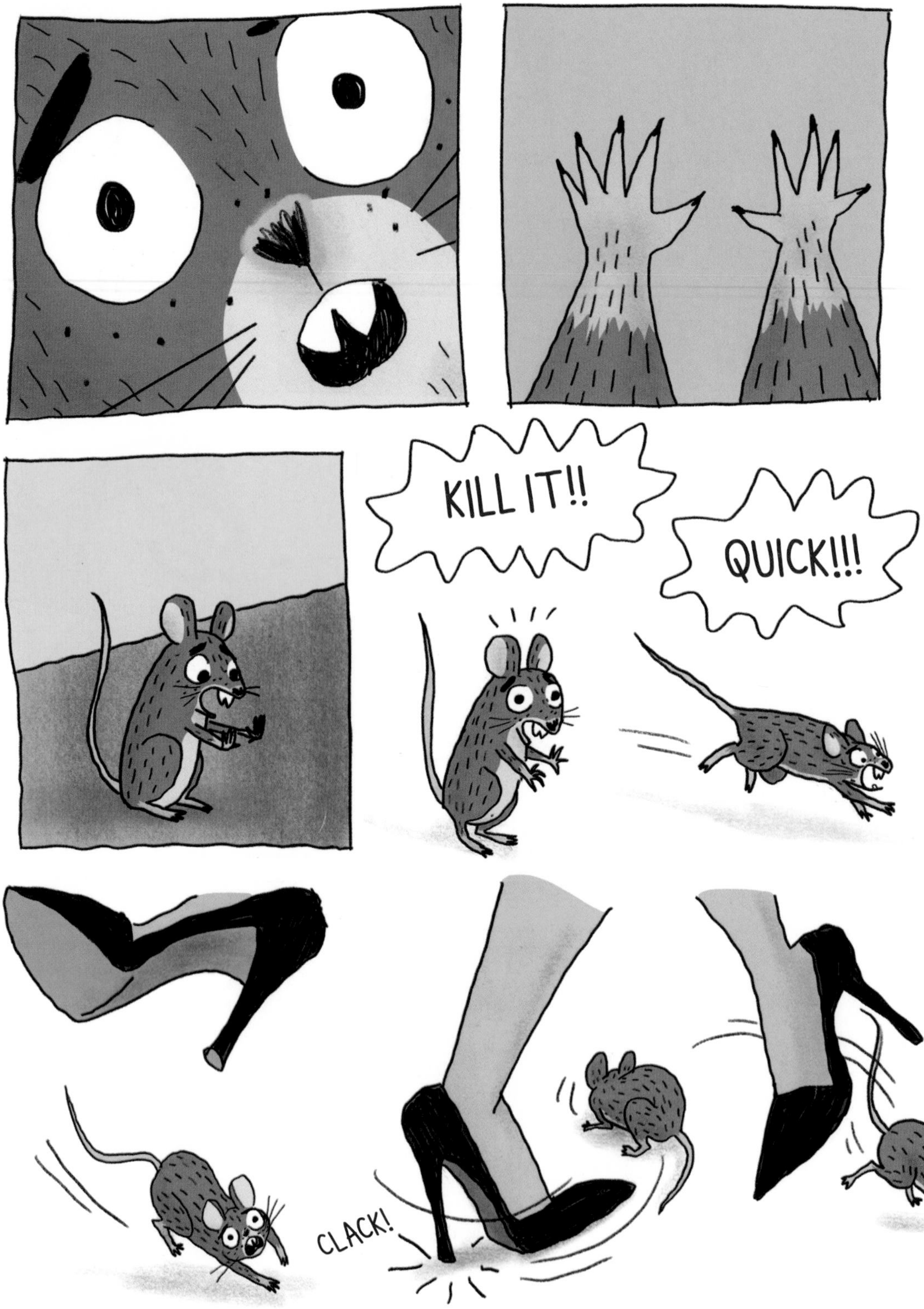
KILL IT!!
QUICK!!!
CLACK!

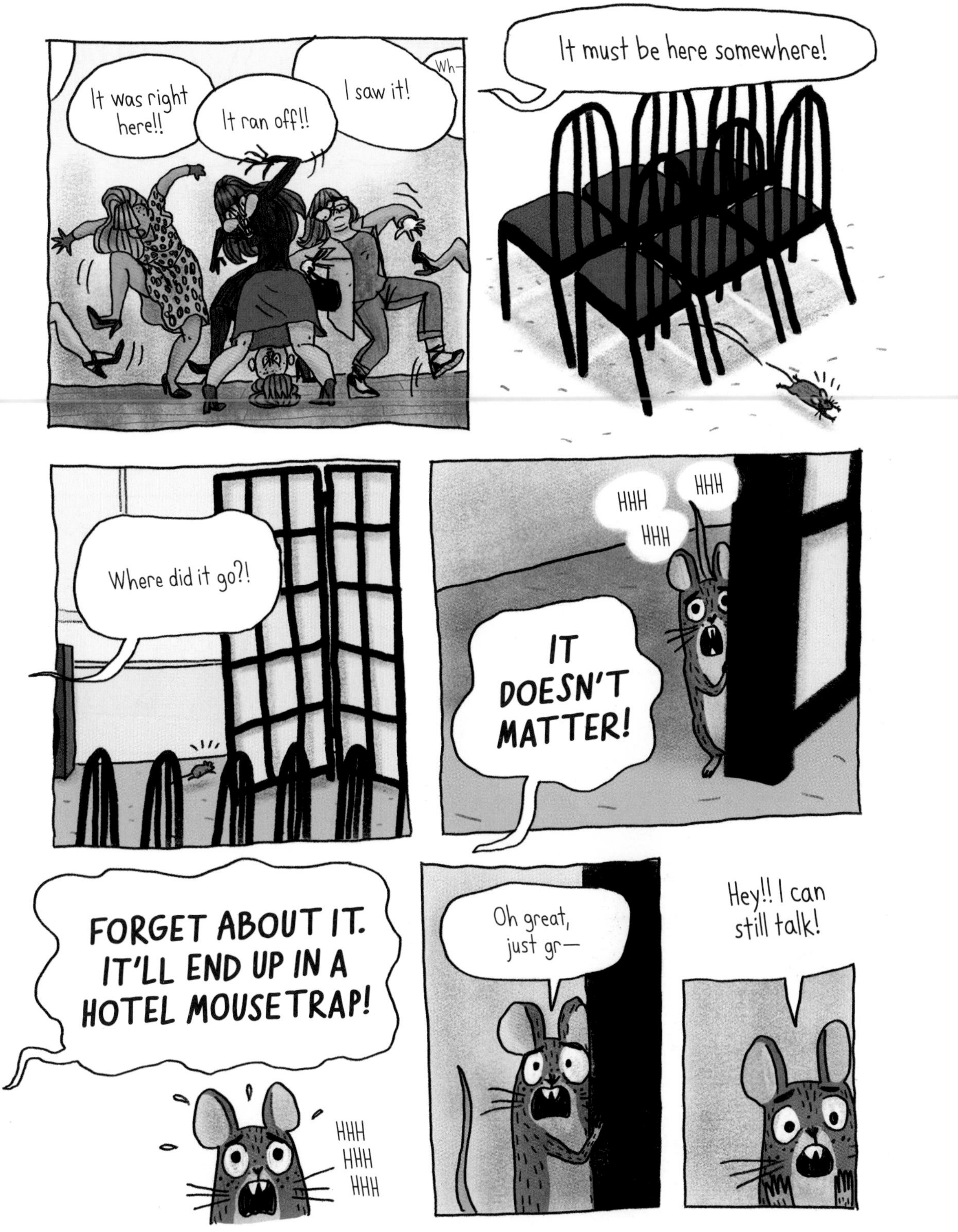
It was right here!!
It ran off!!
I saw it!
Wh–
It must be here somewhere!
Where did it go?!
HHH
HHH
HHH
IT DOESN'T MATTER!
FORGET ABOUT IT. IT'LL END UP IN A HOTEL MOUSETRAP!
HHH
HHH
HHH
Oh great, just gr—
Hey!! I can still talk!

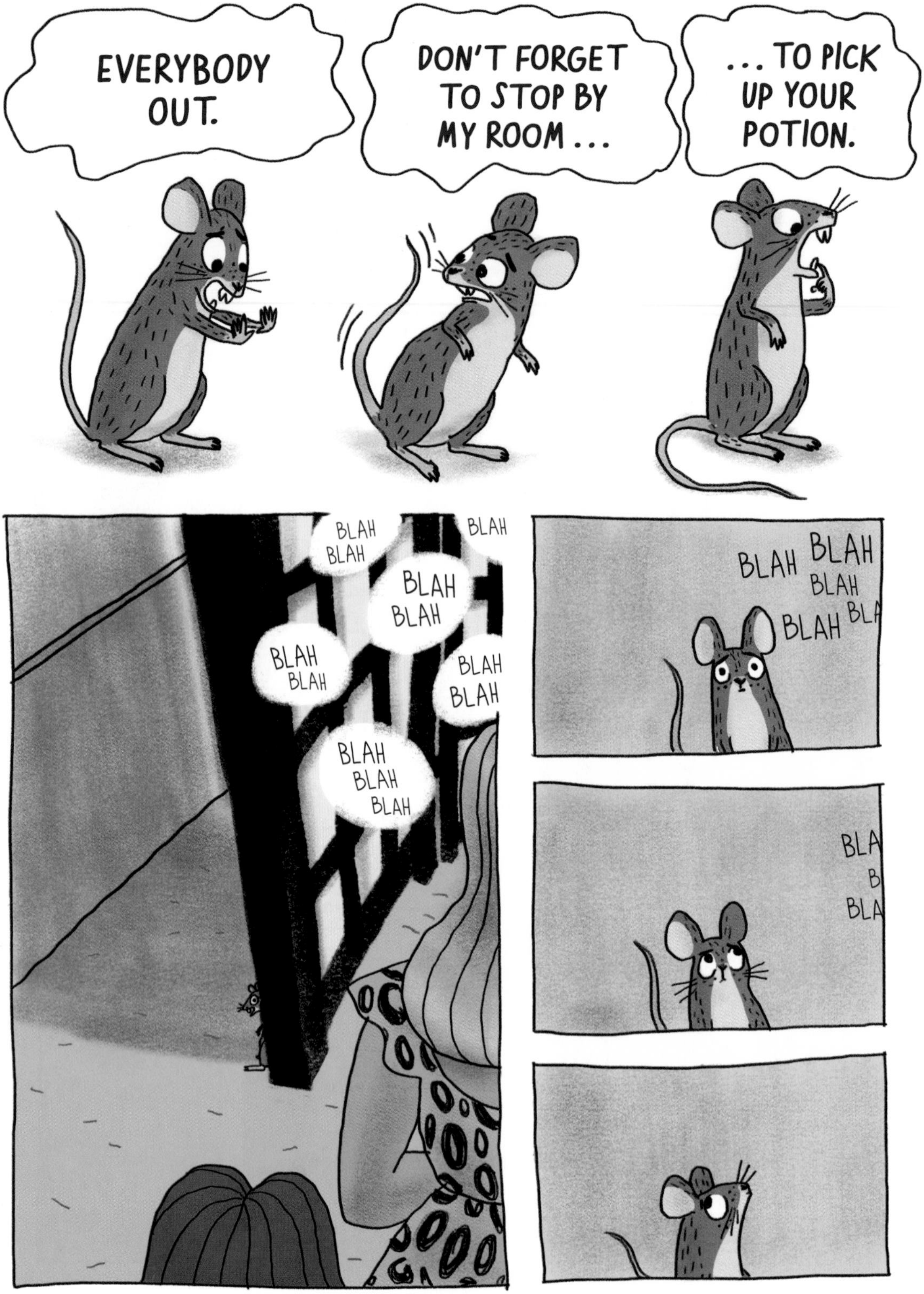
EVERYBODY OUT.
DON'T FORGET TO STOP BY MY ROOM . . .
. . . TO PICK UP YOUR POTION.
BLAH BLAH
BLAH
BLAH BLAH
BLAH BLAH
BLAH BLAH
BLAH BLAH BLAH
BLAH BLAH BLAH BLAH

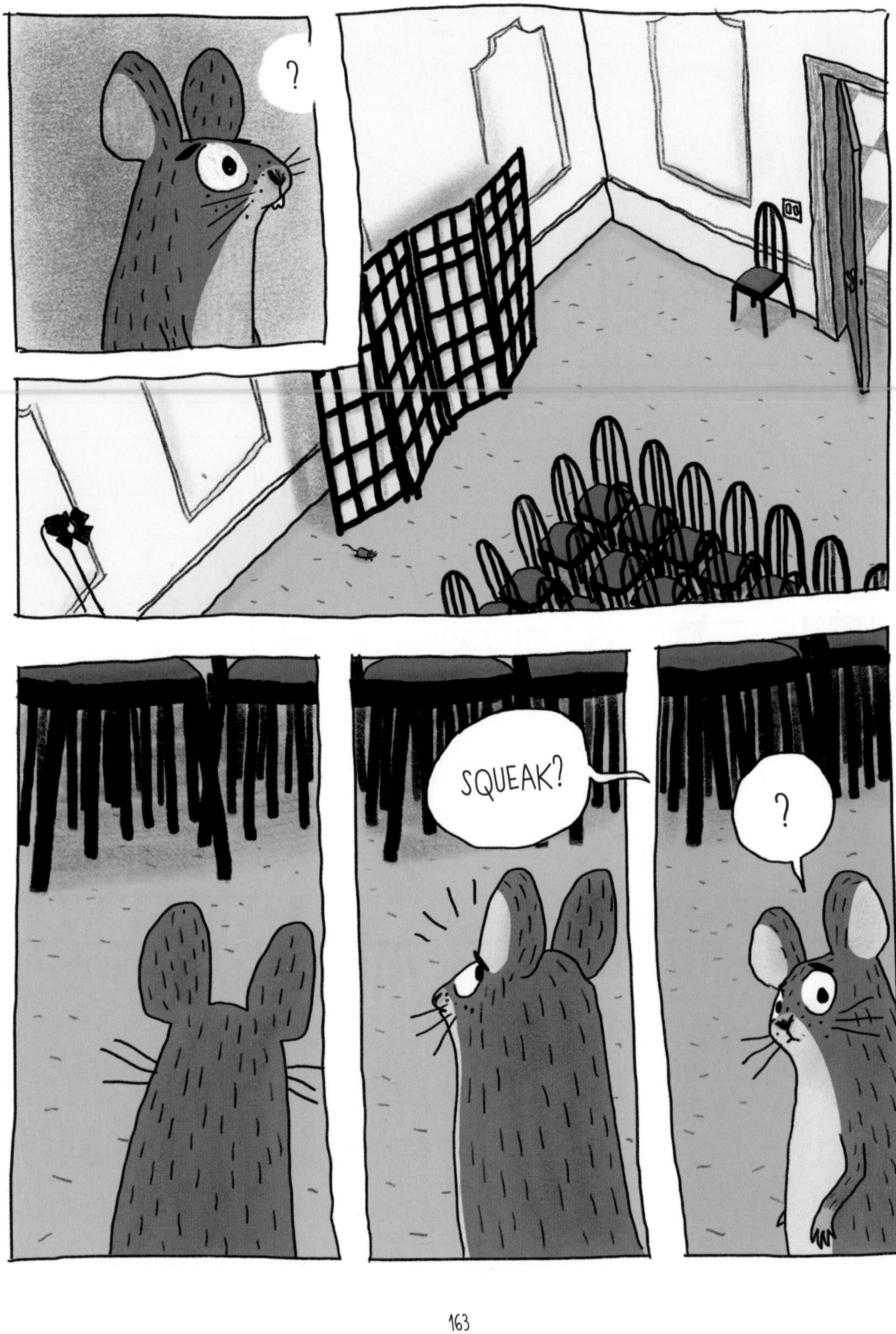
?
SQUEAK?
?

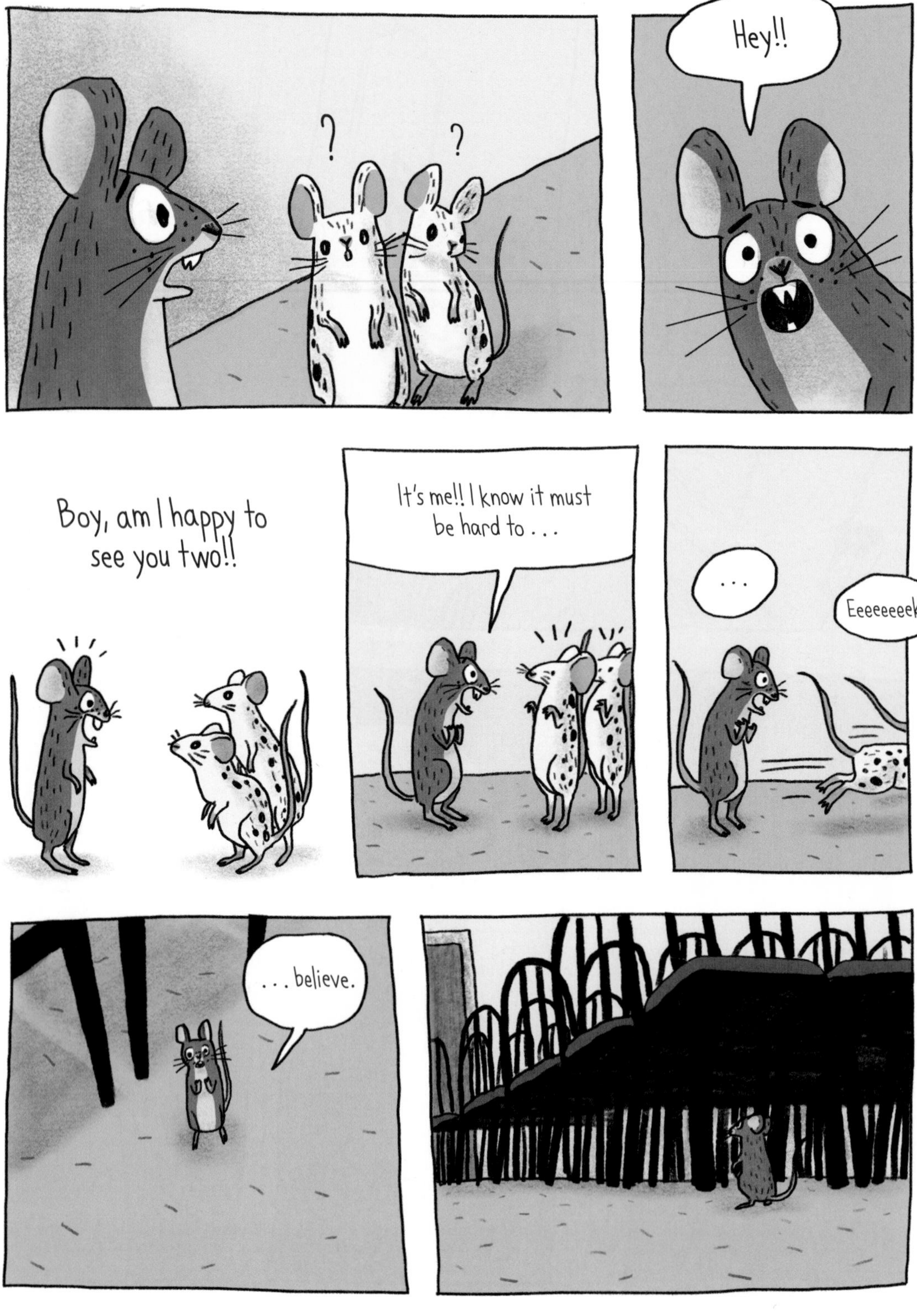
?
?
Hey!!
Boy, am I happy to see you two!!
It's me!! I know it must be hard to . . .
. . .
Eeeeeeeek!!!
. . . believe.

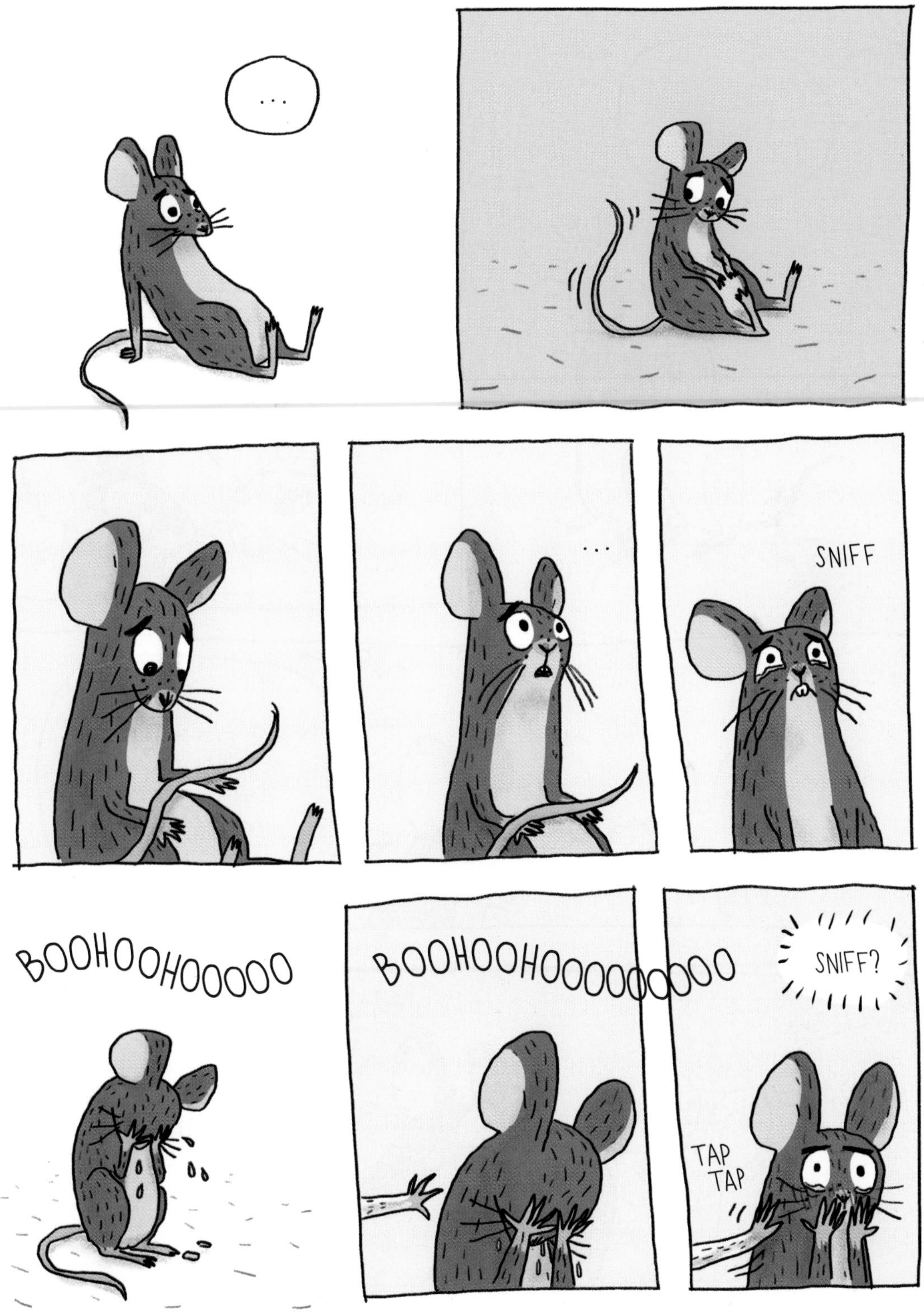
...
...
SNIFF
BOOHOOHOOOOO
BOOHOOHOOOOOOOOOO
SNIFF?
TAP
TAP

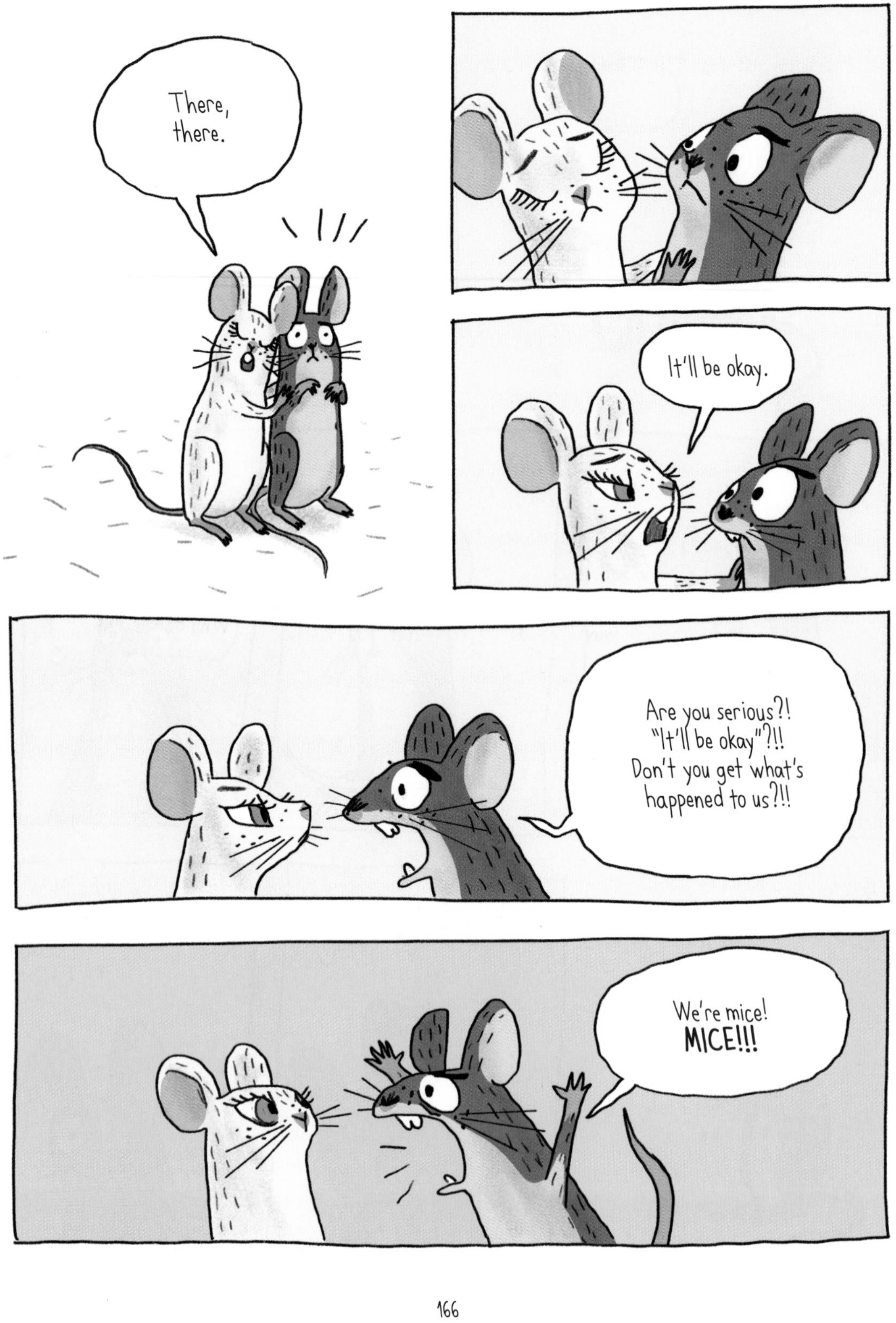
There, there.
It'll be okay.
Are you serious?! "It'll be okay"?!! Don't you get what's happened to us?!!
We're mice! **MICE!!!**

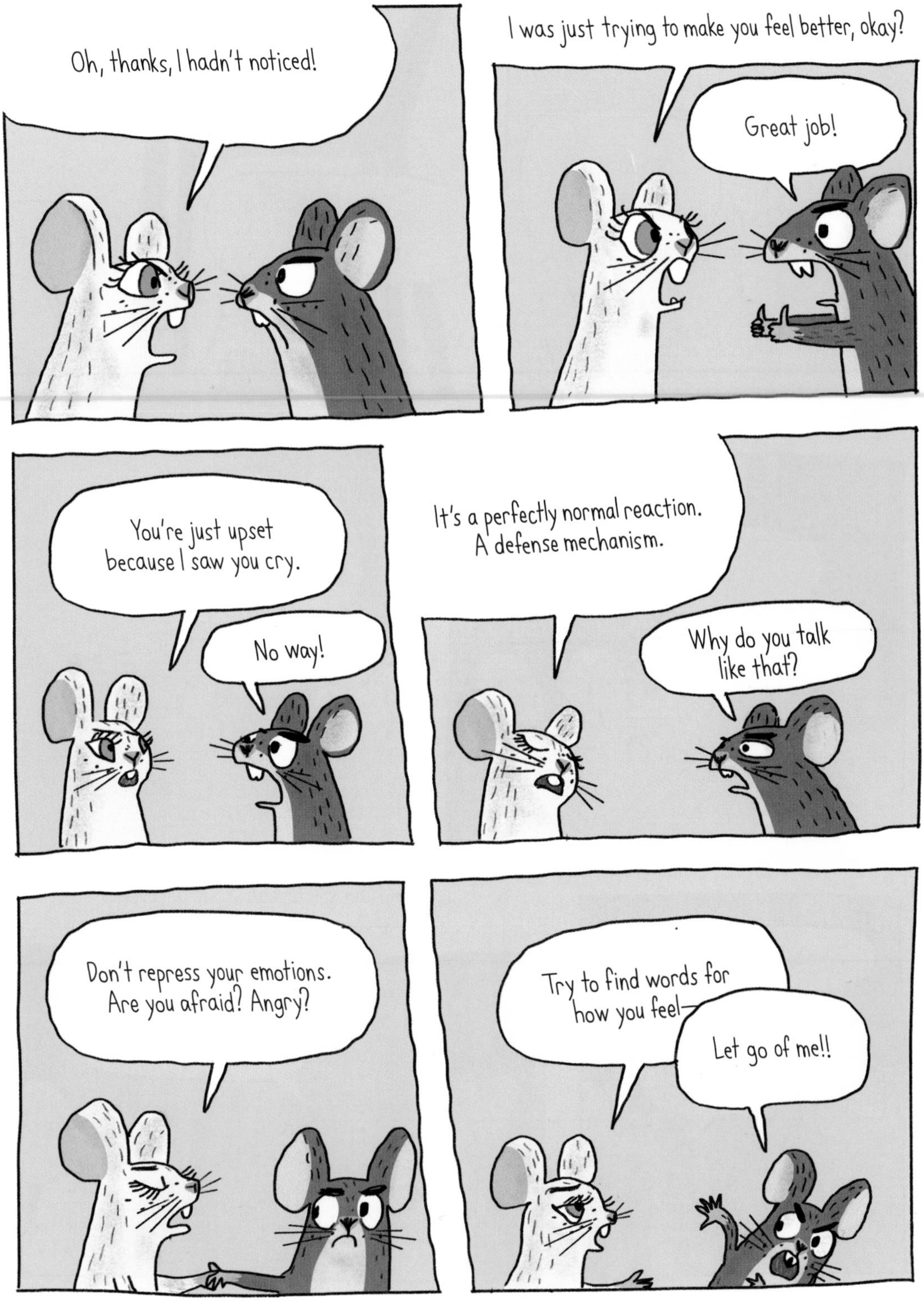
Oh, thanks, I hadn't noticed!
I was just trying to make you feel better, okay?
Great job!
You're just upset because I saw you cry.
No way!
It's a perfectly normal reaction. A defense mechanism.
Why do you talk like that?
Don't repress your emotions. Are you afraid? Angry?
Try to find words for how you feel—
Let go of me!!

It's no use panicking!

What else is there to do?

"No use panicking"! Seriously?

But . . .

Maybe we could talk to the lady from before . . .

. . . and try to get her to turn us back into kids?

The lady?

Yes! The one with the chocolate!

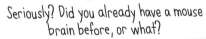

Seriously? Did you already have a mouse brain before, or what?

THE GRAND HIGH WITCH??

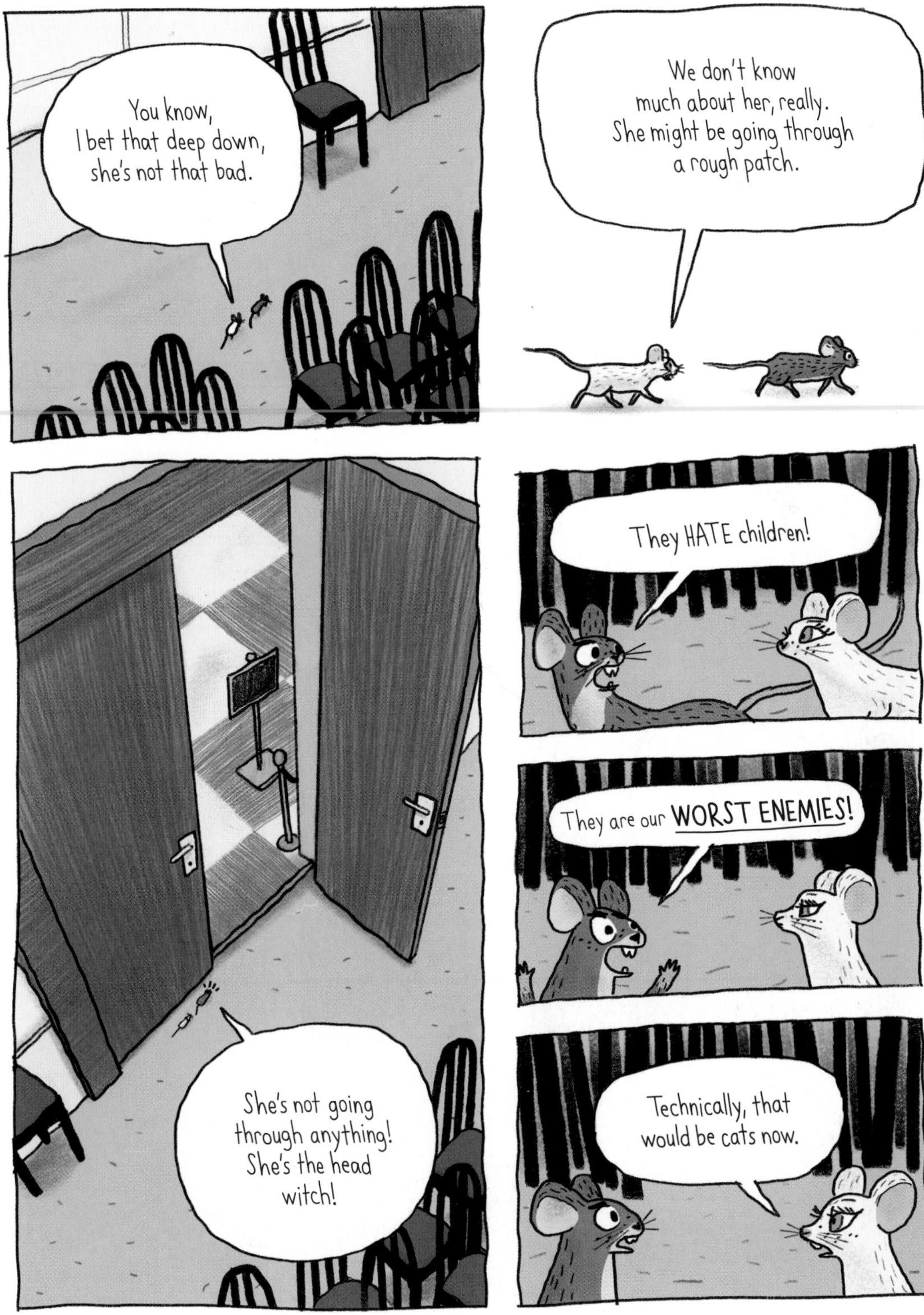
You know, I bet that deep down, she's not that bad.
We don't know much about her, really. She might be going through a rough patch.
She's not going through anything! She's the head witch!
They HATE children!
They are our WORST ENEMIES!
Technically, that would be cats now.

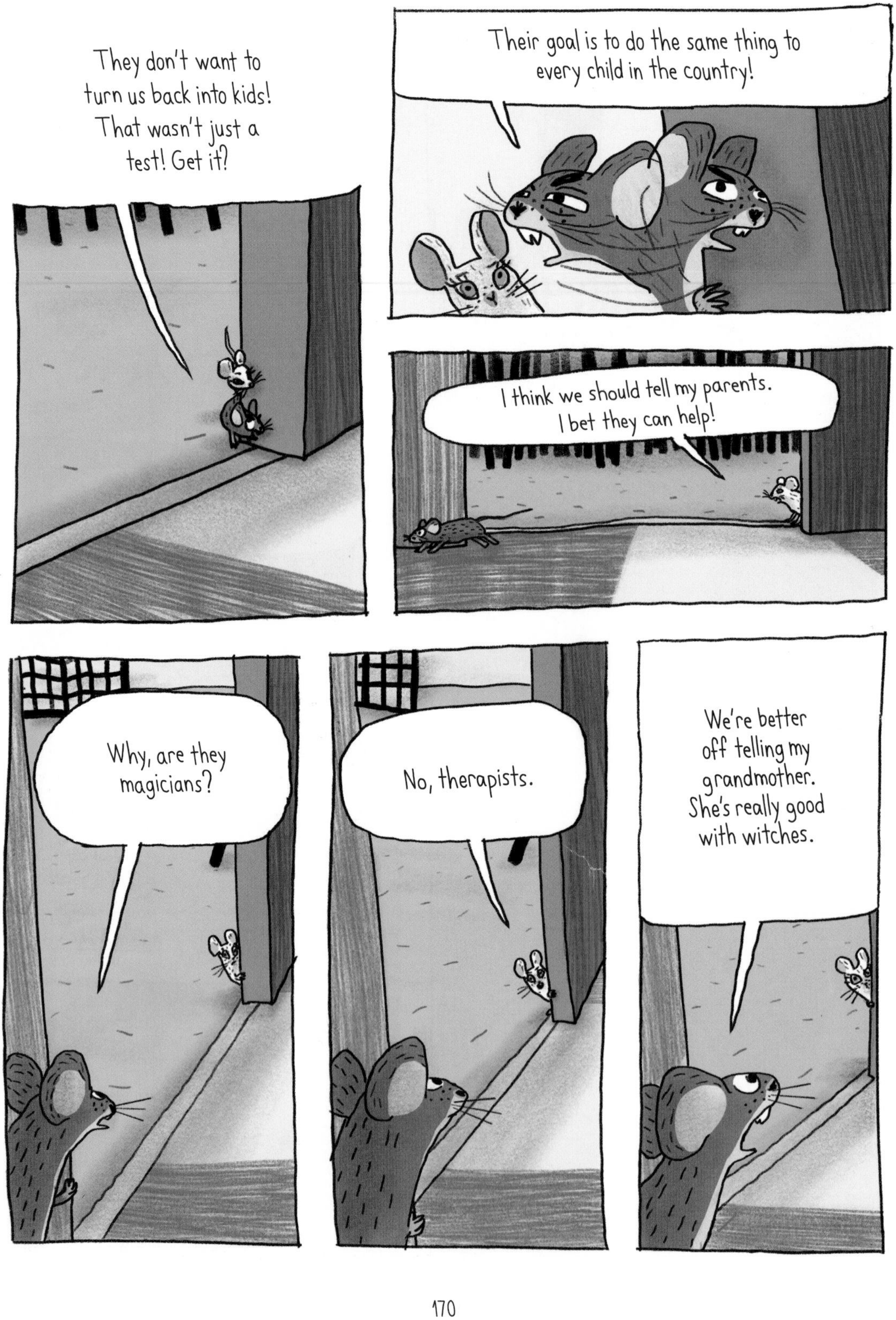
They don't want to turn us back into kids! That wasn't just a test! Get it?
Their goal is to do the same thing to every child in the country!
I think we should tell my parents. I bet they can help!
Why, are they magicians?
No, therapists.
We're better off telling my grandmother. She's really good with witches.

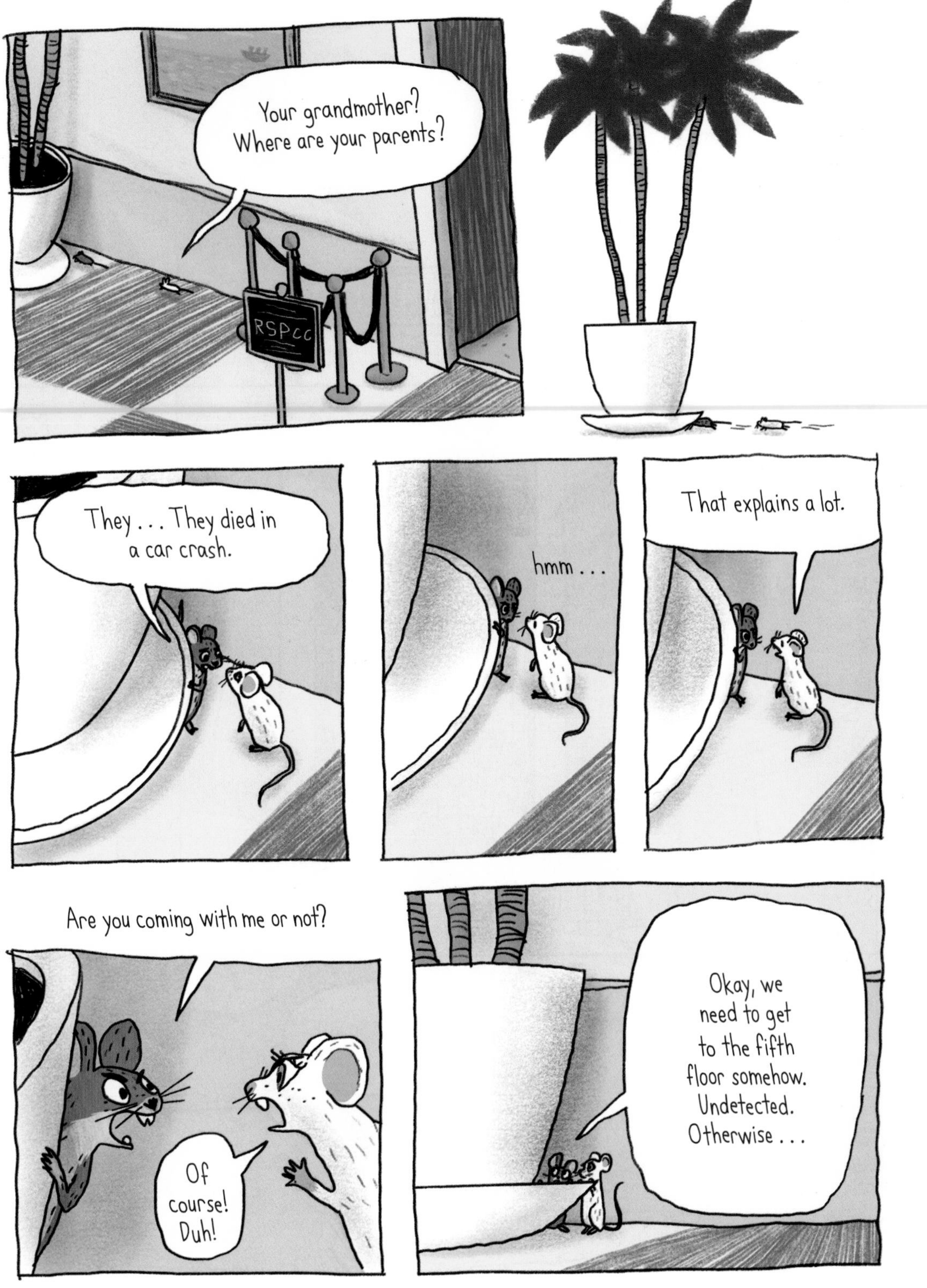
Your grandmother? Where are your parents?
RSPCC
They . . . They died in a car crash.
hmm . . .
That explains a lot.
Are you coming with me or not?
Of course! Duh!
Okay, we need to get to the fifth floor somehow. Undetected. Otherwise . . .

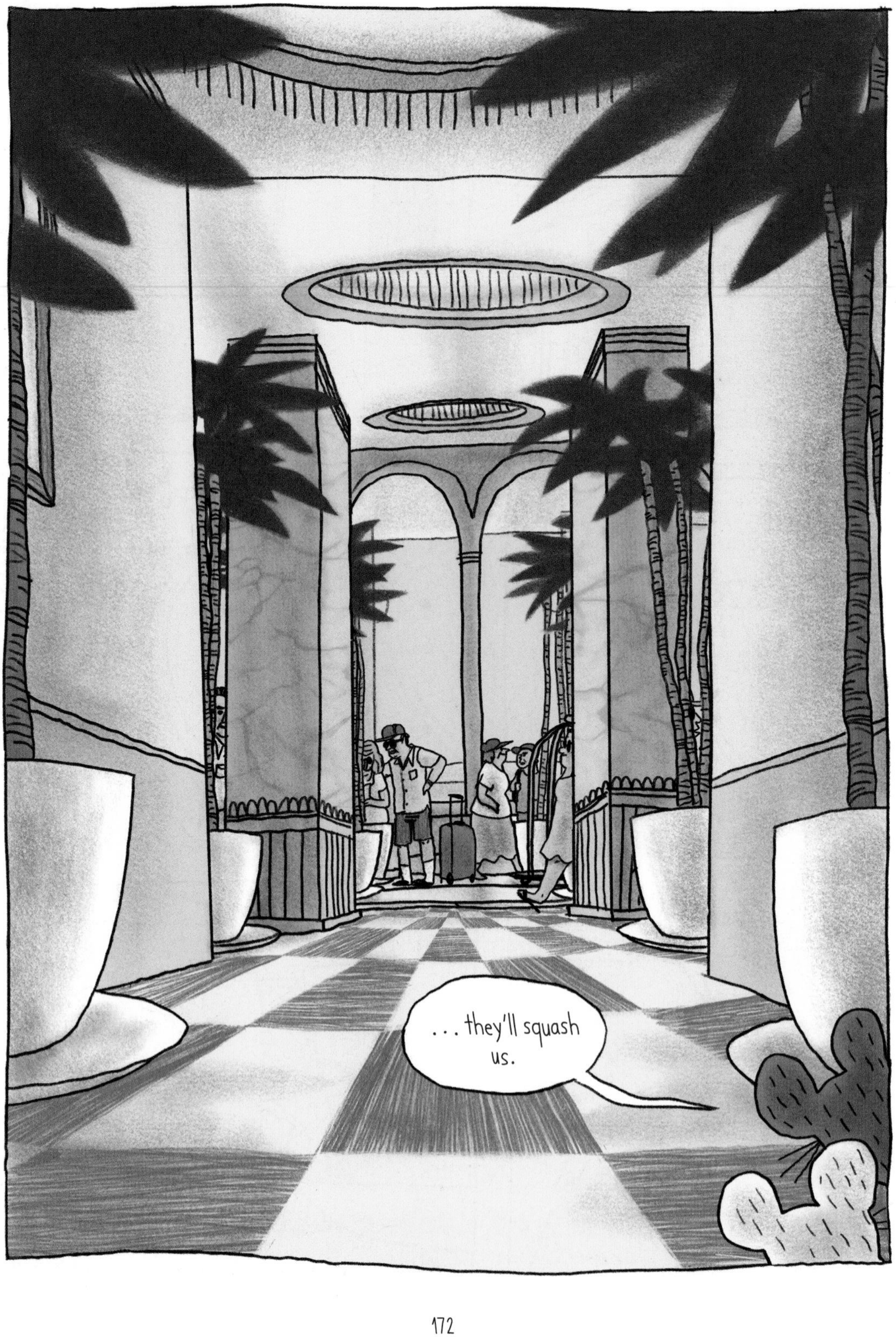
. . . they'll squash us.

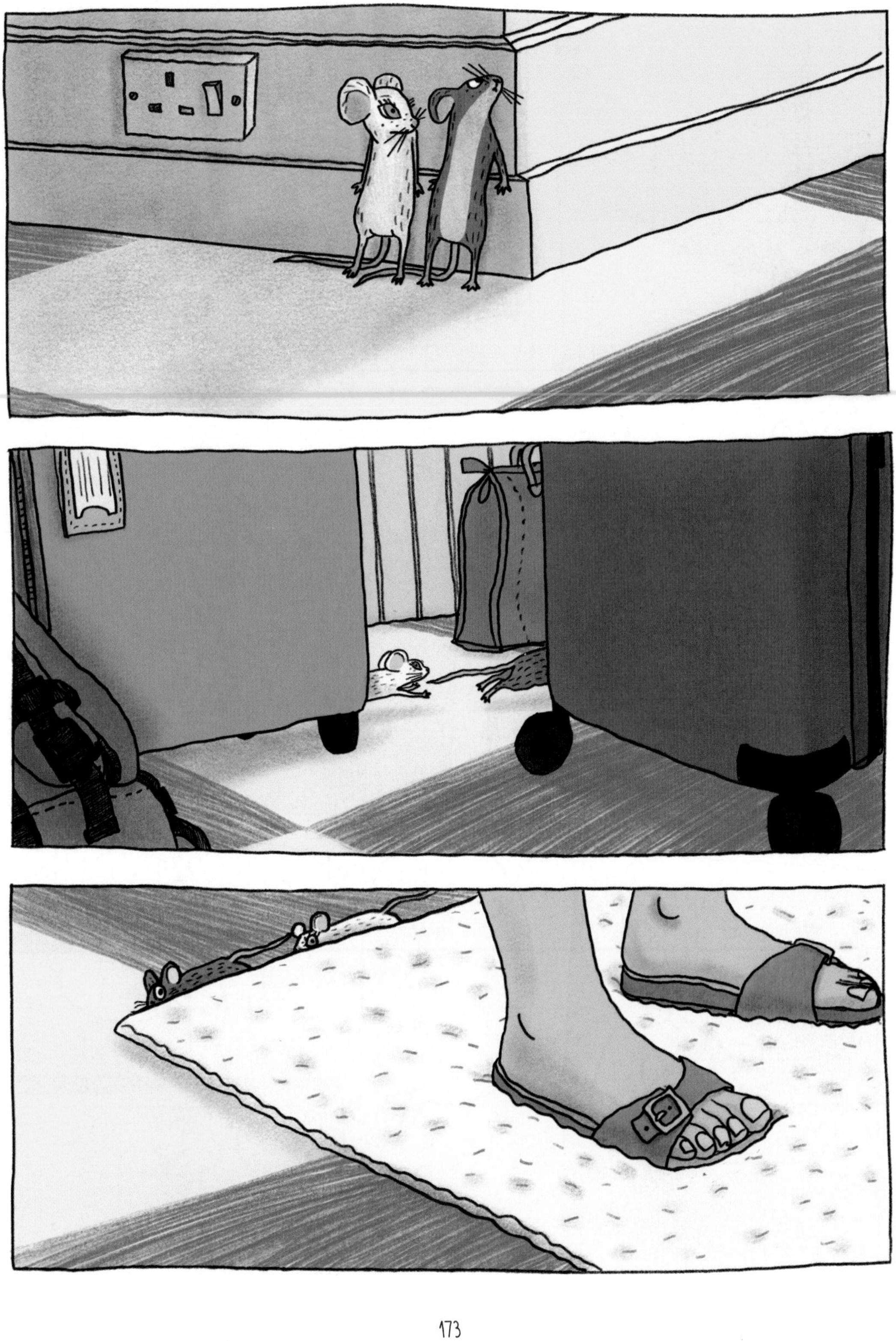

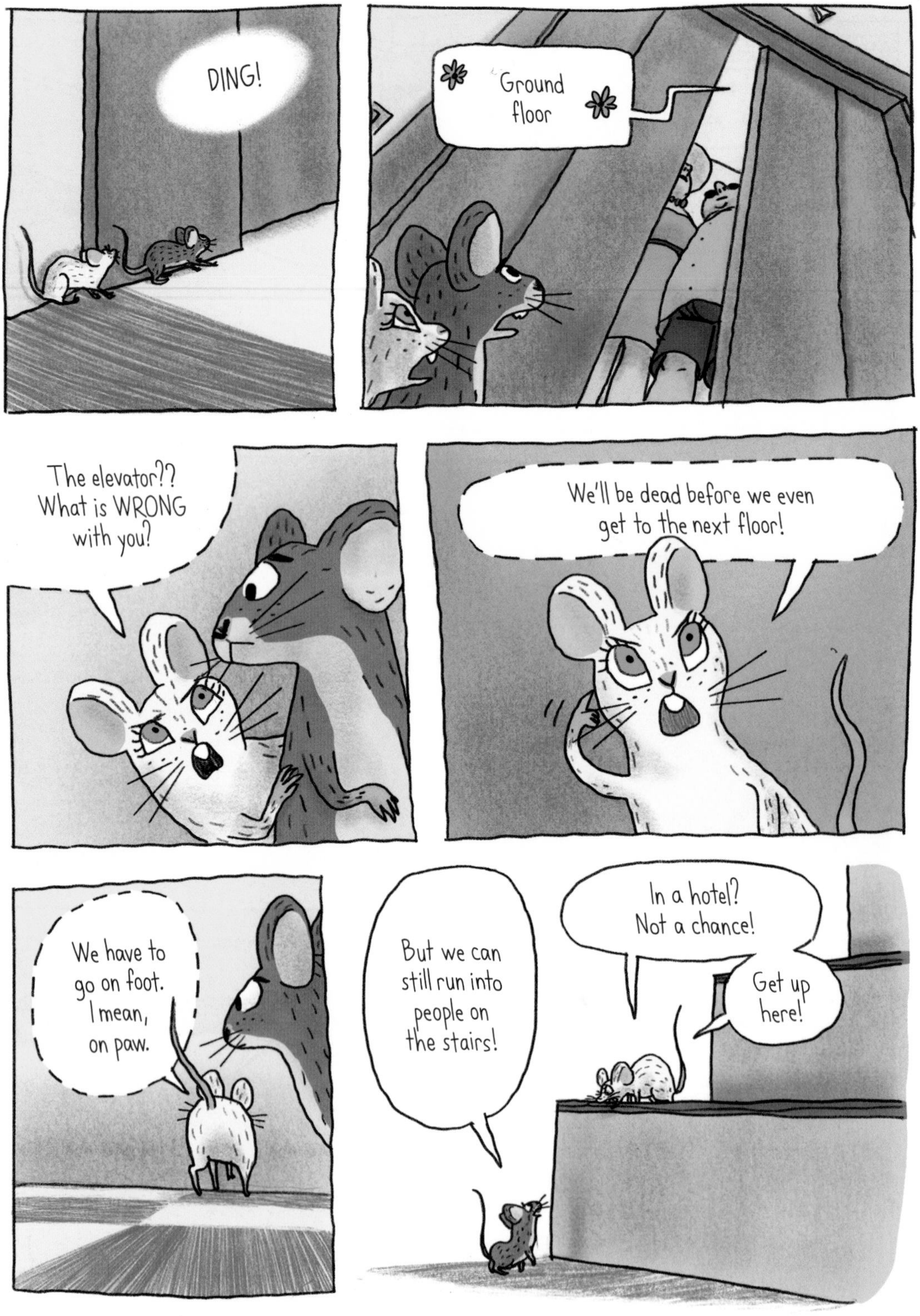
DING!
Ground floor
The elevator?? What is WRONG with you?
We'll be dead before we even get to the next floor!
We have to go on foot. I mean, on paw.
But we can still run into people on the stairs!
In a hotel? Not a chance!
Get up here!

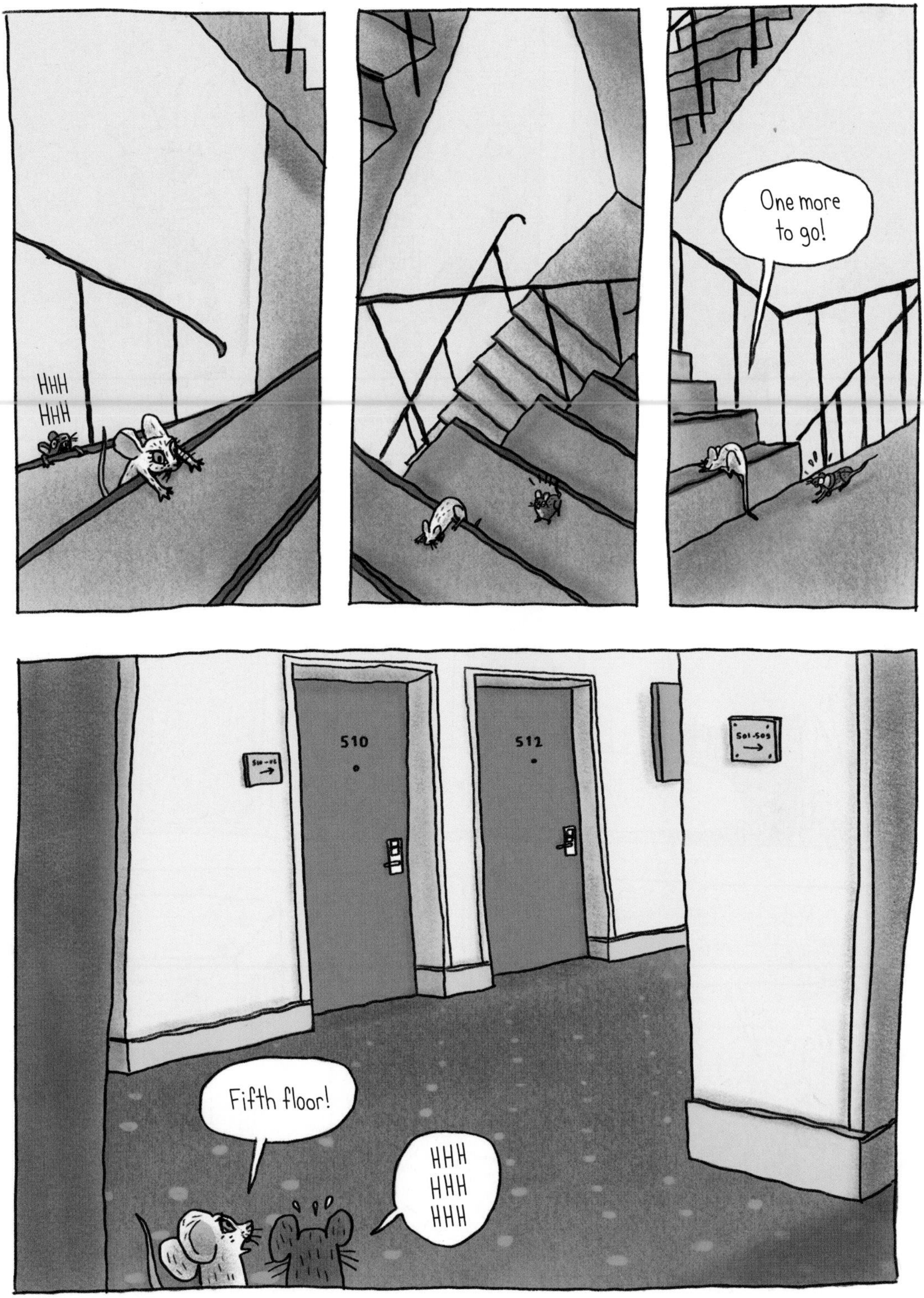
HHH
HHH
One more to go!
510
512
Fifth floor!
HHH
HHH
HHH

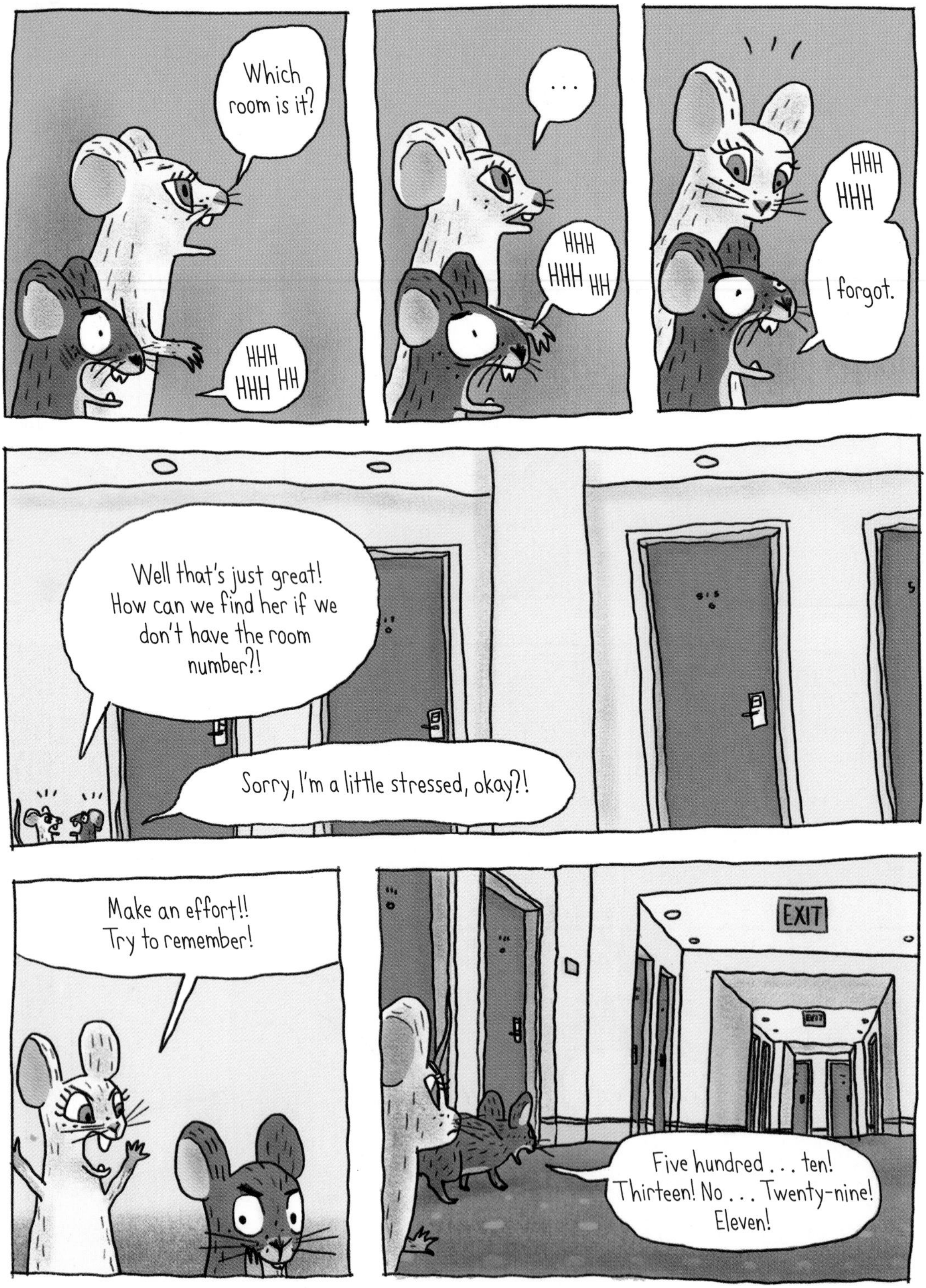
Which room is it?
HHH HHH HH
. . .
HHH HHH HH
HHH HHH
I forgot.
Well that's just great! How can we find her if we don't have the room number?!
Sorry, I'm a little stressed, okay?!
Make an effort!! Try to remember!
EXIT
Five hundred . . . ten! Thirteen! No . . . Twenty-nine! Eleven!

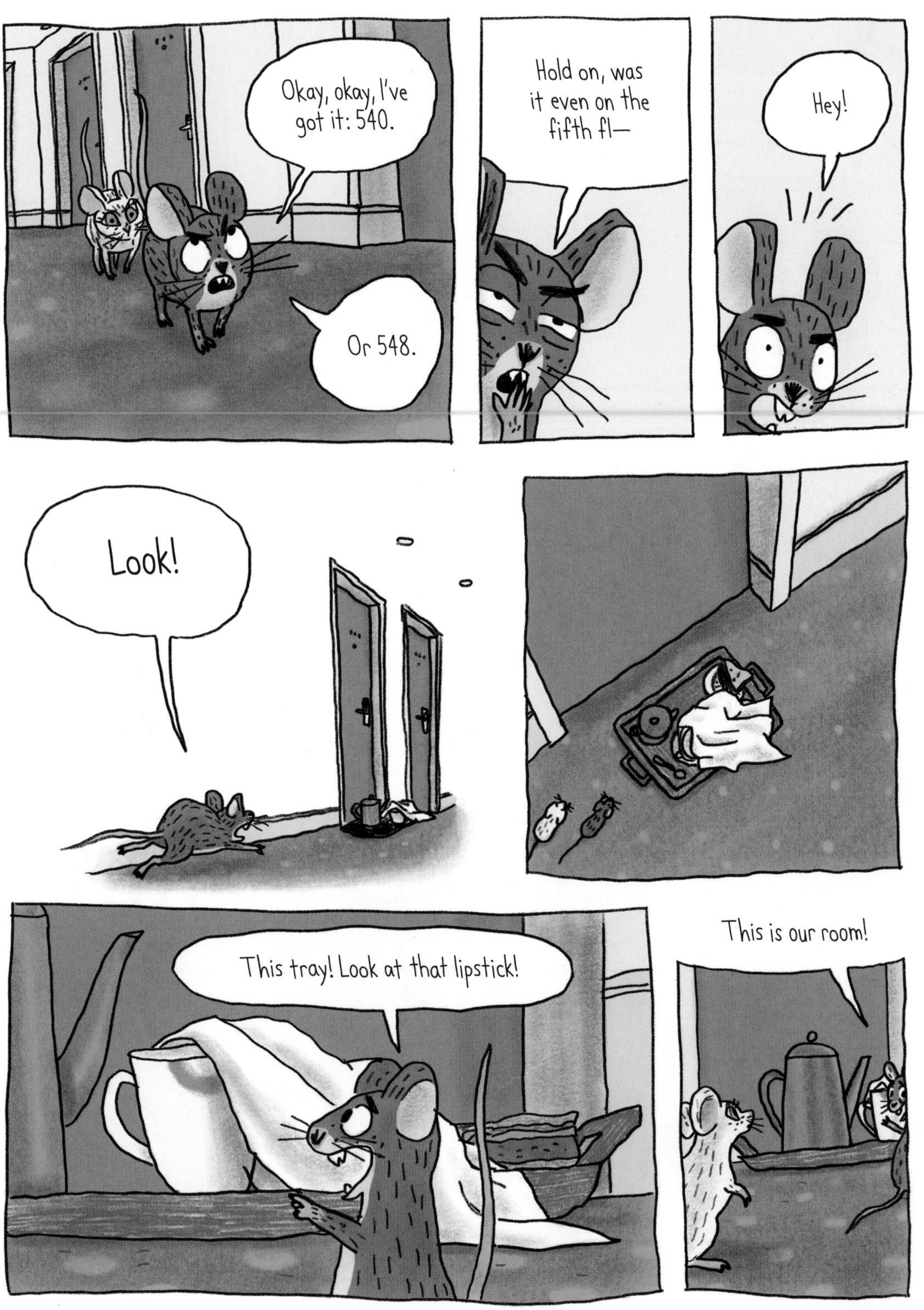
Okay, okay, I've got it: 540.
Or 548.
Hold on, was it even on the fifth fl—
Hey!
Look!
This tray! Look at that lipstick!
This is our room!

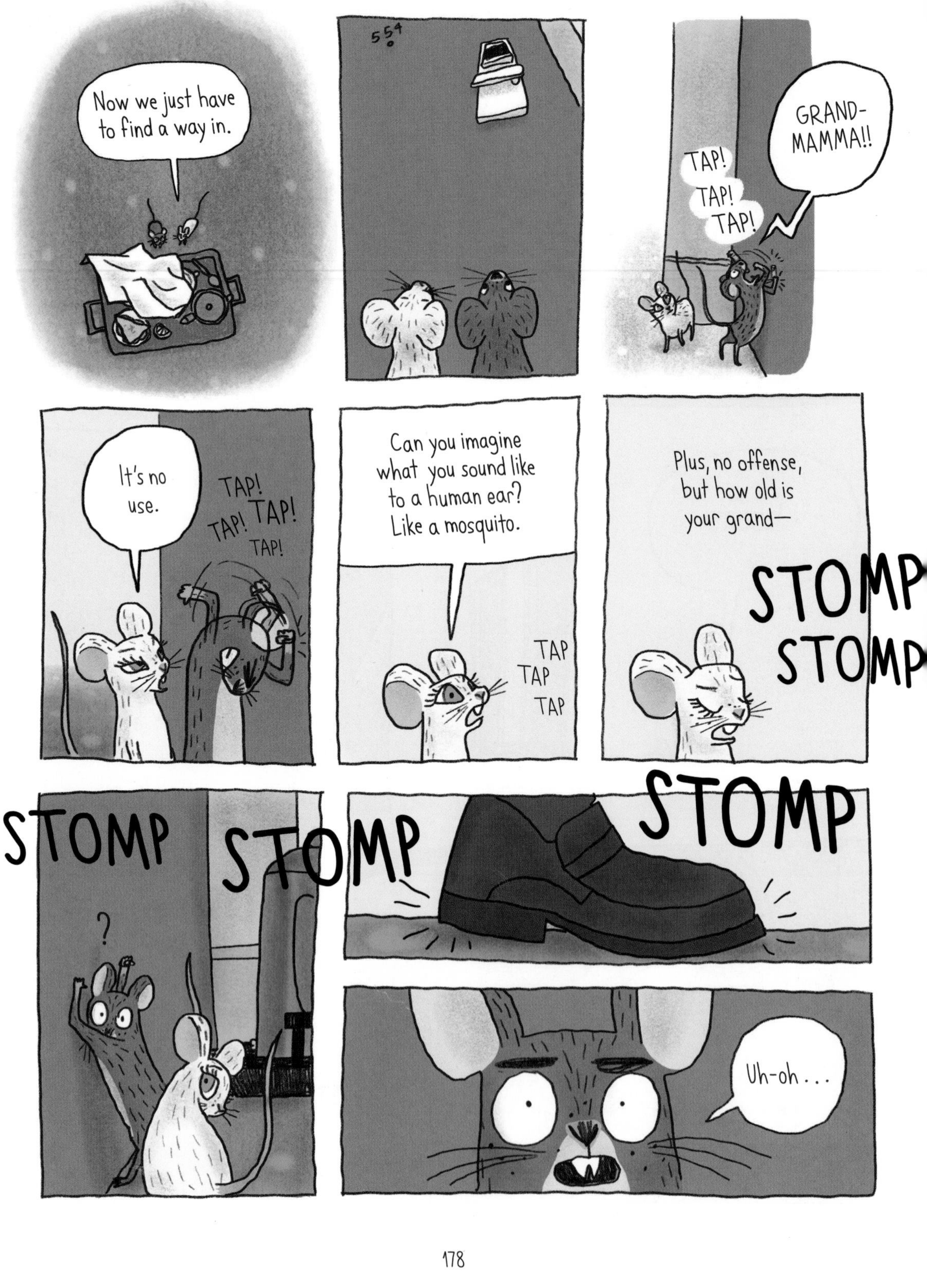
Now we just have to find a way in.
554
GRAND-MAMMA!!
TAP! TAP! TAP!
It's no use.
TAP! TAP! TAP! TAP!
Can you imagine what you sound like to a human ear? Like a mosquito.
TAP TAP TAP
Plus, no offense, but how old is your grand—
STOMP STOMP
STOMP STOMP
?
STOMP
Uh-oh . . .

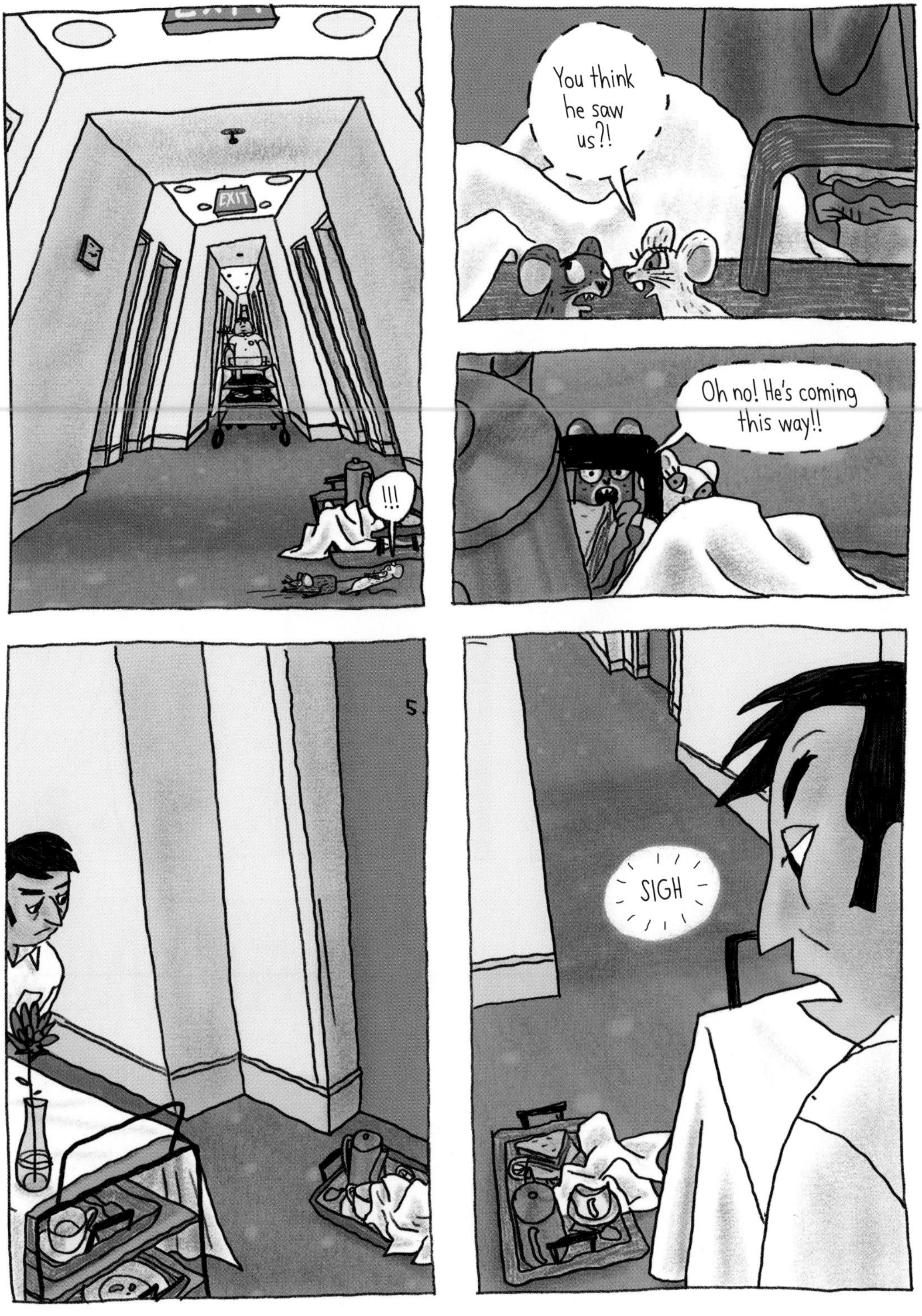
EXIT
!!!
You think he saw us?!
Oh no! He's coming this way!!
SIGH

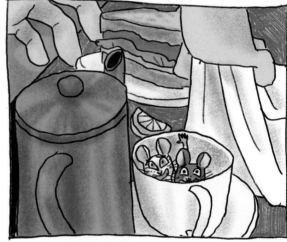

AAAAAAA!!!

180

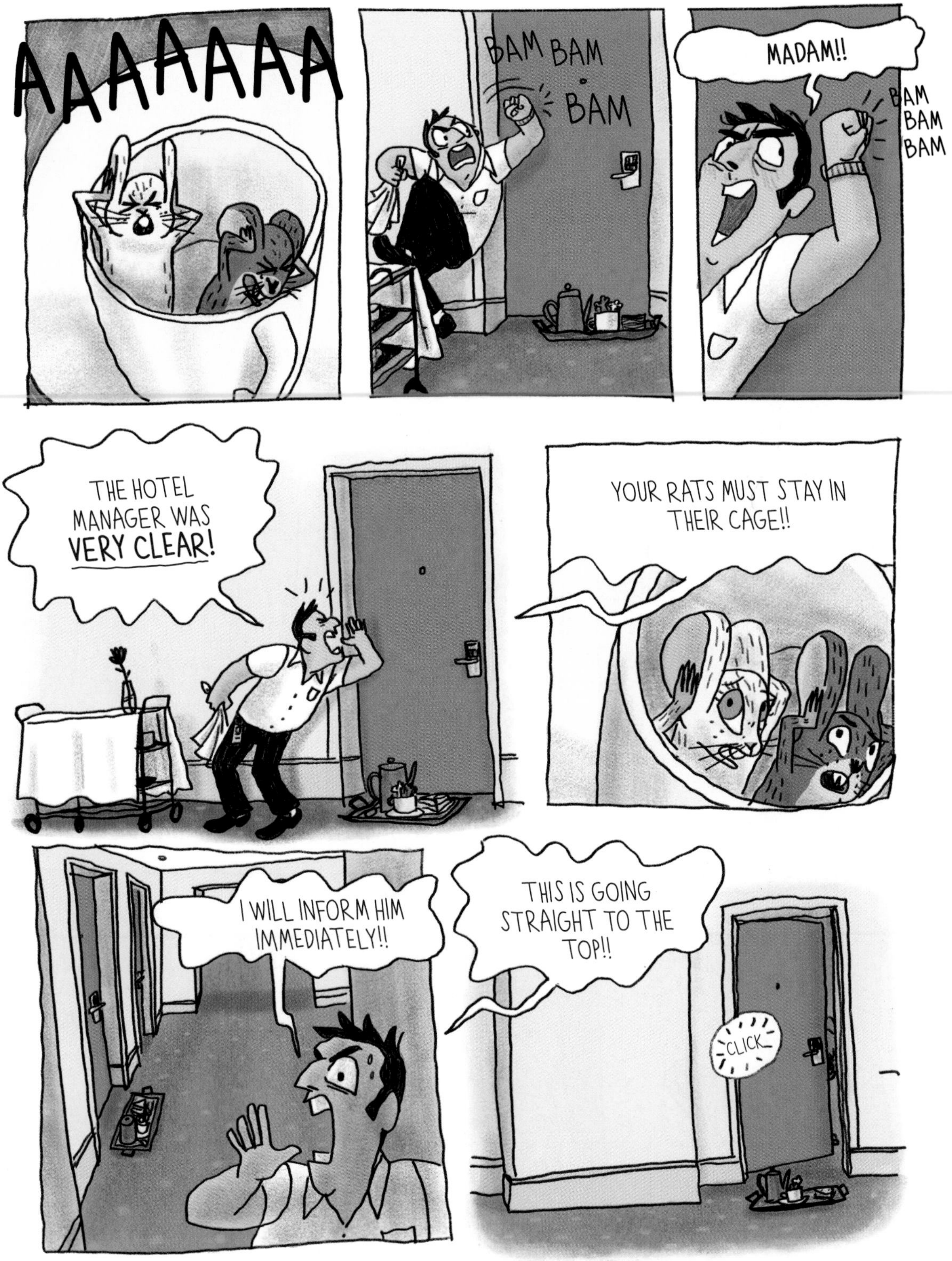
AAAAAAA
BAM BAM BAM
MADAM!!
BAM BAM BAM
THE HOTEL MANAGER WAS VERY CLEAR!
YOUR RATS MUST STAY IN THEIR CAGE!!
I WILL INFORM HIM IMMEDIATELY!!
THIS IS GOING STRAIGHT TO THE TOP!!
CLICK

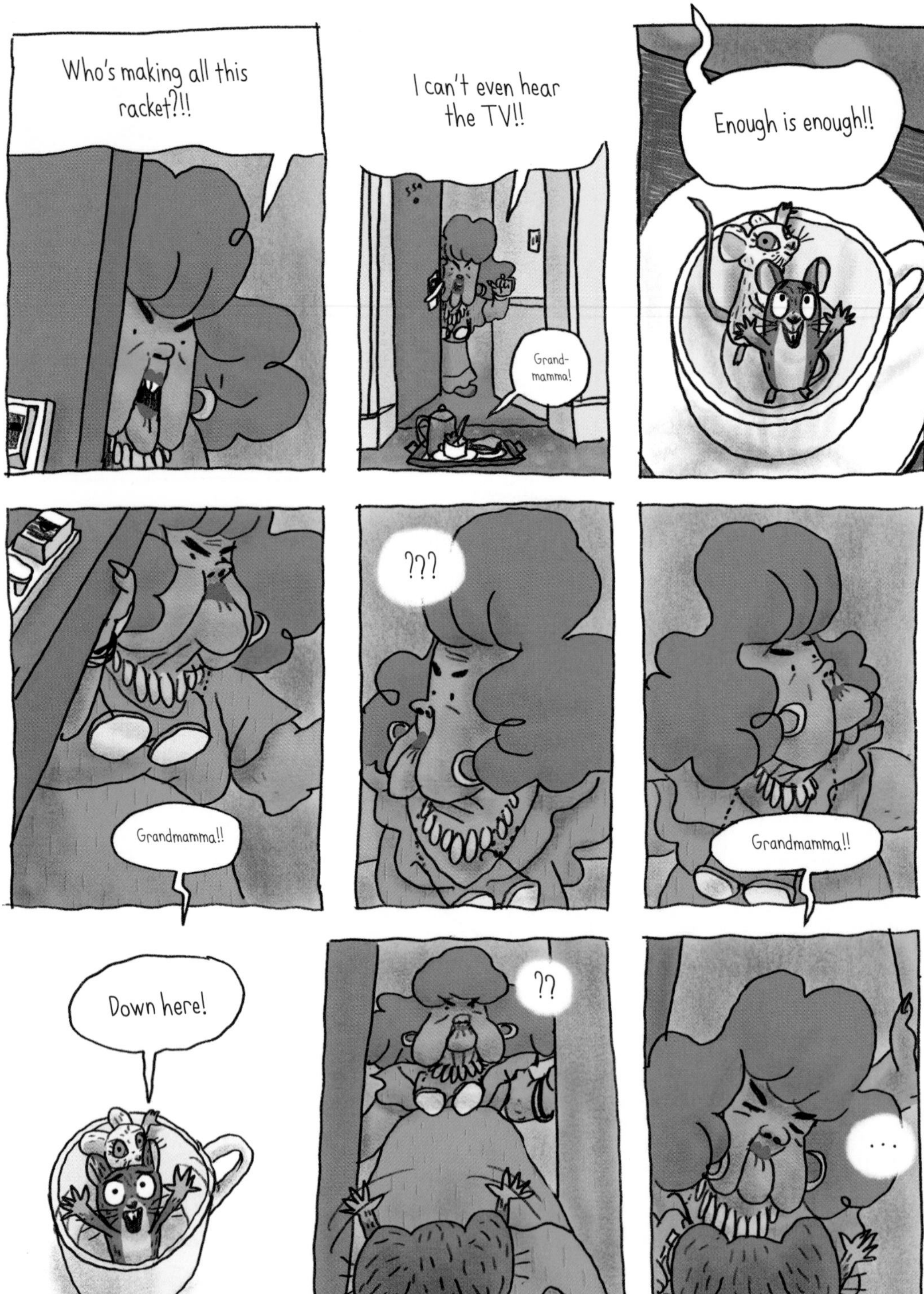

Who's making all this racket?!!
I can't even hear the TV!!
Grand-mamma!
Enough is enough!!
Grandmamma!!
???
Grandmamma!!
Down here!
??
...

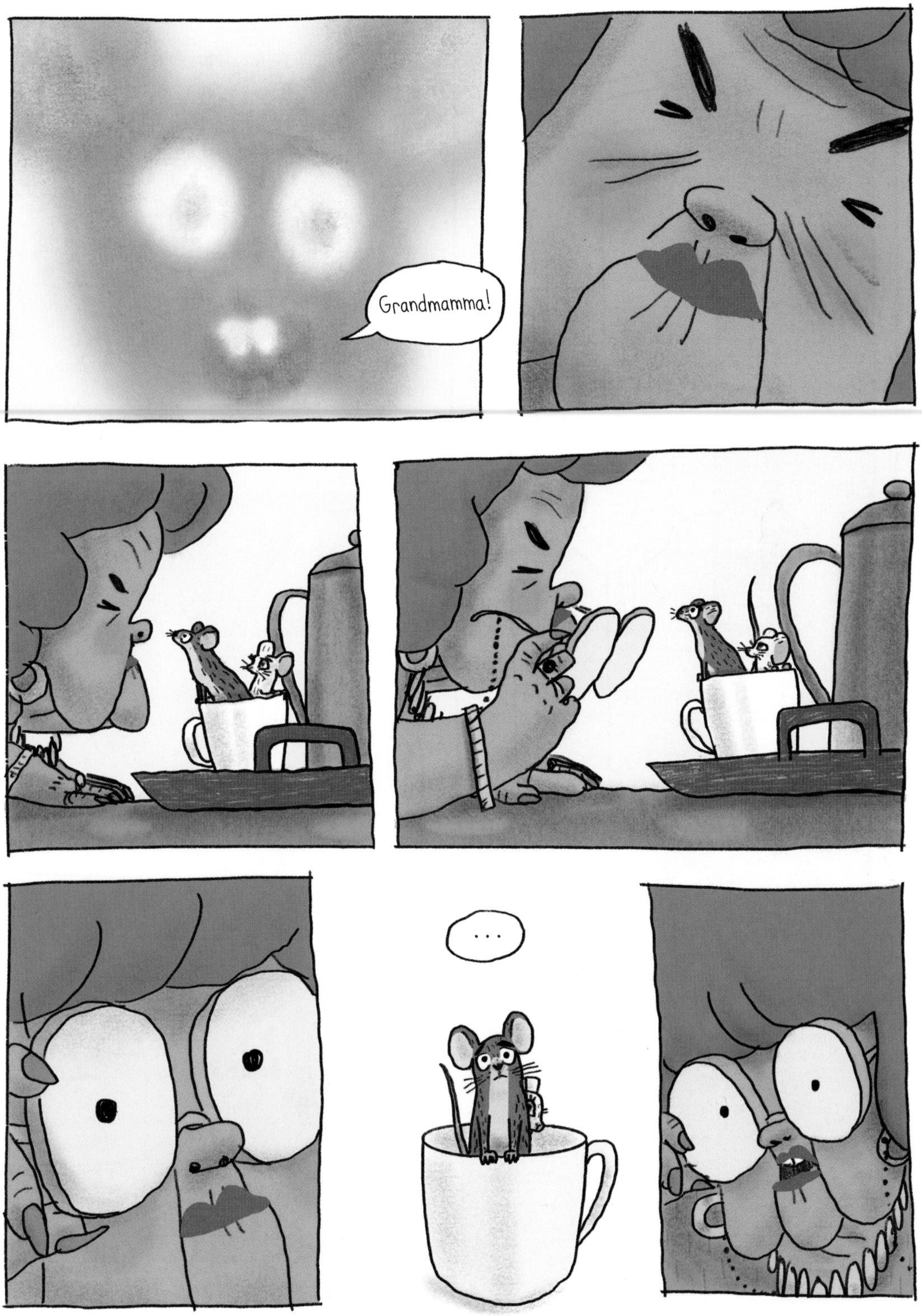
Grandmamma!
...

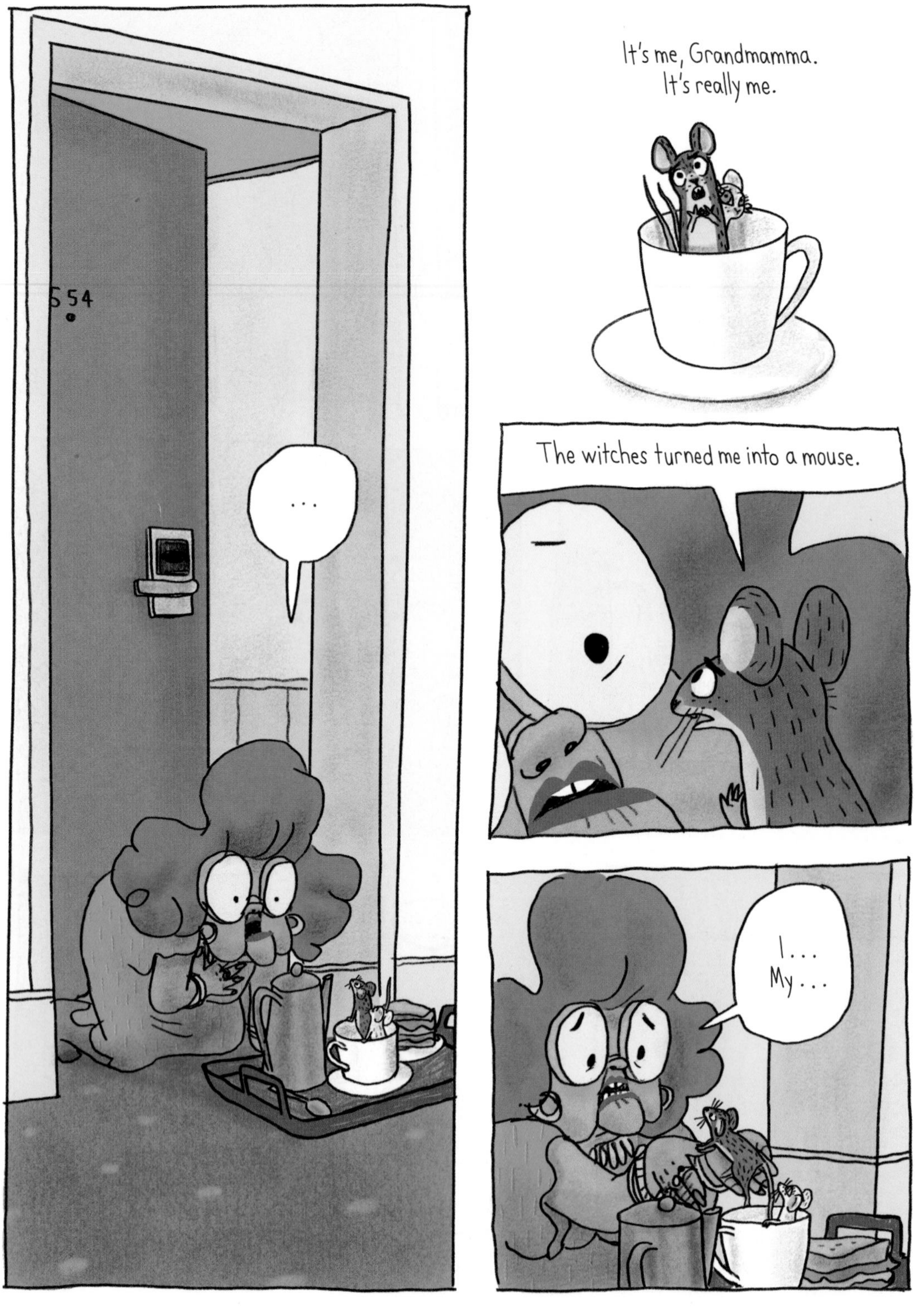
. . .
It's me, Grandmamma.
It's really me.
The witches turned me into a mouse.
I . . .
My . . .

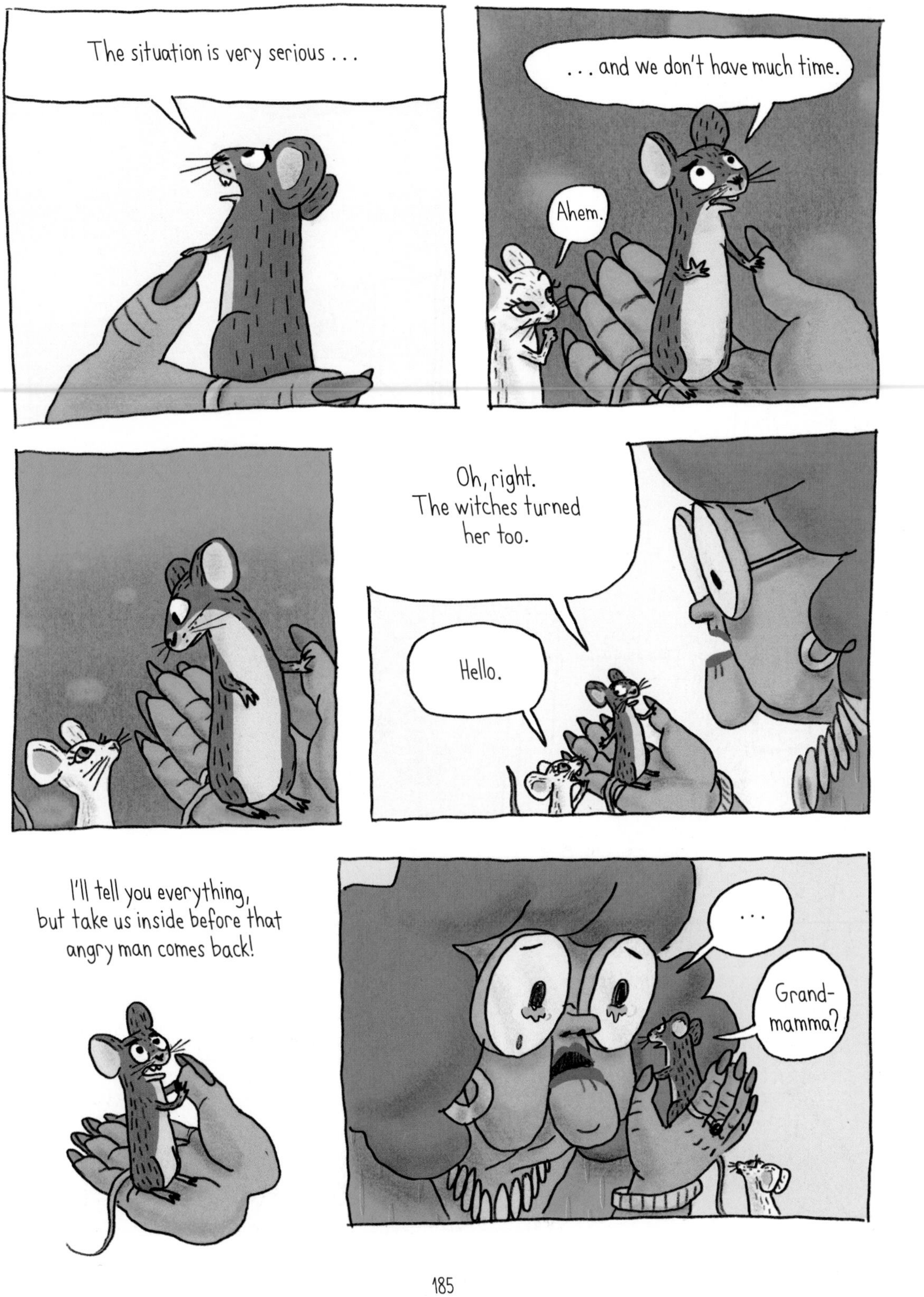
The situation is very serious . . .
. . . and we don't have much time.
Ahem.
Oh, right.
The witches turned
her too.
Hello.
I'll tell you everything,
but take us inside before that
angry man comes back!
. . .
Grand-
mamma?

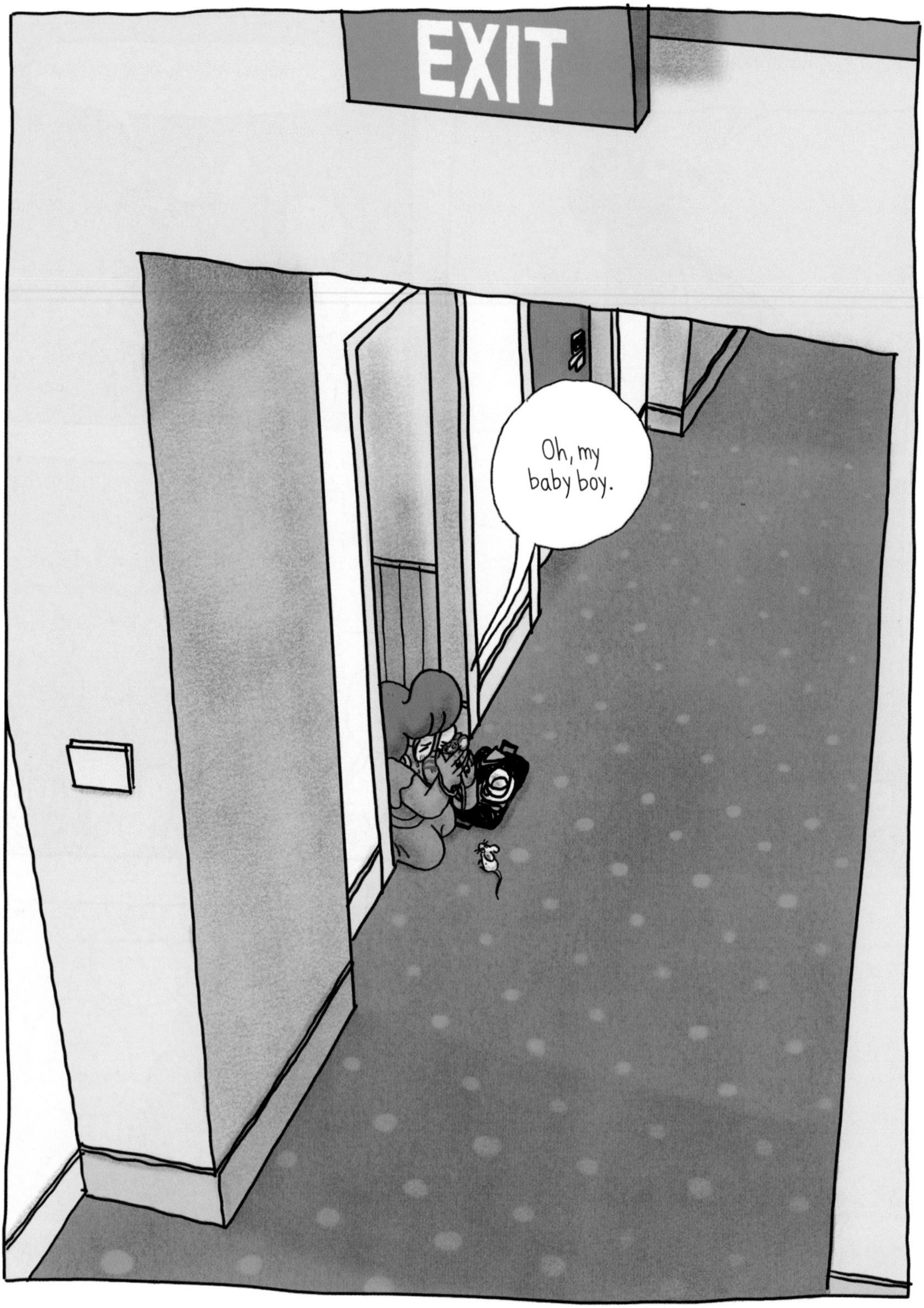
EXIT
Oh, my baby boy.

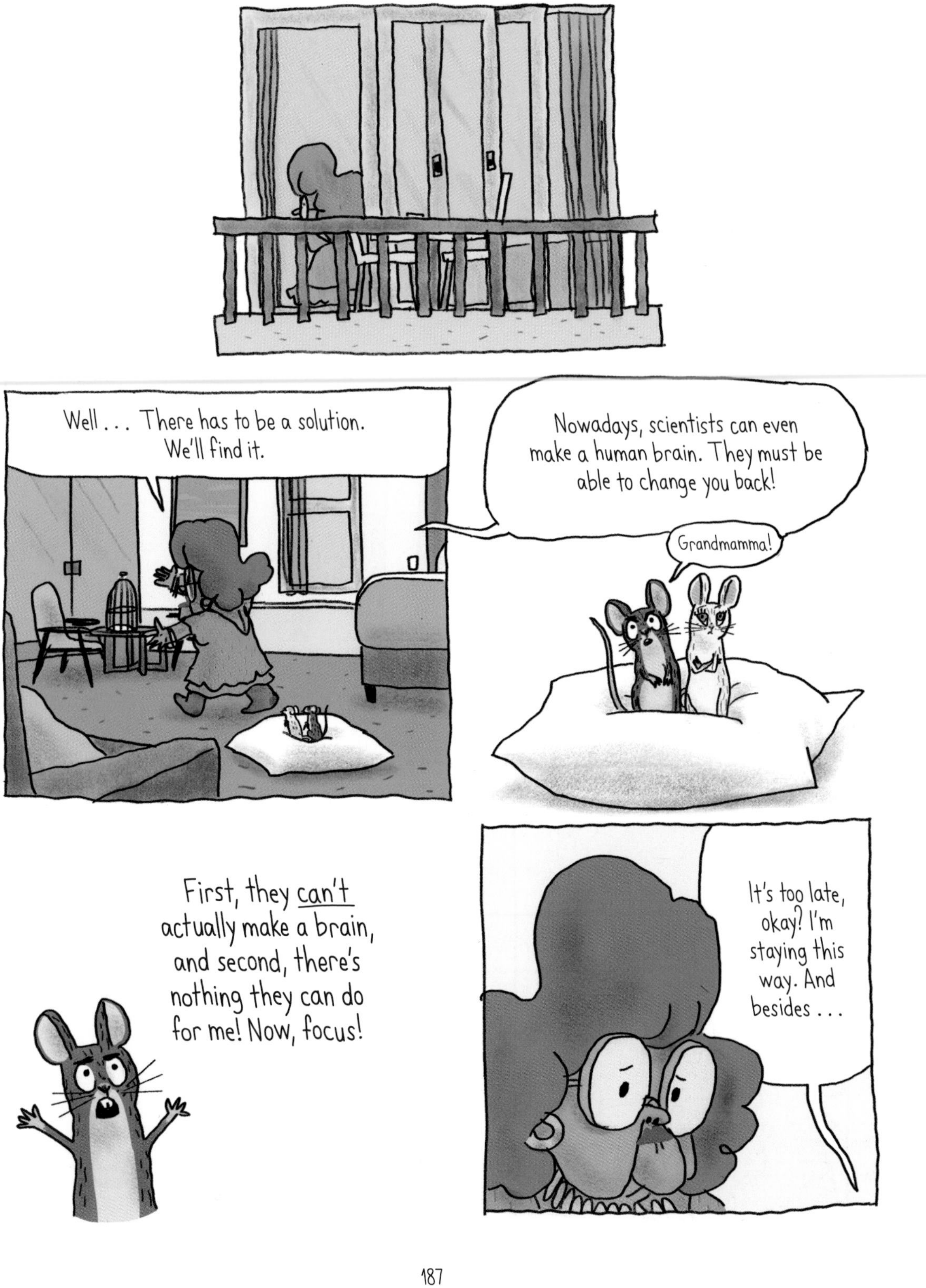
Well . . . There has to be a solution. We'll find it.
Nowadays, scientists can even make a human brain. They must be able to change you back!
Grandmamma!
First, they can't actually make a brain, and second, there's nothing they can do for me! Now, focus!
It's too late, okay? I'm staying this way. And besides . . .

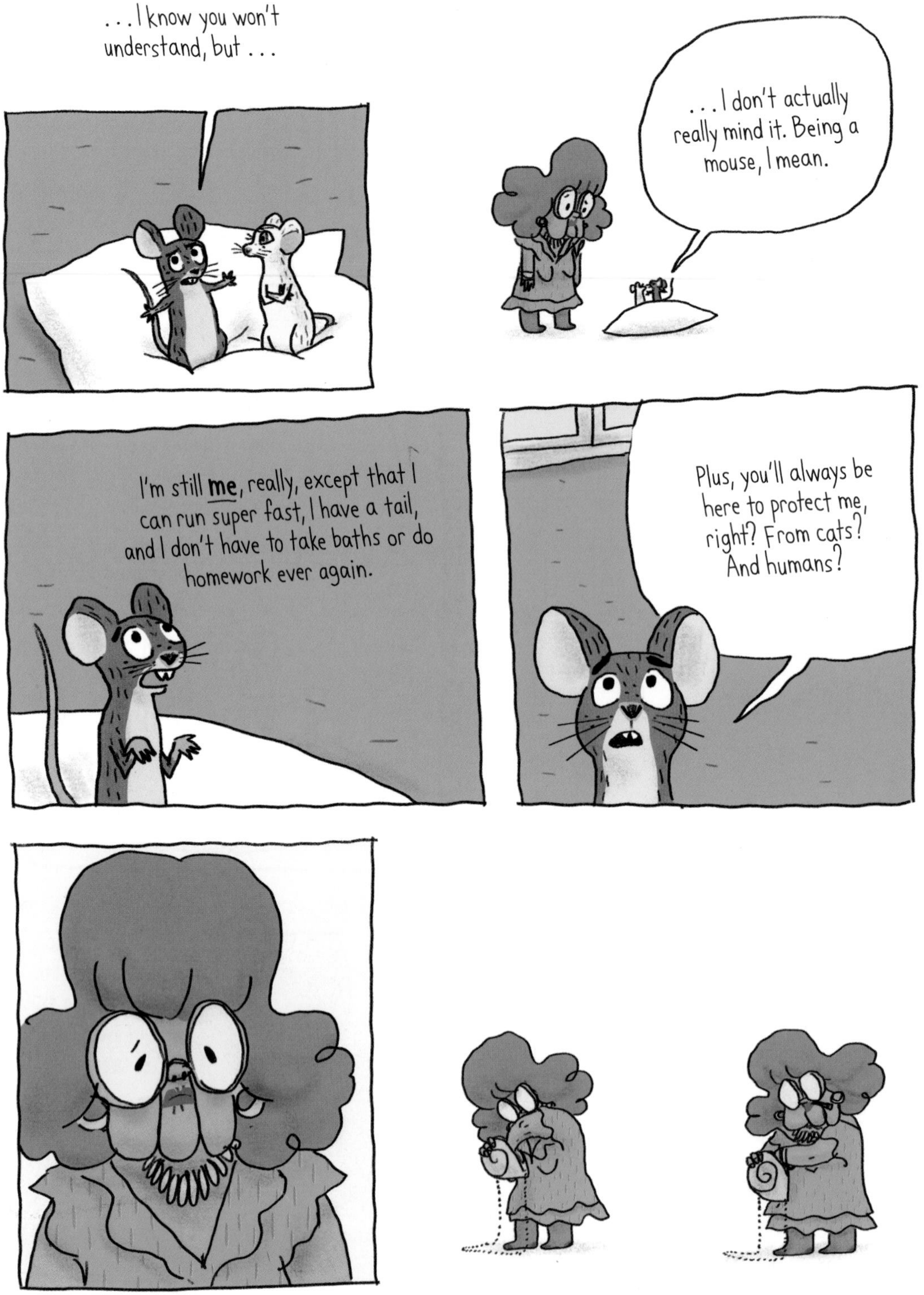
. . . I know you won't understand, but . . .
. . . I don't actually really mind it. Being a mouse, I mean.
I'm still **me**, really, except that I can run super fast, I have a tail, and I don't have to take baths or do homework ever again.
Plus, you'll always be here to protect me, right? From cats? And humans?

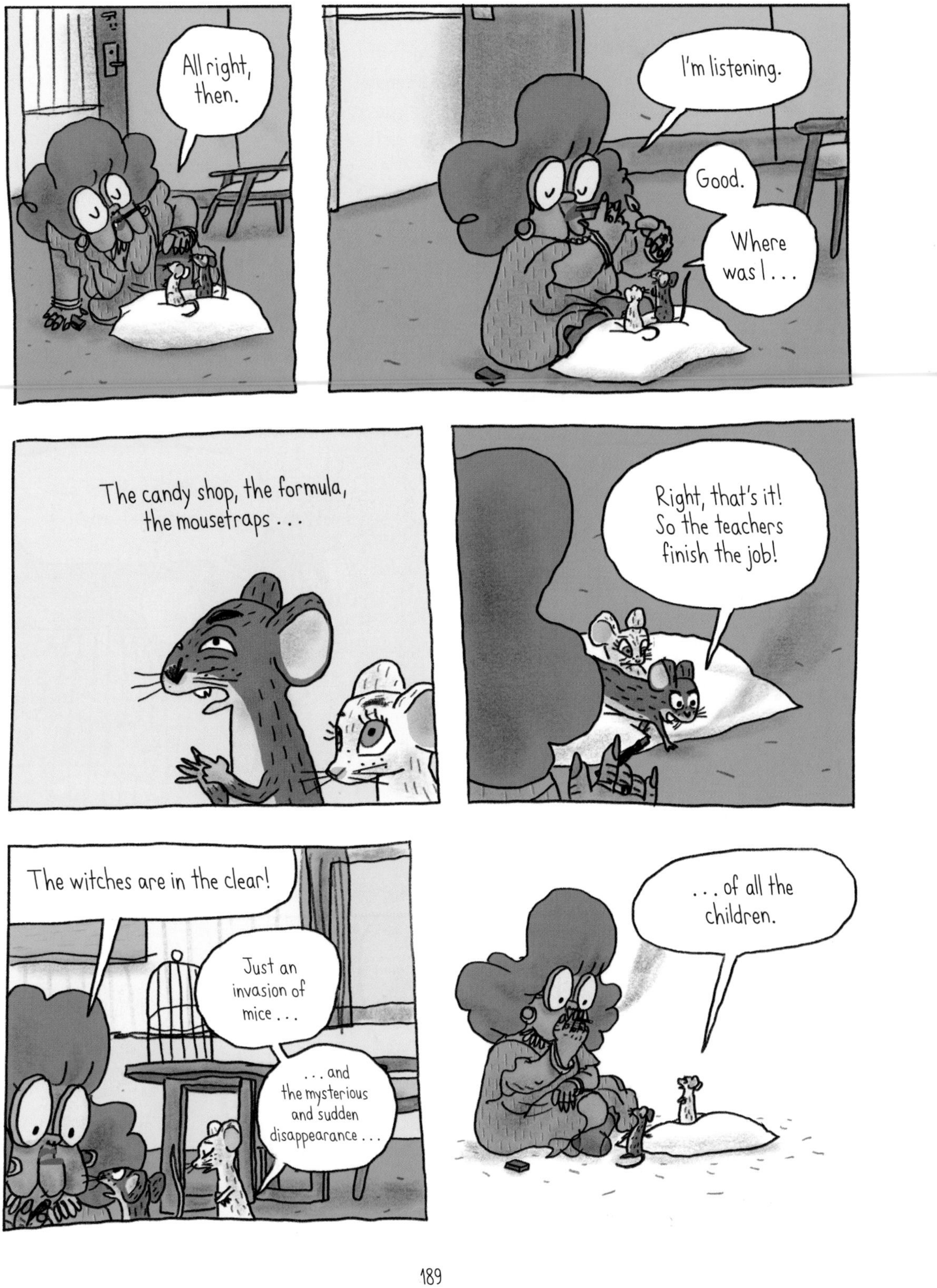
All right, then.
I'm listening.
Good.
Where was I . . .
The candy shop, the formula, the mousetraps . . .
Right, that's it! So the teachers finish the job!
The witches are in the clear!
Just an invasion of mice . . .
. . . and the mysterious and sudden disappearance . . .
. . . of all the children.

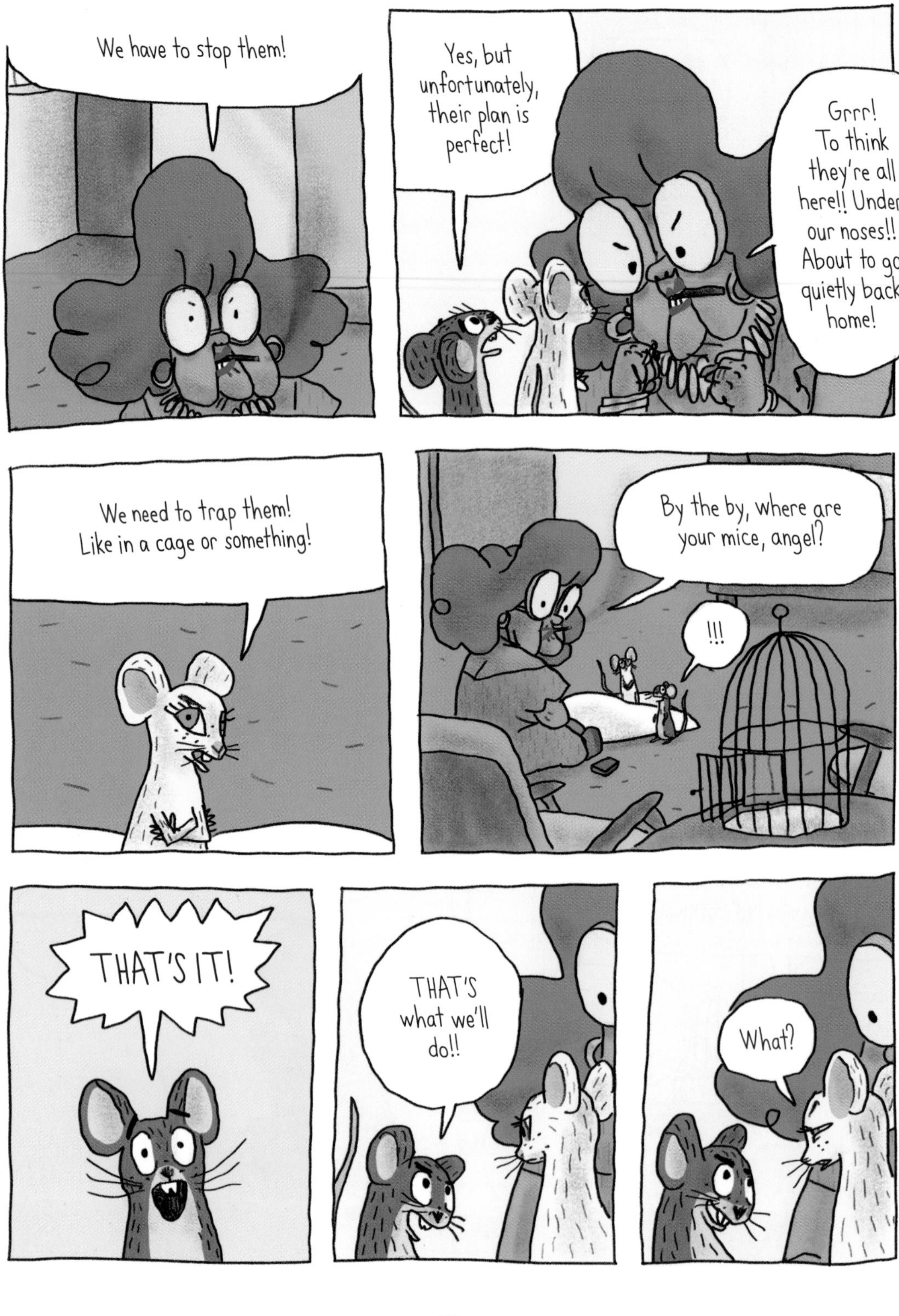
We have to stop them!
Yes, but unfortunately, their plan is perfect!
Grrr! To think they're all here!! Under our noses!! About to go quietly back home!
We need to trap them! Like in a cage or something!
By the by, where are your mice, angel?
!!!
THAT'S IT!
THAT'S what we'll do!!
What?

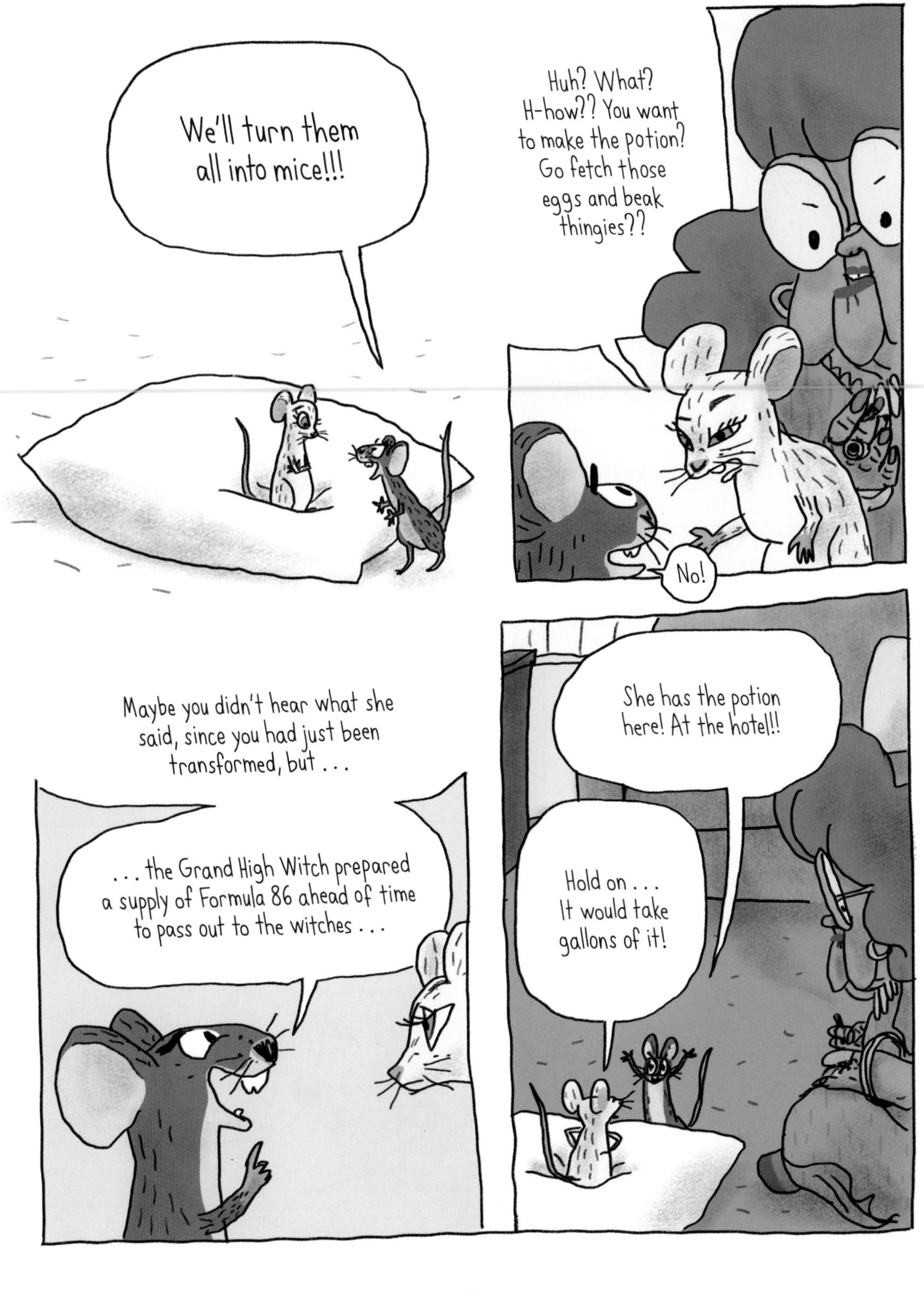
We'll turn them all into mice!!!
Huh? What? H-how?? You want to make the potion? Go fetch those eggs and beak thingies??
No!
Maybe you didn't hear what she said, since you had just been transformed, but . . .
. . . the Grand High Witch prepared a supply of Formula 86 ahead of time to pass out to the witches . . .
She has the potion here! At the hotel!!
Hold on . . . It would take gallons of it!

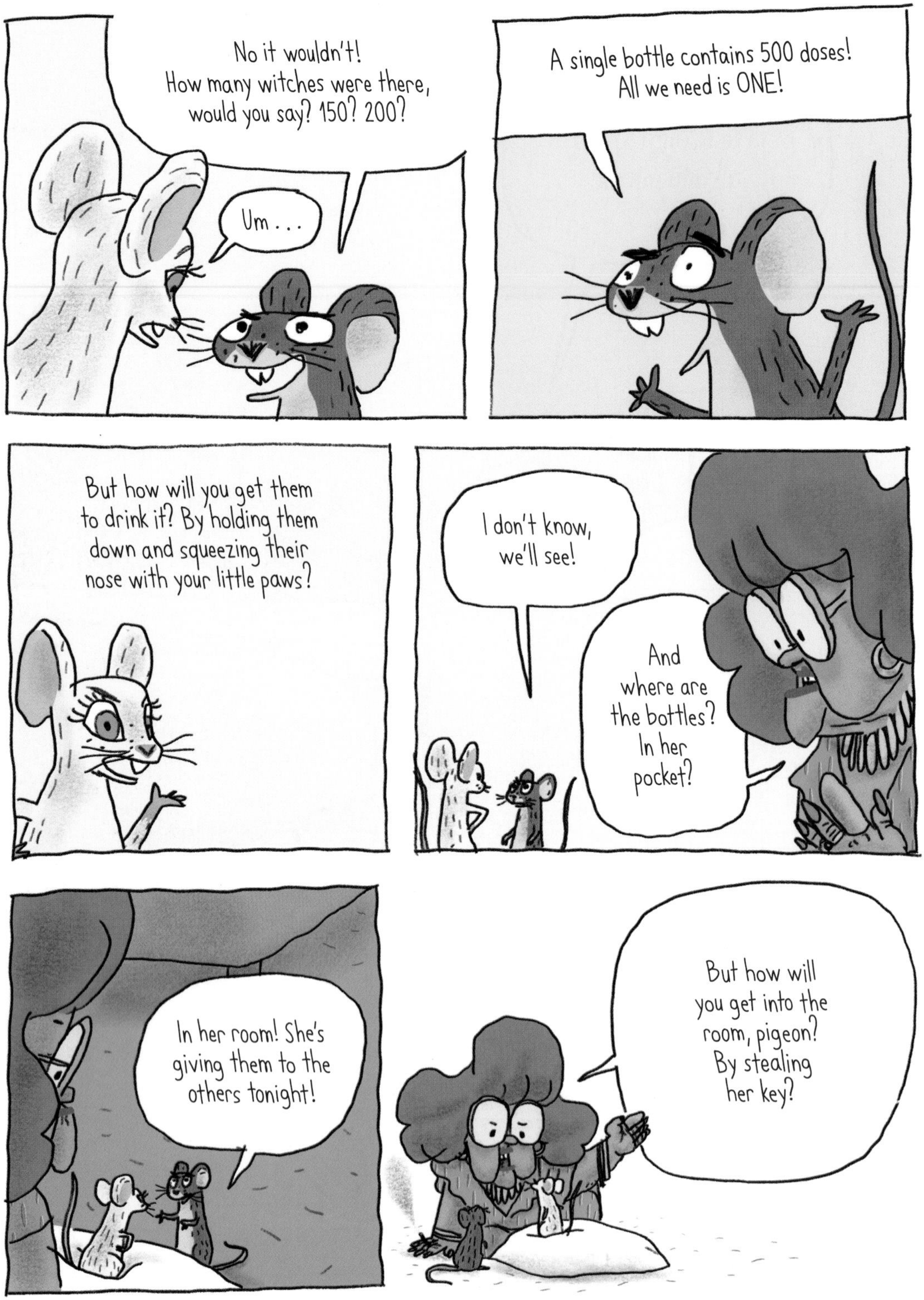
No it wouldn't! How many witches were there, would you say? 150? 200?
Um . . .
A single bottle contains 500 doses! All we need is ONE!
But how will you get them to drink it? By holding them down and squeezing their nose with your little paws?
I don't know, we'll see!
And where are the bottles? In her pocket?
In her room! She's giving them to the others tonight!
But how will you get into the room, pigeon? By stealing her key?

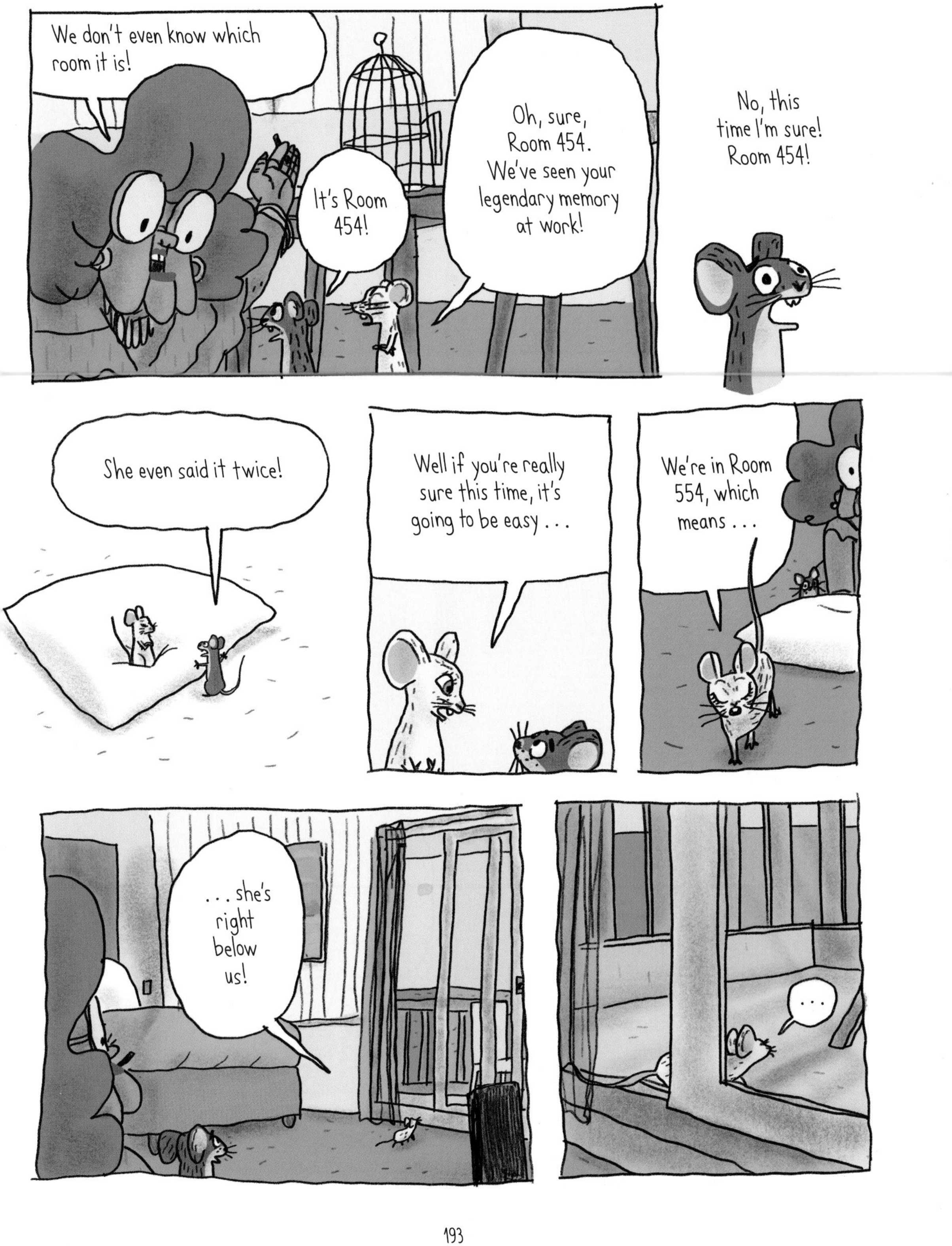
We don't even know which room it is!
It's Room 454!
Oh, sure, Room 454. We've seen your legendary memory at work!
No, this time I'm sure! Room 454!
She even said it twice!
Well if you're really sure this time, it's going to be easy . . .
We're in Room 554, which means . . .
. . . she's right below us!
. . .

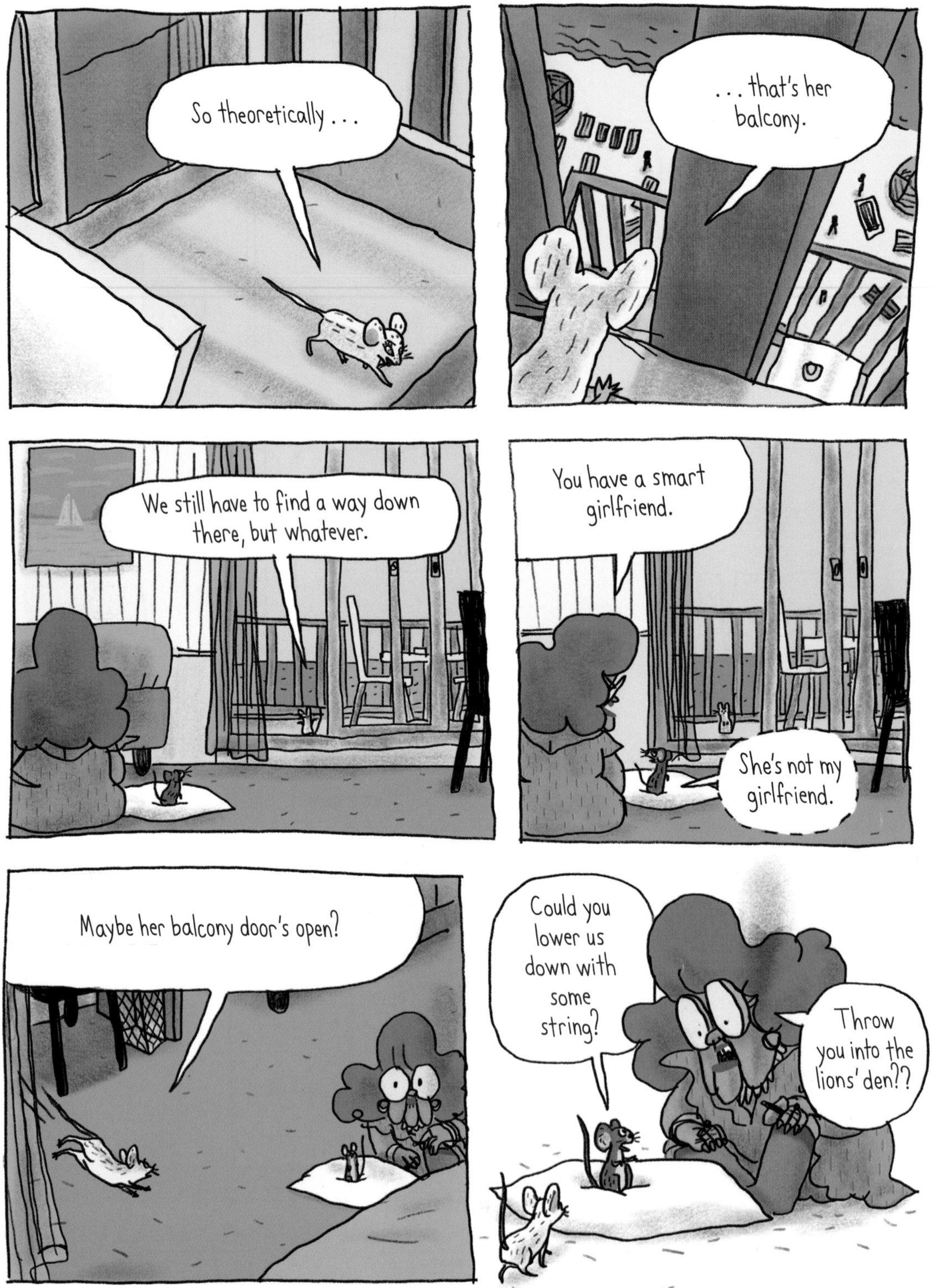
So theoretically . . .
. . . that's her balcony.
We still have to find a way down there, but whatever.
You have a smart girlfriend.
She's not my girlfriend.
Maybe her balcony door's open?
Could you lower us down with some string?
Throw you into the lions' den??

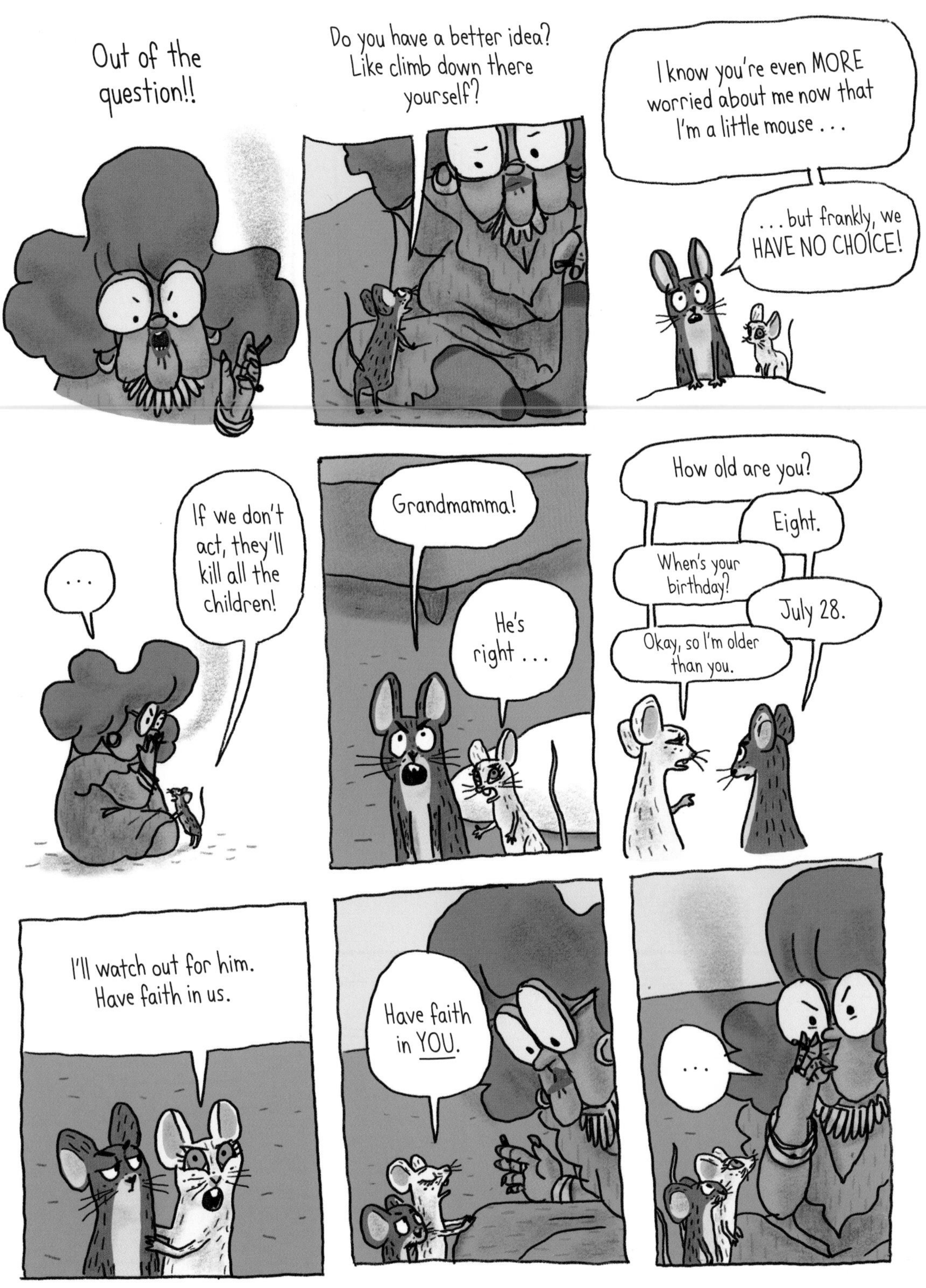

Out of the question!!
Do you have a better idea? Like climb down there yourself?
I know you're even MORE worried about me now that I'm a little mouse . . .
. . . but frankly, we HAVE NO CHOICE!
. . .
If we don't act, they'll kill all the children!
Grandmamma!
He's right . . .
How old are you?
Eight.
When's your birthday?
July 28.
Okay, so I'm older than you.
I'll watch out for him. Have faith in us.
Have faith in YOU.
. . .

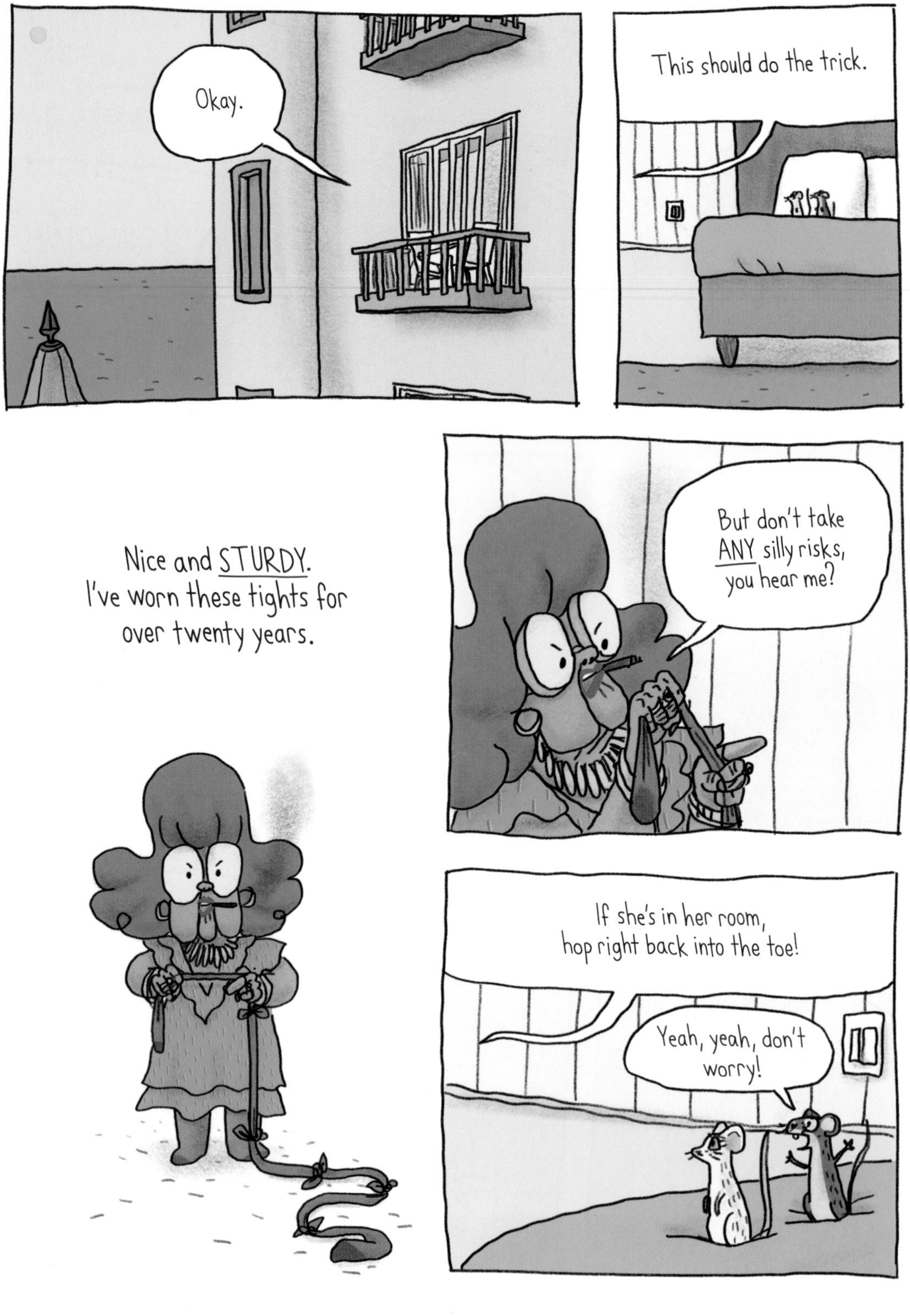

Okay.
This should do the trick.
Nice and STURDY. I've worn these tights for over twenty years.
But don't take ANY silly risks, you hear me?
If she's in her room, hop right back into the toe!
Yeah, yeah, don't worry!

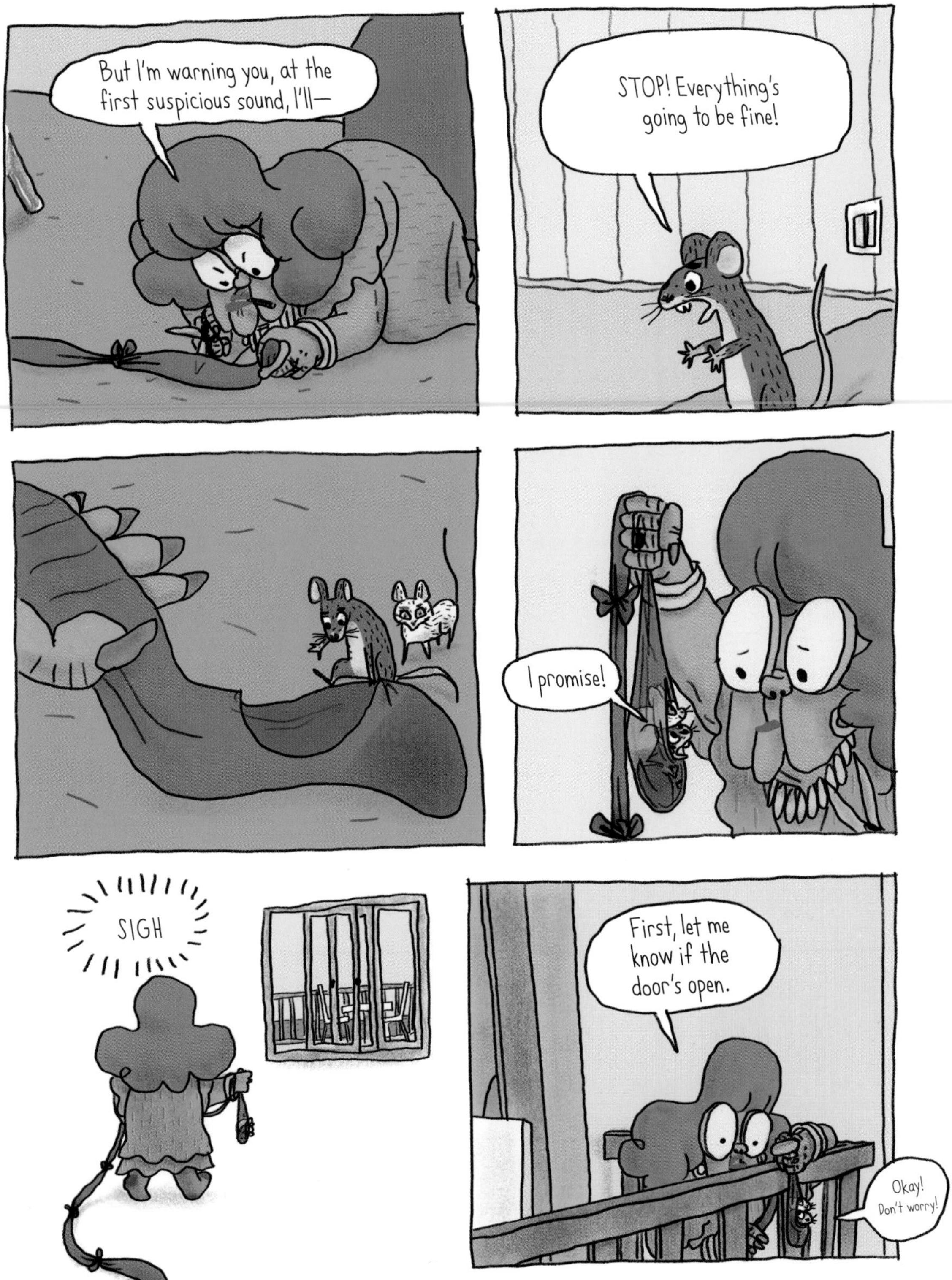
But I'm warning you, at the first suspicious sound, I'll—
STOP! Everything's going to be fine!
I promise!
SIGH
First, let me know if the door's open.
Okay! Don't worry!

Oooooh my gosh . . .

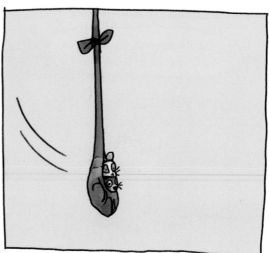

For real?
You're not scared?

I'm scared to death.

That makes me feel better.

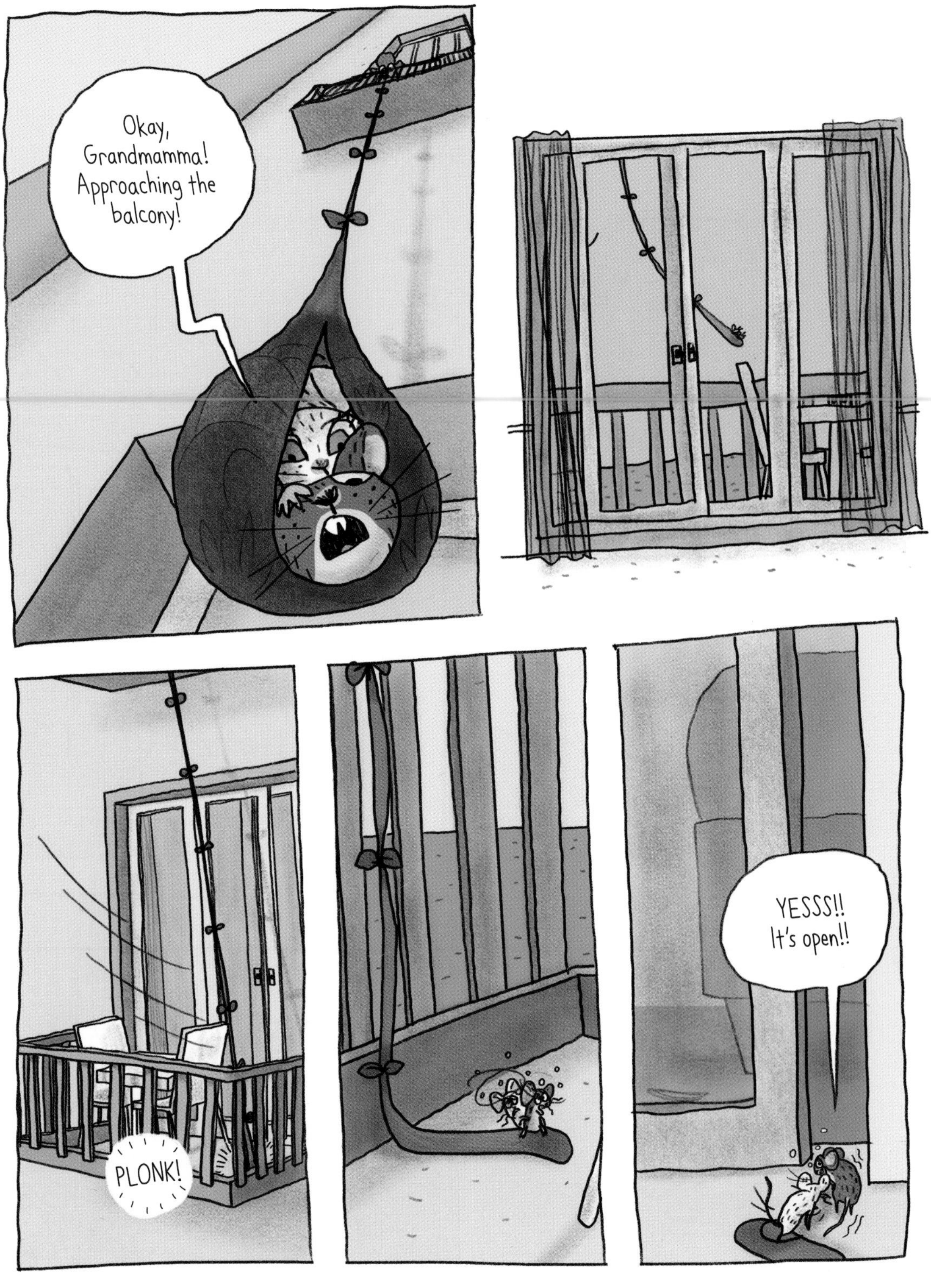
Okay, Grandmamma! Approaching the balcony!
PLONK!
YESSS!! It's open!!

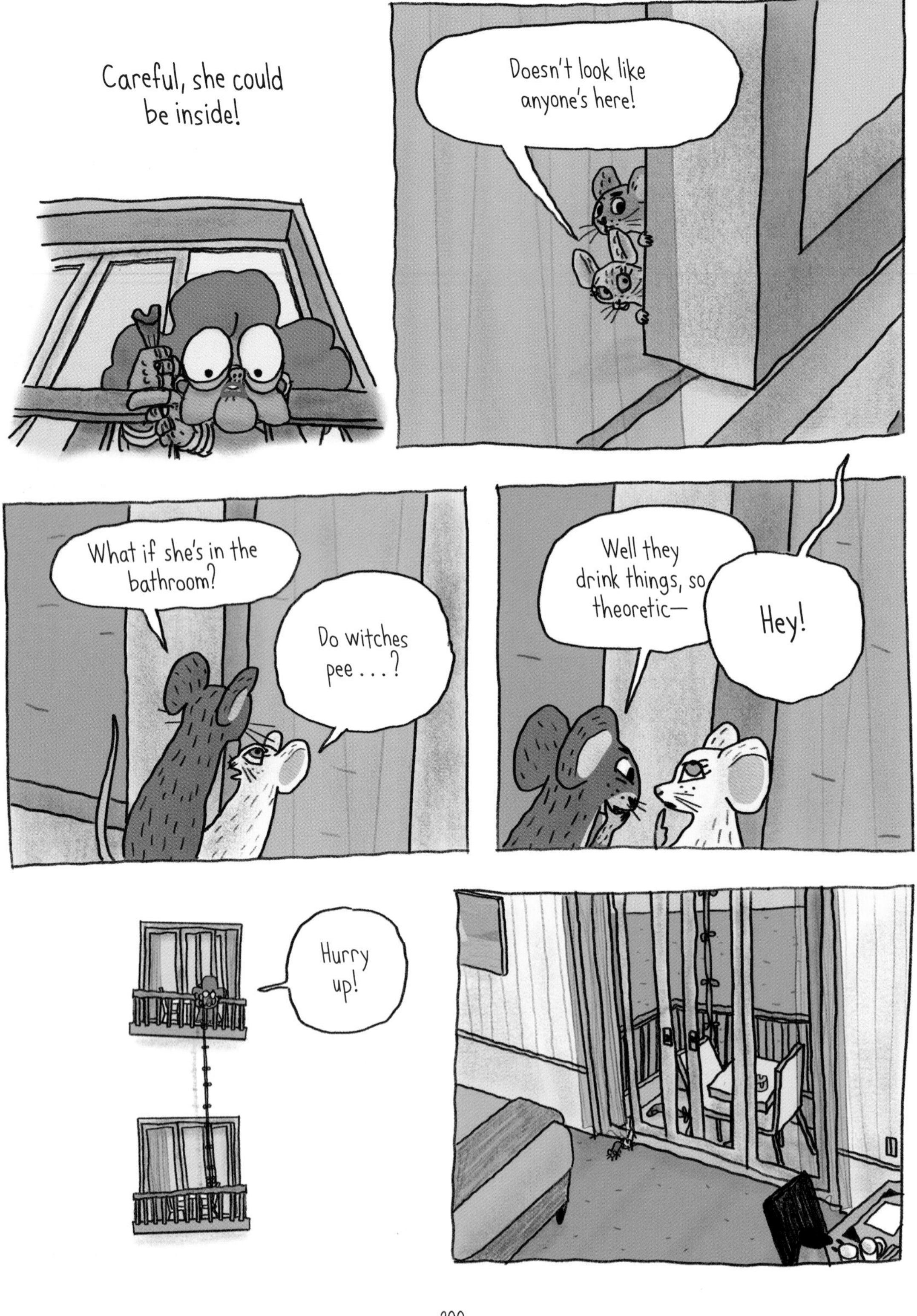

Careful, she could be inside!
Doesn't look like anyone's here!
What if she's in the bathroom?
Do witches pee . . . ?
Well they drink things, so theoretic—
Hey!
Hurry up!

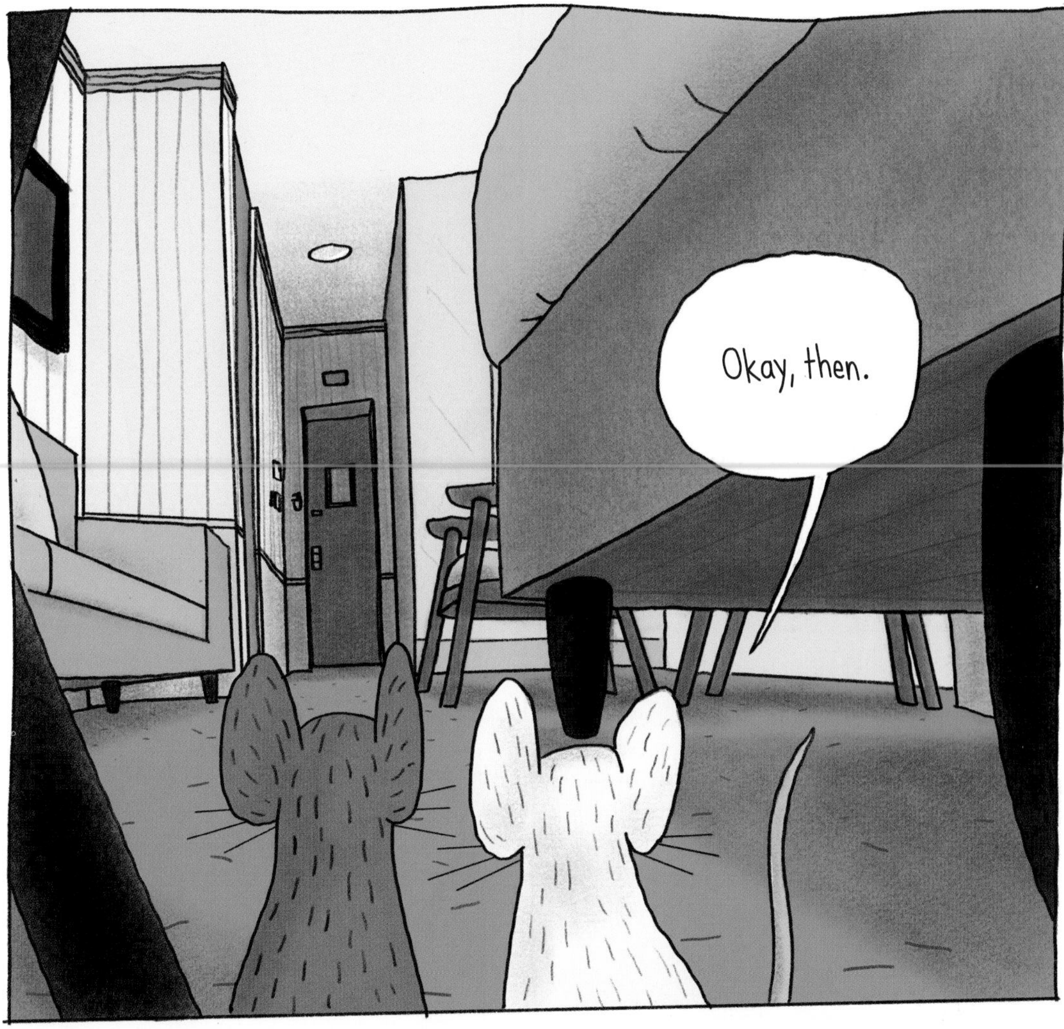
Okay, then.

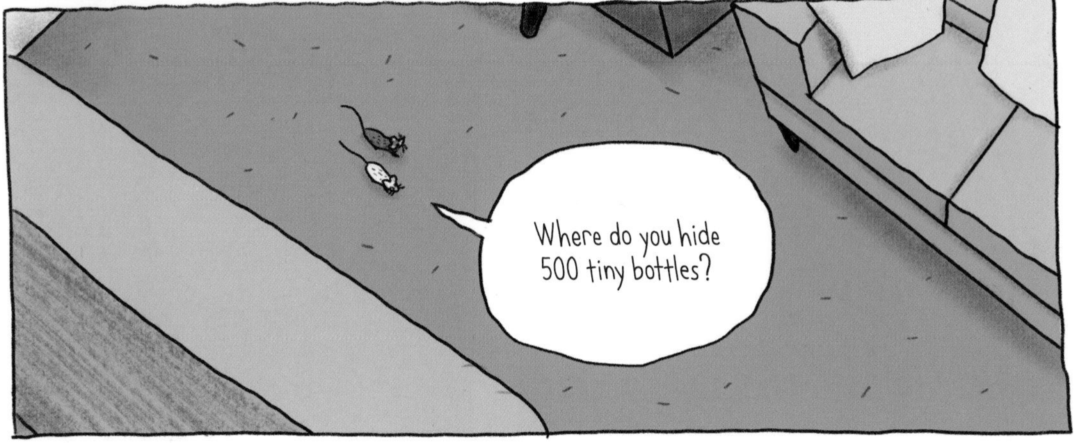
Where do you hide 500 tiny bottles?

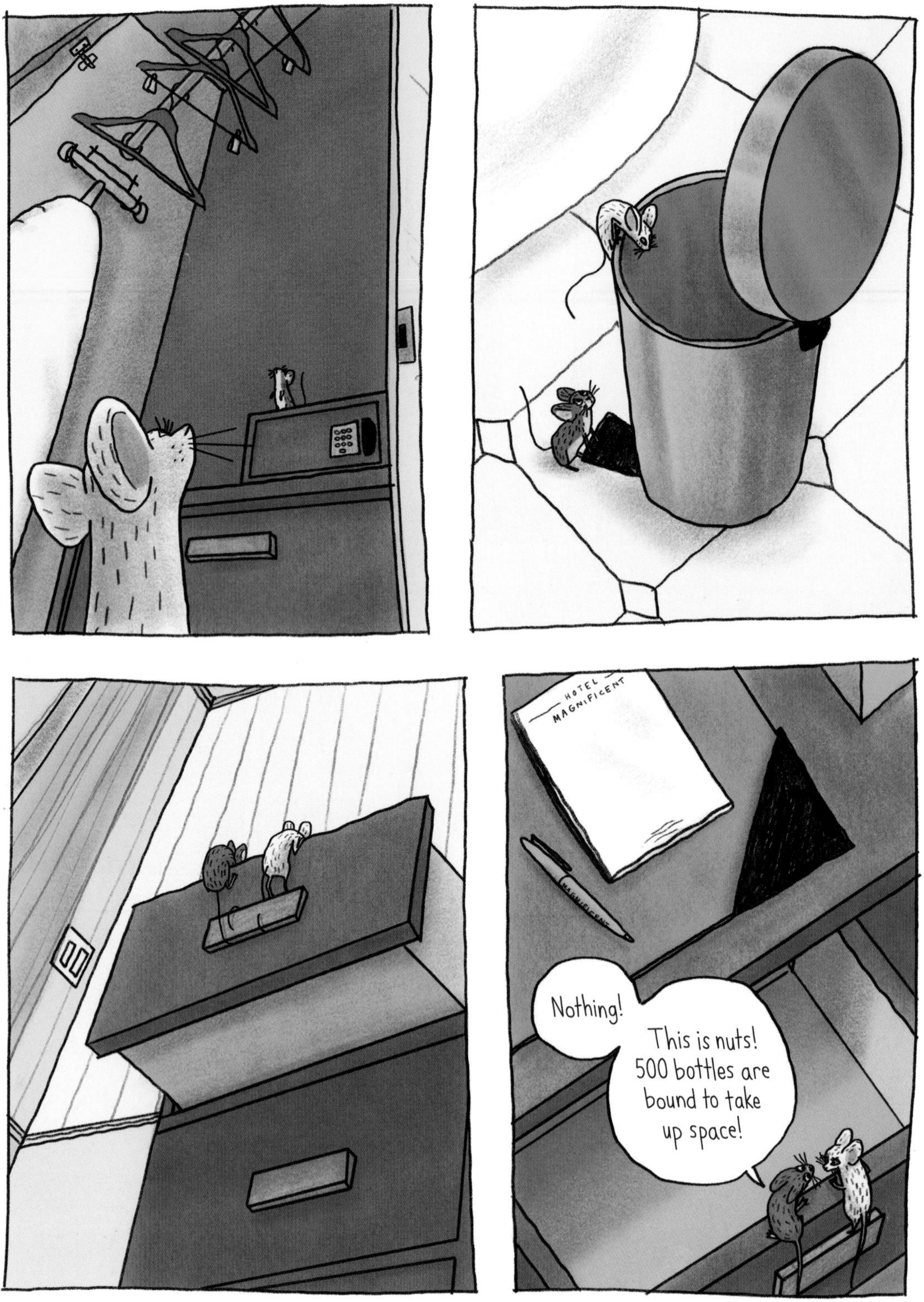
HOTEL MAGNIFICENT
MAGNIFICENT
Nothing!
This is nuts! 500 bottles are bound to take up space!

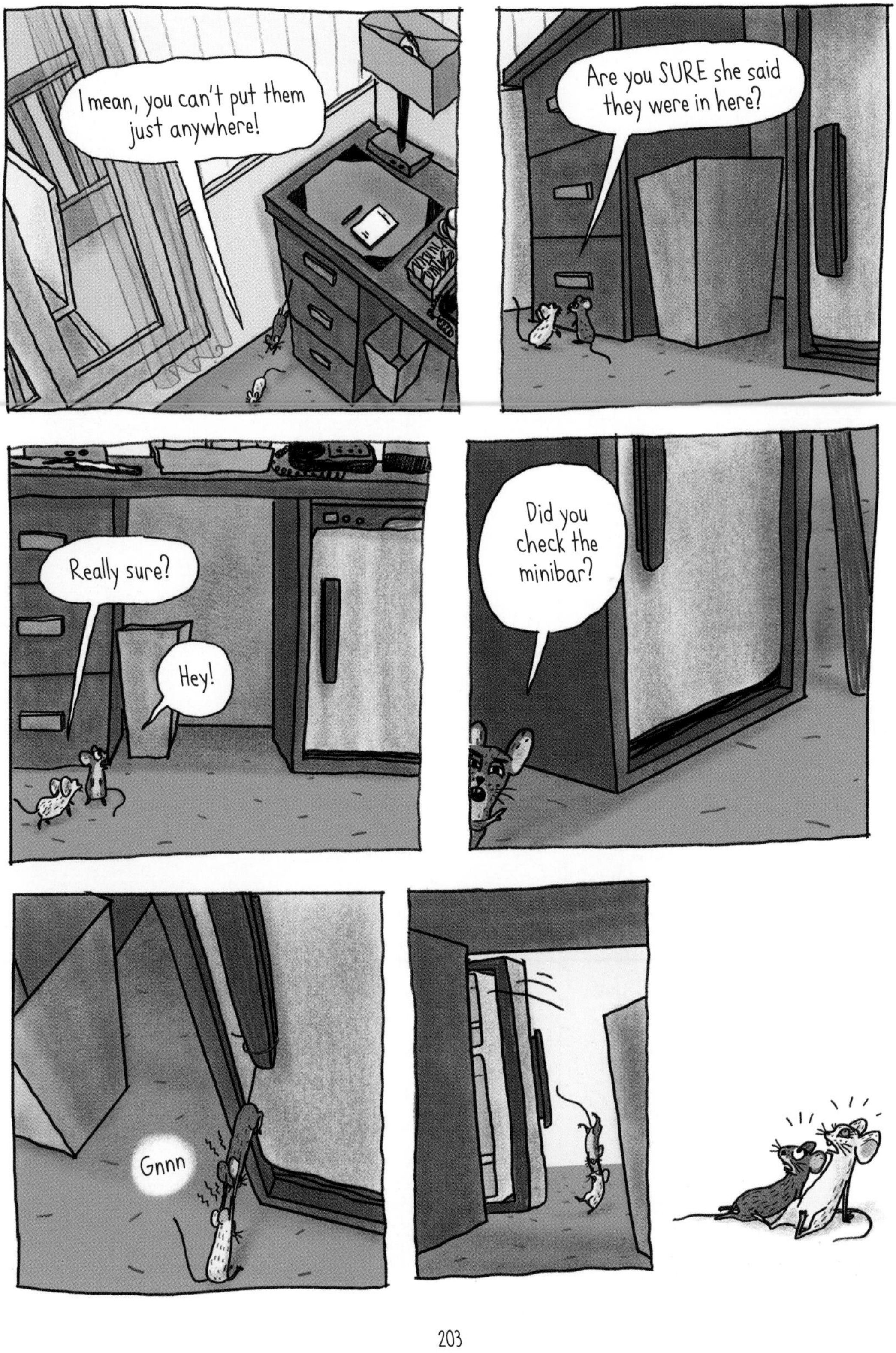
I mean, you can't put them just anywhere!
Are you SURE she said they were in here?
Really sure?
Hey!
Did you check the minibar?
Gnnn

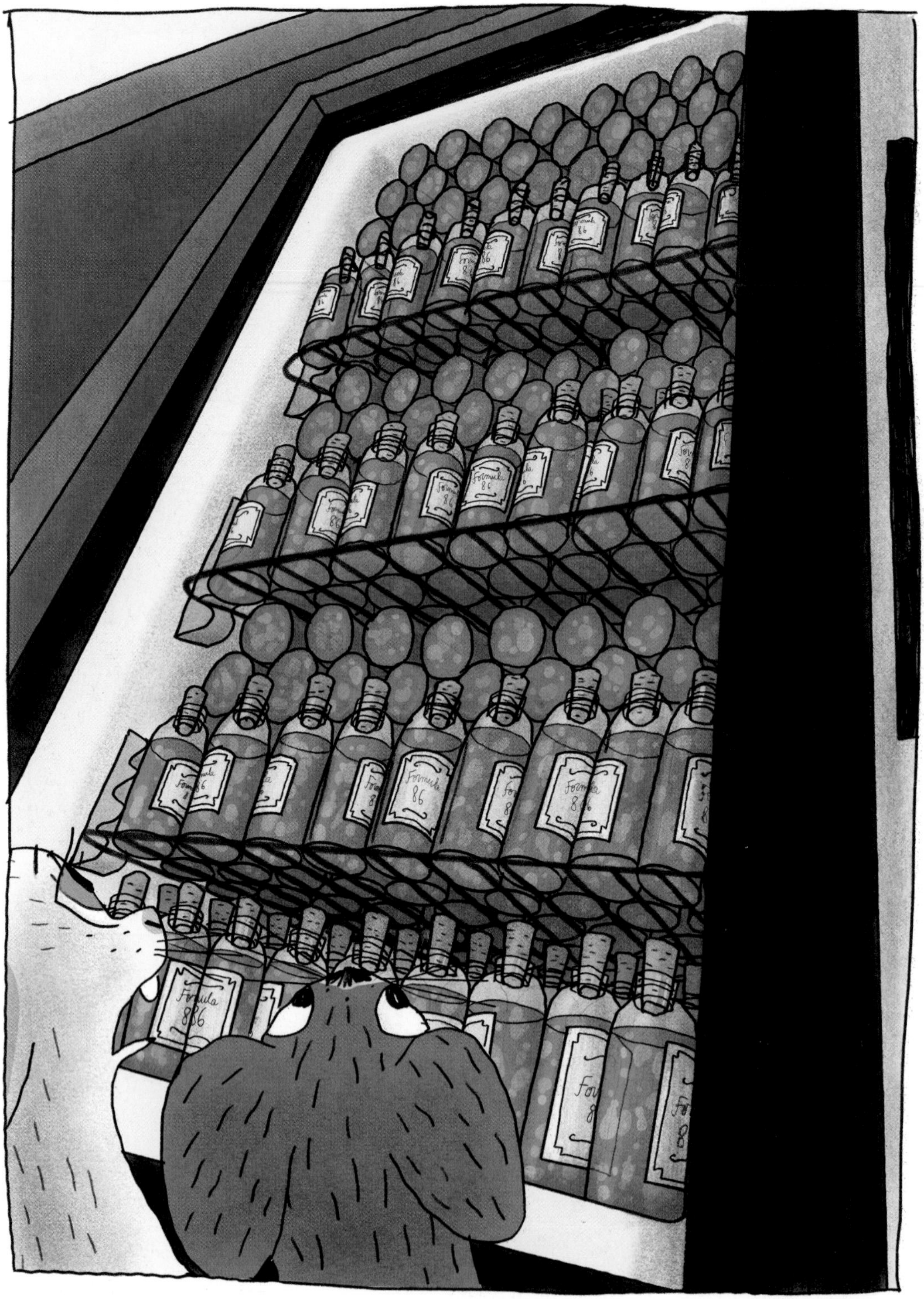
Formula 86

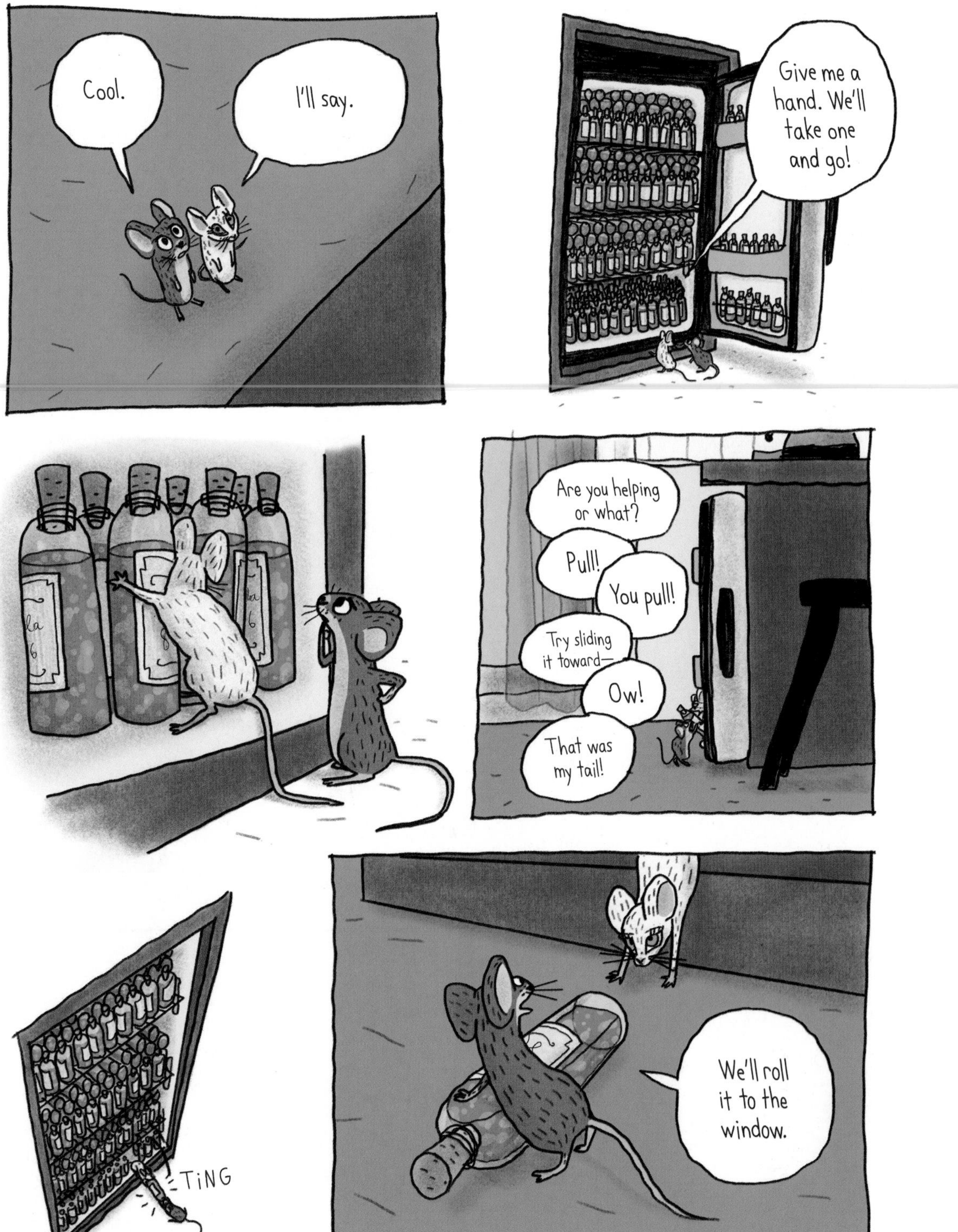
Cool.
I'll say.
Give me a hand. We'll take one and go!
Are you helping or what?
Pull!
You pull!
Try sliding it toward—
Ow!
That was my tail!
TiNG
We'll roll it to the window.

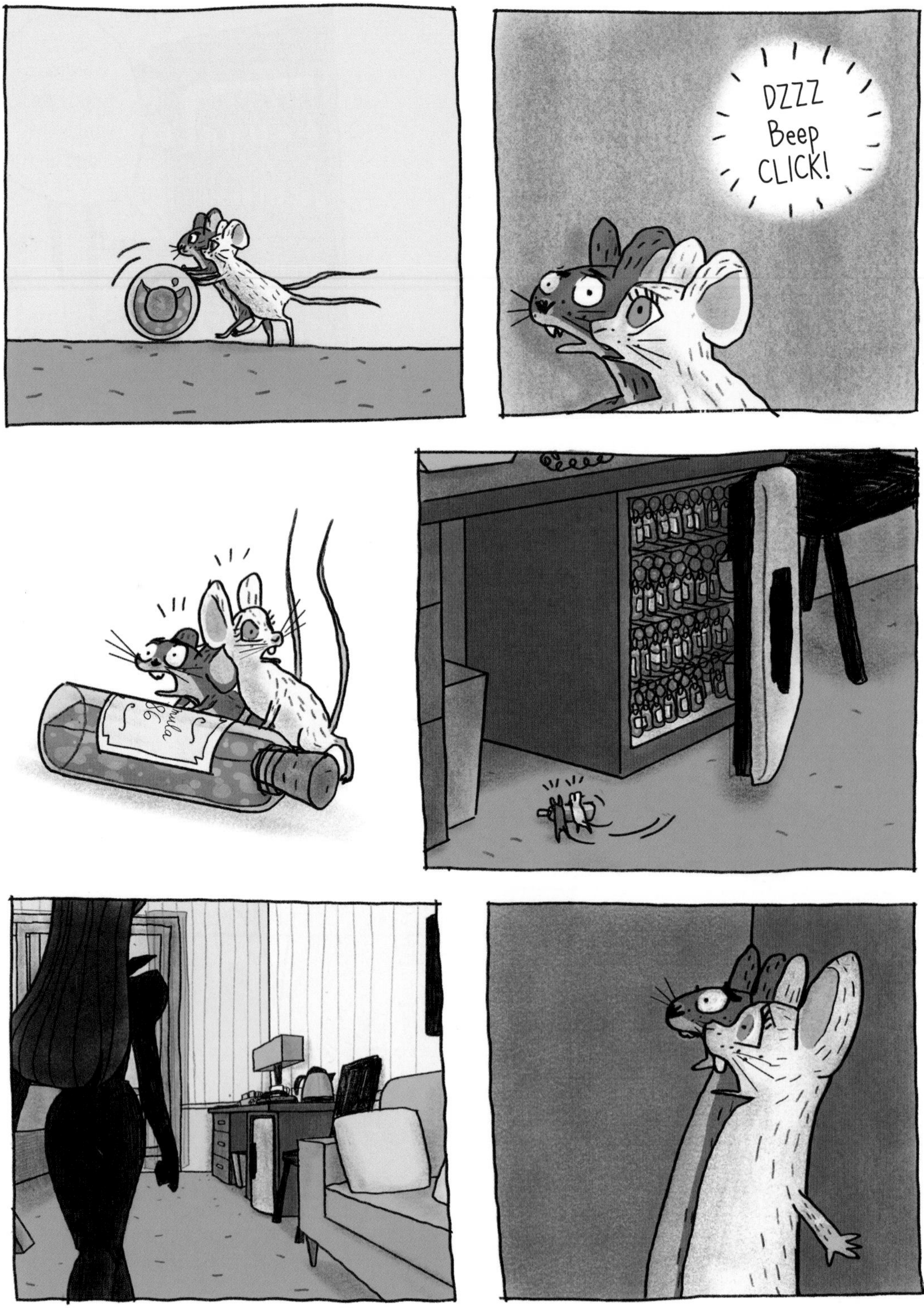
DZZZ
Beep
CLICK!

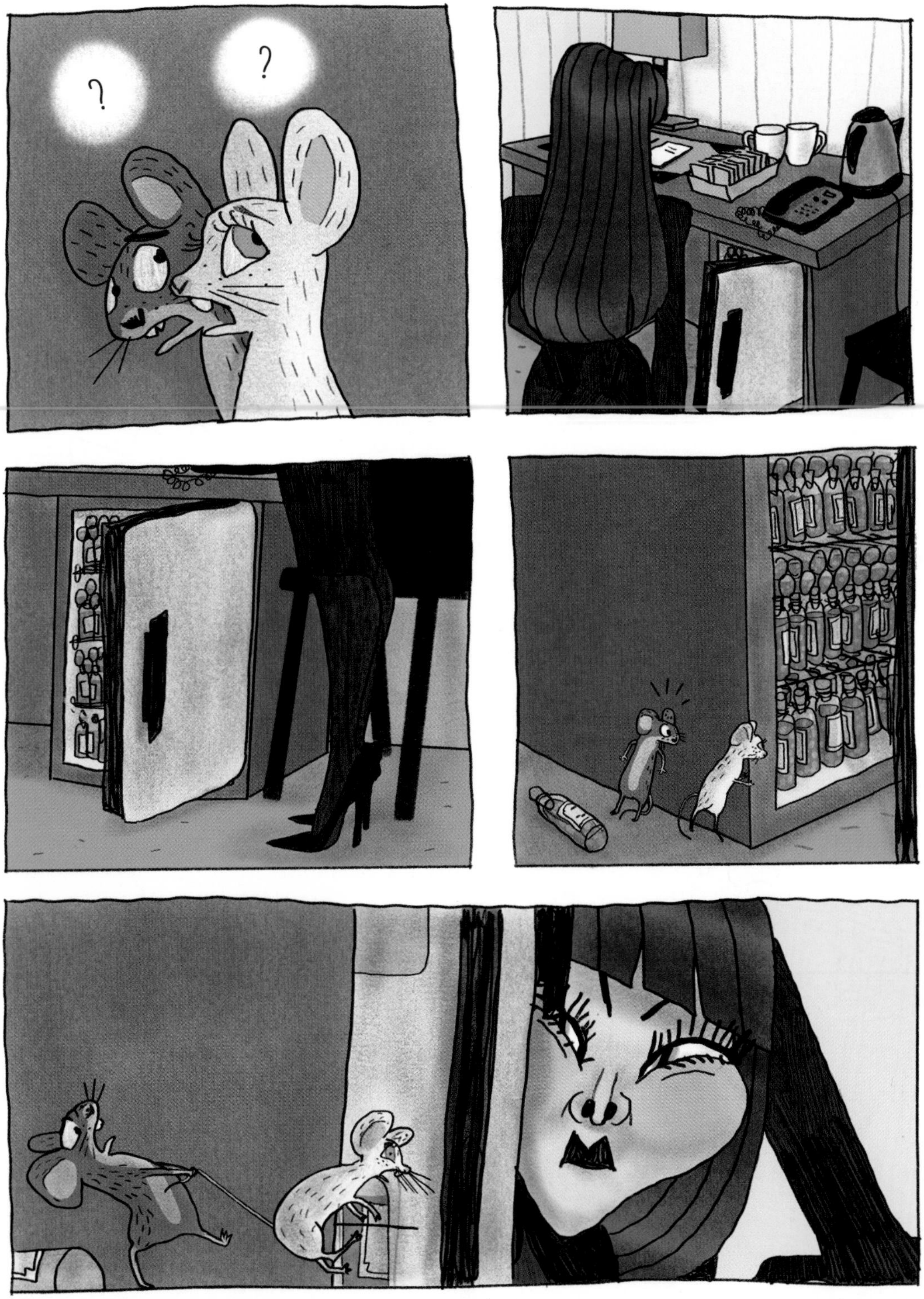
?
?

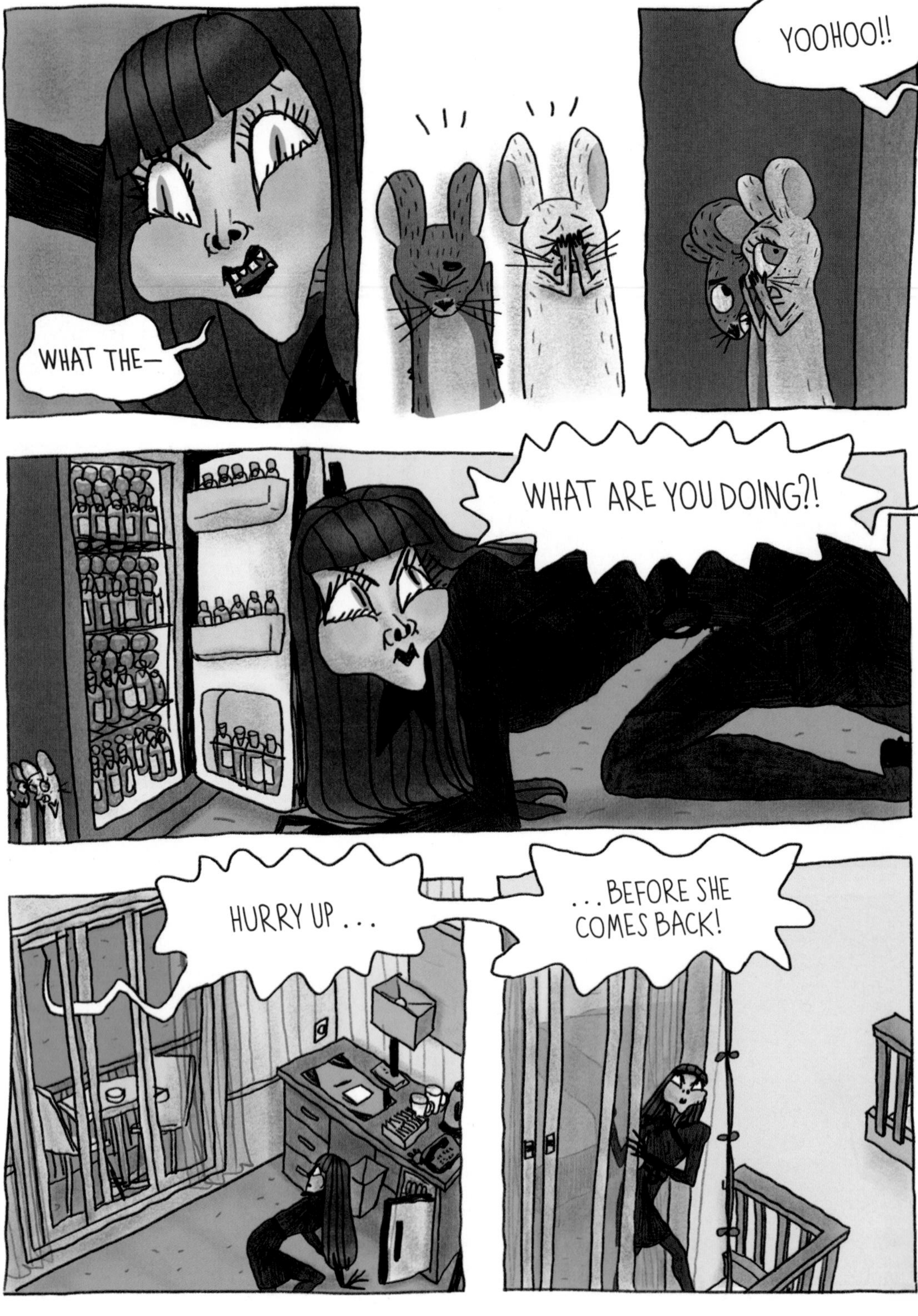
WHAT THE—
YOOHOO!!
WHAT ARE YOU DOING?!
HURRY UP . . .
. . . BEFORE SHE COMES BACK!

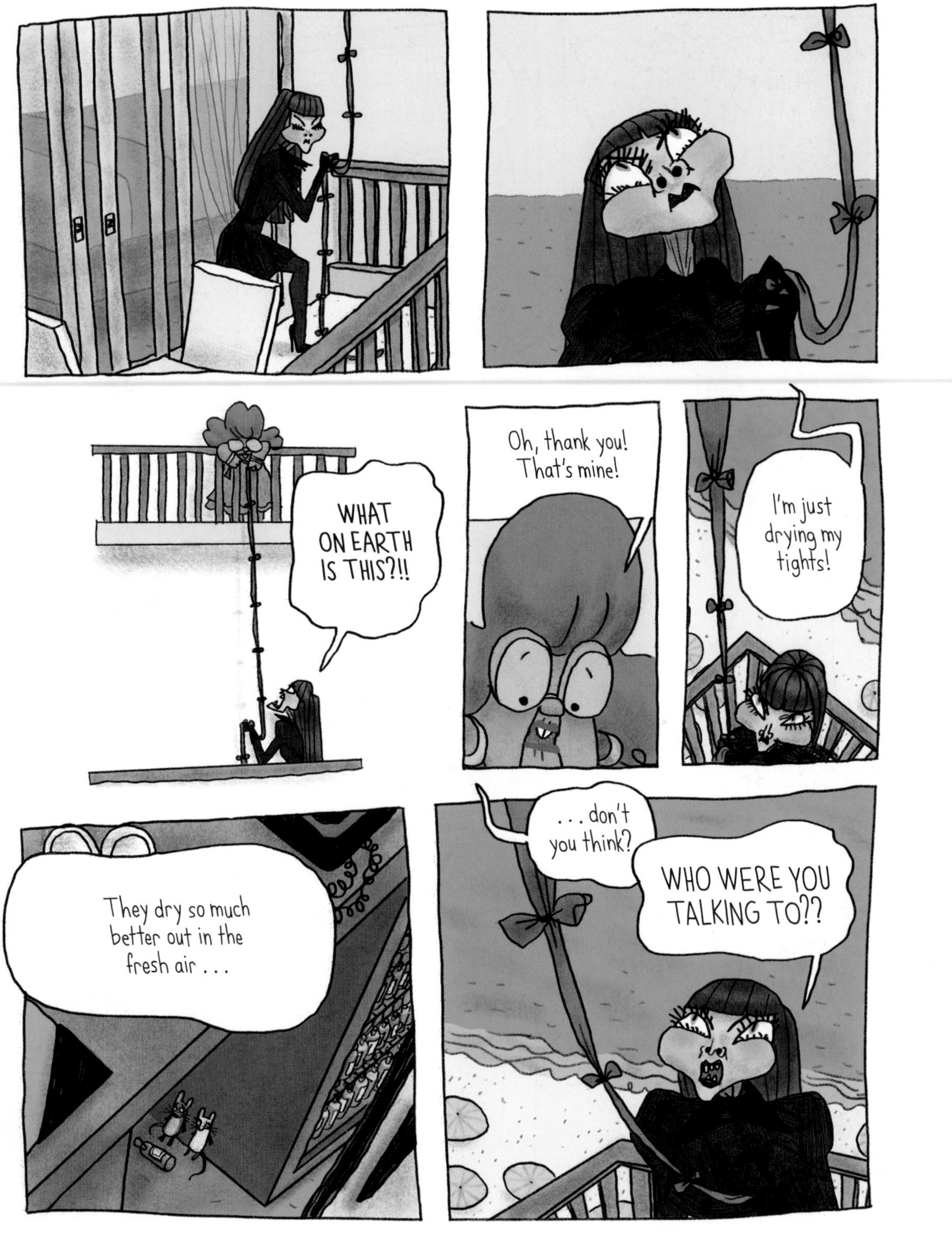
WHAT ON EARTH IS THIS?!!
Oh, thank you! That's mine!
I'm just drying my tights!
They dry so much better out in the fresh air . . .
. . . don't you think?
WHO WERE YOU TALKING TO??

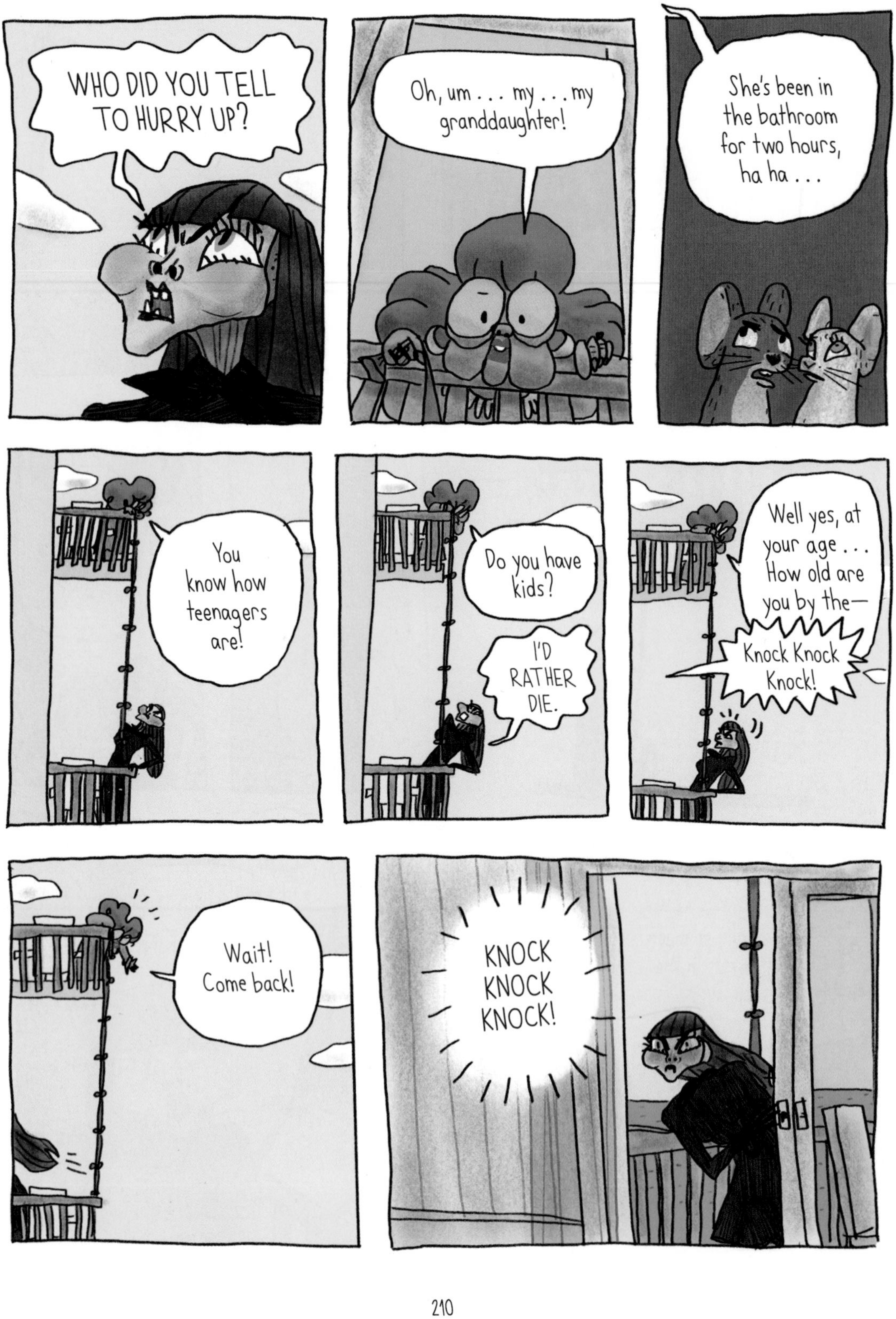
WHO DID YOU TELL TO HURRY UP?
Oh, um . . . my . . . my granddaughter!
She's been in the bathroom for two hours, ha ha . . .
You know how teenagers are!
Do you have kids?
I'D RATHER DIE.
Well yes, at your age . . . How old are you by the—
Knock Knock Knock!
Wait! Come back!
KNOCK KNOCK KNOCK!

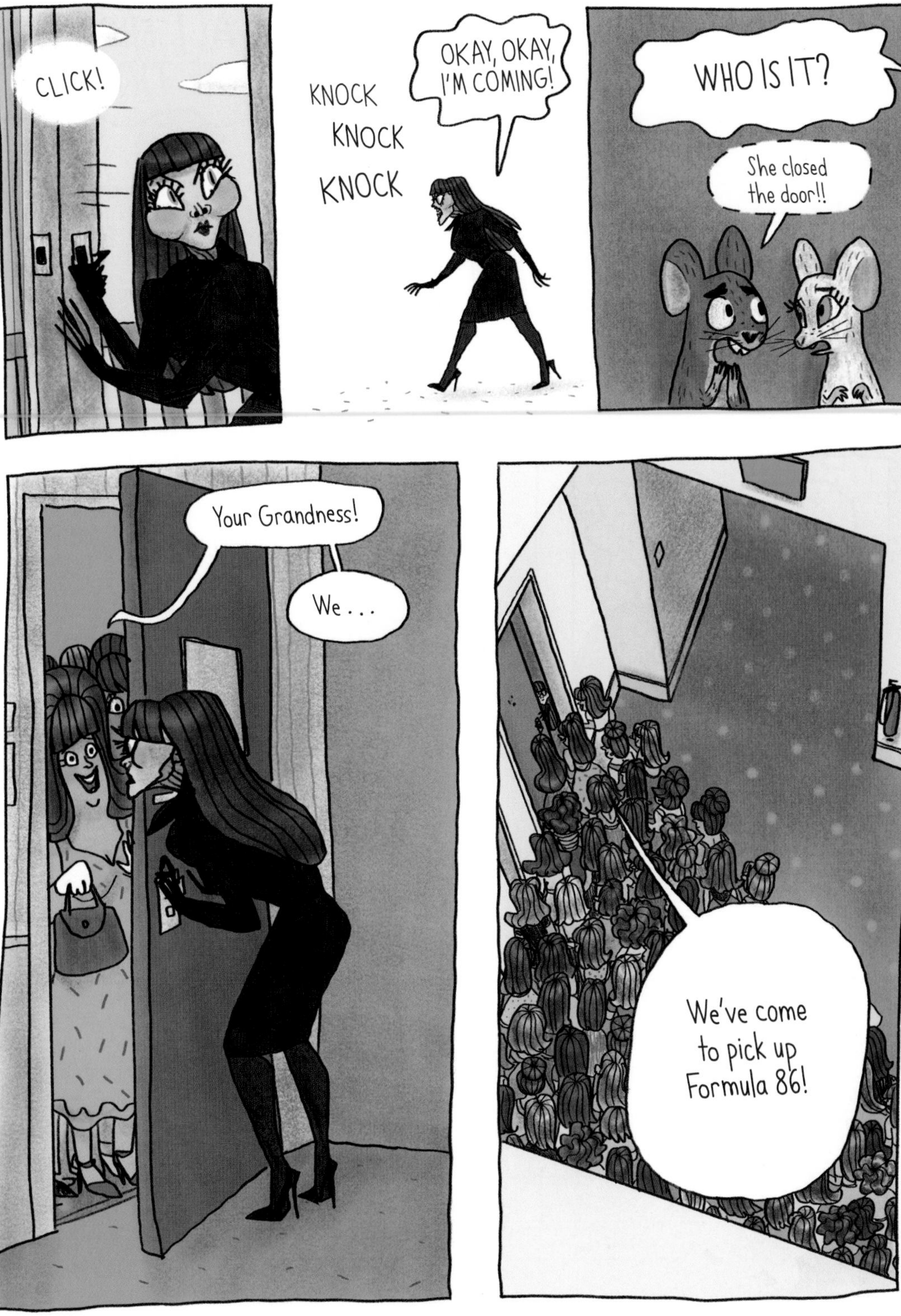
CLICK!
KNOCK
KNOCK
KNOCK
OKAY, OKAY, I'M COMING!
WHO IS IT?
She closed the door!!
Your Grandness!
We . . .
We've come to pick up Formula 86!

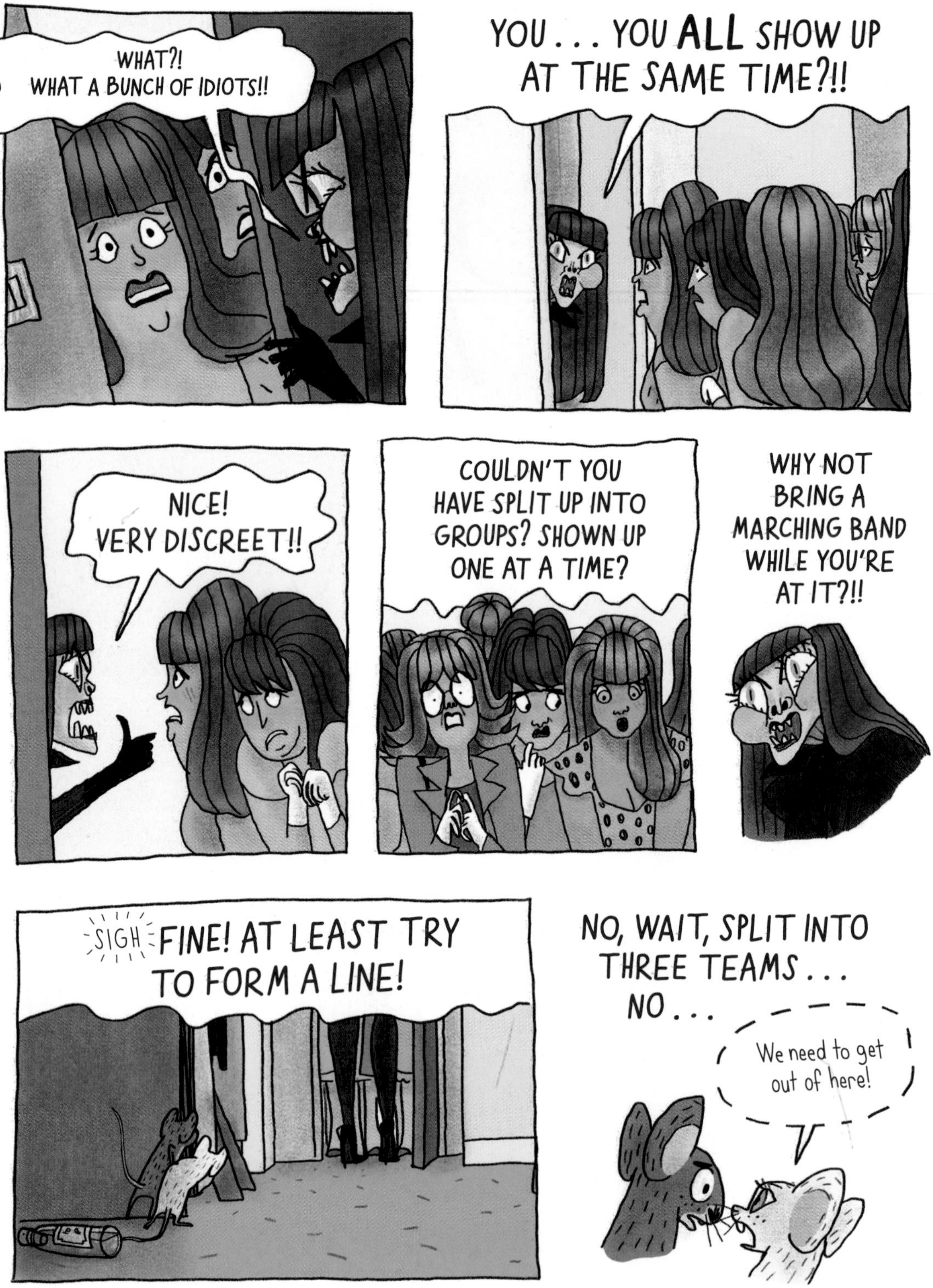
WHAT?! WHAT A BUNCH OF IDIOTS!!
YOU . . . YOU ALL SHOW UP AT THE SAME TIME?!!
NICE! VERY DISCREET!!
COULDN'T YOU HAVE SPLIT UP INTO GROUPS? SHOWN UP ONE AT A TIME?
WHY NOT BRING A MARCHING BAND WHILE YOU'RE AT IT?!!
SIGH
FINE! AT LEAST TRY TO FORM A LINE!
NO, WAIT, SPLIT INTO THREE TEAMS . . . NO . . .
We need to get out of here!

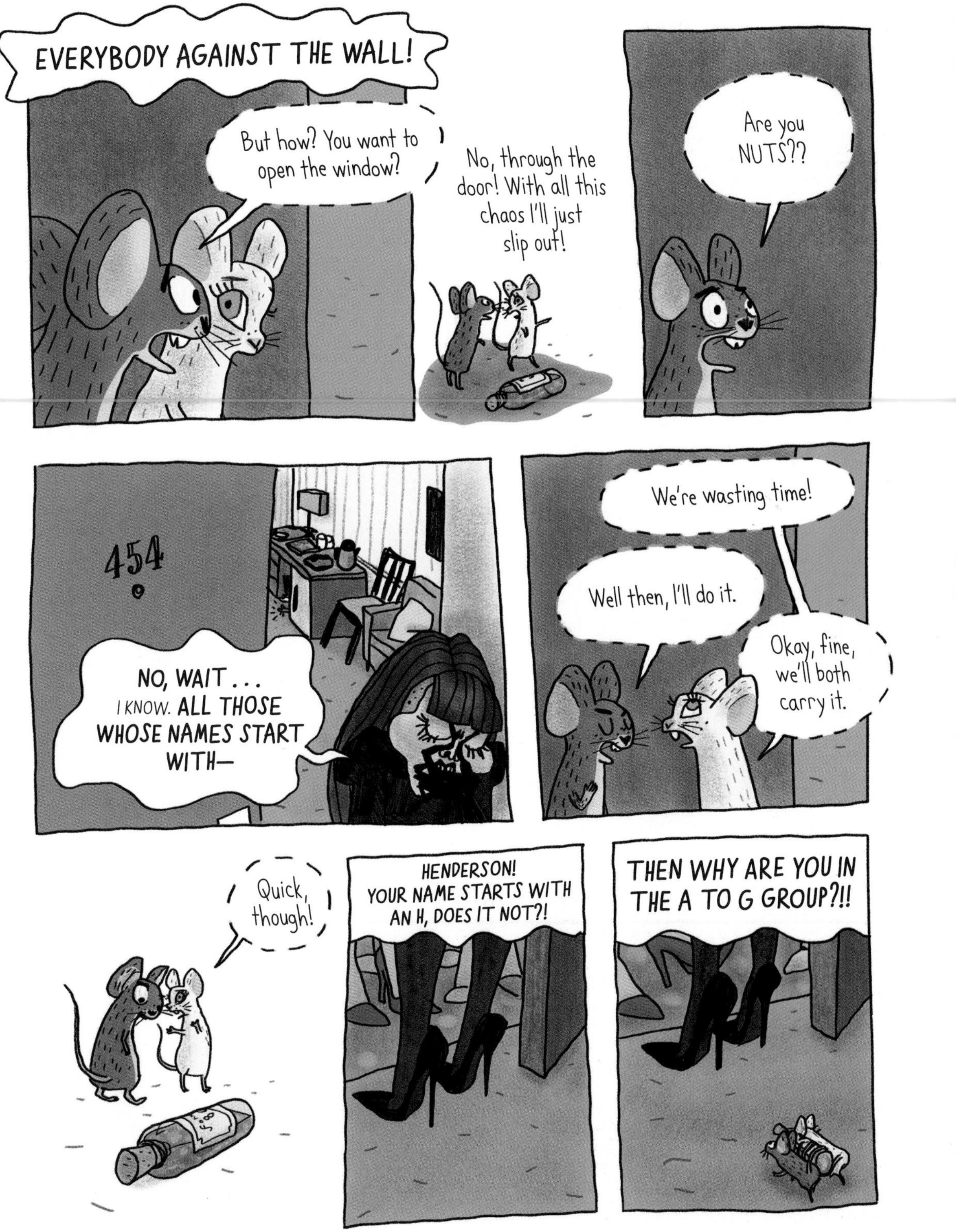

EVERYBODY AGAINST THE WALL!
But how? You want to open the window?
No, through the door! With all this chaos I'll just slip out!
Are you NUTS??
454
NO, WAIT . . . I KNOW. ALL THOSE WHOSE NAMES START WITH—
We're wasting time!
Well then, I'll do it.
Okay, fine, we'll both carry it.
Quick, though!
HENDERSON! YOUR NAME STARTS WITH AN H, DOES IT NOT?!
THEN WHY ARE YOU IN THE A TO G GROUP?!!

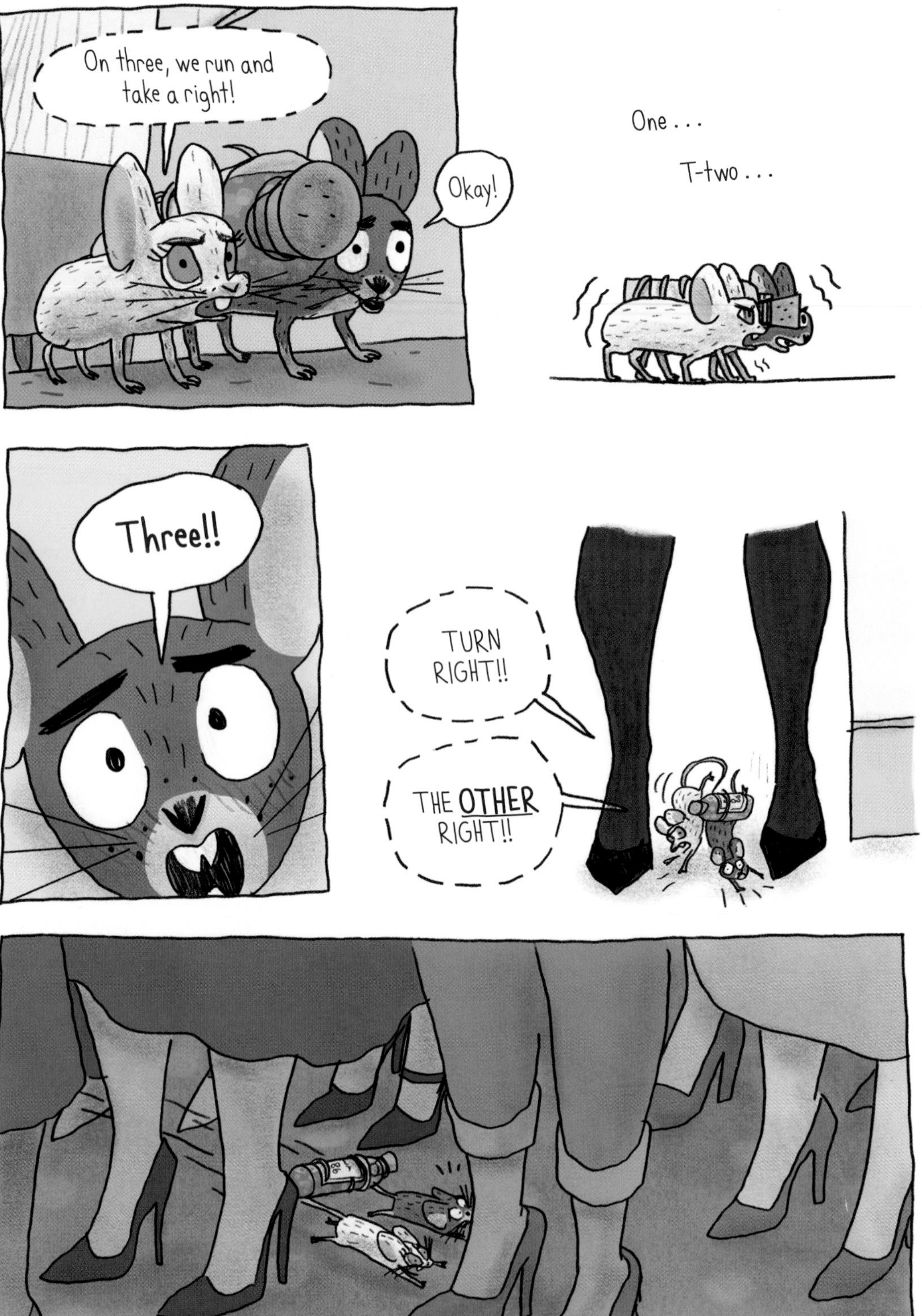
On three, we run and take a right!
Okay!
One . . .
T-two . . .
Three!!
TURN RIGHT!!
THE OTHER RIGHT!!

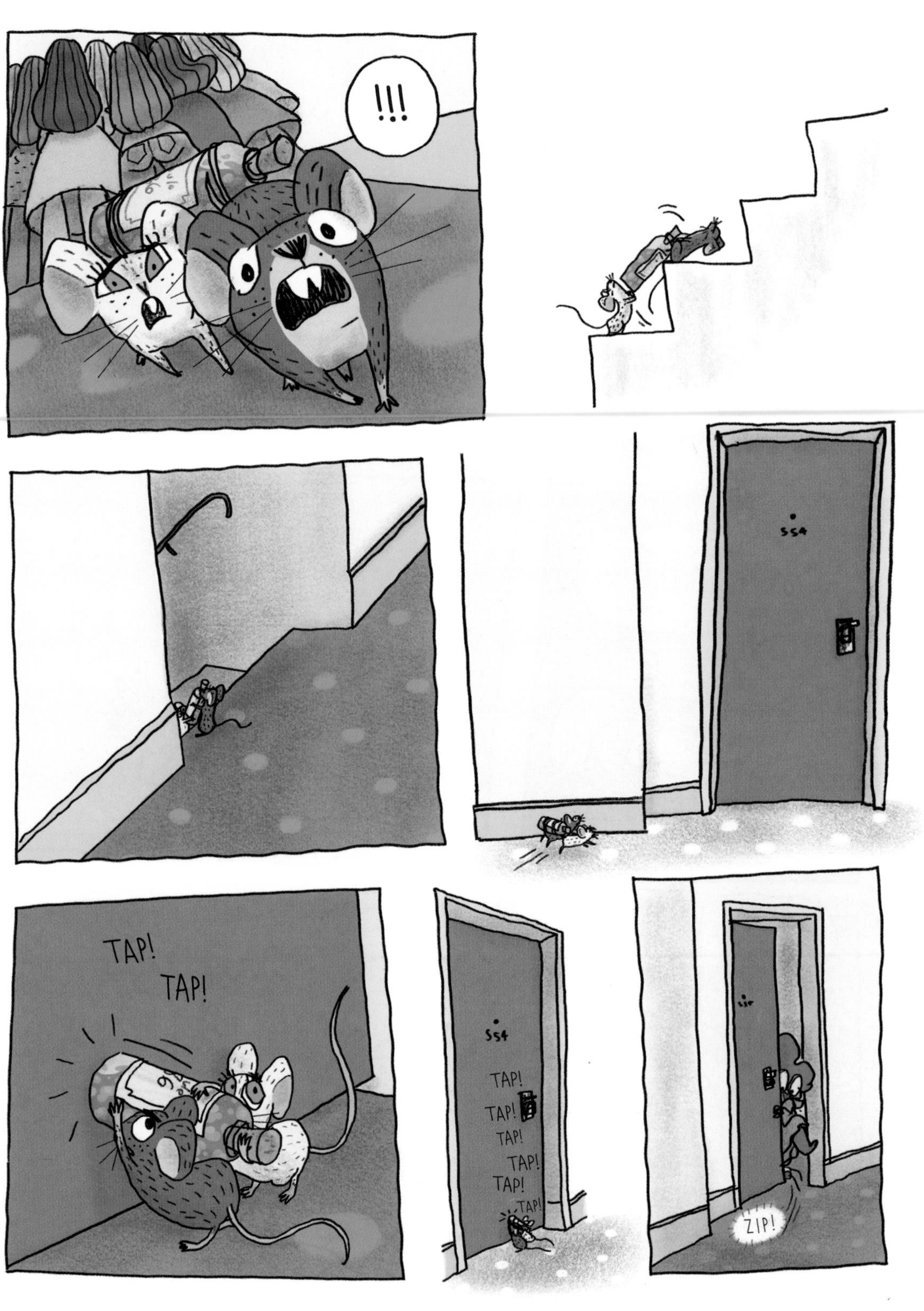
!!!
554
TAP!
TAP!
554
TAP!
TAP!
TAP!
TAP!
TAP!
TAP!
ZIP!

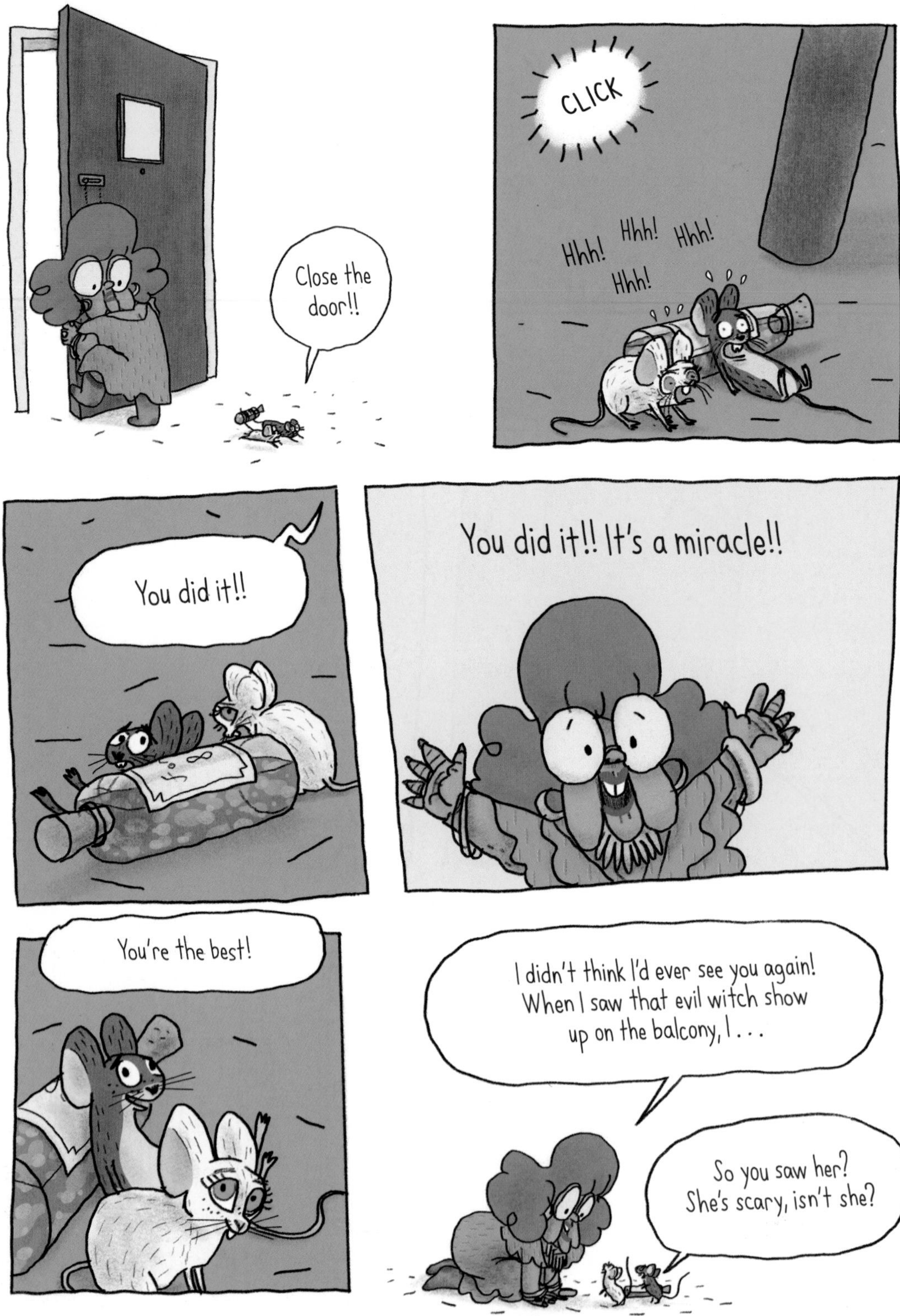

Close the door!!
CLICK
Hhh! Hhh! Hhh!
Hhh!
You did it!!
You did it!! It's a miracle!!
You're the best!
I didn't think I'd ever see you again! When I saw that evil witch show up on the balcony, I . . .
So you saw her? She's scary, isn't she?

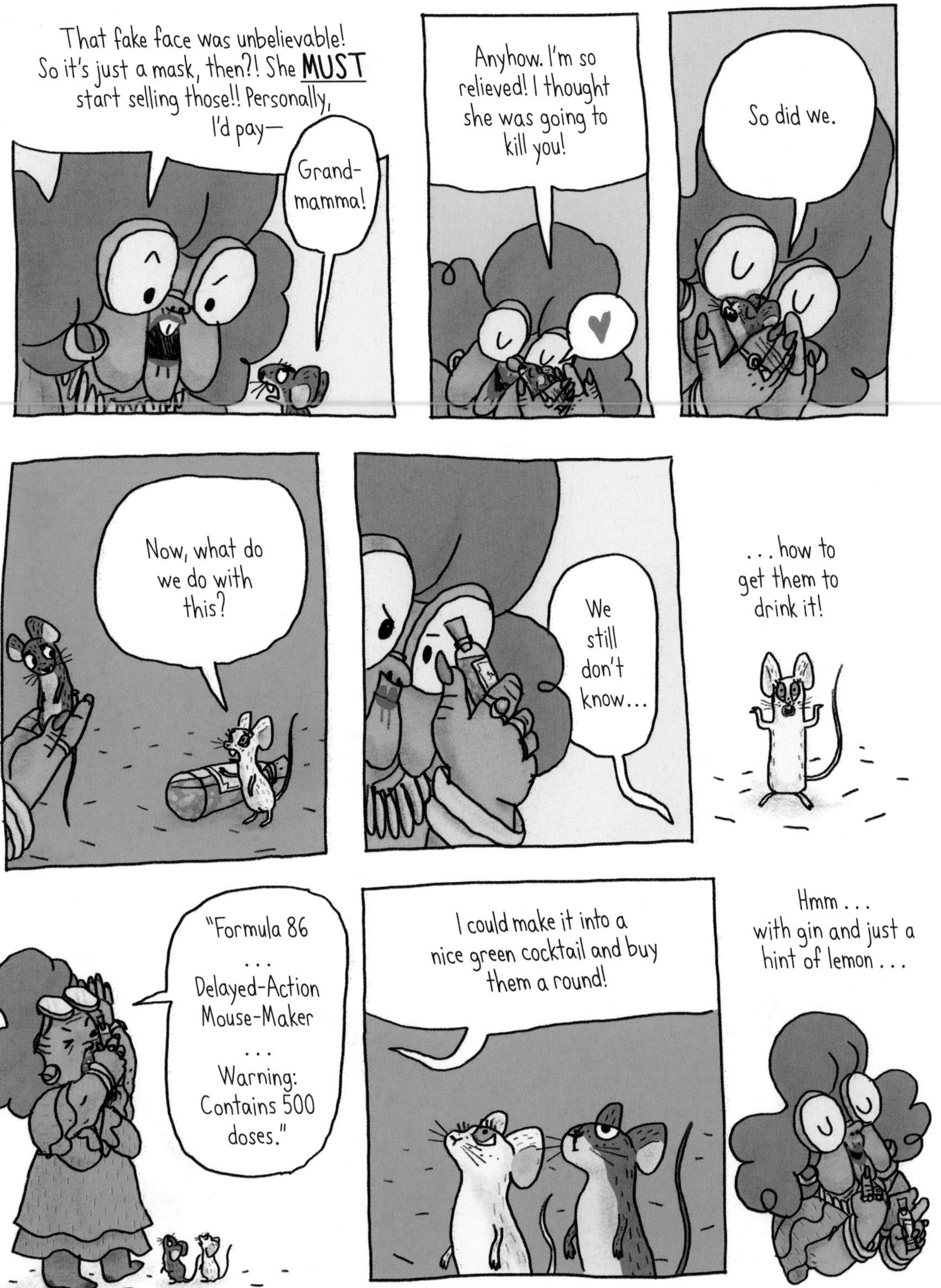

That fake face was unbelievable! So it's just a mask, then?! She MUST start selling those!! Personally, I'd pay—
Grand-mamma!
Anyhow. I'm so relieved! I thought she was going to kill you!
So did we.
Now, what do we do with this?
We still don't know...
. . . how to get them to drink it!
"Formula 86 . . . Delayed-Action Mouse-Maker . . . Warning: Contains 500 doses."
I could make it into a nice green cocktail and buy them a round!
Hmm . . . with gin and just a hint of lemon . . .

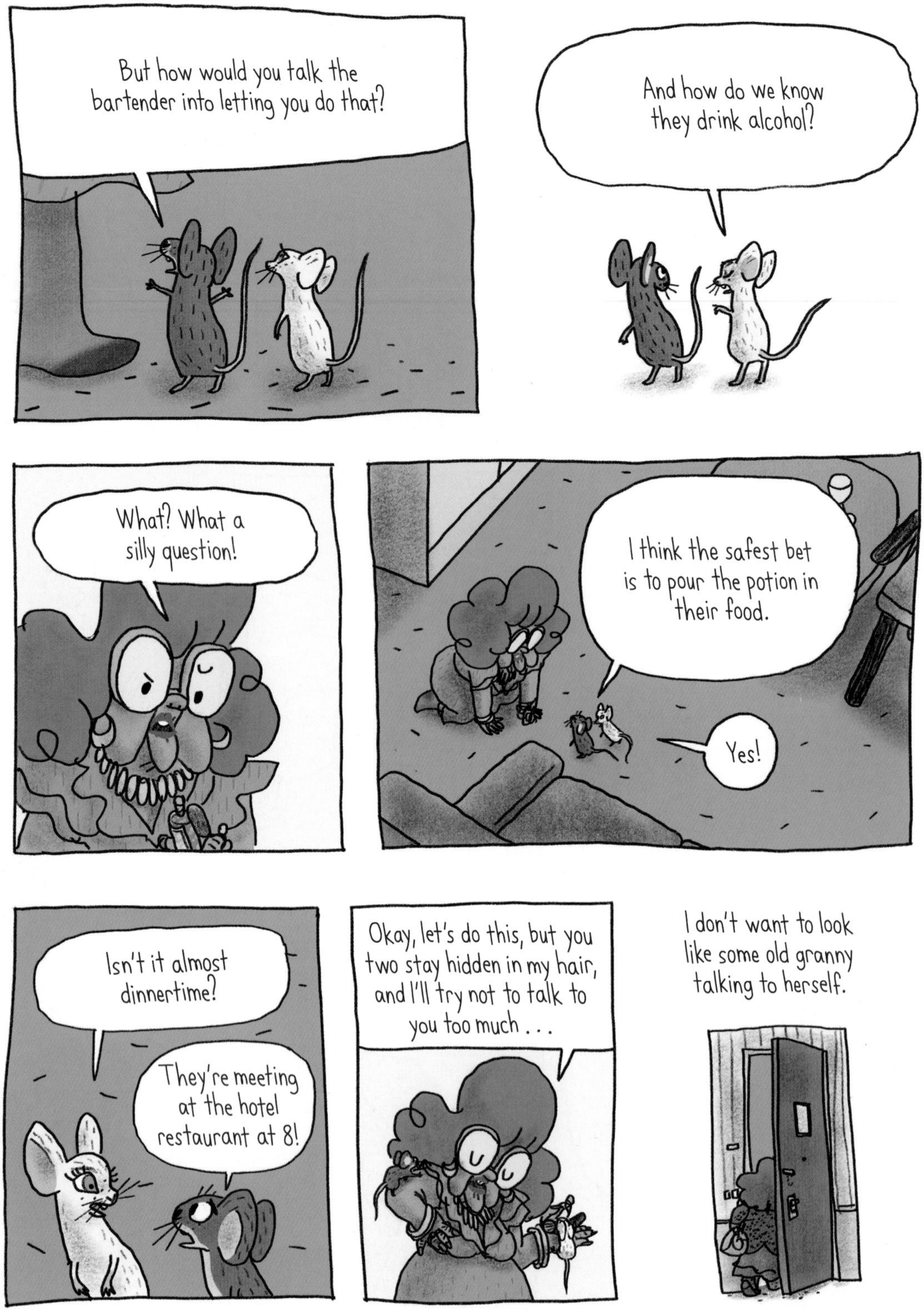
But how would you talk the bartender into letting you do that?
And how do we know they drink alcohol?
What? What a silly question!
I think the safest bet is to pour the potion in their food.
Yes!
Isn't it almost dinnertime?
They're meeting at the hotel restaurant at 8!
Okay, let's do this, but you two stay hidden in my hair, and I'll try not to talk to you too much . . .
I don't want to look like some old granny talking to herself.

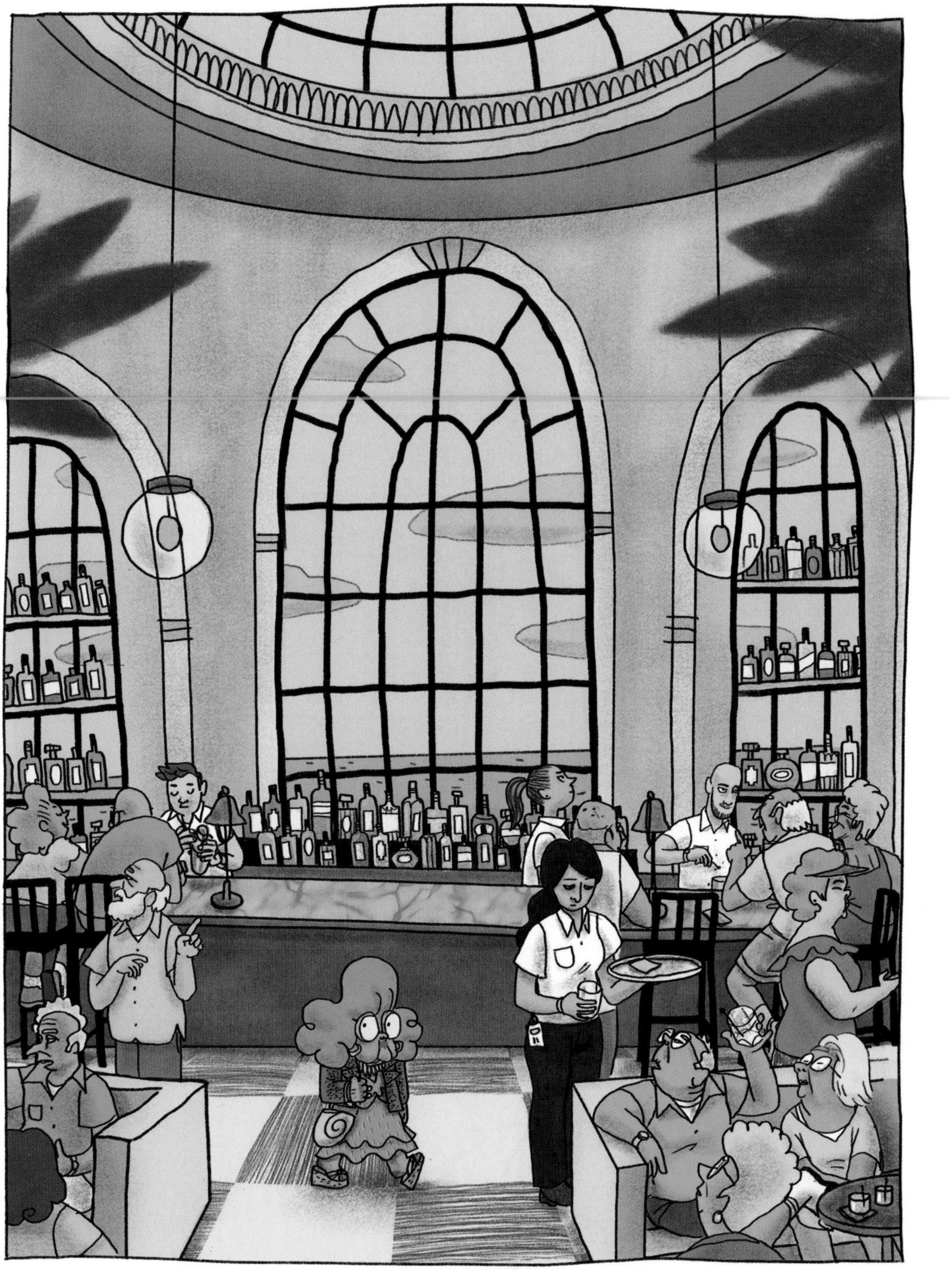

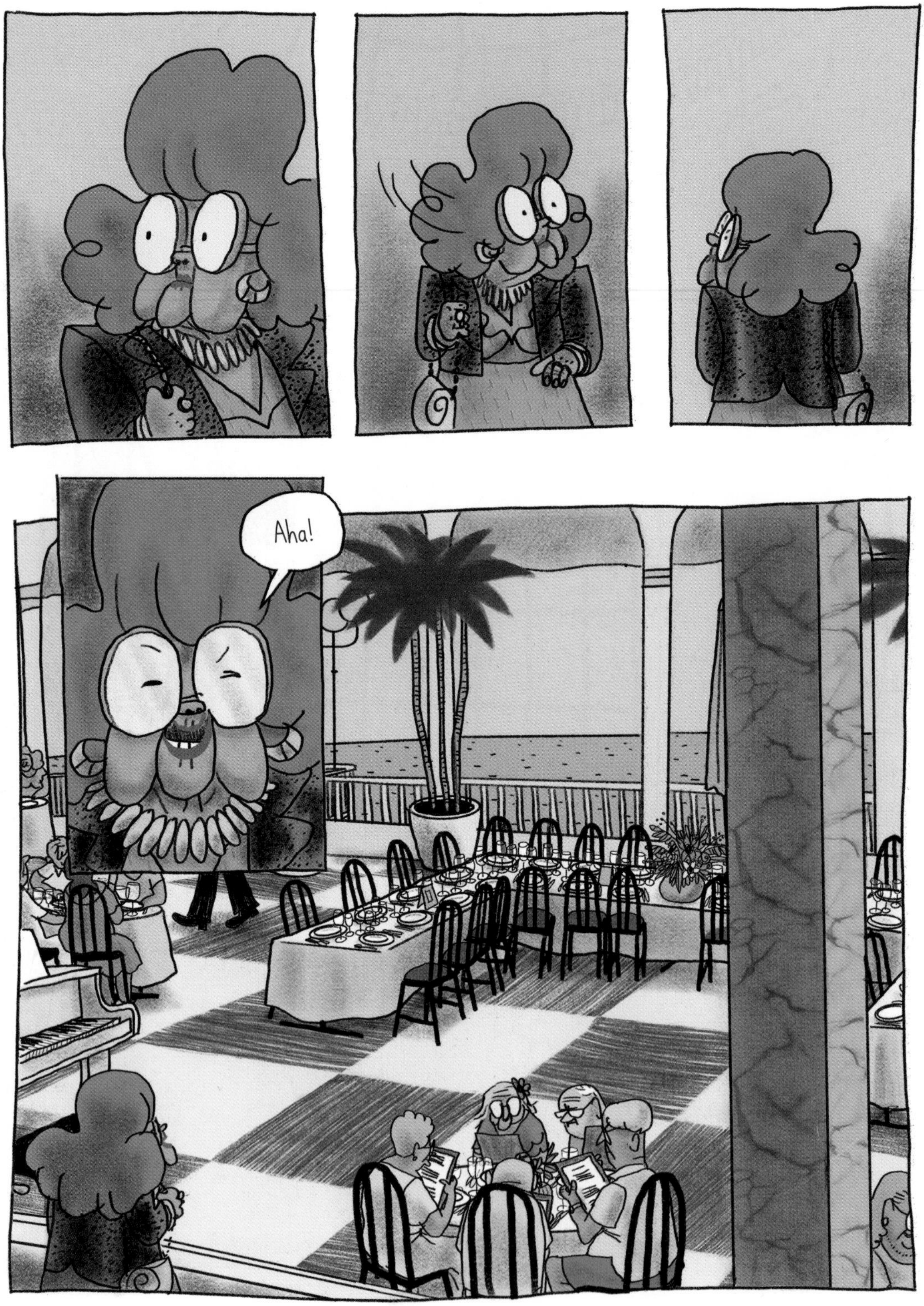
Aha!

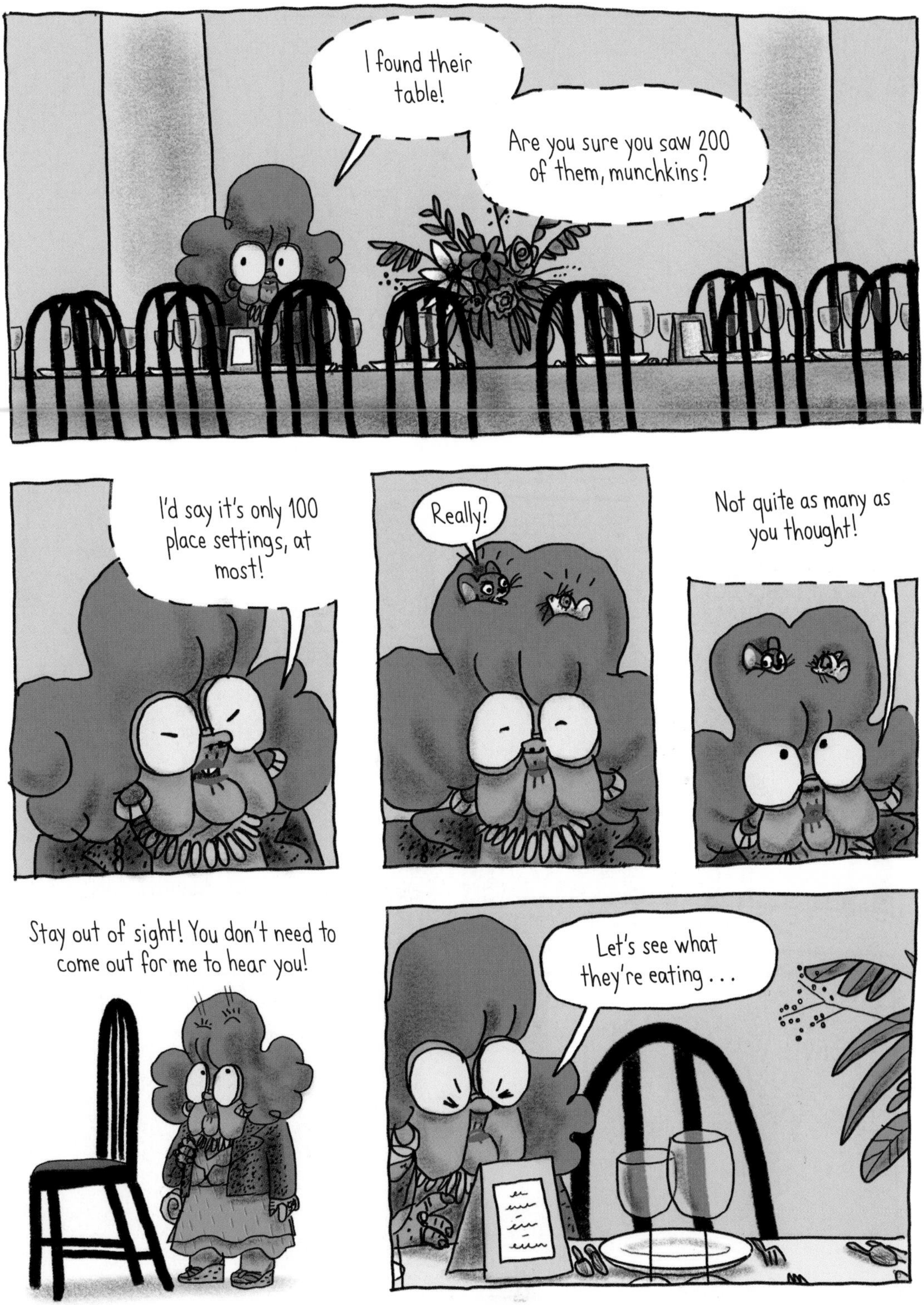
I found their table!
Are you sure you saw 200 of them, munchkins?
I'd say it's only 100 place settings, at most!
Really?
Not quite as many as you thought!
Stay out of sight! You don't need to come out for me to hear you!
Let's see what they're eating . . .

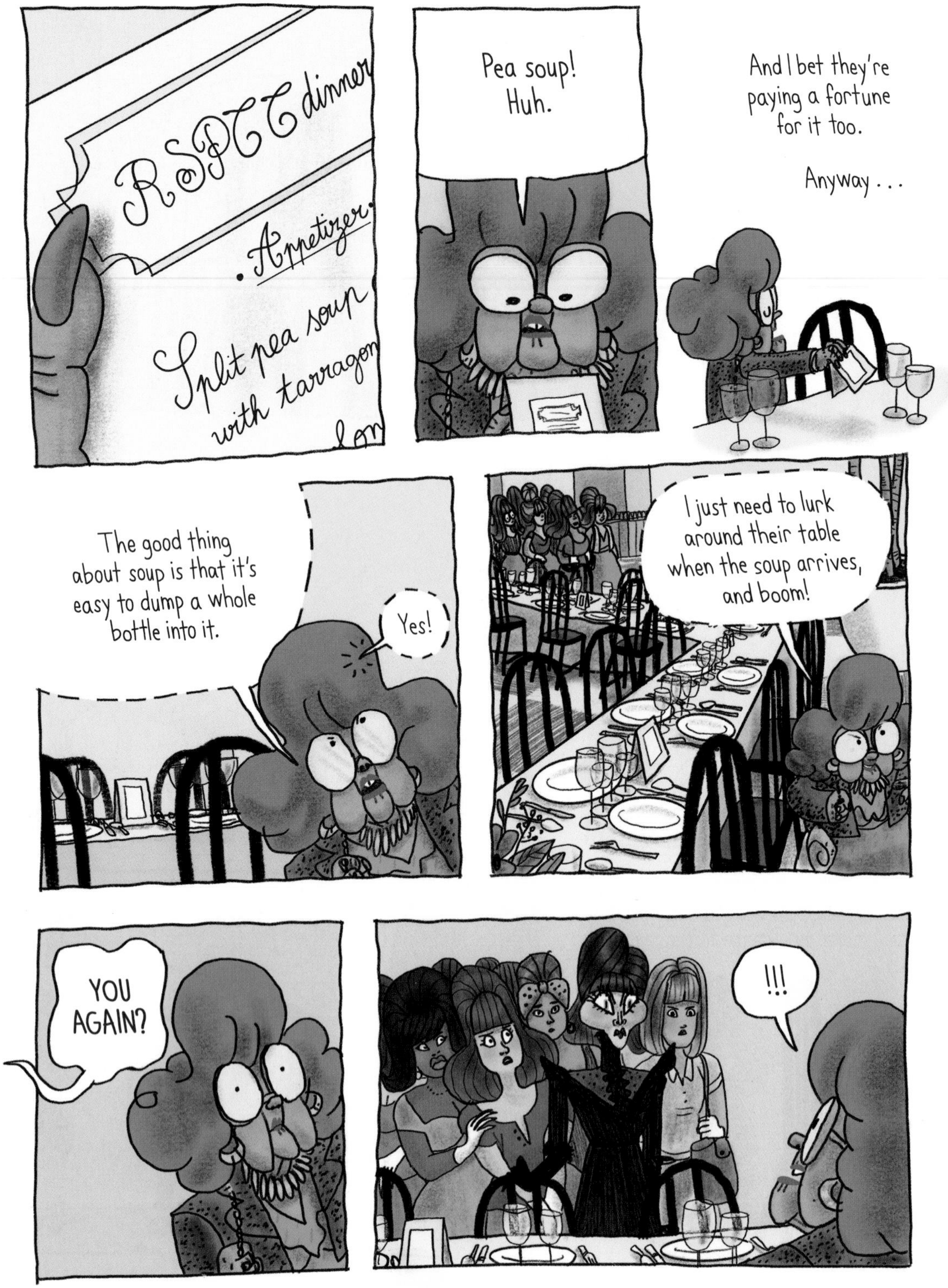
RSPCC dinner
Appetizer
Split pea soup with tarragon
Pea soup! Huh.
And I bet they're paying a fortune for it too.
Anyway . . .
The good thing about soup is that it's easy to dump a whole bottle into it.
Yes!
I just need to lurk around their table when the soup arrives, and boom!
YOU AGAIN?
!!!

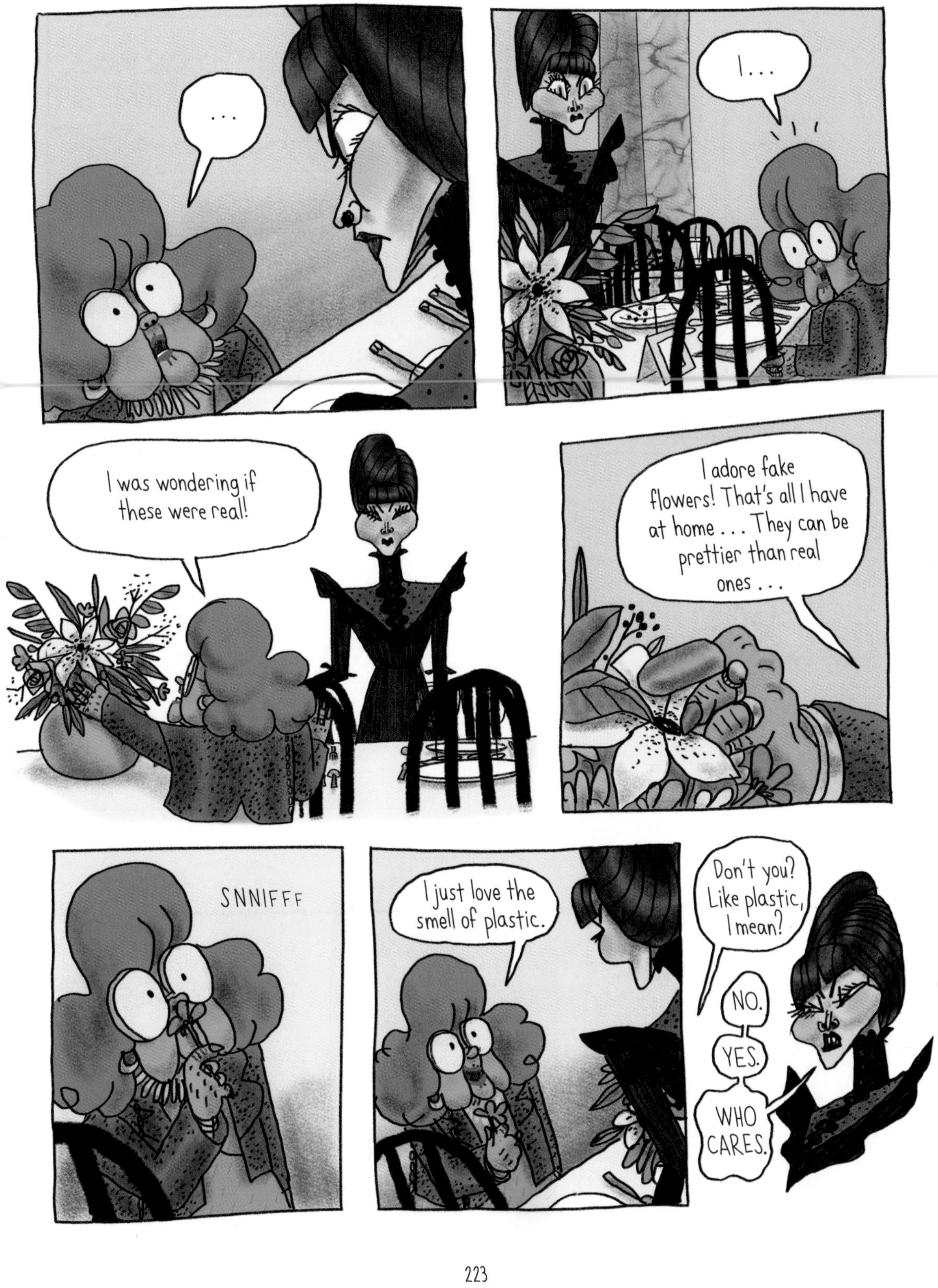
. . .
I . . .
I was wondering if these were real!
I adore fake flowers! That's all I have at home . . . They can be prettier than real ones . . .
SNNIFFF
I just love the smell of plastic.
Don't you? Like plastic, I mean?
NO.
YES.
WHO CARES.

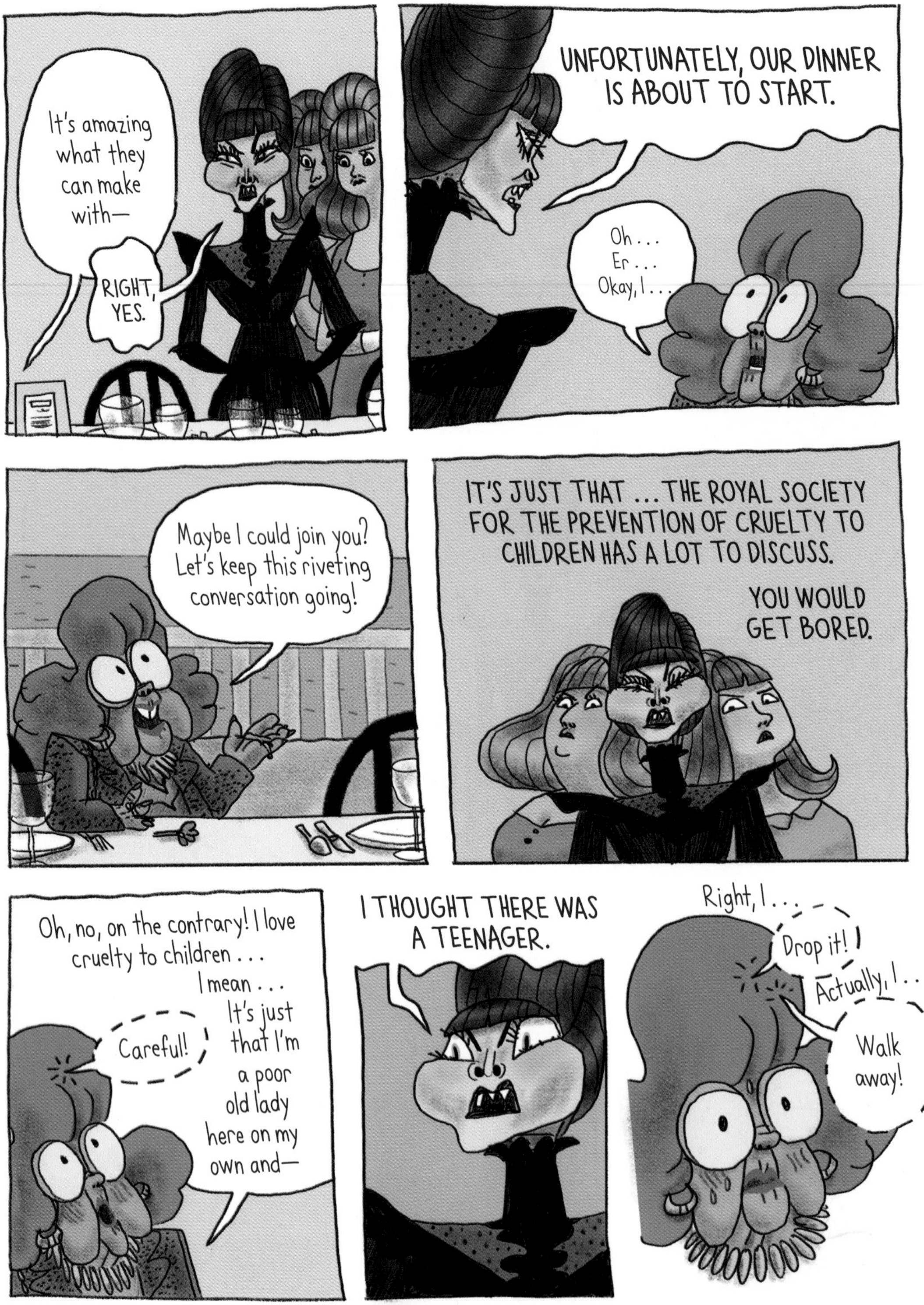
It's amazing what they can make with—
RIGHT, YES.
UNFORTUNATELY, OUR DINNER IS ABOUT TO START.
Oh . . . Er . . . Okay, I . . .
Maybe I could join you? Let's keep this riveting conversation going!
IT'S JUST THAT . . . THE ROYAL SOCIETY FOR THE PREVENTION OF CRUELTY TO CHILDREN HAS A LOT TO DISCUSS.
YOU WOULD GET BORED.
Oh, no, on the contrary! I love cruelty to children . . .
I mean . . .
Careful!
It's just that I'm a poor old lady here on my own and—
I THOUGHT THERE WAS A TEENAGER.
Right, I . . .
Drop it!
Actually, I . . .
Walk away!

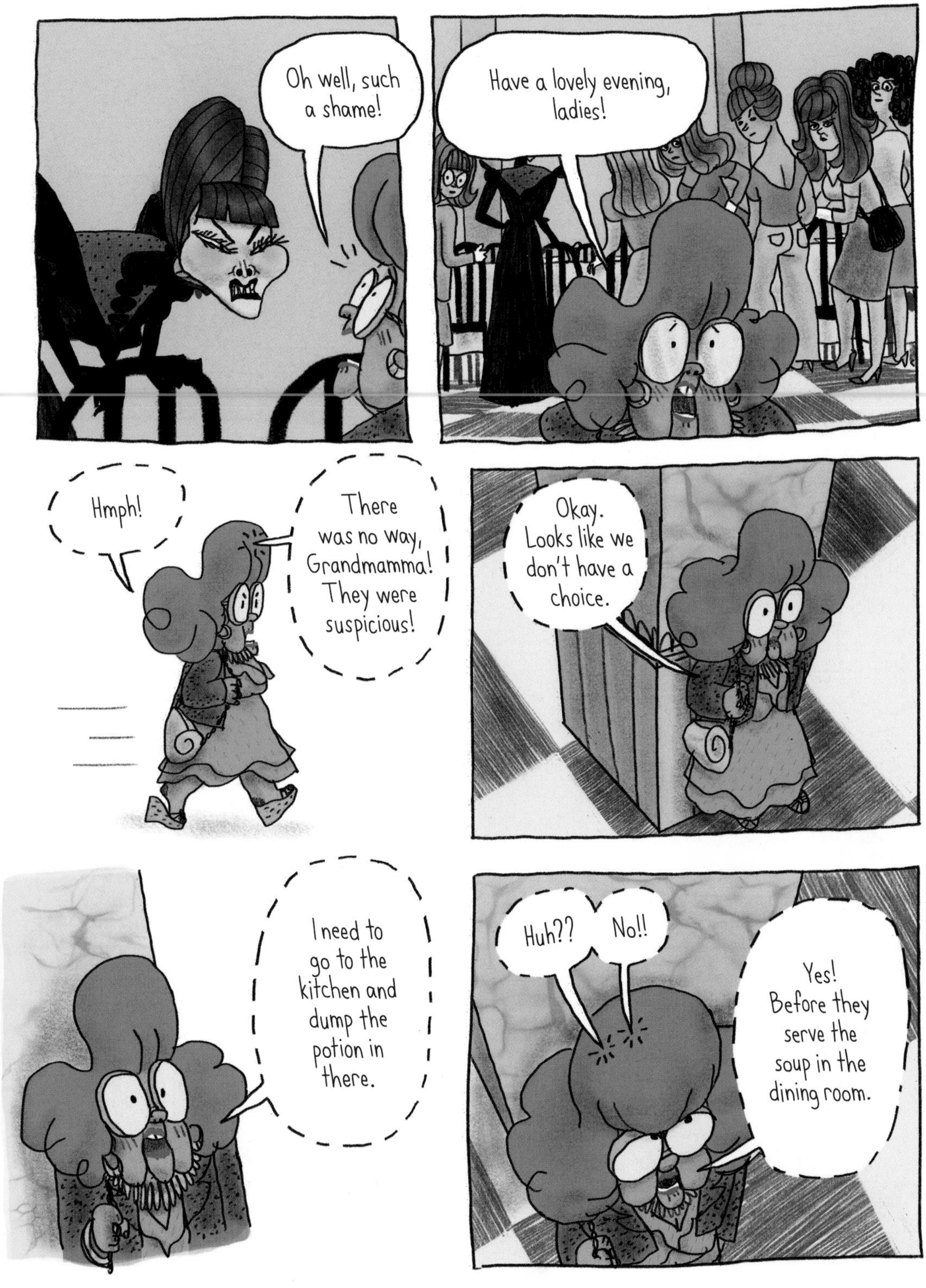
Oh well, such a shame!
Have a lovely evening, ladies!
Hmph!
There was no way, Grandmamma! They were suspicious!
Okay. Looks like we don't have a choice.
I need to go to the kitchen and dump the potion in there.
Huh??
No!!
Yes! Before they serve the soup in the dining room.

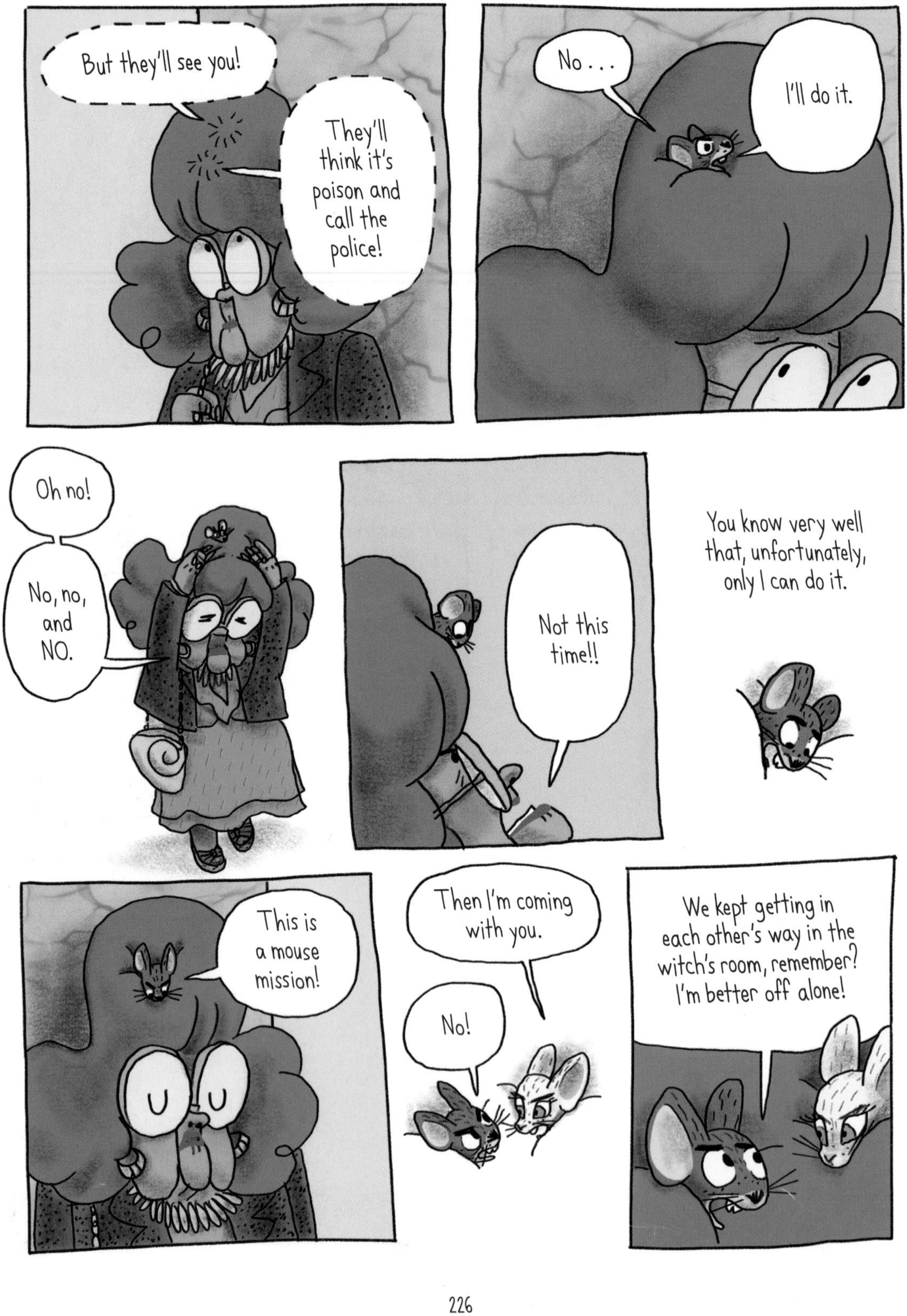
But they'll see you!
They'll think it's poison and call the police!
No . . .
I'll do it.
Oh no!
No, no, and NO.
Not this time!!
You know very well that, unfortunately, only I can do it.
This is a mouse mission!
Then I'm coming with you.
No!
We kept getting in each other's way in the witch's room, remember? I'm better off alone!

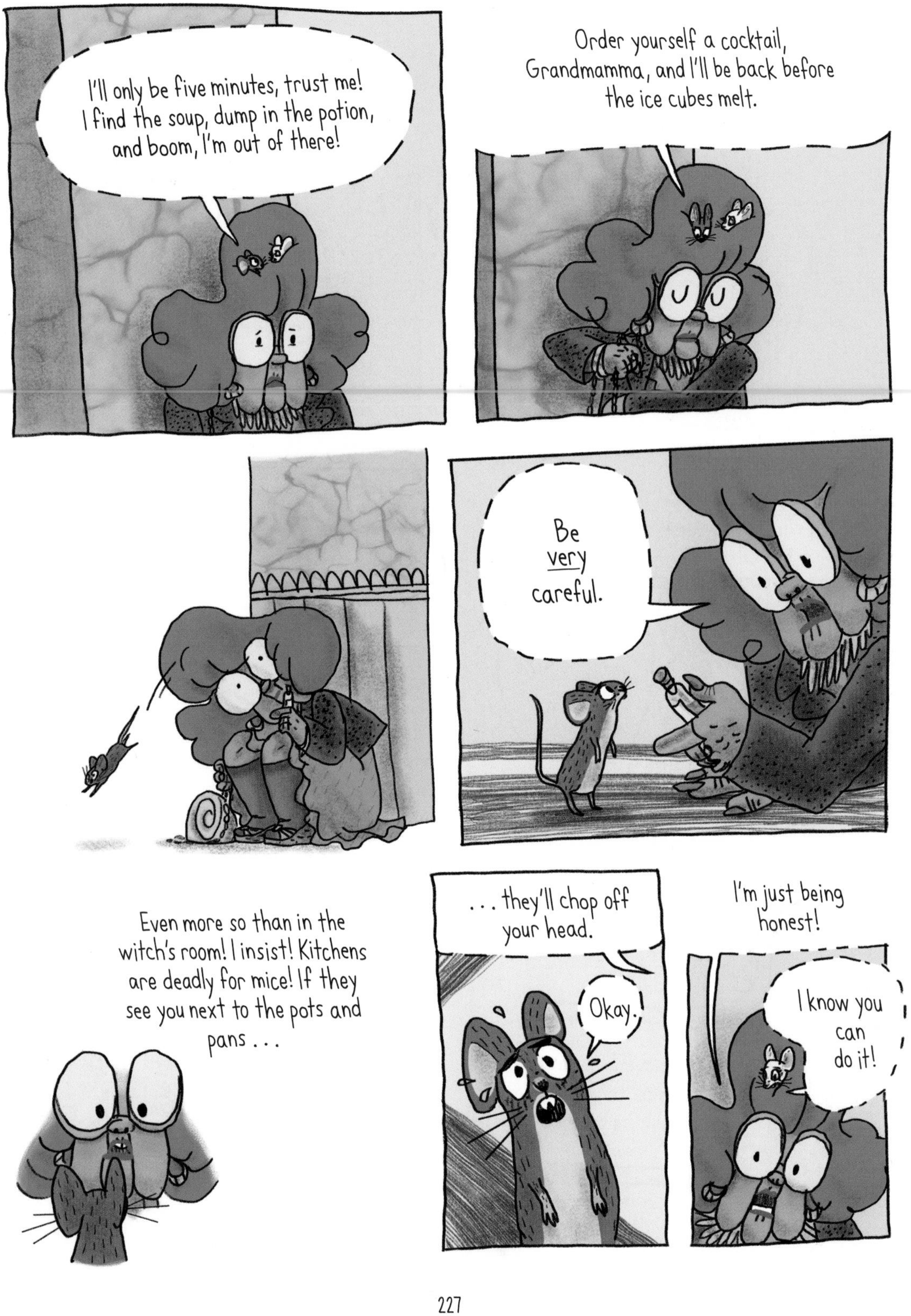
I'll only be five minutes, trust me! I find the soup, dump in the potion, and boom, I'm out of there!
Order yourself a cocktail, Grandmamma, and I'll be back before the ice cubes melt.
Be very careful.
Even more so than in the witch's room! I insist! Kitchens are deadly for mice! If they see you next to the pots and pans . . .
. . . they'll chop off your head.
Okay.
I'm just being honest!
I know you can do it!

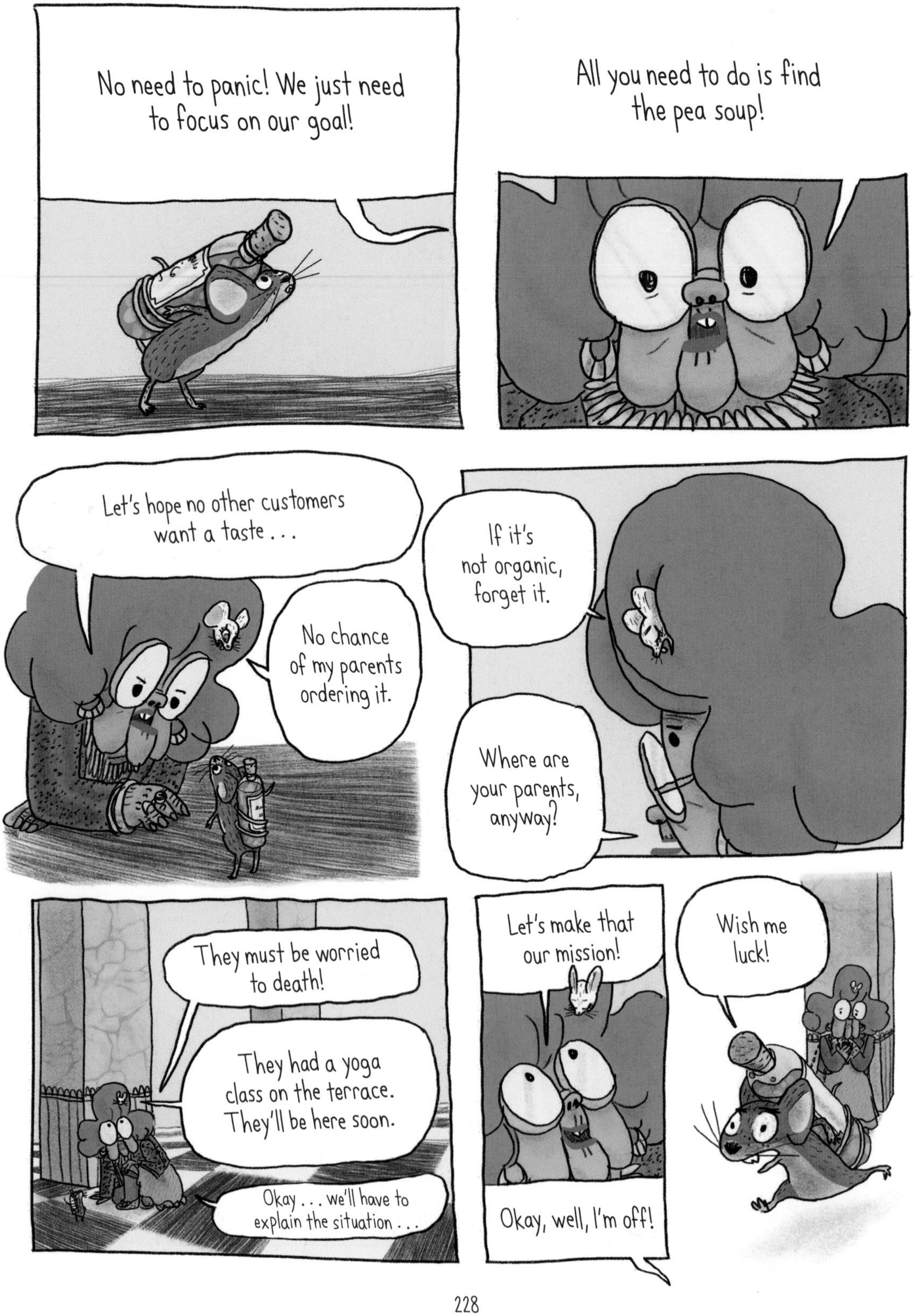
No need to panic! We just need to focus on our goal!
All you need to do is find the pea soup!
Let's hope no other customers want a taste . . .
No chance of my parents ordering it.
If it's not organic, forget it.
Where are your parents, anyway?
They must be worried to death!
They had a yoga class on the terrace. They'll be here soon.
Okay . . . we'll have to explain the situation . . .
Let's make that our mission!
Okay, well, I'm off!
Wish me luck!

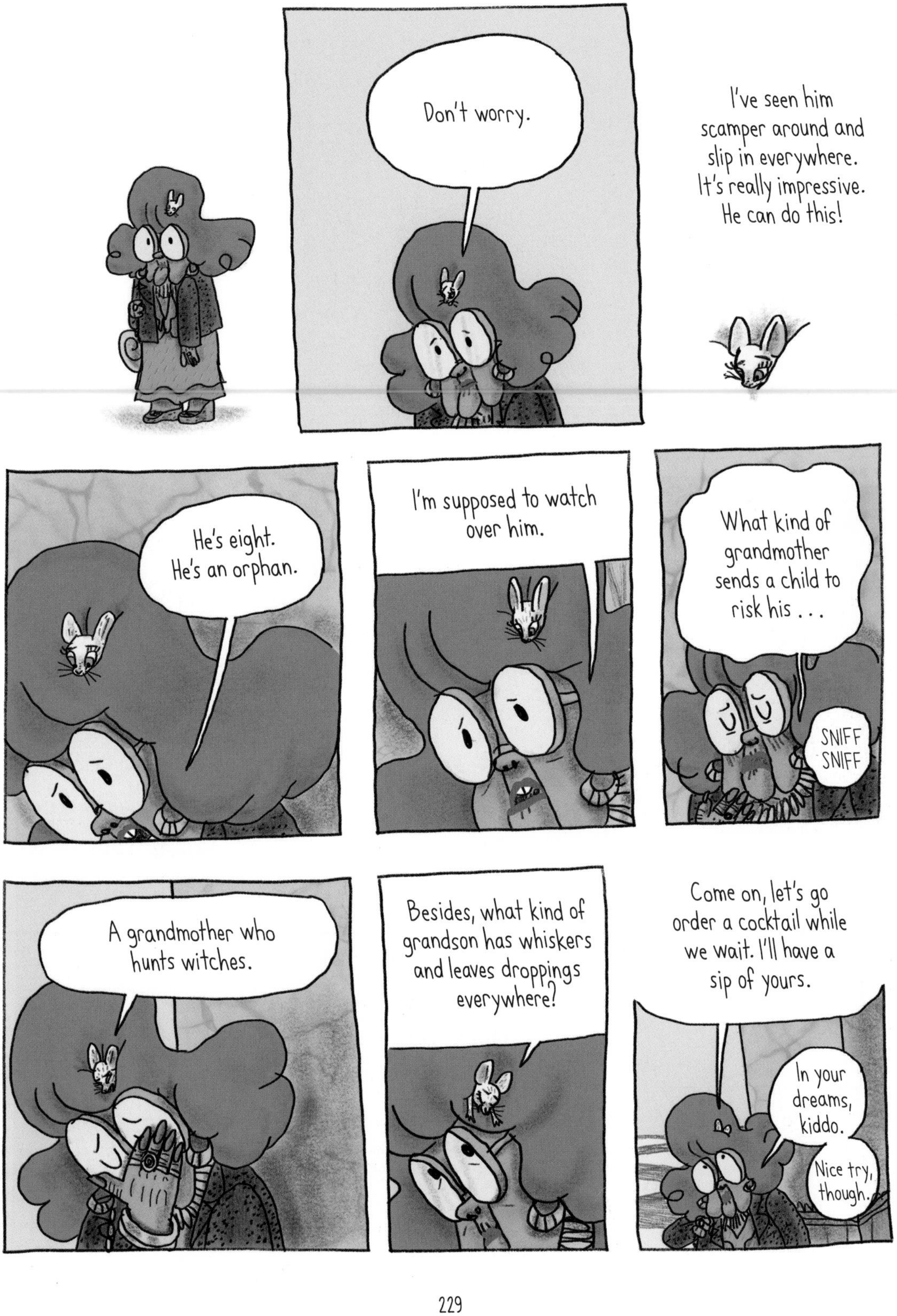
Don't worry.
I've seen him scamper around and slip in everywhere. It's really impressive. He can do this!
He's eight. He's an orphan.
I'm supposed to watch over him.
What kind of grandmother sends a child to risk his . . .
SNIFF SNIFF
A grandmother who hunts witches.
Besides, what kind of grandson has whiskers and leaves droppings everywhere?
Come on, let's go order a cocktail while we wait. I'll have a sip of yours.
In your dreams, kiddo.
Nice try, though.

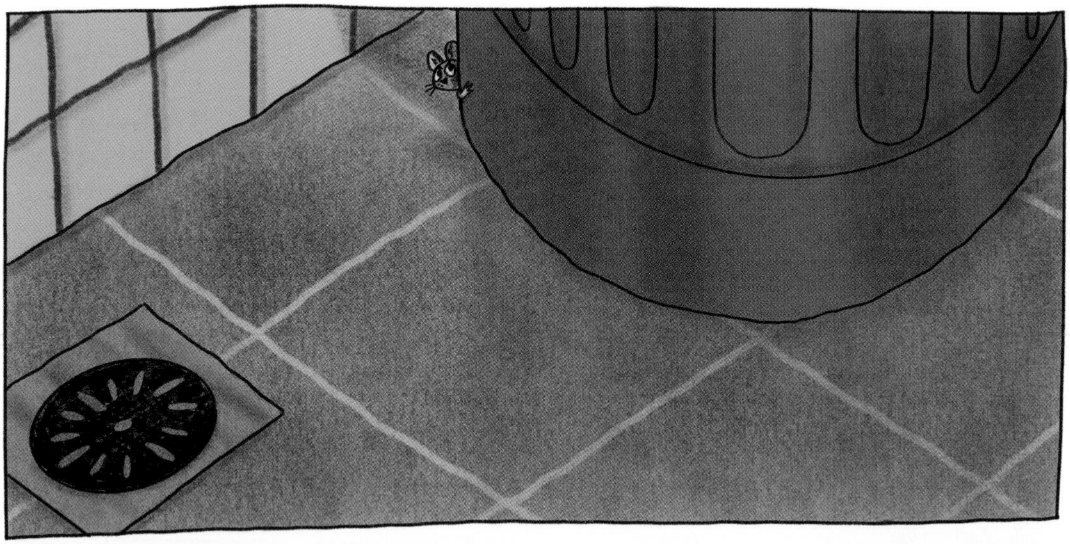

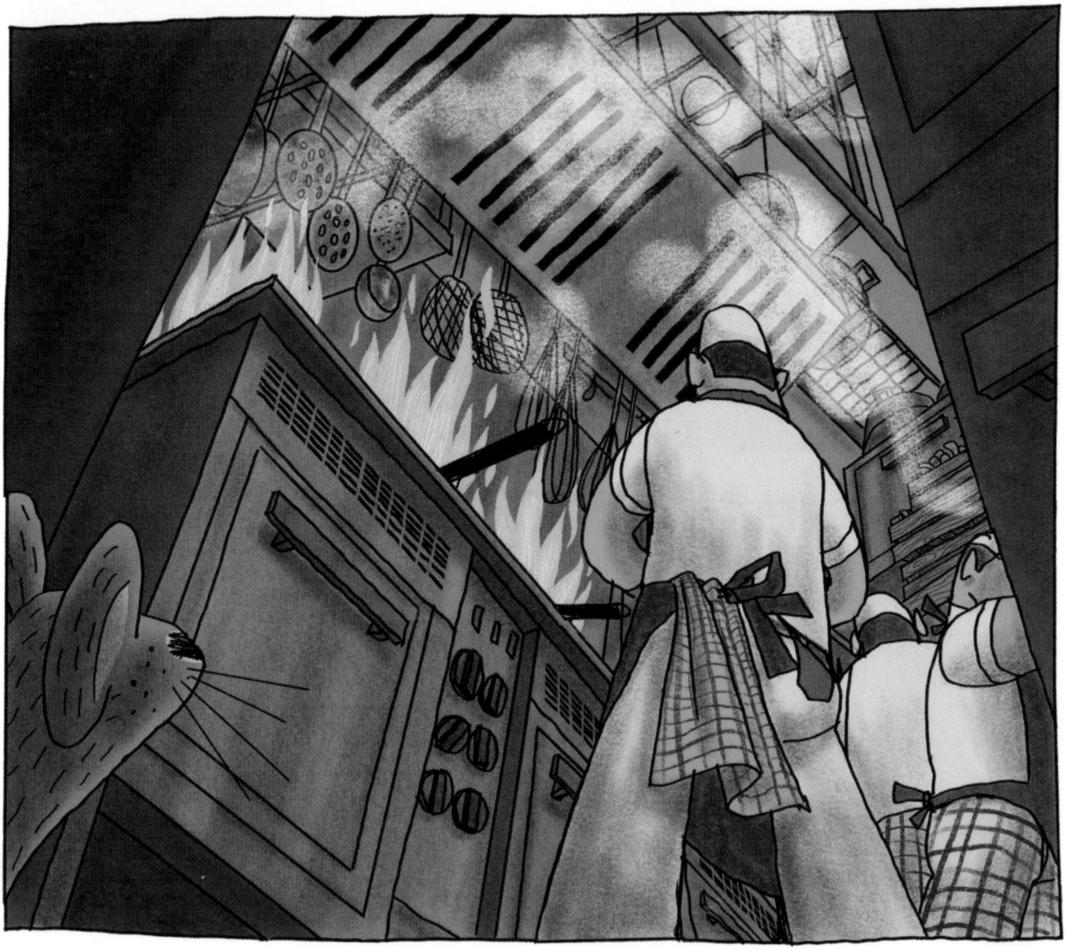

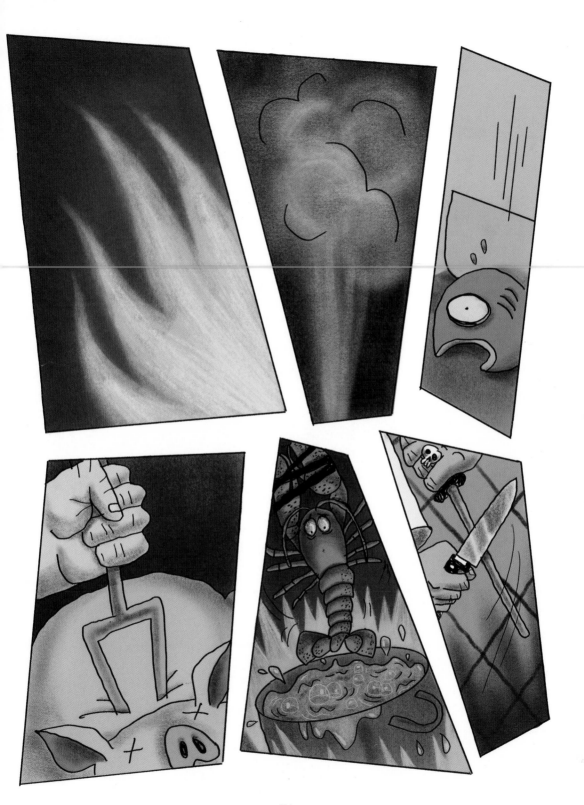

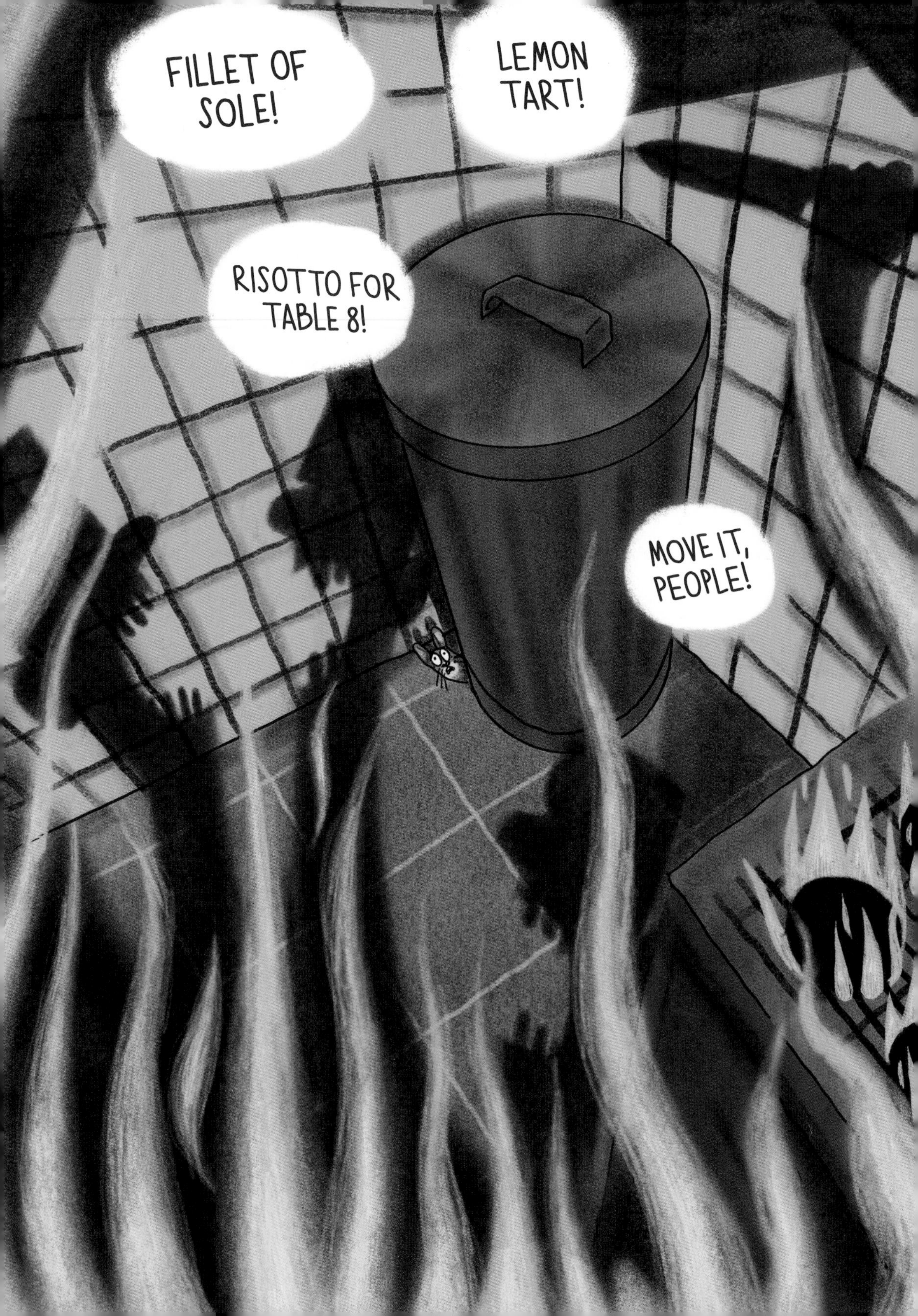
FILLET OF SOLE!
LEMON TART!
RISOTTO FOR TABLE 8!
MOVE IT, PEOPLE!

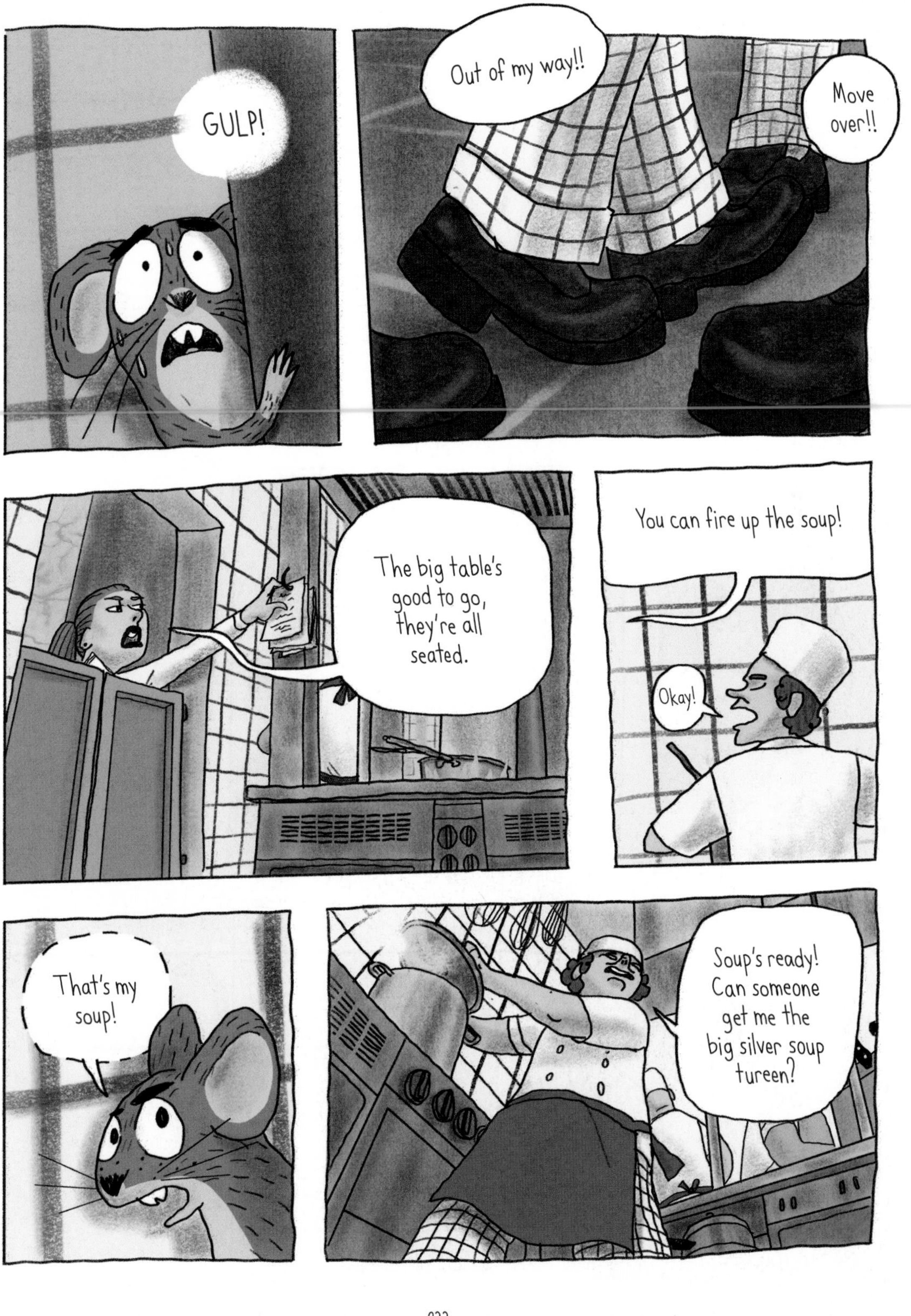
GULP!
Out of my way!!
Move over!!
The big table's good to go, they're all seated.
You can fire up the soup!
Okay!
That's my soup!
Soup's ready! Can someone get me the big silver soup tureen?

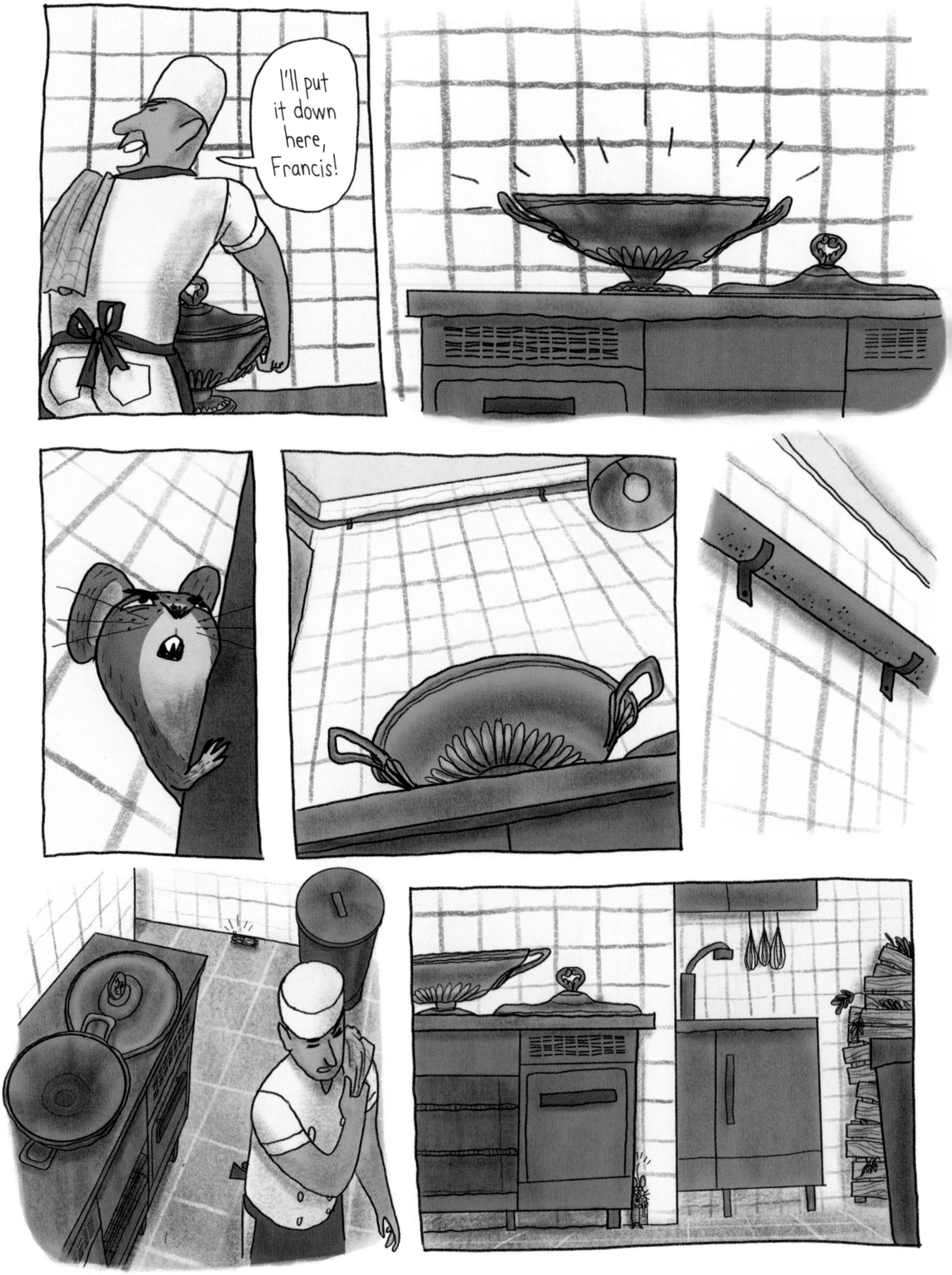
I'll put it down here, Francis!

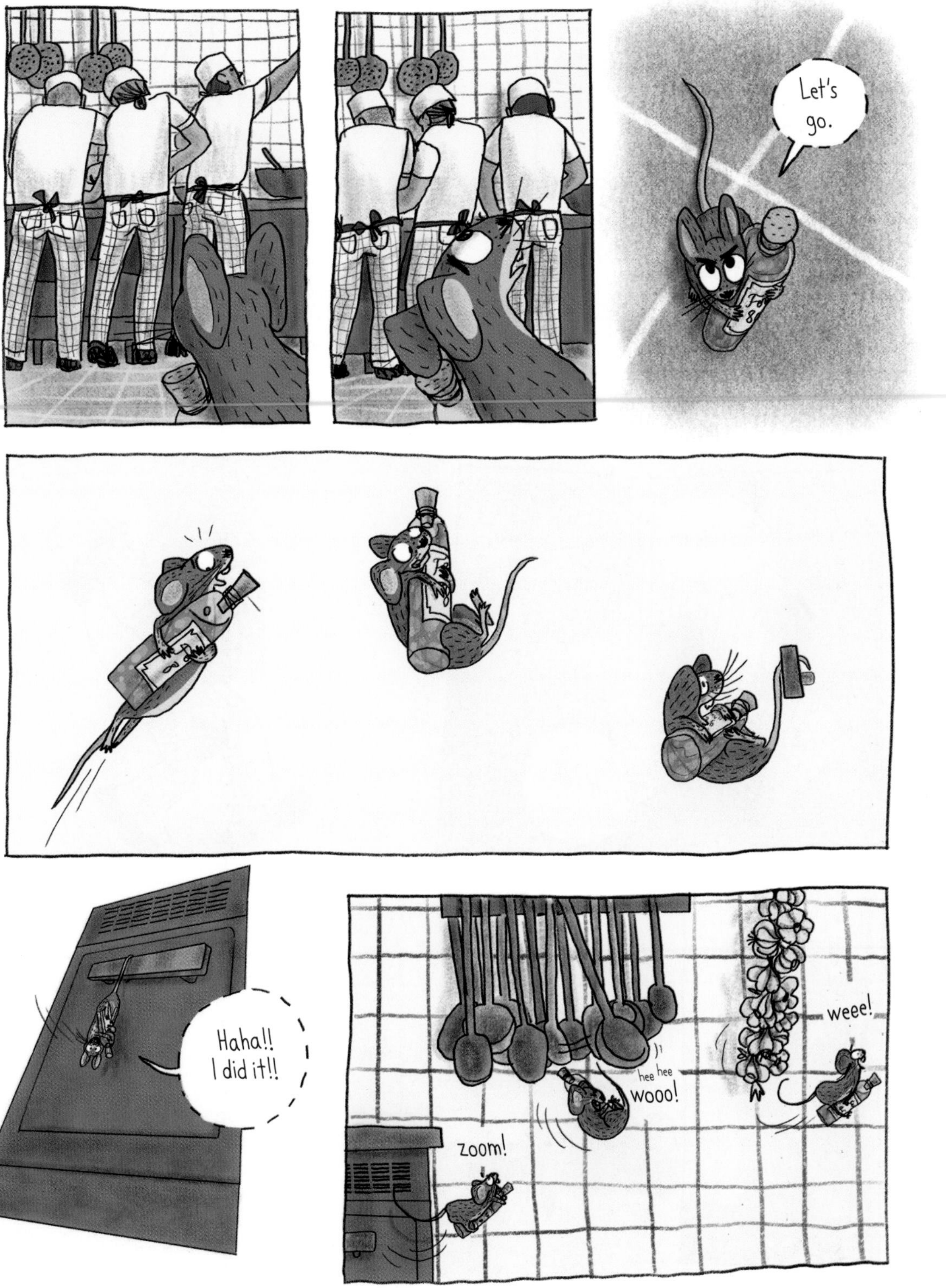
Let's go.
Haha!! I did it!!
hee hee
wooo!
weee!
zoom!

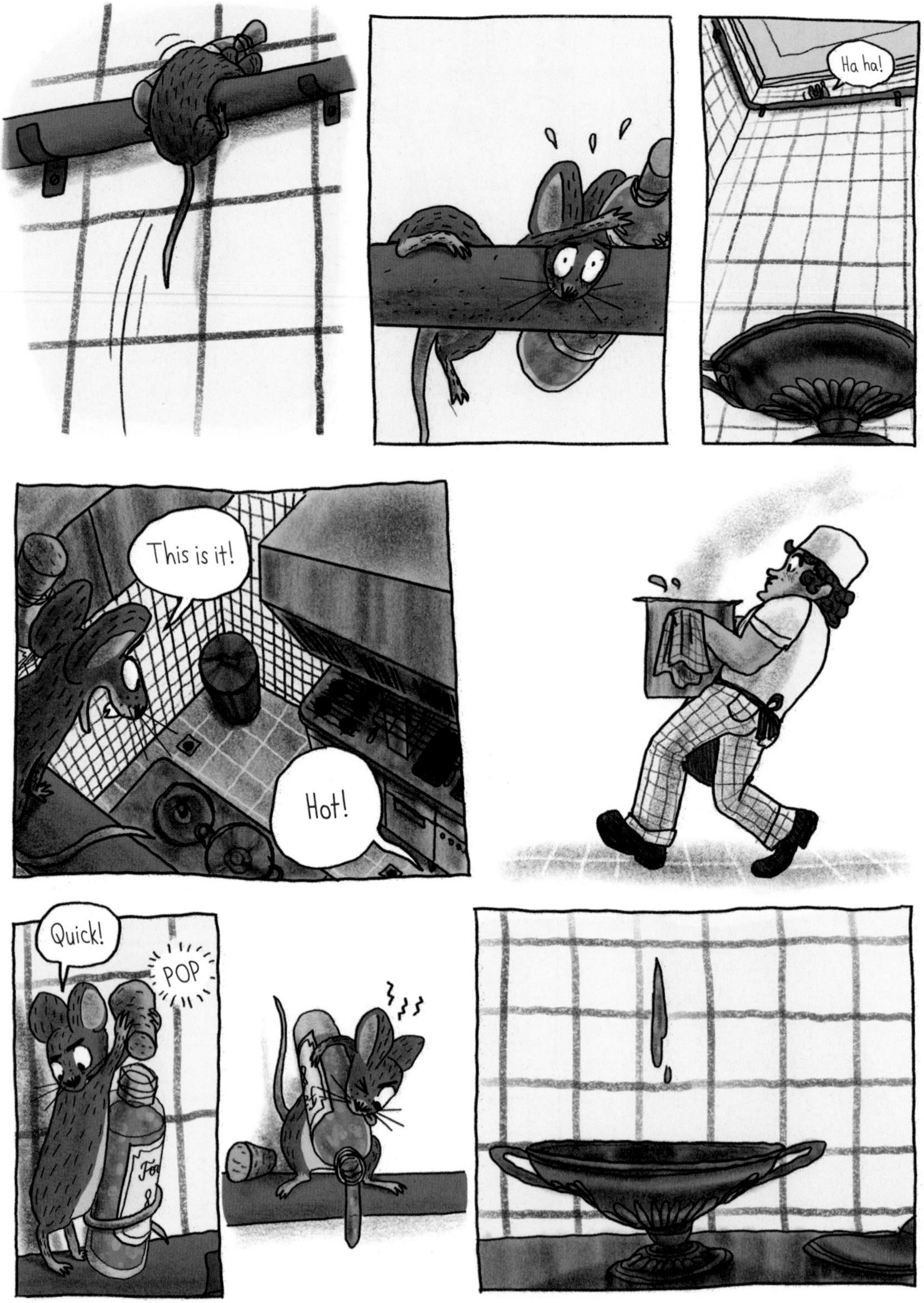
Ha ha!
This is it!
Hot!
Quick!
POP

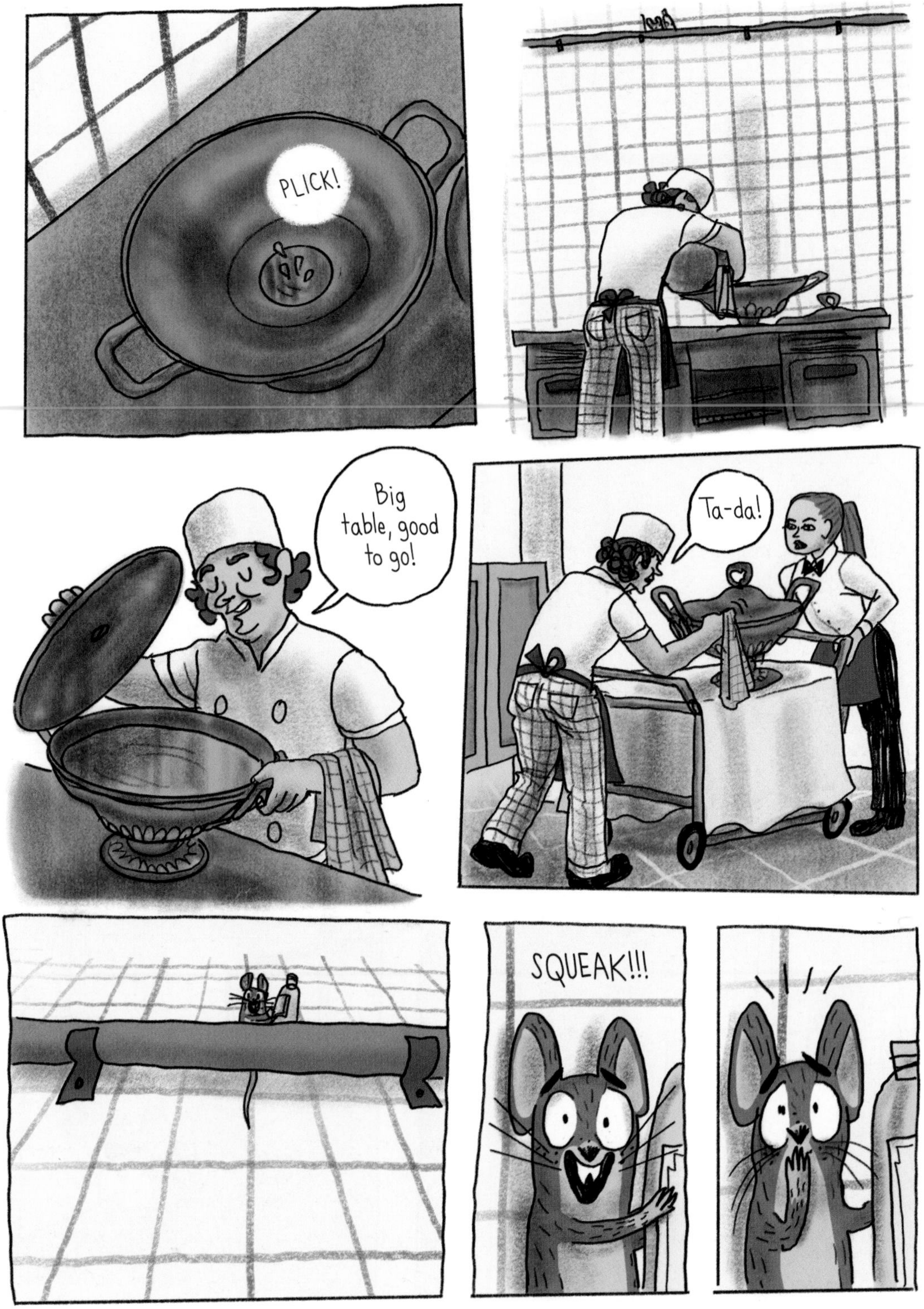
PLICK!
Big table, good to go!
Ta-da!
SQUEAK!!!

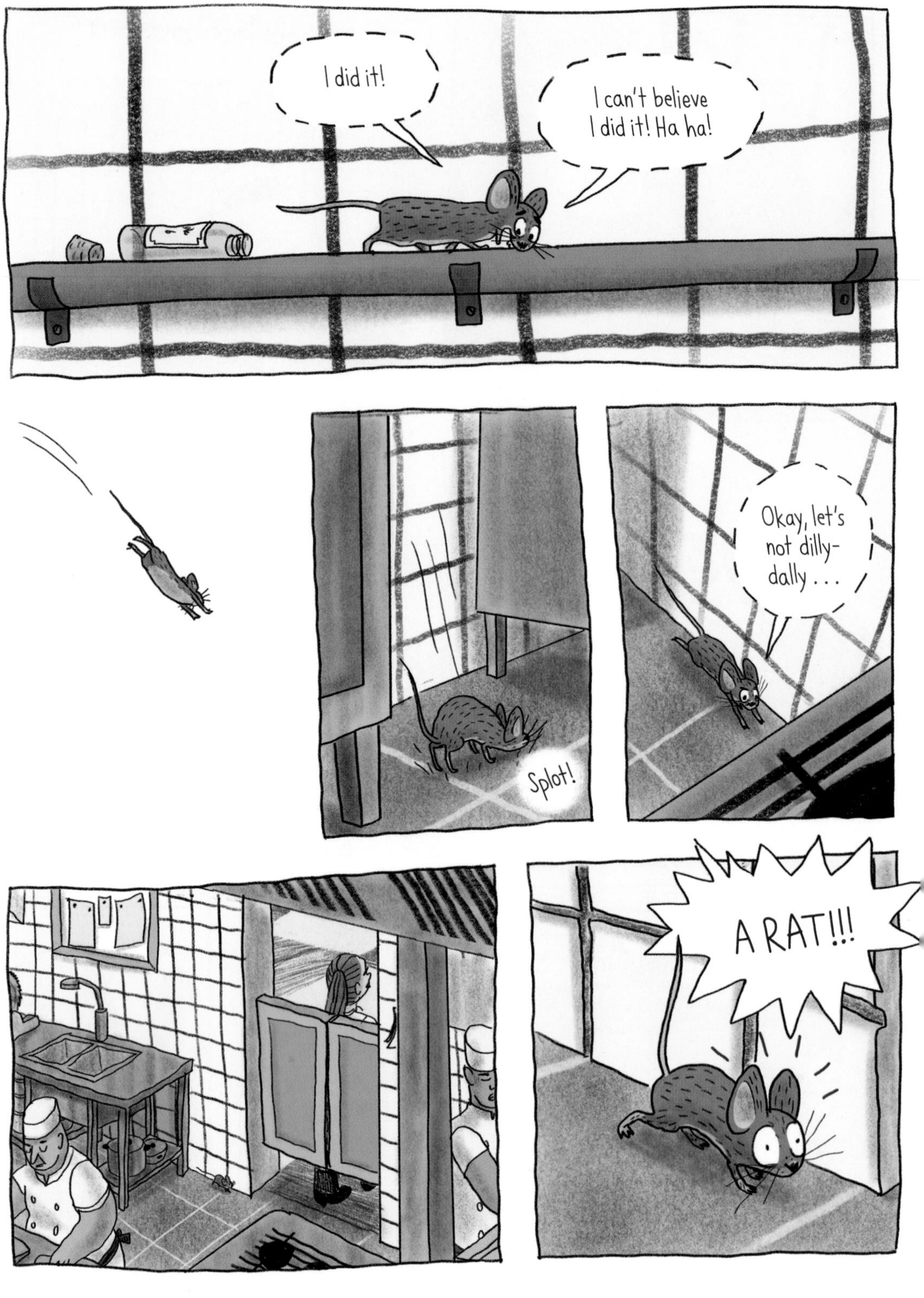
I did it!
I can't believe I did it! Ha ha!
Splot!
Okay, let's not dilly-dally . . .
A RAT!!!

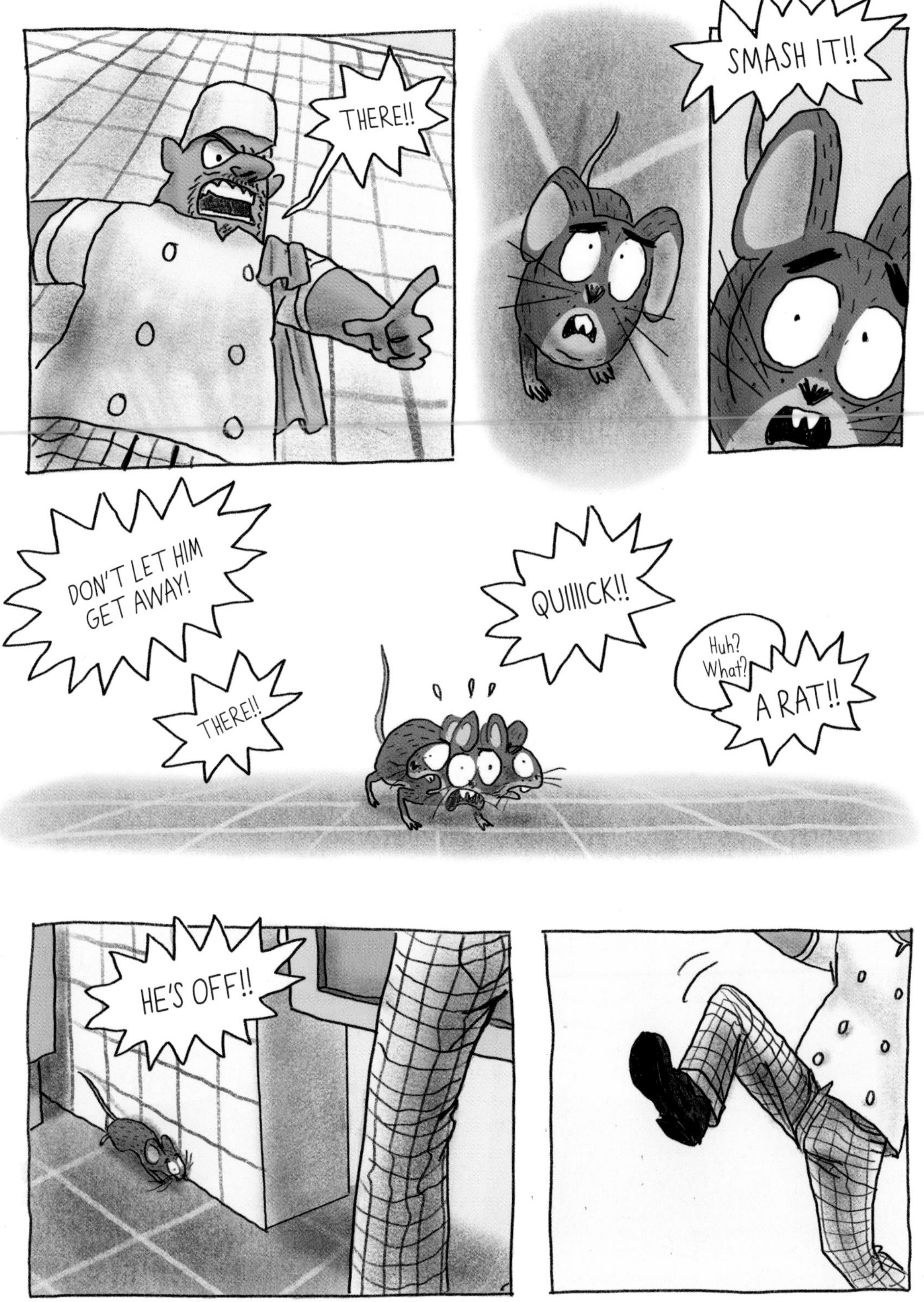
THERE!!
SMASH IT!!
DON'T LET HIM GET AWAY!
QUIIIICK!!
THERE!!
Huh? What?
A RAT!!
HE'S OFF!!

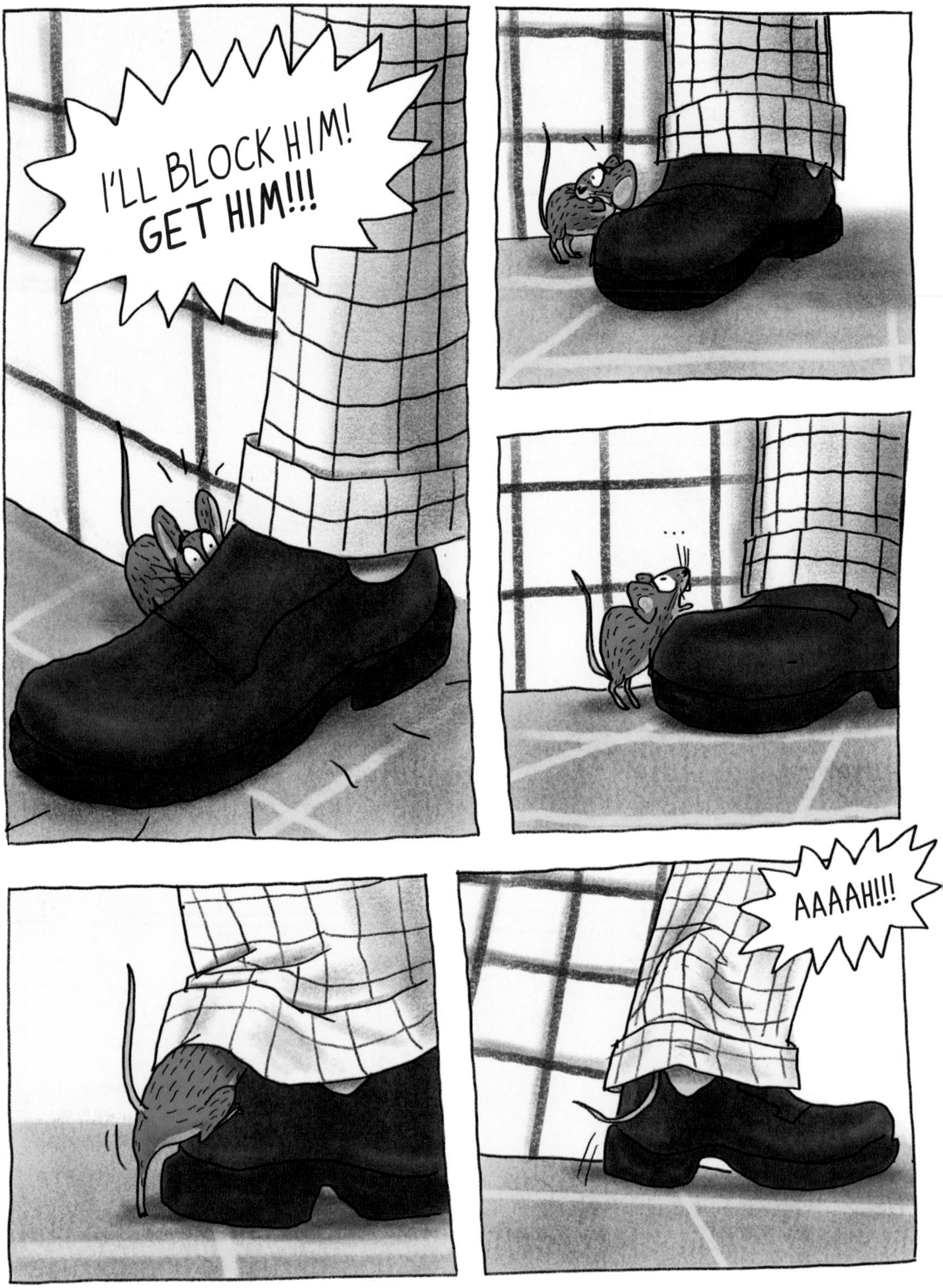
I'LL BLOCK HIM!
GET HIM!!!
...
AAAAH!!!

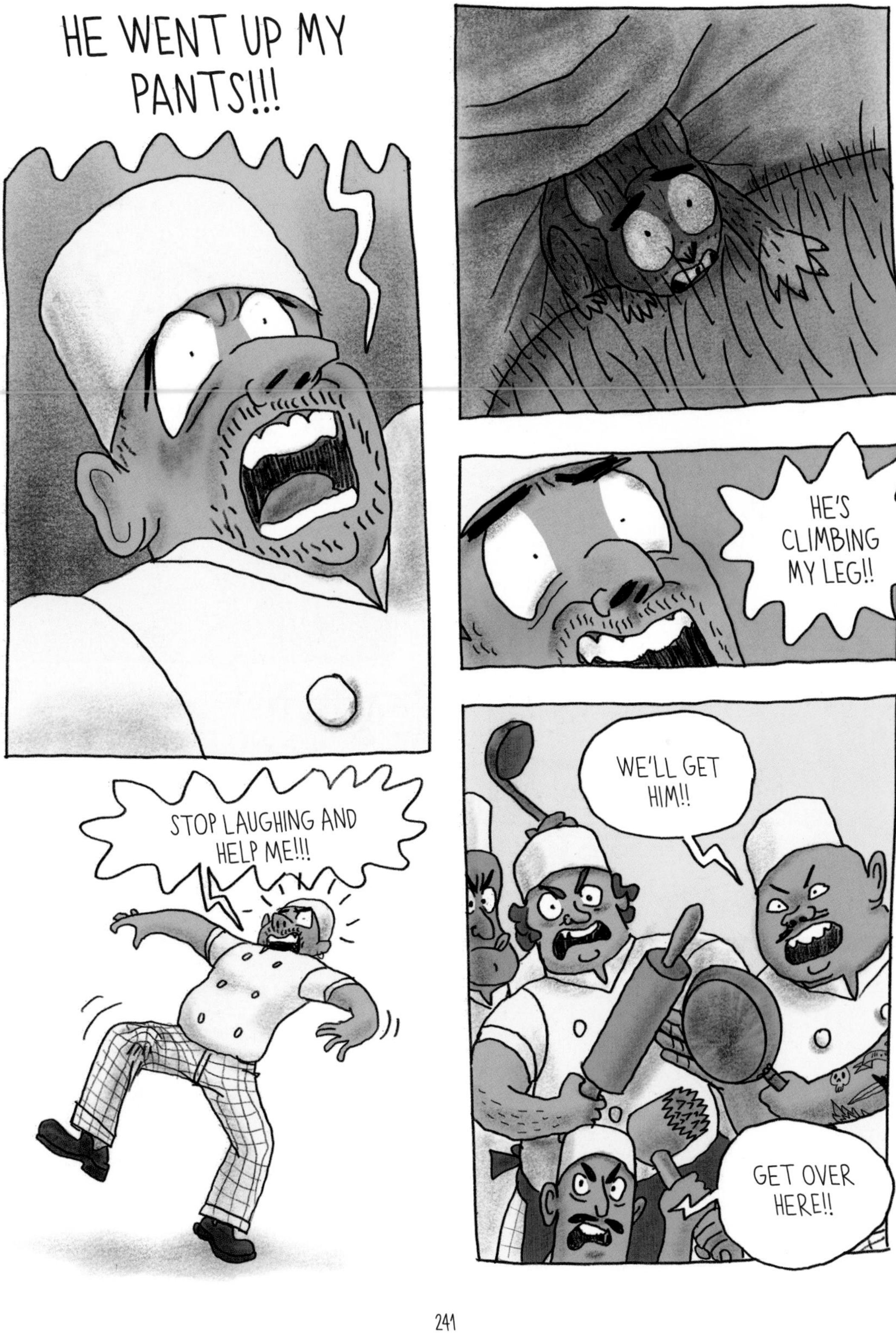
HE WENT UP MY PANTS!!!
HE'S CLIMBING MY LEG!!
STOP LAUGHING AND HELP ME!!!
WE'LL GET HIM!!
GET OVER HERE!!

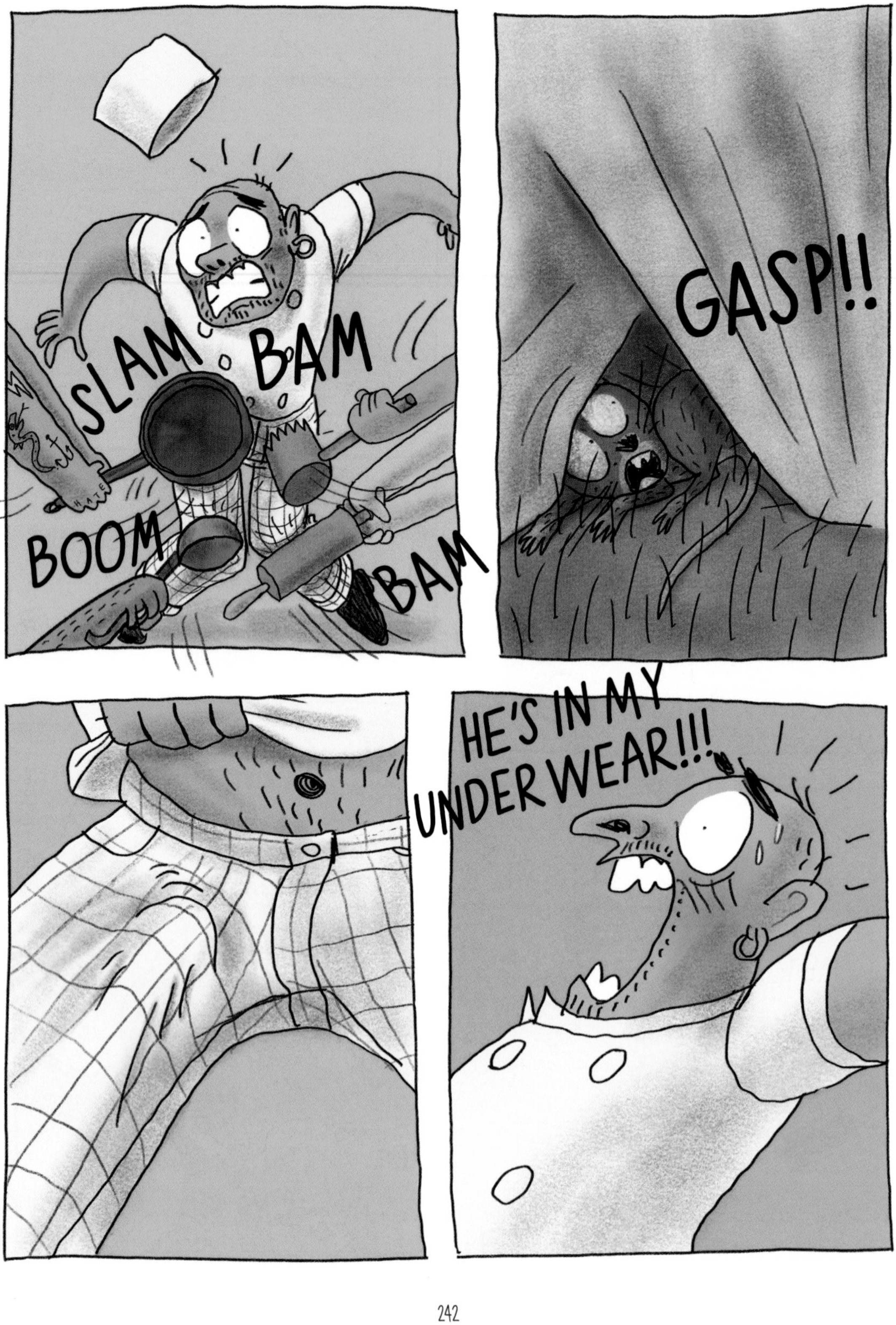
SLAM
BAM
BOOM
BAM
GASP!!
HE'S IN MY UNDERWEAR!!!

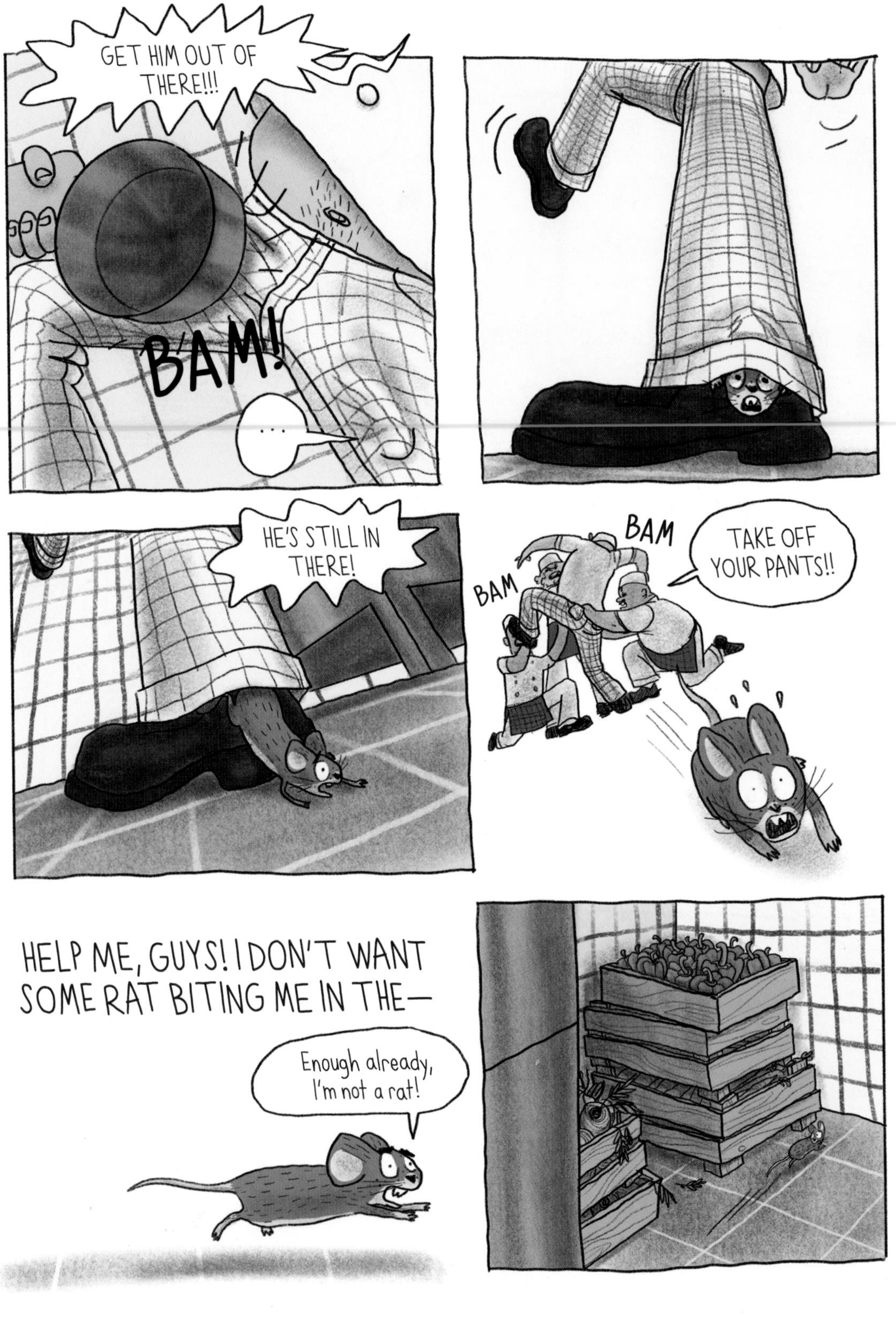
GET HIM OUT OF THERE!!!
BAM!
...
HE'S STILL IN THERE!
BAM
BAM
TAKE OFF YOUR PANTS!!
HELP ME, GUYS! I DON'T WANT SOME RAT BITING ME IN THE—
Enough already, I'm not a rat!

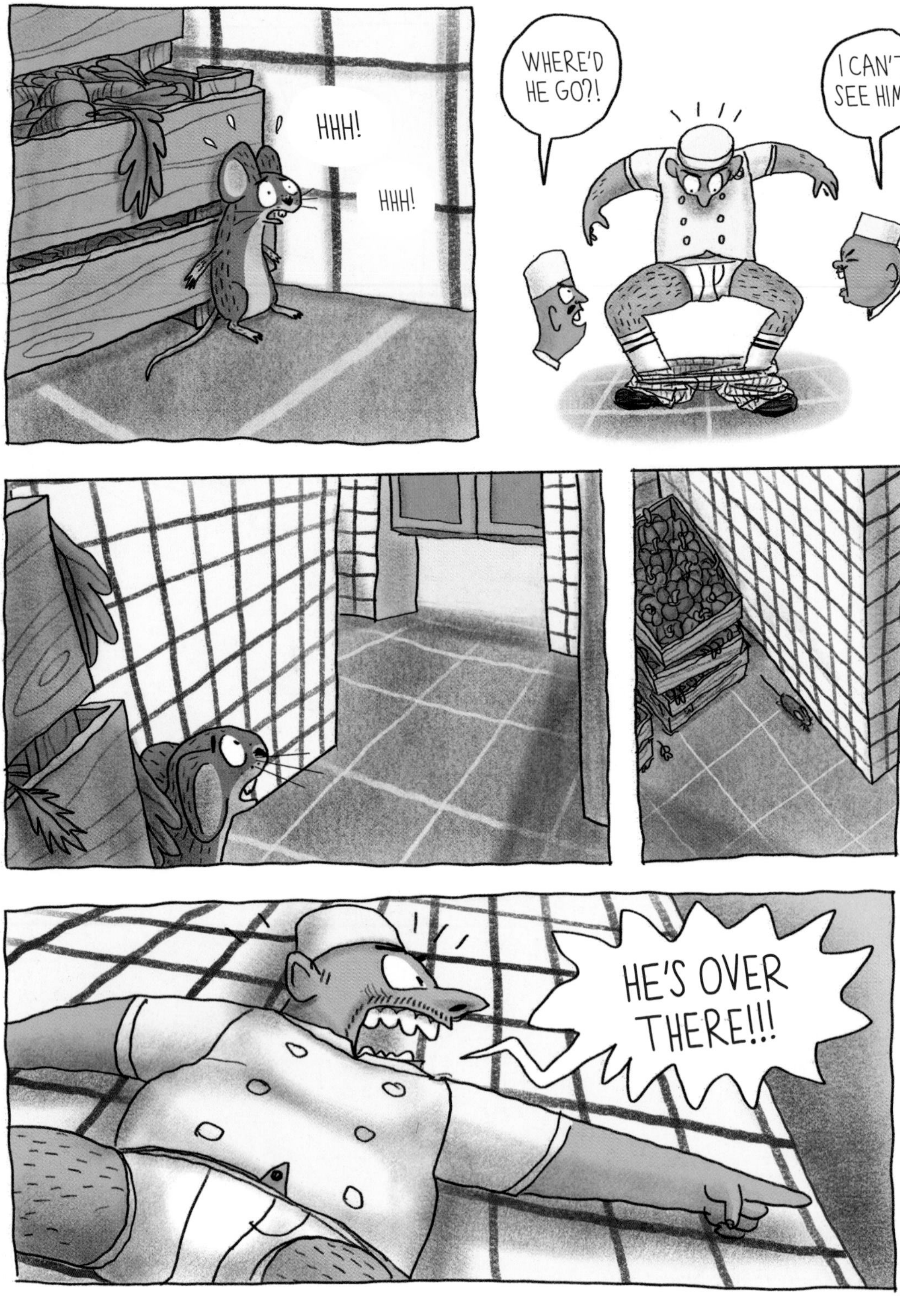
HHH!
HHH!
WHERE'D HE GO?!
I CAN'T SEE HIM!!
HE'S OVER THERE!!!

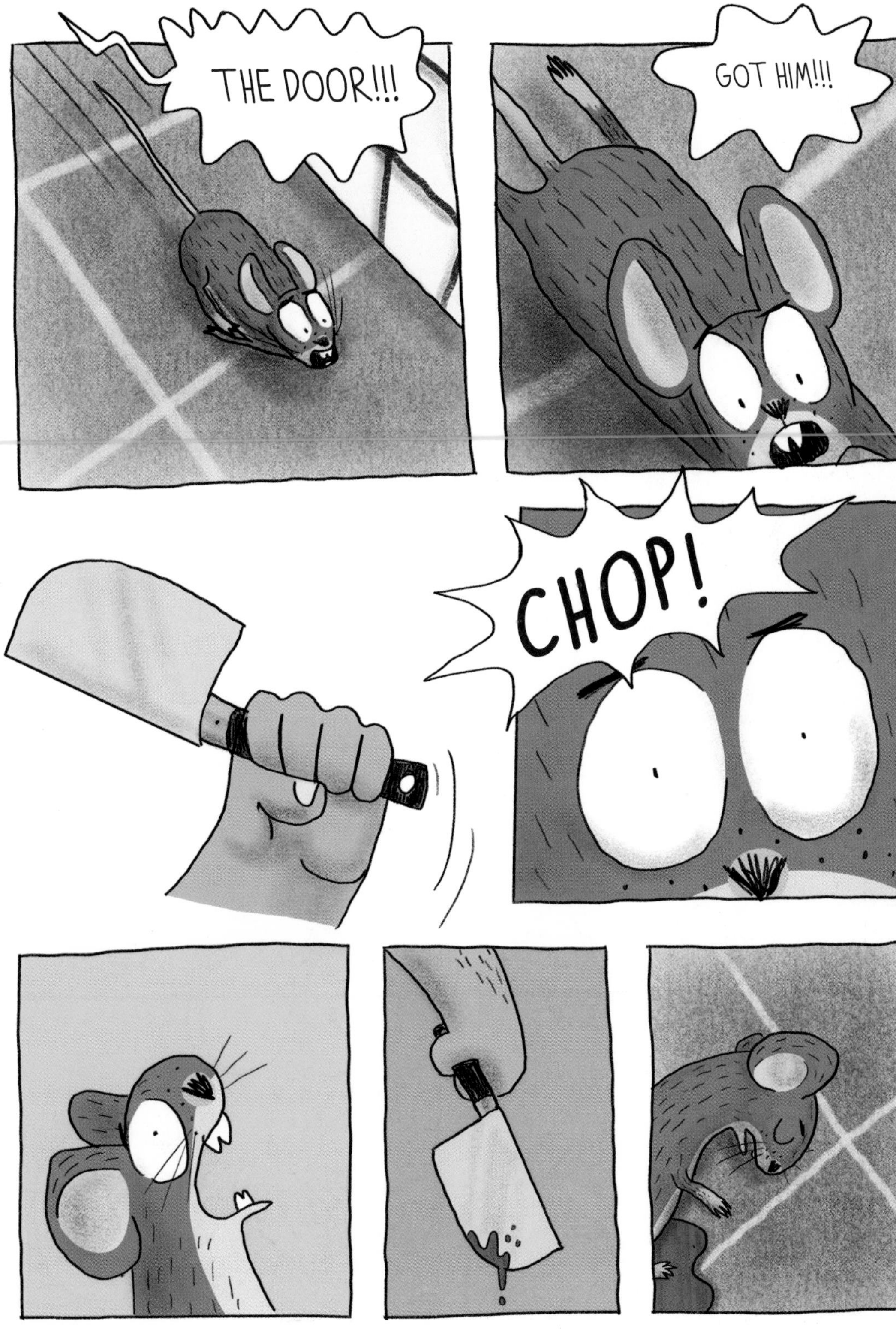
THE DOOR!!!
GOT HIM!!!
CHOP!

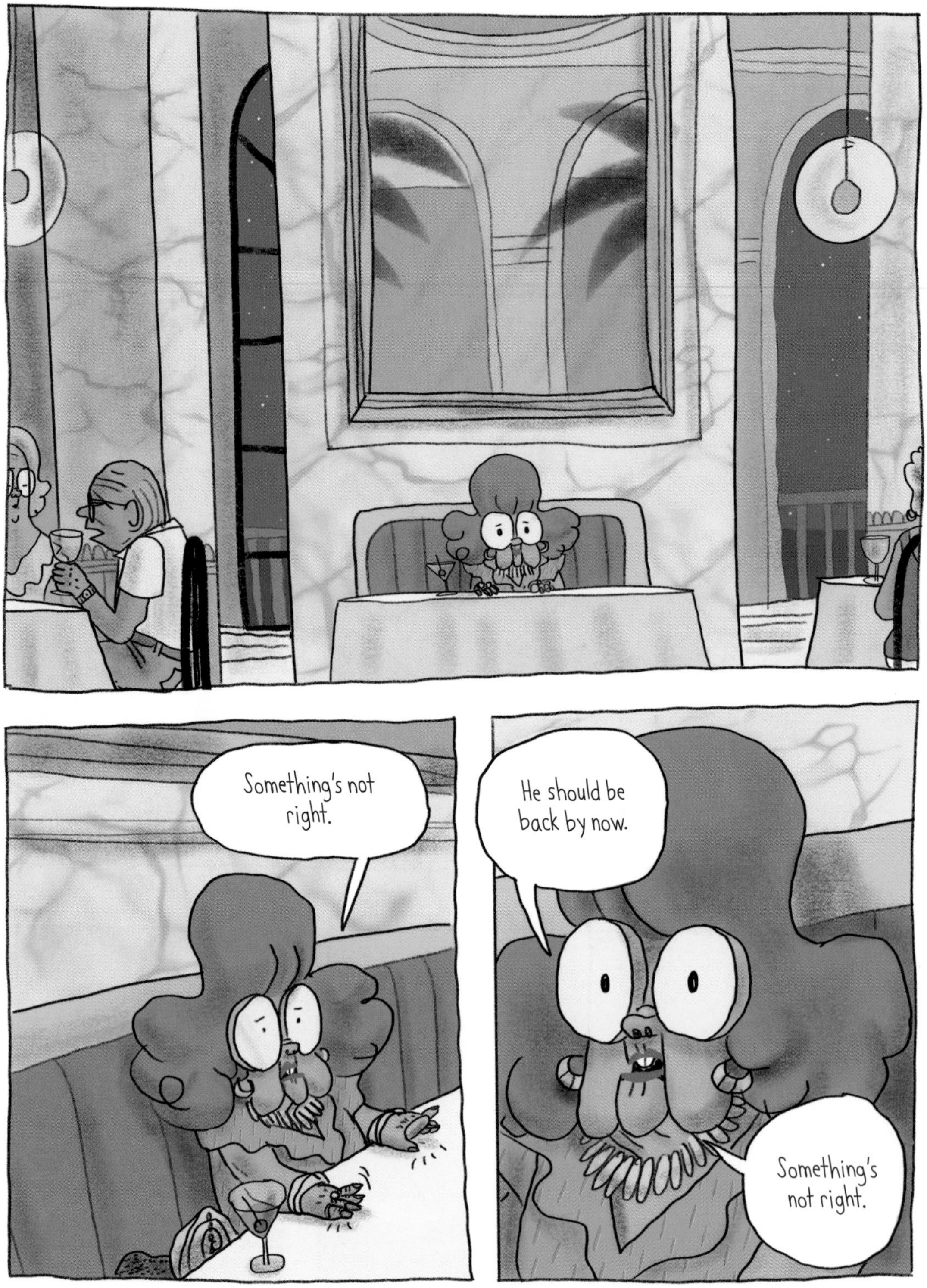
Something's not right.
He should be back by now.
Something's not right.

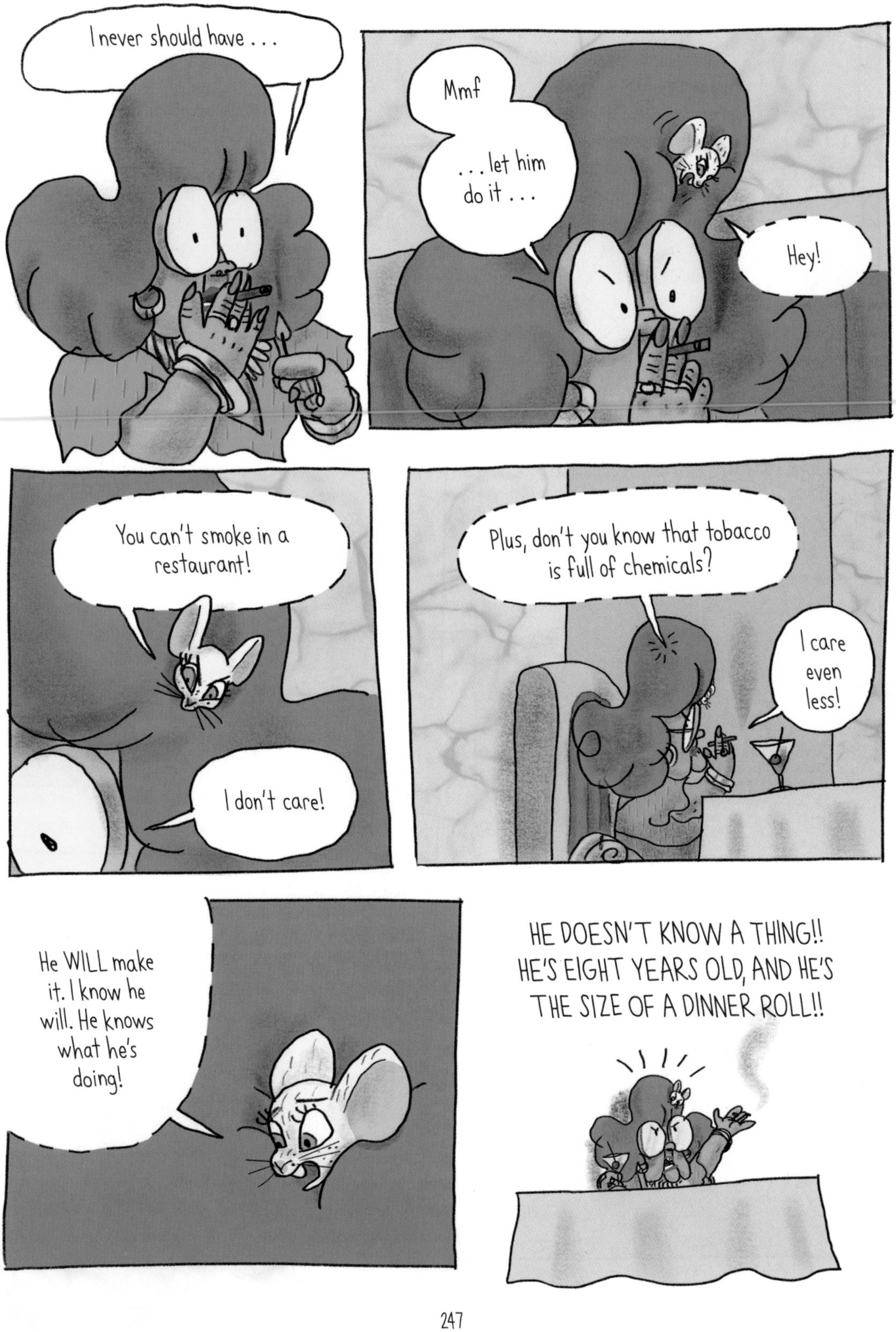
I never should have . . .
Mmf
. . . let him do it . . .
Hey!
You can't smoke in a restaurant!
I don't care!
Plus, don't you know that tobacco is full of chemicals?
I care even less!
He WILL make it. I know he will. He knows what he's doing!
HE DOESN'T KNOW A THING!! HE'S EIGHT YEARS OLD, AND HE'S THE SIZE OF A DINNER ROLL!!

SIGH

What was I thinking?

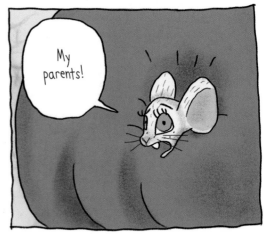

My parents!

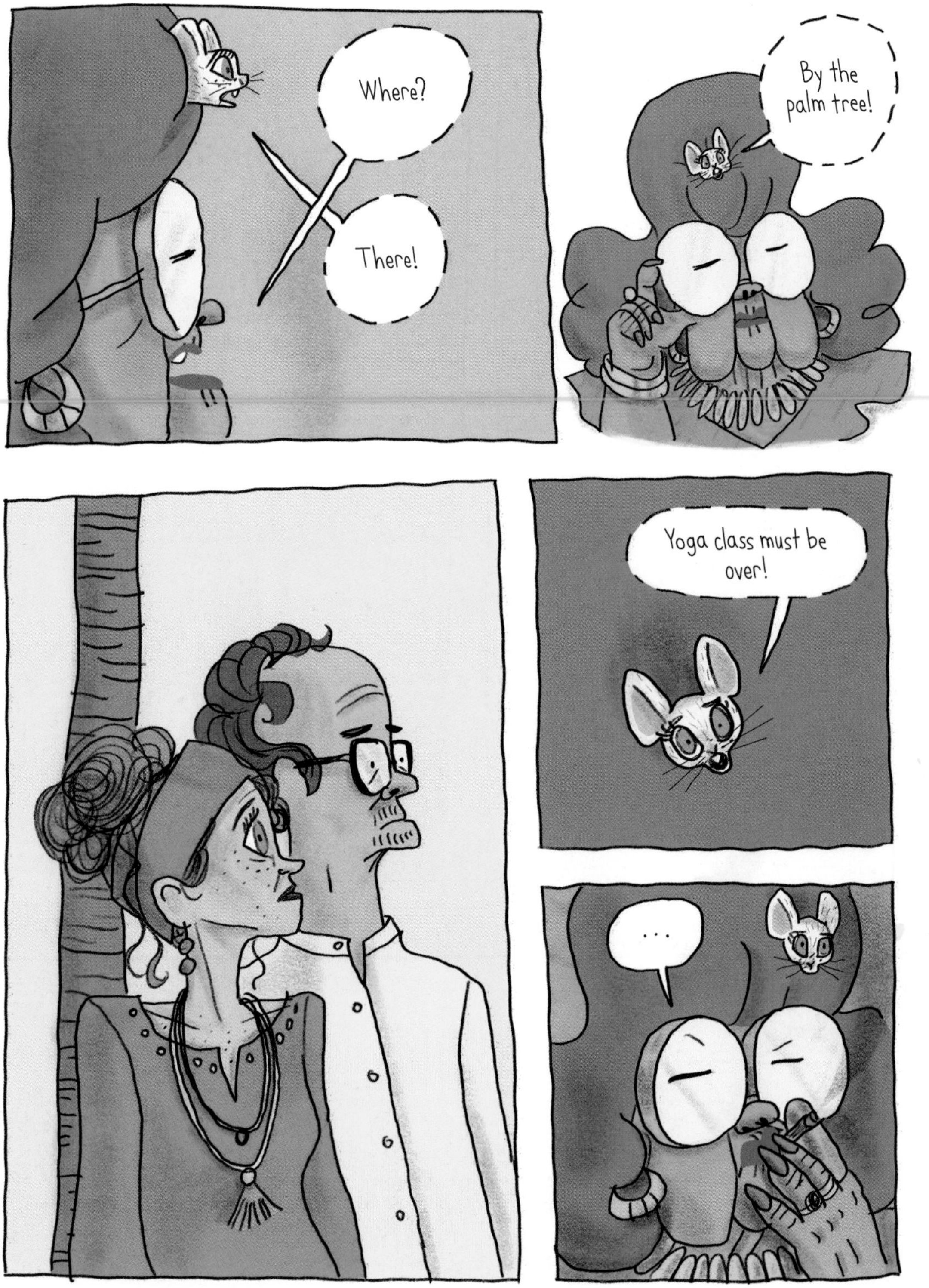
Where?
There!
By the palm tree!
Yoga class must be over!
...

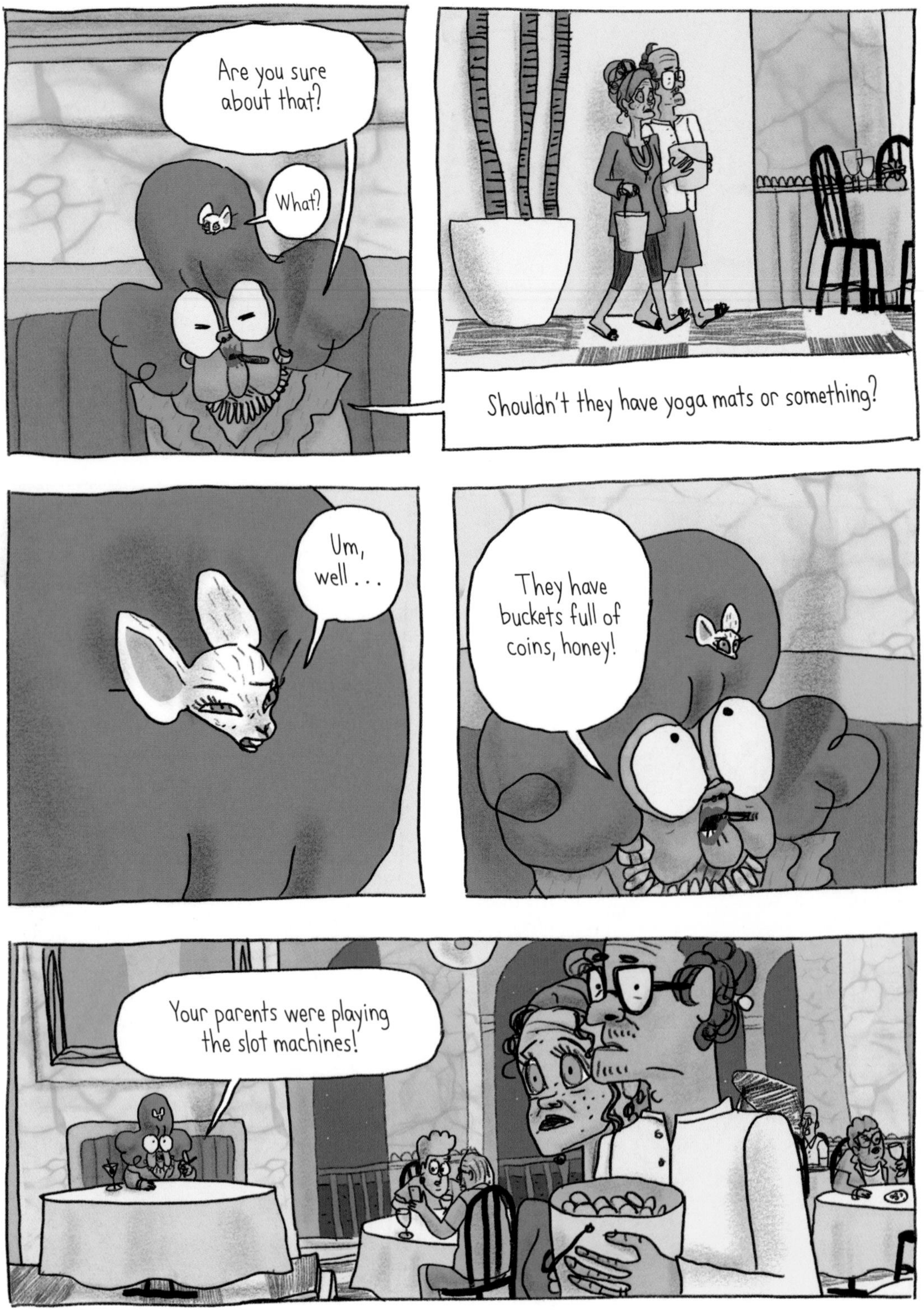
Are you sure about that?
What?
Shouldn't they have yoga mats or something?
Um, well . . .
They have buckets full of coins, honey!
Your parents were playing the slot machines!

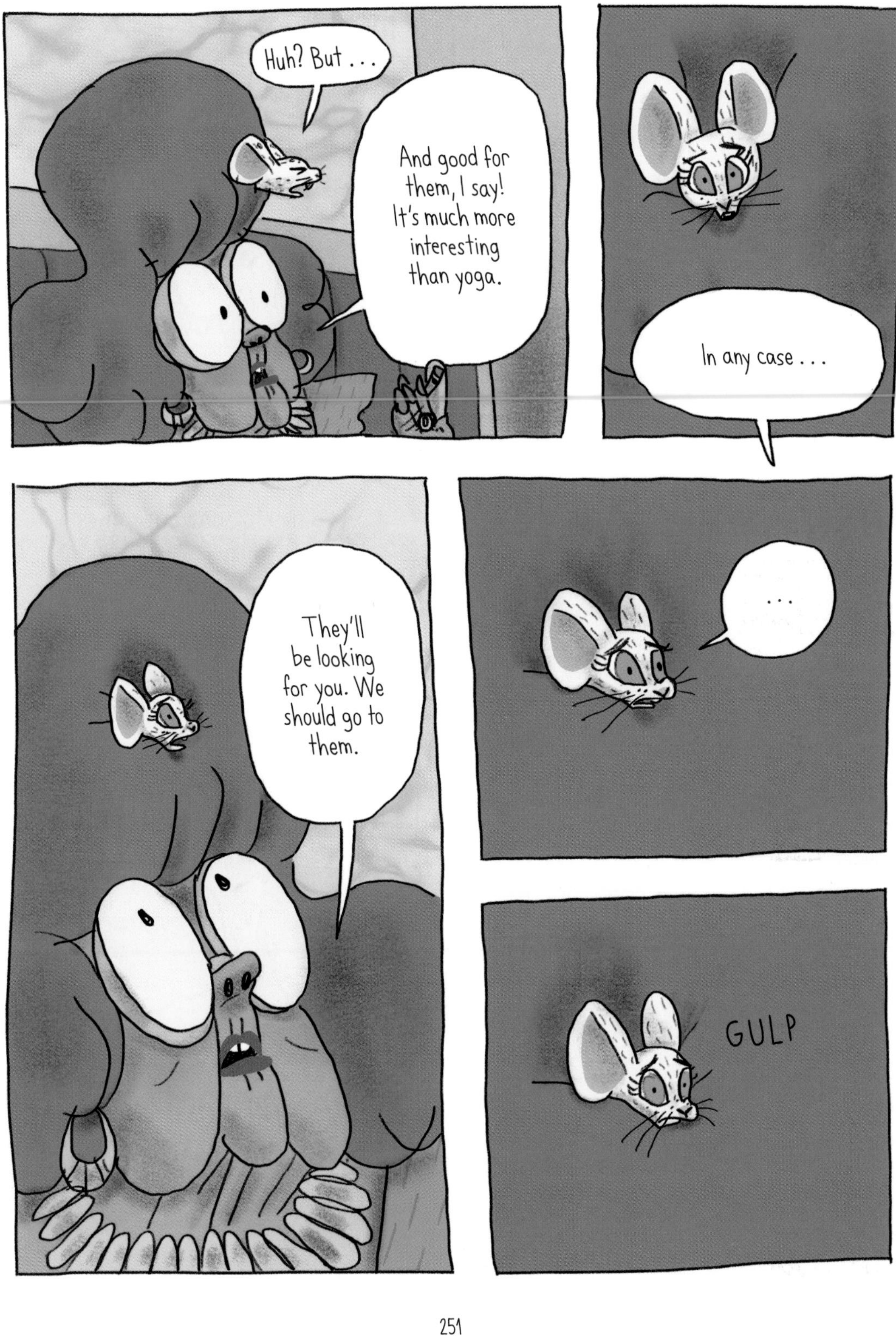

Huh? But . . .
And good for them, I say! It's much more interesting than yoga.
In any case . . .
They'll be looking for you. We should go to them.
. . .
GULP

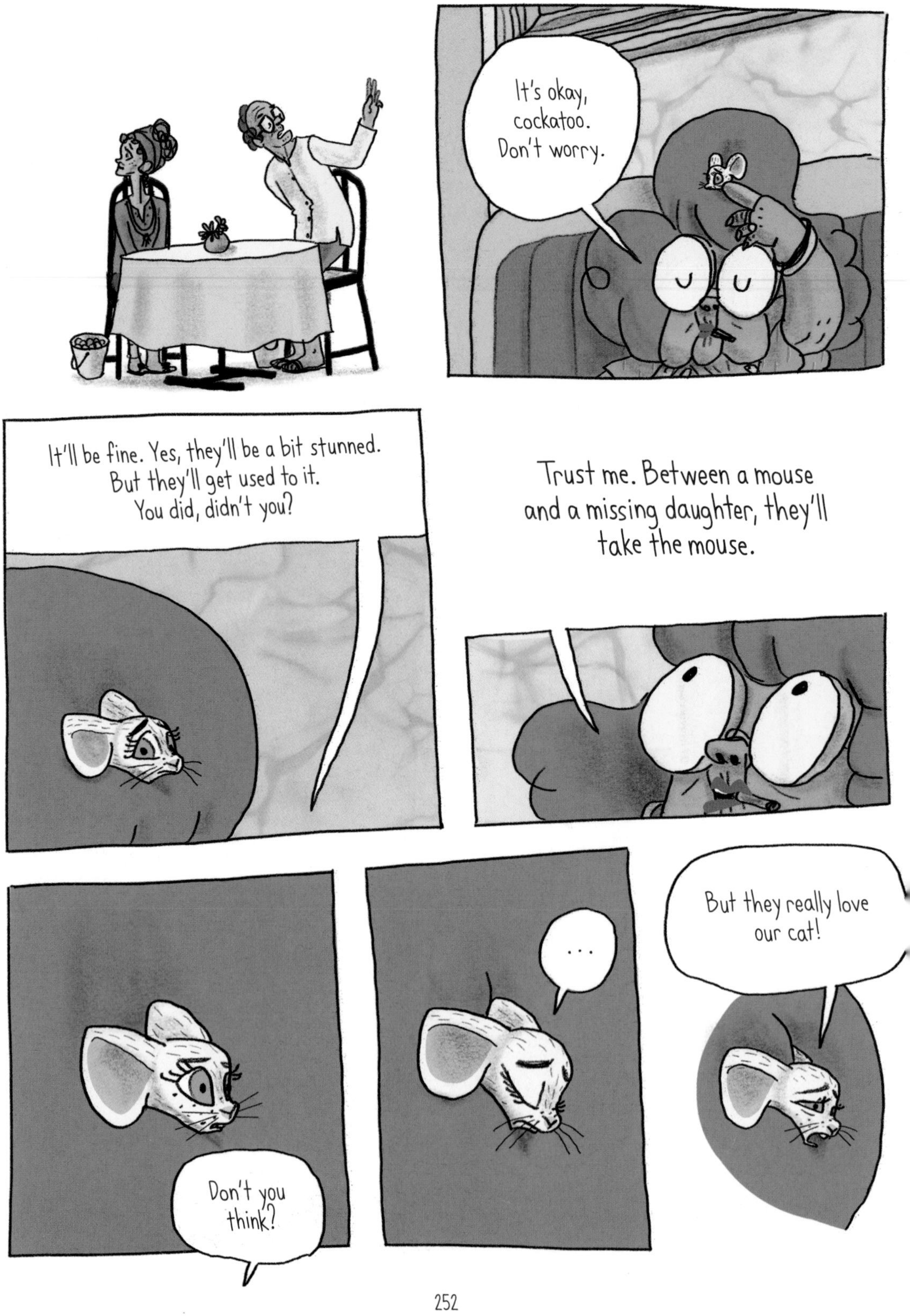
It's okay, cockatoo. Don't worry.
It'll be fine. Yes, they'll be a bit stunned. But they'll get used to it. You did, didn't you?
Trust me. Between a mouse and a missing daughter, they'll take the mouse.
Don't you think?
...
But they really love our cat!

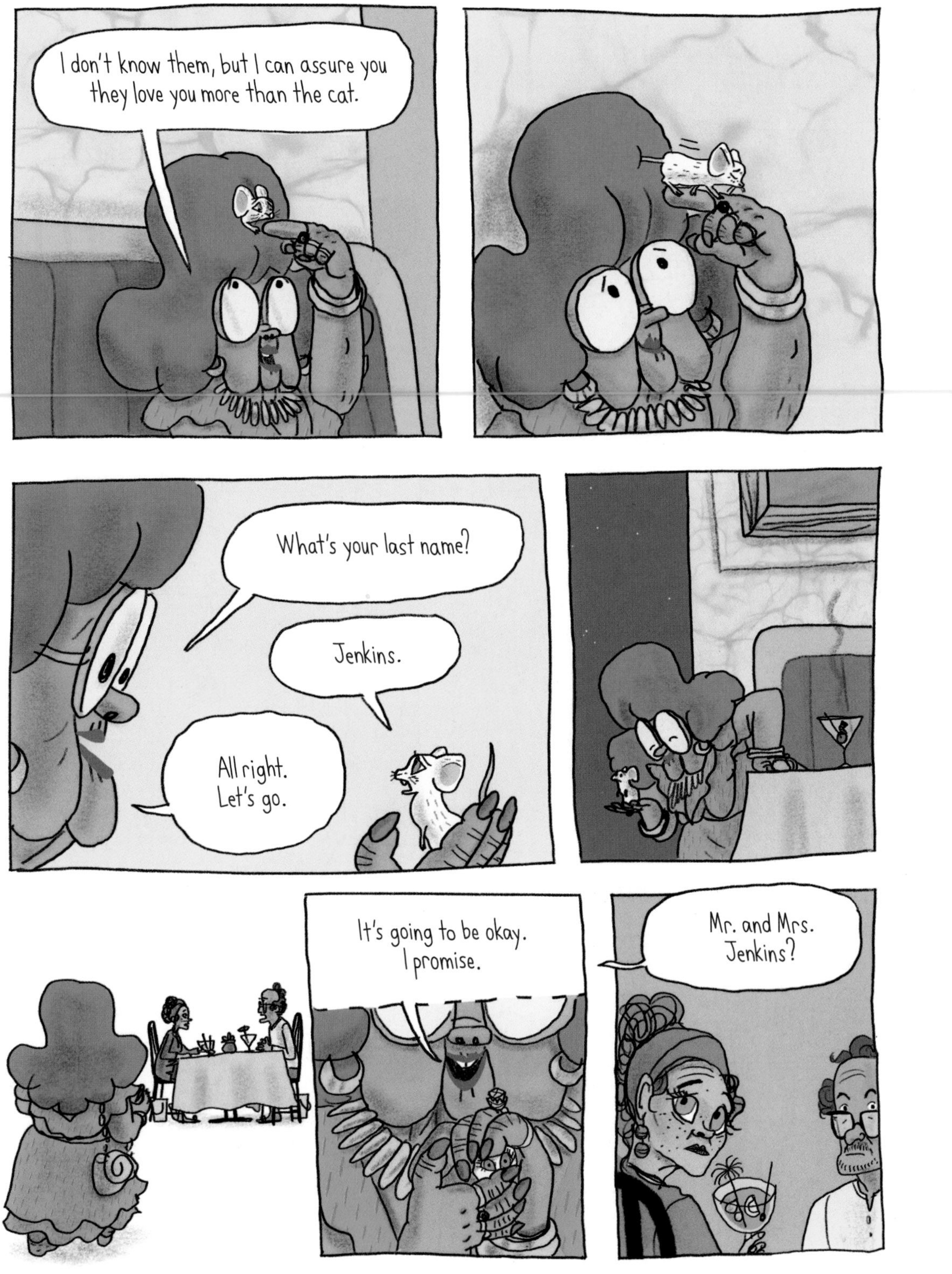
I don't know them, but I can assure you they love you more than the cat.
What's your last name?
Jenkins.
All right. Let's go.
It's going to be okay. I promise.
Mr. and Mrs. Jenkins?

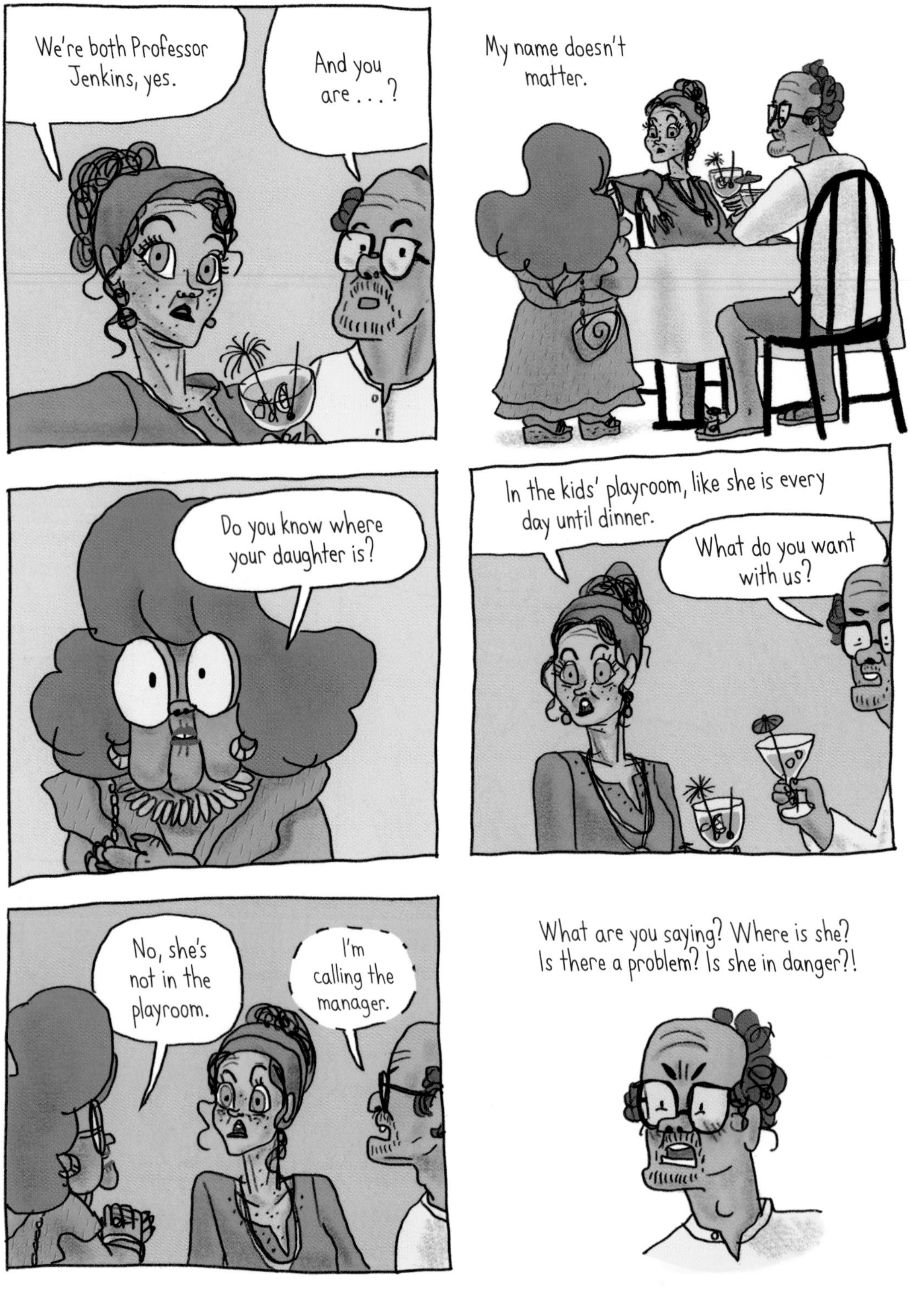
We're both Professor Jenkins, yes.
And you are . . . ?
My name doesn't matter.
Do you know where your daughter is?
In the kids' playroom, like she is every day until dinner.
What do you want with us?
No, she's not in the playroom.
I'm calling the manager.
What are you saying? Where is she? Is there a problem? Is she in danger?!

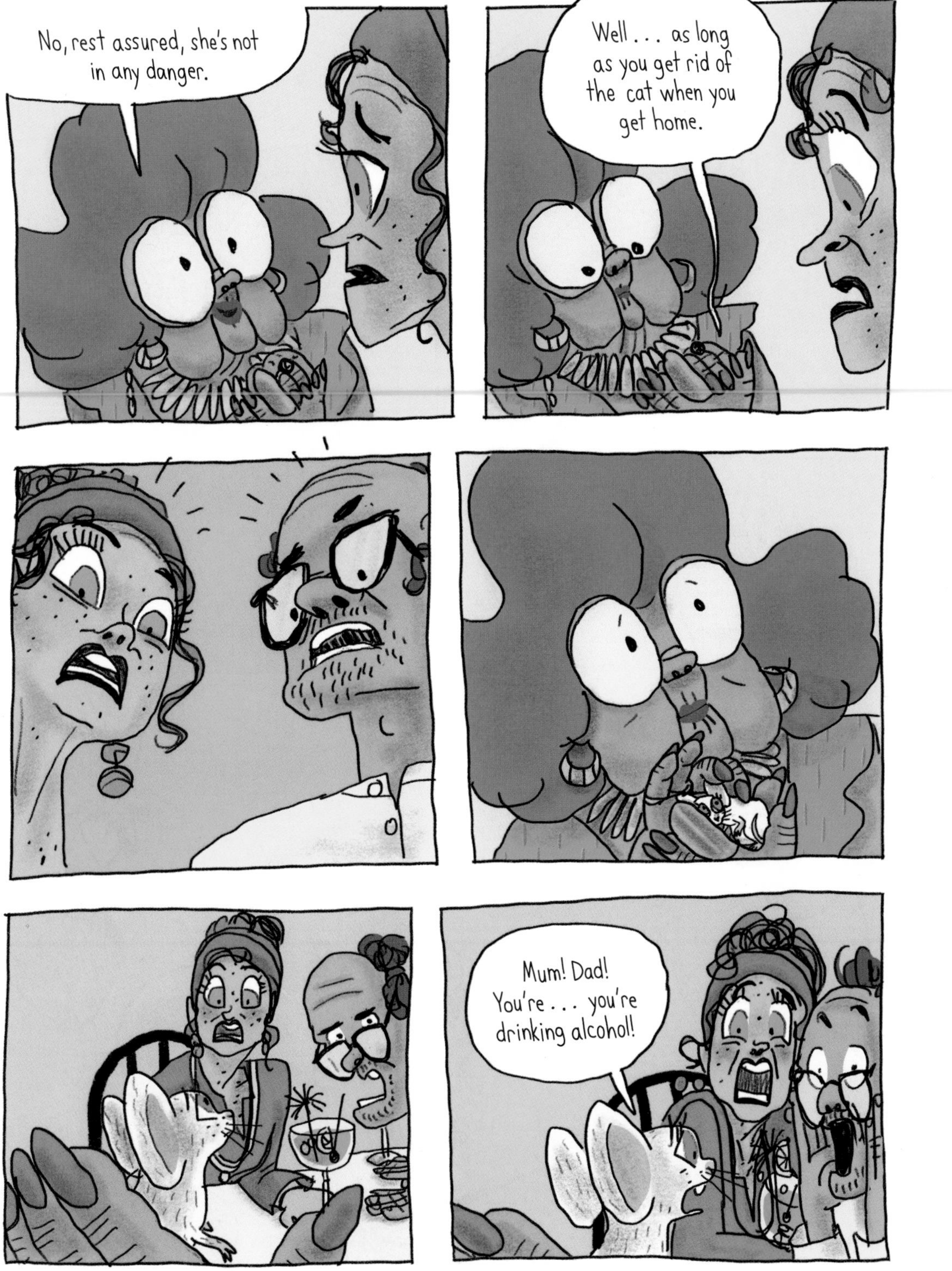
No, rest assured, she's not in any danger.
Well . . . as long as you get rid of the cat when you get home.
Mum! Dad! You're . . . you're drinking alcohol!

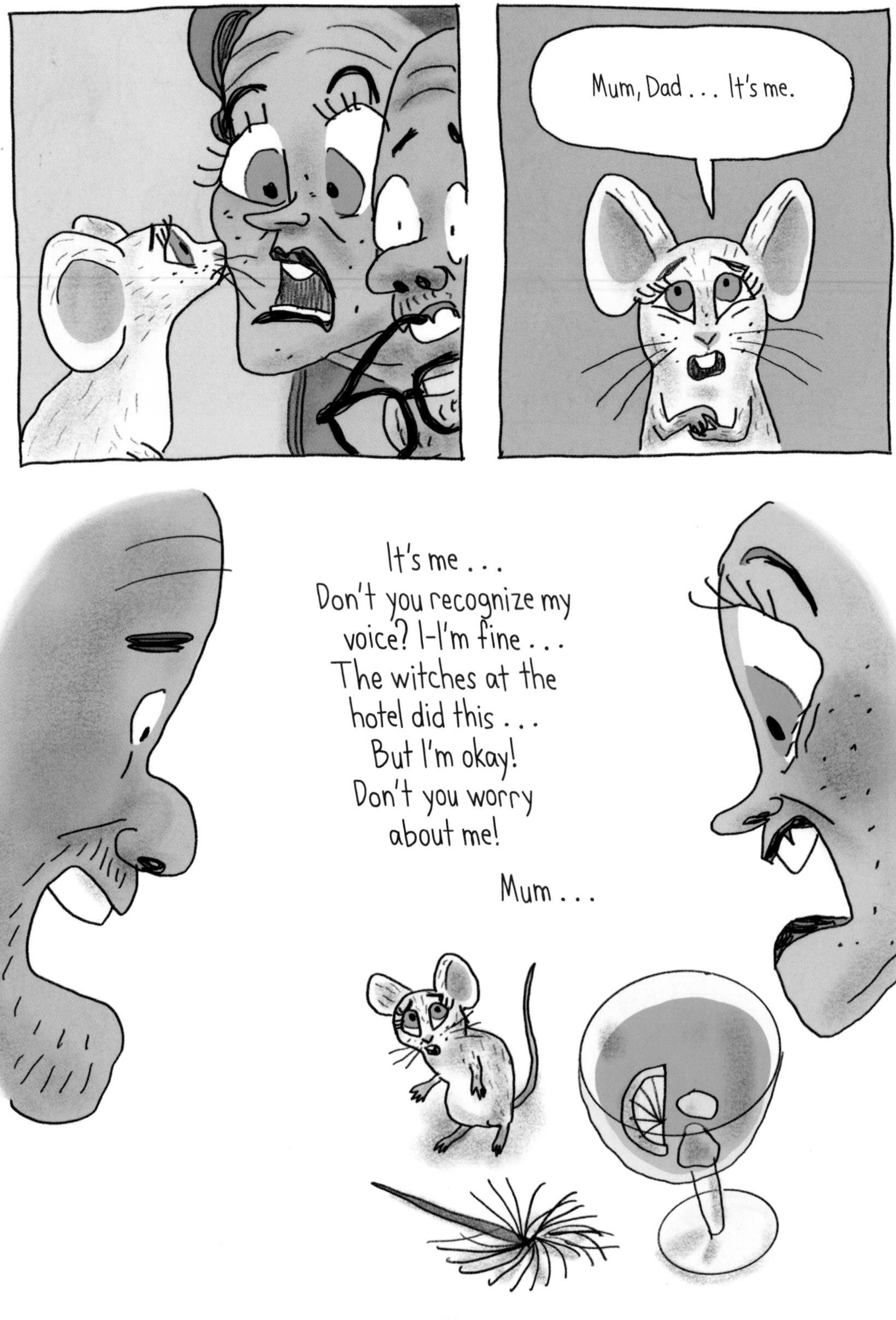

Mum, Dad . . . It's me.
It's me . . . Don't you recognize my voice? I-I'm fine . . . The witches at the hotel did this . . . But I'm okay! Don't you worry about me!
Mum . . .

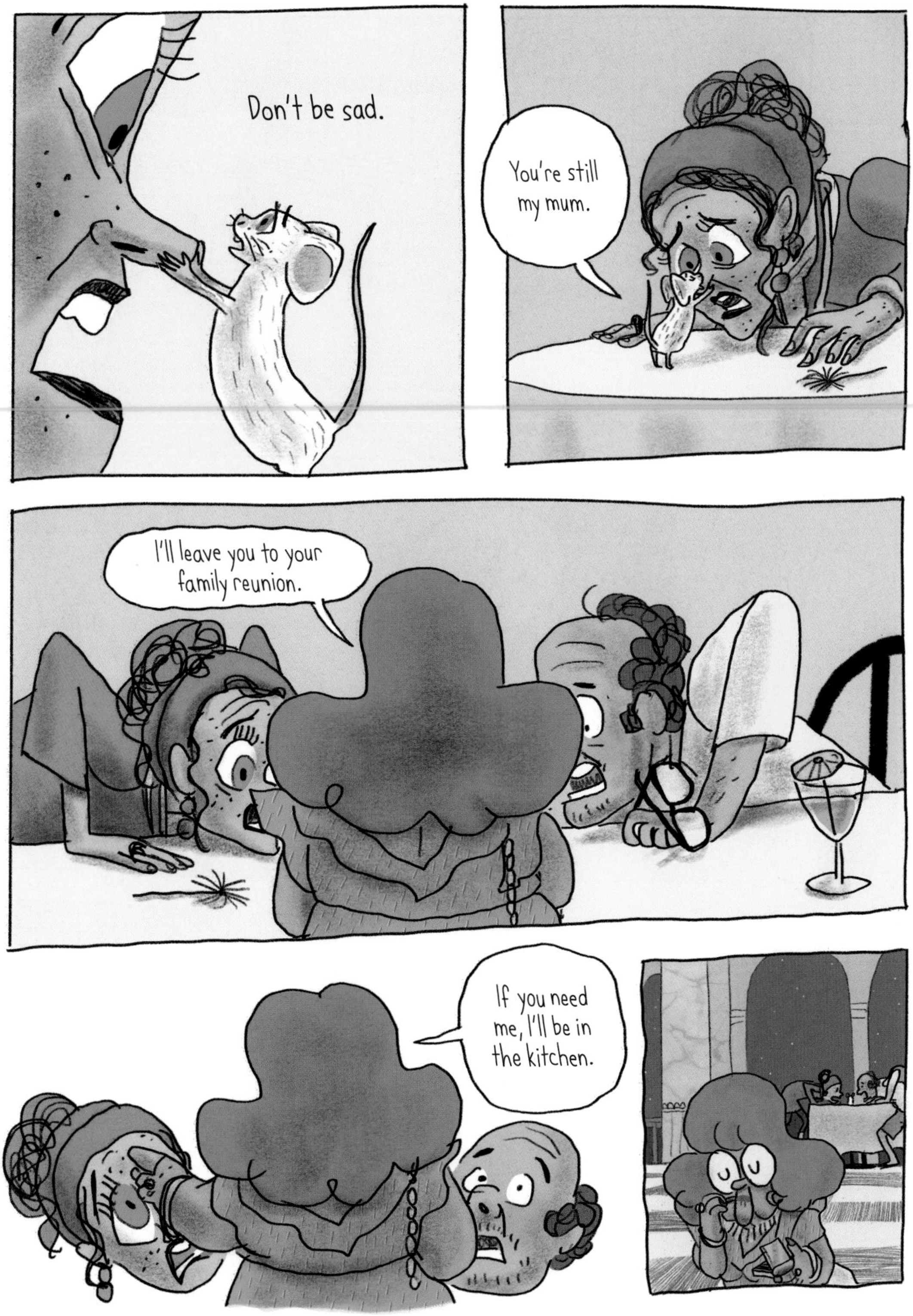
Don't be sad.
You're still my mum.
I'll leave you to your family reunion.
If you need me, I'll be in the kitchen.

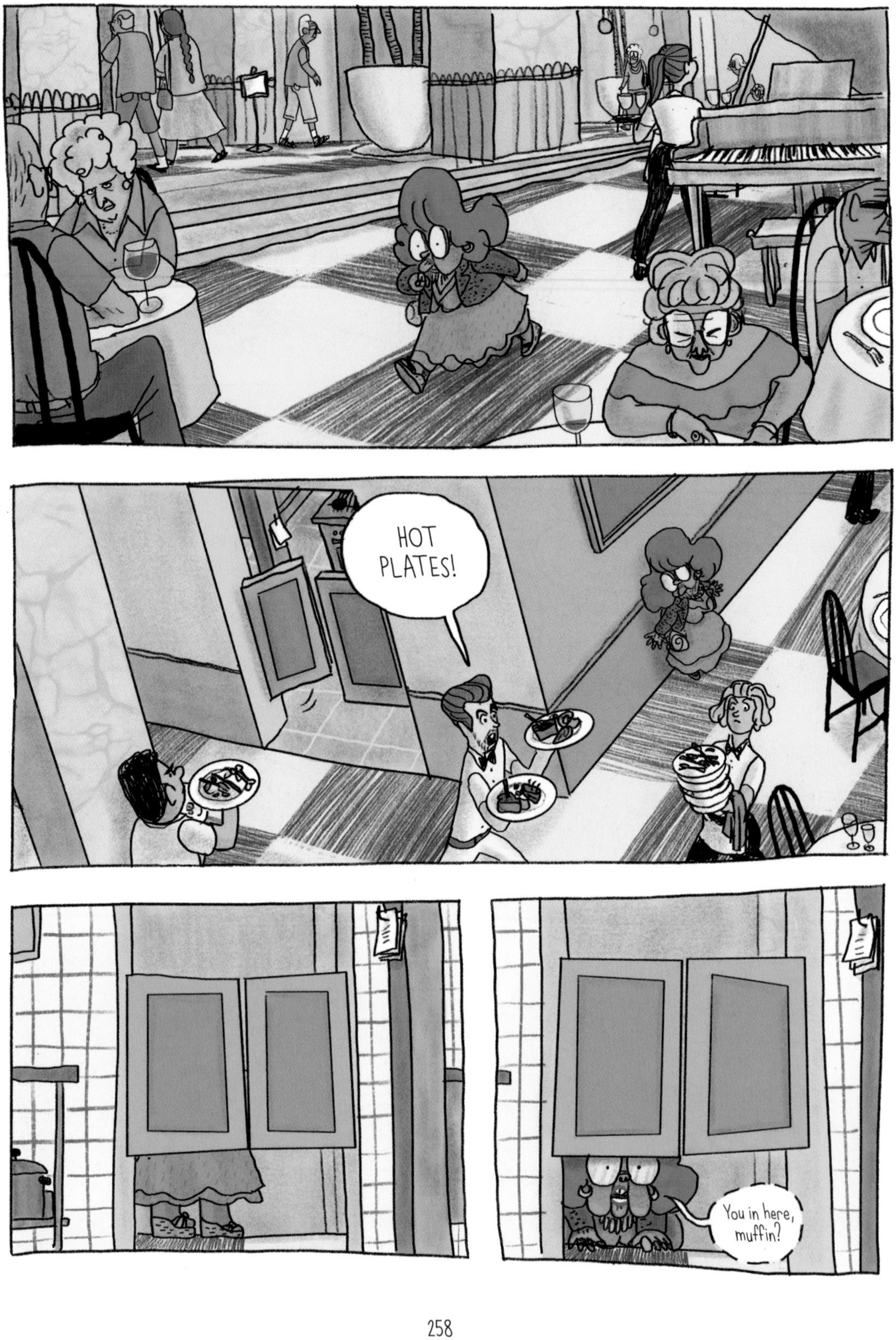
HOT PLATES!
You in here, muffin?

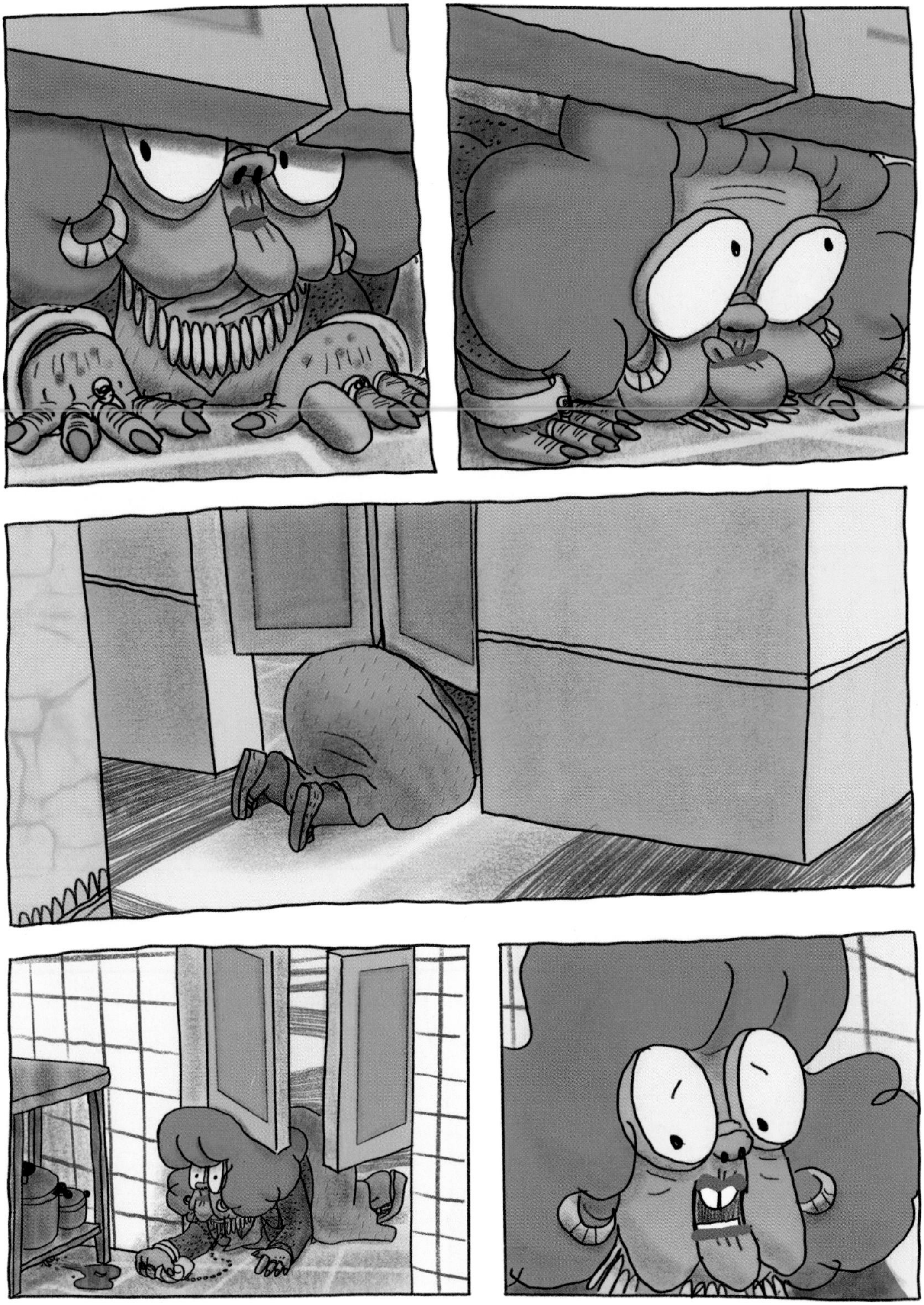

No!!

Gr . . .
Grand-
mamma?

My baby
boy!

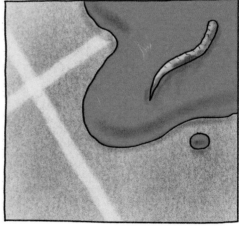

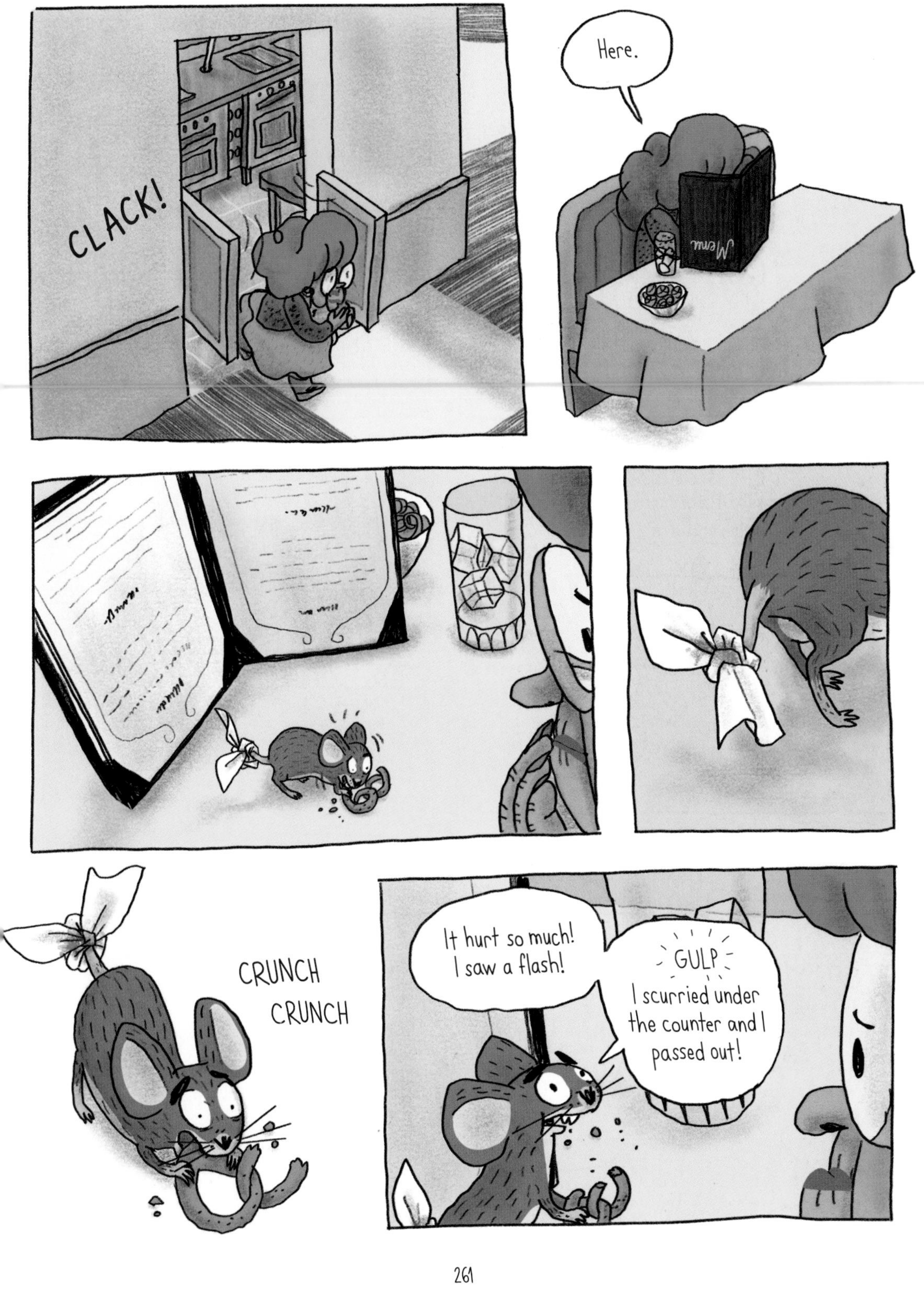
CLACK!
Here.
Menu
CRUNCH
CRUNCH
It hurt so much!
I saw a flash!
GULP
I scurried under
the counter and I
passed out!

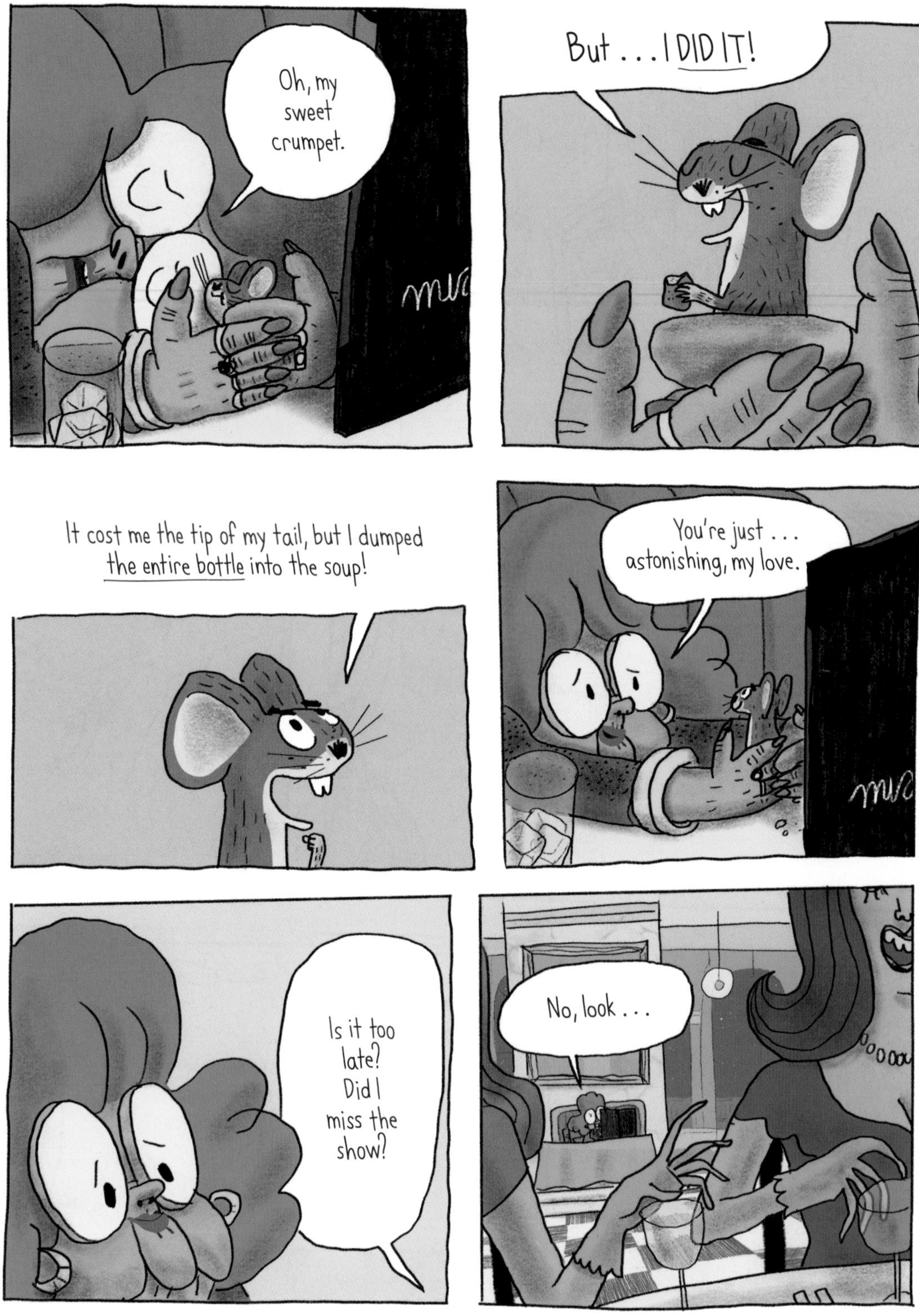
Oh, my sweet crumpet.
But . . . I DID IT!
It cost me the tip of my tail, but I dumped the entire bottle into the soup!
You're just . . . astonishing, my love.
Is it too late? Did I miss the show?
No, look . . .

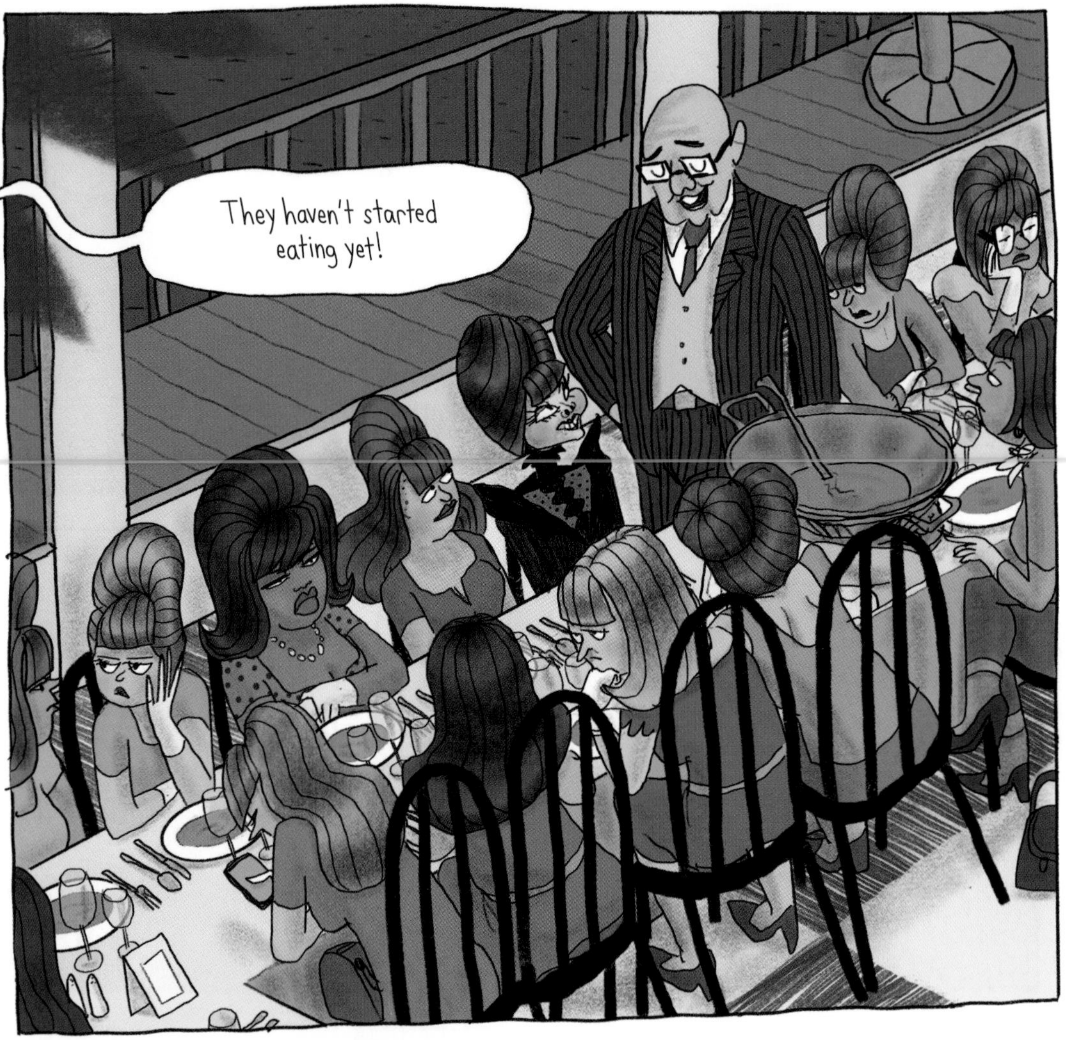
They haven't started eating yet!

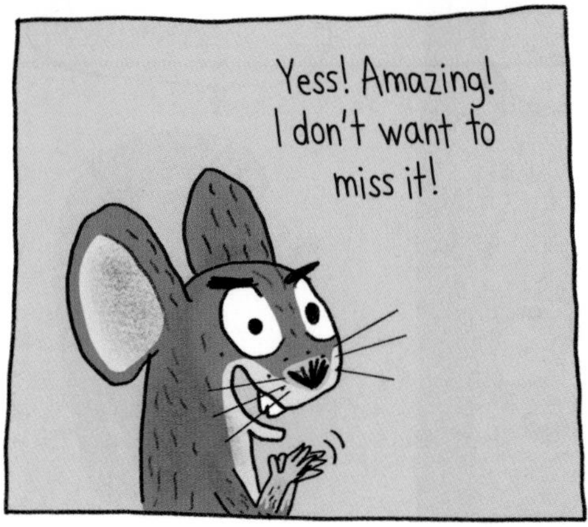
Yess! Amazing! I don't want to miss it!

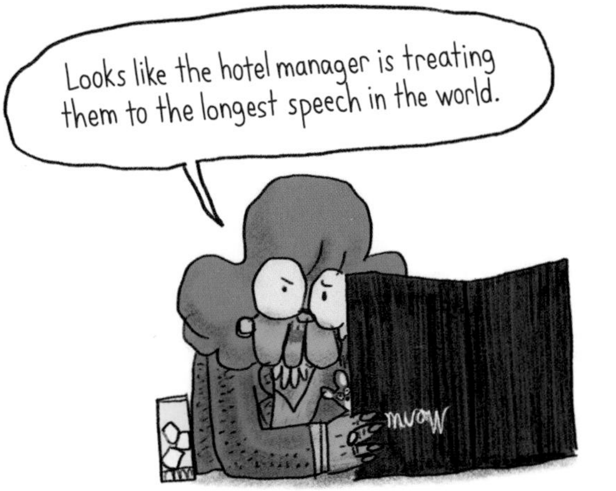
Looks like the hotel manager is treating them to the longest speech in the world.
mvaw

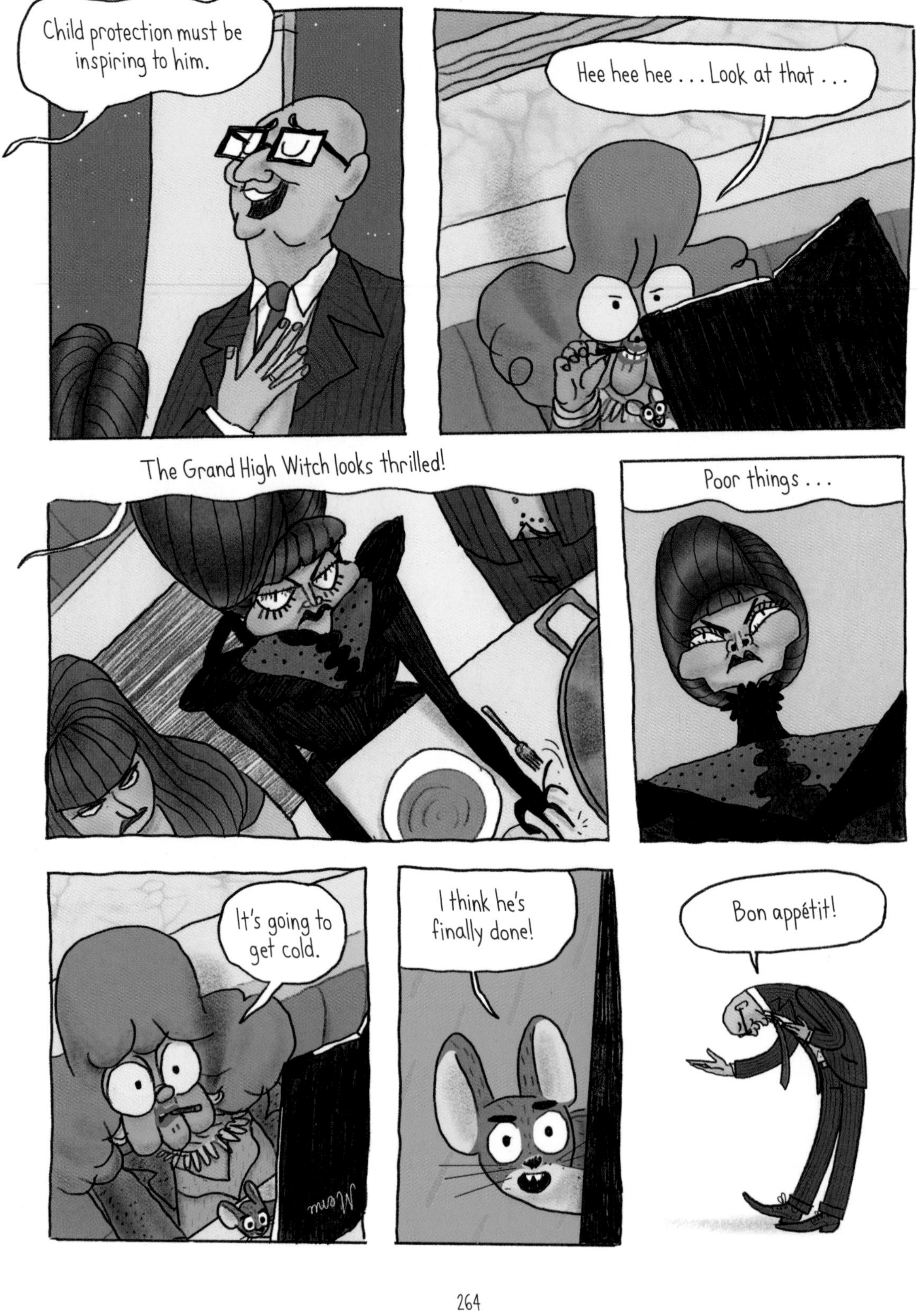
Child protection must be inspiring to him.
Hee hee hee . . . Look at that . . .
The Grand High Witch looks thrilled!
Poor things . . .
It's going to get cold.
I think he's finally done!
Bon appétit!

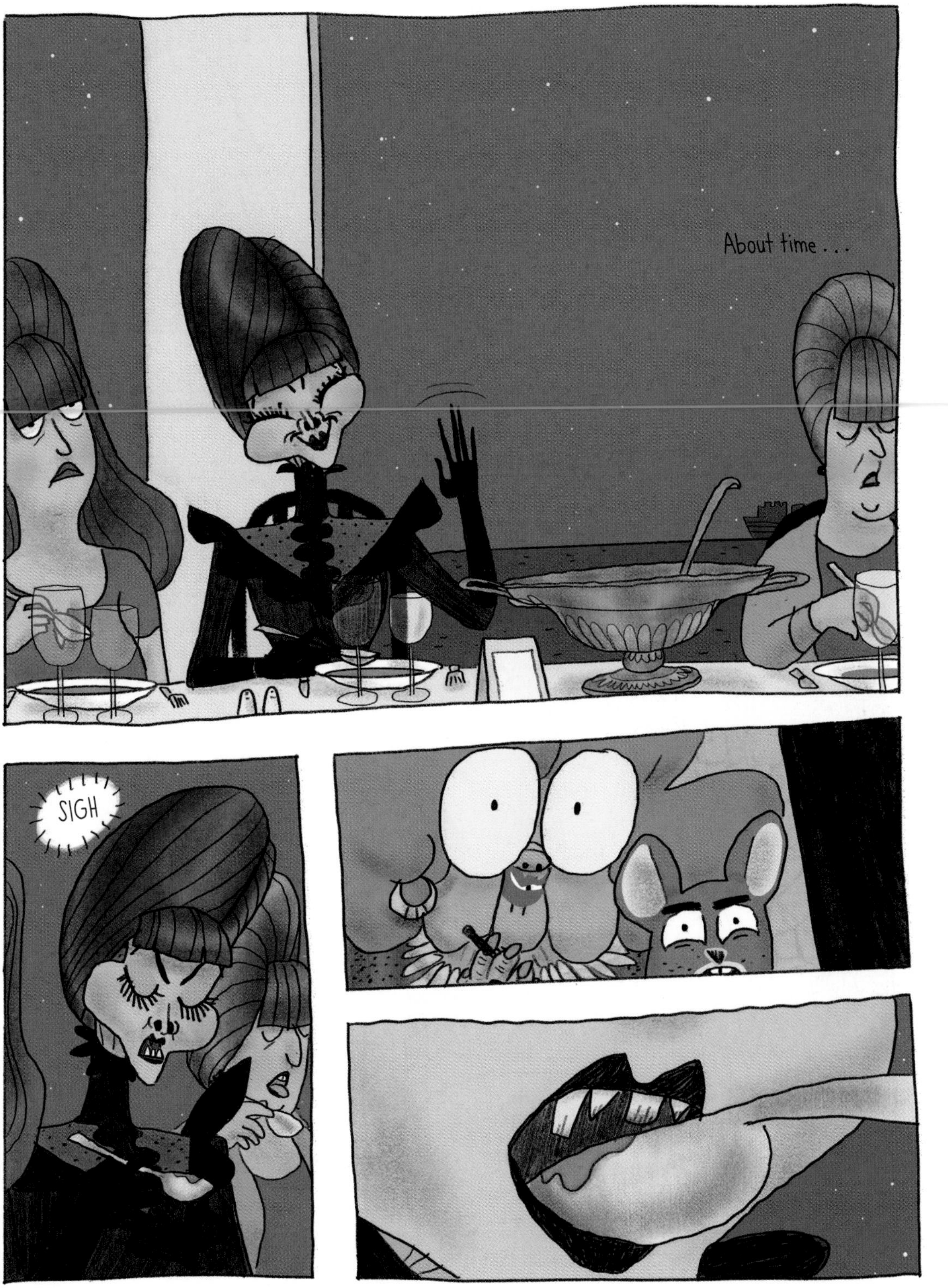
About time . . .
SIGH

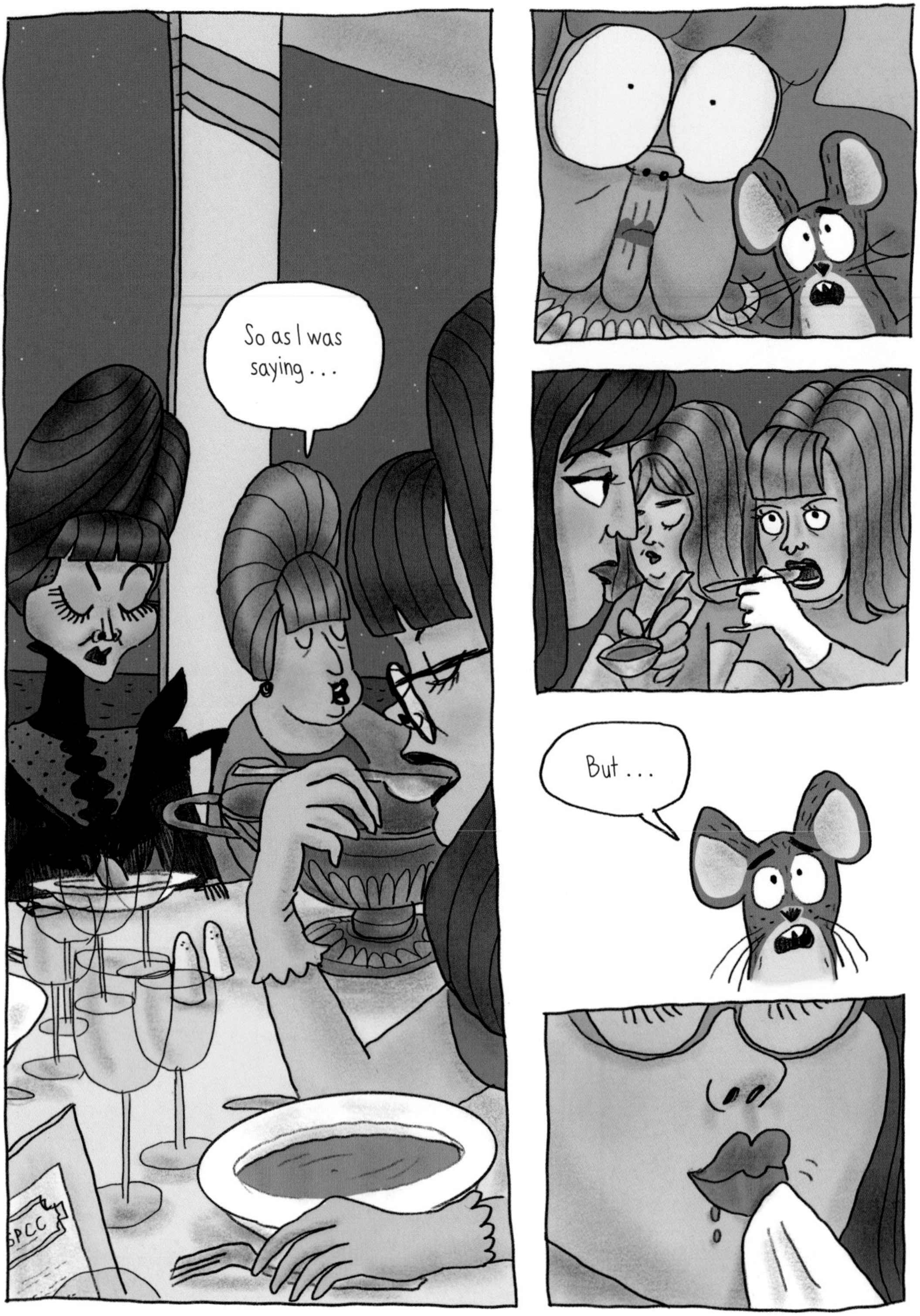
So as I was saying . . .
SPCC
But . . .

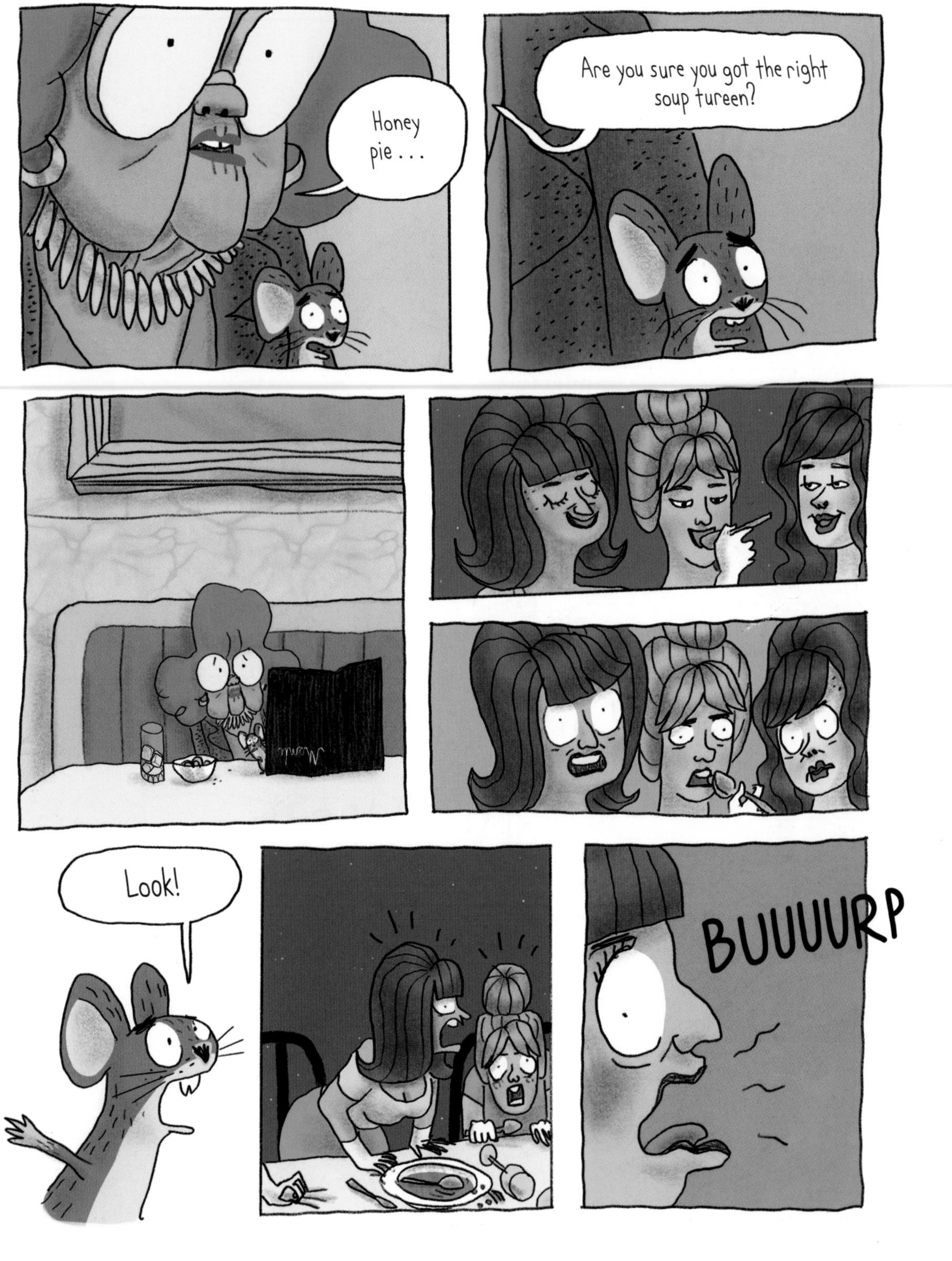
Honey pie . . .
Are you sure you got the right soup tureen?
Look!
BUUUURP

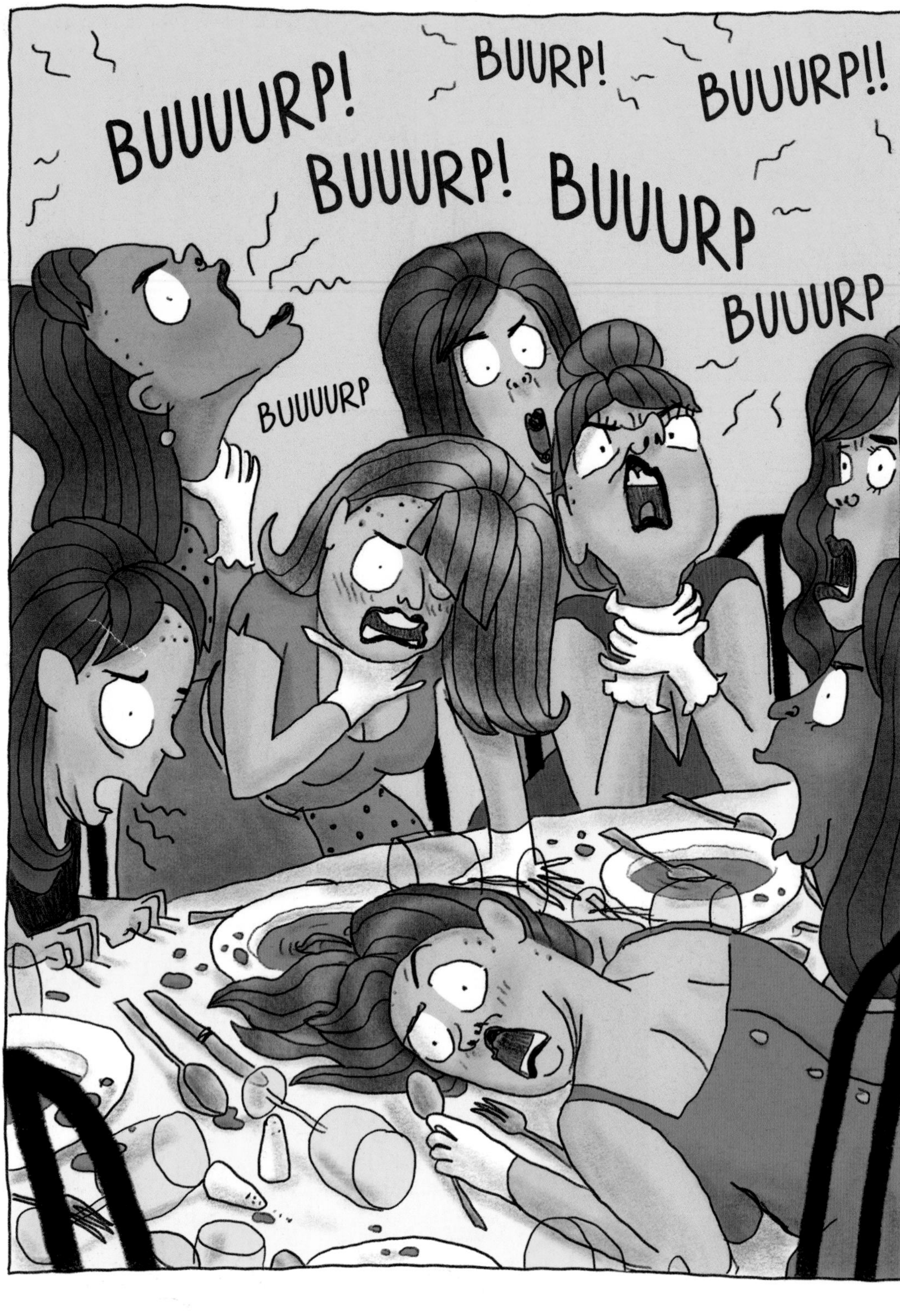
BUUUURP!
BUURP!
BUUURP!!
BUUURP!
BUUURP
BUUURP
BUUUURP

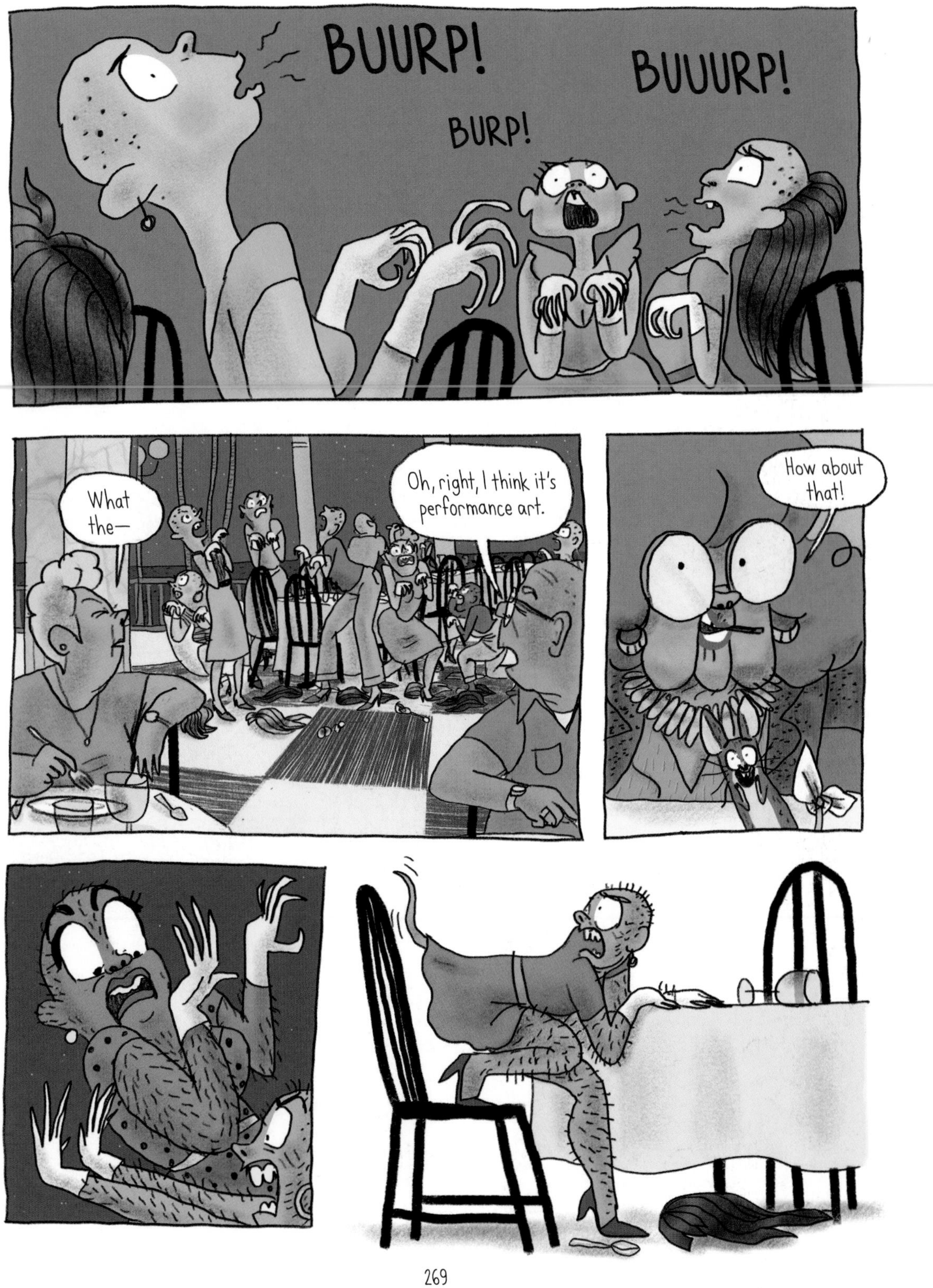
BUURP!
BURP!
BUUURP!
What the—
Oh, right, I think it's performance art.
How about that!

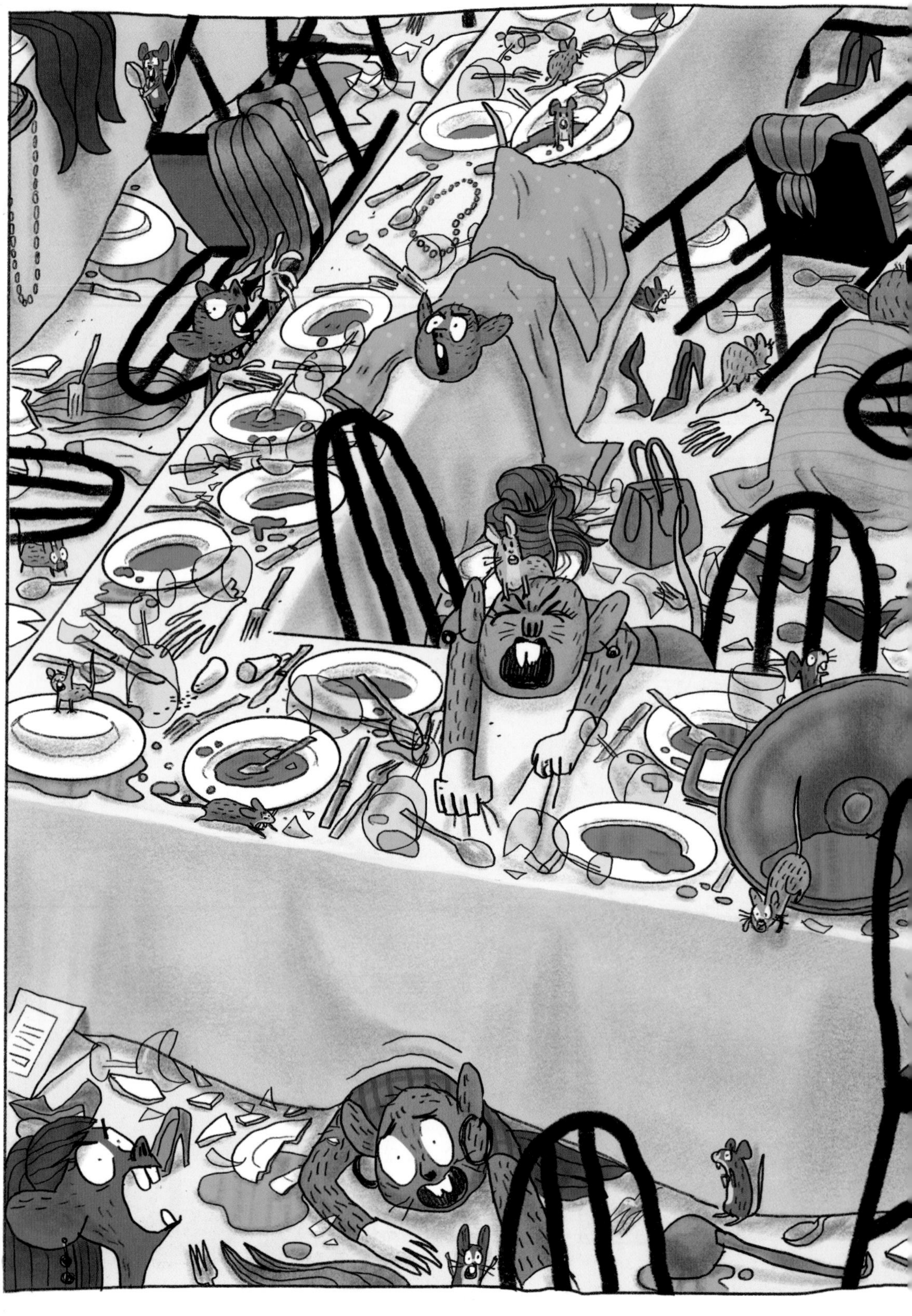

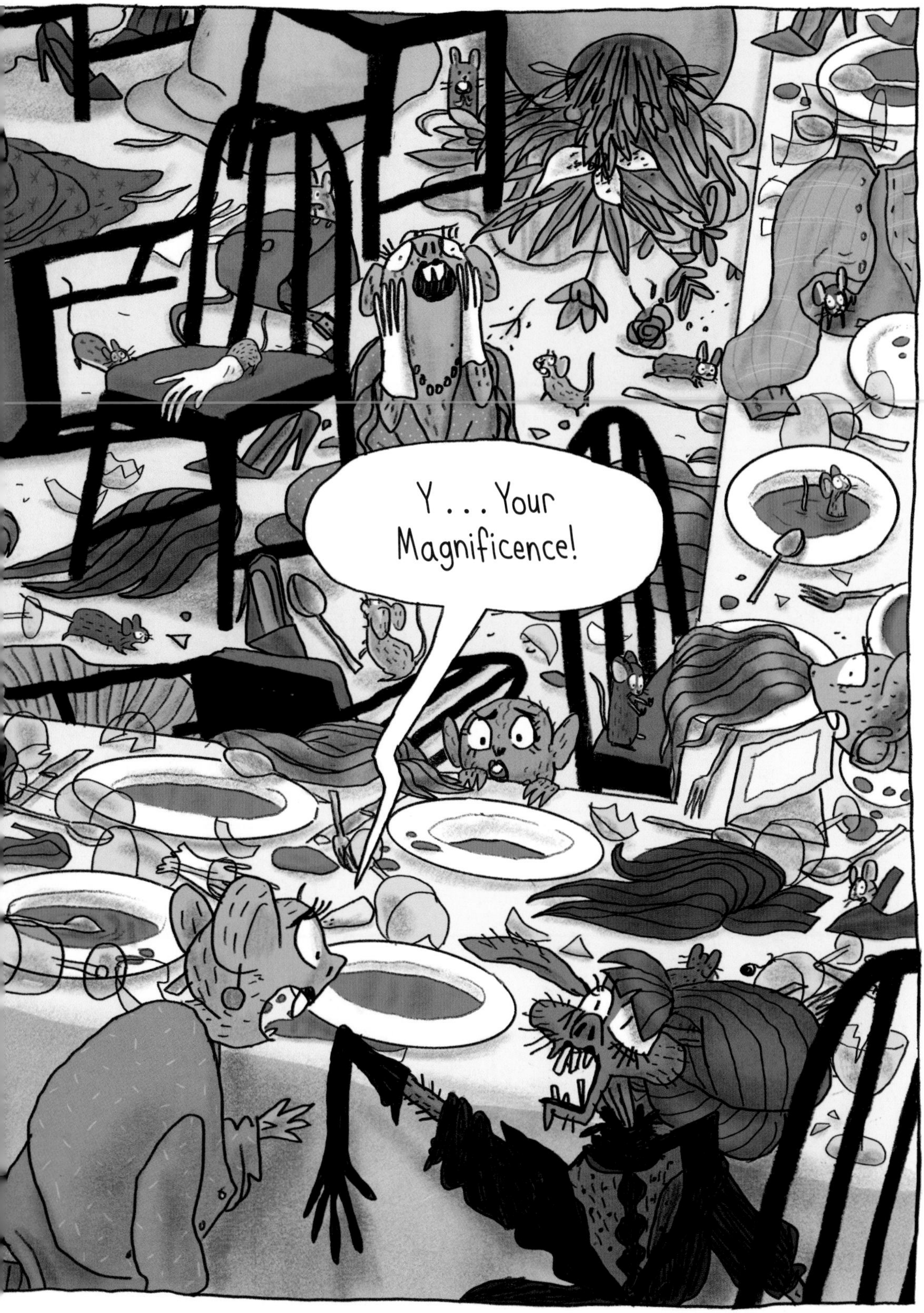
Y . . . Your Magnificence!

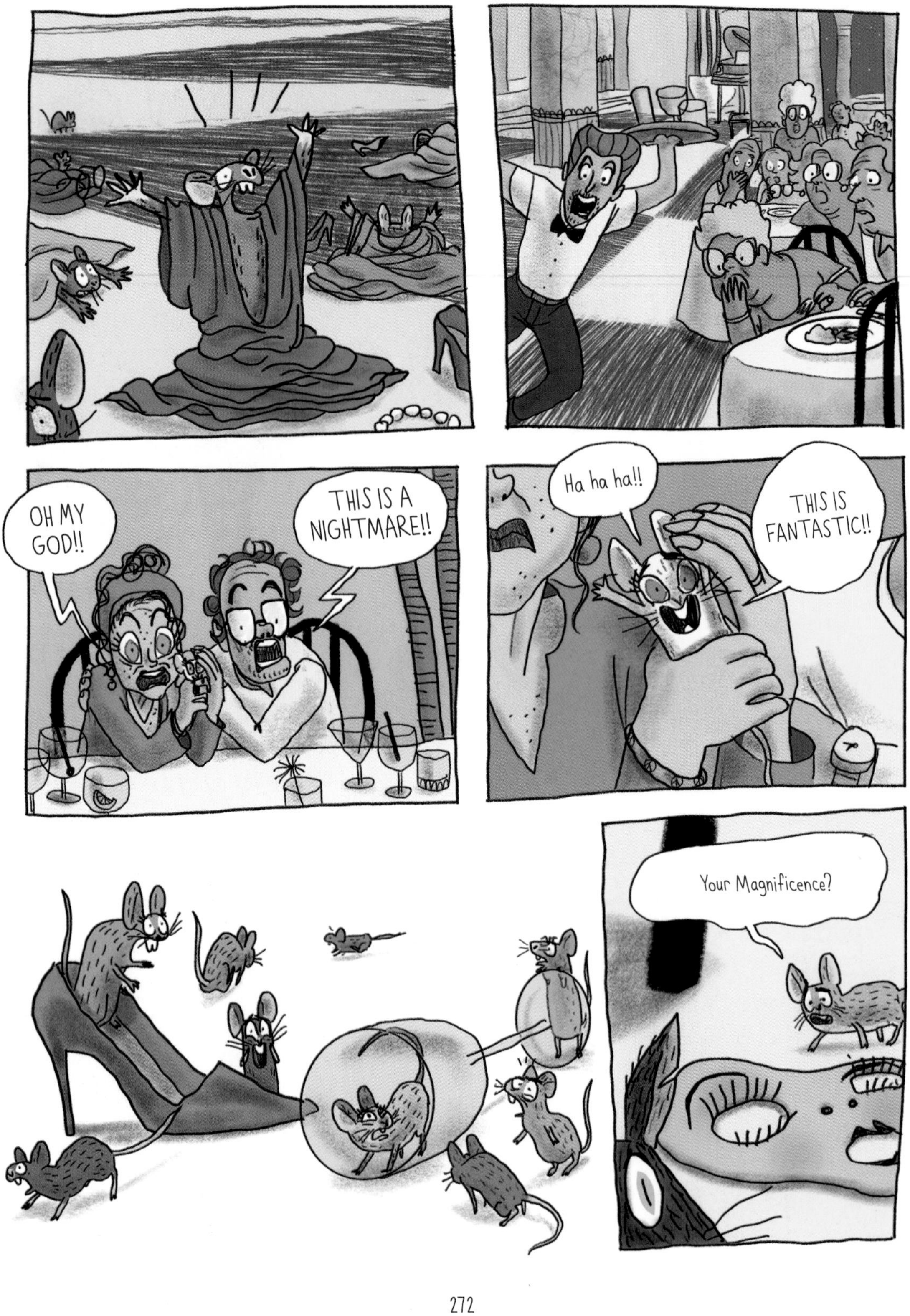
OH MY GOD!!
THIS IS A NIGHTMARE!!
Ha ha ha!!
THIS IS FANTASTIC!!
Your Magnificence?

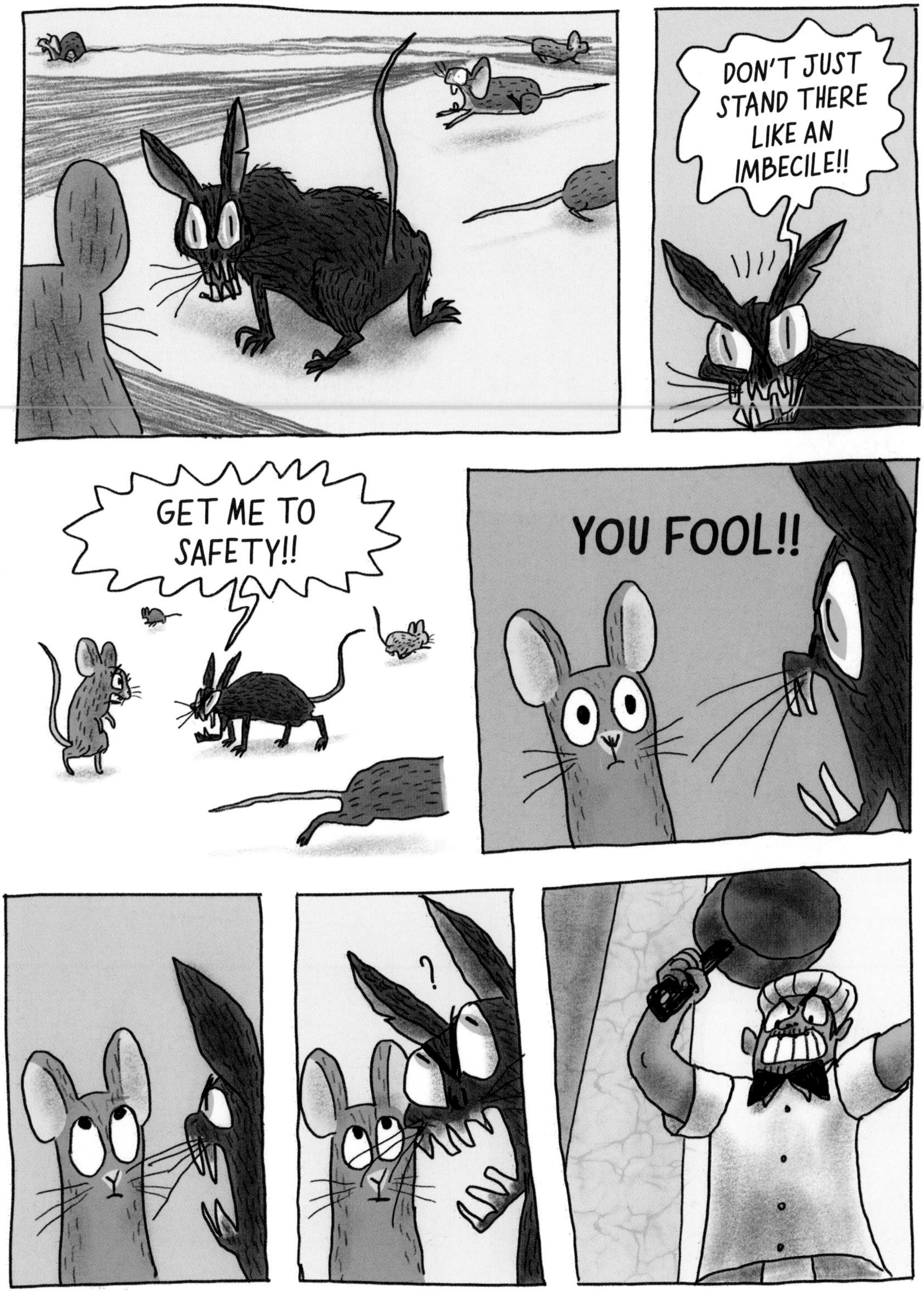
DON'T JUST STAND THERE LIKE AN IMBECILE!!
GET ME TO SAFETY!!
YOU FOOL!!
?

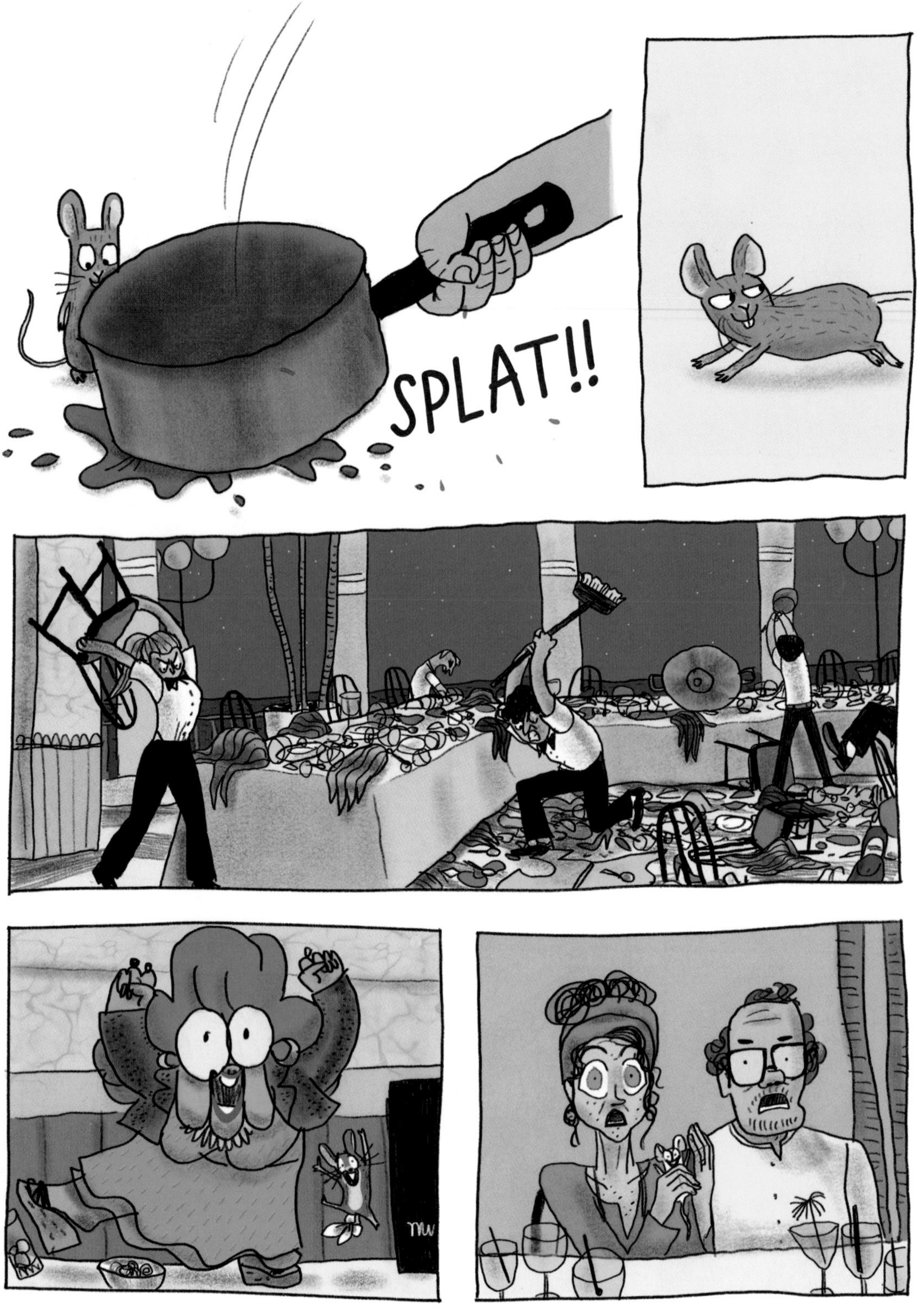
SPLAT!!

THEY'RE MINE!!

SLAM!

I'd say the evening's taken an ugly turn, darling.

Yes.

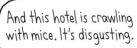

And this hotel is crawling with mice. It's disgusting.

Shall we go home?

Okay.

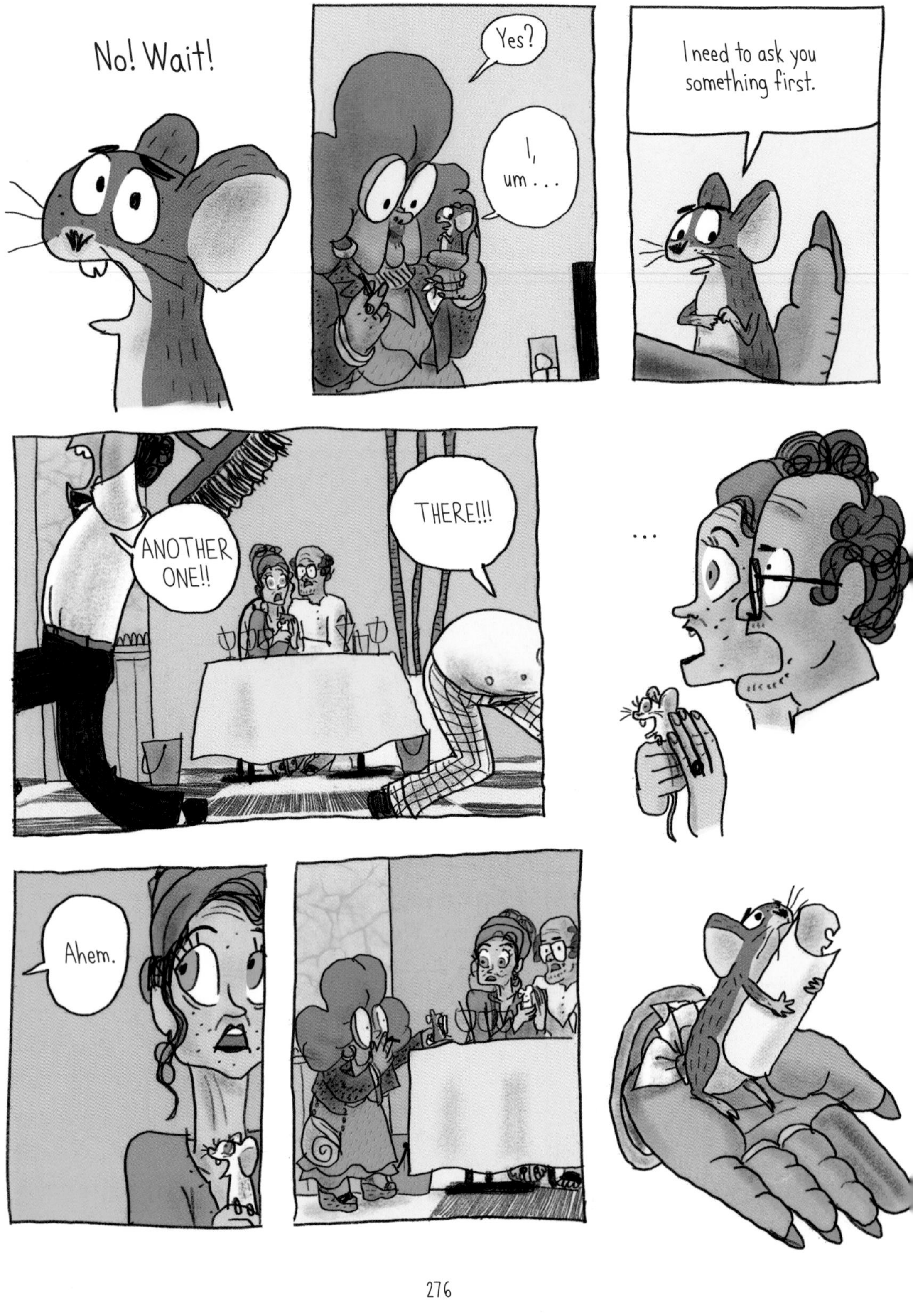
No! Wait!
Yes?
I, um . . .
I need to ask you something first.
ANOTHER ONE!!
THERE!!!
. . .
Ahem.

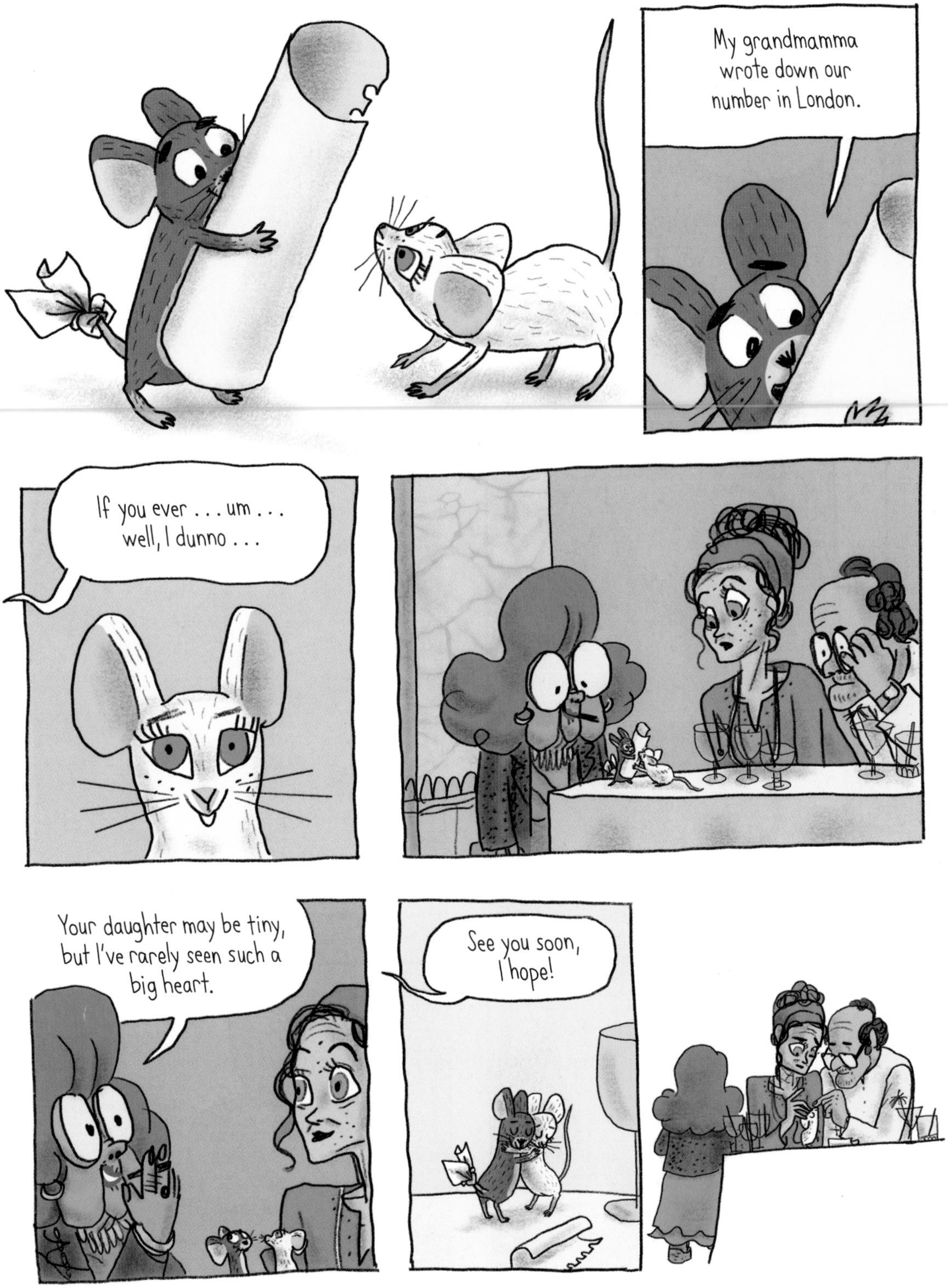
My grandmamma wrote down our number in London.
If you ever . . . um . . . well, I dunno . . .
Your daughter may be tiny, but I've rarely seen such a big heart.
See you soon, I hope!

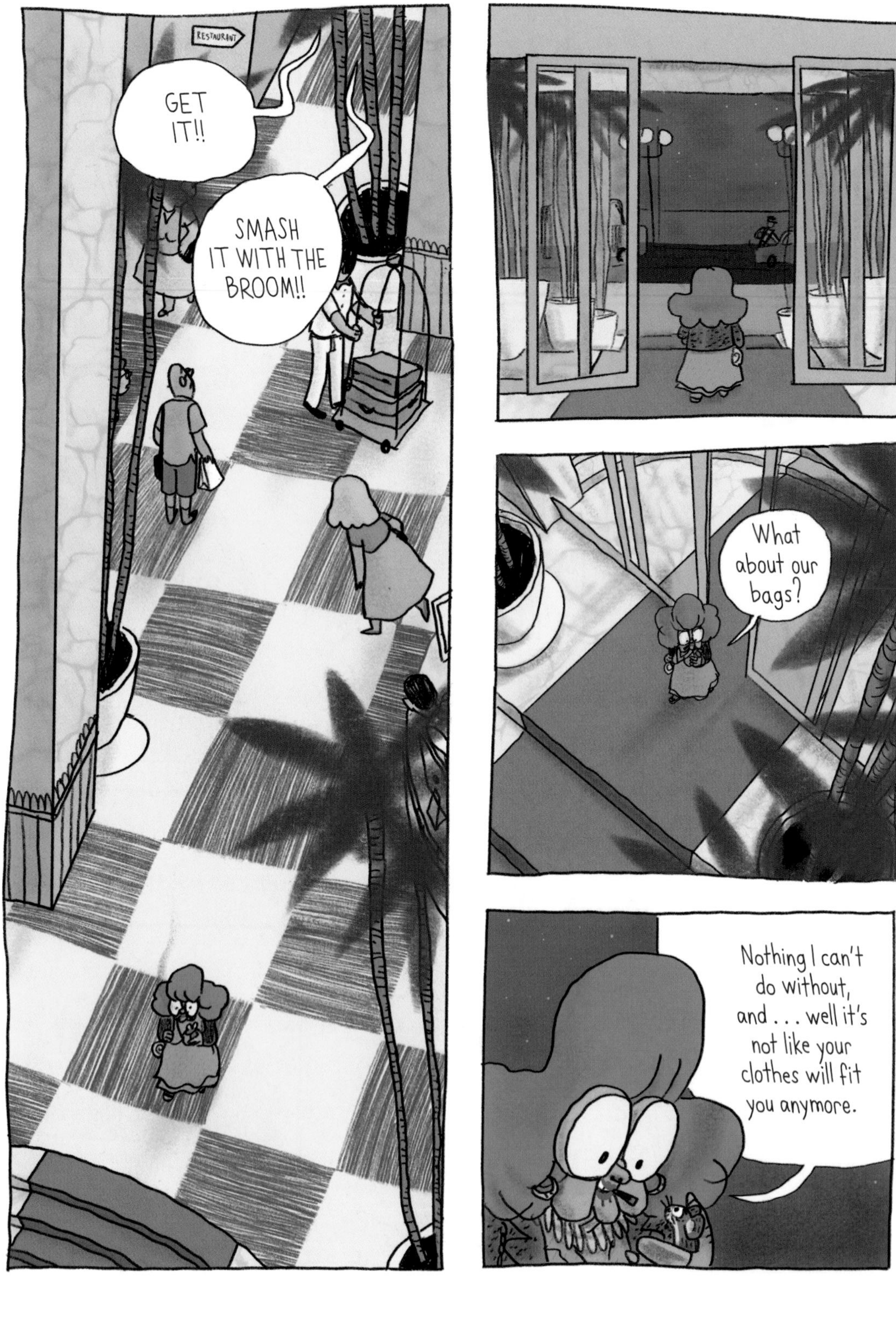
RESTAURANT
GET IT!!
SMASH IT WITH THE BROOM!!
What about our bags?
Nothing I can't do without, and . . . well it's not like your clothes will fit you anymore.

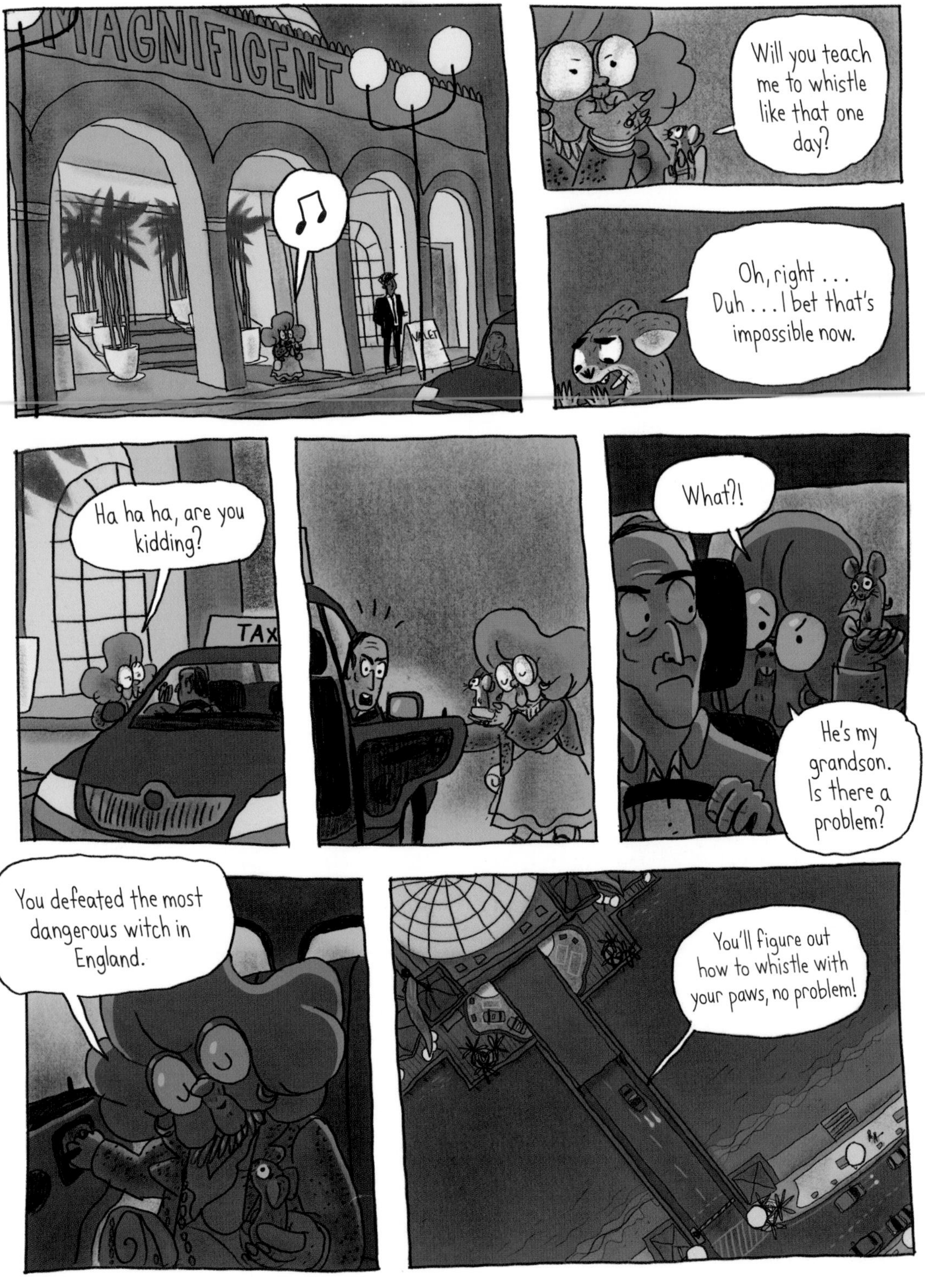
MAGNIFICENT
♫
VALET
Will you teach me to whistle like that one day?
Oh, right . . . Duh . . . I bet that's impossible now.
Ha ha ha, are you kidding?
TAX
What?!
He's my grandson. Is there a problem?
You defeated the most dangerous witch in England.
You'll figure out how to whistle with your paws, no problem!

One month later . . .

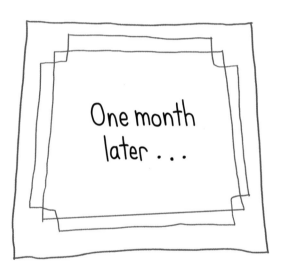

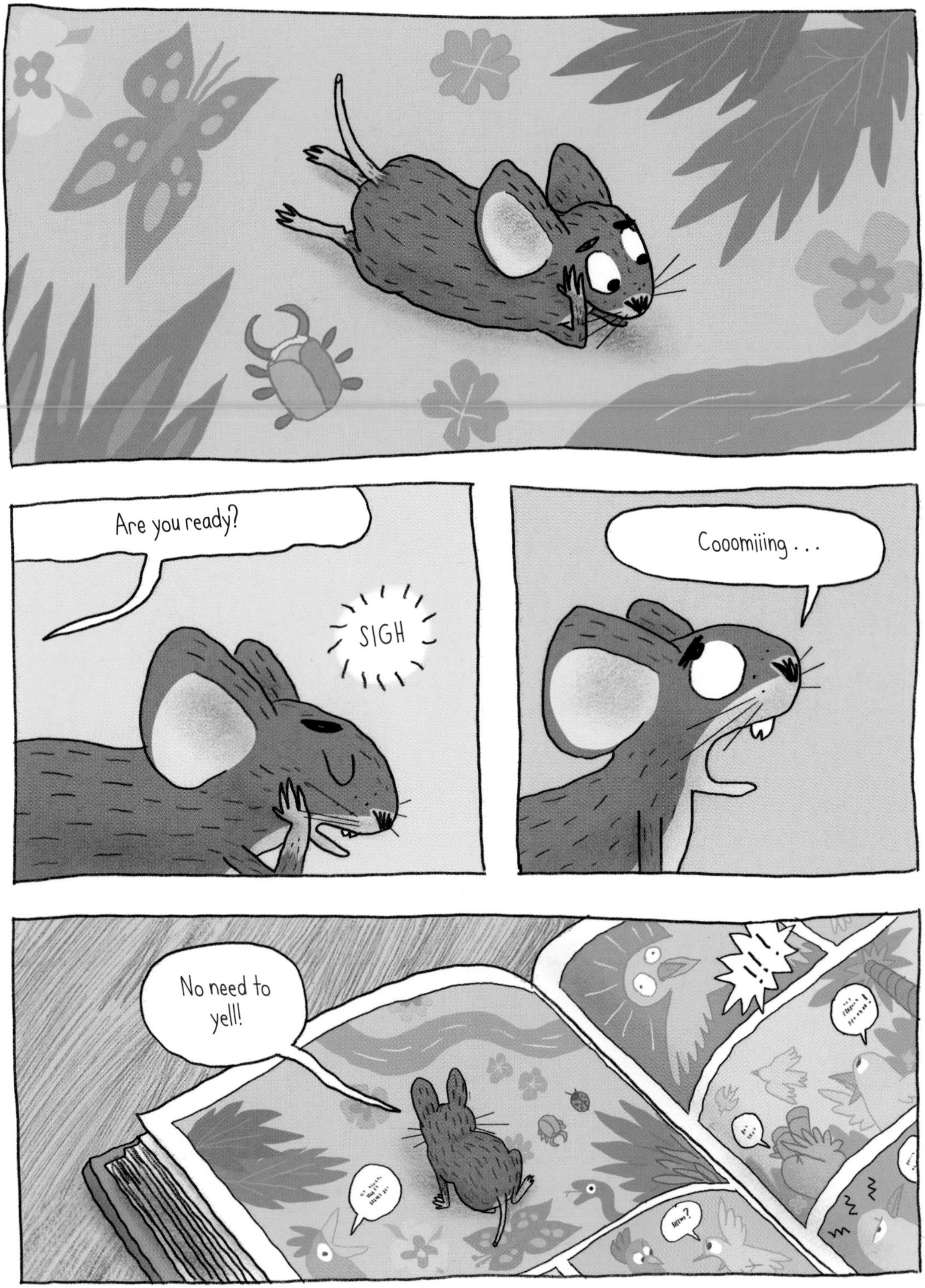

Are you ready?
SIGH
Cooomiiing . . .
No need to yell!

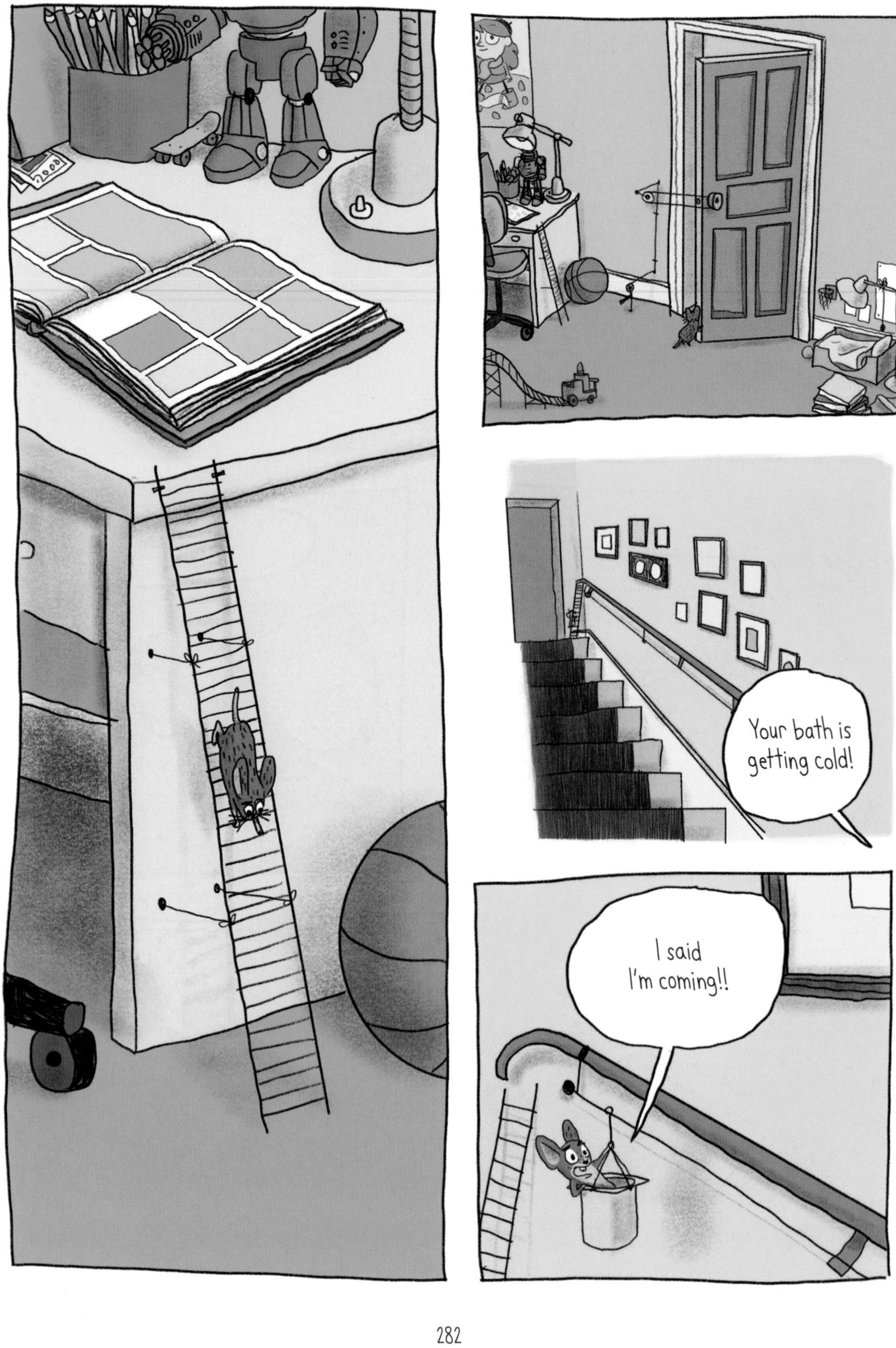

Your bath is getting cold!
I said I'm coming!!

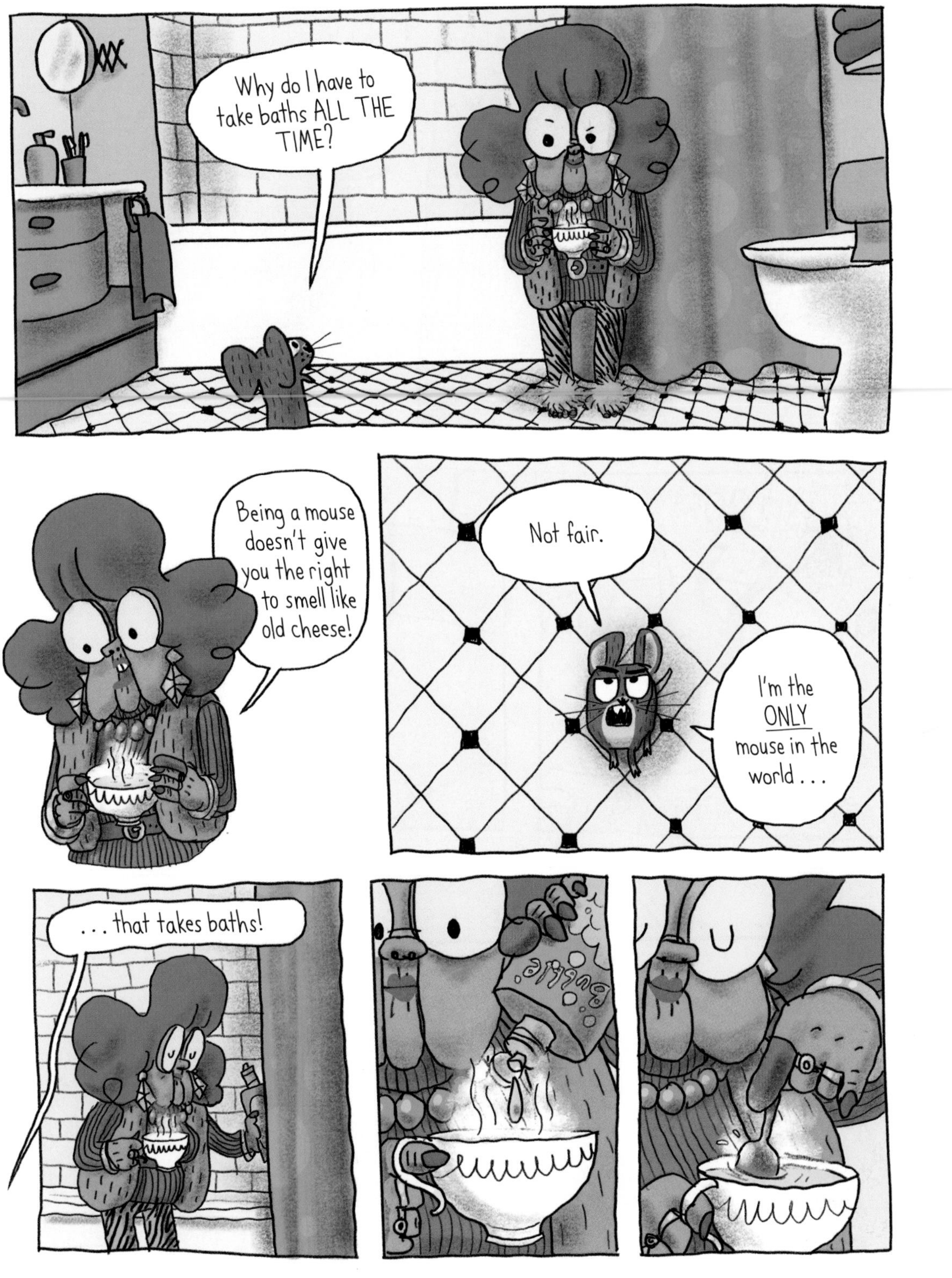

Why do I have to take baths ALL THE TIME?
Being a mouse doesn't give you the right to smell like old cheese!
Not fair.
I'm the ONLY mouse in the world . . .
. . . that takes baths!
Bubble

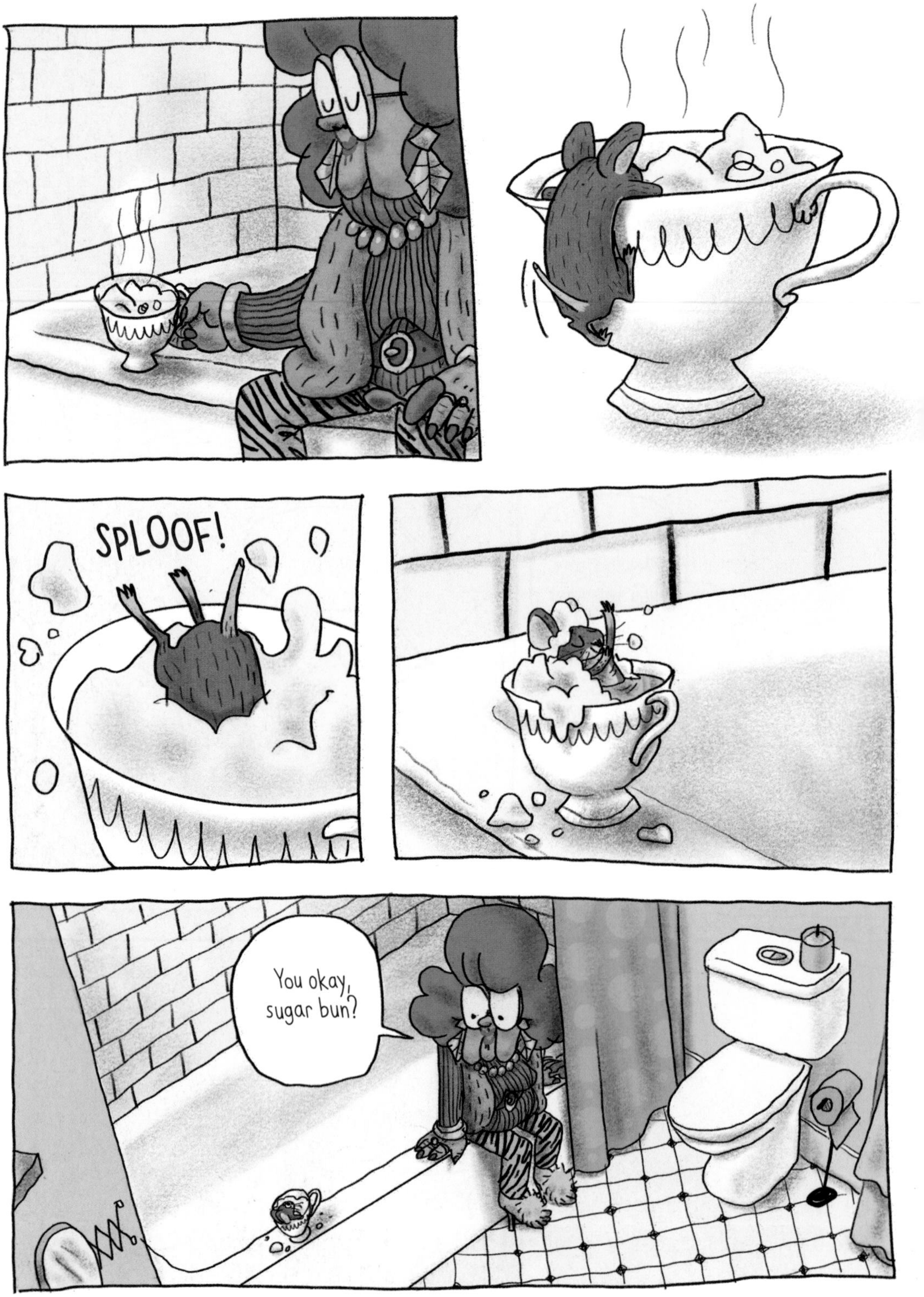
SPLOOF!
You okay, sugar bun?

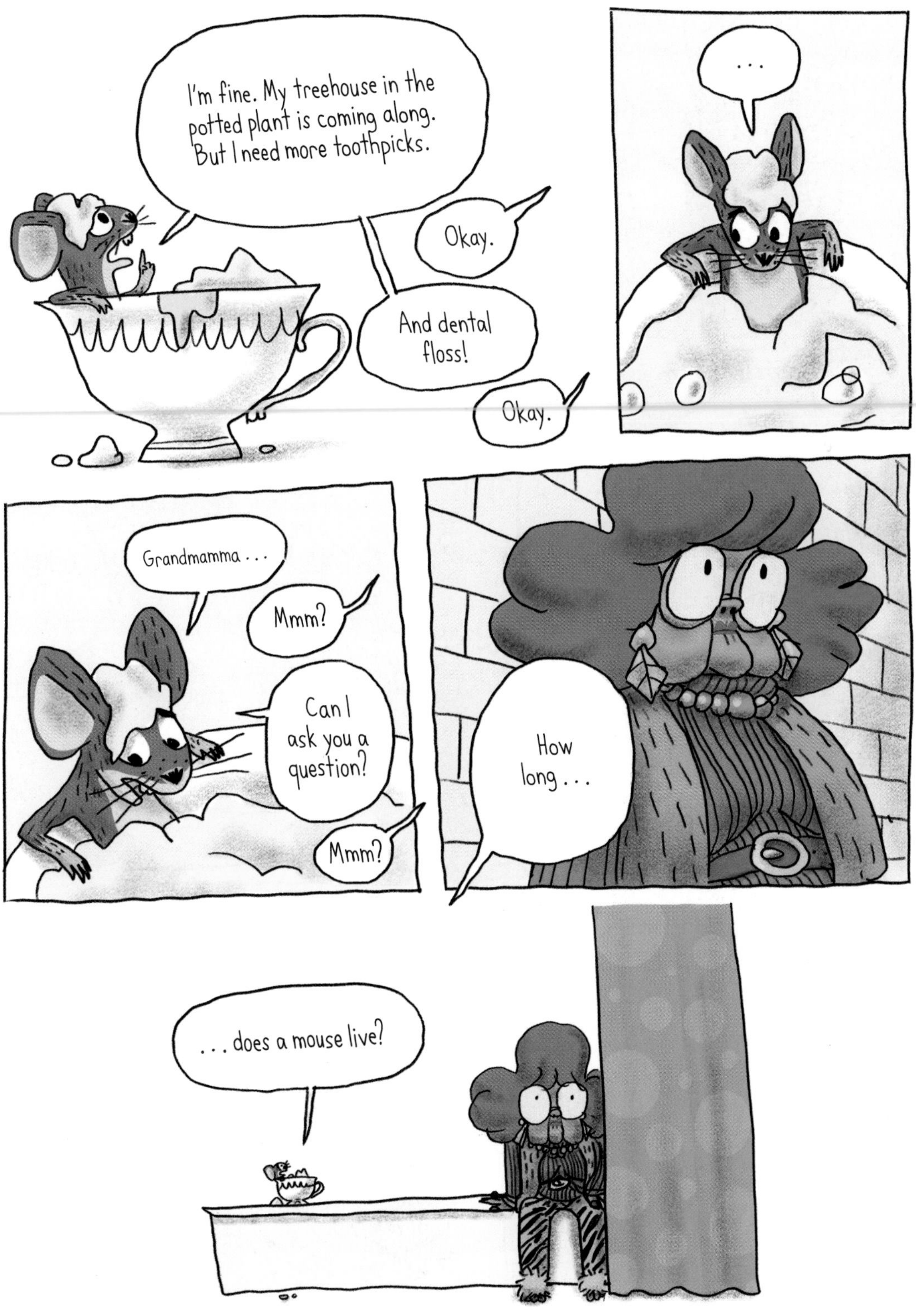
I'm fine. My treehouse in the potted plant is coming along. But I need more toothpicks.
Okay.
And dental floss!
Okay.
. . .
Grandmamma . . .
Mmm?
Can I ask you a question?
Mmm?
How long . . .
. . . does a mouse live?

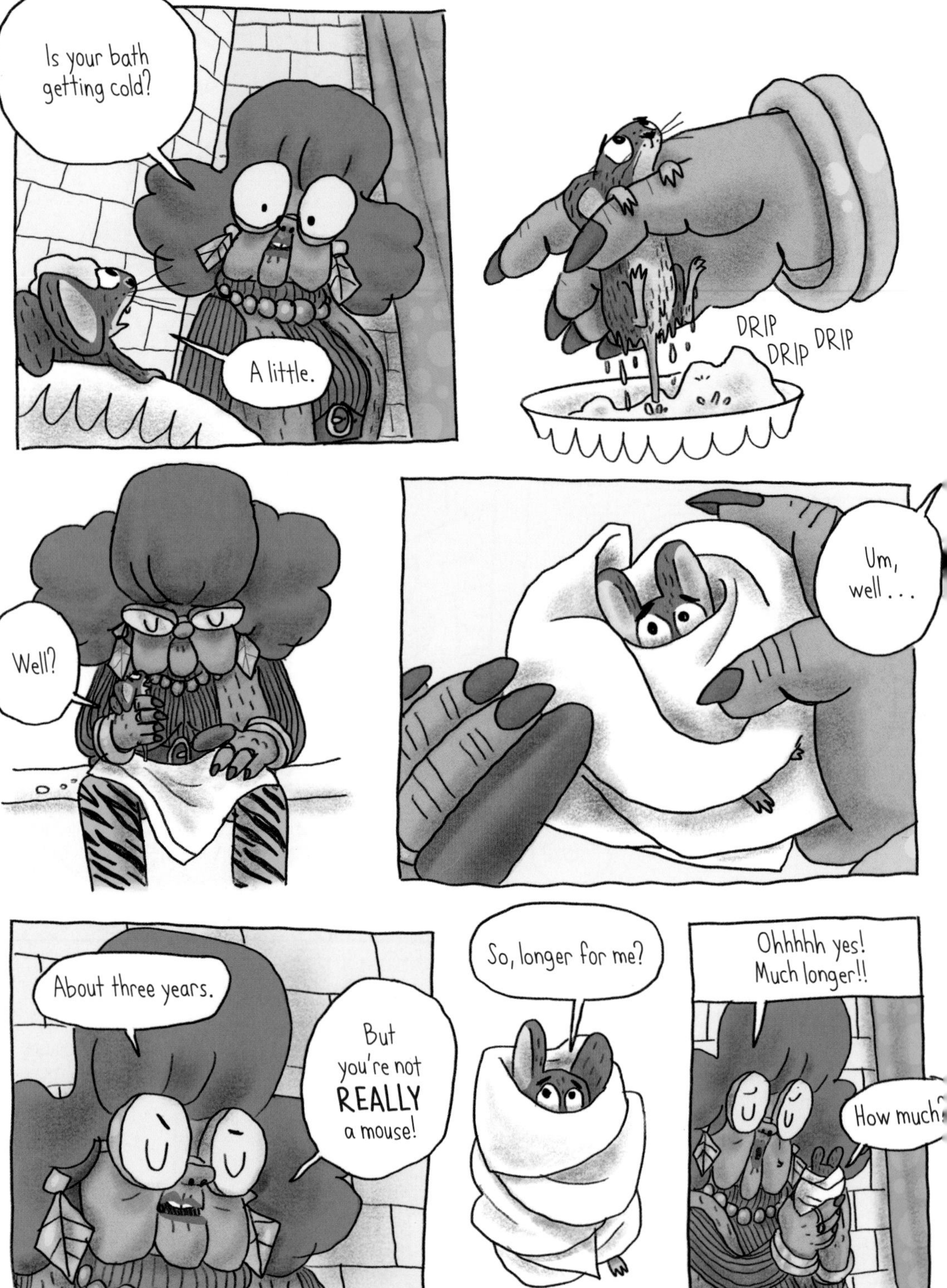

Is your bath getting cold?
A little.
DRIP
DRIP
DRIP
Well?
Um, well . . .
About three years.
But you're not REALLY a mouse!
So, longer for me?
Ohhhhh yes! Much longer!!
How much?

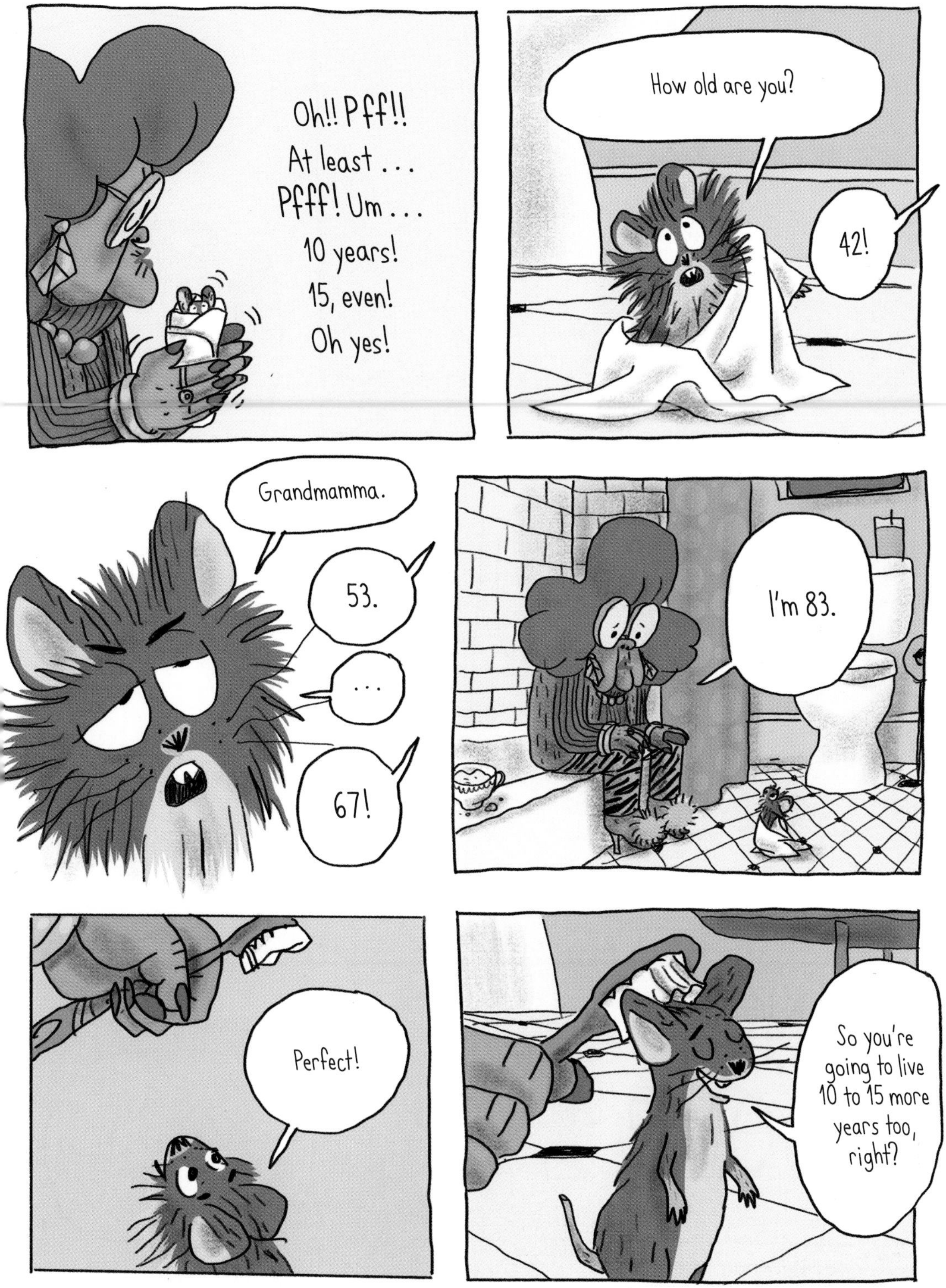
Oh!! Pff!!
At least . . .
Pfff! Um . . .
10 years!
15, even!
Oh yes!
How old are you?
42!
Grandmamma.
53.
. . .
67!
I'm 83.
Perfect!
So you're going to live 10 to 15 more years too, right?

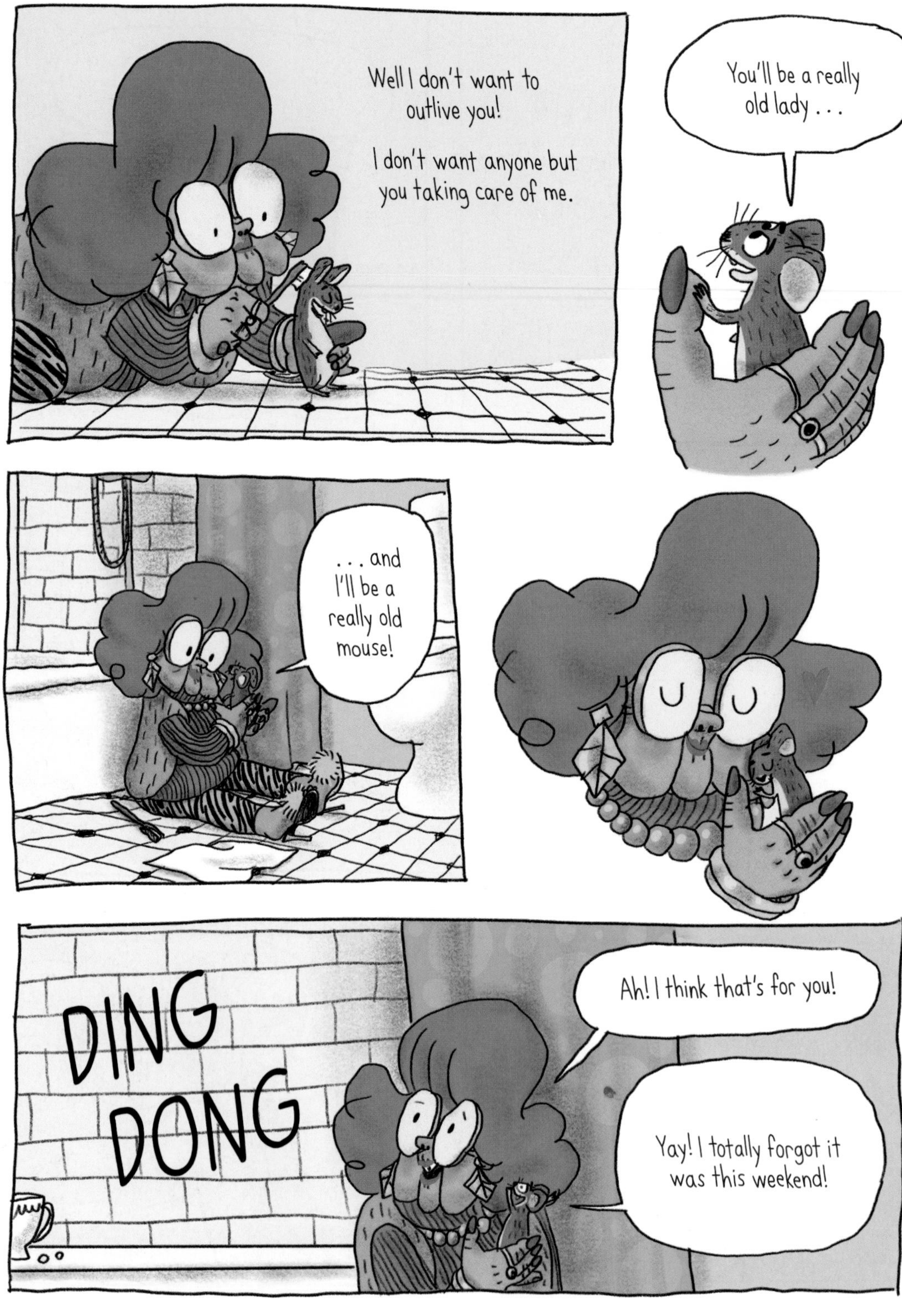
Well I don't want to outlive you!
I don't want anyone but you taking care of me.
You'll be a really old lady . . .
. . . and I'll be a really old mouse!
DING DONG
Ah! I think that's for you!
Yay! I totally forgot it was this weekend!

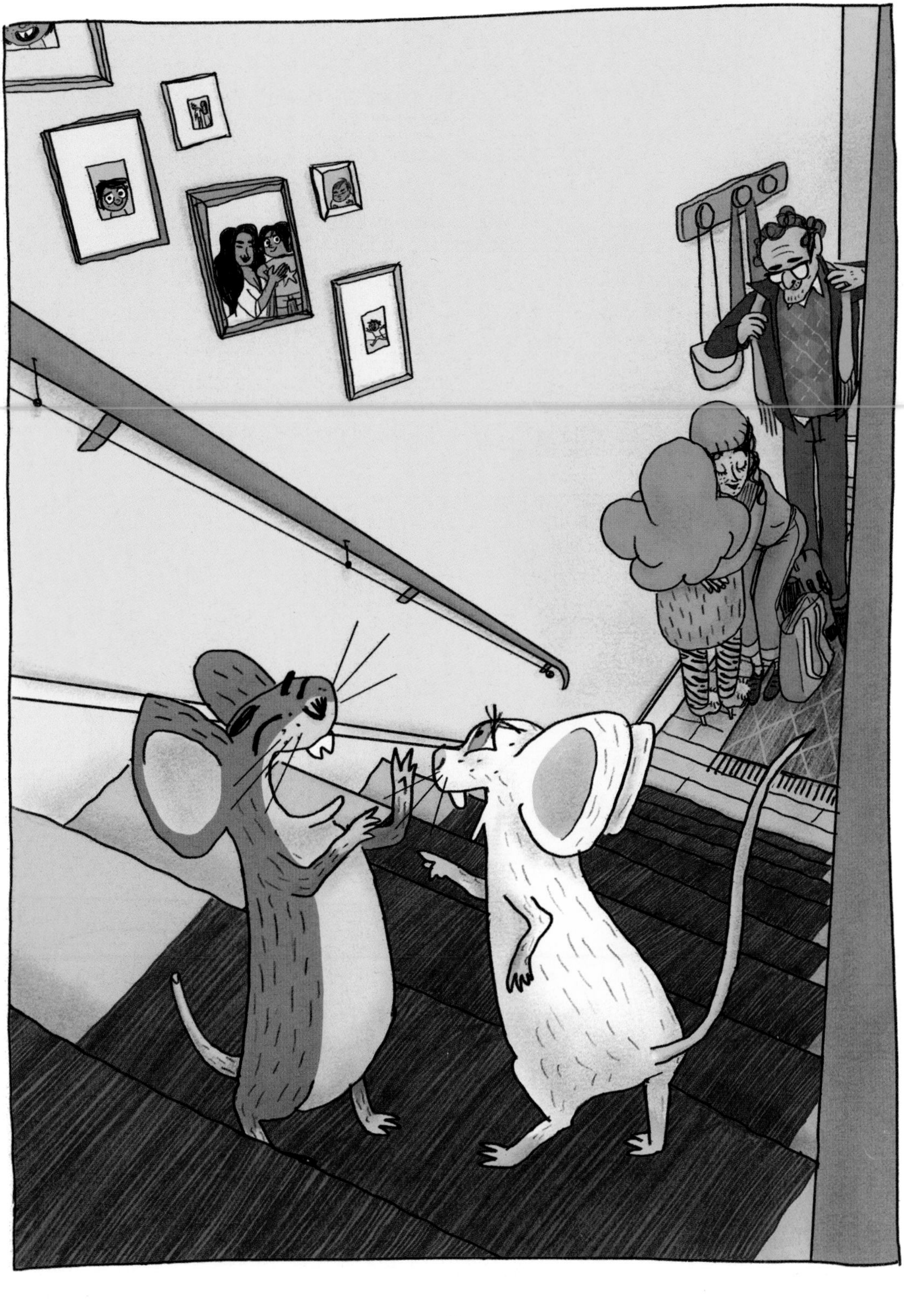

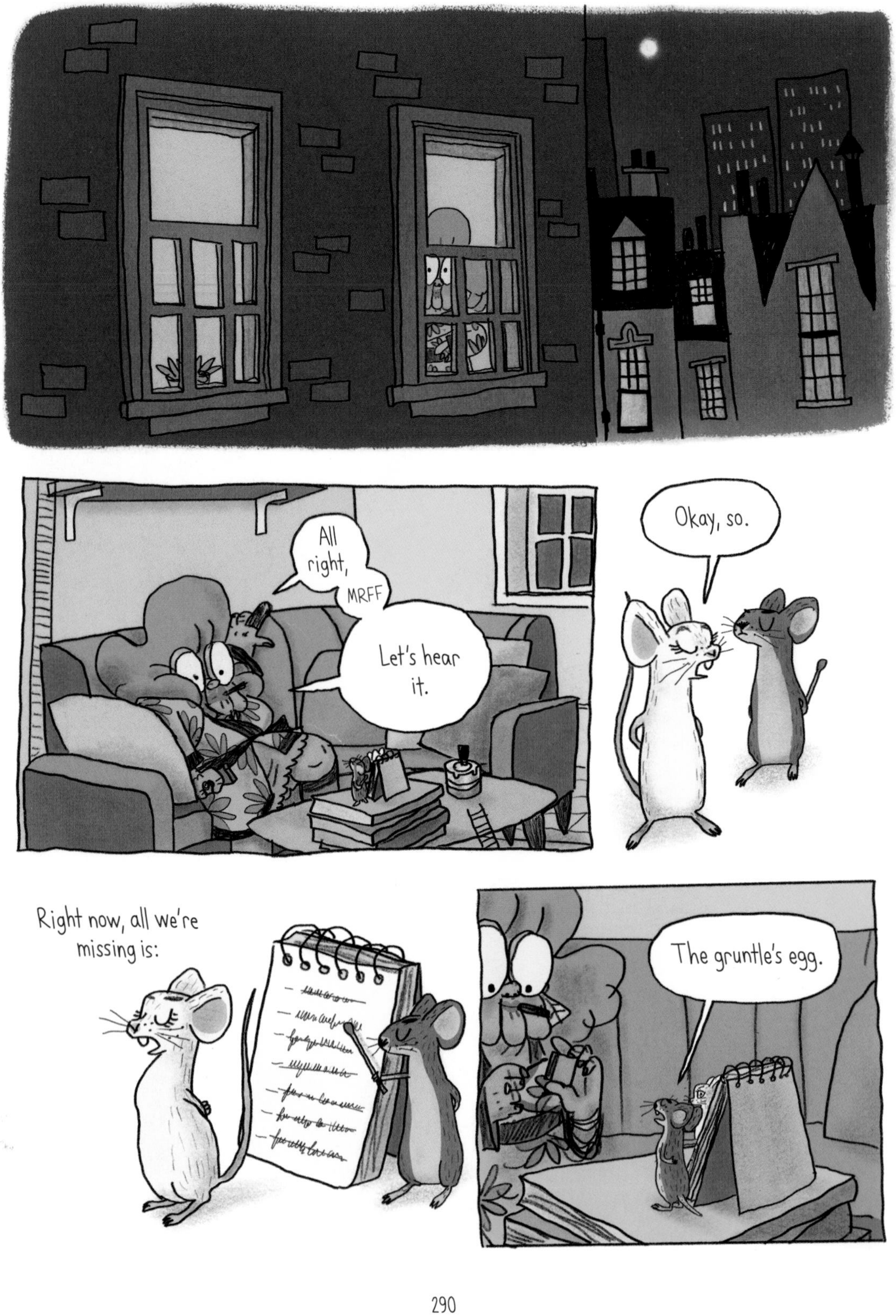
All right,
MRFF
Let's hear it.
Okay, so.
Right now, all we're missing is:
The gruntle's egg.

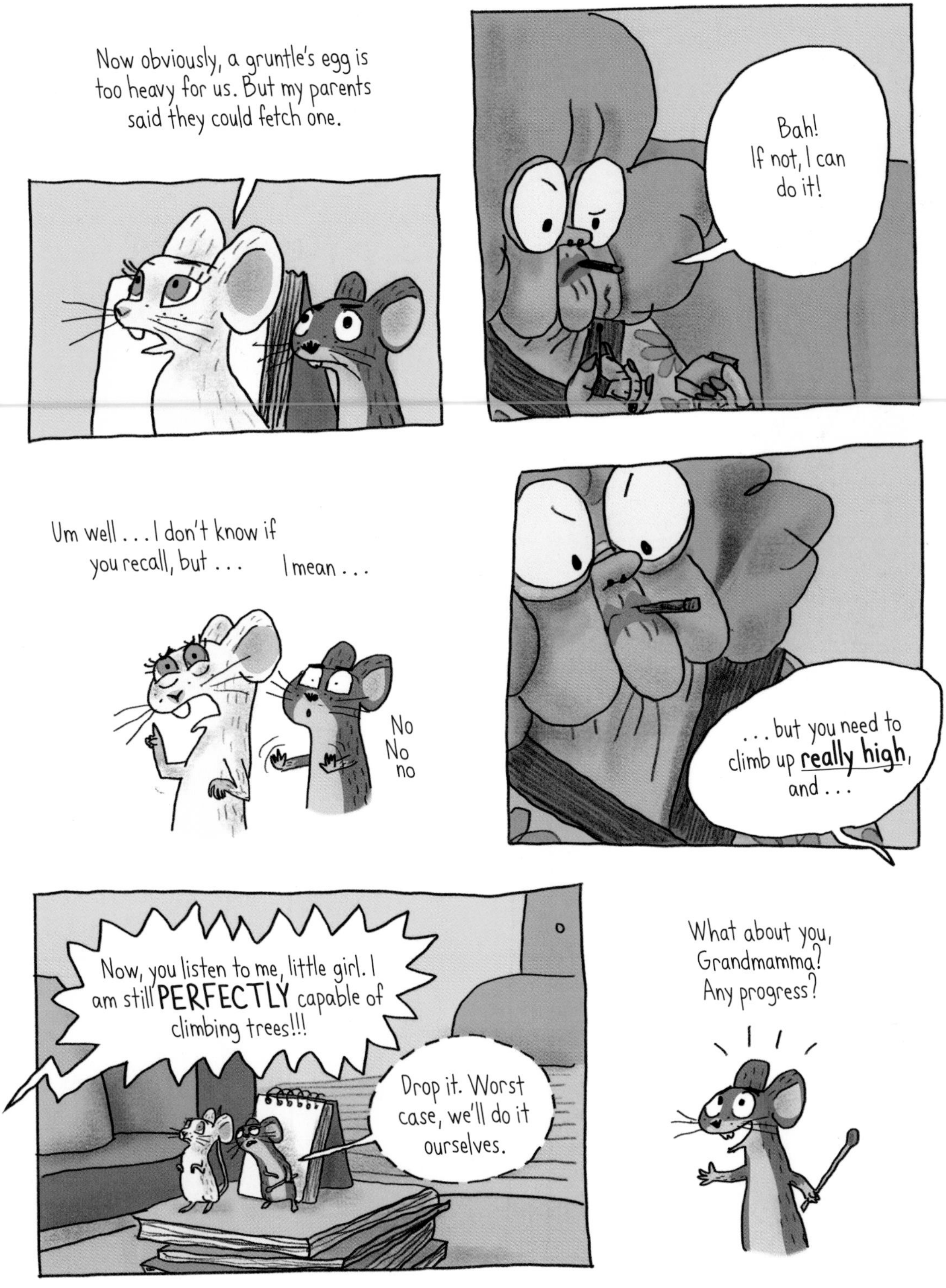
Now obviously, a gruntle's egg is too heavy for us. But my parents said they could fetch one.
Bah! If not, I can do it!
Um well . . . I don't know if you recall, but . . . I mean . . .
No No no
. . . but you need to climb up **really high**, and . . .
Now, you listen to me, little girl. I am still **PERFECTLY** capable of climbing trees!!!
Drop it. Worst case, we'll do it ourselves.
What about you, Grandmamma? Any progress?

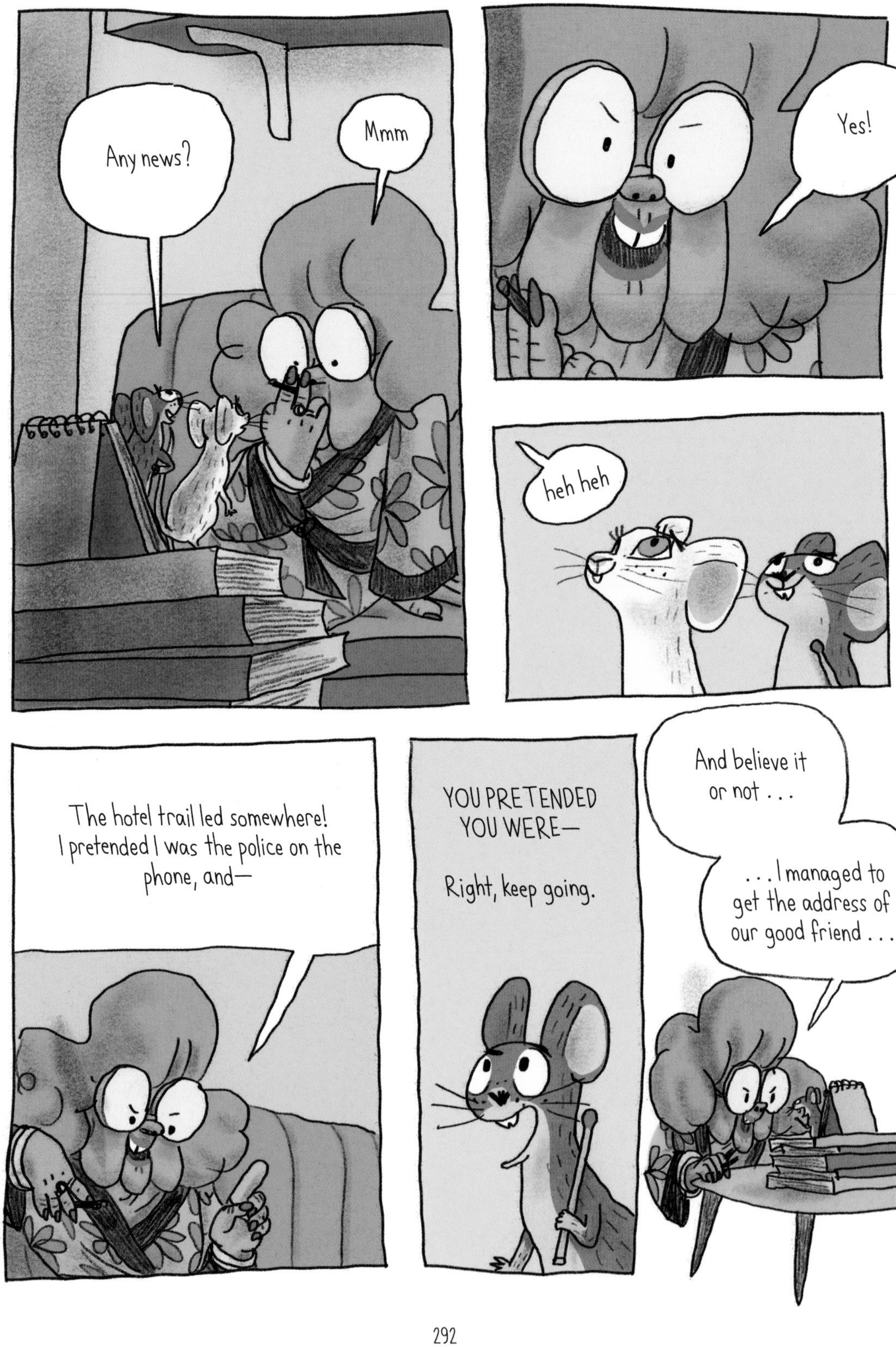
Any news?
Mmm
Yes!
heh heh
The hotel trail led somewhere! I pretended I was the police on the phone, and—
YOU PRETENDED YOU WERE—
Right, keep going.
And believe it or not . . .
. . . I managed to get the address of our good friend . . .

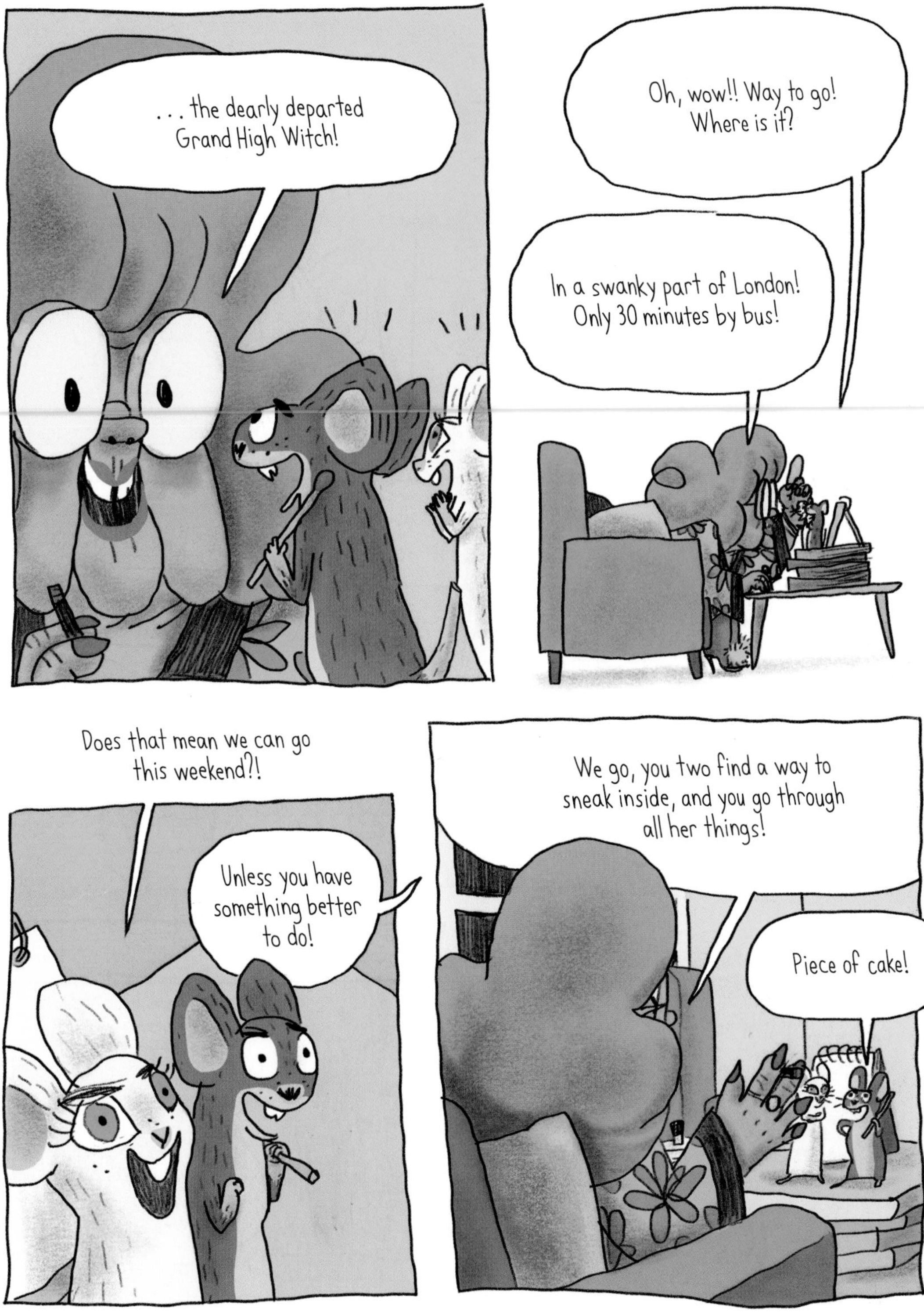
. . . the dearly departed Grand High Witch!
Oh, wow!! Way to go! Where is it?
In a swanky part of London! Only 30 minutes by bus!
Does that mean we can go this weekend?!
Unless you have something better to do!
We go, you two find a way to sneak inside, and you go through all her things!
Piece of cake!

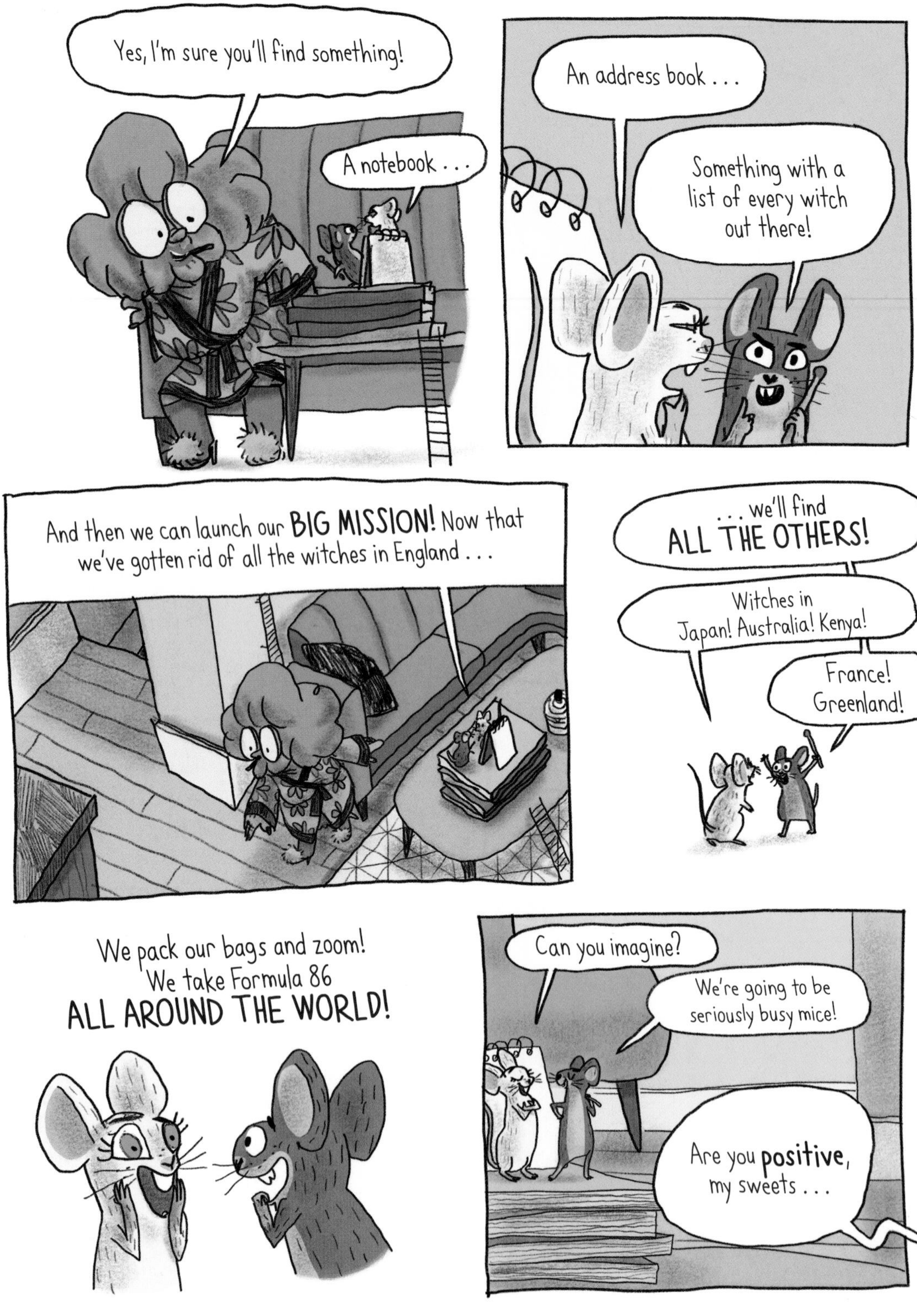
Yes, I'm sure you'll find something!
A notebook . . .
An address book . . .
Something with a list of every witch out there!
And then we can launch our BIG MISSION! Now that we've gotten rid of all the witches in England . . .
. . . we'll find ALL THE OTHERS!
Witches in Japan! Australia! Kenya!
France! Greenland!
We pack our bags and zoom! We take Formula 86 ALL AROUND THE WORLD!
Can you imagine?
We're going to be seriously busy mice!
Are you positive, my sweets . . .

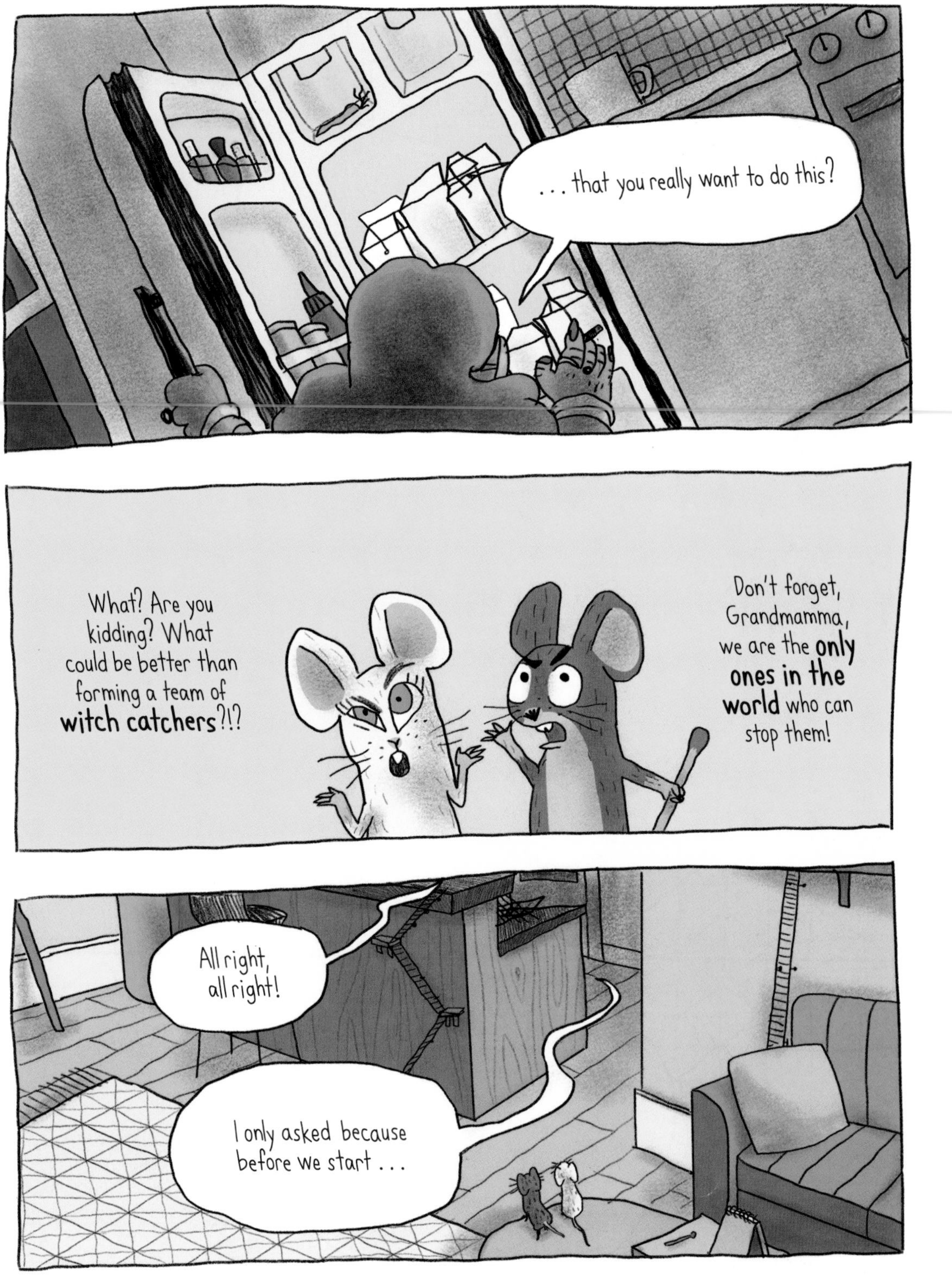
. . . that you really want to do this?
What? Are you kidding? What could be better than forming a team of **witch catchers**?!?
Don't forget, Grandmamma, we are the **only ones in the world** who can stop them!
All right, all right!
I only asked because before we start . . .

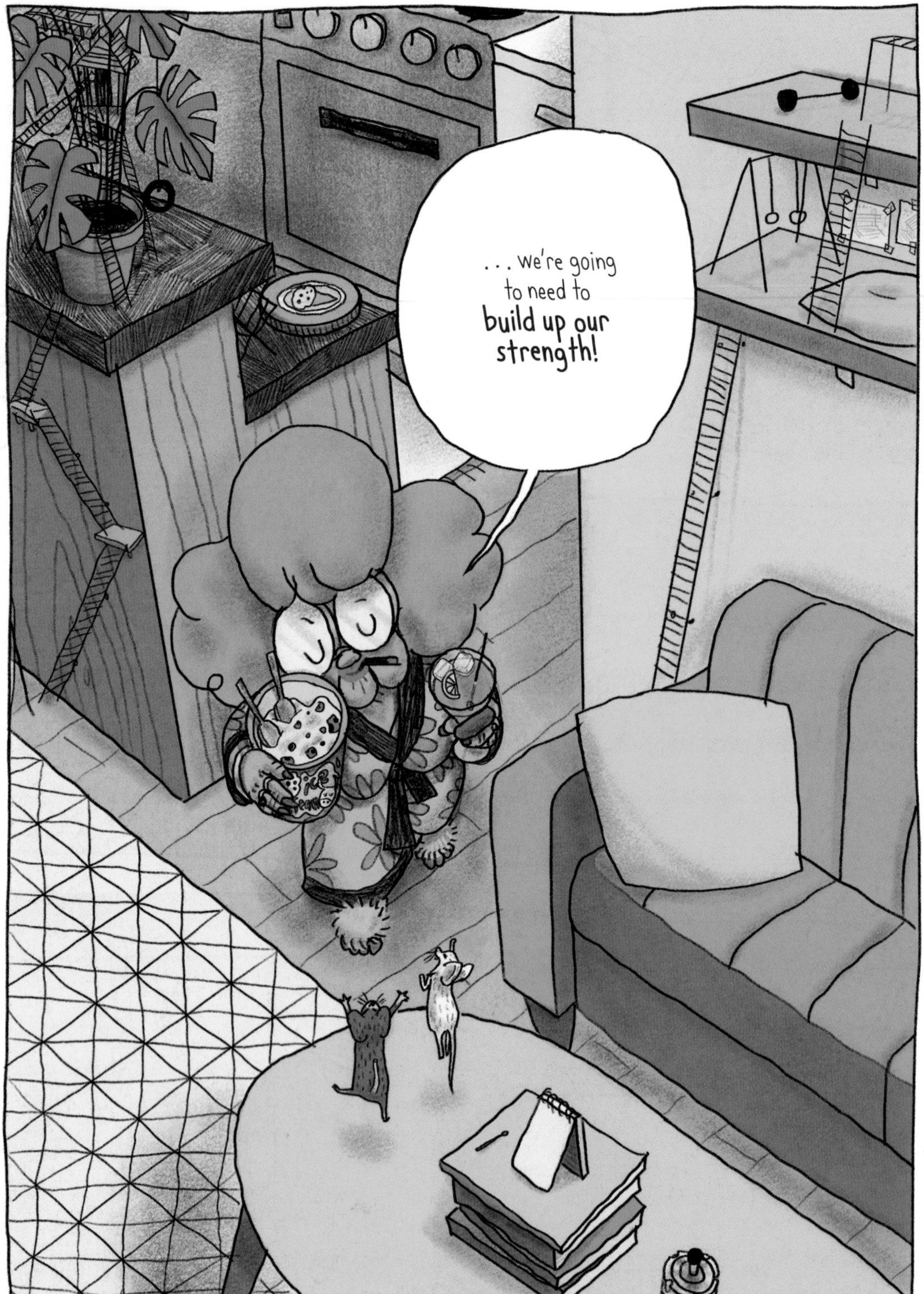
. . . we're going to need to **build up our strength!**
ice cream

THE END

ROALD DAHL was a spy, ace fighter pilot, chocolate historian, and medical inventor. He was also the author of *Charlie and the Chocolate Factory*, *Matilda*, *The BFG*, and many more brilliant stories. He remains the World's Number One Storyteller.

PÉNÉLOPE BAGIEU was born in Paris in 1982, a few months before the original publication of Roald Dahl's *The Witches*. She is the bestselling author of several graphic novels, including the Harvey Award winner *California Dreamin'* and Eisner Award winner *Brazen: Rebel Ladies Who Rocked the World*, which has been translated into seventeen languages and adapted into an animated series. Pénélope Bagieu lives in Paris.

This book would never have existed without the help of Gallimard Jeunesse, and notably Christine Baker, Muriel Chabert, Sandrine Dutordoir, Thierry Laroche, Nicolas Leroy, Olivier Merlin, and Hedwige Pasquet.

Thank you to Luke Kelly and the team at the Roald Dahl Story Company.

Thank you to Mona Challet for her invaluable eye.

A big thank-you to Drac for the coloring, and to Camille, Salomé, Reiko, Zora, Maureen, Robin, Elliot, and Louna.

Thank you to my friends and my family for their support and their advice, especially to my mother, to Victoria, and to Sophie Thimonnier.

And finally, huge thanks to Benjamin.

— P. B.

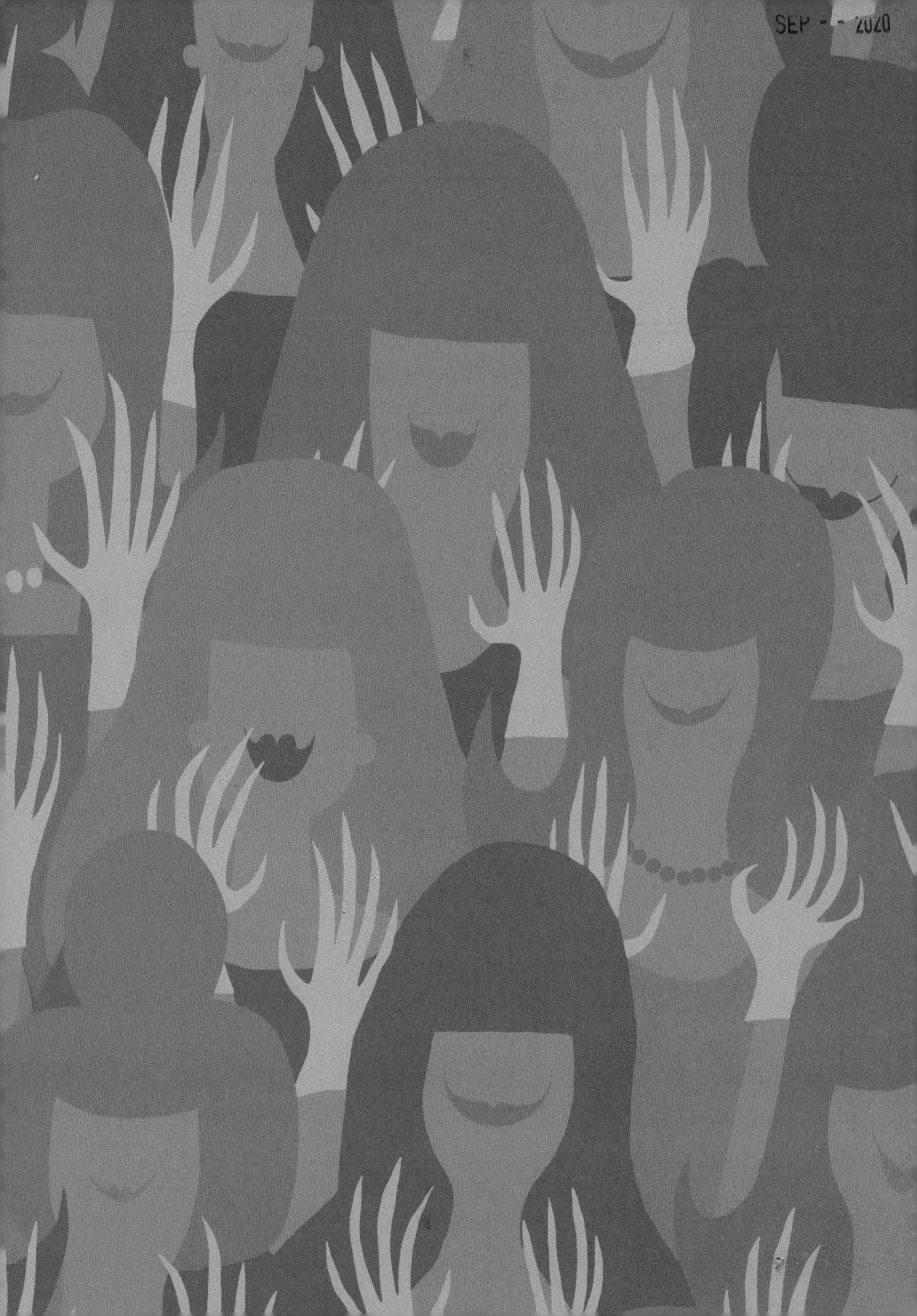